PINKERTON'S SISTER

Peter Rushforth

MacAdam/Cage

MacAdam/Cage Publishing
155 Sansome Street, Suite 550
San Francisco, CA 94104
www.macadamcage.com
Copyright © 2005 by Peter Rushforth
ALL RIGHTS RESERVED.

Library of Congress Cataloging-in-Publication Data

Rushforth, Peter, 1945—
    Pinkerton's sister / Peter Rushforth.
        p. cm.
    ISBN 1-931561-99-0 (hardcover : alk. paper)
    1. Young women—fiction. 2. Mental illnes—Fiction. 3. Eccentrics and
eccentricities—Fiction. 4. Characters and characteristics in literature—Fiction.
New York (N.Y.)—Fiction. I. Title.

    PR6068.U76P56 2005
    823'.94—dc22

                                                                    2004030306

Manufactured in the United States of America.
10 9 8 7 6 5 4 3 2 1

For
my father and mother
Sam and Emily Rushforth
with love

. . . a little cloud out of the sea, like a man's hand.

I Kings, Chapter XVIII, Verse xliv

Contents

One

THE MADWOMAN IN THE ATTIC

I could not help it; the restlessness was in my nature; it agitated me to pain sometimes. Then my sole relief was to walk along the corridor of the third story, backwards and forwards, safe in the silence and solitude of the spot . . .

Charlotte Brontë, *Jane Eyre*

I

The madwoman in the attic was standing at the window.

Something about the slant of her body – slumped, drooping to one side – gave her a look of Mariana-like weariness. Her right hand was gripping one of the vertical iron bars almost at the limit of her reach, and she rested her bowed head – too heavy to hold upright – against the upraised arm, her face hidden, her eyes closed. Her left arm hung loosely against her nightgown, drawn down – it appeared – by the weight of the hairbrush she was holding. It was as if she had been standing there all through the night, struggling against sleep and dreaming, waiting to glimpse the first glimmerings of light in the low winter sky.

I am aweary, aweary.

Yesterday she had been on display at 5 Hampshire Square, and Mrs. Albert Comstock and all her guests had studied her, eyeglasses raised, spectacles specially polished, elbows vigorously nudging each other in a see-what-she-says sort of way. "Oh joy, oh rapture," she had muttered to herself beforehand, without enthusiasm, distinctly aweary at the prospect of an afternoon with Mrs. Albert Comstock and her farting Pekinese stretching endlessly in front of her like a prospect of the wind-chilled steppes. In the small pond of Longfellow Park Mrs. Albert Comstock, sharp-toothed, ravenous-eyed, was the big fish – the very big fish – big, and growing bigger. If she'd been on the menu at the feeding of the five thousand they wouldn't have needed a second fish, and the five loaves would have been entirely surplus to requirements. They'd have had to leave a note for the baker's boy. *No bread today, thank you.* She was quite sufficient for a feast all by herself, tasting foul, but undeniably filling. The five thousand could have come back for second helpings, and brought their hungry friends, brandishing baskets they just happened to have with them. "For later," they'd mutter vaguely, raking in as much as they could with both hands. "For later", they'd repeat, grabbing feverishly, with the air of men seizing their chance to stock up with fat celebratory cigars to commemorate some monstrous birth, piling them up one on top of the other behind their flapped-out, generously accommodating ears.

Mrs. Albert Comstock was one of those Lazarus-pale, white-fleshed, grotesquely shaped creatures drawn up from deep below the surface of cold dark water where light never penetrated, drawn up toward the shallows where the children paddled with their thin bare legs. When she had swallowed everything around her she would munch her way southward down the rest of Manhattan.

Munch. Munch. Munch.

The mighty Comstock teeth — with onomatopoeic avidity — could crunch through cast iron, through glass, through granite, and nothing would impede their irresistible advance.

The madwoman's name was Alice Pinkerton, and she would soon be thirty-five years old.

She continued with what she had been doing, holding the hairbrush in her left hand as she brushed the left side of her hair. The awkwardness of her stance, the halting clumsiness of her movements, showed that this was not the hand she would normally use, *gauche* because she was dexterous. With her right hand she continued to grasp at the iron bar in the window, her back bent as if she was hanging there, supporting the weight of her body with this one hand.

"One, two, three . . ."

She tugged fiercely at the hairbrush, not as if she was angry about something, but more with an attempt at precise control, with determination, as if she had been given new energy after a pause. With each downward pull she swayed a little to one side and back again.

". . . four, five, six . . ."

It annoyed her that they thought she was mad, but it annoyed her even more that they were wrong about the attic. The mad wife in *Jane Eyre*, Dorian Gray's portrait, and herself: all were thought to be locked away in an attic, and not one of them was. If anyone wished to say such a thing about her, he or she could at least take the trouble to get the details right. Of the two pronouns "she" was by far the more probable, always excepting the Reverend Goodchild (Halitotic Herbert, as she thought of him, entirely without affection). She did not feel anger, she did not feel grief or shame (she had had enough of grief and shame); *annoyance* was the word to describe her feelings. The mistake was an irritant, like the lack of an apostrophe in the name of Jacksons Bluff, or a missing question mark at the end of a question, leaving her wrong-footed and itching to correct it. If she was a madwoman, she was a pedantic madwoman.

Charlotte Brontë was quite specific about where Bertha (Alice sometimes thought of Mrs. Rochester by just her Christian name, as if she knew her well) was: in a room on the third story, the floor *below* the attics. In Chapter XI, as Mrs. Fairfax showed her around Thornfield, Jane Eyre stood near this room for the first time, in the low narrow central passage like a corridor in some Bluebeard's castle. She heard, in the dimness and stillness, a preternatural, mirthless laugh. Months later, on the night of a full moon, Rochester summoned her to a room off that same corridor to tend Richard Mason, his arm soaked in blood where he had been stabbed and bitten by his deranged sister.

"Carter – hurry! – hurry!" Rochester said to the surgeon. "The sun will soon rise . . ."

It was as if they were all in Castle Dracula, ruled by the powers of a vampire.

"She sucked the blood," Richard Mason told them, "she said she'd drain my heart."

Bad things happened when the moon was full, and the moon would soon be full. Sometimes there seemed to be several nights in a row when the moon could be described as full, and she was not confident in describing which of the moons was the moment of near-perfect fullness, the most complete circle. She looked up toward it, as if – she sometimes felt – from the bottom of a deep, dark well, holding her hands up, trying to shield her eyes from the circular glimmer of unattainable daylight far above her. She did not consult an almanac to discover when the full moon would be due; the moon-dial clock beneath the mirror warned her when the nights of cold light had come. She avoided seeing it when the time came close, turning her eyes aside. Perhaps she ought to have tried draining Mrs. Albert Comstock's heart yesterday, just to cheer herself up. It would certainly have enlivened the proceedings: Mrs. Goodchild would have alased and alacked fit to bust (well, she had done this in any case), Mrs. Alexander Diddecott would have hurtled backward off the divan (ditto, one of her more spectacular efforts), and Mabel Peartree (now here was an incentive) would probably have burst into enthusiastic applause. However, she doubted that she'd have found much blood in that withered organ (if it existed), massive though the body was that contained it. She'd barely have been able to wet her lips and tongue: no refreshment there.

". . . seven, eight, nine . . ."

("... Light your lamp at mine.
Ten, eleven, twelve –
Loosely hold the helve.
We're the merry miner-boys,
Make the goblins hold their noise . . .")

(The words came to her uninvited from long ago, from *The Princess and the Goblin*, as Curdie sang to drive away the goblins. The goblins couldn't bear singing. The chief defense against them was verse, for they hated verse of every kind.)

She was to go to church this morning. She should be thinking elevated thoughts – heaven knows, you needed to when the

Reverend Goodchild was your clergyman (this was a test of faith that would have had Job struggling) — and purifying her mind. Here she was — before breakfast, on a *Sunday* — thinking of slurping at Mrs. Albert Comstock's lifeblood, licking at her palpitating heart. She should never have read *Dracula* when Charlotte — Charlotte Finch, her best friend at school, and still her best friend — pressed it upon her. What a corrupting influence that woman was. ("Is it horrid, are you sure it is horrid?" This variant of Catherine Morland's line in *Northanger Abbey* was Alice's usual question when Charlotte enthused about an enjoyably frightening novel. Charlotte had assured her that it was, indeed, horrid.)

Think of something else.

Grace Poole had been Bertha Rochester's keeper.

Poole.

There was another character in another novel who had been given the name Poole. . .

Which novel was it?

(The reflection in the pool: clouded, dark, malformed.)

Poole . . .

Poole . . .

Poole . . .

Poole . . .

No. It was no good. She still preferred thinking about the slurping. She poised her lips as if about to down an oyster. She liked to live the moment to the full.

Slurp. Slurp. Slurp.

2

Alice, like Bertha Rochester, was in a room on the third story. This seemed entirely appropriate. The first story was about Jane, the second story was about Rochester, and then there was the third story. On the third story was Bertha Rochester's room, and her room was described as being an inner room, a room without windows, its door concealed beneath a tapestry, hidden, kept apart, a room where it would have been dark, and difficult to breathe.

Alice and Dorian Gray's portrait were even more closely linked. They were in the *same* room, a room right at the top of the house, but it was not the attic. It was the schoolroom. That was why the square-edged bars were there. They were there for safety, so that children could not fall from the window. It should rightly have been called the nursery (it had been used as such for her and her sisters) but she had started to call it the schoolroom when she was a girl, after reading – in some of her mother's English novels – about lonely governesses and grand houses. This was what she had remembered best about these novels. It hadn't happened in *Jane Eyre,* and it hadn't happened in *Agnes Grey*, but it was the image that remained: the picture of a young woman going out into the world to make her way alone, sitting in a chair made for someone the size of a child, surrounded by the possessions of others, writing letters home. Jane possessed no home to which she could write: her home was memory and imagination, her search for someone to love, and these she carried about within her.

The detail Alice most admired in *The Picture of Dorian Gray* was the decision to locate the hideous portrait – the painting that bore upon it all the visible traces of damage and sin – in the locked and disused schoolroom where Dorian Gray had been an unhappy and lonely child, the room especially built for a hated grandson. This seemed to her to be, psychologically, profoundly and powerfully true, an insight of real genius. This was the room in which a monstrous thing had been created, long before the portrait had ever been painted. To place the portrait in the attic would have been to miss the whole point; the portrait *had* to be in the schoolroom, and the portrait *had* to be covered, and hidden from sight.

The rest of the novel had not impressed her as much. She had been unconvinced by Dorian Gray's professed evil, and had felt – as she read the novel (it had to be a surreptitious reading) – that she was being slowly suffocated by rose petals, like the victim of a Roman emperor with depraved and specialized tastes. (What was the name of the emperor who had actually done this?) Adjectives proliferated in *The Picture of Dorian Gray*, an æsthetic thesaurus, but there was a coy evasiveness at the heart of the novel that weakened it, and the reader's imagination – instead of expanding to fill a central void – was stifled, and withered away. "Is that all he's done?" she had caught herself thinking. "Is that *all*?" She'd thought the same about Doctor Faustus. She was demonstrably decadent, corrupted by unsuitable literature, clearly capable of far greater excesses than had ever occurred to Wilde or Marlowe, with lots of helpfully enthusiastic suggestions to offer, all tried and tested (some of them several times, just to make quite certain), all thoroughly enjoyed.

If only.

It was a phrase she sometimes used with Charlotte, when they were trying to make themselves believe that they were being daring about something. *If only*. Charlotte (yet more corruption) had smuggled the Wilde novel in to her in the same way that she had later smuggled in *Trilby*, and it had made her think of the time when they had seen Oscar Wilde at the theatre during his visit to the United States about eight years earlier.

He had been a poet when they had seen him, and then he had turned to prose. *The Picture of Dorian Gray* was nothing like as powerful as *The Strange Case of Dr. Jekyll and Mr. Hyde*, a novel that must have influenced Oscar Wilde's, both set in the same fogbound nighttime city, the city of Dr. Conan Doyle's detective, his cab rattling over cobblestones as he pursued murderers – their capes billowing open, their shadows long, unnaturally thin – past spluttering gas-lamps. Mr. Hyde was *The Picture of Dr. Jekyll*, a portrait given solidity and form, a deformed and dreadful statue brought to life like Frankenstein's creature by an unhappy, tormented Pygmalion. Oscar Wilde had asked for the novels of Robert Louis Stevenson when he was in prison. As he stood in court and faced his accusers, had the words she always remembered best from Stevenson's novel come into his mind: "My devil had been long caged, he came out roaring"?

9

Wishing to be loved, wishing to be wanted, Dorian Gray had wasted away the hours of his unlived, unloved childhood in that schoolroom, ignored by those he wished would be affectionate toward him. In that schoolroom, the picture that was his hidden self had taken shape within him and he had not known that it was there, the Mr. Hyde of his sub-conscious. (She felt quite modern as she made use of this last word.) She thought of her younger brother, Ben, when he was a little boy – his small, neat handwriting, almost like printing: it hadn't changed, it was just the same now – showing his school work to his father, his careful notes and diagrams, the Latin verbs, the cross-section of the human eye, the map of Massachusetts, which were never praised or noticed. When Dorian Gray grew to adulthood (when his *body* grew to adulthood: that which was within him had withered, had never grown properly, taking strange shapes), the schoolroom remained unchanged. The dog-eared schoolbooks still filled the satinwood bookcase; on the wall behind it the ragged Flemish tapestry still hung, with a faded king and queen playing chess in a garden, while a company of hawkers rode by, carrying hooded birds on their gauntleted wrists.

The mediæval women bent over their tapestries, like so many Ladies of Shalott looking out at the world through mirrors, all those pale-faced women half sick of shadows.

> *On either side the river*
> *Lie long fields of barley and of rye . . .*

She saw the Lady of Shalott plainly, in the same pose that she had seen Mariana assuming in a painting (she, also, had been working on embroidery, filling the empty hours), standing – as if weary after a day laboring in those very fields of barley – her hands pressed supportively against her spine, arching herself backward in the low time of the day, the late dark afternoons, aweary, aweary. The same woman, with a different face, floated in her boat down the river, dying in the world for which she had so longed, killed by contact with it, her hair long and tumbled, blown by the wind.

The women wove tapestries, sewed alphabets like school exercises, lions, unicorns, stylized open-petaled flowers. The arras was green, dull gold, crimson, rich with horseman, hawk, and hound. Stags fell, pierced by arrows; wolves pulled deer to the snowy ground; lords released their hawks, and birds – caught in mid-air – fell, fluttering to earth in clouds of feathers: scenes of death and dying, the slaughter of men and animals, beautifully embroidered, thread by thread.

She imagined the colors of their silks – would they have used silk, or would the material have been wool, cotton? – as being the same as those of her watercolors, the little squares of brightness within the wooden box with the brass hinges. She could visualize them with perfect accuracy, as if matching colors for a gown, or fabrics in a room: Chinese White, Viridian Green, Cadmium Yellow, Ultramarine (a Mediterranean light, sea-reflections playing across ruinous white Greek columns: each color had its own little picture), Magenta . . .

As then, so now.

Women bent over their cross-stitch, bent over their canvases, wasting the hours in filling wildernesses of whiteness, as if somehow attempting to occupy the vast unused vacancies of their minds with the bright gleam of a needle, the stitch-stitch-stitch of the endless holes puncturing the plainness. Stitch-stitch-stitch, as they sat unseen in the corner, sewing all day long. Beneath the tapestries were the locked and hidden doors that led into the rooms where the madwomen were imprisoned. Manganese Violet, Raw Sienna, Gamboge, Brown Madder . . .

They should know all about *Madder*.

Stitch-stitch-stitch.

The hands didn't tremble, but kept up the same action over and over, like well-tuned machines, automatons designed by Isaac Singer, automatons with placid, unchanging, Dr. Coppelius human features, massed Coppélias, girls with enamel eyes. Sometimes she confused Coppelius with Copernicus, and planets swam unseen in their orbits around a night sky, above the bowed backs. They were sin-free Hester Prynnes, always sewing, always stitching, embroidering shrouds for burials, embroidering baby linen, the vestments of ceremony. They never embroidered bridal veils.

Stitch-stitch-stitch.

". . . eighty-seven, eighty-eight, eighty-nine . . ."

You became bored with embroidery, after a while. She and Charlotte had spent many happy hours of their childhood in devising different methods of killing Mrs. Albert Comstock. Heaven had indeed lain about them in their infancy. Well spotted, Wordsworth!

The high stone narrow-windowed walls of the dark castles seemed designed to keep the women in, as much as to keep enemies out. Outside the castle walls, beyond the moats, the young men marched about, looking stern, bearing falcons on their arms like feathered musical instruments that they were about to play. Troubadours, minstrels, minnesingers, and trouvères strummed on lutes, or lyres, or halberds, or whatever it was they strummed on. It was quite difficult to concentrate on the tapestries with all that strumming. It was all the women ever seemed to do, work at tapestries, or wave goodbye to departing knights from the battlements of their castles, wearing tall white conical hats like dunces' caps. "My life is dreary,/He cometh not," they chorused as they stitched. The rusted nails fell from the knots that held the pear to the garden-wall. The broken sheds look'd sad and strange. "My life is dreary,/He cometh not."

Stitch-stitch-stitch.

The stitches were small and neat, barely visible, like stitches sewn by a surgeon after he'd ministered to a mind diseas'd, his well-washed hands rearranging the contents of the sleeper's head in a more harmonious pattern, the pale skin smoothed and sewn back into place where the incision had been made.

Best men are molded out of faults. That's what Mariana had said.

On long, empty winter evenings, with the winds whistling around them and rustling the wall hangings, flaring up the torches, they'd sit about competitively comparing the number of lachry-matories they'd managed to fill with their tears to show how much they missed their absent husbands or courtly lovers, those of them who had husbands or courtly lovers. It was their one excitement.

"I'm on my twelfth bottle. I've had to send out for fresh sup-plies," My Lady Sibylle would announce as her opening gambit, skillfully managing to temper quiet pride with a reasonable stab at overwhelming grief, and crushing all opposition. This was a woman who spent her afternoons, a peeled onion in each hand, lis-tening to sentimental ballads – specialized performers catered for this market – with a lachrymatory applied to the inside corner of each eye, rather like a heavy smoker with two pipes. These were carefully held in place by specially trained maidservants to ensure that not one tear was wasted. The balladeer strummed with syrupy skill, his voice stressing the sad bits so that she'd be able to recog-nize them.

> "Out in ye churchyarde ye wilde breezes blowe,
> Seeming to echo ye heart's griefe and woe.
> Softly she murmurs, while chills o'er her creepe,
> 'Why did they dig Ma's grave so deepe?' . . ."

"Sniffle, sniffle!" sniffled Sibylle in record time, snapping her fingers as she sensed saturation approaching in her left lachryma-tory. Time for a fresh container, Eleanor. (Number thirteen! That would show up My Lady Mabelle.) A row of the little glass bottles would be lined neatly across the top of her mediæval mantelshelf like a well-filled salt-tasting miniature-bottled wine cellar if the absence was an extended one, twinkling in the candlelight on assertive display. *I've wept more than you've wept! I've wept more than you've wept!* That's what they were twinkling. That Hundred Years War had been hard going, squeezing them dry like ferociously twisted lemons. Enterprising entrepreneurs had offered ready-filled bottles for sale, with reduced rates for bulk purchases.

"I've just started my ninth."

"My eleventh is nearly half full."

"I've only managed seven so far this week. I've not been very well."

"My life is dreary!"

"He cometh not!"

"He cometh not!"

(They had to remember to repeat these last three lines at regular intervals, an antiphonal woeful chanting. When they couldn't think of anything else to say, these were the lines to repeat.)

The dunces' caps leaned forward as they bent to their tapestries, back to the lions and unicorns, the kings and queens, the games of chess, the hooded hawks, the arrow-pierced stags. The unmarried were excluded from such conversations. The unmarried had no one to cometh not (if you couldn't have a man who cometh, you were automatically excluded from having a man who cometh not), nothing about which to boast, and no reason to weep. The unmarried had extra-large tapestries to stitch as compensation. Another night of stitching lay before them. When they were completed, they would be hung upon the bare stone, and then they would begin more tapestries. There was always enough bare stone for more tapestries. There could never be enough tapestries. There was no one left to whom they might wave goodbye, and so they stitched, the married and the unmarried. They were like monks in a silent order, stitching away at illuminated manuscripts, bent over as if seeking out a brighter source of illumination in the candlelit gloom, day after day, night after night, words of prayer, words of renunciation.

Stitch-stitch-stitch.

"One, two, three . . ." she began again, tugging at her hair with the brush, with the grimly determined expression of a keen gardener pulling up strong-rooted weeds. You spent hours getting rid of them, and back they came again the following day.

She'd been fond of gardening when she was a very little girl, doing her stint as Miss Spade, the Gardener's Daughter. Miss Spade was one of the cards in Happy Families, the English children's card game that Miss Ericsson had given her, and Miss Spade wielded her hoe with a look of murderous malice. All fifty-two members of the Happy Families looked like maniacal potential killers, and most held convenient weapons in threatening postures. It made you worry about English methods of child-rearing.

She'd been no Mary, Mary, Quite Contrary (though she'd been willfully contrary herself, and had known a distinctly contrary Mary).

She hadn't nurtured silver bells, or cockleshells, and she had most certainly *not* nurtured pretty – *ha!* – maids all in a row. She'd hadn't so much been fond of gardening, as fond of weeding, not quite the same thing. What she had nurtured had been weeds, carefully sought out, encouraged, and hoarded for the pleasure of uprooting them. That was how her garden grew. It was not so much the planting she enjoyed, as the pulling up, the ripping away until every inch of earth was free of weeds, and there was nothing there that should not be there, nothing there but disturbed and freshly turned soil, dark and damp beneath the surface like a newly dug grave. It was the way she kept the schoolroom, or tried to – everything in its place, everything angled precisely in position – battling unceasingly with her untidy and unco-operative sisters. (That hyphen in "unco-operative" was one of her acts of rebellion against the dictates of Webster. This was a word that *needed* its hyphen.) The first thing she did, each time she entered the room, was to walk around straightening pictures and shifting objects – half an inch this way, a quarter of an inch that way – like someone with an image of perfection in her mind in which there was a pre-determined area of unfilled space, definite as a cast shadow. She had followed the gardener about during his mornings in the garden, jealously insisting that all weeds were there for her to destroy.

"There's one," he'd indicate helpfully.

"Pluck from the memory a rooted sorrow!" she'd declare, plucking away with a two-handed will.

"There's another one."

"Pluck from the memory a rooted sorrow!"

"What rhubarb, senna, or what purgative drug . . . ?" said the gardener, a young man with a literary frame of mind. "There's another."

They plucked away from the memory effortlessly, scarcely rooted at all, little crumbs of earth adhering, falling loose, pattering down. She sometimes suspected that the gardener planted the weeds there especially, just to give her pleasure. They always pulled away so easily – she preferred the sensation of tugging, grappling with tenacious roots, the breathless struggling – and the earth around them always seemed so watered and fresh, like that of plants for sale in an expensive florist's shop, all the arts of horticulture devoted to their careful nurturing. Undaunted, she tugged away, plucking furiously, someone preparing a chicken for an emergency meal. She didn't care what she plucked, as long as she was plucking. If there'd been silver bells or cockleshells they'd have been hurled into a heap, jingling. The pretty maids all in a row would have blazed in the biggest bonfire she could build, glamorously unarmored Joans of Arc sizzling en masse like an ignited beauty contest.

"And another."

"Pluck from the memory a rooted sorrow!"

She preferred to *feel* the doomed weeds in the palms of her hands as she plucked – quailing, wilting, vainly resisting – though sometimes she employed a hoe, becoming more like Miss Spade than ever, a Lady Macbeth bringing the daggers down with considerable force (she'd have had one in each hand), the impact jarring all the way up to her shoulders. This Lady Macbeth would have elbowed Macbeth aside, trampled over him, eager to have the pleasure of killing all to herself. "Give *me* the daggers!" she'd have bawled, before he'd ever set foot in the bedchamber. This Lady Macbeth would not have been shaken from her purpose by the resemblance of the sleeping Duncan to her father. It would have spurred her on to enthusiastic excesses. She'd have stabbed away, hacking his beard off and stuffing it in his mouth if she'd felt like it. And she'd have felt like it. The whole sinister-faced Spade family massed together – Miss Spade with her hoe, Mr. Spade and Master Spade with their differently shaped sharp-edged spades, and Mrs. Spade with her devilish three-pronged fork – looked like a peasants' revolt (rarely had the peasants appeared so revolting) bursting through the palace gates and thirsting for blood, agitating their agricultural implements with threatening intent. The Royal Family would not be a Happy one for much longer. When she held a hoe she'd say, "Hoe, hoe, hoe, hoe," as she dug out the weeds, the lugubrious laugh of the unamused murderer. This would be after an afternoon listening to Mrs. Albert Comstock's humorless ha-ha-ha-ha-ing, when she was still feeling furious.

"Hoe . . ."

Stab!

– the thin silvery blade of the hoe would shoot into the earth like the thrust of an assassin's dagger –

". . . Hoe . . ."

Stab!

". . . Hoe! . . ."

Stab!

". . . Hoe!"

Stab!

(*STAB ES.*

(She had seen the sign, this emblazoned summons to slaughter – *STAB! STAB!* – with its huge painted Belshazzarian writing on the outside wall above the entrance to Carlo Fiorelli's studio. Who *was* this *ES* she was bidden to stab by the writing on the wall? There was only one possible *ES*, although there would soon be many others.

(*ENORMOUS SIBYL.*

(That was who it was.

(*STAB ENORMOUS SIBYL!*

(That was what was implacably demanded.

(*STAB ENORMOUS SIBYL!* That was what was meant.

(That was what she *wanted* it to mean.

(The only difference between "slaughter" and "laughter" was the letter "s," and "s" was for Sibyl.

(It was so clearly, so unmistakably, a *portent* — she was all in favor of *portents* — that it would have been impolite not to obey it. Apart from the pleasure in the naughtiness of stabbing Mrs. Albert Comstock, there was the pleasure in the naughtiness of calling her Sibyl.)

Stab!

The hoe-hoe-hoe-hoeing and the stabbing were enormously satisfying, as if she'd achieved some hard-won victory against great odds, an Horatius of the kitchen garden.

The gardener — who spent his afternoons working in Mrs. Albert Comstock's garden (she was an exacting employer, quick to find fault, never praising) — enjoyed the hoe-hoe-hoe-hoe, and would encourage her stabbing, with shrewd advice on the best technique, like a coach inspiring his team. She'd hear muffled snortings and gigglings behind her (more authentically amused than Mrs. Albert Comstock's hectoring ha-ha-ha-ha) and when she turned round — suspicious and accusing, the hoe held at a threatening angle — he'd always try to look serious, clutching his trowel with an earnest and professional technique, though his bright eyes betrayed him. He would eagerly produce the hoe unasked at every opportunity, an enthusiastic challenger in a duel — "Go on," he would say, alluringly. "You can scarcely miss when you're this close!" (his literary proclivities had left him with a keen eye for Symbolism) — but Alice preferred "Pluck from the memory a rooted sorrow!" It was a more impressive demonstration of her Shakespearean expertise.

"Another."

"Pluck from the memory a rooted sorrow!"

"Another."

There was almost always another.

In those days it had seemed so easy to minister to a mind diseas'd.

"Another."

It had been utterly painless to raze out the written troubles of the brain.

"Another."

18

To find some sweet oblivious antidote.

". . . thirteen, fourteen, fifteen . . ."

Tug!

She pulled hard at her hair.

Tug! Tug!

Pluck from the memory a rooted sorrow.

Tug! Tug!

The roots grew deep within her, coiled around her mind like sleeping serpents.

To make something grow, you buried it deep.

She often mused over this. It was something the young gardener had told her, imparting tips to improve her horticultural skills, as if attempting to convert her into a nurturer, discreetly displacing her destroying self.

For some reason – she'd no recollection of ever having been told to do this, but it had become a necessary ritual – she brushed each section of her hair one hundred times each morning and night. It did nothing to improve its look, but she kept on doing it, becoming anxious if she failed to complete the necessary number. Perhaps she should increase her number of brushings, until the air crackled blue with static electricity, buzzing like a dentist's illuminated electric sign, and her hair trebled in volume, rising up from her head as if in horror at some appalling sight. One look in the mirror should have the same effect – it would beat any sight seen by Dr. Jekyll – and save a lot of effort.

Looking-glass, looking-glass, on the wall.

She always thought of "looking-glass" as being written with a hyphen, in the English style, because of *Through the Looking-Glass*, and because – to her – all things she saw were looking-glassed, or so she felt, transformed into things that were unfamiliar, a reversal of what they ought to be.

(Alice, the other Alice – the Alice Through the Looking-Glass Alice – was talking to the black kitten.

("*. . . and if you're not good directly, I'll put you through in to Looking-glass House. How would you like* that? *Now, if you'll only* *attend, Kitty, and not talk so much, I'll tell you all my ideas about Looking-glass House . . . Well then, the books are something like our books, only the words go the wrong way. I know that, because I've held up one of our books to the glass, and then they hold up one in the other room. How would you like to live in Looking-glass House, Kitty? . . . Oh, Kitty, how nice it would be if we could only get through into Looking-glass House! I'm sure it's got, oh! such beautiful things in it!"*)

She had this sensation of reversal most of all when she gazed into her own reflection.

What she saw was not who she was.

Other people did not seem to have this feeling. Allegra — laughing Allegra — seemed perfectly happy with what she saw in the mirror, reassured by the confirmation of her prettiness. She preened. She posed. She pouted.

But not Alice. Alice had Dr. Jekyll's mirror, not Dorian Gray's, and the looking-glass was not her face. There were no beautiful things in Looking-glass House when she saw into it.

You'd pull away the tapestry — *Tug! Tug!* — and there would be the reflection.

Behind just such a tapestry Mrs. Rochester was hidden away, like Dorian Gray's portrait behind its coverlet, like Mr. Hyde. Beside just such a tapestry Dorian Gray stood with a mirror in front of the portrait on the wall, comparing the face in the painting with the face in the polished glass, just as the emperor Domitian had looked at the reflections in the polished marble-lined underground corridors, looking for the face of his assassin creeping closer to kill him, the glint of a knife. This, to her, was an image of the novel: it was all polished surfaces, the mirror in the locked schoolroom as important as the portrait, like the mirror in Dr. Jekyll's cabinet, in which he sought for the moment of change.

". . . sixteen, seventeen, eighteen . . ."

She paused, becoming very still.

Gently, she laid the hairbrush down on the windowsill, the handle precisely aligned with the edge. She did this even when she placed things down – as now – only briefly, wishing objects to be carefully positioned within a space.

She had recognized that familiar feeling again, like the gradual build-up to an uncontrollable sneeze. It was not, however, a pocket-handkerchief that she required. She walked across to her bed and once more took up her fountain pen and her writing journal from where she had left them. There were the three sentences she had been studying before she had begun brushing her hair, something she had written late last night. It was the beginning of a story, or perhaps something longer. She knew that.

I saw another ghost last night. They come at twilight, the in-between time, not in full darkness, gathering like starlings in a public square as the light falls. They live in the mirrors.

She crossed out *falls* and substituted *fails*. She was not conscious of thinking about this. *Falls* was clearly the wrong word to use here. She must have been thinking of *fails* when she wrote it, or of darkness falling. She changed the period after *falls* into a comma, wrote in an insertion arrow, and added *but in silence, with none of the gregarious noise of the birds.* She wrote in another insertion arrow before *noise* – the page was covered in little symbols and crossings-out, like a wordy mathematical problem – and added *groupings &.*

She paused for a moment, and then wrote again, as fluently as if taking dictation.

Sometimes – & always one at a time – they emerge from the mirrors, & walk into the room.

She waited.

She waited a little longer.

Then she screwed the cap back on the fountain pen – tightly, like someone fearful that the black ink would leak out and stain the sheets – and replaced the pen and the journal exactly where they had been. She returned to the window, picking up the hairbrush again.

". . . nineteen, twenty, twenty-one . . ."

It was as if she had been briefly called away to deal with something.

To dream of seeing yourself in a mirror, denotes that you will meet many discouraging issues, and sickness will cause you distress and loss in fortune.

The drapes brushed against her.

She felt the rough, dusty underside of the Thornfield tapestry against her face, like the underside of the imperially colored gold-embroidered purple coverlet under which Dorian Gray had hidden the picture. Here she was in the schoolroom: the picture of Dorian Gray.

If she were the picture, was her real self out in the world somewhere, living a life that she had never lived, someone young, someone bright and beautiful, someone popular, someone dazzling in society, with the irresistible allure of an illuminated mirror in a darkened room, a Blanche Ingram to her Bertha Rochester? The self she knew – unlike Dorian Gray – had not remained young and beautiful. Unlike Dorian Gray she had never *been* beautiful, and she could not remember ever feeling that she was young. *The princess was a sweet little creature, and at the time my story begins was about eight years old, I think, but she got older very fast.* That was how the second paragraph of *The Princess and the Goblin* – one of the books Alice remembered best from childhood – started, and, though certainly never a sweet little creature (*sweet!*), Alice felt she was as one with Princess Irene when it came to getting older very fast. She was – she felt on the bad days – the cowering soul locked in a darkened room, a soul rotting from within, a withered thing.

3

When Miss Ericsson had called her The Woman in White, that was all she had been thinking about: the figure of a woman dressed in white. It was just a phrase she knew: she hadn't thought of Anne Catherick when she said it. It would never have occurred to her – she was a woman without guile or unkindness – that she had mentioned a character in a novel who had been imprisoned in a lunatic asylum.

So many of the novels owned by Alice's mother contained scenes of madness and the asylum. Lady Audley's secret: madness, and the fear of madness. Those final scenes at the private lunatic asylum in Belgium: the windows shrouded by a scanty curtain, the dark shadow of a woman with a fantastic head-dress, a restless creature who paced perpetually backward and forward before the window. Perhaps that was why she was drawn to them, as she was drawn to Jacobean tragedies, those plays of ghosts, madness, and revenge. She had never seen one of them performed – just as she had never seen an Ibsen play performed – but she read them, those she could find, as she read Ibsen, acting out the events within her head, hearing the voices, seeing the richly clad figures hurtling to their appalling fates, seeing it happen within the rooms around her, these the places in which they lived and died. The Jacobean plays seemed to have been totally forgotten. The reprinted texts themselves, on crinkled, brown-spotted paper, appeared to be hundreds of years old, with old-fashioned spellings, words – she had the feeling – that had not been spoken for centuries. With their elongated letter esses, with their unutterably ancient smell of old books, it was as if they had been lost in some long-ago library, never opened, never read, never acted, but they lived as she read them, setting the events in motion, as if she had spoken the words with which to open a hidden and long-locked door. They were, she felt – as she sometimes felt about some of Shakespeare's plays (*King Lear*, *The Tempest*) – plays that lived best within the mind, where everything could become internalized and intense.

Another of the novels, the Charles Reade novel – *Hard Cash*, the one that had always frightened her – in which flames consumed the asylum as the lunatics shrieked with laughter, often came into her mind. Most people seemed to know *The Cloister and the Hearth* – she'd confused the title with *The Cricket on the Hearth* – when it came to Charles Reade novels, but for her it had always been *Hard Cash*. Some people read certain books over and over to comfort themselves, as if hearing the words of a story read at bedtime long ago, the voice of a lost mother or father, the time when everything was safe, and someone was there to look after you. She read *Hard Cash* to discomfort herself, to feel a fear that had somehow become necessary.

(Bertha swayed on the roof above the battlements, waving her arms, her long black hair streaming against the flames. Rochester ascended through the skylight to save her. He called her name, and she sprang from the roof to her death on the pavement.)

Miss Ericsson had asked Alice if she dressed in white the way she did because of Emily Dickinson. "No," Alice had replied, "because of Miss Havisham." This name — unlike Anne Catherick's — Miss Ericsson had known, and Alice had had to explain — at great length — that she was not being serious. Once she'd worn colors; now she wore white. It had been something to do with reaching thirty-three. That was when the whiteness started.

Nor would Miss Ericsson have realized that *The Woman in White* contained Marian Halcombe — the joy she had felt when she discovered her! — Alice's favorite moustachioed heroine in fiction. She remembered Emmerson Columbarian making jokes about Mrs. Alexander Diddecott's moustache, and Linnaeus Finch — Charlotte's much younger brother — joining in. "Don't be so cruel, Emmerson," Linn would say. "I happen to think it's a particularly attractive moustache. Very erotic." He'd use such words as "erotic," eager to appall his spinsterly sister and her spinsterly friend, and if they were in the right sort of mood (they were usually in the right sort of mood), Charlotte and Alice would utter shocked tut-tutting gasps to please him. She never thought that — within a few years — she would, in her turn, begin to develop one. She was (and always had been) frizzily dark-haired and sallow-skinned, and it slowly occurred to her — as she examined her face in the mirror (if it was one of her dauntless days) — that what were unquestionably hairs on her upper lip were beginning to achieve the status of a full-grown moustache, as flourishing and twirlable — she felt — as that of any villain in a novel or play.

". . . Come, my Trilby, look a little lower down, between the houses on the other side of the river . . ." — the voice was wheedling and insinuating, with a strong foreign accent, not fully fluent in English — ". . . There is a little light glimmering yonder — it is light of ugly little building – and inside are eight marble slabs – all in a row . . ." – Svengali twiddled and twirled the lank hair that hung down the side of his face, at his moustache and his beard, twisting them counterclockwise around his fingers as if creating small, tight curls – ". . . It is called the Morgue . . ."

She had been a patient of Dr. Wolcott Ascharm Webster (the – *nudge, nudge* – mad-doctor) for *over seven years*. First the seven years of dithering and denying, the various experiments, and then the seven years of treatment. More experiments. Mrs. Albert Comstock had recommended, had virtually *insisted*. She'd heard so much about him. Surely some prince was poised to rescue her, lopping his way through the forest of bearded sentinels with his upraised sword? Her hair had become a little too faded and thin for her to let it down, Rapunzel-like, for him to climb up to reach her tower. It would have to be a not very impressive two-feet-high tower, and – even then – the hair would snap when he was half way up and he would fall to his death, skewered on his own sword. She would have to plait her moustache: it would then bear the weight of armies, and stretch the height of the Flatiron Building. Lines of young princes, their newly polished armor gleaming, would form to make the Jack-in-the-Beanstalk ascent to the schoolroom. They would use the window at the front of the house, facing out across Chestnut Street. She could imagine the expression on their faces when they straddled the window ledge and had a close-up view of what they had climbed up, and of the woman they had risked their lives to claim. The air would be black with princes hurtling to their doom, throwing themselves down like aristocratic lemmings – "Don't climb up, chaps! She's absolutely frightful!" – from the cliff-edge of the schoolroom window, a flock of falling wingless Icaruses thudding earthward.

No prince was on his way to rescue her, that was for sure.

She would have to organize her own escape. She'd do it through her writing, she'd do it by finding the right words, the Ali Baba "Open, Sesame!" to fling open the locked doors. Like the pupils of St. Cassian of Imola, she'd find an unsuspected power in the nib of her pen. Cassian was a Christian schoolmaster who had refused to make sacrifices to the heathen gods, so he had been handed over to his pupils, who had leaped upon him and stabbed him to death with their iron pens. All it took was a little imagination from the relevant authorities, and going to school could so easily be transformed into a positively enjoyable experience.

Stab!

Stab!

Stab!

(*STAB EVIL SINNER!*

(If it wasn't *ENORMOUS SIBYL* it was *EVIL SINNER*. There were, in fact, several candidates for stabbing, *many* candidates, a crack-of-doom line of them, and – on her good days – she felt *tireless*.)

4

She had been sleeping in new cotton sheets, and little knots of whiteness clung to her hair, her top lip, her eyebrows and eye-lashes, like unmelted flakes of snow in a cold room. Absentmindedly she began to pick at the tiny cotton balls. The hairbrush, in her other hand, was as white and ready for spinning as a flax-packed distaff. How very appropriate. When she had accu-mulated enough material she could dye the cotton with her watercolors and perfect her Lady of Shalott impersonation, weav-ing a magic web with colors gay, watching shadows of the world appear in the mirror hanging before her. English authors seemed to have spent most of the last century gazing into mirrors, more and more searchingly as it drew to its close.

Colours.

That should have been the spelling. *Colours gay.*

She tried to observe English spelling for English authors, but sometimes forgot. Best men are *moulded* out of faults. *That's* what Mariana had said. (Though – a vague memory, this, of something she might once have read – hadn't Shakespeare originally written "molded," and wasn't it the English spelling, not the American, that had changed? She wasn't sure. Attempts at consistency were beset with hazards.) She was becoming thoroughly Websterized, Websterized in her spelling by Noah Webster, and Websterized – if she wasn't careful, and relaxed her vigilance – in everything else by Dr. Wolcott Ascharm Webster, proprietor of the Webster Nervine Asylum in Poughkeepsie, as echoing and clangorously guarded as one of those mediæval castles crammed with stitch-stitch-stitching women. "Webster" meant "weaver." Spider-like, they spun their sticky webs, and tapestries – like mirrors for entrapment – hung in narrow angled corridors all around them. The web had flown out and floated wide; the mirror would crack from side to side. It would be quite relaxing to float down the river, lying robed in snowy white, freed from the oppression of reflection by the breaking of the mirror. Websters were everywhere apparent. If you weren't careful, you'd find yourself licking the back of a Webster as you prepared to apply a postage stamp.

"Hello, Ben," she'd said yesterday morning, seeing one-cent stamps on some of the letters that had just been delivered, looking at Benjamin Franklin. This was what she sometimes said when she came across any representation of the man whose name had been given to her brother. No wonder Benjamin Franklin was colored green, finding himself on the lowest-valued stamp. William Henry Harrison might be purple in the face, but at least they'd put him on the thirteen-cents stamp! That's what Benjamin Franklin was thinking. It would be worth it to be blue in the face, as long as – like James Madison – you were on a stamp worth *two dollars*. *Huh!* from Benjamin Franklin. *Two dollars!* Then she'd seen that some Websters had been pushed invasively through the mail slot as well; not Noahs, not Dr. Wolcott Ascharms, but Daniels, all in a chorus-line row on ten-cents stamps on a package, tanned and weather-beaten in brown, clearly men who were at one with nature, rarely without their hoes in their hands, and used to dealing with farm animals. Websters were pressing in upon her spelling, her brain, her *tongue*.

"Liberty *and* Union, now and forever, one and inseparable!"
That's what Daniel Webster had said. That's what Miss Hayergaal
had written on the blackboard, and the whole class had recited it in
unison. You knew he'd shouted it, because Miss Hayergaal had
written an exclamation point.

"One and inseparable!"

That's what they'd shouted, the same words at the same time,
learned by heart like arithmetical tables. They'd sounded like a
multiplicity of the Three Musketeers, all for one, and one for all,
rapiers twitching to thrust into Cardinal Richelieu. If the same
opportunity presented itself to Mrs. Albert Comstock and the
Reverend and Mrs. Goodchild — killing a cardinal must feature
high on their list of priorities — they'd be there with their umbrellas lethally positioned for action, vigorously have-at-thee-varleting.

All the needles gleamed in the little light that penetrated the
narrow windows.

Needles will make you better.

Needles will effect a cure.

Stitch-stitch-stitch.

The curse would be on her soon enough. She had no loyal knight
and true, and Mrs. Albert Comstock stretched before her like a
mountainous subcontinent. She might have spent the whole of yesterday afternoon with the dreadful woman, but that did not grant
her immunity from future visitations.

(This last word, with its implications of suffering and affliction,
was a good choice of noun. Plagues made visitations. She also
thought that Mrs. Albert Comstock's occasional description of her
"At Homes" as "gatherings" was — for her — eerily prescient.
Gatherings were suppurating swellings, boils on the point of bursting. The word described 5 Hampshire Square with forensic
exactness, captured that unforgettable atmosphere of hedonistic
jollity.)

At least she hadn't also spent the whole evening with her as Ben
had — afternoon *and* evening with Mrs. Albert Comstock: his per-
ilous voyagings on the oceans of the world must hold few fears for

him after this — hauled along to the theatre as a member of her party. Her brave seafaring brother!

As she picked out the cotton with her right hand, she stored the harvest in her cupped left hand, beside the hairbrush handle, humming to herself.

> "I wish I was in de land ob cotton,
> Old time dar am not forgotten;
> Look away, look away, look away, Dixie land!
> In Dixie whar I was born in,
> Early on one frosty mornin'. . ."

With her ready grasp of modern history, Mrs. Albert Comstock had been heard to remark what a pity it was that the Civil War had ended slavery, as the darkies — she used this word (at least, in public) instead of "niggers" to demonstrate her daringly liberal views for the benefit of Mrs. William Boemer — had been having such a good time on the plantations. She visualized the plantations as rather like well-tended orchards: regular sun-dappled rows of identically shaped trees, ripe red fruit, apples, cherries, glowing in the soft, fresh greenery, stretching neatly away to the horizon, a darkie Paradise before the Fall as they — laughing for sheer delight — gathered clumps of cotton that were as clean and white as washing laid out to dry. In the fall the leaves would turn red and gold, and shrivel, become thin and papery and blow away, leaving the branches bare. There would be music at dusk as the trees darkened, and big white grins — they were like thoughtless, carefree children — would gleam like the fruit that had once been there in the daytime as they sang and danced in their joy.

> "Some folks like to sigh,
> Some folks do, some folks do;
> Some folks long to die,
> But that's not me nor you . . ."

They were as happy as the day was long, and the day was long in Dixie.

> ". . . Away, away, away down south in Dixie!
> Away, away, away down south in Dixie! . . ."

"What a shame . . . What a shame . . ."

Regular visitors were already beginning to nod their heads in agreement. Others would sense an announcement coming on. Mrs. Albert Comstock tended to announce something rather than merely state it; it was surely a mere oversight that she had failed to install liveried trumpeters in her household, all lined up tidily in a neat line, ready, at a moment's notice, to produce a fanfare before her every utterance.

(Deep breaths, inflated cheeks, puckered-up lips.)

Tarantara!

"I believe I'm correct in saying that it's not as cold today as it was yesterday."

(Breathe, inflate, pucker.)

Tarantara!

"I don't like Mrs. Italiaander's new hat."

(Breathe, inflate, pucker.)

Tarantara!

"What a shame that the war spoiled it all."

She nodded to herself at the picture she had created in her mind, the lost prelapsarian wonderland.

"What a shame . . ."

Jewelry rattled as heads nodded in polite — or enthusiastic — agreement, earrings swaying, feathers vibrating.

Sometimes Alice wasn't sure whether what was being regretted was the loss of Dixie as a place of perpetual darkie jollity, or the appearance of more and more darkie faces on the streets of New York. Mrs. Albert Comstock — Alice was convinced — was under the impression that minstrel shows were performed by genuine darkies, and not by white men with burned cork on their faces, and this had colored – how apt a word could be – her picture of them. She had once met Booker T. Washington at Mrs. William Boemer's in Gramercy Park, and – naturally – assumed that he was being introduced to her, and not she to him. She was equal to the occasion. She knew how to speak to such people. "Have you been black for long?" she asked him chattily, in that informal way she had with the lower orders. She prided herself on her ability to put people at their ease. It was a gift granted to the naturally aristocratic. She later confided to Mrs. Goodchild that Booker T. Washington was not as authentic-looking as some of the other darkies she had seen. He wasn't *very* black, not really black enough to be totally convincing, and there had been – she'd no doubt remarked, suspiciously – a distinct lack of tambourines and bones. (By the by, wasn't it rather – er – presumptuous of him to call himself "Washington"?)

She saw what her mind wanted her to see, and she saw little else. She would have interrupted a performance of *Othello* to request – with her steely glacial smile (her requests were more in the line of an order) – a rendition of "In the Evening by the Moonlight," with Othello playing the banjo, and Iago and Desdemona enthusiastically grinning as they cakewalked.

"In de ebening by de moonlight, you could hear us darkies
      singing . . ."

– Othello sang –

". . . In de ebening by de moonlight, you could hear de
      banjo ringing.
How de old folks would enjoy it . . ."

("Put out de light, and den put out de light," Mrs. Albert Comstock's Othello would soliloquize as – well, what did you expect? – he prepared to strangle Desdemona. "I hab done de state some service" – a likely story! – he would claim, later, when his

31

crime was discovered. All those nasty black fingerprints on Desdemona's nice white nightie!)

There came that deep sigh again.

"What a shame . . . What a shame . . ."

Had she sometimes wondered where they all disappeared to after each minstrel show? Back to Dixie, perhaps, unable to bear missing all the fun?

On her expeditions into New York City Mrs. Albert Comstock counted the number of black faces she saw in the street, and reported back to her daughter Myrtle.

(There were certain things that de old folks did not enjoy much at all.)

"Twenty-seven today," she'd announce as she arrived back home: the day's total would be the first words she spoke, as if she were giving a constantly changing password in order to achieve entrance.

"Only nine today!"

This could clearly be regarded as one of the better days: the lower the score, the more pleasing the result. Mrs. Albert Comstock was not biased. Negroes, Jews, Roman Catholics, foreigners (the rest of the world, most of the United States, whole neighborhoods in New York City, everywhere, really, that was not 5 Hampshire Square), the poor: she disliked them all equally.

5

The crop from her upper lip mounted: several sacksful here, surely.

"I have a son," their father had said, laughing humorlessly (Bertha Rochester to the life; no, that was unfair: she understood and pitied Bertha Rochester), sneering, "who is prettier than any of my daughters."

Ben — who had been about ten at the time (she'd have been twenty: she was the eldest of the three sisters) — had blushed at the words, a deep, painful blush. She wasn't sure whether Papa had said this to hurt her or to hurt Ben — he enjoyed hurting both of them, it was one of his more important hobbies — but Ben had shown the hurt more. It was strange — unsettling — to see so young a child blushing, as if blushing — by all the rules of normality — came later, one of the blood-led manifestations of maturity, and a normal child should be incapable of blushing. There had been something disturbingly knowing about a blush, a knowledge that should not have been possessed. "Papa! Papa!" Allegra had protested at his comment, not so much outraged for Ben's sake, but outraged that her superior prettiness had not been acknowledged. Edith had said nothing, and *she* — as usual — had said nothing. She tended to let things build up inside her.

Alice was sure that Maggie Tulliver and Jo March (dark-haired, dark-complexioned, both, other heroines she had adored as a child) possessed moustaches: George Eliot and Louisa M. Alcott had somehow forgotten to mention them. At the end of the Wilkie Collins novel, Marian Halcombe was not — unlike Laura, Lady Glyde — safe and protected in the arms of a husband. She was the plain one who looked on and smiled as her friend married the hero, the honorary maiden aunt of the children of the marriage.

She had a moustache of her own: what need had she of a man?

"An old maid, that's what I'm to be. A literary spinster, with a pen for a spouse, a family of stories for children, and twenty years hence a morsel of fame, perhaps." That's what Jo March had said, and Alice had always regarded this as an admirable ambition. She had been born in 1868, the year in which the first part of *Little Women* had been published, and that was what Papa had called her for a time, for a short time: "My Little Woman." She had, briefly, modeled herself on Jo — rather halfheartedly saying "Christopher Columbus!" once or twice — though she had never been able to bring herself to address Mama as "Marmee." Even Jo had ended up as a wife and mother, a Laura, Lady Glyde, and not a Marian. If it had not been quite like Dorothea Brooke marrying Mr. Casaubon in *Middlemarch*, Jo March accepting Mr. Bhaer was very much like

Lucy Snowe accepting Monsieur Emmanuel in *Villette*, an equal betrayal. (No Rochesters, they.)

There was no Mr. Bhaer in prospect for Alice – a considerable relief: his accent made him sound worryingly like Mrs. Webster, loyal helpmeet of Dr. Wolcott Ascharm Webster – so perhaps she might concentrate on the possibilities of becoming (she would be more single-minded than Jo March had ever been) "a literary spinster." To be a poet, to be a writer, she needed two things: an appropriate name, and a beard, so that – whatever the qualities of the poetry – her name would at least *sound* right, and her face *look* right. Alice Pinkerton possessed neither the name – the syllables fell sadly short – nor the beard for success. She thought of the names of some of the poets in the poetry book – *An American Anthology* – that Miss Ericsson had given her for her thirty-third birthday in 1901: St. John Honeywood, Fitz-Greene Halleck, Francis Orrery Ticknor, Mirabeau Bonaparte Lamar . . .

(Miss Ericsson stood diffidently in front of her, with *An American Anthology* – the size, weight, and color of two bricks side by side – pressed against her bosom. It was one of the things that women were supposed to do with poetry books. The sunlight caught the gold laurel wreath embossed on its front cover, and Alice expected to see a small, quivering reflection floating on the ceiling, like light from water, or the curved glass face of a pocket-watch. She was holding it out toward Alice, smiling rather shyly.)

She could not recollect a single line that any of these poets had written, but their names (curious how minor talents – she excluded Mrs. Browning from the observation – insisted on having three names) had a music, a – well, *poetry*, she supposed – that in itself inspired confidence. She had no doubt that all four would sport magnificent beards, clinching proof of their poetic credentials. "Francis Orrery Ticknor!" she had chanted, as she spun herself around the pillars in the schoolroom, as if enraptured by the magical harmoniousness of the name. "Francis Orrery Ticknor!" Thirty-three years old, and cavorting, chanting! (For some reason, that *thirty-three* had sounded like a knell of doom.) They may have been wrong about the attic, but perhaps they had a point about the madness. Once she started on Mirabeau Bonaparte Lamar, there'd be no holding her.

There was an awe-inspiring display of beards (all male, only a male could become one of The Bearded Ones: no bewhiskered female had smuggled herself in front of the camera) in the photograph opposite the title page. Many of the poems in the book – too many of them, those written on subjects such as America, Freedom, or Slaves – made her think of some of the groups of statuary silhouetted across the roofs of buildings in the business districts of the city, awkwardly posed, symbolically gesturing. Surprisingly – she had searched assiduously through the volume – there were no poems in praise of beards, though Helen Keller and Shakespeare (with one beard between them) had inspired several eulogies.

She thought she had found a reference in the poetry of William Cullen Bryant, than whom no one could be more appropriate: his beard was the size of Birnam Wood, a monstrosity on a scale epic enough to inspire terror in Dunsinane, panic-stricken flights, mass pallings in resolution. *Macbeth* – it may have been why the image came to mind – was a play populated almost entirely by beards; even most of the women had them. The witches flourished theirs at Banquo and thoroughly confused him ("You should be women": these were pre-Marian Halcombe days), and Lady Macbeth clearly hankered after one of her very own. "Unsex me here," she'd boomed in her deepest voice, keen to get the sprouting started. She wasn't too fussed about being top-full of direst cruelty, about having the access and passage to remorse stopped up, or about having the spirits that tend on mortal thought come to her woman's breasts and take her milk for gall (a passage mysteriously missing from the edition of Shakespeare used at Miss Pearsall's School for Girls). All that she really wanted was the beard. The only beard-free inhabitants of the play – struck down by the beardie murderers – appeared to be Lady Macduff and her son, though this child certainly displayed a precocious beardsomeness in his manner.

When she looked at the words more closely — *In these peaceful shades — peaceful, unpruned, immeasurably old* — they turned out to be describing not a beard but an untracked forest, one of those trackless silences in which Chingachgook and Hawkeye still wandered, looking for signs, listening for danger, the books that Ben had loved as a child.

There was only one thing for it: she clearly needed to develop her moustache — it was a promising beginning — in order to increase her chances of achieving success as a writer, compensate for the paucity of syllables in her name by sprouting a colossal growth of facial hair. At least she chose to write in prose and not in verse. Perhaps this afforded some small possibility of publication, despite her lack of the necessary qualifications. Some women novelists were widely acknowledged to be — er — quite good, really, all things considered.

To dream of a beard on a woman, foretells unpleasant associations and lingering illness.

6

Charlotte had once tried to think of the name of the composer of a particular piece of music. She bent over, banging her forehead against one of the brass candlesticks projecting from the upper frame of the piano, lost in the agonies of thought. She was in a permanent state of near-impalement, and had scars on her forehead the way boys had them on their knees and elbows.

"Brahms . . .?" she muttered doubtfully. "Bizet . . .? B . . .?"

She wavered for a moment, seemingly on the point of considering Byron or Botticelli as possibilities, before adding, "Tchaikowsky?" Her knowledge of different composers and their styles was not very extensive, though her knowledge of Gilbert and Sullivan was second to no one's. At last, inspiration had dawned upon her.

"You know whom I mean," she'd said, challengingly. (*Whom.*

Charlotte was a stickler for grammatical correctness.) "*One of those Bearded Ones!*"

They had developed their own gesture whenever they wished to make a discreet reference to The Bearded Ones, the gesture a man made when he was trying to decide whether or not he was in need of a shave, the insides of the fingers and thumb of their right hands grasping the chin and pulling downward, feeling for bristles. As the beards grew, so did the gestures, and they began to use both hands, making a descending down-down-down gesture from the sides of their faces as far as they could reach to encompass the immensity of the outgrowths. At the bottom, they moved their hands outward and then together, and it looked as if they were making some kind of scooping, gathering movement, drawing something – a large puppy, a tentative tottering toddler experimentally attempting its first steps – protectively in toward them. Alice sometimes wondered if this gesture meant something in the language of the deaf – she kept forgetting to ask Rosobell about this, years later – and was always careful to use it when no one else was looking in her direction. It was a secret gesture.

By then, the phrase "The Bearded Ones" had come to mean far more than just men with beards.

"Speak with respect and honour
Both of The Beard and The Beard's owner."

They'd chant Samuel Butler's words in unison – they'd added the capital letters in the second line as a sign of their deferential esteem – essaying a tone of humble supplication as they made their worshipful Masonic movements.

She had made a precocious attempt to enter the very heartland of The Bearded Ones. It was during her Jo March period, when she had insisted – as a small girl – upon being taken to Grandpapa Brouwer's office for the first time. Alice had been oppressed with the thought that Longfellow Park was a place of women during the day, a place of pale-clad figures strolling irresolutely, without purpose, dawdling, drifting from place to place, gazing into or (more often) out of windows, waiting for their men to return to them from the world outside, like the dunce-capped mediæval women peering shortsightedly from battlements. This was in the days when New York City was a far distant place, before it expanded northward and began to engulf them.

"The day is dreary, / He cometh not," they chorused — the women of the olden times often had to speak in chorus, as if an individual voice was too faint to be heard — "I am aweary, aweary . . ."

(". . . / I would that I were dead!")

Then she had read the chapter almost at the very end of the second part of *Little Women* — "Under the Umbrella" — in which Jo had gone out into the part of the city where women did not belong, the world exclusively inhabited by men. It came shortly after Jo's declaration that she was to be a literary spinster, and she had gone into this unknown — oh, fickle, unreliable, malleable, untrustworthy Jo! — to walk with Mr. Bhaer, with whom she had fallen in love. She addressed him as "Sir," as "Mr. Bhaer," like another Jane Eyre, another Emma Woodhouse, formal with the man she knew she wanted to love her. Jo had wandered far from the dry-goods stores — the area in which the women belonged — and into the area where the gentlemen most do congregate, the area of counting-houses, banks, and wholesale warerooms, and Alice had been seized with the desire to do the same, and at a far younger age than Jo March. In New York it would be on a much larger scale than anything in Jo March's New England town, with not one area but many, street after street after street of congregating gentlemen, beards abristle, shouting loudly, gesticulating. She would do it by going to see Grandpapa's business, the Occidental & Eastern Shipping Company, on South Street. This was where Papa worked, but she always thought of it as being Grandpapa's office, not Papa's, and it was because of Grandpapa (as well as Jo March) that she had wanted to see the office, not because of Papa.

"Will you take me, Grandpapa? Will you take me?" and Grandpapa – of course – had taken her into work for the day. (She had shamelessly employed all Allegra's arts of wide-eyed flirtatiousness.)

She wanted to examine engineering instruments in one window and samples of wool in another with most unfeminine interest; she wanted to tumble over barrels, and be half smothered by descending bales; she wanted to be hustled unceremoniously by busy men, who would ask – out loud – "How the deuce did she get here?" (This last part particularly appealed.)

She had her reply all ready.

"My Grandpapa brought me!"

Pert and self-possessed, that's how she'd be.

"And *who* are you?" That's what she should say next, slightly challenging, far stronger than love-changed Jo, weakened and made foolish, no longer – *sigh!* – the woman she had once been.

She stood in Grandpapa's office with Lumpety, her despised doll – they thought she loved it – clutched under one arm. It was not very long afterward that she had disemboweled Lumpety, inspired by the stained glass window in All Saints' Church depicting the martyrdom of St. Erasmus. Most satisfactory.

"This is your great-grandpapa," Grandpapa had said, indicating the bearded – of course – figure in the huge dark oil painting on the wall of his office, a fearsome-faced unjolliest of Santa Clauses.

"This is my desk," Grandpapa had said, demonstrating how it worked by tugging the roll-top up and down, the inner drawers and compartments whitened by countless slips of paper, their loose ends flapping in the draft.

"This is my spittoon," Grandpapa had said, but he had not – rather disappointingly – demonstrated it in action.

(*Hacht-pertong!*)

There were maps covered in red on the walls, though the red was coloring not the land but the seas, showing the routes of the Occidental & Eastern Shipping Company's steamships, as if this was the element he controlled. "He's in his element," she thought –

pleased with such an exact use of the phrase – as he ran his fingers across the Pacific Ocean with practiced ease, spanning the globe with a sweep of his hand. It was like being in the headquarters of some great general, the place where he planned his battles and conquests. "We shall attack *here*!" he would say, his finger decisively stabbing in an X-marks-the-spot sort of gesture at the place he had chosen.

The streets had been strangely dark, dark with the clothes of the men and youths who were everywhere, dark with the shadows from the new high buildings blocking out the sun. The only women were women made out of wood, women made out of stone, not like objects of veneration, but like sacrifices. They were mythical figures, symbolic groupings, veiled and draperied allegories, lining the edges of the roofs and occupying niches, poised in the postures of those about to jump to their deaths. Sailing ships lined the East River, jammed in so closely that it was as if they were permanent structures, and would never leave, fluttering with so many flags that they seemed to be commemorating some special day of celebration. Their bowsprits projected right across the street, carriages drove past beneath them, and she looked down on them from Grandpapa's high window at the top of the building. There were men in the air above the center of the street at her eye level, working in the rigging above the horses and the laden wagons, the piled barrels, the great sound of shouting. She felt that she could reach across and touch them. After the acrobats, there would be elephants.

She had come across the ships suddenly.

She had been walking hand in hand with Grandpapa beneath the curve of the elevated railroad in Coenties Slip, and there was the thunder of a steam train rattling around overhead, its tall chimney like that of a train out in the West, its whistle shrieking out across the prairies, startling the great herds of buffalo. Whoever had later designed the roller coaster at Luna Park must have often strolled around there, finding his inspiration in the juddering sway of the carriages, the lurching curves, the held-in screams of the helplessly thrown-about passengers. There were shanty-like booths that seemed to belong beneath a Coney Island ride — she half expected the hiss and smoke of fairground lighting, the crack of rifles at shooting-galleries — and there were boxes under tarpaulins as if in an open-air warehouse, with high-sided horse-drawn wagons drawn up beside them, spilling out straw on to the cobble-stones. There was a transient, temporary air about everything — this fair was a traveling fair about to move on elsewhere — and men in dark suits strolled about, lounged, leaned and propped themselves up. No one said, "How the deuce did she get here?" No one appeared even to notice her, as she stared about, beneath their eye level.

On South Street, as they approached Grandpapa's office, she found herself walking beneath the beautifully carved figureheads as they jutted out across the sidewalk between the gas-lamps. The elaborately painted women were lapped by looped chains, and bore the names of goddesses and virtues. He pointed them out to her, and told her their names, just as he told her the names of the Occidental & Eastern Shipping Company vessels in the photographs in his office.

"That one's *Pandora* . . ."

Tap, tap on the glass.

"That one's *Persephone* . . ."

Tap, tap.

"That one's *Eurydice* . . ."

Tap, tap.

His fingerprints left clouded whorls upon the surface of the glass, and it was as if the ships were becalmed in a rapidly descending mist, their sails drooping. Through the mist, through the snow, the not-yet-ancient Mariner's ship sailed, and it grew wondrous cold. And ice, mast-high, came floating by, as green as emerald. She had just been reading the poem.

"That one's *Psyche* . . ."

The albatross, its wings creaking as ponderously as the timbers of a fully rigged sailing-ship, drew down close to the mist-enveloped vessel.

. . . In mist or cloud, on mast or shroud,
It perched for vespers nine . . .

The worshipers gathered on the deck by the light of the evening star, their heads bowed, their faces covered, the silent reaches of the ice all around. Thick snow fell upon them, icicles hung from the rigging, and they held out neatly shaped pieces of food between their thumbs and index fingers as if about to administer communion.

Hide thy face from my sins, and blot out all mine iniquities.

This was what they repeated in chorus, their voices muffled.

One side of the muddy street was all constructed of wood and taut rope, like the elaborate networks of wires – for electricity, for telephone and telegraph – that would later span the lower streets of the city; the other side of the street was of brick and stone, but with all the canvas apparent everywhere else it might as well have been painted scenery. All the figures in the crowded street – all the *living* figures – (Jo March had been perfectly correct) were congregating men, though not all of them were gentlemen. She saw it all, like something beneath glass, like a tiny detailed model, or a photograph, the nearer figures standing stiff and posed, their shadows hard-edged in the bright sunshine, so that they would appear sharp and focused; the further figures ghost images, blurred and half-formed, mistily caught against the walls and streets behind and beneath them, more solid than they were. Everywhere there were wooden carts, pulled by hand or by horses, capstans, thick coiled ropes, piles of merchandise, a smell like that of new sacks, a sewery whiff from the dark water, what Mrs. Goodchild would describe as "a not very polite sort of smell." Such smells had been all around her (she was fearless in her quest) – human waste, horses' (you had to watch where you stepped) – though it had not been a high summer's day. It would have been a distinctly *high* summer's day. Perhaps the beards were designed to be utilized as filters when it became unusually – ahem – unpleasant, a Darwinian evolution to protect the species, the *male* species. Thus equipped, men could survive the worst that the sense of smell could throw at them. Clutching Grandpapa's hand, she leaned out to look down into the East River. She had recently read about the holy River Ganges in India, and had the thought that she might see bodies floating past beneath her and heading out to sea, bobbing against each other like Halloween apples, all facing upward and displaying their still, sad faces. What she saw in the windows across the street were not window displays of the sort she had been used to, but goods piled up as if in a warehouse, or the cargo hold of a ship, and all the goods were those that would be needed on board.

There was *Cordage* painted across the brickwork above the windows, *Chandler, Sail Makers* — and there was *Occidental & Eastern Shipping Company.* There was an area of different-colored stone in front of the entrance to Grandpapa's office, like ballast from the hold of a cargo vessel used to pave it after a long voyage. It was greenish, and cold-looking, ice from around the not-yet-ancient Mariner's ship transported there, crashing down on deck from high above. She bent down and touched it when Grandpapa was not looking. It *did* feel cold, slightly, and as smooth as something polished. She had a sense of somewhere foreign and far away, a land elsewhere, a stateless visitor resting her hand upon the floor in the dim interior of some embassy. Outside, the polished brass plate on the wall glinted dully. This, also, would feel cold, slightly.

> *. . . Whiles all the night through fog-smoke white,*
> *Glimmered the white Moon-shine . . .*

That was the expression that Papa used when she thought out ideas like this.

Moonshine.

He said the same thing, his fingers making dismissive take-them-away gestures, if he came across any of her ideas for stories, any of her scribbled beginnings. She usually hid them away now, and no longer left them — inviting favorable comment — wherever she had been sitting in the house.

Moonshine!

Starveling the tailor played Moonshine in the play at the end of *A Midsummer Night's Dream*. It should have been Snug the joiner. A familiar feeling of rebelliousness was coming across her. Snug would have had access to tools, to potential weapons – saws, hammers – far more powerful than Starveling's needles and thread. She would have fought back, sawing and hammering with an inspired creative frenzy, though demolishing rather than creating. She'd see Papa, and then she'd saw Papa. *See-saw, Margery Daw, Alice shall be a new master.* Here was another of the Happy Families bursting out of hiding to commit slaughter, loitering in a cupboard all day, waiting for the dark. She'd be Mr. Chip, the Carpenter, kneeling on Papa with her right knee, pushing well in as she sawed away, with her bottom lip protruding in concentration with the air of someone enthusiastically constructing a coffin. She'd saw Papa, and then she'd hammer Papa. She'd be Mrs. Chip, the Carpenter's Wife, lashing out with a hammer that was the size of her whole body. She'd – *Tap! Tap! Tap!* – her back arched well back to get in the full arc of hammering, drive home the nails in the coffin-lid, at long last completing the construction of a favorite piece of furniture. There'd be plenty of chips off the old block, no doubt about that. There wouldn't be much *left* of the block when she'd finished.

Well shone, Moon!
Well sawn, Mr. Chip!
Well destroyed, Snug!
Well hammered, Mrs. Chip!
Moonshine!

She straightened up, but still had a sensation of coldness when she walked into the dark interior of the Occidental & Eastern Shipping Company. It did not just permeate her from her fingers; it crept up through the soles of her feet, also.

Ice.
Mast-high.
As green as emerald.

Outside there was a painted board above the first-floor

windows — oddly like a misplaced family heirloom hung above the chimney piece in some vast baronial hall — depicting a steamship plowing confidently through the sea, white foam boiling away to illustrate its effortless speed. And, on the ledge outside Grandpapa's office on the third story, there were the figures of the waiting women gazing out to sea.

All the figures on the ledge were from Greek or Roman mythology, just as the sailing ships in the early years of Grandpapa's business — the years of the child-hating Santa Claus — had borne the names of women from classical mythology. She had imagined the ships' figureheads carved in marble, cool and white and aloof above the spray, like blind-eyed busts in a Roman museum. Standing at Grandpapa's office window, seeing the backs of the stone figures, she had (it seemed thematically appropriate) imagined the Dibbo Daughters lined up on the ledge and about to jump.

"Jump!" she should be yelling encouragingly from below through cupped hands. "Jump!"

She had recently quarreled bitterly with Euterpe Dibbo, and was in vengeful mood. The first four of the Daughters had appeared by this date, the promising start of Daddy Dibbo's idiotic and doomed attempt to produce (with a little incidental assistance from his wife) a complete set of nine daughters, and name them after the Greek muses. It was strange what the writing of overambitious poetry could do to you. Polyhymnia, Terpsichore, and Urania lined up on the ledge next to a still-scowling Euterpe. The muse of music and lyric poetry (and flute playing)! Any sign of a flute, and she'd snap it in half with a disgruntled grunt and stab you with it, the mood she was in.

"Jump! Go on, jump!"

She demonstrated her support to fillip their confidence a little. It was the sort of person she was.

If they leaped too far out, they'd become entangled in the rigging of the nearest ship, and there they'd dangle — boing-boinging up and down, sourly complaining in mid-boing — like the myth of Arachne gone all too horribly wrong.

She didn't know the names of all the women depicted in the statues, some of them seated, some of them standing, all of them gazing out in the direction of the sea, shielding their eyes to see better. Perhaps some of them did not have names. Penelope – now there was a woman who knew about tapestries – was certainly there, searching for a first glimpse of Ulysses returning home after his twenty years of wandering. Next to her was Iphigenia. Perhaps she was hoping to see Achilles. Her father – Agamemnon – sent her to Aulis, pretending that she was to be married to Achilles there, but she was really sent as a sacrifice – Diana had insisted – so that the Greek fleet would receive a favorable wind and could sail to Troy to recover Helen. Her father had led her not to her bridegroom but to her death. She would have known what was going to happen to her, when they dressed her as a sacrificial victim, not a bride.

"I was cut off from hope in that sad place . . ."

– that was what she was saying –

". . . Which yet to name my spirit loathes and fears:
My father held his hand upon his face;
    I, blinded with tears,

"Still strove to speak: my voice was thick with sighs
    As in a dream. Dimly I could descry
The stern black-bearded kings with wolvish eyes,
    Waiting to see me die . . ."

You just knew that The Bearded Ones would have been there. It was the sort of thing they'd have hated to miss.

Papa had not been there on that day – it had been just her and Grandpapa – and she had peeped into Papa's empty office, feeling as she did when she peeped into his study at home, feeling that she ought not to be there, seeing a place without him and realizing that such a thing was possible. Without him, the place should not exist.

It was dark in the office, a feeling of blinds drawn down in mourning, the views from the window partially obscured by the statues, the backs of the women facing away from him, and it smelled of him, the smell of a tobacco-smoke impregnated beard, as if he were announcing his hidden presence.

I am here in the room.

Can you find out whereabouts I am?

I shall leap out.

I shall pounce.

There were maps in his office, also, as there were in Grandpapa's, but the maps in his office were of the world as it no longer was, the world as it had been before the Civil War (*Civil!*), the world as he wished it to be once more. Papa lived in a time of his own creating, where even the clock — *tick-tock* went the wall-clock ponderously, as big as a clock at a railroad station — moved at a pace he dictated. He would tick the time when it was allowed to tick-tock. Without his say-so, the hands of the clock would cease to move, the pages of the calendar would not be ripped away, and there would be an unbroken shaded silence in which nothing moved. Some strangers were named Mr. Robertson or Mr. Faulconbridge or "the man at number seventy-three;" some strangers were named Papa.

Iphigenia had been the name of one of the earliest of the wooden sailing ships of the Occidental & Eastern Shipping Company, and the figurehead of the ship was in Grandpapa and Grandmama's garden. There was what Grandpapa called his "quarterdeck" at the back of their house, and here — at the end of a long, narrowing wooden piazza — was the figurehead, with the ship's wheel mounted in front of it. She would lie on the lawn beneath it, looking up at the calm, sad, downcast face surrounded by drifting clouds, imagining that she was floating in the air beneath the rooftop sculptures of the office, trying to induce a feeling of weightlessness, of vertigo, rather like the way in which she tried to lose her sense of direction by turning round in the darkness beneath her bedclothes. Sometimes she lay on top of the figurehead on the warm, smooth wood, in the afternoon summer sun, looking down through half-closed eyes at the grass beneath her, trying to see the waves beneath, trying to feel the undulation of the ship's movements, herself moving away from the place where she was. She could hear the wind in the branches of the trees, the snapping of the flag on the flagpole. It was the sound of the sea nearby, beyond the bottom of the garden.

7

The bearded faces were blurred. The photograph of the bearded poets in *An American Anthology* was covered by a protective sheet of tissue paper, like the illustrations in her Bible, and The Bearded Ones peered through, a caravan of Old Testament prophets stranded in a sudden desert sandstorm.

(What *was* the collective noun for prophets? A clairvoyance? A prognostication?)

They hovered in the air above her, a mirage in the desert air, far from the oasis, clouds covering the sun. The air became cooler, chillier, and a cold current rippled through the room like wind across a cornfield, rustling the curtains.

Only Edgar Allan Poe and Walt Whitman looked directly into the camera. Henry Wadsworth Longfellow, William Cullen Bryant, and Oliver Wendell Holmes were all photographed in profile, giving them the appearance of suspects posed by a police photographer: *THIS POET IS WANTED!* Bryant and Holmes, like shortsighted duelists, stared into each other's eyes almost nose to nose. They couldn't possibly miss at this range. The remaining three poets – John Greenleaf Whittier, James Russell Lowell, and Sidney Lanier – favored the kind of expression employed by men faced by someone whom they did not wish to acknowledge, eyes focused evasively to one side, gazing intensely into the middle distance, but seeing nothing. It was the expression people were increasingly starting to assume when they were being photographed, pretending that the camera was not there, and had caught them unaware. Whitman – clearly no gentleman – was wearing a hat, and no necktie, but this was to be expected of a man who matily abbreviated his name to Walt, insisting upon familiarity. Billy Bryant? Olly Holmes? Sid Lanier? Not even the biggest of beards could possibly compensate for such summarily clipped forenames. It would compromise the integrity of the very poetry, threaten the meter, imperil the rhymes.

Seeing these beards fluffily flocked together, like an illustration for *Far from the Madding Crowd* – Gabriel Oak, you felt, was just out of sight, grasping his crook like a Good Shepherd (odd to link crooks with goodness) – you could understand why altocumulus clouds were sometimes described as sheep clouds. They crowded the sky with baa-baa bossiness, three bags full with self-importance. Black sheep brought storms.

Beards and three names were not compulsory for composers, as they were for poets. Most of the greatest of composers – Beethoven, Mozart, Handel, the list could be extended almost indefinitely – seemed to thrive frugally with one name and no beard, though there were those who, poet-like, were possessed of enormous beards, especially if they came from Russia. It must have been because of the severe winters of their homeland, but the great Russian composers – like the great Russian novelists – seemed to have thick beards like detachable accessories hanging down over the front of their fur coats in an attempt to keep warm. The novelists wore them proudly, like Siberian sporrans, in Highland homage to Sir Walter Scott, their distinguished predecessor in their chosen profession. Some of their beards were so huge that they gave the impression that packs of starving wolves – drawn out from deep within the mystical Russian forests – were hurling themselves at their throats.

Perhaps, like St. Wilgefortis, she should pray for a miraculous beard. Unlike St. Wilgefortis, she did not need a miraculous hairy outgrowth in order to repel the unwanted attentions of men. She seemed to manage this effortlessly with no help whatsoever from God. It was one of the many gifts she possessed.

All Saints' Church contained some appalling sights (not least the Goodchilds and the Griswolds: some churches featured gargoyles, All Saints' had the Goodchilds and the Griswolds), but the stained glass windows took some beating. St. Wilgefortis – with a beard like a large hairy apron she had inadvertently tied around herself in the wrong position prior to washing the china – was a mere commonplace sight, someone you would pass in the street without a second glance, compared with some of the other saints depicted: St. Erasmus, St. Pharaildis, St. Bartholomew, St. Agatha . . .

The things that were happening to them! The things they were pictured doing!

There was such richness from which to choose, and she had spent most of her Sundays studying them. This had helped to block out the voice of Dr. Vaniah Odom, and then – in more recent years – the Reverend Goodchild's voice.

The artist who worked on them had been a Bearded One with another three-ring circus of a name (they appeared to be compulsory, a different act in each ring – bespangled elephants trumpeting, high-wire acts spinning in mid-air, plumed horses bowing their heads – too much action for the eyes to take in all at once): Elphinstone Dalhousie Barton (the surname did not really live up to the two preceding names, and rather weakened the effect), the father of Mrs. Alexander Diddecott. Elphinstone Dalhousie Barton not only took the name of the church all too literally (trying his utmost to include – with pedantic correctness – a representation of every possible known saint), but proved to be equally literal-minded in his depiction of their symbols and their instruments of martyrdom. He reserved the largest expanses of glass for the saints who had met the goriest ends, and depicted their spectacular demises with an unflinching detail that would not have been out of place in one of the more advanced medical textbooks. They made the most luridly illustrated edition of Foxe's *Book of Martyrs* seem tame and tentative. Sunday after Sunday she had examined them with a sprightly interest, effortlessly replacing the face of her chosen saint with the face of Dr. Vaniah Odom or the Reverend Goodchild, lingering over the depiction of his disemboweling, his decapitation, his death by swords, by arrows, by axes, by lions. It was an impressive illustration of the consolation that could be found in art.

Soon – for the greater glory of Goodchild – the congregation would be moving to a new church, and today would be the last service in the original All Saints'. She would miss the bizarre sights in the windows of the old church.

"A special service," was the way that the Reverend Goodchild had described today's planned events, "a very *special* service," and something in the way he had stressed "special" (evil cackling held at bay, one felt, solely by the exercise of strict self-control) seemed to suggest – at the very least – that human sacrifice might be involved. She wouldn't put it past him. She would probably be the chosen victim, selected like some unfortunate cabin boy clutching the crumpled *X*-marked piece of paper, another black spot with an implacable summons, as the starving shipwrecked survivors of the crew edged salivatingly closer in the overcrowded boat. Ah well, selection as a scapegoat would make a morning in All Saints' more interesting than usual. She certainly possessed the whiskers for the part, William Holman Hunt's painting startlingly given shape. She would be a living reenactment of one of the more obscure martyrdoms in the stained glass windows, like a tiny extract from a mystery play in mediæval England. She liked to see the positive side of things.

"There was a guzzling Jack and a gorging Jimmy . . ."

– she hummed to herself –

". . . There was a guzzling Jack and a gorging Jimmy,
And the third he was little Billee,
And the third he was little Billee . . ."

The first mate and the – how appropriate! – ship's cook closed in on the cabin boy, smiling with unconvincing friendliness, trying not to show their teeth too much, their fingers starting to edge into the pockets where they'd secreted their knives and forks, conveniently close to hand. With the very tips of their fingers they discreetly eased up the flaps, their smiles broadening, gorging Jimmy exerting his every power of gorgeousness. Little Billee — looking deeply suspicious — eyed their approach unenthusiastically, bracing himself to repulse their advances, clenching his fists and scowling. His mother had warned him about this sort of thing.

Many of the windows had already been removed in preparation for the demolition of the church, and were piled in packing cases along the aisles; saints prepared for shipping like some esoteric export line. For the past few weeks members of the congregation had had to contend with the hazards of ill-stacked saints as they made their way to their pews, barking their shins, catching their elbows. Workmen — there was another big top, the pale crowded faces staring upward, hands pointing — would soon swing across to saw at the wooden angels in the roof, and they would come crashing down to earth like a scene from *Paradise Lost* as the church fell, shooting stars plunging downward.

Make a wish! Make a wish!

Years ago, as a little girl, she had once seen angels being jerkily hauled up into the air in a department store (had it been A. T. Stewart's?) one morning about a month before Christmas. It was a scene that ought not to have been visible during shopping hours, and — when she had suddenly come across it, holding her mama's hand — it had been like seeing behind the scenery, pulling aside the striped front of the booth at a Punch and Judy show, or (it had occurred to her more recently, as she read *The Wonderful Wizard of Oz* to her niece Mildred) tipping over the screen to reveal Oz, the Great and Terrible, to be a little old man with a bald head. There had been a rotunda rising the full height of the building — four or five stories — to a glass roof, and it was toward this glass, darkly silhouetted against the gray November light, that the angels were ascending, rotating slowly like life-size wind-blown tree decorations.

Above its sad and lowly plains
They bend on hovering wing;
And ever o'er its Babel sounds
The blessèd angels sing.

On the ground floor, like formally attired tug-of-war teams, young male assistants in dark suits were heaving away together on ropes. "Yo-ho-heave-ho! Yo-ho-heave-ho!" This was the Babel sound in the heart of that temple of commerce.

Hauling up angels was such a change (the opportunity all too rarely presented itself) from their usual dull routine that the young men (there were dozens of them, freed from the close attentions of the floorwalkers) were becoming noisy and excited, competitively eager to see their angel reach the roof first. The Babel-like babblings were rising to a roar. Bets were probably being exchanged. Angels and archangels may have gathered there,/Cherubim and seraphim thronged the air. Bells should be ringing out in mighty peals as they ascended, as the ropes were pulled. There was something nautical and yo-ho-ho — though not very well drilled — about the young men pulling on the ropes in unison, rather like the group of men disemboweling St. Erasmus in the stained glass window to the right of their pew in All Saints'. Hooray, and up she rises! Hooray, and up she rises! Huge white sails should be unfolding like enormous wings, snapping out and bellying in a strong north-by-north-west wind. Eight or nine angels, spaced out around the central light-well, lurched bumpily upward, swaying from side to side, their heads leaning too far forward, like a gathering of feathered suicides deciding where to jump, or — already dead — the dangling corpses after a mass hanging, crows shot by a farmer to deter other scavengers.

More young men were waiting high above them on the top floor, leaning out into the central space, clutching brooms commandeered from the janitor or (they looked pale and pristine) from elsewhere in the store, all ready to maneuver their chosen angel into position with the bristled heads. She had to bend right back in order to see them, as if she were looking up at Dr. Vaniah Odom in his pulpit.

"My angel! My angel!" they were shouting encouragingly, their voices echoing, fervent suitors glimpsing the girl of their dreams.

With the combination of brooms and flying angels it was like an incongruous mixture of Halloween (she dithered on the verge of thinking of the word as Hallowe'en: it was a word that seemed to demand an apostrophe) and Christmas, midway between the two dates. The wings of two of the angels became locked, and the more the young men tugged, the more the angels began to tip upside down. If they plummeted earthward, would the store's employees be insured against death from falling angels? If anything qualified as an Act of God, this was surely it. Alice had tried to walk challengingly beneath the nearest angel — an impulse for a glamorous death had suddenly seized her — but Mama had clutched her hand tightly, and dug her heels in. She was not taking any chances.

Two of the young men on the top floor had become bored after waiting too long for their log-jammed angel, and had reversed their brooms and started a sword-fight, prodding challengingly at each other's chests with the blunt wooden handles, like a safety-conscious d'Artagnan and Lord de Winter.

"*Touché!*" they shouted. "*Touché!*"

Others began to join in. If this had been a few years later, some of the young men would not have been able to resist utilizing their brooms as crutches in Long John Silver impersonations, wincing slightly as the stiff bristles dug painfully into their armpits, and mutineers uttering frightful imprecations would have swung across that central space on hastily improvised rigging. Skewered musketeers and pistol-shattered buccaneers would have hurtled to earth from between the creakily swaying angels. A morning in a department store rarely produced such heady excitement.

8

When she was a small girl – anxious to improve her literary credibility – she had been drawn to the name Pharaildis: Alice Pharaildis Pinkerton had an undoubted poetic ring to it, and would certainly have improved her syllable count. She wasn't sure whether St. Pharaildis was a man or a woman: with their penchant for long, flowing garments, it was difficult to distinguish the sexes of saints. This was an occasion on which beards might have served a useful purpose – making allowances for the unhelpful blurring of the boundaries from the likes of St. Wilgefortis – but, as with clothing, so with names: if you were a saint your name could be used for either sex. Half the nuns at The House of the Magdalenes had men's names. The Reverend Goodchild had his own theories about this, and enjoyed many a good snigger about it with Mrs. Albert Comstock.

St. Pharaildis was pictured with an enormous hen on either side of her, if she *was* a her. Elphinstone Dalhousie Barton – like some of the illustrators in the Lindstrom & Larsson catalogue – had no conception of perspective (grouped rather incongruously in a free-for-all freemasonry with Japanese and mediæval artists), so it was difficult to make out whether the hens were meant to be in the foreground, or whether they really were – as they appeared to be – bigger than she was. Alice, knowing nothing about the saint, was puzzled by the hens, but decided that they must be the instruments of her martyrdom. Here she was, being pecked to death by giant hens unleashed by some evil despot, because . . . because she . . . she defied his cruel edicts and his imperious mien by distributing eggs – from a willow-woven basket – to the starving poor within his evil domain. She pictured just two hens – as there were two in the window – outlandishly large, advancing menacingly, towering over Pharaildis.

Old MacDonald had a farm, E-I-E-I-O!

Their heads – like the pistons of the Coketown steam engines in *Hard Times* – worked monotonously up and down, the heads of elephants in a state of melancholy madness.

And on that farm he had some hens, E-I-E-I-O!
Peck. Peck. Peck.
With a peck-peck here, and a peck-peck there.

Pharaildis (not yet martyred, not yet pecked into sainthood) staggered back a little each time, a girl being pushed in the shoulder by a schoolyard bully, her basket held before her — base forward — like a fragile protective shield, a Basque (a Basque with a basket) playing jai alai. Mabel Peartree had just such a big basket, square with a central handle, and carried it looped over her arm on her way to the shops. It was exactly the sort of basket you imagined being carried by Little Red Riding-Hood, with a piece of cake, a bottle of wine, and a bunch of flowers tucked neatly into one side of it.

"Oh, Miss Peartree! What big teeth you have!"

Miss Peartree opened her mouth to reveal — gigantic and glinting — the mighty fruits of G. G. Schiffendecken's labors. He was a dentist who created on the epic scale of a Michael Angelo sculpture. (This could very well be the only known occasion on which startled comment had been made about the size of her teeth, rather than the size of her — *Ye gods!* — enormous nose.)

"All the better to eat you with!"

Munch. Munch. Munch.

Pharaildis's feet crunched on the hens' eggs, incensing them further. After the *crunch, crunch, crunch* came the *peck, peck, peck* and after the pecking came the *munch, munch, munch.*

Alice had really liked the name Pharaildis — there was nothing exotic about *Alice* — but the hens had put her off.

Had St. Wilgefortis specified the sort of beard she had in mind, or had she to make do with the one she was offered? Alice rather pictured her in front of a mirror, browsing through a selection (ready-to-wear rather than custom-made) offered by a diffident angel, deciding which beard suited her best, trying them on, a fashion-conscious client choosing a bonnet, turning sideways to view herself from different angles, fluffing them up becomingly, judging the effect of threading them artistically through her necklace.

Here was a useful Beauty Hint: she should make a feature of her moustache, thread it with beads, bedeck it with little silken bows, make the most of what she had until the beard came along, bedazzle Mrs. Albert Comstock with her frivolous femininity.

9

Her hand was aching. She had been clutching the bar too tightly, and lines were impressed across the center of her palm, glowing red above the accumulated buds of cotton. The clouds were massing above the Hudson, level upon level, heavy with more snow. She watched them for a while.

It was like the ending of *Villette* (Charlotte Brontë was certainly pushing her way forward this morning): *The skies hang full and dark — a rack sails from the west; the clouds cast themselves into strange forms — arches and broad radiations.* She saw figures unfurling slowly above her, moving with large, stately gestures, and reached up toward them, straining for a direction in which she might begin to move. Sometimes she would watch them for hours at a time from the window, or lying on her bed gazing up through the skylight, languid and irresolute, like a Victorian lady, an Elizabeth Barrett Browning, suffering from the vapors or consumption. She was, after all, born a Victorian (surely, even the most patriotic of Americans born during the presidency of Andrew Johnson would not think of herself as a Johnsonian?): her childhood, her young womanhood, had been *last century*. Though it was now more than three years into the twentieth century, difficult though this was to believe — 1900, 1901, 1902 — she still found herself — when she wasn't concentrating — beginning to write the year with an *18* instead of a *19*. She left a trail of scribbles and crossings-out on checks and bills, and disliked the untidiness. Harry Hollander had written a song about the beginning of the new century: "Let's All Be Naughty in the Naughts (Do All the Things We Really Shouldn't Oughts)." Grammar sometimes took second place to rhyme in Harry's songs.

The clouds – it was oddly soothing – formed and re-formed, and the wind was howling round the house as it had been howling all night. This was not soothing.

She concentrated her thoughts back onto the clouds, as if she were at 11 Park Place, trying to read shapes in the clouds, with Dr. Wolcott Ascharm Webster scribble-scribble-scribbling behind her.

Tell me what you can see in those clouds, Miss Pinkerton.

There was his voice again, telling her what it was she had to do.

He was in the room, voyeuristically loitering in this Eve-of-St.-Agnes weather, hiding away and waiting to see her, like Porphyro spying on Madeline in her chamber, tantalizingly spreading out his seductive feast of candied apple, quince, plum, jellies, manna, dates, as she slept, as she dreamed. . .

> *We must not look at goblin men,*
> *We must not buy their fruits . . .*
> *"No," said Lizzie: "No, no, no . . ."*

In the subterranean caverns of the mountain upon which the palace was built, the goblins lived. They were dwarfed and mis-shapen, they had strength equal to their cunning, and they planned to dig their way up into the palace and carry Princess Irene away to be a mate for their grotesque prince.

Alice watched the shapes, shifting and changing, never at rest.

The Shape of the Clouds.

It could be the title of a novel.

She tried to hide this away in a corner of her mind, to remember it, and moved Annie's ring – she always thought of it as Annie's ring, as if it were something she had borrowed in perpetuity, not something she had been given – from her middle finger to what she thought of as her wedding finger, to nudge her memory. Sometimes, if an idea came to her in the night, she would do this, or drop her handkerchief onto the floor, so that she would know – when she awoke – that there was something to remember. Annie's ring, the little mirror, reminded her of what she ought not to forget. She collected titles, names for characters, ideas for her writing.

Below her, in the early-morning darkness at the back of the house, lines of gas-lamps stretched away through the snow, marking out the lines of the streets that had not yet been built, the new developments where the fields and orchards had once been. It was strange to see the gas-lamps there before the houses had been built. They seemed to stretch away in a long perspective to infinite distances, and – because they were lit – they made the empty streets that were not yet streets emptier and lonelier than ever. The great emptiness outside the window was not as great as the emptiness she felt inside herself. Here – in the outer emptiness, in the inner emptiness – was an unformed place of desolation and shadows, a place to populate with Dr. Jekyll and Mr. Hyde, Dorian Gray, and Sherlock Holmes. There they hid, there they scuttled and squatted, just out of sight of the corners of the eyes. It was as if it was night, and not morning.

> *My tea is nearly ready*
> *   and the sun has left the sky;*
> *It's time to take the window*
> *   to see Leerie going by;*
> *For every night at tea-time*
> *   and before you take your seat,*
> *With lantern and with ladder*
> *   he comes posting up the street . . .*

A Child's Garden of Verses had been published the year before *The Strange Case of Dr. Jekyll and Mr. Hyde* and she had bought a copy for her little brother. She must have been about seventeen or eighteen, and yet – when she had read it – there were lines that were as deep and as dark as anything in the later adult novel. It was a book *about* children, rather than a book *for* children: this was how she had tried to explain away the painful effect it had had upon her. It had awoken memories that she had wanted to remain undisturbed, memories in which she had partly been herself gazing at the little girl she had once been, and she had partly been the little girl, aware of being gazed at by someone older.

She had opened the book at random. "The Lamplighter" was the first poem she had read, and this – like so many of the other poems in the book – had awoken very powerful memories.

> *For we are very lucky,*
> *with a lamp before the door . . .*

The opening lines of the last verse had proven what she had already known, that the poem was about 7 Chestnut Street. There she was in the front parlor, sitting in the darkness, waiting for the lamplighter to bring light. Gradually, one by one, the lights would be lit, coming closer and closer toward her, the street brighter and brighter, until the ladder clunked against the lamppost – she heard it distinctly – outside their house. A glow sent the pattern of the windowpanes across the floor, and light crept a little way into the darkness of the room.

> *O! before you hurry by*
> *with ladder and with light,*
> *O Leerie, see a little child*
> *and nod to him . . .*

– Or her. Or *her* –
> *. . . to-night!*

If he saw her face at the window, the lamplighter never showed that he had noticed, as if she wasn't really there.

The second poem had been "Windy Nights."

The book had not been illustrated. Why hadn't the publishers commissioned Arthur Hughes to illustrate it? After his illustrations for the Christina Rossetti books *Sing Song* and

Speaking Likenesses, the George MacDonald novels she remembered so well, *The Princess and the Goblin* and *At the Back of the North Wind* (why hadn't he, another puzzle, illustrated *The Princess and Curdie?*), and *Tom Brown's Schooldays*, he would have been the perfect choice. There had, however, been no lack of illustrations in her mind as she read the poems; they had been drawn up from within her. She saw the scenes in front of her like pictures on a page.

> *Whenever the moon and the stars are set,*
>   *Whenever the wind is high,*
> *All night long in the dark and wet,*
>   *A man goes riding by.*
> *Late in the night when the fires are out,*
> *Why does he gallop and gallop about?. . .*

This was not a man who brought light with him; this was a man who brought darkness. This was a man with the face of her father.
If you tell anybody, the wind will get you.

These were the words her father had said to Annie. It was the sort of thing an adult would say to frighten a child, and Annie had been a child. Her father had known it when he had done what he had done to her. The use of these words proved it.

This was a man with the voice of her father, the voice that had made her frightened of the wind and the moon, frightened of many things. Thoughts of *Sing Song* brought the words of one of its poems into her mind.

> *Who has seen the wind?*
> *Neither you nor I:*
> *But when the trees bow down their heads*
> *The wind is passing by.*

She shivered, as at the touch of the cold wind.
Curse him! Curse him! Curse him!

These words — the words of Alfred Hardie in *Hard Cash*, also addressed to a father — were words she often whispered, as if they were secret endearments that no one should overhear.

Outside, the wind-blown snow gusted within the little pools of light, and the whole window seemed to groan, the loose pane in the top left-hand corner rattling. The weather had been like this on the day that her father died.

> *. . . Whenever the trees are crying aloud,*
>   *And ships are tossed at sea,*
> *By, on the highway, low and loud,*
>   *By at the gallop goes he.*
> *By at the gallop he goes, and then,*
> *By he comes back at the gallop again.*

In the wind, and in the darkness, the unnamed man galloped past, but he always turned around and came back. He never stayed away for good.

10

It was time to wander about the house, ignite a few bed-curtains, rend a few wedding-veils, that sort of thing. Another busy day in the life of a madwoman. All this, and the Reverend Goodchild too. Mrs. Albert Comstock yesterday; the Reverend Goodchild today. *And* Dr. Vaniah Odom! *What wond'rous Life in this I lead!/Ripe Apples drop about my head;/The Luscious Clusters of the Vine/Upon my Mouth do crush their Wine . . .* She might even manage an enthusiastic demoniac laugh as she staggered berserkly about, though it would be wasted in the absence of visitors. If she had never started the attempts at finding some sort of a "cure" for herself (she heard the quotation marks click cozily into place around "cure" like comforting hands patting shoulders) — Dr. Severance of Staten Island, Dr. Wolcott Ascharm Webster (above all, Dr. Wolcott Ascharm

Webster) — perhaps she would not have been thought of (by some people) as being a madwoman. She was surely well within the permitted range of strangeness, particularly when she paused to compare herself with some of the people she knew, the acquaintances around her, the neighbors? (The word "neighbors" had something folksy and apple-pie about it that was at odds with the reality.) Mrs. Goodchild had chattily informed her that there was madness in the family — watching her reaction closely (you could tell that she had been saving this up for quite some time as a little, well-deserved treat) — as if mentioning a propensity to freckles or premature baldness. She could never lapse into broken inertia, as Lady Audley had done at the end of the novel, as she looked around the suite of apartments that was to be hers for the rest of her life in the private lunatic asylum, dreary in the wan light of a single wax candle. She really ought to have a candle in her hand as she went downstairs, to continue the Lady Macbeth motif that had come into her mind earlier.

Yet who would have thought the old man to have had so much blood in him?

The solitary flame of Lady Audley's candle, pale and ghostlike in itself, was multiplied by paler phantoms of its ghostliness, which glimmered everywhere about the rooms; in the shadowy depths of the polished floors and wainscot, or the windowpanes, in the looking-glasses, or in those great expanses of glimmering something which adorned the rooms, and which my lady mistook for costly mirrors, but which were in reality wretched mockeries of burnished tin. They were fake mirrors, in which the reflections were blurred and indistinct, as fake as the fake books in *Hard Cash*, and made of the same material. Lady Audley would look into them, and she would not be able to recognize herself, just as Alfred Hardie would not be able to open those books, books in which no words were printed.

Looking-glass, looking-glass, made out of tin,
Whose is the face that I see within?

63

Amid all the faded splendor — *splendour* — of shabby velvet, and tarnished gilding, and polished wood, the woman dropped into an armchair, and covered her face with her hands. The whiteness of them, and the starry light of diamonds, trembling about them, glittered in the dimly lighted chamber.

Rochester had told Jane that the Bertha Rochester she had seen in her bedchamber had been the creature of an overstimulated brain. Alice had the same problem. It was what she had been told over and over. A woman should not overexcite her brain. It was injurious. It — ahem — interfered with her — ahem, ahem — womanly functions. Ahems sometimes overwhelmed everything else in any discussion of this — ahem — delicate matter, particularly if it were Dr. Twemlow doing the talking. He was a man who'd blush if a woman removed her hat. There were more throat-clearings than in a consumption clinic. Books should be laid aside for the health's sake. Dr. Severance of Staten Island and Dr. Wolcott Ascharm Webster had both agreed on this. They set down what came from her, to satisfy their remembrance the more strongly.

What's done cannot be undone.

To bed, to bed.

And not to read.

And not to write.

To bed, to bed, to bed.

And not to think.

And not to talk.

To bed, to bed, to bed.

And not to sew.

No stitch-stitch-stitch.

Just sleeping.

Just dreaming.

Drifting listlessly away.

Like the Lady of Shalott down the river.

She has a lovely face.

That was what Lancelot had said.

You thought that he'd have said "hath." That's what knights in poetry tended to say.

Drifting.

Nothing else.

Because nothing else mattered.

She could talk about the clouds.

She could talk about the pictures.

She could talk about the dreams.

Scribble, scribble, scribble.

She talked, and they wrote.

If she talked she would be better.

The thump, thump, thump of Rosobell preparing the fire in the parlor rattled up through the schoolroom fire-grate. Alice had kept this fire burning all night. Hearing Rosobell meant that it would be a little after 6.30. She had forgotten to wind her pocket-watch the night before – it was usually the last thing she did before going to bed – and it had stopped in the early hours. She had noticed the silence from her watch-stand, the absence of the *tick, tick, tick*. She would take it downstairs with her, and set it from the kitchen clock.

She picked up the tongs and added one large piece of coal right in the middle of the fire, one that would slowly burn through in the course of the morning, so that the room would still be warm when she returned from church. The little Old Testament figures on the Dutch tiles around the fireplace flickered, appropriate small-scale animation on a Sunday morning. Adam and Eve stood hand in hand at the side of the tree, as if choosing the best fruit to pick for a pie. Noah and his wife stood on the deck of the tiniest ark imaginable – probably just large enough to save two white mice and a small and solitary rabbit from the flood – as the dove flew toward them, weighed down with an olive leaf the size of a tree. Like Breughel's biblical scenes, like Shakespeare's Romans, they were dressed in the fashions of the time in which they were created. If she listened at the fireplace, she could hear whereabouts people were in the house. It was especially clear in the summer, when no fire was burning.

As a little girl, she would kneel down, looking at the crumpled newspaper pages in the grate, the engravings of bearded faces, soot whispering and trickling down, gathering in the rucks, and listen to Mama playing the piano, Annie singing, fragments of conversation. Sometimes she'd hear sobbing, far away, suppressed. Sometimes it was Annie, and sometimes it would be Mama. Mama cried in the same way that she played the piano, quietly, shyly, hoping not to be overheard. Alice had lain awake and heard her, in the evenings, in the small hours of the darkness. Knowing that you had heard someone else cry gave you a special feeling toward that person. She'd dab her fingers in the soot, wipe them across her face, and look at her minstrel-like face in the mirror above the mantelpiece, moving her mouth like someone singing. "Oh, Dem Golden Slippers." She'd open her mouth very wide, flare her eyes. "Oh, Dem Golden Slippers." She used to imagine that Joel Chandler Harris and the writers of coon songs applied blackface make-up before they began writing, and that their manuscripts were marked all over with burned-cork thumbprints.

There was a burst of fire as she jiggled the poker, and the figure of Isaac in one of the Dutch tiles seemed to writhe in flames as he lay bound on the altar upon the wood. Abraham leaned over him, enthusiastic to slay his son with the knife. The angel, peering out from the middle of a cloud, did not appear inclined to do much to interfere. This was one of the Bible stories that seemed designed to test the faith of the reader as much as God had tested Abraham's. It made it difficult to like God very much. She did not feel guilty for thinking this. This made her feel guilty.

"Don't do it, Daddy!" the little boy pleaded. "Don't do it!" But Daddy wasn't listening. He had his mind on quite other matters, and sharpened the keen edge specially, vigorously stropping the blade on the sole of his sandal like Shylock whetting his knife, keen to start carving Antonio, wolfish, bloody, starved, and ravenous.

"Typical!"

You could just hear Mrs. Albert Comstock commenting loudly in the theatre, her head nodding up and down in delighted disgust.

(How on earth had Ben survived an evening crammed into a box with her and the others? She could only hope that the music had been *very* loud. That might have given him a chance.)

"Typical! Just as I expected!"

("It only goes to show!" That would be her next comment, unless she opted for "You can't be too careful!" It would be one or the other.)

". . . wolfish . . ."

Nod.

". . . bloody . . ."

Extra-enthusiastic nod on this.

". . . starved . . ."

Slightly more dubious nod here.

". . . ravenous . . ."

Enthusiasm resumed for this nod.

The head went up and down so rapidly that (a merciful release, you couldn't help thinking) all the features blurred, all chins and wattles wobbling. It was rather like seeing her in her automobile – well trussed-up in plaid blankets and impenetrable veils, like a kidnapped Scottish beekeeper the size of Ben Nevis – as the engine was cranked up (if that was the correct expression), vibrating vigorously, with considerably more than one pound of flesh in mountainous motion. Every part about her quivered. Alice had once seen – it was just before Mrs. Albert Comstock's fortieth birthday, the day on which her ten-year-old self had destroyed Sobriety Goodchild with the words of Shakespeare – a sign with the words *Youth Restored By Electricity While You Wait*. Mrs. Albert Comstock would not have been able to resist, and Alice had visualized her plugged into the mains, shuddering in just this way, with the added bonus of sizzling sounds, and smoke rising from some of her outlying regions. When, more recently, the electric chair had been introduced as a means of execution, the image had returned to tantalize her, the murderous instincts of childhood not yet fully quelled. "Just sit here, Mrs. Comstock," she'd say, soothingly, as her victim gazed dubiously around her at the unsumptuous surroundings of the execution cell. "Just sit here, and your youth will be restored. All I need do is pull this switch. Just sit here." It would soon be Mrs. Albert Comstock's sixty-fifth birthday. It might be a good time to sing of the wonderful benefits that could be obtained by the application of electricity. *Powerful* currents of electricity. Mrs. Albert Comstock had recently re-read *She*. She'd be in receptive mood for any talk of miraculously eternal youth. She'd just sit here with no hesitation whatsoever. She'd be urging, "More power! More power!" as the great arcs of electricity pulsed blue-white around her. Franken-stein's creature had been lonely for far too long. It was time for him to meet his mate.

Mrs. Albert Comstock had been the first person in Longfellow Park to possess an automobile (she'd made quite sure of that), and had taken possession of the vehicle well before Samuel Cummerford had arrived to set up his business to cater for fashionable automobilists. Alice couldn't remember the name of the manufacturer of Mrs. Albert Comstock's automobile, but its owner had been careful to inform everybody that it was *exactly* (invariably in italics) the same as the one Edith Wharton — the authoress of *The Decoration of Houses* and *The Greater Inclination*, a woman of impeccable pedigree — had purchased. Whatever its correct name, Mrs. Albert Comstock invariably referred to her automobile as Dimmesdale, investing the word with all the grandeur of Mrs. Elton boasting of her sister's barouche-landau in *Emma*. The name was possibly a provocative literary reference to Hester Prynne's secret lover in *The Scarlet Letter*. "I shall climb aboard Dimmesdale," she would announce grandly whenever a visitation was threatened, as if the guilt-ridden minister hadn't suffered enough already. Imaginations buckled with boggling.

A gust of wind blew down the chimney, and sparks flew as in a blacksmith's forge. Different patterns in the pieces of material in the quilt on her bed were clearly distinguishable. She could not see the colors, but she knew what they were. That patch with a narrow stripe was from a dress she had worn when she was ten years old. That polka-dot patch was from one of Annie's old shirtwaists.

The brief brightness died down, and the bed was lost in shadows.

I have a little shadow that goes in and out with me . . .

She saw him jump before her, when she jumped into her bed, as if leading the way, and then waiting there for her to join him. "Maggie Tries to Run Away from Her Shadow" was the title of Chapter XIII in Book First of *The Mill on the Floss*. She'd run away to join the gypsies because she was unhappy. She and her brother Tom had quarreled. She told the gypsies that she could tell them about anything there was in her books, because she'd read them many times, but one of them had taken her back to her father. She'd wanted him to do this.

I I

She wrapped her kimono around her — it had been a present from Kate, after she had admired hers — and left the room. She felt as if she were a figure in one of Grandpapa's Japanese photographs.

"An oddly accidental oriental occidental," she said to herself, as she fastened the sash. She liked the rhythm she had found in the words.

She should offer this line to Harry Hollander for him to use in one of his songs. She walked down the steps onto the top landing. Later, the first cold faint light would be struggling through on that side of the house. The colored glass in the windows would have stained her first blue, and then green. Down on the next landing the wind sounded louder than ever. She would have been stained first green, and then red.

When she walked here in daylight, it was like being at Mrs. Albert Comstock's, in that Masque of the Red Death interior, where the redness of the decorated panes made the whole room scarlet at certain hours in the afternoon. Everyone walked around like a mass gathering of Lady Macbeths, with not just their hands but their whole bodies, faces and all – these Lady Macbeths had been messy with their daggers, gilding more than just the faces of the grooms – incarnadined. "Will these hands ne'er be clean?" they'd ask each other chattily, wading through blood, wringing their hands like fawning, blood-bolted Uriah Heeps, exchanging tips on stain removal in the intervals between gossip about neighbors. It was a spattered assemblage of Mrs. Dip, the Dyer's Wives – polygynous Mr. Dip had clearly shifted to a Salt Lake City perspective when it came to matrimony, no wonder his hair was so wild, no wonder he soaked that suspiciously red-stained sheet so vigorously – and all the identical Mrs. Dips held up their stained hands scowlingly in front of their contorted Punch and Judy faces. These Family members did not look at all Happy. These hands would *ne'er* be clean. They'd tried *everything*. She should recommend Pinkerton's Champion Stain Remover – as if loyally supporting a family enterprise – so enthusiastically endorsed by Washington Otis in "The Canterville Ghost," the go-ahead American vigorously erasing the bloodstain of the wife murdered by the man whose ghost now haunted the English mansion in Oscar Wilde's short story. "The Thane of Fife had a wife; where is she now?" Knowing looks, lingeringly tapped noses.

Mrs. Albert Comstock and Mrs. Goodchild actually performed these sorts of gestures, which Alice had thought existed only in novels. That – with half of their vocabulary – was probably where they found them. There was an illustration in *Oliver Twist* of that very nose-tapping gesture, Noah Claypole and Fagin both striking the sides of their noses with their right forefingers like incompetent nose-pickers – missed again! – and grinning knowingly. Mrs. Albert Comstock and Mrs. Goodchild performed them with overlarge movements, as if they were shouting in the language of the deaf. They probably twiddled their thumbs with the palms of their hands placed carefully on a flat surface, and the designated digits conscientiously extended, circling round and round as far as they could reach, bones cracking as they strove ambitiously for ever-more distant circumferences. Their screwed-up, shortsighted eyes were jammed against the hugely magnified black lettering of the first two rows of the sight-test at the optician's, and the gibberish of these nonsensical words was all that they could speak, all that they knew.

"*A HKL!*" Mrs. Albert Comstock squawked urgently to Mrs. Goodchild.

(*A HKL* were the first two rows of the chart at Alice's optician's, Mr. Brczin. He sometimes economically utilized his own name for a sight-test when the usual letters palled. He was on the second floor, above the chiropodist on Indian Woods Road.)

"*A HKL!*" Mrs. Goodchild squawked back urgently to Mrs. Albert Comstock, eager to share the knowledge that they'd both spotted a hkl.

(You could recognize Mr. Brczin's by the heaving pile of patients, all wearing their new spectacles with bifocal – bi-focal? – lenses for the first time, who'd – *Aaaaghhhh!* – fallen all the way down the flight of steps leading to his consulting-room and spilled out through the door.

("A hkl!" they called faintly, everything around them blurred. "A hkl!"

(It was the only thing they could think of to say, their only means of summoning assistance. The chiropodist chose to ignore them, whistling "The Streets of New York" to drown their cries as he grappled with a bunion. His first loyalty was to feet.)

They watched Alice, half amused, half interested, when she conducted signed conversations with Rosobell, the Pinkertons' deaf servant, as if to pick up new ideas. Half behind her back – it seemed to be a part of their pleasure that she should catch glimpses of what they were doing, and they took no care to be discreet – they exaggeratedly, with convulsed silent mirth, mimicked her actions, like little-known obscene gestures. They lolled their heads from side to side, and rolled their eyes, economically mocking a deaf woman and a madwoman simultaneously in one seamless series of actions. If Alice turned to look at them – she'd tried this – they stared back at her with challengingly bold, bright eyes, proud of their saucy naughtiness.

"Are you interested in dactylology?" she'd asked Mrs. Goodchild once, all bright and beaming — she'd looked up the word for finger language especially — and the use of five syllables had briefly defeated Mrs. Albert Comstock's tittering toady. She hadn't wanted to admit that she didn't know the word, and hadn't wanted to give an answer until she knew what the word meant. After a pause — eyes glazing, fingers still tangled in complex knots — she employed the Mrs. Albert Comstock technique of completely ignoring the question and changing the subject. She also made use of vigorously soggy harrumphing. She certainly modeled her methods on those of her like-minded mentor.

Mr. Pinkerton would never have hired a deaf servant. That was the gist of what they were saying. Things would have been very different if Mr. Pinkerton were still alive. Mrs. Pinkerton always seemed to choose servants for their novelty value. Mr. Pinkerton had been far more sensible. He, like them, had had certain standards.

Though there had been that darkie girl.

Snigger.

"A hkl."

"A hkl."

Their voices had become quieter now, a barely audible bottom-line whisper, the tiniest of tiny lettering — just above *Printed by Charles Gouvernear & Nephew, New York* — unfamiliar words that Mr. Brczin hardly ever heard in his empire of the shortsighted. His eyes filled with nostalgic tears. They were speaking familiar words of greeting from his long-lost homeland — *May your balalaika always be well polished! How brightly the tracks of the troika gleam in the light of the morning sun!* — words that he had not heard spoken for half a century, hearing them only in memory.

"Gracious!" Mrs. Albert Comstock effortlessly switched to English. Her voice rose, in the tone of someone fearlessly giving voice to universal truths that must not be denied utterance. You couldn't stop her talking. You could never stop her talking. Mrs.

Albert Comstock said what had to be said. "My word! If I might be permitted! Darkie!"

"Whatdoyoumacallit?" Mrs. Goodchild agreed. "Thingamajig! Whatsit? Darkie!" (Mrs. Goodchild varied her exclamation points with the occasional question mark.)

Sometimes they appeared to spend entire afternoons of conversation in employing no other words but these, bound by the rules of some strict order. You could rely on Mrs. Albert Comstock and Mrs. Goodchild for intellectual stimulation.

There was no sound from Mama's or Ben's rooms.

This afternoon, her brother would be leaving for Japan.

12

She looked down the long final flight of stairs into the hall, and saw Annie, the little servant girl she had last seen twenty-five years ago.

These things happened without any warning.

Mrs. Alexander Diddecott talked with the dead every Tuesday at a house in Harlem, from seven to eight-thirty, her dead restricted to a certain place, and to certain hours, as if they lived in a museum. Alice seemed to see them at all times, and in all places. The memories were vivid, happening in front of her for the first time. Contrariwise, when real things happened they sometimes felt like something being remembered, a memory of something once read a long time ago, not as if they were happening for the first time then. As she drew nearer, she recognized the moment she was remembering. She had been ten years old. It was nothing special, and yet she had remembered it, as she remembered – with Emily Dickinson – a certain slant of light, or a tree against the sky, looking down at her feet on a beach, a red parasol.

She was not aware of Annie at first.

It was a summer morning, very early, and the hall was suffused by a red glow. In the evening it was green, blue, an underwater color. The hall was tiled, and sounds were sharper there — the heels of boots and the tips of umbrellas and walking sticks click-clicked, dresses swished and hissed, beaded braiding rattled like dogs' claws — echoes close, enclosed. There were patterns on the tiles. No one ever appeared to notice them, but she walked with her head down, and was aware of them all the time she was there, as familiar to her as the Dutch tiles around the fireplace in her room. The tiles in the hall did not represent human figures. They had a look of the Low Countries, with their differently colored tulip-shaped designs, though — despite the blue-figured schoolroom tiles — she would always think of Dutch tiles as being black and white, like those in the cool, tranced interiors of Vermeer and de Hooch. The kitchen floor was like this.

From the eighth step up she could see the newspaper lying on the tiles, neatly folded at an angle across them, placed there carefully, and when she lifted her eyes she saw Annie. Her white apron absorbed the redness of the light. She was standing in front of the mirror in the hall, with the front door and the inner door wide open, to give her more light.

(There should be snow blowing into the house, there should be the heightened sound of the wind as it entered, an intense coldness — Alice was vaguely aware of thinking this — but there was no snow, and no wind, just mild early-morning sunshine.)

Annie was peering intently into the glass — holding her breath, her mouth wide open, very still — and was grasping one of the kitchen carving knives with its bright blade some considerable way into her mouth; down into her throat, it seemed to Alice.

Annie was fourteen, tiny, and the handle of the knife was huge. It looked as though she were about to pin herself to the floor, from the inside. Alice froze, not wanting to make a sudden noise, and stood irresolutely, wondering whether to attempt a silent retreat, or whether — by some discreet and silent sign — to let Annie know that she was there. Colors slanted across the tiled floor from the stained glass of the inner door, green, gules — was this the right word from "The Eve of St. Agnes," the casement high and triple-arch'd? – and blue. Annie shifted the angle of the knife, and the sunlight caught the blade. Alice held her hand up to shade her eyes, dazzled, as if she were gazing out across a sunlit sea, and Annie saw the movement, saw the light in Alice's spectacles. Her eyes, reflected in the mirror, looked up toward Alice, though she could not see Alice's eyes, just two circles of light. With a sigh she pulled the blade out of her mouth. Several inches emerged.

"I did check that I didn't feel like sneezing before I started," Annie said, as if that explained everything. She walked across to close the outer door, and then the inner door. The colors became more intense.

"Are you training to be a sword-swallower?" Alice asked hopefully. This could add interest to her hitherto humdrum life.

Annie shook her head.

"No. This isn't long enough."

There was a disappointingly prosaic answer for the sight that Alice had seen. Annie explained that, not possessing a small enough mirror, she was using the polished blade of the knife to inspect the back of one of her front teeth, where she thought a hole the size of the Grand Canyon (that was the expression she used) was developing. This seemed a perfectly reasonable thing to do. Alice would have preferred the sword-swallowing.

"I kept breathing, and losing the reflection."

"Breathing can be a problem. Would you like me to put my head inside your mouth, rummage about a bit, and check your teeth for you."

"I'm training to be a sword-swallower, aren't I? Not a lion in a lion-tamer's act. Anyhow, you don't want to see my tonsils, not close up, and that big dangly thing."

"I promise I won't attempt to swing upon the big dangly thing."

(A brief, rather pleasing, picture of a possessed Quasimodo – the most grotesque of all the gargoyles of Notre Dame – flinging himself upon the bells, swinging high above a dark abyss on big Marie, his favorite of them all. Even more pleasing was the picture of

Quasimodo flinging himself upon even bigger Sibyl. The appalled squawk. The grimly disapproving "Gracious!" The reticule and fan brought into action as defensive weapons.)

Annie flourished the knife.

"I'll wash it before Cook uses it to cut the meat. I almost always wash the sausage scissors after I've cut my toenails with them, though I may have forgotten last night."

"The sausages were particularly delicious yestere'en," Alice retorted loftily.

"E'en so. Verily, the sausages were suspect. They were – I am afeared to report it – from Comstock's Bargain Counter."

"Oh, horror, horror!"

Annie began to sing.

> "Oh where, Oh where ish mine little dog gone;
> Oh where, Oh where can he be?"

Alice ignored this, adding, "You should refer to me as 'your ladyship,' menial one. I am the young mistress of the house and thou a mere varlet."

This was a game they often played when there was no one else around to hear them. Alice wasn't too sure about "varlet." She had an obscure feeling that it was used only in reference to males. She liked to get things right.

Annie performed one of her spectacularly servile curtsies, arms reaching far out on either side of her, head bowed.

"Forgive this humble underling, your ladyship," she begged.

"I am minded to be merciful on this occasion."

"Your ladyship is all too gracious to one as insignificant as my groveling self."

"And there are few as insignificant as thou art."

"As thou hast often commented."

Annie wobbled from side to side. She was almost doing the splits. Alice had seen a woman acrobat like this, high up on a tightrope, her parasol quivering in her right hand as she tried to keep her balance.

"Your groveling is to be particularly recommended this morn."

"Your ladyship — as ever — is all too kind."

Annie disappeared, clutching the knife, into the dining room, hurrying like someone remembering something urgent. She was in the middle of blackleading the grate. The shutters had all been opened, the doors unlocked, and the dining room would have been swept, and the grate emptied. Annie kept to a meticulous routine. A moment later, the door opened again, and Annie's head reappeared, leaning out at an angle, time only for a few hurried words.

"I didn't waste any time looking at my tooth when I should have been working," she said. "I woke up early this morning, and started work straightaway."

Her usual time to begin work in the summer was six o'clock. The door closed again. It was as if she needed to explain herself. Papa must have said something again. Her hands and the lower parts of her arms had been dusted pale with ashes. Alice imagined her right hand inside her mouth holding the knife, cinders dropping down into her throat, a victim of Vesuvius, lying still in some inner room in Pompeii, curled up amidst her buried possessions, choked with ashes. She would be kneeling down on the cloth she had laid over the carpet, her housemaid's box on one side of her, and the cinder pail on the other side, leaning over into the grate to brush on the blacklead. Sometimes, after she had done this, her hair and forehead were marked with soot. Alice thought of her as Cinderella, and herself and Allegra and Edith as the Ugly Sisters, one more than usual for added ugliness. When did Cinderella's stepsisters become ugly? In her version of the story they were described as "fair in face, but foul at heart," like something out of *Macbeth*, which was rather more interesting, and — she had thought, with considerable venom (Allegra had been annoying her again) — rather more accurate where Allegra was concerned. Allegra (no hesitation whatsoever in her case) and Edith could both be described as pretty. Alice — how appropriate an expression could be — was undoubtedly the cuckoo in this particular nest.

Cuckoo!

Cuckoo!

Allegra and Edith shook two dishes of peas into the ashes. "Pick them all out in one hour's time and you can go to the ball," they said to Annie, and all the little birds under heaven flew down to help her.

As Annie fled from the feast she dropped her left golden slipper upon the stairs.

Oh, Dat Golden Slipper.

13

She remembered the expression on Mrs. Albert Comstock's face when she had first seen Annie, and registered the fact that their new maid was black. She had heard her, another time, making some sophisticated and amusing comments about soot and blacklead upon Annie's skin. Again the jewelry had rattled, the earrings swayed, the feathers vibrated. Teeth had come into view to denote how much her wit had been appreciated. Mrs. Albert Comstock had never seen Annie with dirtied skin – Annie was always fastidious about how she looked when she answered the door – but she found the idea entertaining.

Alice decided that – enjoyable though it was to think about – it was not Allegra who cut off her big toe, and Edith who cut off part of her heel so that the golden slipper would fit their feet when the prince called, but Mrs. Albert Comstock. Her feet were so large – all of her was so large – that she would have had to hack away considerable chunks of flesh with an extra-sharp knife. They could have fed Chinky-Winky – her cacophonous canine (the name she had ha-ha-ha-ha-ingly selected for her Pekinese revealed the good taste for which she was so noted) – for several months. He'd have wolfed it down, and howled for more. Dogs were such loyal pets.

The blood streamed so from the shoe that her white stocking was quite red. At the wedding of Annie and the prince, all the little birds under heaven flew down again to here a peck, there a peck, everywhere a peck, peck, peck, and this time they pecked out the eyes of Mrs. Albert Comstock. Alice did enjoy a good story with a happy ending. It cheered her up no end. All the birds of the air wouldn't be a-sighing and a-sobbing on this occasion. They'd be cheerfully chirping away, licking slurpily at their blood-spattered beaks so that no drop of nourishment was wasted, a dawn chorus of well-nurtured twitterings. Feed birds regularly, supply a good source of water, ensure that household pets are safely out of the way, and they'll bring a great deal of pleasure to your garden with their singing and their colorful plumage.

To Alice, the darkest thing about Annie was not her skin. It was her eyes.

They looked into hers, deep, far-seeing, serious, as Alice read to her, stories, poems, extracts from newspapers, her brother's letters, the words of songs, the meaning of dreams, because Annie couldn't read.

Her eyes were as dark as the pips of a pear.

The sentence came into her mind. She had heard it in a song once, and it was the only line she could remember. It had been about a girl. There was a girl's name in the song title, and the word "green" was also in it somewhere. The words of another song – a nonsense song – drifted into her mind.

Her age it was blonde, and her hair it was nineteen.

Something like that. She must have heard the words when she was at the Calbraiths' house, being sung by someone coming out of the park. She liked the different spellings of "blond" for a man and "blonde" for a woman, and always differentiated. There were so few adjectives in English with this sort of distinction.

She could hear Annie working in the dining room. When she had blackened and then polished the grate, she would dust and polish the furniture. There would be no fire to light from today onward, as summer had now officially arrived. Alice had once regularly talked to Annie as she worked, but now she had started to feel awkward about doing this, even when Papa was not in the house. It had begun to seem wrong, somehow, to be chattering away to Annie's bent back as she cleaned and polished. She saw herself talking to Annie as she swept the stairs, moving down step by step in front of her. She saw herself following her into the parlor – this was still before breakfast – and watching her pushing and tugging all the furniture into the middle of the room, covering it with dust sheets, and sweeping the floor. She would not let Alice help her.

She stood outside the parlor, waiting for Annie to emerge, hoping she would have time to talk to her before she began to lay the breakfast cloth.

"Would your ladyship care to venture into the servants' quarters, and hazard a small cup of coffee and a cookie purchased from Thoroughgood's?" This is what she was hoping Annie might say to her, even though Annie rarely seemed to have a moment when she was not working.

"Gracing our humble domain with her noble presence," Alice would prompt her.

Annie's next obeisance would be even more spectacular, her skirt making a perfect circle on the tiles around her. It had happened many times before. It would happen again.

"Yet again I beg forgiveness, your ladyship. Gracing our humble domain with her noble presence. Wouldst thou care to undertake a Thoroughgood cookie?"

"I wouldst."

She'd enjoy the cookie, though the coffee – it would most certainly need to be a *small* cup – was a more hazardous undertaking: dark, bitter, headachy, a drink for adults. This, of course, was its appeal. She'd sip at it – not really enjoying it, but enjoying the idea of it – her face as puckered up as if she were swallowing down some foul-tasting but essential medication, or as if guiltily indulging in some illicit addiction to alcohol.

Annie turned back again, as she began to walk toward the kitchen.

"I've had a letter from Reuben with some more songs. I'll sing you some of them."

Reuben, Annie's brother, was sixteen, a singing waiter in a restaurant on West 48th Street. She'd asked her about Reuben. She liked to hear about brothers. Annie had been with them for a year, and seemed even smaller than when she'd first arrived. Every time Reuben saw her, he'd pick her up and put her over his shoulder. Annie had told her this. Reuben wouldn't have been allowed to come to the house.

When she told Alice that she had had a letter from her brother, she was asking Alice to read it for her. Alice would read it to her over and over, until she knew it more or less by heart. Sometimes, when she was feeling homesick or unhappy, and if she had completed all her work — she would work ferociously all morning to free fifteen or twenty minutes for herself so that she would be able to do this — she would ask Alice to read parts of old letters to her, so that she would feel closer to Reuben. If Papa were not in the house, Alice would play the music for the songs, and teach Annie the words. All the time, Annie would be on edge, thinking that she was doing wrong, that she'd be caught.

Later, listening by the fireplace in the schoolroom, Alice would hear Annie singing as she worked downstairs. She had a beautiful voice. It had never occurred to her to ask Annie if she would like to be taught how to read. There was some embarrassment, some awkwardness, about the idea — a belief that it was somehow insulting — that had made her unable to suggest it. She wished now that she had thought to at least ask Annie what her reaction would be to the idea.

She saw her holding an envelope containing her brother's latest letter, smoothing it carefully between her hands. Reuben always used the same deep-blue envelope and paper, but Annie would have recognized his letters by his handwriting, whatever the color of his stationery. Alice always read the address on the front of the envelope before she read the letter inside it. "Miss Annie Clement . . ." She discovered Annie's surname when she first read one of the envelopes.

"Miss . . ." Annie would repeat. "Miss . . ."

("Annie *Clement*," Alice repeated to herself. "Annie *Clement*.")

Sometimes, there would be a sheet from a newspaper spread out on the kitchen table, as carefully smoothed as one of Reuben's letters. Alice looked at the flattened, rough-edged paper, still mottled with dried mud from the potatoes or carrots around which it had been wrapped, and imagined Annie's dark hand on the white paper, moving over it again and again, as if she was ironing cotton sheets. Whenever she recognized a page of personals she kept it for Alice to read to her. The ones she liked to hear were the ones from fortune-tellers, mediums, clairvoyants, anyone who professed to be able to offer guidance for the future.

"'Madame Etoile,'" Alice would read, "'the celebrated French Clairvoyant, can tell you all you want to know. She was born with a genuine gift, and can guide you in all aspects of life with her professional skill. She can see the past, the present, and the future.'"

("*Ze past, ʒe present, and ʒe futaire,*" Alice would say, attempting a French accent, to add to the authenticity. Mrs. Albert Comstock's aversion to anything *French* – a word almost always accompanied by a shudder when she spoke it – was a definite incentive for this unsuspected naughtiness.)

Annie would nod her head, as if this was what she had been hoping to hear.

"'She can bring together those long separated, show you an accurate likeness of your future husband . . .'" – ". . . *your futaire 'usband* . . ." (the French had a tendency to drop their aitches with democratic carelessness) – "'. . . and give you his name . . .'" – ". . . *geeve you 'is name* . . ." – "'. . . She has never been known to fail. She also gives lucky numbers. Ladies only. No gentlemen admitted. Consultation fee, fifty cents to one dollar. She sheds light on the tenebrous.'"

"'Tenebrous'?" Annie asked.

"Dark, shadowy, hidden by fog."

"Tenebrous." Annie nodded her head. She liked to learn new words.

Sometimes she asked Alice to write down an address for her,

and Alice would scrape away the dirt with her fingernails so that she could read it, and print it out carefully. Annie had never responded to any of the advertisements, but she had a list of addresses, just in case. Alice had never told her that Madame Etoile was probably about as French as Madame Sylvie, who owned the Human Hair Emporium and Salon de Beauty from which Mrs. Albert Comstock purchased her Jumbo-sized wigs. Phineas T. Barnum had certainly missed an opportunity where she was concerned. Madame Sylvie's accent was Brooklyn at its most unabashed – it made Mary Kinkeldey sound positively genteel – and to hear her pronounce "Salon de Beauty" was to experience all the thrill of living in a city that was truly cosmopolitan.

Sometimes it was "I've had a letter from Reuben," sometimes it was "I've found a new page of personals," and sometimes it was "I had a dream last night." When Annie said, "I had a dream last night," she would be asking Alice to read the interpretation for her from her Dream Book. She would produce the book, wrapped in a special silk scarf like something precious, describe her dream, and Alice would read out to her what it was said to signify. It was a curiously skewed prefiguring of what was to happen twenty-five years later, when Alice found herself describing her dreams to Dr. Wolcott Ascharm Webster. She had become the one who was unable to read, she who needed to have the meanings explained to her.

("I dreamed a dream tonight."

("And so did I."

("Well, what was yours?"

("That dreamers often lie.")

Whatever books he consulted were not consulted in her presence, but locked away behind the glass of his bookcases, the key safely hidden in his vest pocket. He was like an alchemist jealously guarding the arcane rituals of his craft. She could not remember the title of Annie's book. It had been far flimsier than either of the two books Rosobell owned, more of a pamphlet than a book, far too insubstantial to contain all the possibilities of dreams, though Annie believed in it utterly. She listened to Alice's readings with rapt concentration, staring into her eyes, willing her to tell the truth. The fact that the interpretations were written down in words, something she was unable to read, somehow made them more mysterious to her. When she particularly wanted an interpretation to come true, she would close her eyes, and clench her hands, like someone praying.

Alice was sometimes tempted to embroider what she read, to add undreamed-of future happiness (that "undreamed-of" was used absolutely precisely here), a life in which someone loved her, cared for her. She did this just once, and Annie had known that she was inventing what she pretended to read. Many of Annie's dreams were dreams obscured by clouds, dreams in which Annie was surrounded by impenetrable fogs, lost in caverns, corridors deep underground, Annie dreaming Alice's dreams for her, foretelling her future. She had looked up the meanings of some of the dreams she could remember in Rosobell's books – years later – but they did not give the same meanings as the ones she could remember from Annie's book.

For a young woman to dream of being in a fog, denotes that she will be mixed up in a salacious scandal, but if she gets out of the fog she will prove her innocence and regain her social standing.

Sometimes she'd catch Annie staring repeatedly at something as the day drew to a close, some object fading in gathering darkness, and knew that she was trying to make herself dream of it, to make a particular thing happen. It never worked. She didn't have the dreams she wanted to have. Once, throughout the whole of a summer's day, Alice had watched her hurrying out repeatedly – whenever she could snatch a moment, still holding a brush or a cloth – to study a geranium in a pot on the kitchen stairs, as if trying to memorize every petal, every leaf. It was the way Chardin must have looked at his subjects as he painted *la vie silencieuse*. To dream of geraniums – Alice remembered this, she had looked it up – was to become more beautiful, to be loved and respected.

This was what Annie had wanted.

In the echoey kitchen Alice looked out across the *Through the Looking-Glass* chessboard of the floor. She was high up, looking over the country divided into black and white squares by the brooks and hedges. Sir John Tenniel's illustration of this view — the foreground trees on a rocky eminence, the distant converging parallel lines of the landscape — was rather like how she imagined the view of Manhattan would be, viewed from the tower of the Shakespeare Castle on Hudson Heights, the grid pattern of the streets fading mistily away. She was not Alice; she was the Red Queen, still suffused by red light, dragging Alice along with her.

It was as if Bertha Rochester were hauling Jane Eyre behind her, never letting go, escaped from that dark inner room.

The kitchen was deserted.

Alice looked at the kitchen table, expecting to see Annie's Dream Book, still wrapped in its silk scarf, ready for consultation, the printed words of songs on carefully folded paper, or the torn-out page of an out-of-date newspaper. She knew, by the color of the crockery on the dresser — it took as little as that — that she was in the kitchen as it was now, not as it had been then, but she still half expected to turn around and see Annie smiling at her, standing on a chair to reach the coffee beans.

Coffee would be risky if made at the wrong time.

Papa would sniff the air.

"I can smell coffee," he would say. "Who has been drinking coffee?"

Sniff. Sniff. Sniff.

"Who has been sitting on my stool?"

(He'd cozy his buttocks wigglingly, enjoying the telltale residual warmth.)

"Who has been eating off my plate?"

(He'd sniff up the crumbs he'd spotted, filtering them through his nostril hairs.)

"Who has been picking my bread?"

(He'd . . .)

"Who has been meddling with my spoon?"

(He'd . . .)

"Who has been handling my fork?"

(He'd. . .)

"Who has been cutting with my knife?"

(He'd . . .)

"Who has been drinking my wine?"

(He'd do all kinds of things. What they were he knew not, but they would be the terrors of the earth.)

The seven dwarfs found the little girl lying asleep on the bed, just as she would lie later within the glass coffin as they wept around her. No more sitting. An end to eating, picking, meddling, handling, cutting, and drinking.

He'd be licking the end of his index finger next, and drawing it across the top of the kitchen table, and around the inner parts of plates, as if seeking to find dust with which to confront a slovenly housemaid. He was searching for telltale cookie crumbs not yet sniffed into the cavernous interior of his head, silently holding out the evidence challengingly on the shiny damp tip of the digit.

("Well?")

(Pause.)

("*Well?*")

(It was not well.)

Someone had been drinking *his* coffee. (He'd be peering deep into the dimness of the coffee tin.)

Someone had been eating *his* cookie. (He'd be counting the cookies.)

The servants were clearly completely out of control.

Surely it wasn't expecting too much, that his wife could cope with them? He didn't ask for much. The little that he did expect should surely be carried out competently? He had more important things to do than inspect coffee and cookies. *Far* more important things. *He* was the one who worked to bring the money into the house. *He* was the one who worked all the hours that God sent. (You imagined God beside him, nodding supportively, on *his* side.)

Sniff. Sniff. Sniff.

He sniffed so strongly that his moustache was sucked upward and inward toward his nostrils. Alice hoped on such occasions — *how* she hoped — that he might make a fatal error one day, inhaling with such angrily incautious power that his entire beard might rear up into the air like a bear on its hind legs, force itself up into his nose and mouth, and suffocate him to death. It would have been like — this thought had occurred to her just recently, all these years later, after the publication of the novel — a dramatic scene from *The Hound of the Baskervilles*, the prostrate figure writhing in agony (she could hope) on the floor, and the gigantic hairy beast worrying away at his face. (He would have been worried all right.)

The Shepherd's Son would wander in from *The Winter's Tale* to describe to his father how the bear tore out his victim's shoulder bone as he cried — too late — for help.

"Thou met'st with things dying, I with things new-born," the Shepherd would say, and after the cold winter years of suffering and unhappiness, the destruction of a family, good things would begin to grow in the world again.

The ewers from her, Mama's and Ben's rooms were the only things on the table, standing ready where Rosobell had placed them. Water was hissing a little as it bubbled in the tin side boiler of the stove. The slight sound made the kitchen appear larger. It seemed emptier than usual now that Annie had gone again, the clock loud. She drew her watch out of her kimono, set it, and wound it. She'd take her mother's water up later, when she was all ready herself. She, not Rosobell, washed her mother, cared for her in her infirmity. Sometimes, to the sound of trickling water, her mother's silent head bowed over the bowl, she thought of times when her mama had bathed her face, soothed her when she was ill. She was careful not to get soap into her eyes, dabbed gently with the towel.

Alice turned the tap on the boiler, filled her ewer, and went back into the hall, still Comstocked into redness. As the morning progressed, the color would creep across the hall, and begin to climb the stairs, one by one. Alice preferred the green light of the afternoons, when the hall seemed cool and lonely, like a deserted house deep under water, or abandoned in the depths of a dense forest. Sometimes — not very often — she would peer through the green glass on one side of the door, and see a green-faced Mrs. Albert Comstock in a green coat walking up a green path. When the frog-faced Goodchilds and Griswolds came calling — this happened more frequently — their green-faced closeness was almost too alarmingly froggy to bear. She always looked through the blue glass if she thought it was they who were approaching: this lessened the shock as they came hopping, croaking, rustling across the tiles, darkening the sky like locusts stripping the crops bare, to confuse the plague imagery somewhat.

The red glass would have been inviting nightmares, red-blent figures locked in a cycle of hell, like something out of a luridly illustrated edition of Dante, too dreadful even for Doré to contemplate. "Gules" — she had thought correctly — *was* the word from "The Eve of St. Agnes." Charlotte had accidentally read it as "warm Giles" — Giles was the Christian name of Mr. Tilleard, Miss Hayergaal's fiancé — and the whole class had sniggered. (Like "blond" and "blonde," there was "fiancé" and "fiancée." You could imagine Mrs. Albert Comstock's appalled inhalations. Trust the French to bring — ahem — sex so blatantly into their spelling.)

("And threw warm Giles on Madeline's fair breast."

(*Snigger. Snigger. Snigger.*

(It had been like one of the saucier misprints in a Reverend Goodchild novel.)

They had sniggered more loudly when Charlotte — realizing what she had just said — had begun to blush, more gules than Giles herself. Miss Hayergaal had looked somewhat thoughtful at the image the choice of words brought to mind, sharpening her pencil lingeringly, with a certain emphatic twist to her wrist action. After she had left to be married, Miss Swanstrom had replaced her. This had not been a good swap.

She saw again the newspaper she had seen lying across the tiles earlier, the *Hudson Valley Chronicle*. To buy this once a week had been a sign of gentility, a conscious rural distancing from the encroachment of New York City, though Papa had also bought a New York newspaper.

She walked across the tulip designs: the dull red, the charcoal, slate-blue, matt sand, and malachite. She had thought, when she first heard the name of the color, that – surely – malachite was the name of one of the Old Testament prophets, battling alongside Habakkuk and Obadiah, and had gone to her Bible to check. Like the Complete Works of Shakespeare, the Bible was full of lines – whole passages – you'd never found before, or had read and completely forgotten about. Lines and meanings altered as you altered, and they became new. In both books, every line, sentence, and section seemed to be accounted for, even the smallest word too precious to lose, and nothing should be lost in the fine net of numbering. She lived in one of the unnumbered places of the city, in a terrain that resisted numbering, and where names were used for the streets instead.

She'd almost been right.

The name was Malachi. It was the name of the last book – very brief, more like a chapter than a book – of the Old Testament, and it *was* the name of a prophet, a prophet who warned about the weakening of faith.

"For, behold, the day cometh, that shall burn as an oven; and all the proud, yea, and all that do wickedly, shall be stubble: and the day that cometh shall burn them up, saith the LORD of hosts, that it shall leave them neither root nor branch."

She had chanted the words out loud for the pleasure of prophesying doom. The hall had such a satisfyingly resonant sound.

"And ye shall tread down the wicked; for they shall be ashes under the soles of your feet in the day that I shall do *this*, saith the LORD of hosts."

She stomped upon the tiles, and swiveled the ball of her right foot from side to side, in the way that men did when they were extinguishing (those who bothered) the ends of partially smoked cigars and cigarettes in the street. She trod down on the proud, and on the wicked, and they were as ashes under the soles of her feet. She had particular people in mind when she did this. She would ensure that the ashes under the soles of her feet were well and truly extinguished, ground to fine powder like snuff all ready for inhalation, ground to nothingness.

Crunch! (on "tread").

Crunch! (on "wicked").

Crunch! (on "ashes").

Crunch! (on "*this*," an extra crunchy *Crunch!* because of the italics).

Her shoes crunched through the ashes toward Papa's study, to the left of the front door as she approached it. She was treading down the wicked, crushing the cinders beneath her as they fell from the darkened sky, pattering down upon her head and shoulders, as if she were in Sodom, Gomorrah, or (again) Pompeii. It was like walking through the layers of wet cinders that remained upon the sidewalks after the snow upon which they had been scattered had melted completely away. The cinders fell pitter-patter upon the folded pages of the *Hudson Valley Chronicle*.

Here were more ghosts.

On the front page was an engraving of the Board of Governors of her old school, Miss Pearsall's School for Girls. All were men. All were bearded. Her father – he had been dead now for fifteen years – was the one on the far left in the second row. If the size of the beard was the standard by which manhood was measured, her father was the man amongst men, the Biggest of the Beards. A double crown was his: the Biggest of the Beards, the Baldest of the Bald. The bald head gleamed with a Humpty Dumpty radiance, as if freshly polished, a looking-glass in which you might discern your reflection, a mirror of all vanities. Self-conscious colleagues or business acquaintances, in the midst of a serious-faced conversation, would be unable to resist discreetly patting at their hair, adjusting the collars of shirts, or tugging at the knots of neckties. They'd forget what they'd been saying, rapt in self-contemplation, striving for perfection in their appearance, an essential implement in the armory of the ambitious.

"Lean forward a little more," powerful rivals would order peremptorily, and Papa — ever mindful of the importance of contacts — would meekly obey, allowing them to check that false teeth had been correctly inserted, and the most capacious of nostrils kept entirely free of æsthetically displeasing lumpish obstructions. They'd grasp his ears firmly, adjusting the angle of the bald head to their complete satisfaction, as if it were a mirror on a swivel stand.

Her childhood was so long ago that there had been engravings in newspapers in those days, not photographs. (Her childhood was so long ago that it had been in a time when all men had sported beards as a symbol of their maleness. Women thrust out their bosoms, and men their beards: thus were the sexes differentiated.) Doré came to mind again, Papa pictured in (how appropriate) some new circle of hell, some lesser-known Old Testament legend.

The faces of the men were as crosshatched as the engraving on a high-value bank note, meticulously shaded, creating an illusion of depth. The beards were money, and smelled of money, rustling against the face with the smell of all the places where they had been, dirty notes crinkled in tightly grasped handfuls, money slapped down and fanned out challengingly like winning hands at cards displayed by someone who had cheated. They were greasy bank notes with ragged edges, money that had been doubtfully obtained, and folded away in wads, hoarded in dark places for far too long. The beards were almost obsessively detailed, individual hairs drawn and differentiated in precise detail, whilst their ears, in contrast, were oddly unfinished, simply rimmed like manufactured objects — ear trumpets, the interiors of gramophone horns, the thin handles of fragile bone-china teacups — rather than something human, blank and featureless on the inside, blurring into smooth shadows. She could daintily grasp the proffered handle between finger and thumb, and tip it toward her mouth, her whole head tilting, drinking down the bitter contents of the head.

They were the faces of long ago, and they were the faces of long to be.

They stretched back not only the twenty-five years to when she was ten, well back into the previous century, but to many centuries before that. Their faces stared out with the implacable patriarchal confidence of obscure prophets from the Old Testament, warning of what must be, what had to be, what would be, carved in rock like the Ten Commandments, to be obeyed without question, ancestral voices. "Behold!" Malachi cried, pushing himself forward, as if what they had to behold was himself, elbowing the LORD aside and appropriating His words. "I shall do this!" He brought ashes without sackcloth, and his beard was as packed as a factory ashpit. Until recently, a beard appeared to have been a necessary qualification for becoming president, and even Queen Victoria — in fleeting memories of photographs — seemed to have the sort of face that ought to have had a beard, in the way that some faces looked incomplete without spectacles. She probably had a beard worn in private, on intimate royal occasions, passed on to her son — like the crown — as part of the royal regalia. There would be a special attachment, tastefully monogrammed by the royal jeweler — coat of arms tastefully displayed — to fasten the beard and crown together. One was incomplete without the other.

The five faces were eminently respectable male faces, like the faces of surgeons around an operating theatre table, or the managing directors of a successful manufacturing company that was the major employer in some small Midwest town. They were the stern upholders of morality and family values, but with a hint of carefully implied warmth and compassion in their eyes.

Bearded as they were, the expressions on their faces were exactly the same as the expressions on the faces of the middle-aged women in the illustrations for corset designs in the Lindstrom & Larsson catalogue.

All around Longfellow Park the five bearded worthies, risen to greet the dawn, gamboled in the freedom and comfort of expertly fitted corsetry, their faces dignified and remote, their gazes untroubled, confident in the rightness of what they were doing. Each had his left hand resting loosely on his left hip, and strolled little distances to and fro, swaying with a natural grace, his womanly poise enhanced by the manly confidence which the possession of a beard confers.

To the sound of their own inner music – whether of Brahms, of Bizet, or (they had the beards for this) Tchaikowsky, Mussorgsky, or Rimsky-Korsakoff – the other Bearded Ones, the men of Longfellow Park, fully armed in the dignity of their corsets, their eyes unfocused, looking far, far away, lost in some world known only to themselves, breathed and moved and had their being.

Tum, tum, tum, tum, ti-tum . . .

Tum-ti, tum-ti, tum-ti, tum . . .

Tum-ti-tum, tum-ti tum-ti tum-ti, tum-ti-tum . . .

There was some other music, just on the very edge of hearing. It wasn't Tchaikowsky. It wasn't Mussorgsky. It wasn't Rimsky-Korsakoff . . .

The music was surely the music of Bizet, it suddenly occurred to her. Faintly at first, and then louder and louder, a pianist began to pick out the opening notes of Carmen's first aria. By the little decorative flourishes, she recognized that the pianist was Emmerson Columbarian, playing at the entrance of Columbarian & Horowitz, his father's music store on Hudson Row.

The five men were Albert Comstock, Dr. Wolcott Ascharm Webster, the Reverend Goodchild, G. G. Schiffendecken, and her father.

G. G. Schiffendecken had never been on the Board of Governors of Miss Pearsall's School for Girls, and had not arrived in Longfellow Park until about five years ago, but there he was with the others, as if he had known them all his life. All five now had acacia flowers clasped in the corners of their mouths, rather like cigars, and moved forward with large bouquets peeping out provocatively from the bosoms of their corsets. Seductive, slow and sleepy in the sunshine, the lotus-lulled lovelies languorously braided their beards, like mermaids lingeringly brushing their hair with underwater lassitude. With a sultry haughtiness they placed both hands upon their hips, and, moving as one, began to sway their bodies erotically, their heads raised in taunting contempt for all the young men who gazed upon them, fascinated and lost. Their voices, as they sang, were superbly true soprano voices, rich and throaty, vibrant with passion.

> *"L'amour est une oiseau rebelle*
> *Que nul ne peut apprivoiser,*
> *Et c'est bien en vain qu'on l'appelle,*
> *S'il lui convient de refuser*
> *Rien n'y fait . . ."*

Now a full orchestra was playing.

As they moved before her, proudly flaunting their magnificent bodies, lost in the rhythm of the music, she vividly remembered the startling illustrations for what was coyly described as "The Winter Package" in the Fall and Winter editions of the Lindstrom & Larsson catalogue, issued at the end of September. It was a part of the mysterious patterns of the seasons, the signs of an approaching winter: squirrels gathered hazelnuts, the great flocks of migrating birds darkened the skies, bears retreated into caves, and the women of America ordered their warm vests and drawers from Lindstrom & Larsson to ensure their survival in the coldness that lay before them. In this catalogue, middle-aged women – decorous and dignified expressions on their faces, no doubt to dispel any misunderstanding about their motivations – held out two woolen vests and five pairs of woolen drawers neatly lined up across their extended right arms, like worshipers with votive offerings, or thoughtful hostesses offering a tidbit to a particularly favored guest. The intended effect was so thoroughly wholesome that you half expected the women to be giving a jolly wave with their free left hands, though this – perhaps – might imperil the precious cargo by unbalancing the pose.

There was a double-page spread of this mass display of drawers – the effect was rather overwhelming – and what she remembered most of all about it, as an impressive example of the high moral tone on which Lindstrom & Larsson prided themselves, was that – although "The Winter Package" consisted of three vests and six pairs of drawers – the women in the illustration, without exception, proudly held out just two vests and five pairs of drawers, to make absolutely clear to the reader that the women – clad in chemises and smiling winsomely – were securely enclosed within the third vest, and the sixth pair of drawers. This, no doubt, was to avoid unseemly speculation on the part of any male (particularly the young, vulnerable, adolescent male) who – by accident or design – had strayed into these delicate pages of the catalogue, and become inflamed, a weakness to which their sex was prone.

Marching in perfect unison, the massed ranks of drawer-displaying Bearded Ones, the corseted Carmens, appeared over the horizon, and began to converge on Longfellow Park, to join the vanguard of their illustrious army in Hudson Row, their right arms extended like the military salute in some South American dictatorship, the fanned-out underwear like playing cards about to be shuffled for some esoteric variation of *vingt-et-un*. With their left hands they caressed the lower parts of their left breasts, a repeated fondling left-to-right gesture, like a coded Masonic signal. The drawers trembled as their bodies vibrated to the perfectly pitched soprano voices of the wanton temptresses they had become, and the young men who lined the streets were driven into a frenzy by their animal allure.

"... *L'amour est enfant de Bohême,*
Il n'a jamais connu de loi;
Si tu ne m'aimes pas, je t'aime;
Si je t'aime, prends garde à toi . . ."

The sun was blotted out as bouquets — still warm with the heat from within the bosoms of the corsets — vests in sets of two, and drawers in sets of five, were flung high into the air to land at the feet of the chosen objects of desire.

It was the music that made them do it.

Albert Comstock looked in fine form for a man who had died a month or so before her father. He favored the Hilda corset, cut especially for the fuller figure, its amply proportioned gussets in a tasteful shade of green, small floral motifs adding a discreet color contrast. With quiet pride he paraded to and fro, far from the haunts of man on the edge of Indian Woods near the Ivansaans' farm, displaying the same neat economy of movement that characterized the way he tipped flour into the scales in his store, or briskly swung paper bags around twice between his fingers when they were filled with apples. His dimpled upper arms were freckled by the sunlight through the branches, and there was a little moue of concentration on his face as he strove to achieve the outward expression of his inner serenity, the low morning light sending long shadows from the trees out across the grass, and glinting on his garters as they swung in the bright air. He was several hundred pounds of pullulating womanhood, more of a woman than his wife would ever be. Across Hilda's ample bosom — tastefully embroidered for a modest extra payment — were the words *COMSTOCK'S COMESTIBLES: "SERVICE WITH SINCERITY!"*

Above *SINCERITY!* his teeth glinted with insincerely exposed fulsomeness.

For several enjoyable weeks, Emmerson Columbarian had striven to convince her — with supportive evidence — that Albert Comstock and his wife were really one and the same person, Humpty Dumpty (to whom each bore a remarkable resemblance) rather than Tweedledum and Tweedledee. There was something unfocused and distant about Albert Comstock's face, as if his surroundings were not really there.

("... We must not look at goblin men,
We must not buy their fruits:
Who knows upon what soil they fed
Their hungry thirsty roots?...")

G. G. Schiffendecken – the hugely false-toothed dentist, all teeth fully on show – moved with co-ordinated grace under the glass canopies of the stores on the west side of Hudson Row. Dr. Wolcott Ascharm Webster, on the opposite side of the street, mirrored his movements, more complex and balletic than those of Albert Comstock. The occasional ambitious essay of an *entrechat* – G. G. Schiffendecken's perfectly reflected in Dr. Wolcott Ascharm Webster's – was interposed between elegantly executed *pirouettes* and *pliés*.

The shadows of the letters on the front of the canopy above the entrance to Albert Comstock's cavernous emporium, the very first in his ever-expanding empire, the same as those displayed across the corseted bosom – *COMSTOCK'S COMESTIBLES: "SERVICE WITH SINCERITY!"* – were thrown onto the sidewalk. Alfred Eakins, one of the assistants, preparing for the day ahead, was briskly sweeping with a stiff-bristled broom. He must have been a very small child when Albert Comstock died, and yet here he was – the same age he was now, a youth, barely a young man – carrying out his duties on a day on which Albert Comstock danced. His first task of the day, every day, was to sand the wooden floor of the store with generously extended Parable-of-the-Sower gestures. His second task was to line up the chairs in front of the counters, preparing for swooning customers overcome by the splendors of the sausages on display, the charisma of the cheeses. His third task – they were always in the same order – was to brush the sidewalk.

He stood respectfully to one side, holding the broom handle like a salute, as G. G. Schiffendecken – executing a particularly dazzling sequence of *arabesques* – danced across in front of the store, his ample figure reflected in the gleaming windows. Every detail of the Carlotta model (its quiet, understated charm, its ageless sense of

97

style, its convenient access in moments of − ahem − difficulty) moved gracefully across the neatly stacked cans and packets of prepared food, and the display ("Come buy our orchard fruits!") of ripe plums, cherries, melons, peaches, and grapes, each single drop of oozing syrupy juice capturing the image of G. G. Schiffendecken, as his reflection moved across its surface from right to left.

> (". . . How fair the vine must grow
> Whose grapes are so luscious;
> How warm the wind must blow
> Through those fruit bushes . . .")

Outside Metheney's Hardware Store, G. G. Schiffendecken paused for a moment, and turned to face Dr. Wolcott Ascharm Webster across the street. At the very same moment Dr. Wolcott Ascharm Webster turned to face G. G. Schiffendecken, gazing at him intently. All he saw in the world was the shadowed letter "S" across his bosom, like the emblem of some hidden sin, a sin that drew him powerfully toward it. He knew what the "S" meant. He − let's be clear about it − was quite keen on what the "S" meant.

"'S' is for . . ." he whispered teasingly. "'S' is for . . ."

He didn't spell out what the "S" was for.

("S" was secret.

("S" was seductive.

("S" was saucy.)

People strolling in the street, picking their way carefully and unobtrusively between the heaped piles of bouquets and crumpled drawers − "Mind those bloomers, Brenda" − moved helpfully to one side.

They were all there, watching the dancing, the people of Longfellow Park: Charlotte and Linnaeus with Mrs. Chirikos; Dr. Twemlow and Miss Swanstrom, with the sour-faced Mrs. Twemlow interposing herself like a fearless bodyguard between her son and his beloved; Myrtle Comstock and Roland Birtle;

Oliver Comstock and Arthur Vellacott; the Renwicks and Bertie; Mrs. Alexander Diddecott; Kate Calbraith's parents; Hilde Claudia, Theodore, and Max Webster; Reynolds Templeton Seabright; Henry Walden Gauntlett; Elphinstone Dalhousie Barton (a trio of triple-deckered monikers grouped helpfully together like a sub-species); Dr. Severance of Staten Island (drawn out of his natural habitat by the presence of Alice); Miss Caulfeild, the senior schoolmistress at the grade school; Dr. Brown; Dr. and Mrs. Crowninshield; Mr. Rappaport; Mr. and Mrs. Scrivener; Mr. Caswell; the shifty-eyed Dibbo Daughters in full force; Miss Iandoli, the piano teacher; Mabel Peartree; Miss Wouldhave; Miss Ericsson; the Misses Isserliss; Miss Stein (there was a whole armada of Misses, all dressed in white, like the maidens in the May-Day dance in the second chapter of *Tess of the d'Urbervilles*; another Miss – Miss Stammers – hurtled past in the background, hauled by her enormous dogs: they seemed to regard her as a conveniently sized snack on legs, nibbling her in a way she liked to believe was affectionate); Carlo Fiorelli; Dr. Vaniah Odom; Dickinson Prud'homme; Harry Hollander; Highland Kinsolvin . . .

Others were pouring in from the adjoining streets.

Somewhere, half hidden in the shadows in an out-of-the-way corner, unnoticed by the crowds, there was Annie.

All of them, like the saints in the windows of All Saints', bore emblems of themselves before them, held proudly forward, pilgrims inviting a blessing from a passing pope. (Not an image that would have gone down well with Dr. Vaniah Odom, the Goodchilds, or Mrs. Albert Comstock. The group of nuns from The House of the Magdalenes – provocatively gathered together behind Dr. Vaniah Odom, who kept glancing nervously around; when he had told Satan to get him behind him, he hadn't meant it quite so literally – would have responded with more enthusiasm.)

Henry Walden Gauntlett wore the leopard-skin rug from his photographic studio slung over one of his shoulders, a Zulu warrior unaccountably carrying a camera instead of an assegai. Hilde Claudia, Theodore, and Max Webster fluttered their semaphore flags, wordlessly soliciting requests for them to spring into emblematic action, glumly enthusiastic to shape themselves into all the letters of the alphabet, and spell out coded messages. Cissie Isserliss carried a little wooden box with a slit in the lid, like a charity collecting box, rattling it in the faces of those around her like a menacing maraca, as Issie Isserliss rang a little tinkling silver bell, and pointed at the box meaningfully. Puns were not allowed *chez* Isserliss. Issie Isserliss rang the little hand-bell whenever anyone made a pun, and shouted, "Pun Warning! Pun Warning!" Cissie Isserliss called herself the Keeper of the Pun Box, and exacted a small fine from the perpetrator of the pun. This tended to inhibit the natural flow of relaxed conversation. Highland Kinsolvin, dressed in all the black solemnity that befitted his position of funeral director, held a huge black-ribboned wreath aloft, all ready to award it to the victor in some competition: the fastest sprinter in some serious-faced race, the sad-eyed poet whose panegyric had called forth the most tears. Dickinson Prud'homme, his beard, hands, and face, his upheld, well-soaked brushes, as pink as a brothel parlor with carelessly spilt paint, had the dazed, slightly dribbling look of a man who had been painting colossal nudes with considerable enthusiasm all night through. With an imperious *Peep! Peep!* – there went his whistle – Dr. Severance of Staten Island moved forward with his notebook, looking eager, pen poised . . .

In the distance the vastness of Mrs. Albert Comstock hove into sight, with Mrs. Goodchild dancing attendance. Behind them, characteristically scowling, was Serenity Goodchild, followed by a whole plague of frog-faced indistinguishable Goodchilds and Griswolds. Their parasols were being used with the same prod, prod, prod motions they employed with their umbrellas when they were out on patrol, the standard-bearers for moral standards, and their flags flew high, snapping in a brisk breeze. They hastened forward, as if late for their big number in *Florodora*.

"Tell me, pretty maiden,
Are there any more at home like you?"

The parasols began to twirl flirtatiously.

"There are a few . . ."

Glances were exchanged.

If you studied Mrs. Albert Comstock carefully you could convince yourself that Emmerson's theory was right, and that she really was Albert Comstock himself, in disguise. Those beefy biceps, those architectural thighs: they were unmistakable, and that Mount Kilimanjaro of a bosom (thick snow on the upper slopes) could readily be improvised.

Nostrils were flared – you could have had *Ben-Hur* chariot races in and out of Mrs. Albert Comstock's Hoosac Tunnel-sized nostrils – and all senses were on full alert.

They'd heard that *French* was being sung, and they all knew what French meant. French meant filth. French meant licentiousness and poor drains. French meant the complete collapse of all moral standards, and the end of dignity and decorum, accompanied by a strong whiff of garlic. You just *knew* it meant something repugnant. Mrs. Albert Comstock had once been to Paris for a week, and was verging on the bilingual. She couldn't actually *speak* French – "*Nong parley Frongsey*, me," she could announce proudly, virtuously, like Justice Hare in *East Lynne* – but she had acquired a few French phrases, some of them from restaurant menus, and used them (shuddering as she did so) more or less at random, when she felt that the occasion required it, a *conny-sewer* of cringing. She spoke them with a nudgingly portentous, threatening note, the voice of someone saying "*Carpe diem*" at the very moment a comet arrived to bring an end to all life on earth. "*Tabble-dhoti*," she would announce warningly, adding the taste of an Indian loincloth to a French meal, and improving the flavor significantly, "*fetter-complee, tetter-tet, garsong, wee, mersewer*" – trust the French to bring sewers into something – "*swarry, sheff der cwiseen, a bean tote, servees non compree, day-core, chick.*" (To be told that she was wearing a very *chick* – her preferred pronunciation – dress was one thing; to be told that it was *chic*, with recognizable French intonation, and flirtatiously straining eyebrows, was quite another. This was the unmistakable signal for the fan to be produced, the bone-jarring whacks to be administered, and the room hastily evacuated.) On her return from Paris (thankful to have survived, that was the message) she demonstrated her cosmopolitan sophistication by stringing what appeared to be whole sentences together, to the wonderment of Mrs. Goodchild and Mabel Peartree.

"*Lah platt dew jewer*," she remarked meaningfully – this was one of her more ambitious utterances – a philosopher detecting a subtle nuance in one of the more obscure passages of Descartes. (Her lips moved with shuddering distaste: this *platt* would not contain anything nice, that was for sure.)

(Applause from oh-my-goodnessing Mrs. Goodchild and Mabel Peartree.)

"*Entry interdite. Ne pas deeranger silver play. Pelouse interdite.*"

(Thunderous applause. Gasps of astonishment.)

It was one thing for Mrs. Albert Comstock to speak French in this effortless fashion. ("Aren't the French *peculiar*?" That was what she was saying. "Why on earth can't they speak *English*?" That was the true translation of all she spoke.) It was *quite* another thing for anyone else to speak French in her hearing. She could, wincing, *sense* when French was in the vicinity. If you whispered *gâteau* or *château* she would instantly recognize that it was French, and her sucked-lemons expression of appalled disgust would spring into action. *Fin de siècle*: sucked lemons (she'd approached the new century with permanent sourness); *ici on parle français*: sucked lemons; *petits pois à la Française*: the taste of lemon completely drowned the flavor of the peas; *plus ça change*: sucked lemons (no change here). If you whispered "apple pie" in a French accent, it would have the same effect.

Mrs. Albert Comstock and her grim-faced guardians of niceness had definitely heard – faintly, ahead of them as they hastened to Hudson Row – the word *l'amour* (a lemon-lemon-lemon slot machine jackpot of an expression from Mrs. Albert Comstock), panicked slightly, and broken into a waddling sprint. Their parasols strained at an identical angle in front of them, hauling them forward like the leashes of eager bloodhounds sniff-sniffily seeking out sin.

L'amour was a single word to these fearless defenders of public morality. They wouldn't have recognized *amour*, but *l'amour* – oh yes, yes, *yes* (simultaneous shudders at this point) they knew *exactly* what that word meant, thank you very much, and they didn't like what they knew. They didn't like it *at all*. When these women were in the right mood, they spoke almost exclusively in italics. The sharp edges seemed to cut at the insides of their mouths, and give them pained, incensed expressions. They'd heard *l'amour* – quite distinctly – *more than once*. There'd been a *une* (this was *definitely* French) and – loud and clear, as if challengingly emphasized – a provocative *je t'aime. Je t'aime!* It was whispered behind cupped hands from ear to ear, a secret pornographic password being passed on. First *l'amour* and now *je t'aime!* Before much longer they'd be hearing a *le* or a *la*, and it was but a small step from a *la* to an *Ooh la la!*, and they were there to put a stop to any hint of *that sort of thing*. They'd arrived not a moment too soon. Alfred Eakins, in his long apron, continued with his sweeping, the stiff bristles moving backward and forward over the same section, as if he were trying to erase the shadowed letters *SIN*. His service was to remove *SIN* with celerity.

From the entrance of Columbarian & Horowitz, two doors away, a complete orchestra began to play the Cigarette Girls' song. The musicians were rather crammed in, at awkward angles, and the necks of cellos and violins protruded untidily above the heads of the woodwind section, which squatted down on the polished tiles just inside the door. Brass glinted from the inner dimness. The elderly Misses Isserliss, who had never smoked in their lives (indeed, smoking, like punning, was a proscribed peccadillo in their house on Hudson Heights), drew expertly on the cigarettes hanging casually from their lips, and began to sing, swaying in perfect unison. Cissie rattled the coins in the wooden box; Issie rang the little silver bell, as an improvised percussion accompaniment to the music.

Mrs. Albert Comstock and Mrs. Goodchild, despite their best efforts, were seduced from their high purpose by the closer proximity of French. Showing an unexpectedly sensitive response to the Spanish setting of *Carmen* (Mrs. Albert Comstock did not have a box at the Metropolitan Opera for nothing) they removed their false teeth, and began to utilize them as castanets, humming along with the music.

Look at us! they were saying.

We can afford G. G. Schiffendecken false teeth! they were saying.

They moved their bodies sensually from side to side — it was not a sight for the easily nauseated — as their grin-filled hands clicked up and down with manic glee, sending sprays of spit flying for yards. It brought a welcome coolness to those in the immediate vicinity, like a gentle summer shower.

> *"Dans l'air, nous suivons des yeux*
> *La . . ."*

There was a *la*! There was a *la*! Expressions of dawning horror spread across the faces of the denture-wielding dancers. What were they thinking of? What madness had possessed them?

> *". . . fumée*
> *Qui vers les cieux*
> *Monte, monte parfumée.*
> *Dans l'air nous suivons des yeux*
> *La . . ."*

Again!

Teeth were crammed back into mouths with gestures of firm resolve, and parasols were once more grasped firmly, leaping forward at the sound of the *la*, seeking out the evils of Frenchness. The bloodhounds snuffled with whimpering excitement, a low, warning growl beginning deep in their throats. They were close. They were *really* close to the fountainhead of filth. They would cry "Havoc!" and let slip the dogs. Mrs. Albert Comstock was not quite sure what this meant – she was not bilingual in Shakespeare – but it sounded the right sort of idea: teeth, blood, ripping sounds, obliteration, that kind of thing. They would not falter in their purpose a second time. They'd lay about them with their parasols, a scything massacre of muckiness *pour encourager les autres*.

Damn!

They'd just used French.

Shit!

They'd just said "Damn!"

You just couldn't *help* being corrupted when these Frenchies were out in full froggy force. Come on, girls! Time to dagger a dago!

> "...*fumée,*
> *La*..."

The parasols were grasped with grim determination, as if they were stakes about to be hammered through the hearts of a whole vault full of vampires. After the stakes through the hearts came the beheadings. There'd be no problem finding the garlic – *Phew!*, *Fah!*, *Faugh!*, *Teuch!*: all the exclamatory sounds of disgust – to stuff in the mouths of the severed heads with all this French around.

> "...*fumée,*
> *La*..."

Filth! Filth!

> "...*fumée,*
> *La*..."

They held their parasols before them like Crusaders brandishing crosses in the faces of the infidels. They would valiant be 'gainst all disaster, get in a few good whacks, and go down fighting against the rising tide of – the italics sprang back into action – *filth*.

The troops of Midian were upon them.

They were prowling and prowling around.

They would strive.

They would tempt.

They would lure.

They would goad into sin.

Onward, Mrs. Albert Comstock!

Ever onward, Mrs. Goodchild!

Get prodding with those parasols!

Fight the good fight with all thy might!

Faint not nor fear!

"... *fumée* ..."

Dr. Wolcott Ascharm Webster moved first. Gazelle-like, he leaped from his position outside the Manhattan & Brooklyn Bank, lingering for a shy moment, as if to allow the Ethel model to display the suppleness for which it was universally noted and respected by the discriminating, and then began to skip out across the street. With a coy grace, G. G. Schiffendecken, like an object drawn to its reflection, moved toward Dr. Wolcott Ascharm Webster, and Dr. Wolcott Ascharm Webster moved toward him.

They met, like creatures mating, in the middle of the street, G. G. Schiffendecken leaping high into the air, spinning around twice – the swinging garters making a sound like a child's paper windmill spinning – and landing with perfect aplomb in Dr. Wolcott Ascharm Webster's confidently upraised hands, to lie calmly on his side like someone reclining on a *chaise longue* in the comfort and privacy of his own home. Dr. Wolcott Ascharm Webster, legs slightly apart, was braced to hold him, and Carlotta rotated slowly and then with increasing speed, above Ethel, until

G. G. Schiffendecken was just a blur, his spectacles a continuous gleam on the periphery, and the sound of the paper windmill became an insistent rattle, a child running a stick along metal railings. War veterans flung themselves earthward – a loud *WHOOP!* from Dr. Brown – in a well-trained automatic response to its machine-gun rat-a-tat-tatting, but this temporary distraction did not break G. G. Schiffendecken's concentration. His voice – rather breathless – could be heard in bursts as he spun around.

"I would . . ."

– *Gasp!* –

". . . recommend Carlotta to anyone. I love . . ."

– *Gasp!* –

". . . to feel her . . ."

– (*her!*) –

". . . silky sheerness against . . ."

– *Gasp!* –

". . . my skin."

The Misses Isserliss (saying their names correctly three times in rapid succession was generally recognized as a reliable test of sobriety in Longfellow Park) moved closer, arm in arm under the same parasol, which was at an angle of forty-five degrees. Estimable ladies – now in their seventies – always dressed identically because they were twins, even though Miss Issie Isserliss was twice the height of Miss Cissie Isserliss, they commented favorably on the firm uplift and support afforded by Ethel, who did not sag and did not crease, even under the most trying conditions, giving rise to universally approving comment amongst discerning friends.

Mrs. Albert Comstock and Mrs. Goodchild gaped and pointed their parasols accusingly.

Prod! Prod! Prod!

Far off, beyond the distant end of Hudson Row as it turned west and began to move toward the upper reaches of Broadway, the Reverend Goodchild, a veritable *prima ballerina assoluta*, was executing a *divertissement* as he *glissaded* south toward New York City. His Dorinda corset – flesh-colored (for those who happened to possess pinkish-white flesh) for discretion when wearing paler garments in the summer season — was partly obscured by the filmy cascades of a Zuleika lace negligee. The Reverend Goodchild liked his little luxuries. The front of the negligee — he was negligent with his negligee, in a disheveled state of dishabille — lazily opened and closed with each stride he took, slowly, like fabric unfolding under water, something being repeatedly washed to remove stains.

His arms were wide open, as if to embrace the whole city, and he was smiling beatifically, like a man who — at long last, after much searching — had found his true self.

17

It was suddenly dusk.

The area under the chestnut trees, where the children played — she thought of the trees as being immeasurably old, trees that had given their name to Chestnut Street — was deserted with the coming of darkness. In the spring, she'd look out each morning, waiting for the first glimpse of the whiteness of the candles appearing in the branches, the blossom one of the signs that winter really was over. Sometimes, in the summer, she stood on a table in the schoolroom under the opened skylight, looking out, and she could hear the voices of the children at play — The Baptist Game; Trials, Troubles, and Tribulations — and glimpse the girls' pale dresses.

Last night she had heard them playing Walking on the Green Grass, a game they did not often play because it needed boys as well as girls, and the boys were reluctant to join in with the girls' games. Serenity Goodchild, the Reverend Goodchild's fearsome grubby-minded granddaughter, must have threatened, or physically assaulted, the boys until they had joined in. She had not been born until several years after the deaths of Albert Comstock and Alice's father, but there she was on this day of dancing, the same age then as she was now. The children's voices were high and piercing in the fading light.

". . . Now take her by the hand, this queen,
And swing her round and round the green . . ."

Any boy who attempted to swing Serenity Goodchild round and round by her hand (she was a – er – big-boned girl) would have been risking permanent damage. There would have been agonized grunts, the sounds of muffled internal explosions, reverberating twangs. The pattern of movement shifted and broke beneath the trees, the procession becoming a circle, the circle becoming two lines, the figures swinging up into the air, as if they weighed nothing at all, and then there were no figures there, just the trampled grass and the darkness.

Papa – completely alone – was pirouetting in the middle of the bandstand in the park, which was illuminated like a miniature stage. The immense polished dome of his bald head emitted a discreet muted gleam that harmonized with his pearl necklace and earrings.

After she had polished the door knocker, Annie – it was an essential part of her daily duties – gave his head and teeth a vigorous rub with Putz's Pomade Metal Polish. He came out and stood on the front step, bending his knees – further, further – so that his teeth were on the same level as the knocker, then bowing his head to allow access. He completely ignored Annie as she buffed his baldness. One did not thank servants.

"When applied to any polished surface and rubbed off," Annie demonstrated to applauding passers-by, "Putz's will leave a luster obtained in no other way. It will take off dirt, grease, or tarnish quicker than any known substance."

". . . I cleaned the windows and I swept the floor . . ."

– Annie sang (it was not Bizet, but Charlotte would be pleased to hear Gilbert and Sullivan) –

". . . And I polished up the handle of the big front door.
I polished up that handle so carefullee
That now I am the Ruler of the Queen's Navee! . . ."

109

". . . She polished up that handle so carefullee . . ."

— the passers-by chorused —

". . . That now she is the Ruler of the Queen's Navee!"

Some of them linked arms, and danced around in time to the music. It was quite a jolly scene.

Papa looked like a gigantic version of the ballerina in the jewelry box that Mama had given her when she was five years old, spinning round and round to an insidiously repeated little tune. He was a massive Mary Benedict, eager as ever to demonstrate her knowledge of all the ballet positions.

First position.

Heels together, feet turned out.

Don't forget the simper.

Second position . . .

He kept lurching over to the right. A loss of balance would demolish the ornate metal balustrade, and several rows of the chairs lined up on the grass beyond.

The tinkling little tune became louder, and the song from *H.M.S. Pinafore* faded completely away. The luster from Putz's Pomade Metal Polish remained, like a tastefully subdued beacon in the darkness.

The music to which he was wobblily revolving — it was being played by his pocket-watch, one of the six tunes in its repertoire — was the melody she had heard more times in the last years of the century than any other, more even than "After the Ball" (a fleeting glimpse of the grotesque little gnomic silhouette pursuing the large black ball that appeared on the sheet music), "Just Tell Them that You Saw Me," or — raising the tone slightly — "To a Wild Rose," or "Rustle of Spring" ("*Frühlingsrauschen*" to those who wished to impress). The melody had been heard everywhere, and it was surprising that the constant repetition of it by her less promising pupils did not have Miss Iandoli hurling herself from her window in despair, driven to madness by something she had once loved, a Lady Macbeth of music. There she would be, impaled on the ace of spades tips of the railings, unable to prevent her feet from waving in time to the music that stumblingly continued to ker-plunk away inside.

Ker-plunk, ker-plunk, ker-plunkety plunky-plunk . . .

This melody was "Narcissus."

"I shall now play Ethelbert Nevin, Opus 13, Number 4," a pianist would announce portentously at a musical evening.

(He or she — shes tended to predominate — would be one of those who announced "Rustle of Spring" as *"Frühlingsrauschen."* They clearly wished it to be understood that they were more refined than the common herd of amateur ker-plunkers.)

There would be consternation as the threatened imminence of culture looked all set to interrupt conversations and spoil the atmosphere. Then, after the first few bars, everyone would relax. Call it what you would, it was only the tinkly sound of "Narcissus" after all.

What a relief!

> *Ker-plunk, ker-plunk,*
> *Ker-plunkety plunky-plunk.*
> *Ker-plunk, ker-plunk,*
> *Ker-plunkety plunky-plunk.*
> *Ker-plunk, ker-plunk,*
> *Ker-plunk, ker-plunk,*
> *Ker-plunk, ker-plunkety, plunk, ker-plunkety,*
> *Plunk, plunk . . .*

Papa revolved and wobbled, revolved and wobbled, a Narcissus reflected in his own inner eye, and liking what it was he saw there.

You're a crackerjack!

That's what he was thinking.

That corset sets off your figure to its best advantage.

Your legs are superb.

"Narcissus" began to play more and more slowly as the mechanism of the pocket-watch – the bandstand jewelry box – ran down, each *ker* separated from its *plunk* by a longer and longer whir-filled silence. An early evening breeze ruffled the frills on the lower part of Papa's Little Missy corset – he liked Little Missies – and fluffed them up. He revolved ever more slowly, ever more jerkily, the ballerina coming to a halt as the clockwork abruptly stopped with a shudder. He was on tiptoe, his arms raised gracefully above him, a still figure of poise and gracefulness, about to perform in *The Tales of Hoffmann*, another sinful French opera.

(The distant parasols, as if alerted, pointed like dogs sensing game – *Over there! Over there!* – quivering with impassioned distaste.)

He was an Olympia – the mechanical doll – the first great love of Hoffmann's life, waiting to be wound up by Spalanzani.

The key in her back would be turned – *Whir! Whir! Whir!* – and she would begin to sing again with mechanical exactness, her singing ever shriller, ever faster.

A voice rang out of the growing darkness. The music of *Carmen* had returned.

It was the voice of the captain beginning to question Carmen after her arrest. Who had wounded the girl in the fight at the cigarette factory?

Papa was Carmen. Saucy, tantalizing, deliberately provocative, he refused to answer.

"Tra la la la la la la la . . ." he sang, teasingly alluring, coquettishly fluttering his hands, Mrs. Albert Comstock letting rip with her fan.

You are completely irresistible.

You ooze ooh-la-la allure.

"You may cut me," he answered (it sounded far worse in French). "You may burn me, but I won't answer! I defy steel and fire!"

Mockingly defiant, his beard and ballet dress rustling, he

repeated the same taunting phrase after each attempt at questioning, his voice higher each time.

"Tra la la la la la la la . . ."

At each "la" the tips of the parasols winced like Julius Cæsar as yet another dagger thrust home into him.

"Tra la . . ."

— *Ouch!* —

". . . la . . ."

— *Ouch!* —

". . . la . . ."

— *Ouch!* —

". . . la . . ."

Casca, Cassius, Decius, Cinna . . .

They all piled in, a starving mob hacking, salivating, into the rotating carcass at a serve-yourself barbecue. Brutus, in need of a nibble, hovered hungrily. Each "la" was a filthy French attempt to sully the innocence that characterized all things American.

He wouldn't tell them what he knew.

He wouldn't tell them anything. What he knew would remain a secret. No one would ever know.

His eyes were bland, his expression mild, his fingers stroking in a slightly suggestive way the letters *SIN* on the base of his left breast. He seemed very happy. His well-polished bald head gleamed.

"Tra la la la la la la la . . ."

What he knew was a secret, and no one was ever going to find out.

("S" was saucy.

("S" was seductive.

("S" was secret.)

18

It was completely dark.

Annie was beside her now, and they were holding hands. Under the trees in the park, in the part at the far end of the lake, furthest away from the houses and the gas-lamps, in the cool light of a full moon, was her father, squatting down in the darkness, not fully visible. Albert Comstock, G. G. Schiffendecken, Dr. Wolcott Ascharm Webster, and the Reverend Goodchild were there with him, though she couldn't see them. The soft cloth coverings of the corsets had been removed, like clothes at bedtime. Whalebone gleamed whitely in the darkness, as though the remains of something dead were lying there, as if Hilda, Carlotta, Ethel, Dorinda, and Little Missy had all met violent ends at the hands of a corset-crazed killer, and the glint of polished metal reflected the gleam of Annie's eyes. Her eyes seemed enormous. A wind had blown up, quite strong, hissing in the branches like falling water, but the loudest sound was the sound of breathing. The ragged breathing – loud, raw, slightly wheezing, like that of people who had been running too fast and too far – gradually co-ordinated into one rhythm, and became louder, like the beginning of a cat's purring, or the contented sound of sun-warmed, sleepy doves.

She tried to move her head to one side, as if what she was seeing was actually in front of her, and not inside her mind.

> (". . . She heard a voice like voice of doves
> Cooing all together:
> They sounded kind and full of loves
> In the pleasant weather . . .")

She had a sense of the coldness of the metal, the rigidity of the bone. There were the fat white hairy thighs, big and meaty, and the stained, gaping undergarments.

The coarse, insinuating texture of the beards.

The smell of tobacco.

Lips.

> (". . . Dear, you should not stay so late,
> Twilight is not good for maidens;

Should not loiter in the glen
In the haunts of goblin men . . .")

The goblins and their misshapen creatures massed beneath the castle as they sought to carry away Princess Irene deep into the darkness. Always there was the sound of digging and digging, as they drew closer to their goal, hollowing out their narrow corridors into the foundations, drawing closer every day. You could hear them if you listened carefully, their furtive pickaxes gouging into the rock.

Alice gripped Annie's hand more tightly. The two sisters, Lizzie and Laura, lay asleep in their curtained bed, their arms around each other, the moon and star gazing in at them. Lizzie and Laura crouched close together amongst the brookside rushes in the evening, Laura bowing her head to listen to the goblin voices.

"No," said Lizzie: "No, no, no . . ."
Laura did not listen.

(". . . She never tasted such before,
How should it cloy with length of use?
She sucked and sucked and sucked the more
Fruits which that unknown orchard bore;
She sucked until her lips were sore . . .")

Alice started to tremble, and the newspaper, which she had been clutching all this time, began to shake, making a tiny rattling sound.

(". . . Their fruits like honey in the throat
But poison in the blood . . .")

Why hadn't Allegra and Edith been able to help?
They were all little girls, but there were three of them. Ben couldn't have helped. He had been a baby.
Why hadn't her sisters helped her to save Annie, as Laura's sister had saved her in "Goblin Market"?

Why hadn't she helped her, all by herself?

Instead, she had found for her the address of Madame Roskosch, the woman who had promised – in her newspaper advertisements – to produce THE DESIRED EFFECT within twenty-four hours. She had thought she was helping Annie, doing what she wanted her to do. Madame Roskosch had offered a SURE CURE FOR LADIES IN TROUBLE in the way that Madame Etoile offered to see the past, the present, and the future, and never to fail. Madame Roskosch had not told Annie all that she wanted to know; she had not guided her in all aspects of life with her professional skill. She offered consultation and advice FREE. She offered ELEGANT ROOMS and claimed not to make use of injurious medicines or instruments.

She had lied.

Papa had destroyed Annie, coldly and deliberately, and she was the only person who knew.

Then, nine years later, during the 1888 blizzard, he had killed himself.

Mama – before she had been struck down into silence and invalidity – had begun to convince herself that there must have been some sort of terrible accident (*ha!*), a very messy one, if it had been, but Alice liked to think that his death was planned, and was because of what he had done to Annie. She tried to convince herself that he had killed himself because he had made Annie pregnant, had driven her away, but he had done it because of problems with money. These, and not a girl of fourteen, were what had been important to him. He would not have killed himself because of a girl, especially years after he had last seen her. Money was what mattered, especially if you did not have enough of it.

He had been struggling for years.

If Annie had never gone to Madame Roskosch, if she had given birth to her child, this child – when Papa died – would have been almost the same age as Alice herself had been during those secret journeys through the wall and to the Celestial City, the time when Annie had been made pregnant. If Annie had lived, her child would now be almost twenty-five, the same age as Ben. But Annie had gone to Madame Roskosch, to the address that Alice had read out to her, and Annie had died because Madame Roskosch had been an incompetent abortionist. She hadn't brought together those long separated, shown Annie an accurate likeness of a future husband, and given his name; she had killed her. This was what Alice believed had happened, what she had worked out over the years, though she did not know for certain.

What was certain was that she had never seen Annie again.

Upstairs, down a long corridor, a door opened, and she heard her father's voice.

"Alice?"

"Yes, P-P-Papa?"

It seemed excessively vindictive of fate that the stutter she had developed should experience particular difficulty with the letter "p." She couldn't say "Papa" without stuttering.

"Has the newspaper arrived?"

"Yes, P-P-Papa."

She couldn't say her own name without stuttering.

"Bring it to me in my room."

"Yes, P-P-Papa."

She wasn't Miss Pinkerton. She was Miss P-P-Pinkerton. She had heard Myrtle Comstock, Mrs. Albert Comstock's daughter – a woman who pushed the frontiers of sophistication ever outward – calling her this to Mrs. Goodchild. "Myrtle! You really are *dreadful*!" That had been the response. Mrs. Goodchild had been *delighted*. Alice ought to join Miss Stammers on her action-packed dog-walking expeditions, Miss Stutters and Miss Stammers – what, precisely, *was* the distinction between a stutter and a stammer? – jerkily advancing, leashed to unruly hounds, the Tweedledum and Tweedledee of speech impediments.

It would take them so long to say the dogs' names that if any dog made a break for freedom it would be off and away before they could call it to heel.

"H-H-Hamlet!"

"H-H-Hans!"

"K-K-Kierk-k-kegaard!"

(You could virtually guarantee that Alice would be the one charged with the duty of summoning Kierkegaard.)

Distant triumphant barks.

Mocking woofs.

A landscape empty of dogs.

The idea was so appealing that she ignored the fact that Miss Stammers did not, in fact, stammer. With Miss Stammers, Chastity Heighton, and Sobriety Goodchild and his daughter Serenity amongst its inhabitants, Longfellow Park was positively awash with the misleadingly monikered. You'd barely recovered from the shock of grasping that the poisonous squat sniggerer in front of you bore the Christian – *Christian!* – name Serenity, when it dawned upon you that her surname was Goodchild.

Carefully, she began to smooth the newspaper where she had crumpled it slightly, Annie saving a page with the names of women who could foretell the future, women born with a genuine gift. She folded it carefully, arranging it with the engraving of the Board of Governors on top, their beards neatly on display, all lined up like an illustration in a sporran catalogue. Gradually, the trembling began to slow.

"Alice?"

"Yes, P-P-Papa."

She began to walk upstairs. The newspaper still shook slightly in her hands, as if from a distant subterranean tremor.

19

She was at the bottom of the stairs, and there was no newspaper lying on the tiles. It was Sunday. There would not have been a newspaper there. Yesterday's newspaper had already been read, and she had used it to wrap around one of her writing journals when she stored it away.

She was conscious of letting out her breath suddenly, as if she had been holding it all that time, breathing suspended for a while. She had experienced one of those moments that sometimes happened when a certain passage in a book was read, a certain picture contemplated. It happened over and over. Time ceased to exist, and she became one with what she read, what she contemplated, within the work of art, like her namesake Alice within the looking-glass. It happened every time she studied Linnaeus's painting in the schoolroom. The water in the ewer was still hot, steam rising. It must be like dreaming was supposed to be, when time was concentrated into a few seconds, or like drowning, when a life passed before the eyes in moments. Maggie Tulliver must have experienced this, clasped in Tom's arms, as she and her brother sank to their deaths beneath the flood water: beating her doll's wooden head against the pillars, cutting her hair jaggedly, Behaving Worse than She Expected, Trying to Run Away from Her Shadow . . .

She looked into the room – glass-enclosed, plant-filled, cold in winter – where the piano was, at the back of the house, overlooking the garden. No fire had yet been set in this room, and her breath whitened. She didn't know why she looked in there; she knew her mother was still asleep upstairs. It was a major undertaking now, to attempt to bring Mama downstairs, and she spent most of her time in her room.

Louis Moreau Gottschalk's eyes looked intensely across at her from the music rack. The last thing she could remember her mother playing on the piano had been not Gottschalk but "Oh, Dem Golden Slippers," and the music for this was still there. It was in a book with several other songs, and the illustration on the cover was for "Carry Me Back to Old Virginny." She hadn't seen it for a while, and seeing it again made her realize how much she disliked it.

It depicted a black man and woman, and the two figures were utterly grotesque. Somehow, they reminded her of an illustration of an elephant she had seen in an eighteenth-century travel book, obviously drawn by an artist who had never seen an elephant. He must have drawn it from a written description, rather in the way that Mrs. Albert Comstock designed her laugh, and the result – like the laugh – was oddly, disturbingly *wrong*. On the cover of the sheet music the theme was more that of crocodiles than of elephants. The two clumsily drawn figures – a man and a woman awkwardly bidding farewell by shaking hands (this seemed a curiously formal gesture: they appeared to be holding each other at a distance, rather than embracing), the man carrying a carpetbag – had bizarrely extended feet, as if they were wearing clowns' boots, long and narrow like crocodile jaws. Continuing the crocodilian theme, they had small pointed teeth in their enormously wide mouths, bared all ready for a dentist's inspection (though G. G. Schiffendecken would not have been enthusiastic: no money here), completely without humor. No smiles, these.

It brought to mind – she shuddered at the recollection – a performance of *Uncle Tom's Cabin* she had seen as a child, in which Topsy had been played by a middle-aged white man – a little, stunted figure with a falsetto voice – in blackface. There had been something nightmarish about this figure.

"I 'spect I grow'd!" it said, drawing out the last word – "grrrooooow'd!" – and visibly waiting for the laughs, which came.

The audience shrieked, and it stood there, rolling its bugged-out eyes, with its mouth wide open. He was famous for playing this rôle. It was the most disturbing thing she had seen in the theatre until Dum-Dum the Dummy came along.

She saw a whole row of blackfaced white people looking like this. They were swaying from side to side, white-gloved hands fluttering like flocks of escaping birds, and tears, crocodile tears, poured down their faces as they sang a sentimental song. It was like seeing Mr. Soot, the Sweep, and his family, with their soot-blackened faces, bursting into a harmonious rendition of some popular minstrel-show favorite, waving their brushes in time to the music as dark clouds billowed Hades-like around them. Their voices echoed hollowly up the soot-encrusted interiors of the chimneys, adding a mournful resonance to their words.

"The sun shines bright in the old Kentucky home;
'Tis summer, the darkies are gay;
The corn-top's ripe, and the meadow's in the bloom,
While the birds make music all the day.
The young folks roll on the little cabin floor,
All merry, all happy and bright;
By-'n-by hard times comes a-knocking at the door: —
Then my old Kentucky home, good-night!

"Weep no more, my lady,
O, weep no more today!
We will sing one song for the old Kentucky home,
For the old Kentucky home, far away . . ."

"Weep no more, my lady, O, weep no more today!" they sang, and the more they sang about not weeping, the more they wept. White tracks ran down from the eyes through the burned cork blackness, their brushes drooped, and the crocodile faces became the faces of zebras. This Happy Family enjoyed a good sentimental snivel. It quite cheered them up. They'd be merry, all happy and bright.

Alice thought again of the moment when Annie had opened the door to Mrs. Albert Comstock for the first time, and Mrs. Albert Comstock had seen that the Pinkertons' new servant-girl was black. It was something she would not forget. It was something she had to remember. Annie had just joined them. It was her first job, and she had been nervous. Annie opened the door, bobbed a little curtsy, and looked up with a smile. Alice had seen her practicing in the kitchen, when she thought no one was around. Mrs. Albert Comstock — who rarely deigned to notice servants, in any case — swiftly overcame her initial expression of surprise, and looked through, beyond Annie, to where Mama had been approaching.

"Gracious!" she had said, indicating Annie with a slight sideways tilt of the head, and the ha-ha-ha-ha sound that she used in place of a laugh. "What a lot of teeth!"

She spoke like someone referring to "Carry Me Back to Old Virginny," the two crocodile-footed monstrosities.

When she returned home, Mrs. Albert Comstock would have greeted Myrtle with the words, "Only one today!" It was a good day, a very good day, but – "Guess where it was!" – that one was rather too close to home. It wasn't there for very long, just over a year and a half, and then it died.

The word "crocodile" stirred other thoughts. She was as haunted by crocodiles as Thomas De Quincey in his opium-induced dreamings, as if she – in her turn – had emptied some dull opiate to the drains. What could she remember about crocodiles? This was an exercise she sometimes performed with herself, choosing topics at random, checking – she felt – for signs of movement in the brain, as if gingerly moving an injured limb to see if there was pain.

"I was kissed, with cancerous kisses, by crocodiles": these words, and one other sentence, were the words from *Confessions of an English Opium Eater* that had stayed in her mind. David Copperfield and Peggotty. Herodotus. St. Theodore and St. Helenus. Robert Louis Stevenson. Christina Rossetti. Oscar Wilde. They'd all been connected with, or had mentioned, crocodiles. The way to escape crocodiles, David Copperfield had read, was to baffle them by constantly turning as you ran away from them, as they found this difficult to do because of their unwieldiness. (But wouldn't this be too risky? Wouldn't it slow you down too much?) Peggotty had formed the impression that crocodiles were a sort of vegetable. Herodotus . . .

She thrust the illustration out of sight, and walked out of the room – half consciously tucking some of her mother's Louis Moreau Gottschalk music under her arm, as if it was something to read in a quiet moment – and back upstairs.

She hurried up the last flight of stairs to the schoolroom, careful not to spill the hot water. It would be almost too much of a surprise for Ben, to emerge half asleep from his room, thoughts of Japan in his head, and see – at the end of the dark corridor – a figure in a pale kimono moving away from him. He had never been to Japan:

he would be imagining scenes from Grandpapa's photographs, a painted landscape, words on a page.

20

The schoolroom ran the full depth of the house, and she stood looking out again at the back, gazing out from her high window.

The fields and orchards that had once spread away, and up to Hudson Heights, were going, had gone. In the dark morning light, deep under snow, what she could see — the gas-lamps obscured by windblown blizzards — had the feeling of somewhere north of anywhere else, cold and gloomy in perpetual twilight, a huddled underground settlement in the Arctic, some Siberian port where the sea had turned to ice and vessels were frozen at their moorings, rigging furred like frosted spiders' webs. The inhabitants, trebled in size with thick clothing, slowly picked their way through streets of frozen mud, their whitened breath like low clouds turgidly unfolding. Everyone was faceless, swathed in mufflers and low-pulled hats, with just their eyes showing, the streets peopled by bank robbers and bandits, gingerly picking their way toward their next holdup in a society where all control had collapsed. It made her think of a map of the world that showed only the unexplored regions, a world with no names, just untouched, unwritten-on whiteness. The Arctic was an unmapped place like this; Dr. Wolcott Ascharm Webster's phrenology skull with no labeled names.

To dream of looking down from high places, or out of windows, or being in a high garret, shows an ambitious mind, curious desires, wandering imagination, and confused thoughts.

She felt — as she had felt all the previous summer — that she could sense New York City moving up toward them, that the city would engulf Longfellow Park, and turn it into another lost community, like Manhattanville or Bloomingdale Village. On nights, especially the sleepless summer nights (there had been many of these), she had been sure that she could sometimes feel the house shake slightly as explosions blasted the rock of Manhattan for the foundations of new buildings, new streets, whole new areas, and the city advanced north. People began to live in places that were not yet on the map, did not really exist. When there had been too little light to read any longer, she had lain and listened in twilight and darkness. It had been too hot to light the lamps, and the twilights had been long, the objects around slowly thickening into indistinctness in the growing gloom. They would surely not be using explosives at night, but she sensed that the windows rattled, the domes of the lamps vibrated, and her dim reflection shivered in the mirror. Dorian Gray and Dr. Jekyll swayed forward, and then away again. A dull reddish glow burned briefly on the underside of low cloud, and then the house shifted a little. A dull film of dust removed the gleam from the leaves in the garden, and darkened the brightness of glass. When sheets were removed from the clothesline, and when she brushed her hair at night, grains of powdered rock would fall out. The polished surface of her dressing table blurred, and sometimes she thought that the dead gray dust — she stared intently, like someone looking at a first gray hair — came from inside her own head, loosened by the vigor of her brushing.

One, two, three . . .

If I cry, she would think on the bad nights — there were many bad nights — my tears will leave a track down the dust on my face, and everyone will know I have been crying. When the wind — ah, the wind! — blew from the south, she could hear very faint dull explosions like a distant conflict, and birds would whir up into the air, startled, as if expecting to be shot.

In the late summer both sides of Dadenhof Road had been marked out in building lots, and the whole of Heneacher Woods, all the way up to Megoran Hill and Jacksons Bluff (she felt her usual instinctive twitch at "Jacksons," the urge to insert an apostrophe), had been sold. Across the whole of Longfellow Park, fields and farms were vanishing, buildings being demolished, new constructions appearing. It was like the time when she was a little girl, and the Shakespeare Castle had been demolished on Hudson Heights.

Its extensive grounds had been developed, and — in place of the topiary and the peacocks — Pettifar's Orphanage, The House of the Magdalenes, and the North River Lunatic Asylum had appeared, with their Imperial Roman rows of columns and flights of steps, a gleaming white city for the abandoned, the fallen, the demented.

She thought — at various times in her childhood — that she belonged in one of these last two institutions: in The House of the Magdalenes (as one of the nuns, not one of the sinful women), or in the lunatic asylum (this time as one of the inmates, not as a guardian). Women in white, women in black, nurses and nuns, smiled firmly, reached out their hands, capes and cowls obscuring their shadowed faces.

Some of the boys — Sobriety Goodchild always to the fore, the cruelest, the most inventive and insistent — displayed a fondness for deciding (and loudly proclaiming) which girls at Miss Pearsall's School should be dispatched to which of the institutions. They took particular pleasure in urging the orphanage upon girls who had recently lost a mother or father (even better, of course, if it was both): "Got no Ma, Got no Pa, / Time to go to Pettifar!"

The more vulgar boys (Sobriety Goodchild — needless to say — again a prime contender) were fond of loud speculation about which girls should be in The House of the Magdalenes. Alice had not been entirely sure what a Magdalene was, and vaguely thought at first — from what she had heard — that all those young women had somehow lost their way, and were waiting until they could remember the direction again. "Can't they use maps?" she had asked, eager to be of assistance. Sobriety Goodchild would have been the one to ask about maps. The Magdalenes could have consulted him for assistance. "He's *very* keen on geography," his mama had unconvincingly announced a little while earlier. As far as Alice could ascertain, this dubious assertion was based upon Sobriety's saying "Lake — *Snigger!* — Titicaca!" a lot in a loud voice, having — whilst idly browsing in his atlas — discovered this irresistibly vulgar-sounding geographical feature straddling the lands of the clearly uninhibited Peruvians and Bolivians. If it wasn't – *Snigger!* – *titty*, it was – *Snigger!* – *caca* with Sobriety for ages. North Americans had – how superior! – Lakes Superior, Ontario, Michigan, any number of sober-sounding alcohol-free fresh-water lakes. South Americans had Lake Titicaca.

The lost and wandering Magdalenes had long hair that was darkened and clotted with ointment, and they held half-emptied boxes of it in their glistening fingers, as if they were all Maggie Tullivers, innocently caught out in some new enormity. Their elbows were wrapped around with clean white bandages, tidily fastened with neat prim bows. Old bruises and scratches marked hands and arms, and their dresses were dusty and ripped at the knees. They were much given to falling – this much Alice had gathered – and these were the scars of their falling. Perhaps, like Albert Comstock, they were sinfully given to not-so-secret drinking, or – she remembered a comment from Mrs. Goodchild – excessive finery in clothes, keeling over from too-high heels, twisting their ankles as they fell in a flurry of bright silks. Sobriety Goodchild – who else? – had soon clarified matters for her. "Charlotte the Harlot," Sobriety had called Charlotte, and poor, dumpy, innocent Charlotte had sobbed because it had sounded so rude. Alice had always been the favored candidate for the North River Lunatic Asylum: they were nearer the truth with this one, she supposed, than they had been with Charlotte, and they had been unrelenting

She had – for a time – sought to subdue Sobriety with the aid of artfully administered dramatic irony, after she had first come across the concept as she (at the age of nine) worked her way through *Macbeth*, planning her New Improved version of Shakespeare. "A little water clears us of this deed," said Lady Macbeth, her hands soaked in blood. "How easy is it then!" (Dramatic irony.) "Fail not our feast," Macbeth instructed the soon-to-be-murdered Banquo. (Dramatic irony. Banquo did not fail the feast, and his ghost unleashed chaos.) Dramatic irony seemed guaranteed to produce reliable results, and Alice couldn't wait to try it. All you had to do (the Macbeths obviously hadn't realized this) was to say – in your most confident voice – the opposite of what you really wanted to happen, and blank out the words "God willing" from entering your head. (Not even "D.V." should squeeze its way in through the slightest crack of lapsed concentration, and fingers must remain uncrossed, hands splayed out like Struwwelpeter's.) She debated whether or not to employ Shakespearean English to ensure a favorable outcome, vaguely feeling that blank verse (or, at the very least, prose employed for particular dramatic purposes: she was a great reader of footnotes) held out a better chance of success. In the end, she decided on modern English, to avoid suspicion falling upon her as awful things began to happen to the object of her designs.

"I'm sure he'll be absolutely splendid," she would announce in ringing tones whenever it was announced that Sobriety Goodchild was going to be persuaded to sing in front of a cowed assemblage. "I'm sure he'll sing beautifully." "I'm positive that everyone will really enjoy it." These were other sentences she employed on a regular basis. She wasn't sure whether it was the dramatic irony, or whether it was tempted fate (fate succumbed far too easily to temptation in her experience), but it seemed to work with gratifying regularity. The more extravagantly she expressed anticipation (always ensuring that Sobriety heard her), the worse his performance, though everyone applauded politely. Made ambitious by success (*Macbeth* ought to have warned her against the dangers of ambition) she began a plan, by subtle and sophisticated gradations, to lure Sobriety to his doom by the employment of dramatic irony. There would be an extra level of satisfaction in destroying an uncouth oaf by the use of a literary technique. "I'm sure it's quite safe to climb upon the roof," she could proclaim, her tone totally confident, dangling the bait of universal acclaim before his jaw-dangling stupidity. "I can see no possible danger in your launching yourself off into space from on top of the chimney." That sort of thing. Experimentally, *à propos* of nothing whatever, she confidently asserted "I'm sure Sobriety won't spontaneously combust" (this after a first reading of *Bleak House*) or "I'm absolutely certain that Sobriety's head won't fall off," but results were distinctly disappointing. There had — in fact — been no results whatsoever, with no signs of flames or looseness at the neck. "Get a move on, God!" she'd muttered, a little impatiently, presuming that God was the fate she tempted, or the irony that she was attempting to make dramatic, but He hadn't been listening, made sulky by her too-pushy confidence. She'd really been looking forward to Sobriety's leap from the roof of The Old Pigpen, and the instant realization that *this was not going to work*, the look of terror on his face as he plunged, screaming, to a feather-free Icarusian death.

Splat!

She'd particularly looked forward to the *Splat!*

No *Splat!* had been forthcoming, but — after she'd abandoned dramatic irony and put her trust in sheer maliciousness — she'd had her revenge on Sobriety Goodchild after all, *and* with the words of Shakespeare. So — ironically (this seemed the correct expression to employ) — dramatic irony had, despite her scorning its utter uselessness, played a part in the destruction of the wicked and cruel boy. (That's what Jane Eyre had called John Reed. "You are like a murderer," she had said — Alice had cheered her on — "you are like a slave-driver — you are like the Roman emperors!") She'd done what she'd done all by herself, but God — encouraged by her efforts — had eventually done His share. God had bided His time (she'd had to wait *years*), but had at last — (grudgingly, she felt; He could be so petty for Someone capital-lettered and omnipotent: why couldn't He just get on with it instead of moving in a mysterious way all the time?) — punished Sobriety. *Smitten* was probably the verb to use in this context; God seemed very taken with smiting. He had made him the husband of the wispy, the characterless, the virtually invisible, Mrs. Sobriety Goodchild, and the father — strange, still, to think of him as a husband and father, that poisonous little face of his contorted with taunting — of the dreadful Serenity Goodchild, twelve years old now, and already a domineering diva. It had been tempting fate to name her Serenity, and fate had embraced temptation with enthusiasm, crying out "Goody!

Goody!" as it pounced. Perhaps the *Splat!* had arrived after all, wearing a frilly pink dress and a sulky expression.

How pleasurable it had been (and still was, though he had to take his place in the line of contenders) to hate Sobriety Goodchild so entirely. It was very important, very *necessary*, to have someone to hate without reservation, more important – she felt herself thinking – than having someone to love. Love was overrated. This was what she told herself. This was what she tried to believe.

One of the few occasions on which Alice went outside the house (apart from carefully planned outings to Mrs. Albert Comstock's when that lady's insistence finally became too much) was to attend the service at All Saints' on Sundays, as she was doing today. The Reverend Goodchild liked to imply that his spiritual ministrations were the one thing that kept her going (translation: "It keeps the madwoman quiet, but don't go too close"), but she went to see him and his wife for the same reason she went to see Mrs. Albert Comstock: to keep her hatred fresh, energizing. These feelings were dark plants, carefully nourished, lovingly tended.

Oscar Wilde – here he was again – had described her feelings rather well, and supplied some useful expressions: "Get hence, you loathsome mystery! Hideous animal, get hence! You wake in me each bestial sense, you make me what I would not be." She wouldn't agree with that last sentence. The first half was fine – she rather flourished on her bestial sense (her real self, she sometimes felt) – though she tended to feel that what she became was what she wanted to be, not what she would not be. She should try the opening sentences sometime, and see how they went down with Mrs. Albert Comstock.

"Get hence, you loathsome mystery! Hideous animal, get hence!"

That should liven things up in the soporific surroundings of the music room. Teacups and biscuits would fly in all directions, and fans would flick out like lethal weapons. Brontosaurian boomings would rattle windows for miles around, and avalanches would imperil the steeper slopes of Hudson Heights. The shrill cries of startled babies and frightened lunatics would echo around the white-marbled emptinesses.

21

She poured the water into the basin on the hand-wash-stand, tied back her hair, took a deep breath – with the air of someone about to attempt a little adventurous pearl fishing – and immersed her face. If you tired of *Carmen*, there was always *Les Pêcheurs de perles*.

Drowned in a bath of the tresses of Annie.

She began to hum "*Au fond du temple saint,*" imagining silvery bubbles streaming out behind her as she swam deep down into the blue Ceylonese waters.

> "*Au fond du temple saint, paré de fleurs et d'or,*
> *Une femme apparaît! Je crois la voir encore!. . ."*

Time for the symbolic cleansing ceremony – a sort of ritual purification (common amongst primitive peoples) – before she ventured into the unclean realm of the Reverend Goodchild.

Would boiling water be powerful enough for this task?

Should she have recklessly emptied a bottle of Lysol into the bowl, and washed away her face, ceased to be herself, just to be on the safe side?

22

It was on Hudson Heights that she had gone searching for Annie for a while, a year or more after she had gone, circling the new buildings in the way that she had circled the vanished Shakespeare Castle, clockwise and counterclockwise, telling stories to Charlotte, and to Mary Benedict, as if Annie might have become one of the listeners, or a character in one of the stories, abandoned, fallen, demented. She had tried other places, and now she tried these. Annie had disappeared so suddenly — her few possessions had been left neatly tidied away in her little windowless room — that Alice could not believe that she was not coming back. There was the threaded needle carefully tucked into the shirtwaist she had been in the middle of letting out, and a half-eaten chocolate bar — a rare treat — hidden, still fresh, in a decorative box next to Reuben's letters. It had once contained a pull-along iron toy of a father with a baby sitting astride one of his legs, over the shin. It had belonged to Edith. Each time the wheel turned, a bell would ring, and the father would lift his leg high into the air, as if bouncing the baby up and down.

> Hie to the market, Jenny come trot,
> Spilt all her buttermilk, every drop . . .

(Ring! Ring! Ring!)
(Edith would hear the bell, and come running.)

> Every drop and every dram,
> Jenny came home with an empty can . . .

A letter had arrived for Annie from her brother Reuben, two days after she had gone — she had said nothing to anyone, as if expecting to be back before anyone had noticed — and it remained for a while, in its bright blue envelope, propped up where she would see it as soon as she entered the room.
Miss Annie Clement.
"I miss Annie Clement," Alice thought, and felt guilty because wordplay must mean a lack of emotion. It didn't. It didn't. "If he do bleed," Lady Macbeth had said of the murdered Duncan — he bled, he most certainly bled, gallons gushed — "I'll gild the faces of the grooms withal,/For it must seem their guilt." "Gild," "guilt": there were puns at moments of intense emotion. Alice took comfort

in being like Lady Macbeth. It was a definite promotion from being one of the Weird Sisters. Not on her sole, but on her soul, she made her knife keen. That was Gratiano's pun in *The Merchant of Venice*, another pun made as a knife approached a heart.

She began at The House of the Magdalenes, the place of lost girls – though every face she saw there was white – circling in the dark early morning on days when she was not at school, or in the early dusk of evening. It was again a time of winds and snow, as if – by choosing the same weather as that in which she had last seen her – Alice might once more bring her into being. She went out into the coldness, serious and determined – well wrapped up – disguised as a girl about to toboggan or skate with friends. She was a Pinkerton. She should find clues, and follow them up – scribbled lines on a hidden note, telltale prints across fields with unbroken snow (she peered as closely as Good King Wenceslas's page marking his footsteps), a mysterious message – but there were no clues to find.

She peeped in at windows, seeing the girls, the sinful girls with their bowed heads, sitting at tables or carrying out their assigned duties. Sometimes she saw them nursing their babies (mysteriously, they all seemed to have babies; Sobriety Goodchild jeered and sniggered, explaining with crude simplicity, and it was no longer a mystery), and felt as if she was drawing nearer to a truth.

The Magdalenes never appeared in the streets of Longfellow Park with their babies. To carry a child would be to invite a stoning. A large target painted helpfully upon the infant's gown would convert it into an attraction at a traveling fair, with gaudy prizes for the best shots.

"Me first! Me first!"

Mrs. Albert Comstock – eager for all the fun of the fair – lurched forward, swiveling her arm around like the sail of a storm-battered windmill, unleashing a rock the size of a meteorite, still hot from its journey through space.

Oh dear, what can the matter be?

Thwunk!

Dear, dear, what can the matter be?

Thwunk! Thwunk!
Oh dear, what can the matter be?
Thwunk! Thwunk! Thwunk!
She'd be so long at the fair.

Rock after rock hurtled to the target, and Mrs. Albert Comstock was almost buried beneath the tottering pile of tawdry pottery that she'd won by her exertions, her unerring baby-battering bull's-eyes. Rocks! That was what The Bosom was made of; there'd be enough ammunition to keep that bulgy arm whirling for months. The sails spun around until they were just a humming blur. The ground wheat — warm, almost smoking — would keep the city in loaves throughout the winter, flour billowing out like an avalanche. Some were given bread; some were given stones. Man could not live by bread alone, but Mrs. Albert Comstock would thrive on stones.

Alice strained to see figures at lighted upper windows, in the way she had striven to make out the patterns in the clouded stained glass of the tower of the Shakespeare Castle.

After The House of the Magdalenes she tried Pettifar's Orphanage, though she would have been unable to say whether she was searching for Annie's baby, or for Annie herself. At the orphanage there was less to see, and the blinds were drawn for most of the time, the lonely children living in perpetual twilight. "Pettifar's" had the sound of a store about it, the children neatly stacked on shelves, quietly on their best behavior, waiting to be purchased. Customers wrangled for reductions, peering closely to find faults — "This one's rather grubby," "There's a part missing from this one" — to justify their intransigence.

"I'm looking for a little baby," she would say, raising her hand as if she were in school. "I'm not sure whether it's a girl or a boy, but it will be about a year old, with dark skin, and very dark eyes. He'll be called Joshua if he's a boy, and she'll be called Desiderata if she's a girl."

She knew this. She and Annie had talked about children, and the names of children, as if they were playing at Houses, as if the house that Annie was tending were her own house. With her too-long apron, and expression of careful concentration, Annie looked like a small girl tending her make-believe home. They'd both decided that they'd like one boy, and one girl, the boy first. Annie had also volunteered the name she would like her husband to have, as if she had consulted Madame Etoile, the celebrated French Clairvoyant. The capital letters proved that she was important.

"Joshua or Desiderata. It's for a friend," she would add, helpfully.

She would wait, browsing through the selection available, as they checked their stock. The babies would hold up their arms, asking to be chosen, like puppies in a pound wagging their tails. The thought of Pettifar's had always made her shudder, and what she saw in her mind looked very much like George Cruikshank's illustration of Oliver Twist's workhouse: no color anywhere, and the shaded black lines drawn repeatedly, as if they were scribblings-out, covering up some hidden message beneath, especially on the upper part of the blank wall.

Annie *had* left a hidden message — two hidden messages — but Alice had not realized this for some time.

Lastly, and for rather longer than she had at the orphanage, she began circle the North River Lunatic Asylum, the place where Sobriety Goodchild said she herself belonged. Perhaps she'd left it until last for that reason, thinking that they might seize her, keep her there, as they had imprisoned Alfred Hardie in *Hard Cash*, and put an end to her searching. She walked through the entrance, and behind the high walls as boldly as she had walked into the grounds of the Shakespeare Castle, and circled the building in a counter-clockwise direction, the direction she had taken for her darker stories, the ones that made Charlotte go very quiet, and Mary Benedict scream. It was screams she listened for, the sound of the noisy ward. She'd already read *Hard Cash* three and a half times — it was one of her ways of frightening herself — and she knew the horrors that could be expected in a lunatic asylum.

She thought that there was a reason for the close proximity of the three institutions, an efficiency in their positioning. First, the girls would have their babies in The House of the Magdalenes, and these babies would be taken from them after harvesting. She had an image of Mrs. Albert Comstock and Mrs. Goodchild wielding giant, glittering scythes like the pendulum on Mrs. Albert Comstock's clock.

They swung their bodies from side to side, cutting through the crops as if they were imitating the figure of Death, or – in a literary mood (one of Mrs. Albert Comstock's phases) – reenacting a scene from "The Pit and the Pendulum" or one of the more bucolic Thomas Hardy novels. On the chosen morning, the babies would be forcibly removed from the arms of the girls (some prying might be involved, some effortful levering), and transferred to Pettifar's Orphanage, and the girls – walking neatly in line like pilgrims approaching the end of their journey, guarded and prodded by stern-faced attendants – would be removed to the North River Lunatic Asylum, still singing lullabies to the babies who were no longer there, driven mad by the absence of what had once been in their arms.

> "Hush, little baby, don't say a word,
> Papa's going to buy you a mockingbird . . ."

(Mrs. Albert Comstock and Mrs. Goodchild would be fully prepared for mocking. This would be the bit they enjoyed the most. These girls *needed* mocking for the sake of their souls. The umbrellas, the parasols, the scythes, would point at angles as carefully calculated as a diagram in a book of mathematical problems.

("Look at that one!"

("That one's under a cloud!"

("Look at that one!"

(They'd wait until the girl was sobbing – mission accomplished; it sometimes took quite some time with the more hard-faced ones – and then move on to the next one.

("Look at that one!"

("That one's under a cloud!"

("Look at that one!"

(This expression — "under a cloud" — was one of Mrs. Albert Comstock's and it had created the idea of a personal climate in Alice's mind, as if each of the indicated girls had carried an area free of sunshine about with her, a small place of sadness.

(She'd first heard it just after The House of the Magdalenes had opened, when Mrs. Albert Comstock had nudge-nudged Mrs. Goodchild as they stood in front of Twelvetrees & Twelvetrees in Hireling Road, and indicated one of the first Magdalenes to be sighted. They'd been on full alert for several weeks.

("*She's* under a cloud," she had tittered, rather loudly, sounding more pleased than anything else, and she and Mrs. Goodchild — with no attempt at hiding their gawking — had watched the pregnant young woman across the street, walking arm in arm with a friend.

(Mrs. Albert Comstock and Mrs. Goodchild were just like Theodore and Max Webster out loony-spotting, singing their Papageno aria as they pointed.

("There's one!"

("There's one!"

("*Der Vogelfänger bin ich ja . . .*"

(*Cuckoo! Cuckoo!*

(Mrs. Albert Comstock and Mrs. Goodchild had moved their heads gradually across as they watched the young woman's progress down the street, but their bodies had stayed still, rather in the way that certain species of birds observed something of interest, something upon which they were about to pounce. These birds were not cuckoos. These birds were predators, out to kill and eat. The whir of wings. The triumphant squawk. The rending sounds, the flying feathers, the juicy gobbets dangling from the sharp-edged beaks. Nudge, nudge went Mrs. Albert Comstock's left elbow. Nudge, nudge went Mrs. Goodchild's right elbow. The young woman — very young, really a girl — had flushed when she saw that she was being observed, held up her head, and clutched her friend's arm tighter.

("*Brazen!*" had been Mrs. Albert Comstock's considered opinion, and – "*Brazen!*" – Mrs. Goodchild had swiftly agreed. They had clutched their umbrellas tighter to them. There would be some prodding – possibly even some smiting – before the day was through. Busy, busy, busy.

(*Nudge.*

("Under a cloud."

(*Nudge.*

("Under a cloud."

(*Nudge.*

(For a while, Alice had imagined the young woman walking about beneath a small, personal cloud, like an enthusiastic pipe smoker. Rain fell perpetually upon her. It was not a downpour, but one of those damp, dispiriting drizzles that never stopped. Mrs. Albert Comstock's personal climate would have included thunder and lightning to add a bit of excitement, the lightning zinging on the jewelry, and pulsating off the metal parts of her more adventurous articles of underwear. She had seen the young woman walking about with her friend several times after that, and always imagined the impending cloud, the drizzly mist-like descent a veil around her, hiding her from view, dampening her clothes. Perhaps that was why they wandered in Heneacher Woods, seeking refuge from the perpetual rain under the branches of the trees, whispering together as the dripping water from the leaves hissed around them. They sheltered from the wetness and from the booming voices, the jabbing umbrellas; they shivered beneath the trees, imperfectly protected by their new names. When they entered The House of the Magdalenes they were expected to give up their real names, as if they were changing their status like the nuns, and the young women chose romantic names for themselves that they had read in novels and books of poetry. It was as if they were trying to make-believe that they were characters in the love stories and love poetry that they had read, young maidens to whom handsome young men had vowed eternal adoration amidst beautiful landscapes. Somewhere in those same woods, lost in the mist, hidden by the earth-obscuring fogginess – her outline all faded like a partially erased charcoal drawing – there would be Annie, peering forward, straining her dark eyes, trying to find the way.

(Alice wanted to go up and speak to the girl, say something kind, but she vanished, as they all vanished. She would begin to recognize individual girls – sometimes she even looked out especially for some of them – but always, after a while, she would not see them again.

("Look at that one!"

(Mrs. Goodchild's right elbow sank in about three inches.

("That one's come to grief!"

("Look at that one!"

("That one's come to grief!"

(That was another expression they used.

(The girls had come to Grief, a strange, misty cloud-enfolded place of sadness where it always rained, a Promised Land where all promises were broken, a Goshen without light. There they were, looking as if they had been crying, many of them. Perhaps their mamas had died.

> "Hush, little baby, don't say a word,
> Papa's going to buy you a mockingbird . . ."

— Keep moving! Keep moving! —

> ". . . And if that mockingbird won't sing,
> Papa's going to buy you a diamond ring . . ."

— Keep moving! Keep moving! —

> ". . . And if that diamond ring turns to brass,
> Papa's going to buy you a looking-glass . . ."

The girls whose babies had been taken from them sang about a papa who was not there, and not about themselves, because they were of no account.

Alice's circlings must have run through into the summer: she had a distinct memory of pressing her face against sun-warmed stone, grains adhering to her skin like sand, and hearing nothing but a breeze through the leaves of trees, and her own heartbeat, magnified with the sea-wave sound of a seacoast shell. She pressed her ear against the wall, but the place had always appeared utterly silent. She tried to hold her breath, imagining someone in an echoingly empty room on the other side of the wall — also holding her breath — trying to listen to her. Perhaps she might hear Annie's voice, singing a lullaby to her empty arms.

Hush, little baby.

She heard nothing.

Don't say a word.

Day after day she'd wandered through the oddly depopulated, silent grounds, feeling like the last inhabitant of Ancient Rome, dazzled by the light on the white marble. She'd felt as if she had been left — forgotten, crying out "Mater! Mater!" (Maggie Tulliver was not the only girl who studied Latin books) — in an abandoned city, everyone else fled, sandals flip-flopping, from the approach of the barbarian invasion, the head-lopping Visigoths or Vandals.

Ooh, look!

Here they come, the evil swart-faced hordes!

Flee!

Flee for your lives!

The Goodchilds and the Griswolds poured up from the direction of Heneacher Woods — it was like a scene from "The Pied Piper of Hamelin" with frogs instead of rats, or the goblins surging up into the castle in search of Princess Irene — howling threateningly, led by Mrs. Albert Comstock. She was crammed like a bulky Boadicea into her buckle-wheeled chariot, heftily hefting her wide-bladed sword, jammed in with Dr. Vaniah Odom and Anthony Comstock (less than the dust beneath her chariot wheels). Those poor, poor horses. War could be such hell. Dr. Vaniah Odom's little head was straining to see over the top edge of the chariot, like a small child pressing his nose against a candy-store window.

"Smite!" he and Anthony Comstock were urging the frog-faced masses in unison, with venomous glee. "Smite! Smite! Smite! Filth! Filth! Filth!" (When they said it three times it was true.)

They smote.

Their vorpal blades went snicker-snack.

The Jabberwocks – their jaws bit, their claws caught – had seized the weapons from those who had sought to rid the world of them. This was not a frabjous day. It was a day without callooh, a day without callay, and there would be no joyous chortlings.

Flames roared up from Hudson Heights, and the columns of Pettifar's Orphanage, The House of the Magdalenes, and the North River Lunatic Asylum fell in fragments of shattered marble as they were destroyed to the triumphant yells of the barbarians. The black clouds of smoke would be visible for miles, and the fires would rage for days. It was the sort of scene that would lend itself to one of Dickinson Prud'homme's more ambitious quasi-historical canvases, offering ample opportunities for painting large women – in attitudes of extravagant abandonment – deprived of most of their clothing.

The Women of Hudson Heights Lament the Destruction of Their City.

That should draw the crowds at his next exhibition, the men sniggering like Otsego Lake Academy schoolboys, nudging each other, discreetly indicating the best bits with lubricious glee.

"Over there, top left-hand corner!"

– Nudge, nudge! –

"Look at that one bending over!"

– Nudge, nudge! –

"Have you seen *those*?"

Like purchasers of peaches, or the Walrus selecting from the Oysters, they seemed to favor those of the largest size when it came to bosoms, and Dickinson Prud'homme cheerfully catered for the most excessive of their imaginings. The larger his bosoms grew, the larger his houses, his horses, his stomach. Faintly, in the distance, was the rumble of Mrs. Albert Comstock's chariot wheels (now there was a bosom to reduce any bearded nudger to an awed, gaping silence), and the faraway cries of "Smite!" and "Filth!" drew closer, louder.

Alice circled, and she circled again.

She circled The House of the Magdalenes.

She circled Pettifar's Orphanage.

She circled the North River Lunatic Asylum.

Clockwise, and counterclockwise, she circled the white-columned buildings, and she circled their deserted grounds.

She never found Annie.

23

The three little girls walked up to the Shakespeare Castle – built for himself up on Hudson Heights by Reynolds Templeton Seabright, the celebrated Shakespearean actor-manager – in the late afternoon of a day in the summer. Alice Pinkerton walked in front. Behind her, less confident, less willing – they were definitely hanging back – were Charlotte Finch and (even more reluctant, she was almost walking backward) Mary Benedict. They had spent the afternoon in Alice's favorite apple orchard, and Alice had told them that they were going to walk all the way around the castle and look at the terra-cotta panels that depicted scenes from Shakespeare's plays. Alice had done this by herself on the previous afternoon, and now wished to show her findings to her friends. She had seen four Shakespeare plays performed (*Macbeth*, *Hamlet*, *Romeo and Juliet*, and *Julius Cæsar*), and regarded herself as an expert. She might have seen just four on stage, but after she had read them (as if to check that the printed versions had the same endings, and that the actors had remembered their lines correctly), she had read all the others – gripped by them as stories – just as she read Jacobean tragedies and, years later, the plays of Ibsen, hearing the voices, moving the figures around as they played their foreordained parts, spoke their given lines.

No one was as close to her as words on a page. She hugged the books to her, lover-like, and heard no sound but what those words said. She preferred to read in a room by herself, but if she read when other people were in the room – she drew nearer to her book to exclude them – she was always conscious that they did not know the words she read, could not hear what she was hearing, as if a voice was whispering inside her telling her something that only she should know.

Every time they went to Charlotte's house they passed the castle, hidden away behind its wall, but they had never dared to enter the grounds. It was – as Alice had discovered – easy to do so. The castle was close to the road, to take advantage of the views from the bluff, not marooned in the middle of its extensive parkland, and the gates were not locked. There were no signs of life anywhere as they peered – prisoner-like – through the upright metal bars (it was like peering down from the height of the schoolroom): no distant crouching gardeners, no maids with baskets on errands, no ancient strolling actor reciting reminiscing soliloquies as he took advantage of the sunshine.

The gates were slightly ajar, inviting entrance, and Alice boldly pushed them open a little further and marched in, making no attempt to muffle the sound of her feet crunching through the neglected, weed-grown gravel. Charlotte and Mary teetered behind her as if making the first tentative steps across a tightrope, arms out at either side for balance above an abyss. There would – it appeared – be a long way to fall. The battlemented front of the castle rose above them. There was a flag hanging from the flagpole above the tower, but it hung limply in the still, warm air, and the device upon it could not be seen. Gulls squawked above them, giving a sensation of the open sea and of distance, though no sea was visible, and there was no distance. Here, quite close behind the walls, the feeling was just the opposite of that, a feeling of heat and enclosure.

There was – rather disappointingly – no drawbridge or portcullis at the entrance, just a wide shallow flight of steps up to a studded double door.

Alice went straight up to the first pinkish panel, to the right of this main entrance, and stood before it, like a visitor in front of a piece of sculpture in an art gallery. It was about three feet wide and two feet high.

"*Macbeth*," she announced, unnecessarily. The title of the play depicted was inset in the lower edge of the elaborate frame that surrounded the high relief of the molded scene. It seemed to be there just for her alone: the first Shakespeare play she had ever seen performed, the first panel on the castle wall. She knew all about *Macbeth*, and was hoping for some questions. As usual, Mary Benedict did not say anything, but Charlotte did not disappoint her.

"Which one's Macbeth?" she asked.

"That one." This was an easy start. She pointed with complete authority at the figure of the man facing the three figures in long, loose gowns, with their backs toward them.

"And," she added, pointing (she could do with a proper indicator – like a conductor's baton – to give her an air of real authority), "they are the Three Weird Sisters."

"Just like you, Allegra, and Edith," Mary Benedict said. She did not speak often, but when she spoke it always seemed to be as a result of deep thought. Mary Benedict was an only child, and sometimes Alice could not blame her parents for deciding that one was enough.

"Especially Allegra," Alice conceded. Her two sisters were a trial. She bore the burden of her status as eldest sister with – she felt – a certain dignified nobility.

"Especially *you*," Mary Benedict replied, with considerable emphasis. She made it sound like something she'd been saving up to say for ages.

Alice thought for a while, and then decided to ignore this. Such forbearance made her feel righteous, but it would not last for long.

Mary Benedict cultivated (unsuccessfully, in Alice's view) an air of weary sophistication, occasionally — a quick glance around to ensure there was no one else within hearing (this definitely weakened its effect) — employing exotic curse words as a demonstration of this quality.

"Gonorrhea!" she would snap waspishly in a "Very-like-a-whale!" sort of way, and Charlotte would go pink, moving discreetly a few feet to one side to avoid the thunderbolt. Whatever it meant, it sounded absolutely *filthy*, mainly because it sounded like "diarrhea," not a word one would choose to employ in polite society.

("Bosomptious!" Alice felt like snapping in reply, as a correspondingly crushing rudery. It was her and Charlotte's own private rude word — one they never shared with Mary Benedict, with anybody — and it was based upon Mrs. Albert Comstock's mightily unbifurcated bosom. If someone was being "bosomptious," they were being arrogant, condescending, snobbish, or displaying any one of a number of other undesirable qualities. They were — in short — being exactly like Mrs. Albert Comstock. If countless insufferable hairy-faced men could qualify as being one of The Bearded Ones, there was — and could ever be — only one woman who could be referred to as The Bosomed One.

("Rather bosomptious!" they would comment secretly to one another about someone else, feeling greatly daring. Mary Benedict was bosomptious, though they never told her so, and she never knew. "Bosomptious" beat "gonorrhea" any day.)

Alice — as a smaller girl — had longed for "diarrhea" to turn up in a spelling bee, to show that she could spell it (it took advanced skills to get "diarrhea" right), but Miss Caulfeild had skillfully avoided controversial vocabulary, and she had never been given the chance. "Desiccated": that had turned up (an approving tick for Alice Pinkerton: "desiccated" always seemed to her to be a word designed more for spelling tests than for everyday usage); "embarrassment" (*tick*: no embarrassment here), "onomatopoeia" (*tick*), and "graywacke" (*tick*) ("graywacke"!) — all advanced stuff, if of limited use in casual conversation – had turned up (Miss Caulfeild believed in challenging her students), but there was never any sign of "diarrhea." "Graywacke" was a reflection of Miss Caulfeild's interest in geology. Specialized terms for rock strata or the features of underground caves (Alice had soon learned to distinguish between stalactites and stalagmites) regularly featured in spelling bees, alongside "accommodation," "receive," and "fearsome." ("Fiercesome" seemed far more convincing.) Miss Caulfeild, who rattled as she entered a room, seemed to wear most of her geological specimens as jewelry, and her sharp little hammers must have ached to tap-tap-tap experimentally on Mrs. Albert Comstock's Himalayan Bosom, gouging out some of the looser sections, and activating life-threatening landslides. "Graywacke" held no fears for Alice. It was some of the more common words that tended to give her pause for thought, words that failed to feature in spelling tests. The more you looked at "eighth" or "twelfth," the more unlikely their spelling seemed, and she'd once stared at "shelf-ful" for ages – "shelfful" was even worse, verging on the Hebrew – without being convinced of its correctness. After a while, all words looked meaningless. Ennui was so easily induced, as they lurched toward the *fin de siècle*.

Mostly, Mary Benedict (not a very good speller: few ticks for her; she was more of a cross, cross, cross speller: she often looked cross) didn't speak; she just assumed an expression of *knowingness*, and – irritatingly – faint disapproval. If she chose to speak – this was the general impression – she would say things that would render others dumb with astonishment, and pinker than the pinkest pink induced by cursing. Mary Benedict was an irritant who produced no pearl. "Especially *you*" was *very* irritating.

Another irritating thing about her was her middle name, Thérèse. Not only did she actually *possess* a middle name – unlike Alice – but she possessed one with not one, but *two* accents, which smacked of boasting. Mary Benedict was a great one for boasting. Alice had always had a hankering for a name with an accent, and here was Mary Benedict – of all people – with two. A name with two accents outdid even Pharaildis. Give her accents rather than hens, any day.

Ever since she'd read *Jane Eyre* she'd envied Adèle Varens. This was not because she had Rochester for a father, or Jane Eyre for a governess. It was certainly not because she had hair falling in curls to her waist (which made her sound all too like Myrtle Comstock as she had looked in those days, distinctly off-putting). It was – of course – because of the accent in her first name, particularly as it was a grave accent, so much rarer, so much more valuable – she had felt – than a mere acute accent, that little hovering mark that was not a letter of the alphabet adding an exotic touch to the otherwise unremarkable. She understood, all those years later, the appeal of a ligature to Oliver Comstock, the attractions of the "æ" in "æsthetic". For a while – when he was at his most æsthetic – he had always written Linnaeus's name as "Linnæus" whenever he had written to him, little notes, invitations, in the beautiful italic script he had taught himself. Trust Mary Benedict to have both a grave and an acute accent, forming a little protective roof in the middle of her middle name, under which she sheltered with an air of infuriating superiority. It had been uncharacteristically restrained of Mary Benedict not to pile on more accents, until the letters of her name groaned under them, like the chest of an undeserving South American general with more decorations than uniform, his every square inch emblazoned with bright silk sashes, bulletproof with glittering medals. She could surely have weighed herself down with a few randomly inserted apostrophes and circumflexes, breves and tildes, the odd unusual umlaut, her name glinting and jingling like the chandelier-sized earrings dangling from Mrs. Albert Comstock's capacious earlobes. Saint-like she'd die – well, one could hope – scourged with sharp-edged accents, impaled on cruelly-hooked cedillas.

Not only did Mary Thérèse Benedict have the benefit of accents, she also had ballet lessons. She was clearly a cultural beacon, blazing out in a benighted wilderness, a symbol of the higher things in life, *far* too high for the unenlightened masses.

Alice had never been to ballet class. The thought of seeing Mary Benedict and Myrtle Comstock tottering about and assuming graceful postures in the hall above the ice-cream parlor had comprehensively daunted her. *Thud! Thud! Thud!* thundered the Benedict and (enormous) Comstock feet, enclosed in pink silk ballet shoes, and a steady fall of dust and splinters fell through the floorboards to coat the cherries, whipped cream, and chocolate strands in the tall-glassed sundaes on the tables in the parlor beneath, adding an intriguing crunchiness to the treats on offer. No need for nuts with these multi-textured munchies.

Alice looked again at Mary Benedict, not betraying the sourness she was feeling. Mary *Thérèse* Benedict's feet were in the second ballet position. She'd suddenly gone bowlegged, moved her heels a very precise distance apart, looking as if her high standards would have been better served if she'd had the use of a ruler and set square. *My parents can afford ballet lessons*, her feet were saying. *I have acquired social graces. I can dance to Delibes.* A few years later, and they'd have been boasting *I can twirl to Tchaikowsky*. So much could be said with a simple gesture. She'd *en l'air* her. They'd be faced with wobbly simpering-faced *arabesques* next. Not a pleasing prospect. Once Mary Benedict was in balletic mood she could keep going for hours, lumberingly cranking herself into repellent postures, like someone frozen at moments of intense pain. It was a blatant attempt to draw attention to herself, and hog the limelight.

"First position!" she'd announce, sounding like a star pupil eager to demonstrate her abilities to awestruck, envious, less-favored classmates.

"Second position!"

She always announced what it was she was about to do, like Sobriety Goodchild just before he unleashed one of his god-awful dirges. Her mind rested briefly, lightly – not really touching – upon "god-awful," as if the word had never entered her head, and left not a mark behind it. She'd only just heard the expression for the first time, and wasn't quite sure how dangerous it was. She was extremely careful to ensure that she thought of the word "god" with a small "g," concentrating ferociously. She was taking no chances.

("Bosomptious!")

"What are they doing?" Charlotte asked, loyally sounding fascinated, leaning forward, pointing at the *Macbeth* panel. Charlotte was utterly reliable.

"Second position!" Mary Benedict announced belatedly, suddenly noticing her feet, blatantly attempting to turn the attention upon herself. Not only did she invariably announce what she was demonstrating, she also always held her hands as if about to curtsy, like a little ballerina clutching the edges of her ballet dress. Alice ignored this. It was like something by Edgar Degas gone horribly wrong, a disturbingly debased new development in the history of art as they moved into the last decades of the nineteenth century. Art tended toward decadence as centuries drew to their close. In fifteen years' or so time, Mrs. Albert Comstock — in that racily bilingual way she had — would be disapprovingly referring to the scandalous proximity of the *fang de sickle*, as nightmarish *Swan Lake*s, heaving with galumphily *pirouetting* deepwater monsters (these were very dark, very deep lakes, and the swans mutated strangely), sent small and soggy ballet-besotted girls screaming out of theatres.

"They have met Macbeth after a battle," Alice continued, with a friendly, patient expression, not facing Charlotte, but looking Mary Benedict right in the eyes.

(Just you wait, Mary Benedict. Just you wait. She'd get her in the end. She'd look like th' innocent flower — something dark and weed-like, found in soggy ground, in her case — but she'd be the serpent under't. Hypocrisy was much undervalued as a source of pleasure. "Under't" was a most satisfactory word to pronounce when you were in a bad mood, with a hiss and a spit at the end. It was a word to say very forcibly, very wetly, a word like a blow to make people duck.)

"What are they doing?"

This was Charlotte again. Mary Benedict – Mary *Thérèse* Benedict – would not admit to curiosity, preferring to imply that she knew already.

"They are prophesying what is going to happen to him in the future."

"What does happen?"

Charlotte was on incandescent form.

"He becomes evil. He murders people. He has his head chopped off."

"I still haven't found a goatskin." This was a reference to one of their latest plans to kill Mrs. Albert Comstock. It involved decapitation, and they were distinctly keen to put it into execution. What an excellent choice of word "execution" was. They'd found the necessary brass shield, and the sword, but they were experiencing some difficulty with the goatskin. Charlotte displayed an impressive persistence once she had firm hold of an idea. When they were alone, Alice must let her know that they could not possibly carry out their original plan for Mrs. Albert Comstock. How on earth could they dispose of such an enormous body, even one lacking a head?

"A goatskin?" Mary Benedict had been stirred into interest – here was a rare event – but they both ignored her. Her feet were in the third position by now.

"Third position!" Her hands hovered in the about-to-curtsy position, right heel digging away at left instep, as if she were attempting to unbalance herself. The simper appeared, pinging into position. In such a manner, Alice imagined, Papa would stand and recite "The Children's Hour" over and over, the heel of his right foot pressed into the instep of his left foot, his toes turned out as far as they'd go. One push in the chest would have him hurtling to the floor with a thunderous *Aaaaghhhh!*-howling crash.

They ignored this, also.

The panels stretched away around all four sides of the castle. There were nine along each wall, and one of *Hamlet* above the main entrance, though they were arranged in no particular chronological or thematic order, as far as Alice could make out. By the time of their third visit – and these became regular, once the initial uncertainties had been overcome – Alice was using the panels to tell stories, as if they were the consecutive illustrations for a serial, like the installments of a Dickens novel lined up into the distance. She did not relate the stories of the Shakespeare plays, but used the figures in the panels as quite other people in quite other stories, one continuous story each time. She'd relished the thought of being Scheherazade, ever since she'd read *The Arabian Nights*. It was from this book that she'd learned the words "Mameluke," "hammam," and "concubine," though these were not words that Miss Caulfeild ever selected for spelling. They lacked the necessary geological associations, especially the last one. She began to hum an appropriate passage from Rimsky-Korsakoff to get herself in the right mood, "The Sea and Sinbad's Ship."

"Fourth position!"

Mary Benedict began to move one foot in front of the other, concentrating hard to give the impression that she wasn't interested in anything that Alice Pinkerton might have to say. She seemed to be under the impression that Alice Pinkerton's insistent humming was a tribute to her balletic skills, an attempt to tempt her into terpsichorean fireworks. All that mattered was the unparalleled grace – *ha!* – of her postures. She was visualizing the red roses raining down upon her from every part of the auditorium, seeing the standing ovation, hearing the cheers, the orchestra joining in, tapping enthusiastically on their instruments – the percussion-players were going berserk – and the white-gloved applauding hands. (She wasn't *entirely* keen on the gloves; they did tend to muffle the sound too much.) The curtsies were upon them, Mary Benedict's cutesy-cutesy curtsies, the ones with the radiant Oh-I'm-so-modest-please-don't-applaud smile (rapidly supplanted by her rather more insistent Oh-all-right-then-applaud-if-you-must smile), Mary Benedict's GOD-AWFUL curtsies. (Alice had recklessly progressed to capital letters by now.)

It wouldn't be long before the *arabesques* were unleashed. You had to stand well back for these. Once she'd assumed the *pointe* position there was no controlling her, and the air fairly whistled around her scraggy contours. If she and Charlotte were feeling bored, or — a common occurrence, this — in a sadistic mood, they'd develop a sudden fascination with Mary Benedict's ballet positions.

"Show us the first position, Mary!" they'd cry, as if to see it demonstrated would be to have a long-cherished dream come true.

Mary obliged, seizing her opportunity, the daunting simper at full power.

"First position!"

"Now the second position."

"Second position!"

Mary obliged once more.

"Now some *arabesques*."

"*Arabesque*!"

(You could hear the italics distinctly when Mary Benedict said it. The word sounded suitably Scheherazadian for the story-teller Alice was about to become.)

Mary *arabesque*d.

(Alice should *arabesque*, also, draw a veil mysteriously across her features, and assume the rapt tone of voice of a Scheherazade possessed by the power of storytelling. "New lamps for old," she should be saying. "New lamps for old." "What happens next?" King Shahryar would be begging her. "What happens next? *Tell me what happens next!*")

"Now ten *pirouettes*."

"*Pirouette*!"

The lurch to the right was quite pronounced at times.

"Now ten more."

"*Pirouette*!" (Slightly breathless by now, the italics unraveling at the edges.)

Beginning to pant a little, Mary did ten more, the simper losing some of its intensity.

They could keep going like this for ages.

On their more successful days, Mary Benedict would end up racked with cramps, heaving for breath and writhing on the floor, as spasms overwhelmed her. She was incapable of curtsies, incapable of simpers, incapable of speech, utterly overwhelmed, lying there as if she'd just crashed down from heaven.

This was their favorite ballet position.

Just you wait, Mary Benedict.

"Give me a number between one and thirty-seven," Alice would say, once, twice, three times a week, when the ritual had become established.

Macbeth was number one, and they numbered the panels counterclockwise around the castle, until they reached *Hamlet*, number thirty-seven. The chosen number would be the starting point for the story, and they would walk around the building as Alice told a story – a different interpretation each time – as she included the scene on each panel in turn, ending her story at the panel immediately before the one with which she had started. A clockwise walk was a normal sort of story; a counterclockwise walk was a ghost or horror story. There were more of these as the fall and the winter approached, and the days darkened earlier. She beset them round with dismal stories.

Alice began to feel that all of the permutations of literature were contained in those thirty-seven panels, just as all of the permutations of fate were contained in a pack of tarot cards. She had heard of tarot cards from Mrs. Alexander Diddecott, and there were more of these than there were Shakespeare plays, seventy-eight of them. They had the simple gaudy fairground colors of cutout paper theatre figures, or the grotesquely caricatured characters on the cards in a pack of Happy Families, with its monstrous, murderous families of four. There'd be no happy futures if fortunes were read from these families. (Mr. Spade, the Gardener and his family; Mr. Chip, the Carpenter and his family; Mr. Dip, the Dyer and his family; Mr. Soot, the Sweep . . . How many could she remember of the thirteen families?) She'd seen the tarot cards only once, and would have been hard put to name more than half a dozen of them

(Mrs. Alexander Diddecott kept some of the cards away from her, as if they were unsuitable books, the very touch of which would contaminate), though she knew that those with names were named – you might have *guessed*, she could hear Mrs. Albert Comstock snorting (*Typical!*), sensing the nearness of the Black Arts – in *French*. There was *La Maison de Dieu* (The Tower Struck by Lightning); there was *La Force* (Fortitude, a beefy woman who appeared to be on the point of forcing back the jaws of a resisting dog, Mrs. Albert Comstock at last losing patience with Chinky-Winky and attempting – *Harder, Mrs. Comstock, pull harder!* – to rip off the dog's head); there were *Le Soleil*, *La Lune*, and *L'Etoile* (The Sun, The Moon, and The Star). She rather suspected that the illustration of the scandalously naked woman in *L'Etoile* – she'd clearly escaped Mrs. Alexander Diddecott's vigilance, and flaunted her breasts like St. Agatha in the stained glass window in All Saints' – was a representation of Madame Etoile. She certainly shed light on the tenebrous in that position. So that was why no gentlemen were admitted. Kneeling down beneath a star-crowded sky, pouring out water from a pitcher in each hand, her disordered hair falling loosely down over her shoulders – though not far enough down to cover those perkily pointy breasts – she undoubtedly possessed the smugly self-satisfied look of a woman who had never been known to fail. There was *L'Amoureux* (The Lovers); there was *Le Bateleur* (The Magician) . . .

Tarot cards and ballet movements. You couldn't deny that the French led a richly vocabulary-packed life.

La Lune was card number XVIII, and she knew what this card meant. On the card, two battlemented towers seemed to stand guard over the horizon like giant chess pieces, and two dogs howled up at the moon, as a parasitic-looking creature crawled up toward them out of a deep, dark pool. It was not a good card. It meant that a secret would be brought to light. It meant that the imagination was dangerous if it were not controlled. It was a card, Alice felt, to which she would be drawn repeatedly. *Choose a card, any card.* This was what the fortune-teller would order, and this would be the card that she always chose. She wouldn't be able to stop herself. It would be like having a secret never to be told, and being unable to stop yourself from talking about it. "Choose a card, any card," the card-sharp — his eyes obscured by his pulled-down green eye-shade — would urge, fanning out the pack seductively, the identically patterned backs of the cards held out for her to select one, and — every time — the card that she selected would be *La Lune*, just like Carmen always finding death in the cards she drew.

"Any card."

La Lune.

"Any card."

La Lune.

La Lune. La Lune. Seventy-eight moons would blaze down their light from directly overhead with noontime radiance, and seventy-eight creatures would crawl out of seventy-eight pools. This would be no place for shadows. The tenebrous would not survive here. ("*La Loon! La Loon!*" She heard the voices chanting, felt the sharp-nailed fingers as they pointed knowingly in her direction.)

The moon on the breast of the new-fallen snow . . .

All of literature was in the thirty-seven panels, just as the whole of Shakespeare's plays was contained in *Hamlet*. This was her theory. It had occurred to her when Polonius had told Hamlet that he had once played the part of Julius Cæsar at university, and she had the dizzying thought of a character in a Shakespeare play acting another part in a different play. It was just like the moment in "The Eve of St. Agnes" when Porphyro seemed aware of another Keats poem and played "La belle dame sans mercy" (why "mercy" and not "*merci*," the thankless cold-hearted woman without manners who never said "Thank you"?), or the moment in *Don Giovanni* — just before the statue of the murdered Commendatore entered to drag him down to hell — when Don Giovanni listened to music from *The Marriage of Figaro*. If he'd heard the words that should have accompanied the music, he'd have heard the warning that was in them. It was time to say goodbye to pleasure.

Everything around her had gone away for a while, and then

come back. She had read the play to see if she was right. Part of the power of *Hamlet* lay in not fully understanding it. That's what she thought. It was like the interior of a vast echoing building, where the details of the architecture could not be seen or understood, the outlines lost in misty vagueness. You stood within it, dimly aware of the surroundings, sensing vast vaulting arches, distant corridors, hidden levels piled up like a city built on ruins. There was a sense of some great secret, just out of reach, about to be revealed, the tip-of-the-tongue sensation of a forgotten memory on the point of being recalled, that not-quite-remembering the name of a piece of music feeling. The lack of a name for this felt-once-before feeling — she hadn't been able to find one, though she'd searched — made it seem all the more mysterious, something beyond the reach of language. It was like experiencing recollections of a life already lived, seeing things for the first time, but knowing that you'd seen them before. Christina Rossetti's brother had written a poem about this feeling — "Sudden Light" — though it wasn't really *light* that you felt. It was more a *dimming* of the light, a high humming sound in the ears, as you sank beneath deep water, your arms helplessly flailing. *I have been here before.* That was how it began. */But when or how I cannot tell:/I know the grass beyond the door,/The sweet keen smell,/The sighing sound* (he was absolutely right about the sighing sound), *the lights around the shore . . .*

Alice had written this description down, and *The Grass Beyond the Door* had gone onto her list of titles. She had been keeping a writing journal for three years. She was going to be a writer.

24

The three little girls walked up to the Shakespeare Castle in the late afternoon of a day in the fall. Alice Pinkerton walked in front. Behind her, Charlotte Finch was holding on to Mary Benedict. She might have been dragging her unwillingly along, or she might have been clutching her for comfort.

"Gonorrhea!" Mary Benedict said, attempting an air of saucy insouciance, looking closely at Charlotte to see if she turned pink. Charlotte – as ever – did, one of her darker shades, blending quite nicely with her red muffler.

For a moment Alice toyed with the idea of snapping "Don't be so bosomptious!" at Mary Benedict, and seeing what effect that would have on her. She wouldn't lower herself to ask what the word meant, and this might nag away at her for hours, with any luck. Then, more cunningly, she thought of asking Mary Benedict to spell "gonorrhea," but then decided against that also. She had something else in mind.

Mary Benedict had been to her ballet class the previous day, and was attempting to assume the third position, but her heart wasn't in it. She hadn't even remembered to announce what it was she was doing.

"Number one," Charlotte said, and they took up their positions in front of *Macbeth*, looking at the backs of the three figures in the flowing robes facing a single, similarly attired figure. It was the first time they had started with the very first panel they had seen.

"Counterclockwise," Alice decided, and – gratifyingly – Mary Benedict whimpered. Alice always decided the direction the story was going to take. They had been talking of ghosts for most of the afternoon, as the shadows lengthened, and Mary was already in a receptive mood. This was why Alice had chosen counterclockwise. With luck, she might be able to make Mary Benedict scream and run home again. She had managed to do this in a counterclockwise story the previous week when they had reached the final panel of the day's story, the panel for *Measure For Measure*. She had been on good form. At the end of the story, she was explaining what was *really* happening in front of them, the man reaching across a table toward a woman. Alice had leaned toward Mary Benedict – like the man toward the woman – to hiss the final words of the story and Mary had screamed, and fled. That story had gone into her writing journal.

Tried.

Tested.

Succeeded.

Tick. Tick. Tick.

The scream had been pleasingly loud, a three-tick, three-star scream.

This afternoon's story would be even better.

There would be more stars than an entire pack of *L'Etoile*s. There would be more stars than all the tourist guidebooks for Rome combined. The Colosseum, the Vatican, the Pantheon: all would echo ringingly to the screams as Mary Benedict abandoned herself to total hysteria. She was a girl who knew how to enjoy herself. Flakes of paint would gust like a blizzard from *The Last Judgment*, and tourists would be lost from sight in a storm of leaf-like fall colorings. They would become the fallen angels, thick as autumnal leaves strewing the brooks in Vallombrosa. Several of the damned would permanently disappear from sight, and enter Mary Benedict like an infection of the blood. With this Scheherazade, Alice had firmly decided, any life at risk would be the life of the listener, not the storyteller. Danger was in words. That was what Doctor Faustus had told the Scholars just before Mephostophilis brought in Helen of Troy. You had to remain silent when spirits were about.

"Francesca did not know why her father hated her and her two sisters," Alice started. "They did all they could to please him, but he hated them. Their mother had died when they were babies, and they could not remember her at all. They had a sense of being held, being loved, being sung to — none of these things happened now — but they could not picture her face. Sometimes the words of one of the songs would come to them, and they could hear a voice, the voice of their lost mother . . ."

It was almost forty-five minutes later when they reappeared at the front of the castle, and almost an hour before they stood in front of what was to be the last panel for that particular story, the panel depicting Hamlet contemplating Yorick's skull. Now get you to my lady's chamber and tell her, let her paint an inch thick, to this favor — *favour?* — she must come; make her laugh at that. It had

157

become so dark that they had been unable to see the details of the panels after a while. A little while later, and they had been unable to see the panels at all, but – by now – they knew the order of the panels, and what was depicted on them. Sometimes Alice made them feel the outlines of the figures as she continued her story, as if they were handling the words she spoke, caressing the characters she had created. All were within reach, except for the *Hamlet* panel. Sometimes they had to wait a little, while Alice thought of the next words she was to speak, as if she was straining to hear words being whispered to her, just beyond the sense of hearing. Alice herself did not appear to know what was going to happen next, she – also – hearing the words for the first time as she spoke them, words she had not seen written down.

They had come full circle, and ended almost where they had started, just before the first panel, standing at the bottom of the flight of steps, staring up at the panel they could not see, the figure of the man with the skull in his hand, struggling to discern shapes in the darkness. A chill wind was hissing in the branches of the trees beside them, and the dry leaves fell around them, upon them, scratching across their faces, skittering across the flagstones set into the gravel immediately before the entrance, making furtive little rustling noises in the darkness. Mary Benedict was a trembling wreck. The moon had been clearly visible in the sky for quite some time, but it had not occurred to her to point out the features on its surface, in order to demonstrate her superior knowledge in this area. This was highly unusual. "Ooh, look! The Sea of Vapors – *Mare Vaporum –*" (she invariably gave the Latin names, like a condescending botanist volunteering the Latin names of plants to the ignorant and easily impressed) "is clearly visible tonight," she would say, with studied casualness, whenever any part of the moon could be glimpsed hazily through the clouds, pointing firmly upward. The name of the chosen sea varied, but the finger was ever firm. She was incapable of speech on this night. On this night she was drowning in her very own, personal Sea of Vapors. ("*La Lune,*" Alice was thinking – French rather than Latin – "*La Lune.*"

The battlemented towers, the howling dogs, the creature crawling up out of the depths. *La Loon. La Loon.*) Charlotte had not said a word since they had been halfway along the second wall. The two of them clung together, silent. The only sound was Alice's voice — with no pause at all, as if she were reading from a book open in front of her — moving inexorably onward with the terrible events of her story.

This was the worst, this was the best, she had told so far.

The moon was completely ignored, but the stars . . .

The stars were clustering menacingly.

One star.

Two stars.

Three stars.

They were well on the way to four, five, and six stars.

Perky-breasted Madame Etoile would drop both her pitchers and shatter them once those screams started, and the howling of the dogs would increase unbearably. Ripples would spread from the center of the dark pool, as the creature from the depths heaved itself into sight. The towers would tremble, and the masonry begin to lean groaningly outward.

"Francesca, the last of the three sisters, moved toward the uncurtained lamplit window, to see what her sisters had seen before her, seen and not survived. She had to see what they had seen, though what they had seen had killed them . . ."

Charlotte and Mary braced themselves as Alice moved toward the final words of her story. They might even have stopped breathing in the anxiety not to miss hearing what she had to say.

They held on to each other tightly.

At the exact moment when Alice finished, and Mary Benedict's mouth began to open in horror at what she had just heard, her hands moving up — appalled — toward her face, one of the heavy castle doors silently swung open. It was far more terrifying than if it had creaked. An old, old man stood looking down at them, the flame in his oil lamp flickering in the wind, and making a popping sound, his face appearing and disappearing, glowing then darkening, brightness then skull-like hollows, his shifting shadow reaching down the steps toward their feet.

Mary Benedict gasped, uttered a sobbing cry, and then turned and ran toward the gates, gravel shooting up behind her as if from a skidding wagon wheel. Fragments of stone peppered their faces, punishment for some small biblical failing. Wailing screams echoed back, distorted by the wind. Deprived of Mary, Charlotte convulsively grabbed hold of Alice.

The old, old man gazed down at the two little girls who remained, who looked up, open-mouthed, like silent, out-of-season carol-singers, and then – without saying a word – he closed the door. Years ago he had held crowded theatres rapt and breathless when he marveled, "What a piece of work is a man, how noble in reason, how infinite in faculties, in form and moving how express and admirable, in action how like an angel, in apprehension how like a god: the beauty of the world, the paragon of animals!"

The whole audience – a few pale faces caught in the glow, the majority unseen and shadowed – was held, not only by those words, and by what those words meant, but also by the way in which those words were spoken.

25

The following week Alice made them go there again.

Mary Benedict's attempts to convince them that she-wasn't-in the-slightest-bit-nervous, never convincing, had now been abandoned. It was the word "counterclockwise" that had done it. She was already starting to tremble, and pulling around to her left, waiting for the door to swing silently open, and a figure to emerge, and come down the steps toward them, beneath the figure of the man with the skull. She would not have seen the moon if it had bounced off her head and rattled her teeth. There would be no "Ooh, look!" tonight, though there might be an "Ooh!" There would be no more cursing to turn Charlotte pink, though

Charlotte — any blush would soon have faded — looked as if she could do with a little more color in her cheeks. There would be no ballet positions, whether first, second, third, fourth, or fifth. There would be no *arabesques*, nor even the first stirrings of a pointy-toed *pirouette*.

"Number one," Alice said.

("First position," she thought.)

For the first time, she had chosen the panel at which they were to start. They took up their positions to the right of the steps. Also for the first time, she began a story in exactly the same place at which she had started the previous week, wishing — also — to end in the same place, at the bottom of the flight of steps that led upward to the doors, and the figure of the man holding a skull, the doors that had opened.

"Counterclockwise," she repeated, firmly. Charlotte and Mary, who had *known* she was going to say this, grasped each other tightly. It would be the same panels, the same direction, the same order, but it would be a different story.

It would be horrid.

They were sure it was going to be horrid.

More than horrid, this was going to be really awful, really terrifying.

Good.

"The three little g-g-girls . . ."

It was the first time that she could recollect her recently acquired, intermittent stutter ever revealing itself to a person other than her family or Charlotte. It had happened with no warning, and it made it sound as if she herself was trembling, made fearful by the story she was about to tell. She felt her way warily around it when she knew it was starting to happen — there'd been good days, and there'd been *really bad* days — and chose to be silent on what she knew to be the bad days. "Am I stuttering?" she'd ask Charlotte — "Am I st-st-stuttering?" would be what she said (she was not always able to distinguish between her stuttering and her struggles to express precisely what it was she wanted to say) — and Charlotte would let her know if she was indeed stuttering. "Yes," she'd say, shrugging (ever loyal) in a what-does-it-matter? sort of way, though it mattered to Alice.

"G-g-g . . ." said Mary Benedict, trying to find consolation in this easy target for teasing. "G-g-g . . ."

She said it in a tiny, babyish voice, as if she was about to say "coochi-coochi-coo!" to a tickly infant. (What an adorable child she was.) You just knew that she'd be imitating it all week at school. She acted as if Alice was affecting an out-of-period fashionable lisp, or a genteel accent, and thus inviting deserved mockery. It was like the way Papa tended to react. He did not take at all kindly to "P-P-Papa" as a mode of address. It somehow reflected badly on the dignity of his status, and demeaned him. "P-P-P!" he'd repeat to her, wincing at some pitiful solecism.

"G-g-g!"

She took a deep breath and started again, rather put out, though she tried to give the impression that she'd been feigning a terrified shudder – her teeth chattering with fear – in a sophisticated attempt to deepen the atmosphere of doom.

No problems this time.

"The three little girls walked up to the Shakespeare Castle in the late afternoon of a day in the fall. Alice Pinkerton walked in front. Behind her, Charlotte Finch was holding on to Mary Benedict. They took up their positions to the right of the steps . . ." Alice began.

Her voice was low, almost whispering, and they had to strain to hear her. Light was failing, and a storm was approaching.

No more "G-g-g" from Mary Benedict.

G-g-good.

"Light was failing, and a storm was approaching. No one was near them, no one could hear them, and the door of the castle began to swing open . . ."

The figures on the panel were of *them*.

The story was about *them*.

By the fifth panel along – *A Midsummer Night's Dream* – Mary

Benedict was begging Alice to stop. (This was no dream. It was a *nightmare!*) By the time they reached *The Tempest* — a storm completely out of control, a storm to carry them far away to a place where they did not belong — Mary and Charlotte were *both* begging her to stop.

She did not stop.

It was an hour and a quarter before — in complete darkness — they reappeared in front of the main entrance, looking up into the blackness where they knew there was a figure of a man with a skull in his hand.

Tick. Tick. Tick. Tick. Tick.

The screams were five-tick, five-star this time, a gigantic ten-out-of-ten tick in the brightest indelible red ink. The old man did not appear, though Alice had had one extra line of the story ready in case he did, one that would have lifted the screams to an unprecedented six-star — a seven-star, an eight-star, enough stars to blaze with a radiance that would have eclipsed the light of the moon — and awoken early sleepers in Harlem.

This was the last story she had told at the Shakespeare Castle.

She would have liked to have repeated her counterclockwise circlings for a thousand and one nights (storm-threatening nights, all of them, nights without moons or stars), reducing Mary Benedict (Mary *Thérèse* Benedict) to uncontrollable, incoherent gibbering, but — the following week — she and her family had moved away from Longfellow Park, all the way to Lac Qui Parle (now there was a story) in Minnesota. It was as if she had been drawn to Lac Qui Parle by her lavishly accented middle name, the French drawing the French toward it. (It was a way the French had.) It would have been satisfying to think that she had fled in terror, sleepless with nightmares of the Beast of Shakespeare Castle, but the truth was that her father (a lawyer) had taken up a new position in Madison. Alice had known that her story would be the last one that she would tell to Mary. They were carrying her — her and her accents — back to old Minnesota. She saw her, quite clearly, slung headfirst and gagged over someone's shoulder like a kidnap victim, her feet kicking —

first position, second position, third position (she just couldn't stop herself) – not too keen on being carried.

She had rather hoped that the door would swing silently open again. She would have liked to achieve a six-star scream. It would have been her farewell gift.

"Ooh, look!" a girl would be saying in Lac Qui Parle, over and over, anxious to ingratiate herself with her new classmates, "The Sea of Tranquility – *Mare Tranquillitatis* – is clearly visible tonight."

Her trembling finger would be a blur against the night sky. She herself would not know the meaning of tranquility ever again, even if she could say it in Latin.

26

When she had failed to find anything about Annie on Hudson Heights she had read and reread the personals, linking them in her mind with Annie, as if she might find clues to Annie's whereabouts there. She didn't need to look again to find the address of Madame Roskosch, as she knew it by heart. It was in a fashionable district near Washington Square, an address designed to create confidence, not one of those high-numbered nothingnesses where the city faltered into unpicturesque rurality. She had read the Henry James novel – he was not one of the novelists whose publications were laid out, as if casually, in Mrs. Albert Comstock's music room – and thought of Catherine Sloper, sitting alone in a deserted house, sewing her fancy-work like another Lady of Shalott. She often thought of Catherine Sloper. For a while she had thought of it as a novel that had been written just for her, a novel that only she had read, though there had never been a Morris Townsend in her life, though – unlike Dr. Sloper – her father was incapable of wit. (*"Henry James?"* Mrs. Albert Comstock had queried, seemingly under the impression that Alice had just invented the name, completely unaware that she was referring to a novelist, despite

Daisy Miller. "*Henry James?*" She knew of a *James Henry* – Myrtle had known his daughter well, he was a very good swimmer, big moustache, fond of mulligatawny soup, very well thought of – perhaps Alice was thinking of him.) It was rather the way in which Linnaeus had imagined that the Scandinavian – Danish? (Had he known Hans Christian Andersen?) – artist he admired had painted only for him, a painter of white-doored silent rooms, averted faces. There was no crowded gallery or salon; no jostling behind the cordoned-off canvases, the masses restrained by the thick red ropes on stands; no colored postcard reproductions, or illustrated articles in artistic magazines. There was just Linnaeus, he alone studying the painting in an otherwise empty room, seeing something that seemed to come from within himself, a reflection of his inner state.

In a street just off the quiet square, the trees partially visible behind her (again that seashore hiss of waves; now – at this time of the year – there were no leaves, and the sound of the sea was more of a white-foamed roar as a wind swayed twigs and branches), Annie gazed up at the drawn blinds of number thirty-seven, where Madame Roskosch was waiting for her in just such a room. The whole deserted street was blinded, as if it were a hot summer's afternoon. Elegant rooms had been promised in capital letters. Her savings were in her purse, and she was wearing her "jules," the necklace, ring, and earrings that Reuben had bought her for her birthday. Tomorrow she would return to Chestnut Street, and no one would know, not even Alice, not even Reuben.

Later still – she could not remember the chronology of her reasoning, the journey that was as much about discovering about herself as discovering about Annie – she knew that Annie would never have been anywhere near The House of the Magdalenes, Pettifar's Orphanage, or the North River Lunatic Asylum. She had found no clues, not even the beginnings of a trail. She was not really a Pinkerton, she felt, she was unworthy of possessing the same name as the celebrated firm of detectives. The place in which she should have looked first – over a year ago – was not on Hudson Heights.

She should have gone to the Morgue.

It was modeled on the Morgue in Paris, where Count Fosco's body had been placed in *The Woman in White* after his murder. Crowds pressed forward to view the dead, just as they pushed into Bedlam to view the insane. It was one of the sights to see, shivering with delicious dread.

She had visualized the Morgue in *The Woman in White* as the one in Bellevue Hospital at the foot of 26th Street, a New York City building, not the one in Paris, and imagined that all the bodies within were those of people who had drowned. This might have been because of its position beside the East River, or because of memories of the opening chapter of *Our Mutual Friend*, Lizzie Hexam — with an intense look of horror on her face — and her father rowing upon the River Thames, searching for corpses. She could see the engraving — not one by George Cruikshank or by Phiz, but by Marcus Stone (few knew this name) — clearly in front of her. The father and daughter seemed to be avoiding looking each other in the face. The girl was rowing, glancing back over her shoulder, and the bearded father — clutching the sides of the boat — was gazing down into the dark water, staring as intently as if seeking for a particular face. Marcus Stone had also illustrated *The Uncommercial Traveller*, and the first illustration in the book, the one opposite the title-page was of a woman and a little girl leaving the Paris Morgue. Count Fosco had been drawn up out of the Seine, though he had been stabbed through the heart, not drowned.

(The voice whispered, as if sharing a loving, intimate confidence, and spoke the words it had spoken more than once before. It spoke in exactly the same way as it had done previously, as if no variation were permitted, all the "s" sounds pronounced with a hissing noise. It was a heavily accented, foreign voice, and the English was not quite correct.

("There is a little light glimmering yonder — it is light of ugly little building — and inside are eight marble slabs — all in a row. It is called the Morgue, and be careful, oh, my Trilby . . .")

Cold water trickled over the dead faces, and over the corpses, delaying the beginnings of decay.

("Yes, there you will lie, fast asleep. And all day long and all night long the water shall trickle, trickle, trickle . . ."

(*Treacle, treacle, treacle*: this was the way that Svengali pronounced it, as if a thin golden thread of molasses was shimmering down to coat the corpses, a sweetness to lure ants and wasps, a swarming insect life to devour the glistening dead.

(". . . from your beautiful white face to your beautiful white feet till they turn green . . .")

Too much of water hast thou, poor Ophelia.

Annie's clothes would have hung above her to aid identification, in the drip-drip hollowness of the ill-lit room where the sheet-shrouded bodies were on display for twenty-four or forty-eight hours.

(". . . and above your head shall hang your damp, muddy, draggled rags – Drip, drip, drip!"

(*Dreep, dreep, dreep.* It was like the repeated susurration of something at twilight, something drawn out by dampness and darkness.)

Unidentified bodies were then buried in a potter's field (it was white with tumbled stacks of plates, fanned out like hands of playing cards) – she imagined a mist-surrounded island somewhere in the Harbor, accessible only by boat, like a Venetian island of the dead – but their clothes and possessions were carefully stored away, just as Mama had kept Annie's in a trunk in a storeroom.

Sometimes . . .

Sometimes – if students needed one – the unclaimed bodies of the unknown dead were used for dissection, though members of the public were not offered the opportunity to line up to watch this taking place. Some would have offered ready money, insisting on good seats, close up, quite prepared to risk the potential hazard of spurting blood in order to have an uninterrupted view of the gleaming knives making their incisions. If they were near enough they would be able to *hear* the sound the knives made, a multi-sensual treat. Eager and alert as if in a theatre, all keyed up for the entrance of a favorite performer, they'd press their carefully focused opera glasses to their eyes, and their jaws would rotate as they chewed on perfumed cachous or violet creams. They'd go very still during the best bits, and even their jaws would pause. They wouldn't want their opera glasses to wobble. Sometimes Alice – if she was tired and lost concentration – confused Dr. Jekyll and Mr. Hyde with Burke and Hare, the murderers who sold the bodies of their victims to Robert Knox's school of anatomy. Existing in the same moment of time, companionably facing each other across a bed, Dr. Jekyll and Mr. Hyde leaned over an unconscious woman, her face hidden by the pillow they had placed upon it to smother her. They pressed down, gently, firmly, seemingly making her comfortable, each looking into the face of the other, not at the woman. "Sleep, *ma mignonne*, sleep," Mr. Hyde murmured, sounding as if he was speaking to Dr. Jekyll, and not to the woman. Her limbs twitched feebly, little life left in her with which to fight, her clawed hands reaching up toward their faces, but not reaching them. Annie had been wearing her best clothes when she had gone, as well as her "jules." Alice would recognize them, tarnished, water-stained like something wept over.

("Sleep, *ma mignonne*, sleep. Do you hear me, Trilby? Trilby, do you hear me?"

(This was what Svengali had said, years later – Mrs. Albert Comstock in the theatre, writhing with wholly enjoyable revulsion – and she had thought of her search for Annie when she was a little girl, when they were both little girls.)

Papa had known that Annie was only a child. That was why he had been able to frighten her so easily, to make her do what he wanted.

("Then you will do as I bid you – you will rise. You will go into the dining room and get your cloak, you will wait there till I call for you . . .")

Annie did as he bade her.

She rose.

She went into the dining room and got her cloak.

She waited there until he called for her.

It was probably why . . .

("I will it!")

It was probably why – the idea was a relatively recent one – he had been attracted to her in the first place. She wasn't entirely clear about this, and worried away at the idea from different angles, as if trying to untangle a Gordion knot of a problem, an Ariadne who had lost the means of guiding Theseus away from the monster at the heart of the labyrinth. Perhaps Alice sometimes thought these things because she wished – because she *needed* – to think bad things about her father, needed to believe him capable of such badness.

27

She had helped Mama clear Annie's room – it hadn't taken long – when it became clear that she was not coming back, and they were preparing to hire a new maid. She was hoping she might find a hidden message, something that only she would understand, telling her where Annie had gone to, and why she had gone. Papa had made them check through the house to make sure that nothing was missing. He'd left the door of his study open that morning, and Alice had seen him kneeling down, pulling out the drawers in his desk, peering into the dark spaces at the back.

"Check the cutlery!" he'd shouted at one point, as if Annie had walked out laden down with their knives, forks, and spoons, and they'd be reduced to eating with their hands. He'd probably prefer that.

Hidden in Annie's room, under her bed – next to Reuben's letters, stored away with the chocolate in the Baby Quieter Wheel Toy box – there was Annie's metal clockwork bank, a Dancing Bear Bank, its paint peeled and faded. It represented a country house, three stories high with a mansard window, rather like one of the wings of the North River Lunatic Asylum deprived of its pillars. It had the look of something precious preserved from childhood, not so long ago for Annie, but it seemed to carry the weight of years. On one side – again like the asylum – was a high wall. The oversized organ grinder – his head reached the second-floor windows – stood on the lawn in front, next to his bear. Annie had once demonstrated to Alice how it worked. She had wound up the mechanism, like someone preparing a music box (the ballerina revolved and revolved to the tinkly rhythm, *ker-plunk, ker-plunk*), dropped a cent into the slot on the top of the organ, and pushed a knob to one side. The organ grinder's arm had gone around, and the bear danced to a little Italian tune, something from an opera, as the coin slid sideways into the interior of the house.

"They have tied me to a stake; I cannot fly,/But bear-like I must fight the course," Alice had said. This was what Macbeth had said, just before he met he that was not born of woman. She was demonstrating her knowledge of Shakespeare at every opportunity, and proving quite a trial to her family. Alice had brought cents to her especially, to see it do it again, but Annie wouldn't take them.

Alice had taken out a cent then, sitting on the floor beside the bed as Mama folded the two dresses, and copied what Annie had done. She watched the bear dancing, and listened to the music.

"Have you checked your dressing-table drawers?" Papa shouted to them from the hall.

"Yes, Lincoln," Mama said, though Alice knew that she hadn't. She smiled at Mama, who made a hush-hush gesture, her finger pressed to her lips.

"*La donna è mobile.*"

That was the tune the organ grinder was playing, as the clockwork whirred, the arm turned, and the bear danced. Mama hummed along with it. Alice had heard her playing it on the piano, sometimes singing if she thought there was no one there to hear her. Alice had heard her voice coming up through the chimney.

Women were fickle, like feathers flying in a wind.

"La donna è mobile,
Qual piuma al vento . . ."

There was no money in the bank, only the cent that Alice had just inserted, looking rather small and solitary, but there were various crumpled tickets, and some bright little medals made out of thin-hammered tin, awards for fragile bravery.

One of the tickets was for something called "The House of Dreams," sounding like some brightly illuminated attraction on the Bowery or in sight of a crowded boardwalk. She had held it in her hand, as if it were a visiting card from a long-awaited visitor, brought in on a tray by a servant. How that name would have appealed to Annie. She had read her an advertisement for a company that offered steamer excursions to Rockaway and Coney Island. These journeys were not as exotic as those made by Grandpapa's steamship company – the Occidental & Eastern Shipping Company crisscrossed the world, the routes marked in red like highways that only *their* ships could travel – but the descriptions seemed to fulfil Annie's most extravagant dreams of indulgence.

"The boats are provided with every luxury," Alice had read, "and are famous for their excellent table."

"'Every luxury,'" Annie had repeated, savoring the possibilities, her eyes glowing. "'Excellent table.'"

They held out possibilities not offered by the streetcars, an aura of elegance and sophistication. She had held herself upright, imagining herself gliding like a princess through glittering high-society scenes as her boat steamed down the Hudson, the gleam of silver and crystal on white linen, flickering candles, multi-colored rockets exploding in a night sky. The menus were printed in ornate script on thick cream paper, and she would magically be able to read what it was they offered.

"I shall begin with the Quail Eggs *en Croustade*," she would announce regally, her jules – quotation marks no longer required – sparkling.

These white-gloved hands would not be fluttering in the air as she sang an amusing darkie song, prod-proddingly poked by Mrs. Albert Comstock's parasol to keep her in time.

It was no wonder that she had been unable to resist the attraction of *ELEGANT ROOMS*.

28

She found Annie's hidden messages – if that was what they were – when she returned from an entire cold day of circling the North River Lunatic Asylum, listening at the silent stone. Some people seemed to need to return to a source of comfort, curled up on their side in bed clutching a much-loved favorite toy. She imagined Annie, rustlingly surrounded by Reuben's letters and unable to read them, dropping the same cent – over and over – into her Dancing Bear Bank, in order to hear – over and over – that women were fickle, ever-changing, never constant, like feathers flying in a wind, like stars falling from the sky. She would embrace its sharp edges, warming the cold metal against her breast, as if it were all she had in the world to hold against her.

Alice didn't embrace her playthings. She sought no source of comfort, but seemed – instead – to seek out where discomfort could be found, and this was why – that day – she had gone in search of *Hard Cash*, to complete the fourth reading she had started a year earlier, to begin a fifth reading. All day she had been wandering around the outside of a madhouse, and now she wanted to be trapped inside one again in the Charles Reade novel, feeling the walls closing in, as if it were "The Pit and the Pendulum."

She had last been reading the novel on the day that Annie had disappeared, and then – before they had realized that Annie was not coming back – Charlotte had called with her mother and thrust *The Bride of Lammermoor* eagerly into her hand.

"There's an Alice in it! Another one for The Alice Collection!" she had said, and Alice had started to read this instead.

The Alice Collection had been started by Charlotte, who – from the time when she and Alice had been small girls – had sought out novels and poems that contained the name Alice. (This was The Alice Collection, and there was any number of them to find). She would present the books triumphantly to Alice, with her name neatly underlined in the text. Later, she sought out books for Ben that contained the name Pinkerton. (This was The Pinkerton Collection: a somewhat more select number of volumes.)

This "Alice in it" was Alice Grey, the second Alice Grey they'd come across. (The other one was Agnes's mother in *Agnes Grey*. She later found a *third* Alice Grey when Alice Vavasor – she'd hoped she would – married John Grey in *Can You Forgive Her?*) Unencouragingly, Sir Walter Scott's Alice Grey was blind, an obvious riposte on Charlotte's part to Alice for having given her *Poor Miss Finch*, in which the heroine with Charlotte's surname had also been blind.

"At least," Alice had said, with crushing dignity, as Charlotte handed the novel over, "I have never had corsets named after me."

She had been thinking of the Carlotta model, recently unveiled in the Lindstrom & Larsson catalogue. Corsets – in their baffling complexity – did rather prey on the mind. She'd boggled at the hooks and buttons, the straps and clasps, the steel and bone, like a nervous young squire clutching a shield and apprehensively approaching his first suit of armor. The dawning of womanhood would bring with it some truly awesome responsibilities, a whole new world of serious-faced commitment, a sensation of going into battle with advanced and potentially dangerous weaponry.

It might save time if they didn't bother to read the books, just resorting to hitting each other over the head with them instead (a good incentive to find thick novels), but Alice enjoyed reading too much to do this, and Charlotte really was her truest friend. If she had to be rude to someone, Charlotte would be the safest, but least satisfactory, choice, looking sad, but not retaliating. Slim volumes of verse would be all she could bear to use on Charlotte, gently patting her over the head with a petal-scattering of weightless poetry, the lightest of light verse. *The Brothers Karamazov, Crime and Punishment* (how very apt!), *War and Peace, Anna Karenina*, the thickly bearded, thickly volumed Russians: these would be her chosen weapons with which to brain those she really hated, done to death by Dostoyevski, terminated by Tolstoi or Tourgenieff.

All happy families resemble one another . . .

Thwunk!

Well, she'd be happy.

"Tolstoi is by far my favorite novelist," she could declare ringingly after she'd laid waste to one of Mrs. Albert Comstock's literary afternoons (Madame de Stäel offered no competition whatsoever to these glamorous occasions), tripping lightly over the battered bodies, as horrified survivors – there would be few – stared aghast.

Instead of turning to the place she had reached in *Hard Cash*, she sought for the section with which she frightened herself, the scene in which Alfred Hardie first realizes that he has been tricked into a lunatic asylum. She was so caught up in her search for words that she was barely aware of the ring, wrapped in tissue paper so that it would not damage the pages, propping the book open as if to indicate a favorite passage. She held the little package loosely in her left hand as she read.

Alfred Hardie was trapped – trapped for life, it seemed – inside a private madhouse on his wedding morning, and elsewhere his unknowing bride was waiting for him.

He lay mute as death in his gloomy cell, a tomb within a living tomb . . .

She read the words yet again.

(She may have read the entire novel three-and-a-half times, but she had read certain passages many more times than this. The description of Alfred's entombment was the scene she had read the most. This was the page at which the book fell open, with no need of a bookmark. She'd often mused over *a tomb within a living tomb* as she lay on her back, unable to sleep, her arms down by her side. Then the words of Roderick Usher would insinuate their way into her mind. "*We have put her living in the tomb!*")

. . . And, as he lay, deeper horror grew and grew in his dilating eyes: gusts of rage swept over him, shook him, and passed: then gusts of despairing tenderness; all came and went, but his bonds. What would his Julia think? If he could only let her know! At this thought he called, he shouted, he begged for a messenger; there was no reply. The cry of a dangerous lunatic from the strong-room was less heeded here, than a bark from any dog-kennel in Christendom.

"*This is my father's doing,*" *he said.* "*Curse him! Curse him! Curse him!*"

Here she said the words aloud – *Curse him! Curse him! Curse him!* – keeping her voice low, not wishing them to echo down the chimney, but speaking with intense feeling. She couldn't help stuttering when she said this.

"C-C-Curse him! C-C-Curse him! C-C-Curse him!"

She could hear the "C-C-C" mocking voices as she did this, the "Coochi-coochi-coo" baby-talk of satirical impersonations. She tried to think of the "C-C-C" sounds as the rhythmic sounds of the nails being hammered home into the head, the dagger stabbing repeatedly into the heart.

. . . and his brain seemed on fire, his temples throbbed: he vowed to God to be revenged on his father . . .

This was the part she liked best. It was her source of comfort, her one embraceable doll.

Curse him! Curse him! Curse him!

She didn't stutter when she said the words in her mind.

She didn't stutter when she wrote them down.

"Check the cutlery!" Papa had said. "Have you checked your dressing-table drawers?"

"Yes, Lincoln."

All over Longfellow Park the Happy Families – all resembling one another – checked the cutlery and the dressing-table drawers. The whole area echoed to the rattling knives, forks, and spoons being counted, dropped, spilled across the floor, the slamming of drawers and doors, voices shouting, feet running from room to room. You could hear it in the street, the tumult from inside. They were the Happy Families of a menagerie traveling from town to town, the animals of different breeds living together in the same cage. You paid to look at them living happily together, trying to ignore the smell of the soiled straw, the rank, ungroomed coats, trying to breathe through your mouth. They didn't look much like a Peaceable Kingdom. They didn't look happy. They didn't look *together*. Some were restless, some inert, and all seemed nervously conscious of each other. They failed to cozy up together with affectionate cuddlesomeness, lacking all lavishness with licks and purrings. They were the Happy Families, the card game that Miss Ericsson had given her for Christmas, together with – it had been with the best of intentions – three Elsie Dinsmore novels. She could not abide Elsie Dinsmore, who was up there with Ellen Montgomery and Little Eva in the list of heroines of fiction ripe for assassination (and me-me-*me*, *I* want to wield the weapon).

Miss Ericsson, who had no family of her own, showed them how to play Happy Families, and she sat around the table in the schoolroom with Alice, Allegra, and Edith. Charlotte often played with them.

(A sense of irony had been instilled into Alice early, as she glowered at her two sisters, watching eagle-eyed for attempts at cheating. Allegra always tried to cheat. *Happy Families!*

(With *Allegra*!

(With *Edith*!

(With . . .

(With . . .

(With *Papa*!)

It was very much the same game as Fish, or – a particular recommendation in Alice's eyes – Authors, as you moved around the table, requesting the cards to complete the members of a Happy Family. You had to say "Please" when you asked, and "Thank you" if you were given a card. The English were very polite card players. If you failed to say "Please" or "Thank you" you lost a turn. No mercy if you were *sans merci*. If you were asked for a card – "Could I have Miss Bun, please?" – and you didn't have it, you'd say, "Miss Bun is not at home," as if shutting the door on an unwelcome visitor, and then it would be your turn to ask.

Thirteen Happy Families.

Thirteen . . .

There was Mr. Spade, the Gardener's family: Mr. Spade, the Gardener; Mrs. Spade, the Gardener's Wife; Master Spade, the Gardener's Son; and Miss Spade, the Gardener's Daughter. There was Mr. Chip, the Carpenter's family: Mr. Chip, the Carpenter . . .

Mr. Dip, the Dyer's family.

Mr. Soot, the Sweep's family.

Mr. Bun, the Baker's family.

Mr. Tape, the Tailor's family.

Mr. . . . .

Mr. . . . .

She could remember *six* Happy Families.

"Could I have Master Tape, please?" she'd ask Allegra.

"Master Tape is not at home," Allegra would lie, the pert false-faced housemaid guarding the front door and denying entrance, thoroughly enjoying her power.

Slam!

"Could I have Mrs. Bun, please?"

"Mrs. Bun is not at home."

Slam!

The door would crash shut, and the sound would echo around the hollow spaces of the curiously deserted house from which all families had fled. Inside doors were left open, as if to demonstrate the emptiness of the rooms within, the drapes were drawn back from all the windows, but – if you listened carefully – you could hear the hide-and-seek sniggers of the hidden hosts.

("Has she gone yet?" they'd ask, voices from inside closets, voices from beneath pieces of furniture.

("Has she gone yet?" they'd whisper, voices from the servants' quarters, voices from behind screens and portières.

(The maid, standing on the other side of the front door would shake her head, her fingers to her lips.

("Shhh!" she'd hiss. "Shhh!"

(Alice would rap at the door.

("*Ignore her!*" the voices would order.

(Alice would tug the bellpull.

("*Ignore her!*"

(The maid would smile. This was the favorite part of her job, though she'd enjoy a really hard slam even more.)

"Could I have Mr. Spade, please?"

"Mr. Spade is not at home."

Slam!

Allegra held her cards close to her face to hide her smile, peering over the top of them like a flirt with a fan, defying Alice to accuse her of cheating, so that she could unleash the "Mama! Mama!" sobs of the unjustly accused, the wailing "Why me? Why me?" lamentations. Alice was the guest denied access to all homes, a woman beyond the pale of decent society, and everyone shrank from her defiling presence. A reasonable enough preparation for adult life, Alice supposed. She ought to be grateful to Allegra for the practise. The cards swayed back and forth tauntingly in front of Allegra's face, as if they were the visiting cards from all the other, welcome, visitors, the merry throngs of those who were — unlike herself — found acceptable and crammed inside.

(The Buns were not at home.

(The Tapes were not at home.

(The Spades were not at home.

(The Chips, the Dips, the Soots were not at home, their dust-sheeted furniture — you needed dust sheets when the Soots came to call — shrouded in the empty rooms, dim with drawn drapes, the chandeliers swathed as if with Southern mosquito nets, some insect-haunted bedroom in Louisiana or Mississippi. Dust filtered through sunbeams.

(It was a high summer city, the streets were deserted, and everyone had left for the seacoast or the country.

(Alice rap-rap-rapped at the door.

(Alice tug-tug-tugged the bellpulls.

(The doors slammed in her face.

(They ignored her.)

Papa came to watch them playing. He had the air of someone at a loose end, restless, unable to settle to reading or solitaire, seeking for something to do to occupy the time that hung heavy upon him. He sometimes hovered around for a while, smelling of cigar smoke and *drink*, looking at them as though wondering who they were.

You could tell that Miss Ericsson was frightened of Papa. She clutched her cards tightly, and looked at them very closely, as if there was nothing else to look at in the room, like a reader deprived of a book lingeringly studying the labels on the tins and jars in the kitchen.

Alice asked and said "please."

Allegra said that Miss Tape was not at home.

Alice asked and said "please."

Allegra said that Miss Spade was not at home.

"What game is that?" Papa asked eventually, sounding like someone who thought that there might be money in it.

"Happy Families, Papa," Allegra answered, employing her wide-eyed good-little-girl look, though Papa had been asking Miss Ericsson.

"Happy Families!" Papa had snorted, a man who'd just heard the funniest thing for ages. "Happy Families!"

Miss Ericsson bowed her face closer to her cards. Mr. Dip, the Dyer's family was fanned out in front of her, a winning hand.

"Your turn, Edith," she prompted.

Edith turned to face Allegra.

"Could I have . . .?"

"Don't forget to say 'please.'"

Miss Ericsson sounded like a governess being inspected by her employer, anxious to create a good impression of the way in which she ran the schoolroom, the impeccable manners she instilled into

179

her pupils. She hadn't looked at Papa once. This Jane Eyre knew all about Mrs. Rochester.

"Could I have Miss Spade, please?"

She'd asked and said "please."

"Miss Spade is not at home."

Edith looked suspicious and rebellious. (Edith was definitely showing signs of improvement.)

Allegra appeared to be holding a hand of blank cards, a full complement of absences. Her doors were locked and bolted, and probably barricaded. Members of the Happy Family would be waiting behind the barricades and clutching their weapons, like members of the Paris Commune preparing to resist attack.

"Happy Families!" Papa snorted again. He made it sound like something ridiculous, something impossible.

("*Moonshine!*"

(That's what he was thinking.

("*Moonshine!*"

(The cold white light would creep across the floor and dim the warmth of the lamp. Miss Ericsson would hide her eyes with Happy Families and not see the truth of what was in front of her.)

Alice was Miss P-P-Pinkerton, the Shipping Merchant's Daughter, snapped down upon her back on the table. Mr. P-P-Pinkerton, Mrs. P-P-Pinkerton, Miss P-P-Pinkerton (and Miss P-P-Pinkerton and Miss P-P-Pinkerton: three stuttering misses all in a row), and Master P-P-Pinkerton. *Snap, snap, snap, snap, snap!* as the Shipping Merchant's family were arced out for inspection like a partially opened fan, obscuring each other, masking the faces and parts of the body, two Daughters too many in the crammed-in hand.

Alice was Miss Bun, the Baker's Daughter.

She was Miss Tape, the Tailor's Daughter.

She was Miss Spade, the Gardener's Daughter.

She was . . .

She was . . .

Miss Chip. Miss Dip. Miss Soot.

Six Happy Families.

She needed to remember the names of seven more families.

Whoever she was, she always looked the same. The clothes changed, but it was the same face on each card, and the face beamed happily. The cards were slapped down triumphantly onto the table as a Family was gathered together, the Mr., the Mrs., the Miss, and the Master.

Snap!

Snap!

Snap!

Snap!

He must have known.

He must have known what had really happened to Annie when he had told them to check the cutlery and search in the dressing-table drawers, acting the part of an outraged householder (the term used of the eminently respectable in all accounts of crime). This is what she began to believe, what she wanted to believe. Annie could never have afforded to go to Madame Roskosch. Frightened, she must have gone to tell Papa what had happened to her, what he had done to her, and he must have given her the money to go. She must have told him the name and the address, all the details that Alice had given her. This is what she thought.

Sometimes . . .

Sometimes she thought that he had made arrangements with Madame Roskosch to ensure that Annie did not return. The more she thought it, the more it became real.

From behind the blind, lifted up slightly at one corner, Madame Roskosch gazed down from her ELEGANT ROOMS at the hesitating girl on her front steps, the girl in her best dress with the bare trees behind her.

She was the woman who promised THE DESIRED EFFECT.

With her heavy-lidded eyes, and her large-brimmed hat, she was the figure of *Le Bateleur*, The Magician, from Mrs. Alexander Diddecott's tarot cards, magically transformed into a woman, and — like The Magician — she stood behind the table upon which her instruments were ranged, and in her left hand she held something long, and thin, and golden. With what lay on the table before her, and with what she held in her left hand, she would produce THE DESIRED EFFECT, she would offer THE SURE CURE.

Alice had thought that she had lied.

She had been wrong.

Papa was the man who had given Madame Roskosch the money.

Madame Roskosch had produced THE DESIRED EFFECT.

Madame Roskosch had offered THE SURE CURE.

Madame Roskosch had been as good as her word.

Annie's death was desired.

Annie's death was the cure.

The dollars were counted out on the surface of a polished table, like cards before a fortunetelling.

Snap!

Snap!

Snap!

Snap!

The reflection of each dollar rose up to meet the descending dollar snapping down upon it.

"'Curse him! Curse him! Curse him!'" she whispered again, like a prayer at bedtime ("C-C-Curse him! C-C-Curse him! C-C-Curse him!") . . . *and his brain seemed on fire, his temples throbbed: he vowed to God to be revenged on his father* . . .

Sometimes Madame Roskosch had the face of Dr. Twemlow.

Dr. Twemlow was always in need of money. It was rumored that his fearsome mother took all his money from him, allowing him — with an air of reckless generosity — a little pocket money, handed out each evening as if he were a casual laborer at the end of his day's work. He had to say, "Thank you, Mama," when she gave it to him in coins of small value.

There was a hiss of gas in the room, a bud-like flame, as if something was about to be cooked slowly over a low flame, and the air was as shadowy as a winter evening. Dr. Twemlow moved closer.

He bent forward, his face masked like that of a robber, sharp instruments in his hands, as if he were about to remove teeth, gouging them out bloodily, knives glinting. There was the headachy smell of gas, a wet rubber smell, disinfectant that smelled like the viscous liquid that Annie poured down the kitchen sink . . .

"Desired effect," he announced, explaining what he was about to do. The mask muffled his voice, rendered him faceless. "Sure cure. Injurious instruments." He placed the injurious instruments on the table, spaced out around the unconscious girl laid out in front of him. A pillow hid her face. He held them out one at a time between his thumb and middle finger — suspended just above the surface — and snapped them down with his forefinger.

Spoon.

Snap!

Fork.

Snap!

Knife.

Snap!

He positioned the cutlery neatly and precisely all around Annie, the meal on which he was about to assuage his hunger.

Spoon.

Snap!

Fork.

Snap!

Knife.

Snap!

He seemed especially keen on the knives. There was an especially loud *Snap!* as the knives descended.

"Check the cutlery!"

Papa had given his order more than once. He clearly visualized Annie walking away from them, bowed over, chinking slightly, her pockets bulky with furtively purloined knives, forks, and spoons, filched from denuded drawers, as if she were traveling to a place where she would feast perpetually.

It was the knives Alice wanted most, the knives she would most – and most enthusiastically – have used.

"C-C-Curse him! C-C-Curse him! C-C-Curse him!"

She said it aloud because it had to be spoken to take effect; unspoken desires were as futile as unthought wishes, even if she did stutter when she said it.

> *I never saw a brute I hated so;*
> *He must be wicked to deserve such pain.*

(Those last two lines – from Robert Browning – had often gone through her mind. They had the power of an incantation, a double-double-toil-and-trouble spell cast by a solitary Weird Sister in the flickering light of a fire.)

"C-C-Curse him! C-C-Curse him! C-C-Curse him!"

The more she said it, the more likely it was to come true.

Almost without realizing she was doing it – as if unwrapping a candy – she had removed the rustling paper from around the package she was holding, and held the ring in the palm of her hand. She had recognized it immediately, and had almost hurried straight downstairs to show Mama. It had been too big to fit on any of Annie's fingers, and she had worn it threaded onto the necklace.

Alice had been wrong in imagining Annie approaching Madame Roskosch wearing all her "jules": the ring had been left behind for her to find. Annie had placed it in *Hard Cash* on top of Alice's bookmark (a reproduction of a Mrs. Alexander Diddecott painting), thinking that she would find it that same day, when she continued with her rereading.

The necklace, the earrings, and the ring all had the same matching pattern: ovals of mirror glass set into gold-colored metal. Annie had put them on to show Alice when she had first received them. The miniature looking-glasses caught the light, dazzling in bright sun, and sent underwater rainbow patterns along the walls and ceiling, spinning elongated circles of brightness. Sometimes, during long mornings or afternoons in school, Alice had produced a lesser version of the same effect with the glass of her pocket-watch, or the lenses of her spectacles, watching the rippling radiance around the classroom.

If she focused the beams correctly, she might be able to ignite Miss Swanstrom like a condemned witch, and put an end to the hours of agony with a brief but intense blaze, the kind that had consumed Krook in *Bleak House*, though – admittedly – not quite so spontaneous a combustion. This was another passage she found herself rereading, in the way that others returned – for a quietly enjoyable weep, handkerchiefs at the ready, just like Mama – to favorite death scenes in sentimental novels.

The cinder of a small, charred log of wood sprinkled with white ashes: that was the (not at all sentimental) description of what was left of Krook after the flames had finished with him. It beat the death of Little Nell any time. If she couldn't dispose of Miss Swanstrom as spectacularly as St. Cassian of Imola's pupils had disposed of him in Elphinstone Dalhousie Barton's depiction of his death (though she lived in hope), this would have to do for the time being. The whole class could sing celebratory songs around the bonfire as Millie – this was Miss Swanstrom's Christian name – went up in flames, a ginger-headed Joan of Arc. (It was not advisable to make any reference to the color of her hair. Like the size of Mabel Peartree's nose, certain things were safest not remarked upon. The slightest hint of a stunned involuntary "Crikey!" at the sight of Mabel Peartree would have her rolling up her sleeves and looking murderous.) Euterpe Dibbo was the one who had triumphantly discovered that Miss Swanstrom was in possession of a first name, and some of the more impressionable girls had become quite excited.

They could roast potatoes in the glowing remains, and have a feast. There would be recitations and songs, an atmosphere of celebratory jollity.

"'Tender-Heartedness' by Harry Graham," Alice would announce as the title of her chosen poem, alerting the class – by a subtle shift in her tone of voice – that pocket-handkerchiefs might very well be required by all listeners.

Third position.

Simper.

This was going to be sad, really sad. The last few lumps of roast potato were discreetly swallowed. The more enthusiastic amongst her audience began sniffing prematurely, affected by the atmosphere, dabbing genteelly at their eyes. The pocket-handkerchiefs were big and white, and ironed into neat straight-edged quarters.

> "Millie, in one of her nice new sashes,
> Fell in the fire and was burnt to ashes;
> Now, although the room grows chilly,
> I haven't the heart to poke poor Millie."

She wished that Harry Graham really had published his poetry when she had been a girl. Heartless Homes cried out for Ruthless Rhymes.

Annie had beamed proudly as she displayed her jewelry, and moved the top half of her body from side to side, so that she sparkled with spectrums, the lower part of her face dancing with spangles of light, Ophelia or the Lady of Shalott floating down a sun-speckled stream, and Alice could see little bits of herself reflected in the tiny mirrors.

There was her smiling mouth, one of her upraised hands, her hair . . .

Parts of her were everywhere, but she was nowhere complete.

She put the ring onto the ring finger of her left hand – the wedding finger – and extended her hand out in front of her, as if to check her fingernails. She had to fold her thumb across the inside of her palm to hold the ring securely in place. There was a certain sensation of naughtiness in wearing a ring on this finger, a feeling that it wasn't really allowed until she was older. Her own face gazed back at her in miniature, like a portrait in a locket painted small, or a head cut out from a larger photograph to fit.

It ought to have been like Aladdin's ring, a ring to produce the slave of the ring when it was polished, an enormous jinnee that would say to her, "I am yours to command, mistress! Whatever you ask me for, I shall bring to you." She wouldn't ask it to carry her out of the darkness of the cave, and up to the surface of the earth. She wouldn't ask it to carry her to the part of Africa where the magic pavilion had been transported. She would ask for Annie. She rubbed the ring, as if accidentally, not really aware of what it was she was doing.

It hadn't worked.

Of course it hadn't worked.

She'd known it wouldn't work, and yet she'd tried it.

She lay on her side and lifted up the pillow, looking at her reflection in the mirror of the ring that she'd positioned to face her.

She looked at herself, made small in the distance, reflected in the little oval mirror, a mirror for the tiniest of mermaids.

"Looking-glass, looking-glass on the hand
Who is the fairest in all the land?"

Not her, that was for sure.

The ring – too big for Annie's fingers – was also too big for any of her fingers, and – like Annie – she had worn it around her neck, threaded onto a small gold chain. The chain – given to her by Grandmama – had once held a small cross, and she had held her breath for a while when she had first replaced it with the ring. Nothing had happened, and she had let her breath out in a great gasp, and then held it again in case she had been premature.

It was Charlotte who had pointed out the lettering engraved round the inside surface, too tiny for Alice to have noticed it.

I Belong To Annie.

Charlotte had read it out loud to her, seemingly without any effort – she hadn't even screwed up her eyes – and Alice still could not read it, even when she knew what it said. She had taken Papa's magnifying glass and read the lettering for herself. She knew that

Charlotte would have read it out properly, but she had to see it written down, not just read out to her by another person, the way she had read things out to Annie. She tried to believe that she was looking after it for Annie, keeping it safe until she returned, as she would.

After a while, the ring would fit onto her little finger, and she stopped wearing it on a chain around her neck, but Annie did not return. She'd lost the little cross, and was unable to replace it on the chain, even though she'd looked everywhere for it. She was a total failure as a Pinkerton, an unworthy bearer of a proud name.

A little while later – when she knew that Annie would never be returning – it fitted any finger on her hand, and she began to wear it all the time, on her middle finger.

When she first wore it to Mrs. Albert Comstock's, she had noticed – no doubt she was meant to notice – the nudge-nudges at the cheapness of the ring she wore, and Mrs. Albert Comstock and Mrs. Goodchild had made twinkly, carefully kind-faced (or as near as they could manage) inquiries. The sensation of strain had been exhausting just to witness, quite nauseating. She had remained enigmatic. It was the best way to annoy them, and she wasn't going to tell the bejeweled warthogs that it had been given to her by "that darkie girl," the grinning crocodile. (They would not have recognized "Annie," not known the name.)

Gracious!

Ha-ha-ha-ha.

(Alice heard the sound precisely, the hippopotamus honkings.)

What a lot of teeth!

Sometimes, when she didn't feel up to bright repartee, she turned the ring the wrong way around, so that only a simple gold-colored band showed, and she felt the little mirror and the gouging claws that held it when she clenched her hand. She clenched harder and harder as the afternoon became increasingly unendurable, forcing the little mirror into her mount of Saturn, cutting into her line of heart.

Sometimes, when Alice returned home, she found that there was blood on her palm — she had gripped her hands so tightly — and marks that looked as if some small fierce creature had made them, scratching to escape from a place in which it had been trapped. Blood smeared her need for solitude, and seeped along the feelings of her heart. She had a double heart line, and this meant that she had an unusually developed capacity for love.

Mrs. Alexander Diddecott had talked of such things one afternoon, peering dubiously at the lines and markings of her hands, a woman attempting to decipher an unfamiliar — and not very well written — foreign alphabet. She had held the outer edge of Alice's hand lightly, possibly reluctant to grasp something suspected of grubbiness. She probably had a crystal ball at home, well polished on a nicely brushed red velvet cushion, looking rather like the glass dome that Mrs. Alexander Diddecott had, the one containing the plaster cast of her baby boy's arm.

The left hand was the hand to read first. This was the hand that revealed what was inherent, that which was within you.

The lines on the mount of Saturn made a distinct square. This meant that she was in danger from fire. Perhaps she really was Bertha Rochester after all.

One day she would clench her hand so tightly that the tiny mirror would shatter.

"Gracious!" Mrs. Albert Comstock would exclaim, as the shimmering blood-edged fragments tinkled downward.

"Gracious!" Mrs. Goodchild would exclaim, slightly louder, not to be outdone.

I Belong To Annie.

29

The ring was the first message.

The picture was the second message.

She hadn't seen the picture at first. She'd placed the ring on her finger immediately, to feel some closeness to Annie, and looked at her reflection in the tiny oval looking-glass, thinking she might look different in that particular mirror. She looked the same as she always did, she eventually decided, only a little smaller, a little further away. Some improvement there, then, she thought. She sometimes felt that, of all the looking-glasses in the house, she looked best in the oval mirror — another, larger, oval — at the back of her wash-hand-stand, because — glancing into it as she washed her face — she was not wearing her spectacles when she looked. This was not because her spectacles gave her appearance an ugliness it otherwise would not have possessed; it was because she could not see herself at all without her spectacles.

The picture was in color, a small reproduction of a painting she later knew to be by Vermeer, the girl in blue reading a letter at a window, and was tucked beneath her bookmark for her to find. It was a picture she knew well, and had always been drawn to, though she had never known its title, or the name of the artist. Not knowing anything about it, knowing only the image that was in front of her (something she had always seemed to know, like a memory), somehow made it speak to her in a way that was more personal, a way that was beyond the reach of words. She felt something of what Linnaeus must have felt — years later — thinking that that Danish artist painted only for him. He and Ben were babies when Annie disappeared. They would have no memories of her.

Something about the girl in the picture made her think that it was a portrait of the artist who had painted it, the thought that all paintings were self-portraits, serious-faced artists studying their own reflections in the way that Hamlet studied Yorick's skull, or Aristotle contemplated the bust of Homer. There was something about the smock that made her seem like an artist, something about the firm, clenched hands, the way in which the light caught the knuckles. She'd looked for telltale smudges of paint on these hands, stains on the front of the smock, and then it had occurred to her that everything she was looking at was composed entirely of paint: the reflective face with its lowered eyes, the whole figure, the room in which she stood. Women artists to Alice, as a child, were women who stood in silence all day at their easels in front of paintings by men in art galleries, copying them. The copyists – the public galleries were crowded with them – all seemed to be women, a sex with nothing original to say in paint, one that could only mimic what men had already said. Copying Day was a clarion call – this mediæval instrument linked them neatly with their stitch-stitch-stitching forebears – for all amateur women artists to root out their brushes and watercolors and assume attitudes of artistic endeavor. Those unwilling to thus expose themselves to public scrutiny had to be content with needles and silks, the unceasing stitch-stitch-stitch of the past. Her ideas for her novel *The Life Class* must have been forming far earlier than she had realized.

Vermeer was another artist much loved by Linnaeus. It was he who had given her the name of the artist, he who had identified the painting when she had shown it to him. He didn't grasp at crowded value-for-money canvases, packed with gesticulating figures, and filling the whole of a large wall (they'd have golden frames, elaborately carved); all he desired was the small-scale depiction of the solitary figure of a silent girl in a room. It would have a simple black frame, "Dutch frames" Linnaeus called them. To Linnaeus, Dickinson Prud'homme was a purveyor of pulchritude, not an artist, a man who dealt in bosoms and buttocks, a rival to Comstock's Comestibles as a purveyor of fresh meat.

Because she could not read, Annie had a particular fondness for pictures of people reading, and sought them out. Alice imagined the walls of her room as being lined with such pictures, inward-looking faces angled downward, or turned a little to one side, and the room filled with an intense, concentrated silence like a Quaker Meeting in the moment just before someone felt the need to speak. She had imagined wrongly. On the one occasion on which she had been into Annie's room – a night of snow and storm – the white walls had been bare.

Alice had studied *The Woman in Blue*, trying to understand what it was that Annie had been trying to say, to discover the encoded meaning. Because she could not write, Annie had left the picture to speak for her. The young woman in the blue smock was facing to the left, standing at a window, though the window was not depicted. It was something that you knew was there, but could not see. The whole picture had a sense of things that were not there, things just out of reach, things that yet were central to its meaning. The light flooded her face, and the front of her body, as she stood – utterly absorbed – her head bent slightly forward as she read the letter that she held with both hands, her arms resting against her. She was gripping it tightly, her knuckles clenched. Her mouth was slightly open. It was a depiction of the moment at which a reader or viewer melted into the text, into the play or opera, into the painting, the moment at which breathing halted, time ceased to exist, and Alice found her own mouth drooping open, her breathing slowing, as if it were she who was reading the words in the letter, she who was the woman in blue. The young woman's head and shoulders were in profile against a large map that hung on the white wall like a tapestry behind her, the lines and markings of a place that had been exhaustively explored, its frontiers delineated, all details named, a place that had lost its mystery. The young woman herself was mystery entire; nothing was known about her, and it was what the viewer was that made him (or her, or *her*) see what was seen in that captured moment.

It was in a book that she had first found the picture, and it was in books that she kept it, keeping her place in each book that she read. She always penciled comments in books as she read them, marking passages that particularly struck her, and always read a book with a blank piece of paper folded inside it, jotting down thoughts that opened out from a text. The Vermeer picture she kept next to this, all unfolded musings drawn out by studying it, a silent form that teased her out of thought. When she came across these words in "Ode on a Grecian Urn" she knew exactly what Keats had meant, but she had never known what Annie had meant by the message in the ring, the message in the picture, if messages were what they were. She studied her face in the miniature mirror, looked at the girl reading the letter, and the words of what she was reading became a part of what she saw.

30

Now years had gone by and Mrs. Albert Comstock was a widow, the mother of Myrtle and Oliver; and the Reverend and Mrs. Goodchild were the grandparents of simpering Serenity, fruit of the loins of their son Sobriety and his wife whatsername, though they would prefer not to think of her in these terms, and Alice had long since ceased to be a girl.

She liked to think of the Reverend Goodchild undertaking his grandfatherly duties and unenthusiastically dandling Serenity on his knee at regular intervals. She was a "big-boned child": that was Mrs. Goodchild's description of her, said in a tone that made it sound her proudest boast. She sounded, in fact, remarkably like Albert Comstock had sounded when he had been recommending a particular cut of beef, dangling from a hook in front of him like an ill-treated corpse, as he stood there in his long white apron. A few vigorous sessions of Serenity-bouncing should reduce the Reverend Goodchild's lifespan by a few years, or — at the very least — exacerbate his hemorrhoids.

See-saw, down in my lap,
Up again onto her feet . . .

If she was feeling particularly vindictive — this happened quite frequently — she liked to visualize the Reverend Goodchild gingerly attempting to bounce Serenity up and down on the end of his leg, in the position of Edith's old iron toy, a stomach-churningly life-size version of the Baby Quieter Wheel Toy. The figure of the father seemed to be totally unaware that there was a baby firmly attached to his lower leg, and leaned back in his carriage, his hands nowhere near the baby's, reading his *Evening News*. He had a bald head, like Papa, but no beard. *Baby Quieter* was the headline that absorbed him, a rather disturbing headline in a sensational newspaper that seemed to consist almost entirely of lurid descriptions of crime. A quiet baby in the *Evening News* was unlikely to be sleeping peacefully, cooing to itself as Mama sang a lullaby. *Ring! Ring! Ring!* went the bell, as the wheels trundled round and round, and his leg shot rigidly high into the air, over and over again, like a spectacular nervous twitch, with the unnoticed baby grimly clinging on. It had the exact pose of one of Miss Stammers's embarrassing dogs, the dogs that would clamp themselves to the legs of blushing visitors, and snuffle noisily with eyes-closed bliss at inappropriate parts of their anatomy. They had a particular fondness for the Reverend Goodchild himself — that smell clearly awoke some deep-seated ancestral instincts — and he would clasp his hat protectively in front of his person if he spotted the dogs, Miss Stammers in tow, pounding eagerly toward him, salivating, already starting to sniff, tensing their hind legs as they prepared to hurl themselves ecstatically at his crotch.

"Phew!" they would be saying, in their doggy fashion. "Get a whiff of that, chaps!"

Ring! went the bell.

Ring!

Ring!

Serenity rose and fell with increasing speed, until the bell sounded like a nighttime warning in a fire-threatened city, and hemorrhoids exploded like overheated sausages. If he built up enough momentum, he would be able to hurl Serenity high over his head with a resounding *Kerboing!*, and propel her several hundred yards into the distance, as if she were the terrifying ammunition of some advanced mediæval siege-machine. If this weapon had fallen into the hands of the English or the French, the Hundred Years War would have been over in three weeks.

. . . *Little*

194

— little! —

. . . girl lost her white cap,
Blown away in the street.

Splat!
Splat!
Splat!
The skies would have been black with squawkily descending
Serenity Goodchilds, catapulted over the walls of besieged cities to
explode messily inside and spread plague. City walls would have
collapsed instantly into heaps of rubble (plenty more ammunition
for Mrs. Albert Comstock's thwunking here), pushed down from
inside as panic-stricken, fleeing citizens stumbled across the debris,
and it would have been like a nation of Jerichos at the blasts of the
rams' horn trumpets.

"We surrender!" the English would have cried, emerging shakily, pale-faced, nauseated, hands above their heads.

"We surrender!" the French would have cried (in French, you
wouldn't catch *them* lowering themselves to speak English: "*Nous*
something-or-other!"), still trembling after the impact of the terrible new weapon that threatened all civilization, though — being
French — they would be more used to awful smells, and would not
be so shaken by the appalling stink.

And they utterly destroyed all that was in the city, both man and
woman, young and old, and ox, and sheep, and ass, with the edge of
the sword.

Me first.

This was what Alice found herself thinking, with some enthusiasm.

Me first.

Please.

I'm quite prepared to supply my own sword. I've sharpened the
edge especially. It took me *ages*.

I'm not too bothered about the ass or the sheep (I quite like sheep) or the ox, but I'd like first choice of the man and woman, young and old.

I've got a little list.

Well, it's quite a long list, actually, seeing as you ask, but I'd be quick about it.

I wouldn't waste time.

They never would be missed.

31

If Mrs. Goodchild — the Reverend Goodchild's wife (the other Mrs. Goodchild, Sobriety's wife, was of no account whatsoever: she probably had to remind them who she was before they would admit her into the house) — had had her way, the young women from The House of the Magdalenes would all have been dressed in clothing as distinctive as that worn by the boys of Otsego Lake Academy. She probably visualized dresses in some virulent color, bearing scarlet letter "M"s on their bosoms (Mrs. Goodchild liked to flaunt her literary credentials): not just to emblazon the wearer's shame, but also to protect the innocent male youth of Longfellow Park, who were pure, without exception, in thought, word, and deed, until the provocative closeness of the sinful sisterhood drew them into temptation. She probably thought of it as a sort of visual warning. As the brightness appeared in the distance, like a night-time beacon giving intelligence of invasion, the alerted youths could flee in terror at their approach, with high-pitched, bird-like cries.

"A uniform," she'd said, in that reasonable, steely tone of hers, the one that made you love her, and wish to embrace her cuddle-somely in your arms, "just like the boys from the Academy . . ."

Mrs. Goodchild had thought for a moment. You could see thought happening when she thought. It was like witnessing some-one on the verge of sneezing, and you braced yourself for noise and wetness.

". . . though they'd probably need fewer buttons. Being the sort of creatures that they are."

The Magdalenes were expected to walk around in twos, with their eyes lowered, looking suitably ashamed, massed ranks of Hester Prynnes. Mrs. Goodchild and Mrs. Albert Comstock her – ahem – bosom friend (though "bosom" was the last thing one wished to think of in connection with Mrs. Albert Comstock; even a carefully inserted "ahem" scarcely lessened the nausea) took it upon themselves to rebuke the Magdalenes if they did not look repentant enough. They behaved as if they were members of a team, a prod-prodding moral patrol, marching about with their heels click-clicking like disapproving tongues.

They prissily perambulated, taking the air as they prodded the passing Magdalenes with bossy *touché* thrusts, effortlessly combining healthy exercise with uplifting moral correctness. Healthy-bodied, healthy-minded, they were bold exemplars of the power of prodding. They were so strait-laced – teams of panting servants must have yo-ho-heave-hoed on the laces – that the laces were probably digging deep into their flesh, like the self-imposed punishment of guilty secret sinners, the private scourgings and lacerations. They were the Lord's sandwich-board women, *Repent!* on their bosoms – Damn! That word again! – *Repent!* on their backs. It was as if they themselves had become Hester Prynnes, Hester Prynnes emblazoned with complete words, and not just initial letters. They, however, being who they were, bore righteous embellishments, and loitered chastely for pure-minded Arthur Dimmesdales (rather dim Dimmesdales) to join them for an invigorating afternoon of Upholding Moral Standards, and Slaying the Dragons of Sin. (When they fought the forces of sinfulness, they made full use of capital letters.)

They had no trouble whatsoever in saying "Boo!" to a goose, these goose-girls – *girls!* – of good-goodiness. "Boo!" they'd positively bawl, "Boo! Boo! Boo!" as if at a controversial night at the opera (a shortage of nice dresses and nice hairstyles on stage), when "Encore!"s and "Bravo!"s were not the sentiments that sprang to mind. They'd dig the Magdalenes in the back sometimes with their umbrellas or parasols (they took one or other — depending on the weather — out especially, a prod for all seasons), and tell them to conduct themselves with more decorum. A smile was indecorous. They ought to have had spikes inserted on the ends of their umbrellas. Out they marched, large-minded women on a country walk to botanize and entomologize, their instruments poised in readiness to impale a specimen through its abdomen. They were like park attendants on the alert for unauthorized littering.

"She is more to be censured than pitied . . ."

They surely sang this in deep, vibrant baritones, freshly ironed handkerchiefs, curiously dry, dabbing at the corners of their eyes, as they patrolled the streets in ceaseless search of the sinful. Mrs. Albert Comstock, as so often, was being *strangely moved*.

(Emmerson's voice in Delft Place, from long ago: "How were the prunes, Mrs. Albert Comstock?"

(Linnaeus, in a fair approximation of the hippopotamus-buttocked Mrs. Albert Comstock's fruity enunciation, every cushion from the sofa stuffed in appropriate locations about his person: "I was *strangely moved*."

(Here was Linnaeus again, trying to shock his much older sister.)

". . . She is more to be despised than helped . . ."

Prod.

". . . She is a hussy who has ventured
On life's stormy path, ill-advised . . ."

Prod. Prod.

". . . Scorn her with words fierce and bitter,
Laugh at her shame and downfall . . ."

Prod. Prod.

Some of the girls must have stayed inside the whole time, unable to bear the thought of walking outside when these sanctimonious Mrs. Gamps were on patrol, these priggishly prod-prodding Mrs. Grundys. (Should that be "Grundies"?) Alice had sometimes seen the Magdalenes in the twilight, walking arm in arm in Heneacher Woods: the romantically named Zaydas, Juanas, Constanzas, Madelines, Biancas, Rosamonds, Eleanors, Marianas, heads close together, whispering, as if there were no one in the world to talk to but each other, and all that they had to talk about was handsome strangers, and the shy beginnings of love.

Annie, if she ever been in The House of the Magdalenes, possessed a name that already existed in poetry, without any need of change, though the assumption of a new name was more a form of disguise (the fig leaves behind which they hid their shameful nakedness) than a symbol of a new beginning. Like someone collecting the materials for The Annie Collection — something worthy to stand beside The Alice Collection and The Pinkerton Collection — she had read "For Annie" to her when she had found it, and "Annie of Tharaw." It had been as if Edgar Allan Poe and Henry Wadsworth Longfellow had written their poems about her, she their meaning. To read a poem with the name of someone you knew was like coming across a painting of a place where you had been. You saw more than was in front of you.

She could have learned the poems by heart, and recited them to her when she met her again, a sort of password to tell her who she was.

> ". . . As the palm-tree standeth so straight and so tall,
> The more the hail beats, and the more the rains fall, —
>
> "So love in our hearts shall grow mighty and strong,
> Through crosses, through sorrows, through manifold
>   wrong.

"Shouldst thou be torn from me to wander alone
In a desolate land where the sun is scarce known, —

"Through forests I'll follow, and where the sea flows,
Through ice, and through iron, through armies of
foes . . ."

Annie of Tharaw, her light and her sun, the threads of their two lives would be woven in one. She would say this to Annie, as they walked arm in arm in the woods.

Now the woods had gone, the Shakespeare Castle had gone, and the clouds were massed above where they had been. Sometimes, as she looked toward the place where the tower of the castle had once been visible, she saw Hilde Claudia, Theodore, and Max Webster practicing their semaphore. Max was usually the one who was designated to clamber up the slope onto Hudson Heights, signaling incomprehensible messages to his mother and brother far below, with crisp, mechanical, doll-like precision. He'd enjoy that, performing high against the sky, like a Swiss flag-twirler she had once seen performing in the hall above the ice-cream parlor, a cousin of one of the girls from the ballet class. He had remained completely silent, the only sounds the swish and snap of the flags, far larger than the little flags employed by the signalers, much more dramatic in his gestures, his patriotic slow-motion swirling.

Tell me what you can see in those clouds, Miss Pinkerton.

32

She wandered back to the window as she dried her face.

Clouds . . .

The clouds, like shadows at sunset, were elongated and thin, stretching high into the sky as tall as trees above a child. She was a giant in the world, and her thoughts were clouds. Hmm.

There had been some people in Heneacher Woods in the

summer, when the woods were still there. They had been four shirt-sleeved men, all wearing straw hats. One of them had been holding a red and white striped pole, like a peripatetic barber. He was the youngest, little more than a boy, and he had the inferior, humble look of a beater at a hunt, awaiting orders from his gun-bearing superiors. He hefted the pole from hand to hand, a vaulter about to begin the long run toward the sandpit and the balanced cane on the measured stands. The one who appeared to be the leader stood alongside a telescope on a tripod, and he had the look of John Randel, Jr., stepped down from his stone plinth in The Forum — this was the name for the area at the main entrance to the park — all ready to impose his grid plan upon the north of the island. Bluffs, hills, rivers, woods: nothing would stand in the way of his new world, and Adam-like he would name the newly created. One of the others carried an ax — no tree could make them pause in their purpose — and the last one grasped sheets of paper (unfolded maps, possibly, or perhaps there were no maps, and they were creating them). They were like visitors from a distant country bearing emblematic gifts. A fifth, laden down with generous supplies of explosives, like tall church candles with nice white wicks, would clearly be hurrying on his way to join them. He'd look like a textile salesman entering a dry goods store with his samples, about to unroll the latest fashions in cloth with an abracadabra gesture.

"It's *à la mode*!" he'd announce, with a saucily unsuccessful attempt at an accent.

Boom!

"It's what every woman will want!"

Crash!

The landscape would fall flat before them, as if in worship.

They gathered in a little huddle, consulting on some small, vital detail. Another line might be drawn along here, one of those absolutely straight state lines — firmly held ruler, freshly sharpened pencil pressing into the paper — that ignored geography as resolutely as the grid pattern of the city. It was like coming across Mason and Dixon, or Lewis and Clark, unexpectedly, undaunted men about to stride off into the unmapped wilderness, into areas as yet unknown to Rand and McNally.

> ". . . How could she act de foolish part,
> An' marry a man to break her heart?

> "Den I wish I was in Dixie! Hooray! Hooray!
> In Dixie Land we'll take our stand, to lib an' die in Dixie,
> Away, away, away down south in Dixie!
> Away, away, away down south in Dixie!"

There was Dixie again, for the second time that morning. ("In Dixie whar I was born in,/Early on one frosty mornin' . . ." You'd think there'd never be frost there, there'd never be a morning like today's.) She'd convinced herself that Dixie had — or, at least, *ought* to have — taken its name from the Mason-Dixon Line. What did Charles Mason think — she asked herself — of Jeremiah Dixon's name being chummily appropriated and adapted as the name for the South, instead of his? *His* name came first in Mason-Dixon Line, for heaven's sake! It should be Macie, *Macie*, or — at the very least — Macy, not Dixie! ("Ah is from Macy," Southern belles could intone throatily, proud of their pampered department store existence, where all their needs were promptly catered for. They were in Macy! Hooray! Hooray! Away, away, away down south in Macy!)

There was a colossal painting of Lewis and Clark gazing out across the West in Mrs. Italiaander's dining room, taking up the whole of one wall, the lower edge partially hidden by the sideboard, so that the landscape seemed to emerge from the cornucopia of the silver serving dishes. They were somewhere very high up, and an immensity of landscape stretched below them, as if they were being tempted by Satan, looking out at all the kingdoms of the world in a moment of time.

Mrs. Albert Comstock's term for the irredeemably provincial was to describe someone as being from "one of those straight-edged states," casting into the outer darkness all life west of the Mississippi, states so devoid of interest and variety that rigid lines could contain them. Wyoming, Colorado, the Dakotas, Kansas, all of them, withered beneath her contempt: big-skied, wheat-fielded, cow-filled, peopled by grinning gap-toothed gawks wielding grubby dung-spattered pitchforks, far from the seething metropolitan cut and thrust of life in Longfellow Park. "Straight-edged states" was an uncharacteristically poetic phrase from Mrs. Albert Comstock – her strengths lay more in the tepid and colorless – but the more snottily she sniffed and sniggered, the more inescapably provincial she sounded herself, the suburban frump writ large, and few were writ larger than Mrs. Albert Comstock, whose Bosom and Bustle were sights worth a detour for the more adventurous tourist. If Kodaks could cope with the Flatiron Building, Kodaks could cope with Mrs. Albert Comstock.

If the good Witch of the North had asked Mrs. Albert Comstock if Kansas was a civilized country, and therefore free of witches, she would not have replied, with Dorothy, "Oh, yes." ("That's me," Mildred said, jabbing at the illustration of Dorothy with a well-fed forefinger, her young niece recognizing herself in *The Wonderful Wizard of Oz* as Alice read it to her. "That's me.") Geography revealed that Dorothy was a liar, and that Kansas – quite demonstrably – was not civilized. It was undeniably – almost willfully, one felt – straight-edged, a place never civilized, a country in which witches and wizards were still domiciled, shopping in casually chatting twosomes for their groceries in Garden City and Wichita; and in which sorceresses and magicians browsed through racks of ready-made clothing in Topeka and Emporia (whose very name promised large, well-lit department stores). Macy Land was taking its stand, and marching westward. They didn't just march through Georgia. Away, away, away, 'cross west in Macy!

The conference among the little group in the wood became animated, and there was much pointing northward, with hands gesticulating, oscillating to indicate uncertainty. The youth, increasingly self-conscious as he sensed Alice watching him – perhaps he had been told about her, perhaps he was nervous of The Madwoman in the Attic, perhaps madness was infectious, or perhaps it was just that her spectacles were glinting in the pale morning sunshine (there had been sunshine) – was given instructions and began to march resolutely away from the others, carrying his pole. Perhaps it was not a pole, but a javelin, and she would fall, pierced through the heart as Dracula was by Quincey Morris's bowie knife, a casualty of an over-ambitious school sports' day.

She saw him, throughout the morning, standing in various locations, with the pole held out from his right side, trying to make sense of the instructions shouted across to him. It always seemed to take four or five repetitions before he grasped what was wanted – a megaphone might have been a useful addition to their array of instruments – and his lower lip drooped. He stood with his pole at the side of him, like an artist's model for some heroic piece of statuary of a Greek athlete, incongruous in his slenderness and in his dark suit and straw hat, very still, like someone being photographed. They looked like men in an office lunch hour, picnicking in an urban park, loosening their neckties to indicate informality. There was nothing of the countryside about them.

They brought New York City closer.

Apart from the youth with the pole, they all had identical drooping moustaches, as if they had bought them as a matching set with their identical straw hats. There was something about this fact, and the way they stood with their heads close together, their arms resting informally on each other's shoulders, that gave them the look of barbershop singers – perhaps it was the striped pole that made her think of this – about to perform together in close harmony.

"Woodman, ax that tree!
Spare not a single bough!
In youth it sheltered me,
And I'll destroy it now . . ."

Two of them looked so similar that they might have been brothers, and this made her think of the cover of some sheet music she had seen in the window of Columbarian & Horowitz's music store years ago, when she was a girl. It was in the middle of the window. *Popular Songs Sung By The Du Rell* — or had it been *Du Bell*?; the lettering on some of the covers was as elaborate and difficult to read as Mrs. Albert Comstock's visiting cards — *Twin Brothers*. Displayed to the left of the Du Rells or Du Bells was "Why Did They Dig Ma's Grave So Deep?" Memories of Sobriety Goodchild singing this as a shrill and out-of-key boy soprano were still vivid enough to evoke a shudder: he had specialized in songs lamenting the premature death of a mother, and sang them with great — one might almost say enthusiastic — feeling. Alice's feelings about Mrs. Goodchild were clearly shared by her son. Another song in his repertoire had been "Cradle's Empty, Baby's Gone" (you could always be guaranteed to have a smile put upon your face when Sobriety was unleashed), though — these days — "Bottle's Empty, Daddy's Tight" would, perhaps, be more appropriate. He could sing it to Serenity, and the fumes — with luck — would render her unconscious for hours at a time.

Max Webster had, more recently, snatched his former glory from him (art was sometimes as short as life, Hippocrates), and was now the resident shrill-voiced mother-demolisher of Longfellow Park. All places with pretensions to gentility possessed one. This — no doubt — was: (a) why Serenity Goodchild had been so ruthlessly promoted as the New Improved Infant Phenomenon (and with prettier dresses), and (b) why Mrs. Webster always looked so worried. She must keep the kitchen knives in a locked drawer, and ensure that Max's demands were met in every way. "Why Did They Dig Ma's Grave So Deep?" would be followed by "Mother's with the Angels There" and either "Bringing Pretty Blossoms to Strew on Mother's Grave" or "A Flower from Mother's Grave." (When he wasn't strewing flowers there, he was tugging them up and carting them off.) If Mother wasn't Resting Beneath the Daisies, then Mother was 'Neath the Daisies Sleeping; and if the

Angels hadn't Gathered Mother unto Jesus, then the Angels were busily occupied in Beckoning Mother Home to Rest, or Bringing a Kiss from Mother. Mother Dear Had Gone to Heaven, and it appeared to be the best news that Max Webster had heard for ages. He sang with what could best be described as threatening sentimentality, as he gazed dewy-eyed – as if inspired by her presence – at his visibly apprehensive mother, his arms reaching out and making worryingly ambiguous gestures in her direction.

". . . Why did they dig Ma's grave so deep . . ."

– he inquired of his audience, clearly itching to roll up his sleeves, spit on the palms of his hands, and start shoveling –

". . . Down in the clay so deep?
Why did they leave me here to weep . . ."

– Tears filled the eyes of the women in the audience as he launched for the high notes at this point, and, for rather different reasons, pained tears (*Ouch!*) filled the eyes of the wincing men –

". . . Why did they dig Ma's grave so deep? . . ."

Sweet!
Sniff, sniff!
Sweet!
Mrs. Webster's confidence couldn't have been helped by her husband's vigorous applause. She undertook translations of medical treatises from the German on his behalf – at his *insistence* – and Charm became oh-so short-tempered when she made mistakes. She *always* made mistakes. Some of her translations were more difficult to make sense of than the original German, even when you included those alarming occasions when Gothic script was involved. A few mistranslated werbs, and here he was wociferous for her demise. Oh Charm, Charm, you could be wery cruel! Dr. Wolcott Ascharm

Webster was clearly all in favor of securely buried mothers, well down in the soil, with – preferably – a two-ton stone on top. His mother must have been like Dr. Twemlow's. You could sense Mrs. Alexander Diddecott hovering in the background, panting slightly, eager to illustrate these lachrymose scenes. They were just the sort of thing to get her mixing her watercolors. Max always held "The Angels Took Mama" – those angels never had a moment's rest – in readiness as a threatening encore. Alice quite enjoyed the chorus of this one, the agonized philosophical questioning.

> ". . . Goodnight! Mama, your troubles are over,
> Gone to a home on the bright golden shore,
> Never more your sweet smile I see . . ."

(A tremulous smile from Hilde Claudia as Master Max went down on one knee, clasped his hands to his heart, and stared straight at her, as if encouraging her to die right on cue.)

> ". . . The angels took Mama, why don't they take me?
> The angels took Mama, why don't they take me?"

A good question, this last. She had to fight an inclination to join in at this point, astonish them all by her fervor, her sing-along-with-me enthusiastic gesturings.

Take him! Take him!

On the right-hand side of Columbarian & Horowitz's window was "Poor Wandering One," the very first sheet music Charlotte had purchased for a Gilbert and Sullivan song: this was why she could remember this window display so well, so often had she gazed into it with Charlotte, debating the purchase. If she thought deeply she would probably have been able to remember some of the other songs in the window, but there would be, however, no more appropriate song to sing in Longfellow Park than "The Fountain in the Park," the most popular of the songs sung by the Du Rell or Du Bell Twin Brothers.

As with novels, so with sheet music: Alice did not particularly like seeing the illustrations. The images of the singers if they formed the illustration – stiffly posed in evening dress or costumes, staunchly homely in appearance, most of them, eyes glazed with singing the same song over and over, or saucily twinkling if it was a comic song – would infiltrate the music, interposing themselves between the words and her, a song that could be sung only with their voices, their expressions and gestures.

The twins were pictured side by side, at a slight angle to each other, giving them the appearance of Siamese twins joined at the shoulder, a musical Chang and Eng, the one on the left looking younger than the one on the right, and both intensely serious. You knew that their secret sorrow was that they were not identical, and did not look more like twins. There was something so proud about that vaunted *Twin Brothers*, that refusal to give them individual names, on the cover of the sheet music. "We *are!*" you could hear them insisting, the fact giving them rarity value, an added significance. "We *are!* We really are *twins!*" They seemed unaccountably somber for a song so light-hearted, so frivolous, as if it were they who were deploring the depth of Ma's grave. They may have been demonstrating the seriousness of their art, or discovering some hidden shadows in the words, one of the dark levels that Miss Stein had uncovered to her with such zest at school in "William Wilson," "The Masque of the Red Death," or "The Fall of the House of Usher."

"While strolling in the park one day . . ."

There was no preamble. The four men in the woods – each still grasping his pole, his ax, his papers, his telescope, the twins become quadruplets – were suddenly singing, harmonizing their voices with considerable skill, the boy's half-broken plangency like a bourdon. They clasped their hands to their hearts; they swayed to and fro.

"... All in the merry month of May ...
A roguish pair of eyes, they took me by surprise ...
In a moment my poor heart they stole away!. . .
Oh a sunny smile was all she gave to me . . .
And of course we were as happy as could be . . ."

They began to dance, perfectly synchronized, never changing their expressions of dignified solemnity: they, clearly, had also seen the cover of the sheet music, and the faces of the sepulchral songsters, and knew how to behave appropriately. They all simultaneously took three steps to their left, and lifted their left hands out in front of them. "Ahhhhhh!" they chorused, the word long and drawn-out. Carpenters – they were all wearing folded paper hats like children at a birthday party, giving them a festive air – on the roof of one of the new houses being built alongside Megoran Road, chorused "Ahhhhhh!" in return, and lifted their left hands. They formed a vigorously gyrating chorus-line of Mr. Chipses, playing on their saws and hammers in an uninhibitedly improvising percussion section. A hammer flew up in an arc and plummeted to earth, unleashed by some *gauche* sinistral. (Was this last phrase tautological?) "Heads below!" the unleasher shouted, after rather too long a pause. Grunting and heaving, they'd be laboring to prize the hammer – no prizes for this attempt – from the skull of a stunned passer-by, yet another victim of these lethal Highland Games, kilts akimbo and sporrans spattered. After the javelin came the hammer throwing, and after the hammer throwing would come the caber tossing (a useful utilization of the trees that were about to fall in swathes): the ever-expanding school population must be kept down somehow.

After the surveyors, later in the summer, throughout the fall, had come the workmen to chop down Heneacher Woods, and the cherry and apple orchards on the low slopes beneath Hudson Heights. Day after day she had heard them, and watched them from her window, chopping down the cherry trees like massed clockwork George Washingtons. The echoing sound of trees being chopped down was the sound that had so haunted Hawkeye.

209

The cherry trees and apple trees fell in swathes, and truth was upheld in a fierce bright light where there were no shadows in which to shelter. It was as if the men with the axes were in the employ of Mrs. Albert Comstock and Mrs. Goodchild, shamelessly bribed to destroy the woods and cull the Magdalenes, drive all the names from poetry — bowed down beneath the rain falling perpetually from the clouds — out into the open landscape where they might be more readily hunted down. *There's one! There's one!*

"... My mother ..."

Chop! Chop! Chop!

"... kissed me here,
My father ..."

Chop! Chop! Chop!

"... pressed my hand —
Forgive this foolish tear
And ax that oak tree grand!"

Chop! Chop! Chop!

33

Alice looked across to where the orchard had been, the place where Mrs. Albert Comstock had once fallen on top of her.

She saw her, falling to earth like a — *he! he!* — heavenly body, crashing down, the shadow above herself becoming larger and larger as Comet Comstock approached the point of impact, and the moment of complete darkness as she struck. The apple trees splayed out at angles, their fruit pulped white and ciderized, and tidal waves engulfed New Jersey. Any schoolboy eyewitness — she remembered thinking this at the time it happened – would have seen a provocative variation of Newton's theory of gravity: a human being falling earthward toward stationary apples. This, of course, would not have occurred to schoolgirl witnesses, who would – in their artless schoolgirl way – have thought of little but suitable recipes for crushed apples.

"2 lbs. of good cooking apples." (Considerably more than two pounds would be ready for instant, for *urgent*, use.)

Tick.

"4 ozs. of brown sugar, or to taste."

Tick.

"1 oz. of butter."

Tick.

"The rind of one lemon."

Tick.

This was Alice at the age of ten, inflamed by a recent reading of *The Mill on the Floss*, rather embittered by Charles Kingsley's preface to *The Heroes*, in which he matter-of-factly (and – she had to admit it – with complete accuracy) assumed that only boys would be taught Greek. (He wasn't much better in *The Water Babies*, where he took it for granted that any reader would be a boy. "My dear little man," he head-pattingly addressed him, "My dear little boy." He addressed him in this way so frequently that the dear little man would be patronizingly patted to half his original size, flat-headed, and littler with every passing moment. Was that why *pâté* was named *pâté*, because it had been compressed and squashed by unrelenting patting?) It was just the same in *Alice's Adventures in Wonderland*. As Alice swam about in the pool of tears it was her *brother's* Latin Grammar ("A mouse – of a mouse – to a mouse – a mouse – O mouse!") that came into her mind as she tried to remember the correct way of speaking to a mouse, finally deciding that "O Mouse!" was the appropriate response.

The face of Tenniel's Alice, seemingly on the point of drowning – her left hand raised, water up to her chin, her mouth beginning to open as if for a scream, her long blonde hair trailing

Ophelia-like behind her (she saw Ophelia in a painting, like The Lady of Shalott, like Mariana) — became the face of Maggie Tulliver struggling in the water, calling out for her brother Tom. She saw Maggie at Mr. Stelling's, trying to help Tom with his Latin and being scorned.

The Maggie Tulliver period lasted for far longer than the Jo March. It probably never really went away.

She copied Maggie — what a splendid idea it was — in taking out her anger on a wooden doll, entering into the actual text of the novel. In the absence of Papa or Allegra or Edith or Mrs. Albert Comstock or Dr. Vaniah Odom or Sobriety Goodchild or Euterpe Dibbo or any one of twenty others (she was going to need more dolls: hers would never last out) she hammered nails into its head with tremendous enthusiasm, like a small boy keen on carpentry. She was the sort of girl who was very firm with her dolls, and insisted that they behaved themselves. She held them by their feet and dashed them against beams, battered and punished them, and — most satisfyingly of all — hammered in those nails.

Hammer!

She had barely finished reading Chapter IV of *The Mill on the Floss* before she was sprinting around the house in search of a hammer and a good supply of nails in order to follow Maggie's lead. It had been a *Eureka!* moment. Mrs. Albert Comstock opted for "*Earache!*", but Alice — something of a traditionalist — favored "*Eureka!*" Maggie was clearly a girl who felt things the way that Alice felt things, and she embraced the phrase *that luxury of vengeance* — used to describe the hammering — as a proof of fellow-feeling, humming along in unison with Maggie and Jael as the hammer rose and fell. She was definitely Mrs. Chip, the Carpenter's Wife, and not *Miss* Chip. Miss Chip — daintily dressed, her hair neatly enclosed in a mediæval-looking net — simperingly held a measly little lightweight hammer, flourishing it by its slim little handle as if she was pretending to be a fairy and using it as her magic wand. She was Marie Antoinette playing at being a carpenter. She'd have handmade gold nails, and gilded wood with pre-drilled holes for hammering into – with a prettily assumed expression of creative endeavor – as her big-wigged courtiers politely applauded. Mrs. Chip – leaning back at an angle for maximum whack – looked as if she really meant business, about to explode a bloated bluebottle with a rolled-up newspaper, a messy splat to coat the entire surface of a window with sticky entrails, and block out the view. Nothing would survive when she let rip. *She'd* sort the sods out. She was probably in the middle of constructing a home made guillotine. "*Après nous le déluge!*" That's what she'd be saying with a note of triumph, a Madame de Pompadour – Mrs. Chip didn't have *quite* the right hairstyle – who'd switched sides and was keen to start decapitating. Marie Antoinette would not be Happy for much longer. Her feeble little hammer, her jeweled shepherdess's crook, was for ornament, not for use, and would not protect her from what was to come.

Hammer!

She derived far more pleasure from it than Jael – who'd approached it with the air of someone undertaking a distasteful task; what a waste of an opportunity! – when she drove the tent peg into Sisera's temple.

Hammer!

It ought to have encouraged a lifelong love of camping in her, an eagerness to be the first to put up all tents, the bigger the better, billowing white marquees spreading in all directions like a military encampment. You could always rely on the Old Testament to elevate your mind to thoughts of higher things. (You could always – for that matter – rely on the Old Testament for gruesome detail.) *That luxury of vengeance. Luxury* was the perfect word to describe how she felt.

Hammer!

She *luxuriated* in what she did. Miss Hayergaal had just praised her for learning "The Village Blacksmith" by heart, and here was the ideal opportunity to bring to vivid life the very scene she had described to her less-than-riveted audience. (A groan from the rest of the class at another word-perfect display from Alice Pinkerton,

Euterpe Dibbo positively seething. What greater motivation could there be than this for encouraging her to shine?)

Hammer!

Hammer!

"Under a spreading chestnut-tree"

— he was clearly local, an artisan from this very street —

"The village smithy stands . . ."

Her right arm rose and fell.

Hammer!

Longfellow had described her perfectly. A mighty girl was she, with large and sinewy hands, and the muscles of her brawny arms were strong as iron bands. Her hair was crisp, and black, and long; her face was like the tan; her brow was wet with honest sweat . . .

Hmm.

You couldn't help feeling — on second thoughts — that Longfellow had perhaps been a little *too* keen on the realistic detail.

Hammer!

You'd better be careful, Euterpe Dibbo and Sobriety Goodchild! Be on the alert, Dr. Vaniah Odom and Mrs. Albert Comstock! Flee into the hills, Papa and Allegra and Edith! She had *plenty* more nails for hammering, and Mrs. Chip was not feeling chipper. She had a row of them all lined up neatly in her mouth, her mouth puckered primly like Miss Iandoli's around a line of pins as she cut out a dress pattern. She'd unleash herself upon them as she sought vengeance, and bring her army with her. Like Curdie at the end of *The Princess and Curdie*, she'd attack with an army of Uglies — what more appropriate person than she could there be to lead such an assemblage? — and with her nine-and-forty grotesque and abnormal creatures (yes, she *certainly* qualified) she'd scratch, she'd nip, she'd crush, she'd bite, she'd hammer.

Hammer!

Hammer

Hammer!

The nails may have been bent over at clumsy angles, but all their points penetrated the brain. (The Bible was such a suitable, improving read for a quiet Sabbath afternoon. "Too terrible to speak of here," Charles Kingsley would have said coyly of the story of Jael, as he had said when he avoided describing Medeia's revenge — Medea was Medeia to Charles Kingsley, and Dædalus was Daidalos; he was clearly an awful speller, Ida Brook with a beard — unless, being such a muscular Christian, he thought it was different for the Bible, a necessary toughness, my dear little man made all the manlier by a little deep-voiced sinew-stiffening.)

There actually were two pillars in the schoolroom (she had only just begun to call it this) exactly as in Maggie's attic refuge — here was a sign — and against them (when not hammering) she ground and beat the doll's wooden head in the approved Maggie fashion. When she was not doing this she was binding Allegra and Edith (squirming, wriggling, vociferously objecting) to them with jump-ropes, perusing the windows at All Saints' to discover new methods of martyring them at the stake. She may have been firm with her dolls (well, perhaps rather more than firm: one was disembow-eled; one had a head heavy with clumped nails, splintered as a storm-ravaged tree), but she tried to be even firmer with her res-olutely unco-operative sisters. One day she would demolish the pillars with the fury of her attack, and the whole house would col-lapse with an apocalyptic roar, preferably when all her enemies were gathered together within it, drinking tea and nibbling fruit-cake.

"Yea, yea, mine enemies hath . . ." — *was* "hath" a plural form of the verb? "They hath" sounded wrong, somehow — ". . . perished!" she would chant, planning a victory dance, something involving tri-umphant stomping, and much swaying to and fro with uplifted arms. She might essay the occasional "Whoop!", the rise and fall ululations as she patted the flattened palm of her hand against her open mouth. She had vague thoughts of Red Indians whooping around a blazing, crackling fire, flying sparks, long thin shadows across night-darkened plains, paint-slashed faces fiercely illuminated. Terpsichore Dibbo — despite her ambitious name — was utterly useless at this sort of thing, and no help whatsoever.

"First position!" Terps would chant, attempting to emulate Mary Benedict's ballet demonstrations, and fall flat on her face with an always-surprised squawk.

Even better than "perished" was "perishèd," the grave accent adding an emphatic finality to the destruction of those whom she detested.

(She remembered Romeo being banishèd from Verona, and the actress playing Juliet loudly lamenting.

("Banny-*shed*! Banny-*shed*!" she howled to the Nurse.

(It was a word that slew ten thousand Tybalts.

(It was a pronunciation that had taken Alice by surprise.

(The actress had thumped her bosom, helpfully emphasizing the anguish for the benefit of the dimmer members of the audience, wincing slightly at an off-target thump.)

"Perry-*shed*! Perry-*shed*!"

Alice was not lamenting.

Anything but.

No anguish, and no bosom-thumping for her. It was her feet — in the absence of the necessary bosom — that thumped, and her arms and hair swung like storm-lashed tree branches, whilst — to the sound of her breathless, eager incantations — her enemies perry-*shed* in terrified howling heaps. The unexpected power of an extra syllable. Something perry-*shed* sounded far more satisfactorily obliterated than something merely "perished." One last brief glimpse of the rose-patterned china, the shape of the teethmarks in the half-chewed slice of fruitcake (the last thing they ever saw a *glacé* cherry, two sultanas, a few crumbs) and then darkness, dust, oblivion.

"Nutty as a fruitcake, am I?" she'd shout challengingly to the fruitcake nibblers. It would be the last thing they ever heard, putting them quite off their nuts.

It would be just like Samson obliterating the Philistines. (The *perfect* choice of noun, this last.)

It would be extremely entertaining.

She couldn't wait.

34

Now the trees had all gone, and she looked down on building lots, and half-finished houses, outside work stopped in the severe weather, the ground too solid to dig. Carpenters and plasterers were working inside the houses where work was far enough advanced, and on weekdays — above the gusting of the wind — she could hear whistling, singing, hammering, and see the prints of heavy boots in the snow. Out there Frankenstein's creature would be staggering, lost in the Arctic wastes, searching for Mr. Hyde, searching for a mirror, the picture of Dorian Gray, and here was the madwoman gazing down on him from her high window.

At least — she tried to comfort herself — she didn't have to look out from her window across to the park and the statue of Albert Comstock, as Kate did.

Kate and her parents lived on Park Place, a few doors away from Dr. Wolcott Ascharm Webster. How that statue must haunt her dreams, and bring restlessness to quiet evenings. It had been there for nearly fifteen years, and was covered in enough bird droppings to fertilize every cornfield from Ohio to Nebraska. The crops would be gargantuan and strange tasting, the ears curiously shaped. Exports would plummet. The birds seemed to seek out this particular statue, as if Mrs. Albert Comstock — who displayed a surprising grasp of Symbolism — had trained them especially. It might well be, of course, that Mrs. Alexander Diddecott's doves had a hidden purpose, and were not reared solely to inspire poetry.

Carlo Fiorelli had made the unfortunate change in the style of his sculpture at about the time of this statue — brought on, possibly, by his becoming enamored of *Ben-Hur* ("Is wonderful, wonderful book!") several years after its publication — and decided that boots and buttonholes were inimical to marble, and promptly outlawed modern dress from all his work. As a result, the minor worthies of Longfellow Park were depicted dressed in the way he imagined Ancient Romans would have been dressed. In carefully arranged togas or athletes' tunics, barefooted or sandaled, and most of them wearing laurel wreaths — they were, after all, the cream of local society — the men (they were all men: The Bearded Ones were out in cool, white force) stood around The Forum, just inside the ornamental gates on Park Parade facing out toward the lake, like victors in some great battle surveying a conquered kingdom.

The statue of Albert Comstock — *Albert Comstock: The Spirit of Commerce* — was designed to illustrate, and encourage, the entrepreneurial spirit of the growing community. He was sitting down, a portly figure, hands pressed against the sides of his thighs, and leaning forward at an odd angle. There was a sensation of strain about the pose, an expression of extreme concentration on the face. It was known locally among the young — with their distressing lack of respect for their elders — as *Albert Comstock: The Curse of Constipation*.

Carlo Fiorelli had rather misjudged the length of Albert Comstock's tunic. He had aimed for a dignified simplicity, the innocence of earlier times; what he had produced was a very fat man showing his bottom. This was what Kate saw every day from her bedroom window: the bottom facing toward her, peeping provocatively through the trees like a harvest moon.

"How's Bertie's bottom?" was one of Alice's regular greetings when Kate came to see her.

("Sweet Moon . . .")

(Pyramus, sensing his cue, sprang into action, striding on stage in his manliest manner just after Thisby had sprinted away from the lion. *A Midsummer Night's Dream* was nearing its end.

("... I thank thee for thy sunny beams;
I thank thee, Moon, for shining now so bright ...")

The statue consumed enough marble for a small cathedral, and on sunny days its vast shadow blighted several acres beyond it, inhibiting all thoughts of picnics, suppressing all possibilities of *déjeuner sur* this particular *herbe* in that direction. Manet's paintbrush would have dropped from his nerveless hand. Who could face nibbling on a chicken leg with those gigantic dimpled buttocks twinkling close by?

Albert Comstock had unveiled his own statue shortly before his death, just as she had unveiled the statue of herself and her sisters when she was a little girl. She would have liked to see his face when he saw the bottom. Come to think of it, however, with his butcher's training he would probably have been gratified by such an impressive piece of meat, and automatically assessed its weight and price per pound. His deeply ingrained spirit of commerce — other phrases were sometimes employed by the envious or the spiteful (some had been heard to comment that in choosing to marry whom he did he had been automatically following his usual practice of buying in bulk for cheapness) — was so overwhelming that there was general surprise that the words *SHOP AT COM-STOCK'S* were not engraved in large letters across the toga's front. Surely he could have persuaded Carlo Fiorelli that the mighty Roman eminence was incomplete unless — like another Mabel Peartree, one brazenly displaying her anatomy — it was casually swinging a shopping basket containing a selection of the culinary delights available for those who chose to experience Service with Sincerity and a Good Selection of Bones Available for Dogs of All Sizes? You visualized some tiny minion whose special skill was to measure bones and dogs' mouths to achieve maximum compatibility between the two.

Mrs. Albert Comstock had let it be known — you sensed the pageboy, the velvet cushion, the *tarantara* fanfare of trumpets – that her preferred description of the statue was "noble": an adjective that did not spring readily to mind. Mabel Peartree would have been there at the unveiling, and you could guarantee that she would have seized the opportunity to make use yet again of the word "charming" – *charming!* – the one adjective she knew. This would have been followed – shortly afterward – by "He's used a *great deal* of marble." Like Mrs. Albert Comstock, Mabel Peartree always liked to feel that she was getting her money's worth when anything vaguely cultural was in the offing. Alice – though not within the hearing of Mrs. Albert Comstock – referred to it as The Bebuttocked Behemoth: this captured the essence, she felt. When pressed for a comment by Mrs. Albert Comstock – this, after all, was in the days when she was strange though not yet officially regarded as mad – she (thinking rapidly, overwhelmed by what she had seen, that was the message, struggling to find the words to do it justice) had managed to come out with "It possesses a powerful uniqueness of vision." This had been received with gratified nods, and she had later heard Mrs. Albert Comstock using the same expression to Mrs. Goodchild, with the general implication that it had come to her in a visionary moment. If Miss Pearsall's School for Girls had racily risked teaching French, she could have been a daring pioneer of her sex in the male monopoly of the diplomatic service. "The Spanish have a powerful uniqueness of vision," she'd have been saying, as gunboats clashed. "The Russians have a powerful uniqueness of vision." A glittering career had been denied her because of beardlessness.

Herman Melville, his books forgotten, his days of writing novels over, hurrying to work in the New York Custom House, would have had the twilight of his years warmed as he caught a glimpse of its white vastness through the trees, and taken comfort from the fact that he had been remembered after all. Some lover of literature had erected a statue to Moby-Dick, and his greatest creation – though not seen as such at the time – would be forever commemorated in this New York neighborhood.

"Call me Albert Comstock . . ."

The words possessed a certain rough poetry, though they

presupposed that the whale narrated the novel. As was only appropriate (it was oddly satisfying when unexpected symmetries were discovered) Albert Comstock had been buried in the same cemetery as Herman Melville, who was not too far away from the man whose imperfectly sighted immensity had given him such misguided – but very real – consolation.

On nights of the full moon Mrs. Albert Comstock was of the firm opinion that the lascivious girls from The House of the Magdalenes would be drawn out in droves to marvel – in rapt, sensual abandonment – at the ample white flesh revealed to them, and some fierce inner hunger would be assuaged by the highly charged erotic allure of its shadowed loveliness, as they collapsed in synchronized waves, the hussies. Alice had overheard her complaining to Mrs. Goodchild and Mabel Peartree about the determined – ahem – *assaults* upon Bertie's statue. Sometimes, you could tell – ahem – *parts* of the statue had been – ahem – *touched*. Ahems and italics battled to convey the full horror of what she feared. (There was quite a battle in her listeners' features, also, at this point as they struggled to avoid displaying revulsion too obviously.) For a moment Alice had been a little disconcerted by this, this unexpected link with herself, her belief – which she had shared with no one – that some man or men caressed her statue in *The Children's Hour*, always in the same place, creating a small area of shiny goldness. She placed her hand on her left breast, above her heart, above her pocket-watch, as if checking the double ticking, assessing that both pocket-watch and heart were working. That was the place.

On those nights, the full-moon nights, in the cold moonlit dormitory, the long thin shapes of the windowpanes thrown across the bare floorboards, the Magdalenes would dream dreams of Albert Comstock, shifting restlessly, awoken to suppressed needs, emitting little inarticulate cries. Mrs. Albert Comstock would picture them with unusual vividness. The cries would gradually become one chorused word, chanted like a great convulsive invocation to the gods in a Greek tragedy: "Comstock! Comstock! Comstock!"

35

Alice had been born on March the nineteenth 1868, the day on which Captain Nemo had been the first man to reach the South Pole. The summer that followed had been blisteringly hot, and Mama had gone away with her to Staten Island, away from the heat and the glare, to a hotel near the sea where it would be cooler. Even as far uptown as Longfellow Park (tree-fringed, then, semi-rural) the oppressive heavy air of baked, shimmering, heat-hazed sidewalks seemed to press down suffocatingly. Her first few months of babyhood had been in intense heat, and yet — these days — she seemed always to be cold. She had bought *20,000 Leagues Under the Sea* for her little brother, Ben (she always bought books as gifts) — he would have been about eight at the time — and he had come across the date of her birthday, correct down to the year, in the novel. He had been very impressed, thinking it something she had organized herself, a personal request to Jules Verne written in fluent French. It had been like a development of The Alice Collection and The Pinkerton Collection.

Alice's Adventures in Wonderland and *Through the Looking-Glass* were, inevitably, the first two books Charlotte presented to her, in the year that Ben was born. *For Alice in the — er — Wonderland that is Longfellow Park. Beware of the Queen of Hearts. Dot. Dot. Dot. March 1878.*

"Dot. Dot. Dot" was what she and Charlotte tended to say to each other after significant pauses, as if they were experiencing one of those moments in a novel when a text moved into silence. The printed words came to a close with three printed dots in a row above a space of whiteness, and the scene that followed was not described. It was usually a scene that you were particularly keen to see described in every detail.

("But I don't want to go among mad people," Alice remarked.

("Oh, you can't help that," said the Cat: "we're all mad here. I'm mad. You're mad.")

The third novel in The Alice Collection — more of a Pinkerton, really, than an Alice – had been *Vanity Fair*. Two firm lines were drawn down the first words of the opening paragraph.

While the present century was still in its teens, and on one sun-shiny morning in June, there drove up to the great iron gate of Miss Pinkerton's . . .

(Three exclamation points in the margin.)

. . . *academy for young ladies, on Chiswick Mall, a large family coach, with two fat horses in blazing harness* . . .

There were, on the same page of text, four exclamation points for "*Have you completed all the necessary preparations incident to Miss Sedley's departure, Miss Jemima?" asked Miss Pinkerton herself, that majestic lady; the Semiramis of Hammersmith* . . ."

(*!!!!* enthusiastically in the margin, each *!* two inches tall.)

For a while – she quite enjoyed it, and encouraged this usage – Alice was addressed as "majestic lady" or "the Semiramis of Hammersmith" by Charlotte, though neither of them knew what was meant by "Semiramis," or – indeed – what was meant by "Hammersmith." Consulting *Lemprière's Classical Dictionary* soon solved the meaning of "Semiramis" though "Hammersmith" remained a mystery. The village smith stood under a spreading chestnut-tree, hammering away with his large and sinewy hands, the muscles of his brawny arms bulging like Samson's.

Hammer, smith! Hammer, smith!

Semiramis, a great warrior, became queen and sole empress of Assyria, putting her husband to death to establish herself on the throne, and made Babylon the most magnificent city in the world.

Smite, Semiramis! Smite, Semiramis!

They were a formidable combination. As Charlotte said, their likeness to Alice was positively uncanny.

Miss Pinkerton, that austere and god-like woman – a few sides later – had merited five exclamation points. Alice rather warmed to the idea of being austere and god-like, and had hoped – she had hoped in vain – that perceptive friends might make the sort of comments that they tended to make when they examined a new photograph or (for the more prosperous) portrait:

"It's just like you!"

"A remarkable resemblance!"

"So true to life!"

The fourth novel in The Alice Collection had been *The Wide, Wide World*, and Alice had suffered for an entire afternoon in the apple orchard — though not in quite the manner envisaged by the author — as she made the acquaintance of Ellen Montgomery. Alices had been everywhere, an Alice band of sisters jostling competitively in every circulating library, and on every bookshelf: Alice Mildmay, Alice Knevett, Alice Norton, Alice Bluestone . . . She'd referred to the (carefully selected) fiction shelves in the school library as "the Alician Fields" (she thought this was rather good), hoping to floor Mary Benedict with a pun, but she'd had to explain what it meant — it was something she ought to have realized would happen — rather spoiling the intended effect. ("Oh . . ." — Mary Benedict, cool and unimpressed — ". . . I *see*. It's a kind of play on words, is it? What's the point of that?" Quite.)

When Alice had come across "For Annie" in a collection of Edgar Allan Poe's poetry, she had gone straight to Annie, to read it to her, though — unlike Charlotte — she had sought out no text deliberately. The words seemed to find her.

> "Thank Heaven! The crisis —
>   The danger is past,
> And the lingering illness
>   Is over at last —
> And the fever called 'Living'
> Is conquered at last . . ."

This was how it began, though it made her sad to think of it, later.

Annie had looked at her very intently as she read, as if the poem had been addressed specifically to her.

"... A dream of the truth
And the beauty of Annie —
Drowned in a bath
Of the tresses of Annie.

"She tenderly kissed me,
She fondly caressed,
And then I fell gently
To sleep on her breast —
Deeply to sleep
From the heaven of her breast . . ."

She and Annie would sleep with their arms protectively around each other — this is what Alice liked to think — like the sisters, Lizzie and Laura, in "Goblin Market."

She would be Lizzie; Lizzie the one who saved her sister.

Alice thought of Captain Nemo as possessing the face of her father. It was her father gazing at the ruins of Atlantis, her father whose feet — she heard the icy crunch — were the first to make prints in the trackless snow at the South Pole, her father who was frozen into the iceberg. Jules Verne had described the Antarctic as a volcanic landscape of lava and pumice-stones, an atmosphere of sulfur — like the Icelandic countryside over which Harry Lawson, Professor Von Hardwigg, and Hans Bjelka had traveled in *A Journey to the Center of the Earth* — but she had always seen an endless dazzling expanse of untouched, unspoiled snow, seen by man for the first time on the day on which she had been born.

On this day, in this place, a man with the face of her father had unfurled a black flag, bearing an "N" in gold, and called for a six months' night to spread its darkness over his new kingdom. The night had been longer than six months, and it was not a natural night, as if the moon had interposed itself between the sun and the earth, a permanent eclipse, bringing darkness in daylight. Nemo was the name assumed by Captain Hawdon in *Bleak House*. He lived and died in squalor, mourned by no one but Jo, the crossing-sweeper, and was buried in a filthy cemetery heaped with dishonored graves.

His hair is ragged, mingling with his whiskers and his beard — the latter, ragged too, and grown, like the scum and mist around him, in neglect.

36

The other side of Megoran Road was being prepared for a new area of housing to be named da Ponte: a large signboard had been erected in the late fall announcing this. The use of the name of Mozart's librettist (and the prices) indicated that here was to be a select development. Mrs. Albert Comstock hadn't liked the use of an Italian name (this name meant nothing to her except that it sounded *foreign*), in case it attracted Italians (even Italians with money; she understood that such existed), and encouraged them to settle there.

She had heard, she said meaningfully — the sonorous boom tinkling the chandeliers at 5 Hampshire Square — all about what conditions were like in those areas of the city where Italians were allowed to roam unfettered. She visualized them as the hordes of semi-wild pigs that had roamed on the outskirts of the city.

"The Lower East Side, Mulberry Street . . ."

She spoke with faint distaste, speaking the very names might infect her mouth, hesitating slightly over the pronunciation, enough to make it quite clear that these were words that did not often pass her lips.

"I've been led to believe that it is not at all nice *down there*."

She made a vague ambiguous gesture downward with her hand, like a shy patient making a discreet reference to some intimate female medical problem, displaying the same eyes-lowered coyness as her physician, Dr. Twemlow, who gave the impression of struggling to control his blushes whilst wantonly taking a female patient's pulse. He referred to any embarrassing areas of the female anatomy (the greater part of the body, with the possible exception of well-gloved hands) as "The Ladies' District." You'd have thought a fashionable shopping area were contained within their corsets and drawers.

"Is it – ahem – within The Ladies' District?" was a typical inquiry (there were usually several ahems), his head turned discreetly to one side, apparently fascinated by the photograph of his formidable mother on the wall.

(How on earth could male patients bring themselves to discuss their – ahem – Gentlemen's Districts with the unsmiling visage of Mrs. Twemlow scowling disapprovingly straight at them in sure and certain knowledge that all men were beasts? It was just as well that he was primarily thought of as being a ladies' doctor. This was not a carefully calculated choice on his part – though the more complicated structure of the frail female body offered more opportunities for the financially ambitious – but was mainly because men were driven away by his fey manner, his prudish evasiveness, and by, above all by, Mrs. Twemlow, either in person, or as the wall-mounted Medusa glaring at them with every appearance of revulsion.)

The whole of da Ponte – like much of Longfellow Park these days – looked like a snowbound archeological site, with something being excavated rather than constructed: trenches, wooden barriers, the names of what had once been there, rather than of what was to be there, the Italian names – *Despina, Elvira, Cherubino* – that marked out the site of the new neighborhood. It was what some builders did: they named an area of land after the hometown of Italian or German or Swedish immigrants, and the settlers would arrive – drawn by a familiar name – to find nothing but empty fields, as if the village from which they had come had ceased to exist without them. She imagined them, headscarfed, carrying bundles, standing disconsolately on the edge of nothingness, Israelites without a Moses, waiting for manna that was never going to fall.

The Megoran Road signboard depicted Mozart, fifteen feet tall, gazing out across the trenches and the snow-covered mounds of earth toward New York City. There was no illustration of da Ponte. This seemed a little harsh, as he, after all, was the one who had actually lived in the city. That was the way with operas: those who wrote the words (W. S. Gilbert was one of the rare exceptions) somehow ceased to exist. Only the music mattered. The operas were Mozart operas, not Mozart and da Ponte operas. There was a thought to ponder: the insignificance of the words, the invisibility of the writer, overpowered by the language of the music.

It was strange to imagine da Ponte living in New York, a friend of Clement Clarke Moore: the man who had worked with Mozart talking with the man who had written "A Visit From St. Nicholas." (*'Twas the night before Christmas* . . .) It seemed the wrong time, the wrong place, the collapse of chronology. The St. Nicholas in the poem – dressed all in fur – was nothing like the St. Nicholas in the window at All Saints', or the massed ranks of red-clad jolly-faced chucklers ho-ho-hoing in the Christmas magazines and department stores. Here was a lost opera, words that were words without arias, music that had never been written.

> ". . . The moon on the breast of the new-fallen snow
> Gave a lustre of midday to objects below . . ."

The developer had probably chosen the name of da Ponte because da Ponte had taught Italian at Columbia College, and Columbia University had now taken up its new location across on Morningside Heights alongside where the Cathedral of St. John the Divine was going to be, and St. Luke's Hospital, a huge new area of development, just like Hudson Heights earlier. The general feeling was that Mozart was a little – er – *tinkly* and trivial, a minor figure, and that Beethoven would have been a far more satisfactorily respectable and bourgeois choice if you insisted on linking composers with real estate. A profession of "liking" his music was a (relatively) painless method of signaling intellectual pretensions, and demonstrated acceptable taste and middle-class solidity. He was the Tolstoi or Dostoyevski of music, and went well with dark wood and heavy wallpaper. Even if you didn't fully understand him, you knew that you were getting your money's worth, especially during the symphonies. You could feel *comfortable* with Beethoven. However, he had unaccountably failed to establish a widely recognized link with New York, and so they were stuck with Mozart. With da Ponte. As evidence of his cultural credentials, the artist had painted several hugely magnified bars of music behind Mozart's head: she had watched him copying from sheets clipped to the top of his ladder a month or so earlier, struggling as they flapped in the wind. Inspiration was soaring up behind the young man in the powdered wig, music in the very air.

(Longfellow Park, Longfellow Park,
Where even the signboards sing!)

Which moment had he chosen from the three da Ponte operas? (She used the expression "da Ponte operas" to demonstrate her solidarity with the power of words. Mozart probably wouldn't be too enthusiastic about this usage.) She had mused about it for an afternoon, watching him, becoming intrigued. Was it the sublime trio from *Così fan tutte*, in which the two sisters, with Don Alfonso, pray for the safety of their lovers and their friends after they have watched them – as the women believe – sail away to the battlefield, asking for gentle breezes, calm seas to protect them? Was it from the last act of *The Marriage of Figaro*, the sudden mood of melancholy and sadness, the Countess stepping forward in the darkened garden, the casting away of disguises, forgiveness? Was it the Act One finale of *Don Giovanni*, another garden, another evening, and the sound of a miniature minuet flowing outside from a room inside the palace, the three masked figures entering, pausing for a moment to pray on the threshold? Miss Stein had not only opened her eyes to the darkness within Jane Austen's novels; she had alerted her – a simple matter of a transferring of skills – to the desolation that

could be found beneath the pretty dresses and the wigs and frip-
peries of Mozart. Mrs. Albert Comstock strongly disapproved of
such besmirching, and sought sunshine without shadows, smiles
that were ever bright and beaming. Why *spoil* things, for heaven's
sake, and make it sound like Ibsen? "Ibsen" was spoken with a certain self-congratulatory daring. This was Mrs. Albert Comstock
demonstrating that she was fully conversant with the horrors of
modernity. The Longfellow Park fireworks display on New Year's
Eve 1899 might have featured a spectacular sign with the words
Welcome to the 20th Century! blazing out against the night sky, but
she wanted to know the twentieth century a little better before she
offered it her hand for shaking.

Too shortsighted to read even such gigantic notes – the music
would be deafening – Alice had asked Charlotte to bring her telescope across from the piazza at Delft Place, telling her that she was
devising a method of concentrating the sunshine (there actually had
been some sunshine then, though it had been cold) through the
lenses in order to construct a heat-ray. She had not read *The War of
the Worlds* in vain.

"Alice, where art thou?" Charlotte sang outside the door of the
schoolroom.

It was her invariable greeting. Alice would sing the next line of
the song, Charlotte the line after that, and Alice would open the
door singing the fourth line. Sometimes they varied the pattern.
Charlotte would have been mortified if the door had been opened,
and she had found herself staring at a room full of people who had
heard her singing.

". . . I've sought thee by lakelet . . ."

". . . I've sought thee on the hill . . ."

". . . And in the pleasant wild-wood . . ."

Alice opened the schoolroom door, and Charlotte staggered in.

". . . When winds blow cold and chill . . ."

The next line was so appropriate that Alice couldn't resist adding
it.

"Is this yet another valiant attempt to rid the world of Mrs.

Albert Comstock?" Charlotte asked, rather breathlessly thudding the telescope down on its stand at the window. (It had been there ever since.)

"I have slowly and surely drawn my plans against her. Ever since my attempts at a heat-ray failed to destroy Miss Swanstrom . . ."

"Your spectacles and pocket-watch glass, however expertly focused, could hardly possess enough power to explode Miss Swanstrom into flame. She was so damp and soggy that the best you could have managed would have been a thin wisp of smoke."

". . . I have longed to annihilate Mrs. Albert Comstock. Now, at last, a weapon of sufficient power has been placed within my grasp!"

"You forgot the evil cackle of the mad genius."

"Ha. Ha. Ha. Ha," Alice enunciated carefully, a pedantically exact reproduction of the sound Mrs. Albert Comstock made when she wished to suggest that she was in the throes of helpless girlish laughter. The laugh, like the smile, came in one size.

"All too realistic," Charlotte said, with a shudder, and then indicated the telescope. "Have you not considered the possible effects of your actions, however nobly inspired? The – er – . . ."

"Dot. Dot. Dot."

". . . er . . ."

"Dot. Dot. Dot."

". . . corpse . . ."

". . . gigantic as it would be . . ."

". . . would burn for months. The sun would be blotted out. A perpetual winter would descend upon the world, a new Ice Age."

"It would be like 1888 all over again . . ."

(A brief memory of Papa's death, the snowdrifts blocking the light from the windows, the snowdrifts *inside* the house, the drip-drip-drip of the red grin, the torn papers gleaming in the darkness.)

". . . I must seek out my skates, polish the runners on my sled . . ."

". . . and hasten to the Central Park."

"That could be hazardous. A dinosaur might be roaming down Fifth Avenue."

"I thought I'd just killed Mrs. Albert Comstock."

"But how satisfying to kill a Martian with one of her own weapons."

"Mrs. Albert Comstock is *undoubtedly* a Martian. The description in the opening paragraph confirms it."

"'Vast and cool and unsympathetic,'" Charlotte quoted.

"Mrs. Albert Comstock is unquestionably *vast*."

"*Tick*."

"*Tick*."

"Few living things come vaster."

"Except, possibly, blue whales . . ."

". . . There she blows!. . ."

". . . and the population of China."

"Mrs. Albert Comstock is undeniably *unsympathetic*."

"*Tick*."

"*Tick*."

"Mrs. Albert Comstock is unequivocally *cool*."

"*Tick*."

"*Tick*."

"Three adjectives out of three. *Tick, tick, tick*. There is no doubt whatsoever. Mrs. Albert Comstock is a Martian, and it is our *duty* to destroy her."

"Say that again! Say that again!"

"Charlotte Finch! You are a corrupting influence on my pristine innocence."

It was as if the four of them were together again — herself, Charlotte and Linnaeus, and Emmerson Columbarian — up on Hudson Heights in the music room at Delft Place, singing around the piano, laughing at silly jokes. No, it wouldn't be thirty or forty years before she and Charlotte turned into the Misses Isserliss: the metamorphosis was already almost complete. She and Charlotte edged ever closer to their Misses Isserliss incarnation, the full-fledged deranged doppelgängers. If she accepted Charlotte's invitation to move up to Hudson Heights and share Delft Place with her, there they'd be — side by side, their two houses conveniently within cooee distance of each other (a sort of national park for deranged spinsters, a Yellowstone Park of the peculiar) — the two sets of Misses Isserlisses, the image and the reflection, the fully trained and the trainees. It would be so handy for the North River Lunatic Asylum. They'd make friends with the superintendent, wooing him with homemade cakes and knitted vests, and — as a special friend's favor — he'd lock her in one of the padded cells when she lost control completely on nights of the full moon. She'd shriek unheard all night long, raving dementedly, and the soft walls — she'd caress them for comfort, press her face against them and inhale their dusty urine-scented odor — would yield to her touch like walls in dreams. Padded cells would be like rooms designed for eternal sleep, eternal dreams, with mattresses — ripped, disemboweled — sagging from every surface. She'd emerge in the morning, refreshed and twitching with nervous energy, like a vampire fresh filled with a stranger's blood. She and Charlotte would grow battier with each year that passed, sharing a house and a sense of humor that no one else could understand. It was a rather pleasing prospect. They were already developing the mannerisms of eccentricity, and Charlotte had three cats, each of which had a name that was a private joke. Alice was taller than Charlotte, and so she should naturally take upon herself the part of Miss Issie Isserliss. She'd enjoy lashing out with the bell. She'd had plenty of practice with her leper's bell — she was, after all, the Leper of Longfellow Park — and Charlotte would be in top rattling form as she shook the box under the noses of the perpetrators of puns. She'd put a coin into the box specially, to ensure a satisfactory rattle. The box needed its coin, just like the bell needed its clapper. Let's hear the applause for that clapper! She sometimes imagined Pandora rattling her box in that same way, hopeful of encouraging curiosity, the irresistible urge to lift the lid and peer inside.

Have a care, Mrs. Albert Comstock! She'd certainly rattle her, her tinkles ever deepening toward the mighty death-knell tolling of reverberating ding-dongs. You might be taking on more than you expect. Who would true valor see/Let him come hither. *Valour*. A well-wielded bell could give tongue to death.

"Pun Warning!"

Tinkle! Tinkle!

"Unclean!"

Ding-dong! Ding-dong!

"Unclean!"

Splat!

The bats were swarming.

The next generation of batty spinsters was all lined up and ready to be unleashed, more bats than a night-shrouded cavern swarming with high-pitched shrieks, the insect-like rattle of membranous wings, the night sky loud and restless.

She bent to the telescope, fiddling with the eyepiece, as if to bring the memory into sharper focus, bring it closer, and explained what it was she was looking at.

"Which piece of Mozart, do you think?" she asked. "Which would you choose? Which opera? Which music?"

Charlotte gave the matter some thought, as Alice bent to the telescope, like Kate over her camera, or Henry Walden Gauntlett.

"I . . ."

Charlotte didn't know very much Mozart. Beethoven would have been a better bet.

"I . . ."

She'd much rather that Gilbert & Sullivan had been proposed. The ampersand – Charlotte tended to write an ampersand between the two names – linked them like the proprietors of a long-established business, with signs above plate-glass windows in the main streets of most large cities. "*The Mikado*," she'd have said confidently. "*The Pirates of Penzance*."

"I . . ."

She then noticed Alice's shoulders starting to shake, her fingers tightening on the sides of the telescope.

"None of them!" she said firmly.

"None of them," Alice confirmed, laughing. She straightened up, and looked at Charlotte. "One of Mozart's lesser-known pieces."

"Not one of Mozart's pieces at all."

"Not one of Mozart's pieces at all!"

Charlotte started to bend down toward the eyepiece, and Alice put her hand across it teasingly.

"I know what must have happened," she said. "The sign painter decided to add some music, and grabbed hold of whatever was on his music rack to take with him to copy, the first thing he came across." She smiled at Charlotte. "What piece of music would that be? What would be the most likely? *Don't* say Gilbert and Sullivan! Think back a few years. Any home, any music rack, what do you think is most likely to . . .?"

It was not *Ker-plunk, ker-plunk, ker-plunkety plunky-plunk, ker-plunk, ker-plunk, ker-plunkety plunky-plunk*. It was . . .

"'After the Ball'!" Charlotte was unhesitating.

"*Yes!*"

They began to waltz around the room, together, singing.

> ". . . After the ball is over, after the break of morn,
> After the dancers leaving, after the stars are gone,
> Many a heart is aching, if you could read them all,
> Many the hopes that have vanished, after the ball . . ."

"How could Mozart ever manage to forget he wrote that?" Charlotte asked.

"It has definite thematic links with both *The Marriage of Figaro* and *Don Giovanni*, wouldn't you say?"

"Miss Stein would be proud of you!"

"I hope Miss Iandoli doesn't notice," Alice said. "She'd probably set fire to the sign in protest at the demeaning of Mozart."

"*Mysterious Conflagration in Longfellow Park.*"

"Back to Mrs. Albert Comstock."

"Huge flames."

"Thick smoke."

"The thicker the better."

"Then we wouldn't be able to see her."

37

She brushed her teeth with Dr. Graves's Tooth Powder, wondering how long it would be before G. G. Schiffendecken began to stock an extensive range of tooth products bearing his name, and worthy of the false teeth he rammed into every available mouth. There would be bottles on an epic scale in order to cope with the needs of the gigantic landscape-encompassing grins. In his presence it was wise to keep your mouth shut. One thoughtless yawn in his vicinity, and an unfamiliar set of oversized teeth would challengingly occupy your gums, as if you had been seized with an unfamiliar mood of vivacity. As you goggled vacantly at the invasive grin-grin choppers, G. G. Schiffendecken would begin his patter, informing you – in a spirit of informative informality – that it was well worth paying extra for teeth of such high quality.

Smiles were far more sincere when you'd forked out a fortune.

She wandered back across to the window as she dabbed at her lips with the towel. She clutched the towel to her, feeling like a bather drawn to the edge of a frozen sea.

The not-yet-ancient Mariner's ship came into her mind again. The mist. The wondrous cold. The ice, mast-high. The gale-driven snow on the night of Papa's death, and the fallen telegraph poles lying across the street like the ice-covered masts of a storm-wrecked armada. The bowed heads. The muffled voices. Sins and iniquities.

And through the drifts the snowy clifts
Did send a dismal sheen:
Nor shapes of men nor beasts we ken –
The ice was all between.

38

Now the snow covered the whole of the area that was to become da
Ponte, though the face of Mozart was clear. Snow was not falling,
but the wind blew up gusts from the drifts that had accumulated
earlier, and she looked down on the flurries beneath her, high up
above the clouds.

G. G. Schiffendecken trudged into view on his morning walk with
his dog, bowed over as he walked into the blizzard, the dentist drawn
forth by the brushing of her teeth. He lay in wait, listening, all poised
to pounce. For a moment it really felt like she had brought him into
being by thinking of him, but this was a walk he undertook every
morning. Coleridge had been inaccurate in his description. There *was*
the shape of a man. There *was* the shape of a beast. He'd been right
about *drifts* and *snowy* and *ice*. He'd certainly – when G. G.
Schiffendecken was involved – been right about *dismal*. How could
a man with so many teeth, so lavishly equipped for uncontrollable
mirthfulness, look so dismal and *lowering* most of the time? It was a
sinful waste of material. Perhaps for him – as a dentist – grinning
qualified as work, another exhausting demonstration of what it was
he manufactured. He stood nearby, as his dog – huge, of indetermi-
nate breed, the sort of dog one felt ought to have a miniature wooden
barrel around its neck – urinated copiously on Mozart's feet. G. G.
Schiffendecken gazed away into the middle distance in the opposite
direction, back home, up toward Hudson Heights, strenuously adopting the attitude of someone unaware of what his dog was doing.
Knowing his taste in music, Alice suspected Symbolism.

The dog bore the unexpected name of Olivia, unexpected – not
least – because, Olivia, judging by the – ahem – urinating technique employed, was quite demonstrably not what Mrs. Alexander
Diddecott would have described as a "girl dog." It was probably
some coded reference to the missing Mrs. Schiffendecken. G. G.
Schiffendecken had discovered her *liaison* – somewhat *dangereuse*
when dental equipment was freely available – with that very tall
thin man who played the banjo even more loudly than Dr. Wolcott

Ascharm Webster, and she had decamped to Brooklyn (famed home of Mary Kinkeldey, she of the unacceptable vowels) with her paramour. The Teeth – she, of course, had had a set of her husband's false teeth installed – possessed strange, erotic powers.

"Olivia!"

G. G. Schiffendecken could be heard exclaiming the name each evening, as he took his second walk of the day with the dog, unwinding after a busy day with his arms down people's throats.

"Olivia!"

His teeth – the mighty Schiffendecken teeth – could be seen gleaming in the darkness as he wandered past, calling Olivia's name. It was strangely haunting. New posts, still pale and unweathered, bore the names of the streets that would be built there (names that would hold no meaning for G. G. Schiffendecken): *Almaviva*, *Figaro*, *Giovanni* (surely a rather controversial choice for the more strait-laced), *Dorabella*, *Susanna*. . .

Harry Hollander came into view, walking down the site for Susanna Street, heading straight for Mozart. G. G. Schiffendecken (who was probably singing "O, Susanna!" under his breath: that name he *did* recognize), noticing his approach, began to prepare himself for the ritual of greeting. Alice saw Harry Hollander walking past several times a day – even in weather such as today's – as he worked on his latest song. He was gesticulating now as he strode along, as if conducting. He saw her at the window, and removed his hat, with a courtly bow. He was never too lost in his composing to cease to be a gentleman. She bowed back, and then waved with her hairbrush; though – by then – he had lowered his head again against the wind. He had never achieved a success as great as "O, Susanna!", but he worked away every day, and lived in hope.

He was very modest and down-to-earth about what he did for a living, and they – she, Charlotte, Linnaeus, and Emmerson – had once had a very jolly evening with him years ago, in which he insisted that they should vote to decide which was the very worst song he had ever written. The winner – he had promoted it vigorously by singing it appallingly – had been "There's a Gap in My

Heart where Dorothy Dwelt (For Dorothy's Not There Now)."
"Sensible, sensible, Dorothy" had been his comment. He took his
song-writing seriously: this particular song, clearly, had failed to
achieve some personal standard. ("Dorothy paid for the doctor,"
had been his enigmatic explanation.) There was a sign in his
window at Mrs. Chambers's, where he boarded on the far side of
the park, which read: *Harry Hollander. Songs written.*

At the moment he seemed to be working his way through most
girls' names (toward the end of the previous year he had dealt with
the majority of the city's landmarks), and Charlotte told her of
the latest publications as they appeared in the window at
Columbarian & Horowitz. After Lillian, Gertie, Gladys, "You're
Bet, You're Betty, You're Lillibet (But You'll Always Be Lizzie to
Me)," "Linger Longer, Lydia (Stay Awhile with Me)," there had
been Florence, Mabel (Mabel Peartree had studied it avidly, on the
alert for anything dubiously nasal in its references), Bessie, Dora,
Mildred, Grace, whole crowds of others. A publisher on West 28th
Street, not far from Broadway, paid him ten dollars a song.

She had been slightly anxious in case he got around to using the
name Charlotte, and when he did – Charlotte had arrived flushed
with pleasure, and played it instantly on the piano – he had not only
written a lovely melody, but (obliterating memories of Sobriety
Goodchild) had included, amongst his more-or-less rhymes for
Charlotte, "Louisa May Alcott," "Lancelot," and "Camelot" in a
song about a girl who had loved books as a child. She didn't envy
him if this time he'd reached Agatha. ("Stagger the"? "Swagger
the"? or – introducing an element of drama – "Dagger the"?)
Aggie *might* have been easier, but there were worrying hazards –
"saggy," "baggy," "scraggy" – if he was attempting a love song. It
was only a matter of time before he got around to Alice. Perhaps
she could collaborate with him, unleash her creative side.

> "Look up, there's Alice,
> Dripping with malice,
> Peering out over the park.

It must be traumatic,
Quite operatic,
To be crazy like poor
Lucia di Lammermoor,
To be locked in the attic
All, all alone in the dark . . ."

She was undoubtedly strange.

Mrs. Albert Comstock — with her detailed information about Dr. Wolcott Ascharm Webster and the clinic — frequently told her she was strange (in the tone of voice of someone doing her a tactful favor, as if discreetly informing her that she had bad breath or an unfaithful husband), so it must be true. Mrs. Albert Comstock — who was a mistress of the well placed "er" — invariably referred to it as "Dr. Webster's — er — clinic." (She was clearly longing to say "er — lunatic asylum," so keen that she'd probably dispense with the "er" before much longer.) Alice always felt that the next sentence would be to remark that it was rather — er — eccentric, surely, to rely upon the Webster Nervine Asylum — such an inconvenient distance away — when the North River Lunatic Asylum — she'd manage to slip the phrase in, somehow — was so — er — convenient. She couldn't get it into her head (surprising, when you considered its vast empty spaciousness) that Alice was seeing Dr. Wolcott Ascharm Webster in his consulting room on Park Place, and was not making the journey to stay up in Poughkeepsie.

(Yet.)

Though she would . . .

She would . . .

She would be making that journey soon.

On Wednesday.

Dr. Wolcott Ascharm Webster had insisted.

Today, Ben would begin his journey to Japan, and — three days later — she would be making her shorter journey upriver. "Upriver." The thought frightened her. There was a hint of slavery about the word, a suggestion of being sold into bondage. She was probably thinking of some narratives from before the Civil War, accounts of slaves being taken *down*river to the busier slave markets. There was some such reference, she thought, in *Uncle Tom's Cabin* (or was it *The Adventures of Huckleberry Finn?*), where the word "downriver" was a word to be spoken with fear. Curiously enough, Mrs. Albert Comstock's intelligence sources — a moment's pause here, to consider the incongruity of the word "intelligence" being discovered cheek by jowl (the jowls were pendulous and saliva-glistening, wobbling like those of a dribbly bulldog's) with Mrs. Albert Comstock — had failed to discover the imminence of this departure. It was news she'd be thrilled to discover, and she'd waste no time in informing all her acquaintances. Sides would be sore from vigorous elbow-prodding, spectacles misted and dripping from sibilant whisperings.

She'd feel safer if Alice was some considerable distance away, preferably locked up, even more preferably chained to the wall and wearing a straitjacket in a barred and well-guarded cell. "How *is* Alice?" she used to ask Alice's mother, in her usual tone of mild distaste, like a fastidious doctor driven to make unenthusiastic inquiries about a bowel movement. (Lady Macbeth — with every reason to be a little wary of doctors — would have had no patience with such dainty Twemlowian twemulousness. "When all's done," she would have hissed witheringly, in her most contemptuously are-you-a-*man?* tone of voice, "You look but on a stool," wiggling the chamber pot vigorously right under his averted nose as if agitating a frying pan in mid-omelet.)

Miss Ericsson also tended to use "er" with great frequency, so frequently — in fact — that Alice sometimes thought of her as Miss Er-Ericsson. Miss Ericsson was fully aware of this.

"I *er*. I'm human": this was her summing-up.

"Er was the name of Judah's firstborn": this was Alice's reply. "He was wicked in the sight of the Lord."

Keats's Top Tip to Shelley for poetry writing was to "load every rift" with "ore," piling on the adjectives like a fireman frantically shoveling on the fuel in a coast-to-coast railroad race. Clearly a Keats lacking in confidence, Miss Ericsson hesitatingly loaded every rift with "er." In Miss Ericsson's case – it could hardly be more different from the Comstock Technique – it was her way of trying to avoid saying something unpleasant about someone, as she searched for an alternative word to use. "Mrs. Albert Comstock is – er – a very confident lady in the expression of her ideas" was the sort of thing she would say. Alice would not have used "er" in this sentence. Alice would not have used "confident" or "lady," either. She sometimes thought Miss Ericsson was the most Christian person she knew. She would probably describe Jack the Ripper as "rather too – er – boisterous," and Genghis Khan, in similar terms to those she had employed for Mrs. Albert Comstock, as "very – er – confident in his actions." Here was Mrs. Albert Comstock: Genghis Khan with a Bosom instead of a Beard.

Olivia was still urinating with undiminished vigor. It was as if he – that "he" with the unsuitable name – was there in the summer, hearing "The Fountain in the Park" and being inspired to ambitious emulation, though this little ritual had happened every day since the sign had been erected. Perhaps, as a woman, Alice should avert her eyes decorously, but she was waiting for the day – in a week or so's time – when Mozart, by now quite rotted away at the ankles, crashed down upon G. G. Schiffendecken, as he tunefully informed Susanna that he came from Alabama wid his banjo on his knee, and was gwine to Lou'siana his true lub for to see. She quite looked forward to seeing him being squashed flat, to the thunderous chords of some appropriate climax from toward the end of the *Requiem* or *Don Giovanni*, as Mozart took his revenge, risen like another Commendatore.

"And when I'm dead and buried, Susanna, don't you cry."

She wouldn't. She wouldn't.

39

As Harry Hollander drew toward him, G. G. Schiffendecken began to prepare The Grin, and she witnessed the miracle of its unveiling. Fortunately for Harry Hollander's eyesight there was no bright sun to gleam dazzlingly across the acres of G. G. Schiffendecken's Grin, one of the sights of Longfellow Park, up there with Mrs. Albert Comstock's Bosom and Mabel Peartree's Nose (three stars apiece in all the most reputable guidebooks). Schiffendecken's Smile would have possessed a more euphonious alliteration, and would have sounded more genteel, but Grins were when teeth were involved, and few sights involved more teeth than this one. Alice could never decide whether a dentist with false teeth was a poor advertisement for his profession, or whether – in fact – he was embracing the world of advertising with a zeal worthy of commendation. The Grin was a blazoned paradigm of his dental artistry, and he carried his advertisement about with him like the sandwich-board man who advertised the bargains that could be obtained at Oldermann & Oldermann (*Particularly To Be Recommended For Boys' School Attire!*).

Merchants dealing in small luxury items – jewelry, for instance – were able to produce examples, apparently casually, from inner pockets of their suits. G. G. Schiffendecken went one better than this, and carried a sample of his wares around with him at all times, conveniently inserted into his mouth. Whenever he sensed a potential client, the lips – it was happening in front of her now – began to draw back like the curtains of a theatre, rising slowly to reveal a breathtaking interior: row upon row (so it appeared) of gleaming white teeth. This action combined an air of friendly informality with a practical demonstration, though it never looked much like a smile.

Perhaps a tasteful badge, with a discreet arrow, could be affixed to the lapel of his jacket: *These Teeth May Be Purchased at G. G. Schiffendecken, 43 Hudson Row, Longfellow Park, New York. Smiles Are Our Business! Need Grins? We Got 'Em!* In his more informal moments he probably passed them around for people to insert into their own mouths for a while, to get the feel of them, in a spirit of free enterprise, rather in the way that Washington Thoroughgood urged free samples of cookies on his customers. A giant grin should swing above the entrance to his consulting room, to lure people into his domain of perpetual cheerfulness. Like William Cullen Bryant with beards, he appeared to be possessed of more than the usual number of teeth, as if he stored several sets, stacked one upon another, and his audience was mesmerized, seduced into envious longing for their gleaming magnificence, as they slid slowly into view. The full display took quite some time to appear. Just when it seemed that there could not possibly be any more teeth, the acreage expanded further and further, and even more emerged, "the sinecure of all eyes," as Mrs. Goodchild described them, awestruck. It was like watching a magician producing endless strings of colored flags, though the only color here was a dazzling white, a white to send out rippling reflections across all the walls around, like sunlight on water. The Ichthyosaurus – with its measly one hundred and eighty-two teeth – was positively toothless when compared with G. G. Schiffendecken, whose grin was not like a part of the body at all. It was more like an article of clothing, a new design in well-polished decorative armor; or jewelry, a shiny oversized brooch pinned where it would most catch the light.

40

At the feet of Mozart, G. G. Schiffendecken – all teeth fully on view – descended upon his potential client. He had great hopes of Harry Hollander, ever since the success of "The Wheels on Betty's Bicycle," imagining vast riches pouring in because he had heard the band in the park play it several times. Here was the clincher: some of the audience *sang the chorus*, moving their arms around in unison when they came to the words "Go round and round and round." Harry hadn't the heart to tell him that the riches amounted to ten dollars (which would surely not purchase a smile worthy of the name of Schiffendecken). All that dental sweetness was being wasted on the desert air.

The Teeth hovered seductively in the air like one of William Blake's more puzzling visions, or the Cheshire Cat at the point when it had become a grin without a cat.

(The Cheshire Cat had *very* long claws, and a great many teeth. ("I'm mad," it said. "You're mad.")

How on earth could G. G. Schiffendecken manage to grin so gigantically and speak at the same time? He must sound like a dummy, Dum-Dum the Dummy, wielded by an inadequately rehearsed ventriloquist, half his consonants slurred and swallowed. The dummy, dressed as a ringleted little girl in a party dress, its Schiffendecken Grin maniacally exposed, a Serenity Goodchild helpless on gin, sat on Harry Hollander's lap, looked winsomely up into his eyes, and — in a strangulated accent — begged for a story.

"... 'Why are you single; why live alone?
Have you no babies; have you no home?' ..."

The music was in the air above them, and Harry Hollander sang his reply.

"... 'I had a sweetheart, years, years ago.
Where she is now, pet, you will soon know.
List to the story, I'll tell it all,
I believed her faithless, after the ball' ..."

Harry Hollander and G. G. Schiffendecken — the layers of pale, ruffled silk flaring becomingly, the beribboned hair bouncing vigorously — waltzed together in the snow.

She could still remember the peculiar way Mrs. Albert Comstock had been speaking on the night of The Unveiling of her new Schiffendecken false teeth, concentrating more on displaying the smile than on shaping her words, the teeth demonstrably an inconvenience in the course of conversation, a blockage in the mouth.

You were more aware of her pronunciation than of what it was she was actually trying to say. If she had been so anxious for everyone to see The Teeth to their best advantage, Alice couldn't understand why she hadn't placed them on top of her head like a vivaciously smiling tiara, leaving her able to relax and enjoy a gummy grin-free gossip. This could be an attractive permanent feature of Mrs. Albert Comstock's coiffure, the hard bright smile beaming out its cold radiance from amongst the dead birds which lined her frightening hats, as she went on uninterruptedly talking, talking, talking. There had not been such a massacre of the birds since the tree fell on the aviary in the park during the winter storms, if – that is – it had been the tree that wrought destruction. It may very well have been Mrs. Albert Comstock herself, avid for new materials for her hats, seeking out fresh supplies. The teeth would lie amongst the birds like a clutch of giant eggs, a promise of life to come for the feathered denizens of the air slaughtered upon the nests they guarded.

The exchange of words between G. G. Schiffendecken and Harry Hollander was brief: it was scarcely the weather for long outdoor conversations. There were nods, a few words, then hats were raised. Harry continued on his way, moving across to her left. Olivia, looking refreshed, made after him, and trotted beside him adoringly, like a Shetland pony awaiting a rider. He (rather like Mrs. Schiffendecken) always seemed to find other people more fascinating than his master, and usually had to be forcibly restrained from wandering off with them.

"Olivia! Olivia!"

That cry rose upon the air again.

> "What are the long waves singing so mournfully evermore?
> What are they singing so mournfully as they weep on the
>   sandy shore?
> 'Olivia, oh Olivia!' – what else can it seem to be?
> 'Olivia, lost Olivia, will never return to thee!'
> 'Olivia, lost Olivia!' – what else can the sad song be?

'Weep and mourn, she will not return, – she cannot return, to thee!' . . ."

There were eight verses of this, and every one of them weighed upon G. G. Schiffendecken's bowed back. Mozart gazed down, a god above the petty foibles of the world, serene in the heights of his art, advertising elegant and commodious homes for those with taste and refinement.

41

There would usually be Mr. Chip, the Carpenter sounds of hammering and sawing from Megoran Road by now, but a Sunday morning silence spread over everything. The only sound was the moaning of the wind. The men who worked indoors had been working all hours since the bad weather had set in, as if eager to make up for lost time. If this bad weather continued – who knows? – they might start working on Sundays, also. Sharpen those umbrellas, Mrs. Albert Comstock and Mrs. Goodchild. Prepare for prodding. You may be required for duty, and you know you enjoy it. Alice rather missed the workmen's whistling, just out on the edge of consciousness. Would they be whistling hymn tunes if they controversially labored on the Sabbath? Dear, dear. What was the world coming to?

There was something she must remember to tell Harry the next time she saw him . . .

She remembered.

She had heard a line from one of his songs the previous day. She had been looking out of her window at the front of the house, and had heard one of the carpenters – walking past on his way to work – calling across the street to Miss Iandoli's maid Katherine as she returned from Thoroughgood's with some bread. His friendly overtures were studiously ignored.

"You know how to hurtie, Gertie!" he shouted, sounding

wounded, spotting a good opportunity to quote from the second verse of "Why Are You So Flirty, Gertie? (Why Are You Such a Tease?)."

"The name's *Katherine*!" Katherine had called back to him as she went down the steps to the basement, and the young man grinned, delightedly. It had worked again. He'd be calling her by her name tomorrow. Alice felt that Katherine had rather counted on this.

She had heard the young carpenter – in the lulls in the wind – whistling as he worked. They were not Harry Hollander songs, though the whistler had shown that he knew at least one of them. No – here was culture conveniently positioned not far from Mozart – he always whistled music from opera as he worked. Saturday had been a Wagner day, and she had heard selections from *Die Meistersinger*, *Der fliegende Holländer* and *Das Rheingold* all morning, his hammering in time with his whistling. Siegfried hammered away as he shaped his sword.

> *"Hoho! hahei! hoho!*
> *Schmiede, mein Hammer*
> *ein hartes Schwert!*
> *Hoho! hahei!*
> *hahei! hoho!*
> *Hahei! hoho! hahei!"*

Here was a challenge for the serious whistler. Hammer, Schmidt! Hammer, Schmidt! He'd have to be carried out – scarlet in the face, a hammer still convulsively clutched in his hand – if he over-ambitiously launched himself into *Tristan und Isolde*. For something so lacking in humor, there was a surprising amount of ho-hoing going on in Wagner. It had been like listening to the "Anvil Chorus" translated into German.

She'd rather have stayed and listened to this than gone to Mrs. Albert Comstock's "At Home." It made far more sense than most of what she'd heard there. There hadn't been much ho-ho at

Hampshire Square, though the humorless ha-ha-ha-ha had been sporadically activated.

When she returned home, the carpenter had left for the day, Siegfried's sword shaped, and all the hammering stilled. The day before it had been the turn of *Carmen*, and her lips had moved as automatically as those of the church congregation listening to the music for "The Camptown Races" had.

> "*Sur la place*
> *Chacun passe,*
> *Chacun vient, chacun va;*
> *Drôles de gens que ces gens-là . . .*"

42

G. G. Schiffendecken was walking with Olivia — the occasional regretful doggy glance behind him at Harry's retreating back — past the *Susanna* sign, heading up toward the base of the bluff which arose beyond where Heneacher Woods had been, picking his way carefully through the snow. He was returning to his large house with its fabulous views from Hudson Heights, the spoils of his toothy triumphs. It was strange to have a rear view of him. She had never thought of him as existing without his massive molars being visible. He was somewhat diminished, shrunk by the lack of teeth, and the size of the clouds massing above Hudson Heights. They were huge, architectural, like a many-towered city floating there, dissolving and re-forming, transient as human shapes.

He stood still for a moment, his back whitened by the blown snow, in a curious hieratic posture — positively Goodchildian — as if he were contemplating his pose when the time came (and the time would surely come) for him to be captured forever in polished stone for a statue. When he grinned, a large proportion of him (it seemed the greater part) was, indeed, already statue. The very sight of him should send Carlo Fiorelli hastening for a freshly sharpened chisel. G. G. Schiffendecken, the Reverend Goodchild, and Dr. Wolcott Ascharm Webster were undoubtedly eagerly awaiting the fully deserved public recognition which would reward their labors, when the day came when they – too – should have statues of themselves erected in the park alongside the other local notables. All three would be immortalized in marble for posterity, and achieve an apotheosis far more public and numinous than that afforded the saints crowded together with such unpleasantly democratic closeness in the gloom of All Saints'.

She could visualize the gleaming new statues: Herbert Goodchild next to Albert Comstock – the two Big-Buttocked Berties companionably side by side, like a matching set of grotesquely misproportioned titanic Toby jugs – and G. G. Schiffendecken and Dr. Wolcott Ascharm Webster in the space between Herbert Goodchild and Reynolds Templeton Seabright. There they would be – as was only right – captured in characteristic poses at the scene of their greatest triumphs, the place where they had saved so many souls, bound so many lunatics, inserted so many teeth. All three of them would grin, grin, grin in triumph, free of all false modesty, free of modesty of any kind whatsoever.

("My Herbert has been immoralized!" That would probably be the expression employed by Mrs. Goodchild. Mrs. Goodchild would be so right.)

The neoclassical statues were arranged in a large circle around The Forum, like a rather more sophisticated version of Stonehenge. Perhaps – she had never checked, she must ask Kate – on Midsummer's morning the sun rose to throw its beams directly on to the base (generally a word one preferred not to utilize in this context) of the Bebuttocked Behemoth, and another Tess of the d'Urbervilles would be discovered curled up like a sacrificial victim at the feet of Albert Comstock. Chanting Druids (did Druids, in fact, chant?) and uniformed police officers (humming appropriate airs from *The Pirates of Penzance*, to continue the musical motif) would advance toward her as the new day dawned.

Shortly after Albert Comstock had been hoisted into position — it had been like a scene from the erection of the Great Pyramid, the crack of whips, the groans of slaves — she had almost been floored by an appalling rancid smell as she walked past it. She thought that Carlo Fiorelli was carrying realism to startling new heights until she realized that the figure had been coated in yogurt (from Comstock's Comestibles, naturally) in the belief that this would encourage the growth of lichen, and add a patina of age and antiquity to the too-bright newness.

For several days the picture of the poor soul whose job it had been to rub on the yogurt haunted her. He was probably one of Dr. Wolcott Ascharm Webster's more hopeless cases now, a benighted being who had descended totally into madness. Curled up in a dark corner of a padded and permanently locked room in the Webster Nervine Asylum, an oubliette for the demented, he would move his hand obsessively round and round in a circular clockwise direction, as if urging the clock onward to the moment of his longed-for death. Whimpering, weeping, he would forever be repeating the movements he had made on the day that had driven him into insanity, the day on which he had applied the yogurt in generously dripping layers to Albert Comstock's gigantic buttocks. He was a Harry Lawson who was trapped forever in the darkness of the corridors at the center of the earth, the darkness of the corridors within his own mind, an insane Lady Macbeth forever fondling the buttocks that only she could see. ("I have known her continue in this a quarter of an hour." That was what the Waiting-Gentlewoman told the startled Doctor of Physic. Hubby clutched at the dagger which he saw before him; she clutched at the fatal chubby-buttocked vision.) Perhaps she might be assigned a cell next to his in their Poughkeepsie place of exile and they could strike up an acquaintanceship, hesitatingly attempting to tap out faltering messages in Morse code, but knowing all the time that it was impossible to tap-tap-tap on a padded wall. Instead of a dot, instead of a dash, the only sound from inside the cells — audible above the howls, the laughter, the shrieks — would be the scratch-scratch-scratch of nails upon the dementedly layered scrawled graffiti, and time would pass with infinite slowness.

Kate — then a little girl — had watched strollers in the park veer abruptly to one side, choking, to remain upwind of the awful smell from Albert Comstock.

"And from his statue, as well, I hope," Alice had added, helpfully.

The Central Park might very well have statues that included Shakespeare, Goethe, Sir Walter Scott, Burns, Beethoven, and Giuseppe Mazzini, but Longfellow Park was quite content with the likes of Albert Comstock and Reynolds Templeton Seabright, thank you very much. Carlo Fiorelli seemed to wish his minor status as a sculptor upon himself. He seemed to specialize in virtually unknown classical figures (*Posthumia Faces Her Accusers, Servilius Is Ridiculed by the Soldiers, Claudius Pulcher Dips the Sacred Chickens in Water*), and they languished — dusty and unsold — in his workshop, facing their accusers, being ridiculed, dipping chickens.

Reynolds Templeton Seabright was the best known of the figures. This was not a figure that had been modeled from life: it had been erected some years after his death, when his Shakespeare Castle had already followed him into oblivion, existing only in memory, photographs, and paintings. Carlo Fiorelli had pictured him as Hamlet, his most famous rôle. Unusually, Carlo Fiorelli (*Alas*) had not chosen the most obvious pose — Hamlet contemplating Yorick's skull (the pose in the panel above the front door of the Shakespeare Castle) — but had shown Hamlet at the moment of seeing his father's ghost, rather an unsettling choice for a man not depicted until after his death. Reynolds Templeton Seabright, mouth open, had just reached the last of four tottering steps back: both arms were outstretched in front of him, the right arm slightly higher than the left, both hands with fingers spread and held upward.

He had been an actor of the old school, and this was how one portrayed Terror. He would have looked exactly the same when he played Macbeth, and saw the dagger in front of him, or when he played Julius Cæsar, and saw more than one dagger heading toward him. Shakespeare was full of descending daggers. It was like the carefully designed steps in a ballet: open mouth, four steps back, arms out, fingers spread, freeze.

Count five.

"Angels and ministers of grace defend us!"

The voice swooped up and down far more than in ordinary conversation, the vowels drawn out like stretched elastic.

Thunderous applause.

Open mouth, four steps back, arms out, fingers spread, freeze.

Count five.

"Is this a dagger which I see before me?"

The voice swooped up and down far more than in ordinary conversation, the vowels drawn out like stretched elastic.

Thunderous applause.

Open mouth, four steps back, arms out, fingers spread, freeze.

"*Et tu, Brute?* Then fall, Cæsar!"

If he had been conveying the idea of Searching, he would have held his hand above his eyes, as if shielding them from sunshine, turning his whole head slowly to the right, then slowly to the left, then slowly to the right, always beginning with the turn to the right. This was how Richard the Third would have looked for a horse, how Malvolio would have scanned Olivia's garden for spectators, how Kent would have sought King Lear in the storm. One felt, where Reynolds Templeton Seabright was concerned, that he would have employed this same gesture if he had been looking in a drawer for a fresh pair of socks, or in the larder for a jar of pickles. Hand above eyes, head swiveled to right, head swiveled to left, head swiveled to right.

"Hwhere" — he pronounced it thus — "are the socks, my sweetheart?"

His fricatives, his aspirates, his consonants, and vowels were caressed, were drawn out lingeringly by his teeth, tongue, and throat.

Thunderous applause.

Hand above eyes, head swiveled to right, head swiveled to left, head swiveled to right.

"Hwhere are the pickles, my precious?"

His vowels gave hours of pleasure. You could listen to them all day.

Thunderous applause.

Sock-seeking, pickles-perusing, he had lived his life to the sound of acclamation, up above the world on Hudson Heights.

As Carlo Fiorelli had confusingly portrayed Hamlet in a toga — he stuck determinedly to the consistency of his art (his Reynolds Templeton Seabright statue had been his ringing declaration of a new philosophy of art: *Bare Knees, Not Buttonholes!*) — Julius Cæsar did tend to come into the mind of the spectator, rather than Hamlet. "Let me have men about me that are fat," Cæsar commented to Mark Antony, well pleased with the nearness of Albert Comstock. It may very well have been, of course, that Claudius Pulcher, his outstretched hands deprived of their sacred chickens, had been dusted off and economically pressed into use, at last finding his purpose.

On the other side of Reynolds Templeton Seabright, somewhat unexpectedly, was a statue of John Randel, Jr., the surveyor for the grid plan that was powering up Manhattan, overwhelming everything in its way. But not Longfellow Park. He was depicted facing north with a Pointing gesture that would have met with the full — if slightly jealous — approval of Reynolds Templeton Seabright, a mighty leader indicating new lands to conquer.

All the statues in The Forum — toga-clad and tunic-clad — were caught in similar old-fashioned histrionic poses, striking stylized attitudes of emotion, as if Reynolds Templeton Seabright were but the leading man in a company of actors, traveling players finding their home at last in Longfellow Park, waiting hopefully to be greeted by a properly dressed Hamlet (properly dressed was tights, properly dressed was all in black with a nice white Byronic shirt), the best actors in the world for tragedy, comedy, history, pastoral,

pastoral-comical, historical-pastoral . . . They were like diagrams in a book of acting, demonstrating feelings and how they ought to be conveyed: Triumph, Despair, Arrogance (there were several of these), Joy, raring to be unleashed upon tragical-historical, tragical-comical-historical-pastoral, scene individable, or poem unlimited. Hands were held to heads, to hearts, held in the air in front of the face, their whole body become the image of a mood without the use of words.

Alice felt that here was a true portrayal of the theatre, where her memories of performances – so often – tended to be visual, the gestures remembered, but not the language that had been used. It was the same in life. In the most intense moments, words did not matter.

There were no words.

Emotion was contained within the movements of the body: a head turned to one side, the curled fingers of a hand raised in greeting or farewell, two hands held forward imploringly. They were like the figures on the terra-cotta panels that had been on the walls all around the Shakespeare Castle, and their gesturing was like what she had heard of the cinematograph where there was no speech, where no words were heard, and everything was conveyed by the expressions of the face, the way the body was held. It was what she had seen in so many operas. It was a language like music, beyond words, a language in which words were no longer needed, or no longer adequate. Much of it was to do with the hands, the way they moved, the way they pulled up at the air, striving for expression, like a language for those who could not speak or hear, intense emotions contained within a small, fierce area of silence, Rosobell attempting to convey a great and complex grief.

Mama's . . .

Mama's . . .

Mama's face, now that she could no longer speak.

The faces were like faces seen in electric light for the first time, suddenly brilliantly illuminated, overbright.

43

In their pompous gesturing – they outdid the best that Max Webster and Serenity Goodchild could accomplish – the statues were tempting targets for the unimpressed and the frivolous, and *The Curse of Constipation*, in particular, had suffered numerous indignities. Most recently, at the end of the summer, a tandem bicycle had been crammed between Albert Comstock's buttocks, as if the statue had been an overdesigned storage facility – *Insert Front Wheel HERE*, with a discreet downward-pointing arrow – for the many bicyclists who whirred around the park, a useful and commendable addition to the many services offered for visitors. She had been cruelly delighted to hear of this from Kate, particularly when photographic evidence had been produced.

"Tut-tut!" she had – er – tut-tutted. "How shocking. Tut-tut-*tut!*"

The bicycle had remained proudly in place over a weekend, proving a popular attraction after the last of the year's Sunday afternoon concerts.

Still humming the more well-known airs from *The Marriage of Figaro* (Mozart was insinuating himself in everywhere), *Les Huguenots* or *La Sonnambula*, and singing "Just Tell Them that You Saw Me" or "Break the News to Mother" (the band master had been in nostalgic mood), the crowds had paused to savor the sight once more before leaving the park. The bicycle was so firmly inserted into the cleavage that Daisy Bell and her beau could have pedaled away in mid-air for hours with perfect safety, the bright lights in her dazzling eyes – despising policemen and lamps – illuminating the statue with a soft radiance. This had not gone unnoticed. The last music Kate had heard from the park on that Sunday afternoon had not been Mozart or Meyerbeer or Bellini, but the sound of the crowds spilling out through the gates singing, with enormous feeling:

"Daisy, Daisy
Give me your answer do!

I'm half crazy,
All for the love of you!
It won't be a stylish marriage,
I can't afford a carriage,
But you'll look sweet,
Upon the seat
Of a bicycle made for two!"

The outrage – for outrage it surely was (it struck at the very roots of a civilized society) – remained in place until Monday morning, when two unenthusiastic workmen were detailed to remove the bicycle from Albert Comstock's buttocks. Kate had taken her camera along to record the moment ("for posterior," Alice said, mentally bracing herself for Issie Isserliss to ring her bell for a Pun Warning), and brought the resulting photographic essay along to Alice, showing it to her with a detailed commentary. There were two men involved in the operation, one very much younger than the other. They marched in step, accidentally, rather than by design, but this, and the fact that they were similarly attired in dark blue suits, gave them the air of a vaudeville act arriving on stage to begin their routine. The ladder they carried between them became their prop, in the way that some artistes made use of umbrellas or suitcases.

Whilst the older man carried out his duties with gloomy distaste, the young man – sensing his moment – entered into the spirit of the occasion with a verve which hinted at frustrated theatrical ambitions. He paused in heroic poses on his stepladder as the Kodaks clicked, like a famous engineer captured as he paused before some great structure he had brought into being – a bridge flung across a great gorge, a vast machine in an echoing manufactory – or a fearless adventurer about to plant a flag at the North Pole or on the summit of a mountain. He had the right size of moustache for this latter rôle.

Fired by the success of this – appreciative murmurs, discreet bursts of applause – he added sound effects to his repertoire, producing an impressively graphic sucking slurping (rather too graphic for delicate sensibilities) as – wobbling dramatically at the top of the ladder – he finally prized the front wheel of the bicycle free. He bowed with great dignity, his hand upon his heart, like a tenor taking his curtain call after a triumphant début, a Tannhäuser after dying amidst the pilgrims, an Alfredo after cradling the dying Violetta in his arms: the death roll in opera almost paralleled Shakespeare's. A glittering career with a shrewd theatre owner surely beckoned.

As the applause died away, Oliver thrust his way through the assembled throng.

"Papa! Papa!" he cried, embracing the plinth as if it were a square-shouldered paterfamilias. "I had to be here" – he spoke like one broken, struggling to overcome a deep and painful emotion – "to see your dignity at last restored to you." He paused, as if unable to continue. "When the wheel finally emerged" – here he paused to produce a lengthy and elaborate sound effect, ending with a liquescent plop (the younger workman was jealously alert, sensing an astute seizer of the limelight) – "I felt that my heart could once more be at peace."

It was an affecting scene, somewhat spoiled when it emerged – within the week – that it had been Oliver who had inserted the offending artifact in the first place. Anyone who referred to his father's statue as "Bertie Buttocks" – as Oliver did, on every possible occasion – was marked as a young man somewhat deficient in filial piety. He had committed the vile crime – it was little less than symbolic patricide in the eyes of Mrs. Goodchild, who saw Symbolism in most things and should have interested Dr. Wolcott Ascharm Webster – with the help of Arthur Vellacott. Mrs. Albert Comstock referred to Arthur as Oliver's "friend" (to be absolutely accurate, she referred to him as Oliver's "– er – 'friend'"), the quotation marks – they were pronounced quite distinctly – being a good example of her ability to employ audible punctuation.

("Friend" . . .

("Friend" in quotation marks . . .

(It was . . .

(It was a long time ago.

(Papa and Annie.

(And Papa's "friend."

(She was drawn to the thoughts as if she were picking at a barely healed abrasion, digging the edges of her nails into what ought to have been left untouched, unable to stop herself.

(The smell of new-struck matches and cigarette smoke, the fire and brimstone smell in the suits and beards of the two men. *Beautiful dreamer, wake unto me.* She was one of the girls from the statue. The full moon emerged from between the trees. The trees had gone; the trees had been destroyed.

("Plato, Copernicus, Julius Cæsar, Agrippa, Tycho . . ." Papa's "friend" was saying, as if conjugating an irregular verb, the same words in the same order as he looked up at the moon, rattling off what he said with the monotonous emphases of something he had learned by heart. There were thirty-three wounds in Julius Cæsar's body. His ghost appeared to Brutus at Sardis, and at Philippi, and Brutus knew that his hour was come.

(". . . Aristotle, Archimedes, Kepler, Hercules . . ." The oceans, the marshes, the lakes, the seas, were waterless, arid desert regions of ash and stone: Oceanus Procellarum, Palus Epidemiarum, Lacus Somniorum, Mare Frigoris, Mare Crisium, Mare Imbrium, Mare Nubium . . . They stretched away on all sides of her, and their names infected her, drawn up inside her as she walked upon them in her bare feet: The Ocean of Storms, The Marsh of Disease, The Lake of Sleep, The Sea of Coldness, The Sea of Crises, The Sea of Showers, The Sea of Clouds . . .

(*Then will all clouds of sorrow depart . . .*

(She thought, fleetingly, of the very first performance of *The Pilgrim's Progress*, when she had been ten, of the parts played by Papa and his "friend," their nobility, their virtue. She wondered if Papa's "friend" was dead, like Papa, and wished he were.

(*Scourged.*

(*Buffeted.*

(*Lanced.*

(*Stoned.*

(*Pricked.*

(*Burned.*

(The man had not been a friend. He had been a "friend.")

Er – "friend."

Mrs. Albert Comstock's "er" controversially hovered on the very verge of becoming an "ahem," and contained a whole nudge-nudging world of grubbily unwholesome innuendo. Reputations could be enjoyably destroyed by an efficiently administered "ahem." Oliver was not one to be cowed by an "er" – even an "ahem" would have held no fears for him – and he never failed to introduce Arthur as "my – er – 'friend.'" Such occasions did not present themselves at 5 Hampshire Square. After she had described Arthur as "Oliver's – er – 'friend,'" Mrs. Albert Comstock would go on to comment – without the use of an "er"; no hesitation whatsoever was needed here – that "Arthur Vellacott is rather *French.*" It was the worst thing she could say about anyone.

The younger workman, reluctant to return to his workaday world of weeding planting beds, and mowing lawns, posed with the bicycle for further photographs, as if it were a tiger he had just shot from his howdah. One ambitious photographer posed him beneath the buttocks, pointing upward, a witness indicating the scene of an appalling crime in one of the more lurid newspapers. With his other hand he gripped the handlebars of the bicycle. He avoided touching the front wheel, made fastidious by his own sound effects. The older man, judging by the expression on his face, would have a lot to say to him when they were alone in the musty privacy of their potting shed. "You think you're too grand now for the likes of me," he would complain in the agitated accents of a spurned suitor, emotion causing a wobble in his copperplate handwriting as he carefully wrote out his labels, *Fuchsia magellanica, Rhododendron ponticum,* like a doctor prescribing poison. They would be visible all around the park, like the love poems in *As You Like It* hung upon the trees in the Forest of Arden, for the fair, the chaste, the unexpressive she of Rosalind.

44

As a little girl, during the most intense period of her Maggie Tulliver incarnation, she had thought – standing in The Forum, surrounded by the fruits of Carlo Fiorelli's labors – that this was the nearest she would ever approach to Latin. It was not, she had to admit to her innermost self – as she averted her gaze from Albert Comstock's straining hams – the most seductive of visions (would she really wish to approach any nearer to *that*?) but *that was not the point*. (She could utilize italics with the best of them.)

The first time she looked at her new baby brother, Ben, she had leaned her face alongside his on the pillow, and – to Mama's astonishment – said, "You'll learn Latin," no great encouragement to the mild-natured infant. As she helped to teach him to walk, she would help him with his Latin, as Maggie had helped Tom.

"Latin's a language," she would say, in her most Maggie-like manner, as the toddler tottered toward her. "There are Latin words in the Dictionary. There's bonus, a gift." Maggie was so hungry for the written word that she read the dictionary when there was nothing else available. It would give him a flying start at Otsego Lake Academy, and everyone would be impressed by his fluency.

The nearest they approached to Latin or Greek at Miss Pearsall's School for Girls was when they read translations of some of the more decorous myths in prettily illustrated editions. Charles Kingsley – she had to admit it – had been absolutely right about girls and Greek (and Latin).

"A mouse – of a mouse – to a mouse – a mouse – O mouse!"

She was struggling in the water. She was starting to drown. The water was entering her mouth, being drawn up into her nostrils.

"O mouse!"

No mouse appeared.

"O mouse!"

No mouse came to save her from drowning, or offer assistance with Latin grammar.

The men and women within the books of myths were clad in a plethora of loose, flowing, all-enveloping garments (each fold meticulously delineated), and both sexes seemed to favor matching loose, flowing hair. The occasional knee (male) was the sum total of their raciness. The Judgment of Paris was a parade of winter fashions; The Birth of Venus an object lesson in how to avoid catching a chill. Perhaps some day, as their long-delayed entrance into the Classical World, the girls might be allowed to embroider an Ionic column, or even – if they showed real promise – a Corinthian column.

No danger here – it occurred to Alice in later years – of impressionable girls being confronted by the flagrantly displayed Ladies' and Gentlemen's Districts of the Classical World. She could see the pain of thought in the expressions of Mrs. Albert Comstock and Mrs. Goodchild. Had the Greeks and Romans really experienced such uninterrupted sunshine that clothes were no longer necessary? Carlo Fiorelli's generously carved buttocks were problematic enough, but buttocks were the least of their worries when confronted by brazen wall-to-wall bareness in Greece, Italy, or most of the larger museums. One really did not know where to look; every averted eye found itself confronted by further excesses.

Mrs. Albert Comstock occasionally played at being a gardener at 5 Hampshire Square, an enormous Marie Antoinette pottering about as a shepherdess between neatly sculpted topiary, a gigantic Mrs. Elton (a woman, surely, after Mrs. Albert Comstock's own heart) picking strawberries at Donwell Abbey in *Emma*. In all her apparatus of happiness, wearing a large-brimmed hat in the sunshine (a *very* large-brimmed hat), adopting various picturesque, nurturing poses, she would stand about in the shrubbery like a half-ruined folly erected by an eccentric landowner. She was especially keen on cutting, lopping, and pruning, whatever the time of year.

Snip-snap! Snip-snap! Snip-snap!

This skill would be utilized for a new and even more important purpose: to ensure the tenacious endurance of all that was nice, the destruction of all that was not nice. Niceness was a central concept of Comstockian philosophy.

("Is it *nice*? Is it really *nice*?" Alice imagined her inquiring, quite as enthusiastically as she herself asked "Is it *horrid*?" when Charlotte urged some dubious novel upon her.)

Mrs. Albert Comstock would approach disapproved-of nude statues with that same expression of intense concentration, that same pair of scissors, that same snip-snap enthusiasm. Never had Struwwelpeter looked so nightmarish, the great, long, red-legged scissor-woman so threatening.

Snip-snap! Snip-snap! Snip-snap!

In her wake would be small tinkling sounds, like Christmas tree baubles smashing on the hall tiles, though, instead of sharp silvery shards, there would be white pieces of marble, curled and rounded, like sea-smoothed tropical shells.

Snip-snap! Snip-snap! Snip-snap!
Tinkle! Tinkle! Tinkle!

A well-gloved Mrs. Goodchild would surely not take too much persuasion to follow behind her, gingerly sweeping the – ahem – lopped extremities into a dustpan with an expression of theatrical disgust (Tamora realizing the *precise* contents of the pie she'd so enjoyed polishing off), head shudderingly averted. Reynolds Templeton Seabright would have been hard put to equal it. Here could be the raw materials for a Swiss Garden to outdo G. G. Schiffendecken's *Crikey!*-inducing landscape, one of the sights of Hudson Heights. The genteel ladies of Longfellow Park would line up with sedate eagerness for entry, elbows fiercely angled to prevent latecomers from pushing their way forward. The rumor was that the Swiss Garden on the dentist's "estate" was composed of hundreds of discarded Schiffendecken Grins, the marbled teeth piled high in serried ranks with the alpine plants cascading around them. It would be a terrifying sight in the twilight, with all those hundreds of identical grins gleaming cheekily, like a scene at

5 Hampshire Square just after Mrs. Albert Comstock had unleashed an epigram. It was unnerving, the thought of lips being silently retracted in the half-darkness, and the garden grinning in the gloom. Suddenly, startlingly, they would begin to yodel in unison, to demonstrate that they were Swiss. This must have done much damage to the Swiss tourist industry, and inhibited an entire generation from purchasing cuckoo clocks and learning to ski. Skiing would have been a useful accomplishment on a day like today.

In her travels — Mrs. Albert Comstock traveled far and wide, Kodak clicking, scissors snipping (though Switzerland had so far escaped the clickings and snippings) — she would have a special pocket in her reticule, next to the one for her Kodak, and in it she would keep her scissors. She would leave a white wake behind her like a battleship bashing through marble, and all the world would wonder. ("Who on earth is that *appalling* woman?" That's what the world would wonder.)

She saw no contradiction whatsoever in disapproving of public displays of nudity, and yet at the same time inflicting — in the shapely form of *The Curse of Constipation* — the biggest buttocks in the Northern Hemisphere, the Grand Canyon of the eastern states, on Longfellow Park. She was a Walt Whitman of art critics: "Do I contradict myself? Very well then I contradict myself, (I am large, I contain multitudes.)" (Walt Whitman had clearly been personally acquainted with Mrs. Albert Comstock, and knew what he was talking about, but had he inserted that final period in the right place?) She knew Art when she saw Art, and she knew Filth when she saw Filth. Carlo Fiorelli's Albert was Art; Michael Angelo's David was — Mrs. Albert Comstock was a great believer in the power of italics — *Filth*.

45

G. G. Schiffendecken was scrambling up the slope that led to Hudson Heights, taking the footpath parallel with the road. On his right was the site of the apple orchards, and the George Washington-lopped cherry orchards. It was still very icy, and he slid back a foot or so on his first few attempts. Olivia plodded along behind him. Ahead were the trees above which the tower of the Shakespeare Castle had once been visible, alongside the road that led to the group of big houses. She had seen it every time she had looked across from the school-room window. She had passed it every time she had gone to or from Charlotte's house when she was a little girl. She was conscious of the absence in the air, the sensation of something missing that should still be there even after so many years, like the feeling on the birthday of someone who had died long ago.

She focused the telescope on G. G. Schiffendecken. At the top of the slope, he turned around to look out over Longfellow Park and New York City beyond. His teeth came fully into view, and he was complete once more, a man in every detail. He stood like a mega-lomaniac grinning with salivating glee as he savored his power over the unsuspecting city that would capitulate, and lie defenseless before his toothy rampage, unsubtle as a villain in one of the Reverend Goodchild's novels (and every Reverend H. P. – Heroes Pounded – Goodchild novel had a villain). John Randel, Jr.'s power was as nothing compared to that possessed by cackling, hand-rub-bing, teeth-unleashing G. G. Schiffendecken, the diabolical desperado of dentistry.

It was he who had sold the land to the west of Dadenhof Road to the developers. The mind tried to come to terms with the thought of an area named Schiffendecken just across from da Ponte, savoring the possibilities of Incisor Avenue, Canine Street, Bicuspid Drive, and Wisdom Tooth Way. It would be next to the Hudson River district, where all the streets bore the names of artists from the Hudson River School. The artistic allure of Longfellow Park grew ever more powerful. Connoisseurs of landscape paint-ing could casually announce that they lived on Thomas Cole, Asher B. Durand, or Frederick E. Church Street. Those who could not raise the necessary cash for one of the larger houses with the grander, more well-known names, had to be content with one of the smaller houses in the more closely built side-streets, crammed in more tightly. Here were the streets named after Thomas Worthington Whittredge, Albert Bierstadt (Mrs. Albert Comstock wouldn't like the sound of "Bierstadt"), and John Frederick Kensett. Had these artists painted smaller canvases? G. G. Schiffendecken was waiting for the Misses Isserliss to die, so that he could annex their grounds to his, a second Louisiana Purchase precisely one hundred years after the first, albeit (he liked to imply) slightly larger. Thus, he would consolidate his landholdings in one continuous area. He might even assist with the demise of the Misses Isserliss, informally mixing business with pleasure, creeping up on them with his implements in his hand, his teeth glinting in the darkness as he advanced, grinning.

He already spoke rather grandly of his "estate," and this purchase would treble its size. He said that it took him more than half an hour to walk across his "estate" from side to side, and this was probably true, if he walked rather slowly. She imagined his walking pace becoming slower and slower as he expanded the size of his land, so that it would become worthy of the size of his teeth. He sounded rather Russian, like someone out of Tourgenieff or Tolstoi, like Prince Andrei Bolkonsky referring to Bald Hills (not a name that would have appealed to Papa), when he spoke in a lordly manner of "the estate," someone who owned serfs, and for whom respectful peasants labored, doffing their caps on his approach and bowing deferentially. Those particularly keen to make a good impression would spread-eagle themselves before him, their features impressively impressed — mask-like — into the snow. Mrs. Albert Comstock always referred to Tolstoi as "Count Tolstoi," as if to demonstrate his superiority to mere commoners amongst novelists, the unennobled multitude. More recently, she had started to correct anyone who referred to "Dr. Conan Doyle." "*Sir Arthur*," she would hiss, teeth unleashed in what was intended to be winsome playfulness (rather terrifying). No doubt, his novels had vastly improved since his knighthood, with — *Snip-snap!* — nicer printing and a more aristocratic choice of words.

G. G. Schiffendecken stood on the edge of Hudson Heights, like Eugene Onegin waiting for the next troika home after having shot Lenski in the duel. His dark greatcoat was whitened with the wind-blown snow, and he stood there, half man, half statue, the forerunner of the new race that would soon conquer the world and dominate it dentally. All smiles were G. G. Schiffendecken's. His were the grins and the giggles, all visible signs of glee. The teeth would nibble, chomp, crunch, chew, munch, munch, munch, advancing as the irresistible vanguard of the new world of Schiffendecken.

The New World was well underway in Longfellow Park. Dvořák would be displeased to hear that whenever Alice heard *From the New World*, she did not visualize majestic American rivers, dappled with sunlight; vast unspoiled forests, free of the sound of the ax; or endless rippling cornfields stretching away to distant horizons. What she saw was teeth, enormous teeth, rearing into view as lips peeled back to maximize their magnificence.

Social historians — by a close analysis of the photographs pro-duced in the studio of Henry Walden Gauntlett (the local Photographer of Note) — would be able to date the precise moment at which G. G. Schiffendecken had begun to demonstrate his dental dexterity. With startling suddenness, teeth appeared in the photo-graphs like a sunrise after a long winter night to grin out from the surrounding darkness. It had become the fashion to smile a little in photographs, giving the impression that the past was a — ha, ha — happy place, but the corset-busting guffaws in Longfellow Park photographs were positively disconcerting, and took some getting used to. Once there had been seriousness, expressions of grave resolve, constipational concentration, and now — as they grouped themselves in front of clouded skyscapes around the chair and table (those standing always looking as if they resented not being given the chair), lingered (as if contemplating suicide) on the rustic bridge, sat on the lover's seat (studiously avoiding each other's eyes), or posed (rather awkwardly, especially if they were men) beside the statue of the bouncily bare-breasted Vestal — ahem —

virgin, or the giant urn – his subjects grinned with terrifying glee, anxious to illustrate that they could afford the biggest and best when it came to inserting teeth. The teeth were the prime motivation in having the photographs taken – ("Look what I've just bought!") – and every effort was made to display as much of them as was humanly possible. It was as if, overnight, Henry Walden Gauntlett had suddenly developed an irresistibly hilarious line in behind-the-camera banter, reducing his subjects to helpless laughter as he wittily click-clicked away, the Oscar Wilde of the wet plate. In some of the photographs – those people who had been, perhaps, a little overambitious dentally – there were more teeth than there was face, and – my! – how those dentures dazzled. The Schiffendecken conquest had begun with the people of Longfellow Park, and it would continue with the statues.

Statuary was – without doubt – the glummest of all the arts (second only to pre-Schiffendecken photography, if that could be considered an art), and G. G. Schiffendecken would take it upon himself to have the Schiffendecken Grin inserted into all the statues in the park. His own statue (it would appear soon, *soon*), fittingly, would be the first, and from there they would spread: the first half-suppressed smirk, and then the irresistible tidal wave of titters, sniggers, gigantic grins, and cacophonous guffaws. One by one the statues would succumb: Dr. Wolcott Ascharm Webster (first it would be the turn of the man himself – the gold from his extracted teeth reemployed to produce quite an attractive set of cutlery – and then it would be the turn of the statue), the Reverend Goodchild, Reynolds Templeton Seabright (now visibly pleased to see the Ghost, quite perked up), Albert Comstock . . . It would be as if some new hilarity were being whispered around the circle of the bearded, something spicy and smutty passed from Beard to Beard, the grins spreading out in ripples, the chuckles ever expanding.

". . . Longfellow Park! Longfellow Park!
Where even the statues grin!

268

Longfellow Park! Longfellow Park!
I can tell by your teeth it's your home! . . ."

After the statues it would be the turn of the door knockers, gleaming grins hanging from every door, this new architectural feature announcing to all visitors that they were now in the carefree land that was Longfellow Park, the land of Happy Families. Far more demonstrative than the muted word *Welcome* woven into a doormat, the cheerful choppers would line up in rows down every street, like the servants gathered together in the hall of a great mansion to greet their new master. Smiling hospitably, they would lift the spirits of all passers-by, gladdening the hearts of strangers.

"Rat-a-tat-tats
Outsmile welcoming mats
In Longfellow Park.
Longfellow Park! Longfellow Park!
Where even the doors have a smile!

"When I see mouths crammed with teeth
It's such a relief
To be home!
When those canines emerge
I feel such a surge
Of joy!
You're revealingly toothy,
So, come on, tell the truthy,
You're from there!
Longfellow Park! Longfellow Park!
I can tell by your teeth it's your home! . . ."

A new era of jollity was being ushered in as the grin spread from the statues and the door knockers, out from Longfellow Park and across the sculptures of the world, and Schiffendecken's Grin would become more celebrated than the Gioconda Smile. Carlo

Fiorelli would be commissioned to produce the teeth for the statues, and long rows of workmen – specially trained skilled artisans – would labor all day at their benches to produce rows of identical fierce grins. They would beam out with gladsome good humor from every flat surface, lending an air of cheerfulness to the whole establishment, dispelling the memento mori atmosphere of the death-masked shelves.

It would begin close to home. From her elevated perch above Madison Square Gardens, the figure of Diana would grin above the pleasure-seeking crowds. *Liberty Enlightening the World* would grin an identical grin from Bedloe's Island, beaming out across New York Harbor with teeth large enough to construct spacious and affordable homes, gleamingly lighthousing ships packed with awed, pointing immigrants. The huddled masses would visibly unhuddle at the sight of such cheerfulness, such beaming transcendental dental-work, toothsomely welcoming them – *Grin! Grin! Grin!* – to the Land of the Grin.

Then it would spread, its pace increasing. After the activities of Mrs. Albert Comstock, compulsorily inserted Schiffendecken Grins would be as nothing to international statuary. Good heavens, the statues *needed* something about which to grin after she'd been snipping.

David, The Discus Thrower, The Kiss (the two heads swinging together, the teeth meeting with an audible clunk, like the thick-lensed spectacles of shortsighted lovers colliding as they abandoned themselves to passion), *Venus de Milo, Laocoön* (the Trojan priest and his sons demonstrating remarkable good humor as they wrestled with the giant sea serpents that were devouring them), *The Dying Gladiator* . . . All of them would grin, grin, grin – as if caught by a Kodak – with the same maniacal rictus grin, the grin of Mrs. Albert Comstock, the grin of Mrs. Goodchild, the grin of the Reverend Goodchild, the grin of half of Longfellow Park, and the Schiffendecken conquest of the world would have begun.

46

G. G. Schiffendecken wouldn't be the only one to hurl himself head first upon *David*. Mrs. Albert Comstock would be there, hot on his heels, panting slightly, scissors snip-snappily activated. For once, the Grin had beaten the snip-snap, and Mrs. Albert Comstock would snarl with the outraged righteousness of the unjustly fore-stalled. She'd soon make up for lost time. There'd be an extra-vigorous *snip*, an extra-crunchy *snap*. Her energy for avenge-ment was fairly sizzling out of her. David was *grinning*. *Grinning*. There he was, as if proud of himself, standing there. In public. Flaunting his – ahem – person. *Look what I've got! Look what I've got!* That's what he was saying, and he was not making a reference to his grin. She couldn't possibly ignore the challenge of his vul-garly exhibitionist flaunting, his obscene absence of drawers. His *grin*. She'd soon wipe that off his face!

Mrs. Albert Comstock in front of Michael Angelo's statue of David in Florence, Italy.

That was how the photograph would be labeled, and there she would be, leaning back, scowling, aghast, her head and shoulders heaped with telltale white dust, as if snow were falling upon her.

Filth!

That was what her face was saying.

Filth!

She held her scissors defiantly in front of her, like a fierce-faced warrior photographed with his well-used weapon, threateningly flourished, or a boxer holding his gloved hands high in triumph after a first round knockout. With these she had done what had to be done. She was not a sloppy lopper, but snipped and snapped with surgical precision, and the white dust fell upon her from the mistreated marble.

"*One!*" she had counted. *She* had no need of a referee.

"*Two!*" she had counted.

She had counted all the way up to ten – with scarcely any pauses for calculation – and her enemy had remained floored, out for the count, and still counting.

"*Seventeen!*"

"Er . . . Er . . ."

"*Eighteen!*"

"Er . . . Er . . . Er . . ."

She faltered slightly at the approach of more advanced mathematics.

I have not stood idly by. I have done what had to be done. I am the irresistible force of niceness. Nothing nasty flourishes in my vicinity.

Her scissors had swung into action.

Niceness gave her power.

First there was *Snip-snap! Snip-snap! Snip-snap!*

Then there was *Tinkle! Tinkle! Tinkle!*

David's new grin – it hadn't been wiped off his face; it hadn't faltered once – appeared ever braver, a breathtaking display of insouciance as he stood ankle-deep in the wreckage of his Gentlemen's District, gazed upon by astonished Florentines. The smooth white remnants were heaped upon the plinth, and scattered down the steps in front of the Palazzo Vecchio, like the debris left behind by a recently retreated glacier.

Mrs. Albert Comstock was waddling off triumphantly back across the Piazza della Signoria, her shadow squat before her. She held her scissors high in the air, snipping them and snapping them, as if to demonstrate how she had defeated her loathed enemy, an Old Testament champion dancing challengingly between opposing camps. She saith among the trumpets, Ha, ha, ha, ha; and she smelleth the battle afar off, the thunder of the captains, and the shouting. She had been too busy snip-snapping David to have noticed the nearby statue of Judith and Holofernes, but her pose (though it would require far more bronze: mass meltings would be mandatory; the faces of gods and goddesses would dissolve and flow) was an exact copy of Judith's, the weapon held aloft in the right hand. After the snips, came the snaps, and after the snaps the tinkles. Verily.

I am the irresistible force of niceness. Tremble, the not very nice!
Panic, the forces of nastiness!

David flexed his sling speculatively.

She was well within range, a gargantuan Goliath impossible to miss with a well-slung stone, the champion of the Philistines.

Smiting time had arrived in Florence.

Her width was six cubits and a span. And she had an helmet of brass upon her head, and she was armed with a coat of mail; and the weight of the coat was five thousand shekels of brass. And she had greaves of brass upon her legs, and a target of brass between her shoulders. David was but a youth and ruddy, and of a fair countenance, but any moment now there was going to be the most tremendous clanging, like the collapse of a fully laden bell tower in mid-peal, as — with considerable enthusiasm — he unleashed his smite.

This day the LORD had delivered her into his hand; and he would smite her, and take her head from her; and he would give the carcasses of the host of the Philistines this day unto the fowls of the air, and to the wild beasts of the earth. There was no sword in the hand of David. Therefore David would run, and stand upon the Philistine, and take her scissors and draw them out of the hands thereof, and slay her, and cut off her head therewith.

The decapitated head in the statue of Judith and Holofernes should have been a warning unto her, though — in an intriguing variation of the original story — it was Judith who was about to be beheaded. David would quite enjoy doing this. He'd been rather bored standing there for all those years, and this was quite like old times again. It would serve her right for making his eyes water.

She had herself provided the ammunition that would destroy her. David looked down, and there — conveniently close to hand — were the smooth stones for smiting with, far more than five. Mrs. Albert Comstock had lived by the snip-snap, and would die with what it was she had snip-snapped. There was a certain rough poetry in this symmetry of slaughter. David sorted five stones of the largest size, and picked out the largest of the lot. She wouldn't like this. She wouldn't like this at all. He would prevail over the Philistine with a sling and with a — ahem — stone, and smite the Philistine, and slay her.

"You killed me with *what?*"

Aghast could not be aghaster.

Good.

"With *what?*"

Whirrr! Whirrr!

He began to whirl the sling around his head. My word, it was heavy.

(An expression of quiet pride came across his face.)

The grin — it had appeared at just the right moment, and he put it to full use — reemerged and broadened.

Whirrr! Whirrr!

Leonardo da Vinci would be so thrilled to hear that sound, to see that blurred cyclonic whirling. He had waited centuries to see it take shape, but at last his sketch for a helicopter had leaped out of his notebooks and soared whirrr-whirrringly into the sky. He'd known it would work! Pshaw! to the pooh-poohers! Admittedly, it was distinctly annoying that he'd had to rely on Michael Angelo for technical assistance (he would have liked to have slung that sling), but — and this was the most important thing — his vision had finally taken flight.

The best bit about killing Goliath had been when the stone had hit the Philistine in his forehead, and the stone *sunk into* his forehead. David had really enjoyed that "sunk into." Goliath had swayed there for a moment, like a three-eyed creature on the point of death — his third eye spouting blood — and then he fell upon his face to the earth with a ground-shuddering thud. It was just as well that they were away from Jericho, or the walls would have crashed down all over again, just after they'd spent all that money rebuilding them, even stronger than before. They were guaranteed proof against the most sonorous of rams' horn trumpets, but damage caused by demolished Goliaths was not covered by the insurance policy.

He had to get her to turn around. Only by doing this could he sink the stone into her forehead; only by doing this could he see her crash to earth upon her face. He wanted the women to come out of all cities of Israel again, singing and dancing, to meet King Saul, with tabrets, with joy, and with instruments of musick, saying, Saul hath slain his thousands, and David his ten thousands. He'd enjoyed making Saul very wroth, all jealous and sulky. The eternal sleepiness of tending sheep had long lost its allure.

He had to get Mrs. Albert Comstock to turn around.

(*Sunk into! Sunk into!*)

What could he do to delay her? What could he say to have the necessary effect? Should he tell her that he was only a *copy* of Michael Angelo's *David*, and that the provocatively unlopped original stood in the Galleria dell'Accademia? Would that make her turn around? No, that wouldn't do. He could do better than that.

She wasn't too far away from him, and he had to act before she became small in the distance. No, on second thoughts, the Piazza della Signoria was nowhere near big enough for her ever to appear *small* in it, no matter how far away within it she was. She wouldn't look *small* in the Sahara Desert, the Great Plains, or the Steppes of Central Asia, humming an appropriate air from Aleksandr Borodin. Pigeons whirred into the air to both sides of her as she Juggernauted through them, and it was as if her hat were given life beyond her control, activated into a bid for freedom.

Might it be worth waiting to see if she ambled across the piazza and accidentally stood for a moment on the plaque that marked the place where Savonarola had been hanged as a heretic and burned, and unleash his – ahem – unusually shaped stone upon her *there*? There could be no better place for a second execution. It appealed to his sense of symmetry. After the beheading there would be a bonfire of the vanities – it would burn for weeks – which would surpass anything that had been seen there in the fifteenth century.

George Eliot came dashing down from the Casa Guida, arm in arm with Elizabeth Barrett Browning – great writers could scorn

chronology; they lived in the same moment, whatever the time —
eager to take notes for her new version of *Romola*, one, this time,
that people could read and survive. This would be so useful for her
research! The Reverend H. P. Goodchild (she ever yearned to equal
the achievement of his oeuvre) had kindly condescended — she'd
been so grateful — to give her numerous helpful hints on how she
might improve her novel writing. *Romola: The Fury of the
Florentines* would be a literary sensation! Under his tutelage, all
her novels could be wondrously transformed! *The Curse of
Casaubon! The Sins of St. Ogg's! The Sorrows of Silas!* If she listened in a true spirit of humility, she might learn how to be as good
as Marie Corelli.

Scribble, scribble, scribble!

Mrs. Albert Comstock was alongside the Loggia dei Lanzi, just
in front of him, and reared suddenly away from it, a distinct list to
starboard, as she caught sight of more statuary uninhibitedly glo-
rying in its nudity, automatically activating her scissors. David
could hear the *Snip-snap! Snip-snap!* distinctly, like the jaws of a
hungry animal sensing the nearness of food. Like Stendahl in
Florence she was overwhelmed and whimpering (though for rather
different reasons), unable to cope with the excessive richness assail-
ing her from all sides.

So much to snip!

So much to snap!

So little time!

Her work would never be done!

The first sideways rear was for *Perseus.*

She lingered, speculatively snip-snapping, definitely tempted.

David's grin was positively wolfish. The shepherd was about to
leap upon the lamb and devour it utterly. No, he wouldn't wait to
see if she stood on Savonarola's plaque. He *couldn't* wait. He did
not need a *Shoot here!* target to focus his aim; he wanted to smite,
and smite mightily, *now*. There would be no clang on the brass of
the helmet, no clang on the brass of the coat of mail, no clang on
the brass of the legs. All there would be would be the smiting of the

forehead – *sunk into! sunk into!* – and *then* the thunderous bell-tower collapse. The fowls of the air and the wild beasts of the earth would be gathering.

He'd do it now.

All that Mrs. Albert Comstock saw in Perseus was his nudity. What she failed to see was that Perseus was holding the severed head of Medusa, a warning – if she could but see it – as to her future fate. Hers was the head and hers would be the scissors with which David would cut it off.

He had to get her to turn around.

What was her first name again?

All he could remember – *ouch!* – was the snip-snap of her scissors. Then he recollected. It was not "Mrs. Albert." It was Sibyl.

The grin appeared once more, and Schiffendecken's handiwork shone out upon the land. He'd lure her into turning around, with the use of the grin and her first name. She'd find it impossible to spurn his seductive use of a Sibyl.

Whirrr! Whirrr!

The helicopter began its ponderous ascent.

"*Theebyl!*" David called enticingly. "*Theebyl Comthtock!*"

Because of the newly acquired false teeth he spoke with a lisp, unexpected, but not unattractive.

"*Theebyl!*" he cooed with a Siren-like allure. He spoke with the voice of Carlo Fiorelli after several glasses of wine too many. It was the voice of the waiter in a Staten Island summer hotel.

Mrs. Albert Comstock – hearing the rare sound of "Sibyl" (all senses were on full alert: it *was* "Sibyl," wasn't it?) – paused, lingered . . .

Whirrr! Whirrr!

"*Theebyl! Oh, Theebyl!*"

She hesitated a little, but then the waddle away from him continued, and with a more determined step. It was as if a malodorous beggar was importuning her, a beggar deficient in underwear, and she had firmly decided to withdraw herself from this lack of drawers. She knew who it was calling out to her in that shamefully enticing manner. You'd have thought that the skillfully employed scissors would have put paid to *that sort of thing*. She hadn't forgotten that ghastly sight, the shamefully ebullient beefiness of that Florentine "meat flasher." ("Meat flasher" – thank heaven for quotation marks! – was a term she'd learned from Mrs. Alexander Diddecott, who had a nephew of seventeen, and so – *shudder* – knew all about slang. It was the sort of expression that Roland Birtle probably employed on a daily basis, flagrantly discarding the necessary punctuation.) She wasn't going to look at *that* again.

Well, if she wouldn't come to *that* – David decided – then *that* would hurtle toward her, and for *that* to finish her off in the most enjoyable manner possible, it was necessary for her to turn around.

"*Theebyl! Oh, Theebyl Comthtock!*"

There was another dramatic list to starboard.

Mrs. Albert Comstock had just caught sight (*Aaaaghhhh!*) of *The Rape of the Sabine Women*, another of the statues in the Loggia dei Lanzi. Hither and thither Theebyl dithered, ahemmed in on all sides by aggressive unsuitabilities, dubious danglinesses. Was she stunned *à la* Stendhal (and, possibly, flummoxed *à la* Flaubert)? Had she lost her sense of direction? Was she going to find herself – in attempting to seek refuge – heading (awful thought) toward the Duomo in her confused and vulnerable condition, blundering straight into the very heart of candles, incense, confessionals, loitering, leering *priests* seductively swinging their thuribles as if in an attempt at hypnosis?

"Eek!" she'd shriek. "Eek!"

She wouldn't eke out her eeks; she'd litter them lavishly.

"*Theebyl!*"

Whirrr! Whirrr!

The seductive voice behind her called again.

"*Theebyl!*"

Mrs. Albert Comstock began to turn around . . .

Choosing what appeared to be the perfect moment, and just the right sort of song for the occasion, Judith and Holofernes, Perseus and Medusa, and all the Sabine Women, launched themselves encouragingly into the chorus of "Throw Him Down, McCluskey," showing an impressive knowledge of one of the rowdier of contemporary American compositions. Any excuse to flash their new gnashers. It'd be "Down Went McGinty (Dressed in His Best Suit of Clothes)" next. The severed heads sang with an unexpected resonance, swaying from side to side in time to the rhythm. The Sabine Women had been members of a well-rehearsed amateur choir, dragged off in mid-recitation, and even included hand movements ("Throw Her Down, David!" they'd be singing. "Down Went Mrs. Comstock!")

The stone – it was the right size and shape – would (*Thwunk!*) protrude from the middle of her forehead. For one brief, fairytale moment – just before she crashed to earth with a discordant clang ("Gracious!") – a unicorn would be seen on earth again, and dreams could come true.

The stone would have *sunk into*, and Mrs. Albert Comstock would be sunk.

("This is a child! We only found it today. It's as large as life, and twice as natural!"

("I always thought they were fabulous monsters!" said the Unicorn. "Is it alive?"

("It can talk," said Haigha solemnly.

(The Unicorn looked dreamily at Alice, and said, "Talk, child."

(Alice began: "Do you know, I always thought Unicorns were fabulous monsters, too? I never saw one alive before!")

(It would not be alive for much longer.)

Whirrr! Whirrr!

"*Theebyl!*"

47

Charles Kingsley – if no great encourager of girls – had his uses. She and Charlotte had found – in *The Heroes* – some extremely useful tips on how to deal with Mrs. Albert Comstock. They had been discussing how to dispose of her *twenty-five years ago*. This – rather like Dr. Wolcott Ascharm Webster's treatment of her – was an inspiring example of tenacity of purpose, but did not speak very highly of the effectiveness of the methods used. When Athene gave her advice to Perseus on how he could overcome the power of the Medusa (who, like Mrs. Albert Comstock, had the strange power of being able to turn people to stone in her presence) they paid careful attention.

You shall take this polished shield, and when you come near her look not at her herself, but at her image in the brass; so you may strike her safely.

This had been Alice's time to *scribble, scribble, scribble.*

And when you have struck off her head, wrap it with your face turned away, in the folds of the goat-skin on which the shield hangs.

This sounded hopeful, this sounded useful, this sounded positively enjoyable. It was one of the most serious things that could possibly happen to one in battle – that was how Tweedledee had expressed it – to get one's head cut off. His words were a source of great comfort to her.

A book, a handkerchief, and an apple had not brought much tranquility the time she had gone into the apple orchard to read *The Wide, Wide World*; for a while she had higher hopes of a brass shield, a sword, and a goatskin, and had polished the coal scuttle to gleaming magnificence in the absence of a shield. This would give a good reflection. She could easily borrow one of Grandpapa's Japanese swords: there would be no problem there.

The statue of Perseus in the Piazza della Signoria gave them an inspiring example of what might be achieved by a well-polished coal scuttle. He looked so proud as he stood there, holding the head aloft, the winner who'd just been awarded the prize for growing the biggest vegetable marrow in that year's competition. The city of Florence had ever been in the forefront of civilized endeavor.

"The Gorgon! She will freeze you into stone," she and Charlotte had chanted, like the maidens in the garden. Alice had remembered this, years later, when she had walked into the park through The Forum. It was as if all the statues had been casually conversing passers-by, frozen where they stood by a vindictive Comstockian glare.

When Alice read the story of Apollo and the Sibyl of Cumæ, she and Charlotte — somewhat shuffling their myth-pack — began to refer to Mrs. Albert Comstock as The Sibyl. It was an enjoyably naughty thing to say to each other, as much for the use of the "The" as for the use of "Sibyl." Whenever Mrs. Albert Comstock boomed out some sonorous banality, Alice and Charlotte would whisper to each other, "Sibylline Oracles! Sibylline Oracles!" and the words possessed all the glamorously forbidden allure of "bosomptious" or — indeed — "gonorrhea." You never again felt as clever or as totally knowledgeable as you did when you were a young child with a new piece of information.

"The Sibyl! She will freeze you into stone! The Sibyl! She will freeze you into stone!"

It had made an enchanting chant, and they had circled the pillars in the schoolroom menacingly in a counterclockwise direction for what seemed like hours at a time, as if they had Mrs. Albert Comstock (eyes bulging, sweating prodigiously) securely pinioned to one of them, and at their mercy, prolonging — with delicious anticipation — the moment of her demise.

(*STAB ENORMOUS SIBYL!*

(*STAB ENORMOUS SIBYL!*)

It would take a lot of rope to lash her down. They would be grappling with the sails of an Indiaman during a storm, belaying her, me hearties, or erecting a circus tent in a tornado. It would be like capturing some wild, ferocious beast for Phineas T. Barnum (hence the tent), but this monster would not be taken alive. Where would be the fun in that?

Decapitating Mrs. Albert Comstock, she wrote in her neatest hand-writing as a heading in her journal — it was healthy for a girl to have an ambition (with or without Latin) — and made a neat list of the requirements beneath it. She felt all the pleasure of fulfillment as she ticked off the items on her list.

It was like collecting the ingredients together for a recipe.

2 lbs. of good cooking apples.

(*Tick.*)

4 ozs. of brown sugar, or to taste.

(*Tick.*)

1 oz. of butter.

(*Tick.*)

The rind of 1 lemon.

(*Tick.*)

That was how the recipe for Apple Charlotte started. They had cooked it especially once, just because of its name.

If she wanted to make herself feel ill — an excuse to avoid an afternoon of Miss Swanstrom slowly murdering George Eliot or John Keats — she would go into the kitchen and read the recipe for Brain and Tongue Pudding. The very name of it could bring on nausea, and turn her convincingly pale. It sounded like something out of *Titus Andronicus*.

The list of ingredients began: *4 sheep's tongues, 4 sheep's brains* — it actually, with the freedom of punctuation more common in sheet music, specified *4 sheeps' brains — 1 hard-boiled egg, sliced* . . . For some reason, it was the addition of the hard-boiled egg (sliced) that started to tip her over into genuine queasiness. Reading the instructions completed what the ingredients had started, and soon had her heaving. *Slice the tongues, chop the brains coarsely, and place them in the basin in alternate layers* . . . it began chattily, and she would be clutching the edge of the kitchen table, with every-thing swimming around her, a distant ringing in her ears. Perhaps there were families who feasted yum-yummily upon this for months.

"Why, there they are, both baked in this pie,
Whereof their mother daintily hath fed,
Eating the flesh that she herself hath bred.
'Tis true. 'Tis true: witness my knife's sharp point."

Stab! Stab!
No Miss Swanstrom today.
(*STAB EMPTY-HEADED SWANSTROM!*)
'Tis true. 'Tis true.
Dispatched like Tamora.

It was one of the cruelties of chronology that *Dracula* had not been published twenty years earlier than it was. It would have given them so much pleasure, far more pleasure than "Is it horrid, are you sure it is horrid?" ever gave them. This wasn't a matter of the horrid, this was entering the realms of the thoroughly entertaining. It would have given them an even more enjoyable list to *tick, tick, tick*, better by far than a brass shield, a sword, and a goatskin, as they planned the far more spectacular doom of Mrs. Albert Comstock, a decapitation (it would have been a real disappointment to have missed out the decapitation) with attractively gruesome added extras, copying the method by which Dracula had been destroyed. The novel gave detailed instructions, and it beat killing the Medusa. It would have been something much better than collecting the ingredients for a recipe, as recipes somehow failed to include instructions on killing the animals whose meat would be cooked.

It would have been – this had occurred to her, years later, when she had studied Ben's carefully written accounts for Dr. Brown – more like describing an experiment in a Chemistry lesson at Otsego Lake Academy. "Experiment" was so much more satisfying a word than "recipe," adding a spurious air of scientific respectability to what was a long-anticipated killing. It would be a challenge to maintain an air of intellectual coolness when so much deeply fulfilling pleasure was involved. Shrieks of delight were out of place in a laboratory. You had to have a serious expression on your face.

Title.
Object.
Equipment.
Materials.
Diagram.
Method.
Observations.

You had to have all these in your notebook, neatly underlined, in this order. Dr. Brown was quite adamant, and his handwriting positively shook with impassioned outrage if Ben deviated from his formula. He was a man whose life possessed little excitement; his obsessive head-down long-distance running about Longfellow Park – he circled and circled, as if seeking a prey he never found – signally failed to expel the demons within him. That handwriting could be really *agitated*, great loops and uprights shooting right off the top of the page.

She had her *Title*.

Decapitating Mrs. Albert Comstock.

She had her *Object*.

Decapitating Mrs. Albert Comstock.

It was an *Object* (all sublime) to which surely no one could possibly object. They'd be encouraging her with cheers, offering helpful suggestions and generous bribes. She'd written the same thing twice, but it was so enjoyable to write that she'd willingly have written it several times more. She'd have written it out a hundred times, as if set some copying task for unacceptable behavior, listening to the echoes as the same words bounced off all the walls around her, each echo as loud as the first cry. What she was about to do was certainly verging on the not-at-all-acceptable.

She wasn't sure what she ought to define as *Equipment* and what as *Materials*, her scientific certainties wobbling slightly at the edges.

Under *Equipment*, she could have made her list.

1. A soldering iron.

Tick.

2. *Some plumbing solder.* (Or was this *Materials*? She did like to do things *properly*.)

Tick. (She hovered on the verge of recollecting some memory of Ben or Linnaeus as she remembered the smell of this.)

3. *A small oil lamp.* (*Definitely* *Equipment*.)

Tick. (This was such an *easy* list of things to find.)

4. *Operating knives.* (No doubt about these, either.)

Tick. (They'd be sure to find various knives in the kitchen that would meet their needs.)

5. *Garlic.* (*Materials*?)

Tick. (The kitchen was going to be a *gold mine*. The fact that Mrs. Albert Comstock viewed garlic with utter revulsion – garlic was *far* too French for her – added considerably to the pleasure of what they were planning.)

6. *A round wooden stake, some two and a half or three inches thick and about three feet long.*

Tick. (She had found the *very* stake in the garden, supporting a bough on one of the more dramatically drooping apple trees. This was meant to be. She'd feel quite in control and masculine, quite Maggie learning Latin, as she hardened one end by charring it in the fire, and sharpened it to a fine point. She'd hum a tune under her breath as she sharpened away, thinking of the joys ahead, like someone preparing a giant pencil for an inspired piece of writing, ideas swarming upon her from all directions.)

7. *A saw.*

Tick.

8. *A heavy hammer, such as in households is used in the coal cellar for breaking the lumps.*

Tick. (They had the very same hammer, used for the very same purpose. This was *surely* meant to be. It was manifestly their destiny to hammer a stake into Mrs. Albert Comstock's heart, cut off her head, cram her mouth full of garlic, and solder her up in her coffin. The fact that they'd enjoy it so much was surely a secondary consideration.)

Even more pleasurable than the preparations – the anticipation would have been wonderful — would have been the actual end of the vampire of Hampshire Square.

Method.

(She'd save *Diagram* as a treat until the very end. She'd sharpen all her red pencils especially, and Science would merge seamlessly into Art. *Blood spurting high into air,* she'd label neatly, drawing the arrows nice and straight with her ruler. *Mouth wide open for scream of agony.*)

1. Lift the lid of Mrs. Albert Comstock's coffin.

Tick.

2. Place the point of the stake over Mrs. Albert Comstock's heart.

Tick. Charlotte takes the stake in her left hand, and places the point over the heart, holding it ready in position for Alice.

3. Hammer the stake into Mrs. Albert Comstock's heart.

Tick. Alice takes the hammer in her right hand — no, no, forget the text, *both* hands — and strikes with all her might. One *Tick* would not be enough.

Tick. Tick. Tick.

There would be enough ticks for a shop full of clocks.

Alice would insist on being the one to wield the hammer. It was, after all, from *her* house. She would bring the hammer down as if destroying a Test Your Strength machine, the bell exploding and whistling across the fairground to cut a swathe through the freak show. (It would spell the end of the Goodchilds and the Griswolds, the depopulation of vast areas of Longfellow Park.) Her capital-lettered Strength would pass the Test with all flags flying.

Tick. Tick. Tick.

She would bring the hammer down as if she were driving home the last bolt into a tie securing a coast-to-coast railroad track. Her arms would rise and fall, driving the stake deeper and deeper, while the blood from the pierced heart welled and spurted up around it. She would wear an apron — her long, cream, floor-length apron — to protect her dress. She would wear her winter gloves to prevent blisters on her hands. She'd be thwunking so hard that there'd be a definite danger of blisters. There would be

no hint of a *Teuch!* There would be no *Faugh!* and no *Fah!* There
would not even be a *Phew!* The only sound, over and over – apart
from the loud cheers – would be a satisfyingly resonant *Thwunk!*
as the blood from the pierced heart – she liked to think of it yet
again – welled and spurted up around it. That's what it said in the
book, and instructions needed to be followed precisely to be certain of success. (Just as *Equipment* had merged into *Materials*, so
Method had blended with *Observations*. She clearly lacked the necessary scientific detachment to become a Madame Curie of
Murder.)

(*STAB ENORMOUS SIBYL!*)

She would sing the "Anvil Chorus" from *Il trovatore* as she
thwunked away. She'd learned the words especially.

4. Sing the "Anvil Chorus."

  "*Chi . . .*"

Thwunk!

  "*. . . del gitano . . .*"

Thwunk!

  "*. . . i giorni abbella? . . .*"

Thwunk!

  "*. . . Chi del gitano i giorni abbella? . . .*"

Thwunk! Thwunk! Thwunk!

  "*. . . La ʒingarella! . . .*"

Thwunk!

"... La zingarella!"

Thwunk!

Charlotte would be permitted to join in.

5(a). Listen awhile to hideous blood-curdling screech from the opened red lips.

Tick.

(b). Listen a little while longer, as it was so much fun the first time.

Tick.

6. Saw the top off the stake, leaving the point of it in the body.

Tick.

7. Cut off Mrs. Albert Comstock's head.

Tick. Alice would insist on being the one to cut off the head. The knives were, after all, from *her* house.

8. Fill the mouth with garlic.

Tick. Charlotte would be permitted to do this, if she asked nicely. They'd need an enormous amount of garlic to fill that cavernous aperture. Charlotte would be shoveling it in with both hands.

9. Light the oil lamp.

Tick.

10. Melt some plumbing solder.

Tick.

11. Solder up the lead coffin.

Tick.

12. Screw on the coffin lid.

Tick.

13. Gather up belongings.

Tick.

14. Come away.

Tick.

They'd sing an extra chorus from *Il trovatore* as they came away, as a form of celebration.

"La zingarella!" they'd bawl triumphantly as they emerged, blinking, into daylight from the cellars of 5 Hampshire Square.

"La zingarella!"

You could keep Apple Charlotte. You could keep Brain and Tongue Pudding. *This* was the recipe to make everyone roar for more. *This* was the recipe for second and third helpings. *This* was the recipe to get the spoons banging on the dining-room table in an insistent, irresistible rhythm, bouncing from wall to wall like deafening multi-layered echoes of the heart-piercing thwunks.

"Please, sir, I want some more."

The master grinned hugely, and plunged his ladle deep into the copper.

"And you shall have some more, Oliver. As much as you want! All of you!"

In the George Cruikshank illustration, Oliver's spoon was huge, as large as his bowl. It was too large to insert into his mouth. He would have to sip his gruel from the side. Here was an artist who read the text carefully.

"As much as you want! All of you!"

With a ringing cheer, the workhouse boys began to bang on their bowls with their enormous spoons, singing the "Anvil Chorus" as they jostled into a line behind Oliver Twist.

"Chi . . ."

Clink!

". . . del gitano . . ."

Clink!

". . . i giorni abbella? . . ."

Clink!

The spoons, like the bowls, were very bright and shiny, where the workhouse boys had licked them in their hunger. They held the spoons before their faces, as if they were hand mirrors – they were the right size and shape for this – in which they were studying their faces, like mermaids, like girls combing their hair late at night, noticing the results of slow starvation, the withholding of love, being unwanted: the sunken eyes, the pale, drawn cheeks, the emaciated bodies. They were — shrunken and bowed down — like a procession of young Dorian Grays or ragged Mr. Hydes lining up for nourishment.

"... *La zingarella!*..."

Clink!

"... *La zingarella!*"

Clink!

She stared at herself in the coal scuttle's curving surface, her face lugubrious and elongated, like a face on the back of a spoon, as she pondered the problem of a goatskin. The goatskin was proving elusive. Charlotte's reflection appeared beside hers, equally drawn-out and doleful.

"Do you think Mr. Gauntlett would let us borrow his leopard-skin?" Charlotte mused. They had remembered seeing one in the photographer's studio, draped informally over the shoulders of the Vestal virgin, massive in marble, with the breasts — "Boo!" — thrusting officiously through. Henry Walden Gauntlett was about the only man in Longfellow Park who employed a naked woman as a rack for clothes, if — that is — you ignored the scurrilous rumors about Dr. Vaniah Odom. "If we explain what it's for?"

"If we explain what it's for he'll insist on doing it himself," Alice objected, "and *I* want to chop her head off. I've been practicing."

The pillars in the schoolroom had been quivering for days. The rooms beneath must be deep in shaken-down dust. They ought to send out a search party for Annie. She was — like Jane Eyre's Alice Wood — such a small servant that she might be lying somewhere under a drift, completely vanished from view, praying for rescue.

They caused considerable concern to their mothers — Charlotte's mother had still been alive then — by, for several weeks, inexplicably speaking to Mrs. Albert Comstock's reflection in the mirror on the rare occasions on which she addressed them, rather than facing her directly.

"Little girl . . ."

"Little girl . . ."

Charlotte had spent one afternoon speaking to a large polished brooch on the left of Mrs. Goodchild's bosom because it reflected — even more grotesquely misshapen than the real thing (and divided into three parts, like Gaul) — the Hunchfront of Hampshire Square.

(Alice had been listening to the older brothers of some of her friends: smart young men with parted hair and vulgar imaginations, smoking cigarettes and laughing together as they exorcised their demons, their remembered afternoons of agony as small boys, desperately fighting their irresistible urge to give way to hilarity as Chinky-Winky's foundations-threatening farts shook the music — *music!* — room around them. She tried not to giggle when she listened to them, because they'd make her go away.)

"Little girl" had developed a positively icy resonance.

Thoughts of the Medusa of Longfellow Park awakened thoughts of the Minotaur, the monster for which she had searched with Dr. Wolcott Ascharm Webster, so many years later.

"You shall not go, to die horribly, as those youths and maidens die; for Minos thrusts them into a labyrinth, which Daidalos made for him among the rocks, — Daidalos, the renegade, the accursed, the pest of this his native land . . ."

This was what Aegeus had said to his son Theseus.

On the ledge outside the window of Grandpapa's office, she imagined the statue of Aegeus staring out to sea, the one man amongst all the women, like a man turned to stone by years of waiting, his blind eyes straining to make the color of the shadowed sails discernible, the first glimpse of whiteness that meant his son was alive. Daidalos had also made statues for Minos, statues that could speak and move. He was like Prometheus in what he could do. He had also invented the plumb line, the auger, glue, wood-working tools, and masts for ships.

When Alice was a little girl the highest things on the skyline of New York had been the masts of ships and the steeples of churches.

It was so long ago, last century.

Daidalos and Icaros – "Daidalos" and "Icaros" were further examples of Charles Kingsley's creative, almost Mrs. Good-childian, approach to spelling – fled from the anger of Minos, having made themselves wings of feathers, and fixed the feathers with wax. So they flew over the sea toward Sicily; but Icaros flew too near the sun; and the wax on his wings melted, and he fell into the Icarian Sea, the feathers falling like snow in summer.

48

She stared at the clouds, striving to see a tiny figure falling to earth, striving to see the first flakes of a fresh snowfall.

Clouds . . .

There was something she had to remember . . .

She reached for the ring on her finger, and realized that it was not there. She ran the first two fingers of her right hand up and down in the place where the ring ought to have been, and then looked down.

She had taken it off before she washed.

The ring, however, had already been moved to her wedding finger. There *was* something else she had to remember . . .

She had been standing where she was now, at the window, hearing a voice in her head – *Tell me what you can see in those clouds, Miss Pinkerton* – and looking at the sky . . .

She found herself opening her right hand loosely and circling it round and round, rotating her wrist as far as it would go, in an attempt to grasp something that was just out of her reach, the memory something tangible, pushing it away with the tips of her fingers as she drew close . . .

Clouds . . .

It was something to do with clouds . . .

She placed Annie's ring back on her wedding finger, as if this would prompt her into remembering.

She looked up at the clouds, attempting to read a meaning in them.

Dr. Wolcott Ascharm Webster had made her believe that everything would change if meanings were found within those clouds, and in dreams. If the clouds were correctly interpreted, they would lift away to reveal limitless sun-filled landscapes. If the dreams were accurately read, there would be nothing to fear anymore; nothing but endless nights of soothing, dreamless sleep would lie before her.

Every movement of the body, every emotion of the mind, is at certain times an omen . . .

She would repeat the words from *Extraordinary Popular Delusions and the Madness of Crowds* to herself — what better place for this title than in the lair of the mad-doctor? — to shut out his voice, as she read the titles of the books beneath the glass, as she stared at the walls or from the window.

Every form and object in nature, even the shape of the clouds . . .

Even the shape of the clouds . . .

Clouds . . .

She touched the ring. The memory was there, something that could be touched.

The Shape of the Clouds.

That was it.

The title for a novel.

She should write it down, add it to her list.

Two

THE SHAPE OF
THE CLOUDS

Every form and object in nature, even the shape of the clouds and the changes of the weather; every colour, every sound, whether of men or animals, or birds or insects, or inanimate things, is an omen. Nothing is too trifling or inconsiderable to inspire a hope which is not worth cherishing, or a fear which is sufficient to embitter existence.

Charles Mackay, *Extraordinary Popular Delusions*
and the Madness of Crowds

"Listen to my voice . . ."

"Be still . . ."

"Empty your mind of all thought . . ."

"Sleep . . ."

She listened to Dr. Wolcott Ascharm Webster's voice.

She was still.

She emptied her mind of all thought.

She slept.

(She spent the years in sleeping and dreaming, the fairy tale seven years, with no sign of a happy ever after.)

Always she heard his voice, and those were the words she heard him speaking, even when they were not the words he spoke.

When the moon was full, she thought – though she tried not to – of her father.

When the sky was full of clouds, when she'd dreamed, she thought of Dr. Wolcott Ascharm Webster, and every day the sky was cloud-crowded, and every night there were dreams. The clouds massed oppressively around her like *Bleak House* fog, blurring the outlines of all that she could see.

Come in, or the fog will get into the house.

(Which novel was it that contained those words? It wasn't *Bleak House*, she knew that. Was it *The Strange Case of Dr. Jekyll and Mr. Hyde*? *Case*. That was the word used. It made it sound like something that Sherlock Holmes ought to have investigated, Holmes accompanying Utterson into Jekyll's cabinet, Holmes looking into the depth of the cheval glass, Holmes – another Pinkerton – searching for clues.)

The fog will get into the house.

All morning she had been thinking of Dr. Wolcott Ascharm Webster.

Dr. Wolcott Ascharm Webster was always with Alice.

She didn't see her skirt or her shirtwaist as she drew them on.

She didn't see her omelet and cutlets as she ate her breakfast, or her coffee as she drank.

It was Dr. Wolcott Ascharm Webster she drew upon her with her skirt and shirtwaist, as if to hug him close about her, patting him smooth, adjusting him into place; she pulled him across the surface of her skin with her stockings; she assumed him with her shoes, buttoning him close across her ankle-bones; she fastened him upon her left breast with her watch, his small weight, the vibration of his ticking; she swallowed him down as she nibbled her breakfast; she drank him down with her coffee, his heat down her throat and deep inside her.

(*I can smell coffee. Who has been drinking coffee?*

(*Sniff. Sniff. Sniff.*)

I have, Papa. *I* have.

I've been sitting on your stool.

I've been eating off your plate.

I've been picking your bread.

I've been meddling with your spoon.

I've been handling your fork.

I've been cutting with your knife.

It's a very sharp knife.

It can cut through most things.

It can . . .

— *Stab! Stab!* —

. . . it can stab.

Alice Pinkerton took a knife . . .

It was time to walk out with Papa.

It is morning.

There is no moon.

I cannot see you.

I cannot *hear* you.

She sounded strong.

She sounded confident.

She'd be drinking his wine next.

Wine with breakfast, decadence completely out of control. She'd be woozy all morning, wandering and forgetful throughout the service, barely hearing a word spoken by Dr. Vaniah Odom and the Reverend Goodchild, giggling helplessly during the carefully calculated moving moments, hurling hymnbooks, and swinging from the pulpit. It was definitely tempting. Three bottles should just about guarantee a sensation . . .

Dr. Wolcott Ascharm Webster sat down beside her — rather too close, mingling breaths, as if about to hypnotize her yet again — as she waited for Charlotte to call in order to walk to All Saints' with her and Ben for the final service there. She was sitting and thinking for a while, musing away the time in between, and he was there all the time, cozily beside her like a fervent wooer.

She didn't see her surroundings as she sat in the back parlor, shivering slightly, surrounded by glass — she avoided the front parlor — waiting, half sensing that there was something missing now that the deep-set eyes of Louis Moreau Gottschalk were no longer there to watch her from the music rack. She didn't see the words of the hymnbook that she'd taken into the room with her, and opened, as if believing that she really was going to read it like a novel to pass the time. She should be browsing through some of the more aggressive cross-rattling heathen-smiting hymns, the sort of hymns favored by Dr. Vaniah Odom and the Reverend Goodchild, great smiters both, tuning herself up into the right mood for what was going to happen in All Saints'. She should be raising her voice, launching herself into song. She should be rhyming "might" with "smite," "Lord" with "horde," donning her armor and flourishing her banner, setting all the glass panels vibrating, and awakening discordant notes in the sleeping strings of the piano. She was reflected in the glass in front of her, and on both sides, the windows turned to looking-glasses by the dark morning.

In the old, warped glass she was blurred and featureless, rising like a strange bloom out of plant-pots that were filled with shriveled-looking, unpromising plants.

"Alice," Mama had tried to say to her over the breakfast tray she had taken into her bedroom, and Alice looked up, as if surprised to see her there.

"Alice," Ben called across the breakfast table, and she looked at her brother, as if wondering who he was.

"Miss Pinkerton," Rosobell had signed to her in the manual alphabet, and she had stared at her fingers, puzzled, as if unable to read them anymore, seeing the silence that Rosobell heard all the time.

She had let the fog get into the house, blurring the lineaments of everything that was around her.

"Tell me what you can see in those clouds, Miss Pinkerton."

Every movement of the body, every emotion of the mind, is at certain times an omen.

She heard Dr. Wolcott Ascharm Webster's voice, sounding quite eager, as if inviting sinful revelations. With his name, the importance of having three names, and not just a parsimonious two, was clearly being emphasized again.

(Wolcott.

(*One!*

(Ascharm.

(*Two!*

(Webster.

(*Three!*

(*Count 'em!*

(*Count 'em!*)

He was, of course, another of The Bearded Ones. This particular beard faltered a little in the middle, as though some central portion had been destroyed in unwisely leaning too close to a candle to ignite a cigar, but gigantic sweeping sidewhiskers more than compensated for this tragic loss, this catastrophic forest fire.

He was . . .

He was . . .

He was her . . .

(*Mad-doctor!*)

. . . alienist physician.

The Reverend Goodchild, in the tasteful way that was his special gift, made it perfectly clear that he preferred to refer to him as "the mad-doctor." The word "mad" here was intended – not with entire accuracy, Alice felt – to refer to the doctor's patients (the inserted hyphen was important), rather than to describe the good doctor himself.

"Tell me what you can see in those clouds, Miss Pinkerton."

Every form and object in nature, even the shape of the clouds . . .

It was as if reading meaning into the shapes of clouds would reveal some mysteries from within the mind. He was a Madame Etoile with a beard, there to shed light on the tenebrous. His consultation fee was considerably more than fifty cents to one dollar. He held the firm opinion that he was born with a genuine gift, and was capable of guiding you in all aspects of life with his professional skill (and could – no doubt whatsoever about this – see the past, the present, and the future) but he understandably failed to bring together those long separated, show you an accurate likeness of your future husband, and give you his name. (Who'd want to marry *you?* That would be the unspoken – possibly, if he were in the right mood – *spoken* question from Dr. Wolcott Ascharm Webster.) Neither did he give you lucky numbers. You were lucky enough to have him treating you, so don't push your luck, don't be greedy. Alice was sometimes tempted to ask him what hers was, just to see his reaction. "Is my lucky number five?" she'd ask coquettishly. "Is it seven? Is it ten?" She would tell him that he needn't speak the number, but could nod his head as a sign when she spoke it, like the educated goat she'd seen as a small girl that had shown an astonishing ability to calculate in arithmetic, nodding its head the correct number of times for an answer. Its beard had had a remarkable resemblance to Dr. Wolcott Ascharm Webster's. "Is it *eleven?*" she should ask, roguishly, apparently seized by sudden insight, as if unexpectedly remembering that eleven was his house number, and she was lucky – my word, she was lucky! – to be there, to be treated by this god-like being. Surely that should stir his beard into confirmatory rustlings?

"Tell me what you can see in those clouds, Miss Pinkerton."

. . . and the changes of the weather; every colour, every sound, whether of men or animals, or birds or insects, or inanimate things, is an omen.

Time after time, she gazed, deep into the depths of the fathomless clouds, telling him what she could see.

(*To dream of clouds with the stars shining, denotes fleeting joys and small advancements.*)

"Tell me what you can see in those clouds, Miss Pinkerton."

Nothing is too trifling or inconsiderable to inspire a hope which is not worth cherishing . . .

He was most insistent. Days without clouds were not days for rejoicing to Dr. Wolcott Ascharm Webster.

Something about her mood of languor, her feeling of exhaustion, listlessness, brought his voice to mind. It was the same tone of voice with which he said – he almost whispered, intimate, confiding, as if he were making a naughty request he ought not to make – "Tell me your dreams, Miss Pinkerton." It was the same tone of voice he would use if he were saying, "Take off your clothes, Miss Pinkerton." She found herself thinking this with no sensation of surprise. It was always, thank goodness, "Miss Pinkerton," never "Alice": she could not have borne it if he had wanted to call her by her first name.

"I c-c-can see . . ."

(*Damn!*)

"I c-c-can see . . ."

Pause.

"I can see . . ." she would begin again.

"Yes?"

"I can see . . ."

"Tell me what you can see . . ."

"I can see . . . I can see a c-c-cloud almost in shape of a c-c-camel . . ."

That's what she nearly said.

She'd actually heard herself saying it.

C-c-cloud and *c-c-camel*.

Her stutters sometimes seemed to cluster uneconomically around the consonants she used the most in a sentence. Why on earth had she thought of speaking to him in a qu-qu-quotation from *Hamlet*, c-c-crammed as it was with c-c-c sounds?

Dr. Wolcott Ascharm Webster would not have recognized it as a quotation if she *had* started to use Hamlet's words as her reply, the scene in which Hamlet was pointing out the shape of a cloud to Polonius. He wouldn't have recognized *Hamlet* if she'd recited "To be, or not to be" and bounced Yorick's skull off his head with a tinkly little laugh. She was tempted to try this the next time she saw him.

"It is like a w-w-weasel . . . Or like a w-w-whale."

(You could guarantee that the stutters would have shifted to the "w" sound at this point.)

"Very like a whale."

This was the expression that Oliver Comstock used when he was expressing disbelief in something someone had just said. "Very like a whale!" he would snort skeptically. But there would be no disbelief from Dr. Wolcott Ascharm Webster. Unlike Hamlet, he was not a man ever likely to wax desperate with imagination, and whatever she said to him he swallowed whole, his gold-weighted teeth slamming shut like a mantrap from Tiffany's. He'd have swallowed a camel. A weasel or a whale would have gone down with a gulp, scarcely shifting his Adam's apple.

"Imagination is an impediment to progress," he had once said to her, in a tone of voice that suggested he thought he had coined an epigram, a Wildean Mr. Gradgrind wandered far from Coketown. What he had been trying to suggest was that he was a true scientist in the examination of the mind, a man unswayed by anything but the empirical evidence of what he discovered, coolly assessing, free from the dangerous unpredictability of emotion, though she would have preferred imagination, she would have liked emotion.

He would probably listen to the words from *Hamlet* with his usual lack of expression, scribble-scribbling in his notebook. *Alice P: "Clouds almost in shape of a camel." Odd grammar. Query: detrimental effect of Harry Hollander songs?* She imagined his amused, patronizing little laugh, the sort of indulgent male laughter she associated with beards, dark clothes, the smell of tobacco. Perhaps he might start to hum one of Harry's songs under his breath as he wrote. "Why Are You So Flirty, Gertie? (Why Are You Such a Tease?)" (An appropriate choice to accompany *Hamlet*.)

That's what she'd do.

She'd confuse him with camels, worry him with weasels and whales.

They'd get him blotting his notebook. They'd snap his pen nib.

She knew Dr. Wolcott Ascharm Webster for what he was, and she was sure that he knew this.

When her attention wandered, as it often did, during her visits to his consulting room — as he urged her to tell him her dreams, or what she could see in those clouds, that picture (week after week, he did this) — she studied her surroundings carefully, whilst maintaining an expression of rapt attentiveness and a steady flow of grammatically correct sentences. This was a skill that had served her well at Miss Pearsall's School for Girls. The books on display in the glazed cabinets alongside the window, the framed certificates and the photographs of the famous (or reasonably well-known locally: Dr. Wolcott Ascharm Webster seized his opportunities where he could) smiling, shaking his hand: all were a statement of his worth, a gown of power.

Lie there, my art.

There was plenty of lying, and precious little art.

She was irresistibly reminded of a fisherman flaunting a large fish for a photographer. *Look what I've caught!*

The books — as books always did — captured her attention most, and she peered shortsightedly in an attempt to read the titles, hoping that light would glint on the embossed gold. Were they real books, or were they — like those in the terrifying scene in the first lunatic asylum in *Hard Cash* — fake books, books made out of metal?

(All unaware, Alfred Hardie walked through the open gate and into the grounds of Silverton Grove House, lured there by the forged note.

(He entered the handsome hall, was directed up the left-hand staircase, and through an open door into what appeared to be a drawing room.

(The servant led Alfred across the drawing room and opened a concealed door that was disguised as a looking-glass, and they walked through the looking-glass into the cold bare room beyond, dirty and cobwebbed, its nearer wall lined with the fake books.)

Every Wednesday morning, as she entered 11 Park Place she imagined herself walking through the looking-glass when the front door was opened, stepping into the reversed, reflected chessboard world of the Jabberwock.

(Mrs. Archbold, the matron of the asylum, walked toward him. She had been hired by Alfred's father to imprison him, to keep him prisoner in the hidden realms of the mad.

("Calm yourself," she said, laying a hand on his arm. "There is no wonder nor mystery in the matter: *you were expected.*"

(She pulled at a gold chain that was hanging around her neck, and drew out an ivory whistle. When she blew upon it, two men came quietly into the room . . .)

"I can see a galleon," Alice would say, fluently, sincerely, all stuttering ceasing, trying to angle her neck to make it look as if she was looking out of the window at the clouds, "its sails billowing out, its flag fluttering . . ." (*Scribble, scribble*) and her hesitations, as she strained to make out letters in the blur, were seen as an attempt to describe what she saw with more accuracy.

The Principles of Psychology. Grundzuge der Physiologischen Psychologie . . .

Many of the titles were in German. Hilde Claudia, his small, frightened-looking, Austrian wife (difficult to imagine her waltzing gaily: the Vienna Woods would be dark and troublesome, a place of nightmares) labored all day translating impenetrable texts for his pursed-lipped approval. Her second name was pronounced "Cloudier," and Alice often thought of her as Hilde Cloudier. The clouds swarmed dark about her, obliterating the sun, and it was cold. She rarely appeared in public, an even more elusive local than Mrs. Alexander Diddecott's husband, and never spoke, utterly silenced by her husband's constant state of irritation or (more usual) heavily facetious amusement at her frequent mistakes in speaking English.

"*Gesundheit!*" he would exclaim, with the heavy jocularity of the humorless, every time Hilde Claudia inadvertently lapsed into German, her own language the symptom of a problem with her health. Poor Hilde Claudia was perpetually under a cloud, perpetually damp and drizzled upon, suffering from colds and sneezing whatever the weather. Theodore and Max were encouraged to be on the alert for the unauthorized use of German, and would shout *Gesundheit!* just like Papa. It would make her speak English. It was a jolly family joke, demonstrating their jolly family funsomeness. It was for her own good. They were very keen. "*Gesundheit! Gesundheit!*" they'd be crowing all the time, fingers pointing triumphantly, even if Hilde Claudia had done nothing more than mispronounce a word. "It has wery cold been, this vinter," she would begin, slowly, agonizing over each word, and — "*Gesundheit! Gesundheit!*" — Theodore and Max would be off like rockets, fingers accusingly angled. (*Wery! Vinter!*) "'Wery' is *not* German!" Hilde Claudia would insist desperately, almost weeping. "'Vinter' is *not* German!" (Unfortunately for Hilde Claudia, "vinter" *was* German. Theodore and Max cock-a-doodle-dood like a farmyard full of roosters.) After a while she stopped speaking altogether, probably thinking it safer. You could tell that Theodore and Max were disappointed about this, slightly sulky at a lost chance of pleasure.

Alice remembered her at Mrs. Alexander Diddecott's once, before she took the veil and vanished, closing as many doors as possible between herself and the world outside 11 Park Place. She'd been sitting in a corner of the conservatory, partially hidden behind a large fern, like some drab-colored moth seeking camouflage to escape capture, visibly nervous at the thought of being forced into conversation. "It is the werbs." That was what she had told Miss Ericsson, when – not liking to see anyone sitting all by herself – she had gone and sat beside her and tried to talk. This was more or less all that she had said, explaining her silence, her crouching in the undergrowth, made tense by tenses. Nouns she could more or less cope with – she could grasp at the person or thing, and, a little more helplessly, at the place – especially if they were common or proper (though abstract nouns opened up worrying areas of ungraspability). She learned lists of vocabulary every night, trying to improve her English, rather in the way that Alice's Mama had tried to learn things to please Papa. Alice thought of her – thought of both women – alone in a room with a book, bent over, lips moving as they repeated things to themselves, memorizing, counting things out on their fingers as if speaking to someone deaf. Dr. Wolcott Ascharm Webster had hauled Hilde Claudia out into the open, after making a determined search, and she had trembled as she was led into the next room to be introduced to someone she was told she ought to meet. Dr. Wolcott Ascharm Webster wished to demonstrate her in action. She was a useful piece of equipment for his office, like a shiny new typewriter or a newly installed telephone. She could speak German. "Speak German, Hilde Claudia," he'd say (giving his imprimatur to an authorized occasion) – you had a sensation of a lever being pulled, or a button pressed – and she'd say something in German, usually the same thing, some comment about the weather, or about being pleased to meet whomever she was meeting. She could use verbs when she spoke in German. There were no problems with "wery" or "vinter." All sneezing ceased.

She'd spent a few evenings looking wretched, and then she had stopped appearing in other people's houses. Alice had pictured her, cowering in a corner, unable to speak, reduced to holding up shakily printed notices to keep potential conversationalists away. *Please at a distance away with werbs be keeping. Please be not speaking. Please aloneness let me be having.* Perhaps it was on such evenings that she had begun to develop her curiously all-absorbing interest in semaphore. A system of communication that did not involve speaking must have held a powerful allure for her. The idea would have grown in her mind to fill all that silence around her as she sought frond-shadowed refuge behind the more distant plants in conservatories, or sat upright and petrified on far-distant sofas in dark corners, with someone's aged half-asleep aunt propped up against her, chin firmly clamped to her shoulder. She would have begun her first tentative signalings with napkins filched from a nearby side table (she tended to hide herself away amidst the stacked appurtenances of the dining room), passing the hours — a napkin in each hand — by learning the different signals, as methodically as she learned her lists of English vocabulary. Rapidly, jerkily, each gesture looking like an out-of-control nervous twitch, a stutter of the whole body, she'd jerk out her right arm — the aged aunts shooting off the sofa to slide across the well-polished parquet flooring on their chins — and her left arm at different angles, mumblingly memorizing the alphabet. Then she'd started to appear, accompanied by her two tall sons — they towered above her, spindly, angled to one side if the wind was blowing, two Ichabod Cranes who'd be much improved by headlessness — in the less populated parts of Longfellow Park, early in the morning, or just before dusk, practicing long-distance signaling. She'd somehow acquired several sets of semaphore flags, and Theodore or Max would be sent as far away as possible — here was a requirement with which Alice could readily identify — to conduct wordless conversations with their mama. Alice could imagine her in the evenings with the red material and the yellow material stitch-stitch-stitching away in her sewing chair by the light of a lamp as she manufactured her flags. Semaphore flags would have been ideal for the mediæval women, a useful method for signaling from between the crenellations in the battlements of the castles that enclosed them, an attractive alternative to arrows or boiling oil. Alice had watched the semaphoring

Websters, borrowing Charlotte's telescope for the purpose, intrigued enough to attempt to work out the code.

There were two signals that were used more than any other, both of them — unusually — involving agitation of the flags. The first — in which both flags were held in the air at an angle away from the body and waved like a jolly greeting — always preceded any signal, and clearly meant *Attention!* or *Ready to Begin!*, something like that. She would concentrate on what followed, once she saw that one. The other signal of this sort was the one that Hilde Claudia seemed to use more than any other, even more than *Attention!* — she always looked frantically worried, as if every signal was a cry for help, a desperate last attempt to seek succor, *Come now! Come now! Come NOW!* — in which she held the flag in her right hand down in front of her, and looped the flag in her left hand around and around as if describing a figure of eight in the air. This, Alice, came to realize, meant *Error!*, and Hilde Claudia would begin her signaling all over again. Even with semaphore flags, it appeared, werbs crept in and caused chaos. *Error! Error!* An expression of unutterable woe came across her face every time she signaled an error, and she sometimes dashed her flags to the ground in despair. Not much comedy in these errors.

Dr. Wolcott Ascharm Webster always referred to her as Hilde Claudia — not "my wife," not "Mrs. Webster" — when he introduced her, using her first name as if she were a child being chucklingly introduced to be cooed over and chucked under the chin. If Alice were Hilde Claudia she'd have chucked him over her shoulder with a vigorous grunt. He made her name sound like one word, as if this were the name of the particular item he had purchased, and jabbed her in the back as he said it.

"This is my telephone . . ."

"This is my typewriter . . ."

"This is my . . ."

— *Thrust!* —

". . . Hildeclaudia. It can speak German."

"Speak German."

Thrust!

"Speak German."

Thrust!

The thrust made her totter forward a few inches, as if she were given to hurling herself at strangers. They wouldn't realize that they were being given her name, and – suspecting some exotic foreign word or phrase (they knew that she was *foreign*) – *Hulles de Clous d'hier? Île de Cloudiérè?* (Was that was where she was *from?* Where on earth was it?) It sounded *French* – they tended to smile in their most cosmopolitan fashion (this involved more teeth than usual), and murmur (to Hilde Claudia's bafflement) *"Bonjour"* or (sometimes accompanied by a self-consciously continental kiss on the back of her hand) *"Enchanté!"* As she politely endured the long lingering kisses – thank goodness she was wearing gloves – she studied the bald patches on the backs of their heads (the kissers tended to have bald patches) with evident distaste. She could still see the red lines where they'd been scratching themselves, and why did that one have a mirror-reversed line of handwriting across it in green ink, as if he'd applied his newly written correspondence to his conveniently situated baldness and employed it as a blotter? She leaned a little closer, interested despite herself, trying to make out what it said, but the man must have had an unusually absorbent head, and all the writing was blurred. There was one phrase, however, just on the verge of legibility, which seemed to say . . .

She leaned closer.

Which seemed to say . . .

If the bowing man had stood up unexpectedly, the back of his head would have caught Hilde Claudia's chin with a painful whack, and hoisted her up into the air, setting the chandelier jingling.

. . . *You saucy boy!*

This was what it seemed to say.

Who was this oh-so-saucy boy, and what was the source of his oh-so-sauciness?

(Much agitation from Mrs. Albert Comstock's fan if she happened to be present. French *and* kissing. *Ooh la la!* crept ever closer. Nowhere was safe.)

It became cloudier and cloudier for Claudia, and the days were always dark.

"Speak German."

Thrust!

"Speak German."

Thrust!

With much the same thrustingly officious tone of voice, Mrs. Albert Comstock imperiously demanded "Speak English!" (with an added exclamation point) of the Renwicks, the young English couple, possibly in an attempt to prevent them from indulging in a predilection for conversing in Hindoostanee. She wanted to hear what English accents sounded like, and – after the Renwicks politely obliged – she commented loudly on how convincing she found them, on the very verge of correcting their pronunciation of certain words. Guests of Mrs. Albert Comstock had to conform to preexisting prejudices.

"How is it now with the weather?" Hilde Claudia asked repeatedly, with increasing desperation, on the occasions on which she was allowed to speak English in public. "How is it now with the weather?" People tended to nod at this, with small smiles, as if what she said was a conversational counter, rather like "How are you?" (to which an answer was not expected) but Hilde Claudia really wanted to know.

("How is it now with the weather?"

(She waited for news of increasing warmth.

(She waited for news of brighter days.

(She waited for news of cloud-free heavens.

(She waited in vain.

("We have been given cold weather," she was sometimes driven to answer herself.

("We have been given dark weather."

("We have been given oh-so-much cloud."

(The oh-so-much cloud grew thicker, darker, ever more impenetrable. Cloudier, today, Hilde Claudia, *very* much cloudier.)

Come now! Come now! Come NOW!

Alice had never heard her refer to her husband by name, and sometimes speculated about how she would address him, though she always thought that — whatever it was — it was sure to be spoken deferentially. Perhaps she abbreviated his middle name and called him Charm. If the Heightons could still straight-facedly address their daughter as Chastity after the Sunday-school picnic, Mrs. Webster could go ahead and address her husband as Charm.

Unless she called him Cotty.

Unless she called him Asch.

Asch would *Tritsch* her, Asch would *Tratsch* her, if she attempted the *Tritsch, Tratsch* polka. ("Opus 214," she would announce solemnly, determined to suppress any unsuitable elements of frivolity in her choice.) There'd be *Donner*, there'd be *Blitz*, there'd be *Wiener Blut* all over the carpet, and the air would be bluer than the Beautiful Blue Danube when *he* let rip. (Yes to Wine, yes to Song, no, no, *no* to Women.)

She saw Hilde Claudia, tentatively, rubbing tired eyes, holding out a translation to her husband after a day of toiling, the pages covered in crossings-out and variant readings.

"Is this meeting with your approval, Charm? Always I am trouble having with the werbs."

Her exhausted arms — barely capable of lifting the flags — jerked into spasmodic automatic action. Somewhere in the distance, *someone* would see her signal, and respond.

Attention!

H . . .

I . . .

Error!

H . . .

E . . .

HELP! FROM CHARM ME BE RESCUING!

HELP! I AM BY COTTY CAPTIVE!

HELP! ASCH HAS ME HERE PRISONERED!

More book titles became legible.

Journal of Nervous and Mental Disease. Asylum Journal. Traumdeutung. A Treatise on the Nervous Diseases of Women. The Borderlands of Insanity . . .

These last two projected slightly forward from the others, as if replaced hastily on the shelf, highly suitable volumes for last-minute pre-Miss-Pinkerton perusings, judging by the titles. They'd supply a few words, a few phrases, sparsely hold the silences at bay as she told him what she saw in the clouds, what she had dreamed. She couldn't see a copy of *Extraordinary Popular Delusions and the Madness of Crowds*. This was a book she *had* read. This was the book whose words she repeated to herself. The title would have appealed immensely to Dr. Wolcott Ascharm Webster, with its promise of crowds of loonies eagerly surging toward 11 Park Place, all clutching hard cash in their hands, eager to thrust ready money at him for listening to their ravings. If only Charles Mackay had stayed in Longfellow Park in the course of his researches as he expanded his findings for new editions. He'd have found mad crowds aplenty, enough material for a multi-volumed masterwork. She'd have had a chapter all to herself, between "Fortune-Telling" and "The Magnetisers" or — more appealing, this — between "The Witch Mania" and "The Slow Poisoners." She'd like to have a stab (a more appropriate expression should surely have come to mind) at being a slow poisoner, though *fast* poisoning held considerably more appeal. "Miss Pinker*rr*ton," Charles Mackay would have called her, rolling the "r" sound to demonstrate his Scottishness skittishly, in case she hadn't spotted the saucily fluttered kilt — *well-formed and smooth knees, predicts that you will have many admirers* — as he skirled his bagpipes. *But none to woo you in wedlock.*

Alice assumed an expression of intelligent concentration, and tried to look as though she was seeing *plenty* in the clouds, a galleon crowded with incident. She thought of Hilde Cloudier.

"I can see . . ."

"I can see . . ."

That was what she should be saying.

"The rigging is lined with sailors dressed in white . . ."

Scribble, scribble, scribble.

At the appearance of dozens of sailors, the pen began positively to leap across the page.

Neue Vorlesungen uber — shouldn't there be an umlaut over that *u?* — *die Krankheiten des Nervensystems, insbesondere uber* — another umlaut, surely? — *Hysterie. Psychiatry: A Clinical Treatise on Diseases of the Fore-Brain. Injuries of Nerves and Their Consequences. Fat and Blood . . .*

What fun bedtime reading must be in the Webster household, as Mama and Papa sat down with their loved ones — the two crumpled-looking scrawny boys — to read the latest installment from *The Treatment of Certain Forms of Neurasthenia and Hysteria* or *Mind and Brain.*

"Read that part about women's inability to deal with the abstract again, Papa!" young Theodore — he knew how to please — would cry. "Tell us about the less development of their frontal convolutions!. . ."

(If this was an example of Hilde Claudia's translation skills, Dr. Wolcott Ascharm Webster's lips would remain firmly pursed, as if perpetually poised for a dry passionless Pharaildisian peck — *Peck. Peck. Peck* — of a kiss. Here a peck, there a peck, everywhere a peck-peck.)

". . . It is by far my favorite section! Perhaps Mama will demonstrate it for us!" He revealed his proud Germanic heritage with an excess of exclamation points.

(One of the men began to speak to Alfred.

("Be calm, my dear young gentleman; don't agitate yourself. You have been sent here for your good; and that you may be cured . . ."

("What are you talking about? What do you mean?" cried Alfred. "Are you mad?"

("No," one of the men answered. "*We* are not . . .")

. . . or a fear which is sufficient to embitter existence.

The first title she had deciphered had been a whole bound series of the magazine *Brain*. At first she had read the word as *Brian*, and something about its pale mauve binding, and its position half hidden in the shadows on the bottom shelf, had led her to uncover the clues — she was after all, a *Pinkerton*, detection was her heritage, she was fully alert to the latest discoveries — that revealed what was hidden within those tenebrous tomes. Sparingly applied talcum powder (finely ground, lavender-scented, smuggled into the consulting room in a china pillbox inside her purse) brought to light what had hitherto been hidden, but long suspected by her: the glass which enclosed *Brian* was made cloudy with the whorls of damp and fevered fingerprints, the pouted imprints of kissing lips. The study of fingerprints — a true Pinkertonian awareness, this — by detectives, this new infant science, this search for uniqueness in order to gather together the evidence against a criminal, seemed like something from the realm of the quacks, the quack-quacking migration of sky-darkening flocks of wild geese out chasing. They were caught red-handed, and hidden in the bloodstained lines of their fingers and thumbs was the evidence that would condemn them to death, captured by the markings on the body that only they possessed. In the fairground booths, doctors and detectives fearlessly donned brightly colored headscarves, and jangled with gold-coin jewelry as they interpreted dreams (if they were doctors), or (if they were detectives) ventured into palmistry and graphology to bring murderers to justice. "The Lower Mars section of your Mount of Venus is flat and undeveloped," the detective would say accusingly, his earrings jangling, as he grasped the killer's especially washed hand firmly. (*Wash suspect's hands thoroughly* was the golden rule in the grubby world of fingerprint reading.) "Your whole Plain of Mars is also very flat, almost a hollow." This — it would be made quite clear — was not a characteristic of which one could be proud. "Are you a man lacking in *confidence?*" he would suddenly ask with meaningful emphasis, gazing with unblinking and suspicious regard into the eyes of the sweating man across the table, daring him to attempt to outstare him, daring him to keep on denying and denying, when his guilt was as clearly marked upon his hands as Lady Macbeth's had been. "Your Line of Life is *very* short." (That always set them trembling, the first words of confession spilling from the frightened lips. "I didn't *mean* to . . ." That's how they would start. "All I wanted was the *money* . . ." It would all come pouring out, another triumph for forensic palm-reading.) Dr. Wolcott Ascharm Webster – for his were the fingerprints, the lip-prints (was a science in these developing, also?) – would have had to lie prostrate on the carpet to achieve the right angle for labial contact; he would probably rather have enjoyed this, the ritualistic humiliation.

The keys to the bookcases – tiny, ornate, golden, like the key to a musical box, "Daisy, Daisy, give me your answer do! I'm half crazy, all for the love of you!" – were kept at all times in the doctor's vest pocket, just above his heart. He – of all people (the reader of clouds, the reader of dreams and pictures) – had to be fully alert to the significance of Symbolism, odd in a man who claimed to eschew imagination. All the bookcases were kept locked, to exclude the unworthy, to bar the beardless. The lack of keys was no problem to a trained Pinkerton: a few deft watch-repairer-like twists with the point of her hatpin, and the bookcase – the only one with its glass covered in prints, the only one kept *double* locked with two different keys (her keen eye had soon registered these significant details) – yielded up its secrets, and the truth could no longer be denied.

To dream of keys, denotes unexpected changes.

The violet volumes were filled – crammed to bursting – with erotic photographs of Dr. Wolcott Ascharm Webster's secret, forbidden love: Brian, a pale, artistic youth, thin and sinuous as an Aubrey Beardsley lily, with a collection of blue and white china, and limpid, sulky eyes.

Between the two of them, a dangerous passion throbbed.

"The sailors are swaying from side to side. They are beginning to sing, and they're waving to two other ships that have just started to appear over the horizon . . ."

Sailors swaying from side to side. More sailors pouring in by the shipload.

Scribble, scribble, scribble.

The nib of the pen almost ripped through the paper. The impression of the handwriting would be legible six pages deep.

For a young woman to dream of sailors, is ominous of a separation from her lover through a frivolous flirtation. If she dreams that she is a sailor, she will indulge in some unmaidenly escapade, and be in danger of losing a faithful lover.

Alone, in the evening — "I need to undertake some research, *meine kleine Nachtmusik*" — fortified by a glass of brandy, Dr. Wolcott Ascharm Webster (reclining in a nightshirt of a color that Brian told him really suited his complexion) would linger guiltily, caressingly, over certain pages, illuminated in flickering firelight, as the voices of Hilde Claudia, Theodore, and Max echoed faintly from around the piano in the room upstairs, the words of the song interspersed with extempore yodeling. A certain frivolity was permitted on carefully designated occasions.

". . . A most intense young man,
A soulful-eyed young man,
An ultra-poetical, super æsthetical,
Out-of-the-way young man!. . .

"A Japanese young man,
A blue-and-white young man,
Francesca di Rimini, miminy, piminy,
Je-ne-sais-quoi young man!. . .

"A pallid and thin young man,
A haggard and lank young man,
A greenery-yallery, Grosvenor Gallery,
Foot-in-the-grave young man!. . ."

Something inside Dr. Wolcott Ascharm Webster broke, and he began to sob. The tears flowed down his cheeks, as he tenderly pressed his lips against Brian's bare shoulder, imperfectly concealed by a loosely clutched sunflower. These were photographs of the kind that could not be entrusted to the post office without dire risk of incurring the wrath of Anthony Comstock, and all the gradations of shame to follow: seizure, denunciation, destruction, vast heaped piles of dirty books and dirty pictures – fluttering, blackening – blazing like a forest fire.

Anthony Comstock, the celebrated – not to say, notorious – moral reformer was no kin of Mrs. Albert Comstock, but he and she were as twin souls in their vindictiveness, their small-mindedness, and their implacable air (worn like Crusaders' breastplates: Mrs. Albert Comstock's would contain enough metal for Brooklyn Bridge) of moral superiority.

"My strength is as the strength of ten," Anthony Comstock probably intoned into the mirror each morning (in the way that other men intoned, "Youth! Health! Vigor!"), "because my heart is pure."

What a tribute it was to his fame, he no doubt remarked – vague, like Mrs. Albert Comstock, about dates and chronologies – that Tennyson should have created so recognizable a picture of him in Sir Galahad. One felt, with Anthony Comstock, that any bonfire of piled up *filth!* – the word spat out, faces dampened for yards around, lightning bolts unleashed from his eyes – would not be complete without the perpetrator (artist, author, purchaser: he was happy to allow considerable leeway on this point) tied to a stake at its summit, screaming dementedly in agony, and dying – hideously disfigured – as the flames consumed his body with exquisite slowness. Anthony Comstock's thoughts lingered sensually on this image. He was a self-appointed scourge of the sinful, and therefore all the keener. He did not seek financial reward. It was payment enough for him – he'd say this with a modest, self-deprecating smile – to drive his chosen victims to suicide. With the quiet pride of a stamp collector arranging and mounting his latest findings, he sat at home of an evening – filling the empty hours – totting up the numbers of those he'd driven to death, and calculating the number of tons of books and pictures he'd been instrumental in burning or dumping into a convenient river. He'd dumped so many dirty books and pictures into the rivers around New York that it was astonishing that they were still navigable, not filth-silted through full fathom five, so crammed with carnality that even a canoe couldn't get through. Every day should be bringing shocking news of ships being wrecked against these rude reefs, or stranded in these salacious shallows. The survivors – not too keen on being saved too swiftly – would gather in giggling damp-bearded groups, making themselves comfy – "Look at *this*! Look at *this*!" – to examine the details of the grubby merchandise on which they'd grounded, breathing their hot breath on the soggy pages to dry them out a bit and make them more legible. They came unto those yellow sands, and then took hands. Bow-wow, the watch dogs barked. "Look at *this*! Look at *this*!" they'd whisper, keeping their voices as low as possible, anxious to avoid making any sound that might be interpreted as a cry for help.

"Look at page one hundred and sixty-three!"

"Page one hundred and eleven!"

"Eighty-nine!"

"*Seven!*"

Any fool who attempted to signal with his shirt, or a hastily improvised fire, idiotically seeking premature rescue, would soon find himself knocked on the head and bound and gagged. You wouldn't have been surprised if lust-crazed pilots had deliberately steered ships to destruction, wreckers seduced by the siren call of smut. You wouldn't catch Grace Darling rowing out to rescue licentious lingerers such as these! Not likely! "Over here, *Darling*!" they'd snigger droolingly, nudging each other with meaningful purposefulness, their baser selves fully unleashed and all raring to go, especially after they'd boggled at page seven. "This way, *Darling*!" She'd biff them over the head with her oars, brain them with a bash. They weren't going to contaminate *her* nice clean rowboat. Mucky mariners! Filthy beasts!

"I'll drown my book!" Anthony Comstock declaimed challengingly, like a pornographic Prospero, rather pleased with himself. (*Deeper than did ever plummet sound.* That's how deep he'd drown it.)

The printed word was bad enough, but the world was crammed with unsuitable works of art, paintings and sculptures athrob with brazen bareness, pendulously wobbling dangliness (hadn't these people heard of sensible underwear?) that quite turned the stomach, and gave rise to potential impurity of thought. Strategically positioned fig leaves were not the answer. Oh dear me, no. They left far too much still – ahem – protruding, giving rise to ribald speculation.

Aprons.

That was what it said in the Bible – Genesis, Chapter III, Verse vii – *they sewed fig leaves* (definitely a plural) *together, and made themselves aprons,* and it was in aprons that their hopes clearly lay for a dangle-free future. Montgomery Ward & Co. produced good-quality mechanics' aprons out of bed ticking at a cost of only *twenty cents* each if their name was stamped clearly on the front. (They cost fifty cents without the name.) These aprons were perfect for their job of enforcing purity. They were thirty inches wide, and thirty-six inches in length, the right size for covering the areas of maximum danger (though some of Rubens's larger ladies – as if employed in one of the messier manufactories – might require to be multi-aproned), and were supplied complete with shoulder and waist straps that – tightly knotted and carefully adjusted – should ensure safety from all angles. *And* they had useful pockets. *Montgomery Ward & Co., Chicago* would be a guarantee of suitability for the family agog for culture without embarrassment, and would introduce a bracing sensation of the outside world of commerce into the too rarefied atmosphere of museums and galleries.

He thought of himself as a man living a thrilling life full of adventures, battling the forces of evil with the upraised sword of purity. Perhaps the Reverend Goodchild could be persuaded to model one of his dreadful historical novels upon his life.

Comstock: Scourge of the Sinners (1903) would be one more to add to the list, the long, long list of ploppily bubbling potboilers, the ones that smelled so bad as they were stirred upon the stove. Inspiration – not the first word that sprang to mind – showed no signs of flagging, and Halitotic Herbert churned them out as if he'd borrowed one of the sausage machines from Comstock's Comestibles, all titles throbbing with sensational overtones, all titles racily alliterative.

"Buy a Goodchild for your Good Child!" was the exhortation above the full list of titles available in The Works of the Reverend H. P. Goodchild (the oeuvre was much recommended as a suitable source for Sunday-school prizes), printed opposite the title pages. "Thoroughly wholesome in tone!" was the puzzling conclusion of *The Poughkeepsie Press*, placed alluringly beneath. (The exclamation points got you panting before you'd even read a word of the first page.) The anxious parents of Vassar students must be hastening – in the vastness of the night – to remove their imperiled daughters to a place of greater safety, if this was what wholesomeness meant in the dark backward and abyss of Poughkeepsie. Poughkeepsie was clearly not the quiet place slumbering in academic quietude that it purported to be. Some freelance contributor, scribbling away in one of the less accessible rooms at the Webster Nervine Asylum (the third door on the left, just past the Fauntleroy Ward), had probably written the enticing recommendation.

Possibly, some time in 1930 – when he would be about a hundred – he would run out of sinful Roman and Parisian landmarks to employ for his settings, and inspiration (*ha!*) would at last fail him. All he would have to offer as his anticlimactic swan-song (here was a swan that Leda would have repulsed vigorously, lashing out with every sign of revulsion) would be *The Slightly Unpleasant Events Just off the Corso*, where even alliteration faltered, and the death count was disappointingly low, only just making double figures. The – *ha!* – thoroughly wholesome in tone oeuvre would grind to a halt, and there would be a crisis in Sunday-schools throughout the land. What on earth could they offer as prizes now that there were to be no more Goodchilds for their Good Children? It would be back to *Ben-Hur*.

"I've already *read* this!" the Good Children – no longer so Good – would complain rebelliously, and there would be a nation-wide revolt. (Not missing a single Sunday-school all year, and then being offered a book you'd already read as a reward!) He wrote at least two a year: forests were laid waste for his meretricious trash, and when the forests were gone the light was blinding.

The scandalously apron-free photographs of Brian would not meet with Anthony Comstock's approval. He did not know much about art and literature, but he knew what he disliked, and what he disliked most of all was any hint of nudity, or any mention of (careful glance around, voice lowered to a thrilling hiss) sex. It would be an extra-big bonfire, with extra-hot flames. Spectators would be encouraged to lob bricks, to engage in antiphonal chanting.

"Wanton Webster!"
"Bottom-Baring Brian!"
"Wanton Webster!"
"Bottom-Baring Brian!"

Opportunities for this kind of thing were one of the many benefits of becoming a member of the New York Society for the Suppression of Vice, and marching behind the banner proudly borne by Anthony Comstock. Bricks and firewood would be on offer at special discounted prices. For a small fee, you could be one of those manning the barricades alongside Mrs. Albert Comstock (a formidable barricade all by herself) and the Goodchilds, another high priest of prissiness, a nabob of niceness, a grumpy mugwump of modesty, flourishing gigantic fig leaves as if taking part in some rural festivities at harvest time in one of the wine-growing regions of the world.

Life had suddenly become unbearable for Dr. Wolcott Ascharm Webster. Shades of the prison-house began to close upon the groaning man. His beard – with painful irony he favored the model worn by Anthony Comstock – rustled against the edges of the page and scratched against the photograph, tickling unsuitable areas.

"Brian . . . Brian . . . I yearn for your touch, but yet it cannot be. I have a family. I must think of Hilde Claudia, little Theodore" — little Theodore was at least five feet eleven — "and little Max. I have my position in society to consider. This is madness, my darling."

The tears flowed through his lank and darkened sidewhiskers and emerged — as if filtered into fresh water — on the other side, dripping from his dampened Dundrearies onto the cover of the book and turning the mauve into — *ooh!* — (the weeping doctor forgot to cry, perked up, and looked with alerted interest) *such* an attractive shade of purple. It would be the ideal shade for that new vase he was contemplating purchasing for the conservatory.

"Tell me what you are thinking, Miss Pinkerton."

He would have been surprised if she had told him, particularly bearing in mind the comments she had heard him make to Halitotic Herbert about Oliver Comstock. Oliver was the only one of the Comstocks Alice liked. He had always made it perfectly clear that he loathed his mother, a most endearing quality to anyone who felt about her as Alice did, and if Charm — *ha!* — felt it was amusing to snigger that Oliver was a Charlotte Anne (this was the expression he used) she was quite prepared to leap to his defense. (Why *Charlotte*? Alice thought, loyally.)

Unseen by the doctor, a telltale trickle of talcum powder ran across the carpet toward his desk, like a gunpowder trail about to be ignited for a massive explosion. Bits of Brians — thin shadowed chests, provocatively angled peacock feathers, sleepily half-closed eyes — would be everywhere. Fingerprinting would open up exciting new career prospects for Chastity Heighton. Lightly dusted with talcum powder, she would be an invaluable source for fingerprints of all the men of dubious morals in Longfellow Park, and would find her rôle in life at last. "Your Mount of Venus is highly developed toward the Lower Mars area, and your Lower Luna is very pronounced," the detective began, accusingly, studying her all-too-eagerly proffered palm, and Chastity nodded excitedly, as if she'd just been paid a great compliment. "I *know*!" she said proudly. Talcum powder would avalanche down like a storm of confectioners' sugar onto pastries: sinful, fattening, impossible to resist. Her parents would be so thrilled. The very mention of her name, for the past few years, had brought an excitedly shocked gleam into the eyes of the respectable women of Longfellow Park, and (silently, and in private) a nostalgic smile to the faces of certain equally respectable men.

Alice had once been startled by a complaining comment she had overheard a woman – on her way to the circulating library – calling across Chestnut Street, at the front of the house, to another through a drizzle.

"Jane Eyre is covered in fingerprints!"

(It was as if Chastity Heighton had found a woman friend at last, one with whom she could share her hobby.)

Jane Eyre covered in fingerprints!

It was an appealing thought.

"Rochester has p-p-pounced at last! Fight back, Jane! B-B-Bawl for B-B-Bertha!" she called to them from the window.

The wet umbrellas had been tilted briefly backward – white, upturned faces – and then hastily moved back upright, clutched more firmly. They had not known what to say.

(*It's the madwoman! It's the madwoman!* They had known what to think.

(*It's the local Lizzie Borden, all set to start whacking!*)

It had been intended as a joke. She knew, of course – *Of course! Of course!*: she should have shouted it at them – that the woman was talking about the condition of *Jane Eyre* the printed book, and not Jane Eyre the character, but they had – conversation abandoned – hastily continued in their different directions, the one bound for the library clutching the maltreated *Jane Eyre* closer to her under her greatcoat, carefully avoiding looking up toward Alice at the window. The lack of punctuation in the spoken word (in the majority of people: Mrs. Albert Comstock somehow managed to use punctuation, where appropriate, as a weapon when she spoke) could so easily give rise to unfortunate misunderstandings.

"Do not be afraid," the book borrower muttered to her bosom. "I shall protect you from Mrs. Rochester."

The words were whispered, the lips pressed against the edges of the pages in the gap between the buttons, a mother comforting a sleeping child.

Here was a borrower who was only too conscious of the awesome responsibilities that were placed upon her each time she removed a book from the premises, her heart going pit-a-pat as she stepped outside the double doors and down the steps. Here was a borrower who nightly intoned the rules that were pasted on the inside front cover of every volume in the library, her lips moving as if in prayer as she tremblingly repeated the Four Commandments of the insomniac bookworm. Here was a borrower whose tastes ran to full-blooded novels throbbing with pulsating passions. Here was a borrower whose life was a little lacking in excitement.

1. *Every precaution must be taken to protect the library book from rain in the event of inclement weather.*
2. *If infectious diseases should break out in your house do not return this book but at once inform the librarian.*
3. *Readers infringing this regulation, or knowingly permitting the book to be exposed to infection, are liable to a penalty.*
4. *Do NOT write inside this book, EVEN in pencil.*

(*Whack!* the maternal mutterer was hearing behind her. *Whack! Whack! Whack!* She could feel the ax whistling past her, just missing.)

"I am taking every precaution to protect you!" she reassured *Jane Eyre*.

Whack!

"I shall at once inform the librarian!"

Whack!

"I shall not knowingly permit you to be exposed!"

Whack!

"NOT!"
Whack!
"EVEN!"
(*Whack! Whack! Whack!*)

To dream that you are in an attic, denotes that you are entertaining hopes which will fail of materialization. For a young woman to dream that she is sleeping in an attic, foretells that she will fail to find contentment in her present occupation.

Propping up *Brian* – she preferred her reading of the word – was a well-fingered copy of one of L. N. Fowler's phrenology heads. Everywhere it was cracked and crazed. Remarkably like her head. Astonishingly like it.

It was mapped in labeled regions, some of them printed in capital letters, the words faded and worn. Was the head possibly a portrait of L. N. Fowler himself, spectacularly bald, amenably posing for the sculptor? Mrs. L. N. Fowler would have shaved him specially, with his newly sharpened cutthroat razor, concentrating carefully as she swept across *Humor*, *Mirthfulness*, and *Wit*, anxious to avoid cutting him and having blood drip down through *Time*, *Measure*, *Color* and *Neatness* into his left eye. She would have marked out the areas of his skull in her neatest printing.

Some of the letters had been rubbed completely away, and an obliterated initial letter *S* above the right ear produced an area intriguingly identified as the one that revealed *ELFISH PROPEN-SITIES*. She remembered – as a child – studying the ear closely (the head had not always been placed in the consulting room), to determine whether or not it was unusually pointed at the tip. She had touched her own skull, as if feeling for evidence of lettering beneath her hair, the mapping that meant an area had been explored and claimed by The Bearded Ones. The left side of the phrenology head – *Love of Sex*, *Amativeness*, *Destructiveness*, *Extermination*, *Secretiveness*, *Reserve*, *Policy*, *Evasion* – was cozily nuzzled up against *Brian* in snugglesome emulation of Dr. Wolcott Ascharm Webster. Perhaps there was something in phrenology after all, though she would like to have seen more detailed evidence of *Destructiveness* and *Extermination* where he was concerned. She should assess its accuracy, run her fingers through her physician's hair around his left ear, expertly caressing the organ, passing off her actions with a bell-like Mrs. Albert Comstock-style laugh. Mrs. Albert Comstock was currently modeling her laugh on the one possessed by Mavis Clare, the heroine of *The Sorrows of Satan*, a novel which was the most outrageous example of a writer making love to herself since Charlotte Brontë had written *The Professor*. Mrs. Albert Comstock was a tremendous admirer of Marie Corelli's novels. Miss Corelli knew everything about everything, and this spoke directly to the heart of Mrs. Albert Comstock, who possessed (oddly enough) these very same qualities. Both women had firm opinions on every subject, and showed little reluctance in letting everyone know this: the best manufacturer of umbrellas, the real meaning of Christianity, the most efficacious treatment for the complexion, the principle of forgiveness (and where it was appropriate). Mavis Clare's laugh was described as "a merry little laugh like a peal of bells," and Mrs. Albert Comstock tried her best.

MORAL AND RELIGIOUS SENTIMENTS was printed across the top of the skull on the right-hand side. She found herself reversing left and right, thinking from the point of view of the pottery head, as if the skull were her own head, and she was a reflection looking into her own eyes. The eyes were without pupils, and she thought of *The Children's Hour*, the bronze statue in the park of herself and her sisters when they were little girls, the blind-eyed children grouped around their father.

(Between the dark and the daylight, / When the night is beginning to lower, / Comes a pause in the day's occupations, / That is known as the Children's Hour.)

For a woman to dream of a bronze statue, signifies that she will fail in her efforts to win the person she has determined on for a husband.

Lower down, just above the forehead, was the legend *INTU-*

ITIVE, REASONING, REFLECTIVE, FACULTIES. (That last comma was surely redundant.) Lowest of all on the side she could see, just above the right eye, the words were *LITERARY, OBSERVING, KNOWING, FACULTIES.* (Ditto.) The only place any of these qualities existed in that office was locked away in a glass-fronted bookcase, printed on the surface of a hollow pottery head. To the left of the door – it was one of a number of framed portraits (all of them men, mostly Bearded Ones, mostly unknown) that lined that wall, a disconcerting phalanx of disapproving faces – there was an engraving of Dr. Gall of Vienna, the physician who had laid the foundations of phrenology. He had adapted the heads from Ancient Greek statues for use in phrenology – she imagined plaster casts of Apollo Belvedere, Venus, Zeus, and Aphrodite – and gods and goddesses bowed down before him as he read the fate that lay encoded within the contours of their skulls. They would wither and die as a new mythology rose to replace them. It would be like a scene from "Hyperion," the Titans lost in lethargy and self-doubt.

"The exploration of the head is a well-established science in Vienna," Dr. Wolcott Ascharm Webster had once announced, as if commenting (a highly unlikely possibility) on the perspicacity of his wife.

(Franz Mesmer – the founder of animal magnetism, the man after whom mesmerism was named – was another one from Vienna. He had studied medicine at the university there, and his portrait was inevitably amongst Dr. Wolcott Ascharm Webster's pantheon of household gods. Alice avoided looking into his eyes, but could feel them on the back of her neck.

(*The sun, the moon, and the stars affect the nervous system of the human body* . . . That was what he was saying in a hypnotic monotone.

(*Turn around!*

(That was what he was saying.

(*Turn around!*

(Mesmer, who had learned much of his craft from Father Hell – a man drawn surely to his calling by the appropriateness of his name, a man who had applied steel to the naked bodies of his patients as his method of treatment — would have been received with open arms at the Webster Nervine Asylum. Dr. Wolcott Ascharm Webster would be able to relax by attempting to outstare Franz Mesmer, looking him challengingly in the white of the eye close up, in the posture of someone about to arm-wrestle. Put in the mood by an exhausting evening of Brian-grappling, he wouldn't leave it at looking. He'd be all in favor of emulating Mesmer's own technique and employing the laying on of hands, vigorously setting to work like a saucy slap-slapping *masseur* let loose on a naughty boy in need of strict discipline. The application of steel — and not just bamboo — was what was required for satisfactory results, and, of course, *chuckle*, a more enjoyable time for all concerned.)

Papa had had a taste for phrenology.

"May I?" he would inquire of friends and neighbors (usually mothers; he seemed a little more wary of fathers) as he placed a hand on the shoulder of a young daughter (never a son), you'd have thought that he was asking to borrow an umbrella, and then — *whumpf!* — everything went black for the girl as she was rammed face forward against him — a stink of tobacco, itching fabric, buttons cutting into the skin — as he began to caress what he wetly referred to as "the organs." The busy fingers would go to work on the half-suffocated child, the dexterous digits — could something dexterous be described as sinister? — beavering away, a man truly fulfilled by his hobby, snuffling excitedly, like a pig rooting for truffles. It was regarded as an endearing eccentricity. It had never happened to her — being unattractive had its compensations — but Kate Calbraith had shown what it had done to her, as if the actions of the fingers upon her skull had changed the contours of her face, when Alice had taken her up to the schoolroom — after he had finished — to show her the sections of stained glass and the terra-cotta figures she had saved from the Shakespeare Castle. Papa had comprehensively investigated her only a few days before his — hurrah! hurrah! — death during the snowstorm. Perhaps the excitement had contributed to his demise: he had certainly gone at it with enthusiasm. There had been snow on the Calbraiths' boots when they arrived: she remembered the wet footprints across the tiles in the hall, the red-tinged snow through the colored glass in the door.

Kate had had the impression of his watch-chain at an angle across her forehead, like a scar caused by some piece of machinery, and the reverse side of the Roman coin he wore on the chain was clearly marked over her left eye. She was a little girl then, a few years younger than Alice's little brother, who had been ten when Papa killed himself. There was the lettering at the bottom of the coin, and the image of the two captives sitting on the ground with their heads bowed, the woman on the left, and the man – his hands bound behind him – on the right. There was desolation and despair in the posture of the two simply portrayed figures.

The red imprint – like a temporary tattoo from Mississippi Mike's Parlor (*TatTOOSE PROFFesionally DONE UpSTARES*) – gradually began to fade. Kate had rubbed at it squeamishly, a child removing someone else's spit from her face.

"The psychological damage, will – of course – take longer to heal," Alice had said to herself, feeling very modern, though Kate was more concerned about the possible damage to her dress.

If this had happened a few weeks later, when Ben had started at Otsego Lake Academy – he and all the Crowninshields' boys had started there after their old school had closed abruptly – she could have asked his Latin teacher, Mr. Rappaport, to come across. If he had been able to read mirror writing he could have had a brief one-word browse – *CÆSAR* – of Kate.

The Reverend Goodchild, long after Papa's death, borrowed that same Roman coin from Mama (tactful twinkle, creepy little caress of the hand) – not, these days, Kate-warmed (though that would have been a bonus for Halitotic Horace: a brief frisson of pleasure) – whenever he launched into his celebrated "Render unto Cæsar" sermon: a source of innocent merriment to all those who knew his taste in food and wine, and other – less categorizable –

pleasures.

"'Shew me the tribute money'" he would declaim, as he began to approach what he regarded as the sensational climax of his oration. (You just *knew* he was saying "shew" and not "show.") "'And they brought unto him a penny. And he saith unto them, Whose is this image and superscription? They say unto him, Cæsar's. Then saith he unto them, Render therefore unto Cæsar the things which are Cæsar's; and unto God the things that are God's.'"

At this point he would pause breathtakingly – so he firmly believed – and whip the pocket-watch out of some inner sanctum several layers within his clothing. There was a certain amount of wriggling and bending, a coy bather slipping out of his bathing suit under an inadequate towel. He held the watch on high, the chain dangling, the coin catching the light, now become a street seller of dubious valuables. (The Reverend Goodchild was many different men.)

"This – *this* . . ." – he shook it, to emphasize his point – "is the *very coin of which Our Savior spoke!*"

He sounded exactly like a seller of fake religious relics, about to unload several hundredweight in pieces of the true cross. His knowledge of history was as shaky as his brain-rotting novels would have led you to believe: he appeared to believe that Julius Cæsar had been the Roman emperor during the life of Christ. Somewhere, in the dim – a perfect choice of adjective – recesses of his brain, he was doubtless convinced that Nero was one of the early popes. Corrupt as the rest of them, sourly indicating with his down-turned thumb that death was all that gladiators could expect when *he* was sitting in the Colosseum, he would be carried across from St. Peter's by whip-lashed slaves, their final indignity before the lions pounced.

"And if you study this coin, if you examine it closely, if you gaze upon the lineaments of this *Cæsar* . . ."

– contempt drenched the first three rows in almost Dr. Vaniah Odom-like quantities –

". . . what do you find?"

(He paused dramatically. This rhetorical question would shortly

331

be answered. The more shortsighted of his congregation would spend the interval in marveling at the image of all these Ancient Romans using pocket-watches as coinage, thinking that this probably explained why so many clocks and watches employed Roman numerals.)

The rhetorical question was answered.

"You find that Julius Cæsar *looks like a woman, and has got a big nose!*"

This obviously summed up all the decadence of the Roman Empire at its vilest for the Reverend Goodchild. He had not come to praise Cæsar.

(Mabel Peartree, whose nose had been an inspiration to the architect of the Flatiron Building, always looked poisonous at this point.

("*Et tu*, Reverend Goodchild?")

Strollers in the park on the afternoon of that same Sunday could be seen studying the statue of Reynolds Templeton Seabright, clearly firmly of the opinion that it was a depiction of Julius Cæsar, taking comfort from the fact that the nose was not big, and the fact that – despite the flowing toga – he did not look like a woman. The Reverend Goodchild's influence was not as overwhelming as he seemed to think. Thank heaven for that!

"Forget not in your speed, Antonius . . ."

– Julius Cæsar chattily instructed Mark Antony, every word audible to the large crowd gathered around him –

". . . To touch Calphurnia; for our elders say,
The barren touched in this holy chase,
Shake off their sterile curse."

You could imagine the crowds, months later, pointing her out in the street with loud whispers.

"That's the one! That's the one who's barren! That's the one with the sterile curse!"

Here was a man with a special skill in making his wife feel cherished and respected, Dr. Wolcott Ascharm Webster in a toga, with the Latin word for *Gesundheit!* ever on his lips. Calphurnia must have smiled gamely, and tried to look pleased.

Barren.

Teeth came into sight.

Sterile curse.

Grin widened.

No wonder Calphurnia had gone to such pains to forbid Julius Cæsar from leaving the house on the Ides of March. She knew this was exactly the way to make him do the opposite. Hadn't Brutus been a little bit suspicious when an unknown extra conspirator had slipped in to join them, one with a well-muffled face, a woman's voice, and the biggest dagger of all of them, the one who elbowed Casca aside to get at Julius Cæsar first, the one responsible for at least twenty-seven of the thirty-three stab wounds? (She'd seen pictures in the clouds. She'd seen fierce fiery warriors fighting in ranks and squadrons.)

How could you explain to the Reverend Goodchild that Julius Cæsar's likeness was not, in fact, on the coin, and that what he was displaying for public vilification – an intriguing reversal of Mark Antony with the body in the Forum: "If you have sniggers, prepare to unleash them now" – was an image of *Venus*. Roman ideas of beauty obviously differed markedly from modern taste. The thought of Mabel Peartree as the goddess of beauty, the mother of love, the queen of laughter, the mistress of the graces and of pleasure, was enough to set those of a nervous disposition whimpering.

He had rather spoiled the effect the last time he preached by accidentally opening the case of the pocket-watch. Of its repertoire of six tunes, "The Camptown Races" was probably the least appropriate for it to have played on this particular occasion ("Narcissus" would have been more acceptable), but everyone listened, serious-faced – perhaps searching for what the Reverend Goodchild tended to call "that which is of Symbolic import" (you could hear the capital "S") – as the first line tinkled tinnily out in All Saints': "De Camptown ladies sing dis song . . ." It was impossible not to think of the words, and she had seen the lips of the congregation moving in silent unison, like those of shy hymn-singers lacking confidence in their singing ability. The more uninhibited amongst them tapped their feet.

"Doo-dah! Doo-dah!" a loud voice added – quite tunefully – when it had finished. "De Camptown racetrack five miles long . . ."

This was Serenity Goodchild, the ever lumpish, ever troublesome granddaughter, with that obstinate expression of hers, as if she was – if she felt like it – gwine to run all night, gwine to run all day.

———

It was the existence of L. N. Fowler's phrenology head in his study that had given her the key to understanding Dr. Wolcott Ascharm Webster, of knowing him for what he was. Her first thought – she *knew* it was true as soon as she thought it – was that if phrenology (long discredited, as outdated as the clothes worn by Lucy Snowe, Jane Eyre, Marian Halcombe, or, for that matter, herself at the age of twenty, friends from childhood, Annie) ever showed the slightest hint of coming back into fashion, Dr. Wolcott Ascharm Webster would be at the forefront, cracking his knuckles and shaking his hands limply from the wrist, an athlete loosening up before an important race, poised for action on the nearest available head, his scrabbling fingers racing across the bumps like crabs on seacoast rocks scuttling toward the nearest pool.

Plop. Plop. Plop.

There was something raffishly disreputable now about phrenology, something that linked it vaguely with fortune-telling, tarot cards, palm-reading. Madame Sylvie's Human Hair Emporium and Salon de Beauty (it had been in business long enough) had probably once supplied (at vastly inflated prices) wigs with gigantically exaggerated Himalayas of bumps – *Amaze Your Phrenologist!*

Impress Your Friends! — in the areas it was thought most desirable to possess. She'd imagined stupid people demonstrating their stupidity by hammering themselves repeatedly on the head to create grossly swollen mounds in the areas that denoted intelligence. Now, the laying on of hands had something distinctly wash-them-now-and-keep-them-clean about it, the faint whiff of lingering perspiration from a (very) high summer chiropodist, gingerly handling corns and bunions, calluses slippery with sweatiness. She'd seen the haggard face of the Indian Woods Road chiropodist when she'd visited her optician last August. There he was, sitting shakily on a white-painted chair beside the front door, inhaling the fresh air as urgently as a firing-squad prisoner drawing on his last cigarette, working up his courage for another deep dive into the murky depths of the lower digits, a man whose nerves were visibly shattered by squelchy summer socks and stockings. Perhaps the Reverend Goodchild had booked in for an extra-long appointment after a good, brisk walk to Harlem and back in his thickest socks that he'd worn all week. That stricken face had interposed itself between her and *A HKL* as she peered mistily at Mr. Brczin's sight-test. The windows had been open in the heat, and she'd — suicidally — sniffed the air. No. Not a whiff of Reverend Goodchild. Things hadn't been quite as bad for the chiropodist as she had feared.

Fashion was what mattered most to Dr. Wolcott Ascharm Webster, if fashion meant more money. Mrs. Albert Comstock showed herself a slave to fashion in the hats with which she adorned her head (she paraded them like the saints in the windows of All Saints' paraded the instruments of their martyrdom, some hats bearing a disconcerting resemblance to some of the more outré instruments). Dr. Wolcott Ascharm Webster's similar enslavement revealed itself in what he chose to do with the insides of other people's heads (a form of martyrdom — alienated to death — unaccountably not given artistic expression by Elphinstone Dalhousie Barton in his otherwise comprehensive coverage of the subject).

Wherever there was a new fashion, wherever there was a new

idea (a faint stir, a distant rumor), there would Dr. Wolcott Ascharm Webster be, straining at the starting line, concentrating on hearing the crack of the pistol, wearing his white knee-length shorts (neatly ironed by Hilde Claudia: the results produced by the maid were not equal to his exacting standards) and white running-shirt (bearing the number 11 – for 11 Park Place, the address of his consulting room – front and back). In any race, Dr. Twemlow was the one to watch carefully. He was a keen amateur runner, and he and Dr. Brown – one of the Science masters at Otsego Lake Academy – often went out running together. They had the best-known knees in the neighborhood. Dr. Wolcott Ascharm Webster's eyes were keenly focused on the finishing tape. It was a short track, but its length was crowded with enthusiastic spectators, those at the back jumping up and down to achieve a better view. Hilde Claudia, Theodore, and Max were there, to cheer Papa on, prominent in the front row, waving little triangular flags (also neatly ironed): they knew what he would say if they were not present. In the race elbows would be utilized, opponents would be tripped, but no one would notice.

All that mattered was to win.

<hr />

She had experienced her first collapse at the age of twenty, not long after her father's death. The Bearded Ones – approvingly – had said it was grief. (*Ha!*) When the grief proved longer lasting than the black mourning clothes, and there appeared to be no remedy, it became an embarrassing problem. *A Remedy for Grief*: it sounded like something from a mediæval tale, something in which simples and dawn-gathered flowers featured. She already had this phrase in her list of titles, and had even written the first few pages of a story.

Anna listened carefully for a moment, locked the door behind her, & stepped out into the street, into the sunshine of a mild spring morning. . .

Several years went by, and The Bearded Ones gathered around her bed, the dark clothes, the beards – black, gray, white, ginger

(Dr. Cortelyou, a man unlikely to rise very high in his profession) — in a circle around the whiteness of the linen, like the elders of a tribe or a mass gathering of exorcists, their faces blurred and indistinct, braced to cast out demons. Some demons were named Mephostophilis or Beelzebub or Asmodeus. The names of her demons varied, and The Bearded Ones called them out, as if to lure them into daylight from the darkness. Sometimes they were named Neurasthenia. Sometimes they were named Hysteria or Dread or a variety of other names. They were exceeding fierce. They would not go away. Tobias had driven Asmodeus away with the awful stench caused by burning the liver and heart of a fish. You'd have thought that the smell of The Bearded Ones would have had the same effect, that smoky, sweaty smell, of cigars and pipe tobacco, of grubby old bank notes and dirty coins.

For a young woman to dream of a physician, denotes that she is sacrificing her beauty in engaging in frivolous pastimes. If she is sick and thus dreams, she will have sickness or worry, but will soon overcome them, unless the physician appears very anxious, and then her trials may increase, ending in loss and sorrow.

"The female is exhibiting various manifestations of hysteria. Note, gentlemen, the obvious agitation as I approach her and take hold of her arm. Perhaps, Dr. Severance, you would care to take hold of the other arm. Ignore her attempts to pull away."

They would join hands like Mrs. Alexander Diddecott's Spiritualist Circle, they would sway from side to side, they would chant, they would hum, they would lull her to sleep and forgetfulness.

"Sweetly she sleeps, my Alice fair . . ."

— Fair! —

". . . Her cheeks on the pillow pressed,
Sweetly she sleeps, while her Saxon . . ."

— Saxon! —

337

". . . hair,
Like sunlight, streams o'er her breast.
Hush! Let her sleep! I pray, sweet breeze,
Breathe low on the maple bough.
Hush! Bright bird, on her window trees!
For sweetly she sleepeth now . . ."

And when she sleepeth, she dreameth.

The dreams were inescapable, filling the nighttime skies like the clouds in daytime.

Dr. Severance — who was always spoken of as Dr. Severance of Staten Island, as if it were his title — was the one who pounced first, and she was carried across to his Staten Island clinic on the ferry in a hailstorm, like the body in an out-of-season Venetian funeral.

Dr. Severance tried electrotherapy.

Dr. Severance tried baths (hot).

Dr. Severance tried baths (cold).

Dr. Severance tried massage.

This went on intermittently for about three years. She saw him so much in echoing glass-roofed, white-tiled interiors, so much through the mist of the steam (during hot baths), and the mist of her breath (during cold baths), that she began to think of him not as a doctor but as the proprietor of a bathhouse or a gymnasium with a strict regimen. Around his neck, instead of a stethoscope, a brightly polished whistle — its shiny surface beaded and misted with condensation — hung on the end of a cord, dully visible through the hairs of his beard.

Peep, peep!

Dr. Severance began to blow his whistle, regular blasts like a system of code, running on the spot as if to urge her into activity by his own good example.

"Arms down for The Beards!"

Peep, peep!

338

Down-down-down!
"Out for The Bosom!"
Peep, peep!
Out-out-out!
"Beards!"
Peep, peep.
"Bosom!"
Peep, peep!
Down-down-down!
Out-out-out!

> "Speak with respect and honour
> Both of The Beard and The Beard's owner."

The arms moved down-down-down, like those of herself and Charlotte, carefully co-ordinated as they worshiped The Sibyl with servile slave-girl bowing movements, bowed down before The Beards, bowed down before The Bosom. They spoke the words in unison, a congregation chanting the responses in an act of worship; they moved their arms in unison, and they bowed down at the same angle of agonized abasement. They knew their place.

> "Speak with respect and honour
> Both of The Bosom and The Bosom's owner."

They wouldn't dream of speaking in any other way. A different tone of voice would be shockingly inappropriate to all right-minded people, and give rise to appalled and disapproving comment.

Out-out-out!
Peep, peep!
"Again!"
Peep, peep!
"Again!"
Youth!

Pant!
Health!
Pant!
Vigor!
Pant!

In strict regimented lines, across wooden floors scrubbed as white and clean as the deck of a sailing ship, the gymnasts – perfectly synchronized – performed their drill, swinging the Indian clubs in front of them, behind them, above their heads, like jugglers lacking in confidence, reluctant to release their implements. The lines of the floorboards stretched away beneath them, the lines of the wall bars on either side of them, the hissing gasoliers cast down a garish, flickering light: all of them – the floorboards, the wall bars, the gasoliers – narrowing and fading into the distance as far as the eye could see. They were the circus performers in one of the three rings: the Elphinstone ring, or the Dalhousie ring, sufficiently important to avoid relegation to the Barton ring. The strong man stood in front of them in his leopardskin, his right arm upraised, the weights at the ends of the bar as shiny and black and spherical as balloons lifting him up on tiptoe. She was there; blinking in the flaring lights, unable to see the faces of the audience tiered up into the tented interior, Phineas T. ("T" is for Tremendous! "T" is for Terrific! "T" is for Titanic!) Barnum's latest sensation, the Bearded Lady on display.

The gymnasts were like the diagrams to illustrate the semaphore alphabet, arms thrust firmly out in precise positions, a flag in each hand, the little figures in naval uniform like her brother, Ben, drawn over and over. The two-color flags were divided from corner to corner, creating a triangle of red and a triangle of yellow. Perhaps Hilde Claudia, Theodore, and Max, with their triangular flags, were passing coded tactical advice to their bearded leader.

"Cortelyou approaching from left-hand side! Severance pouncing on your right! Twemlow attempting a sprint!"

The arms moved with jerky precision, like those of a mechanical toy, manufactured to produce certain repeated actions.

Charlotte had told her that the Pinkerton coat of arms was *a rose gules, stalked and leafed, vert.* Colors had special names in heraldry. *Gules* — there came "The Eve of St. Agnes" again — was red.

(In the windows of All Saints', St. Agnes was accompanied by a lamb on the same Brobdingnagian scale as Pharaildis's hens. It was not a little lamb the size of Mary's, not a lamb one would wish to follow one to school, not a lamb to make children laugh and play: it was a lamb from the island of Dr. Moreau, a lamb for screams and flight.)

Vert — of course — was green, *sable* was black.

ON A FIELD, SABLE, THE LETTER A. GULES.

That was Hester Prynne's gravestone at the end of *The Scarlet Letter,* and she had imagined a long, slanting field — something barren and unplowed — stretching away to leafless winter hedges, with an emblematic scarlet letter *A,* huge as a billboard, catching the last light of a setting sun, the one ever-glowing point of light gloomier than the shadow. Because they were the last words of the novel, the capital letters standing above the blank whiteness of the rest of the final page, she always thought of the gravestone as standing amidst untrodden snow, snow covering the mourning sable of the field, a grave that no one visited.

Charlotte had asked Linnaeus to draw the coat of arms for her, the red rose with six leaves, and the motto beneath it.

The Pinkerton motto was *Post nubila sol.*

After clouds, sunshine.

———❧———

The reader of the clouds followed Dr. Severance of Staten Island, but he brought no sunshine.

Dr. Wolcott Ascharm Webster tried electrotherapy.

Dr. Wolcott Ascharm Webster tried baths (hot).

Dr. Wolcott Ascharm Webster tried baths (cold).

Dr. Wolcott Ascharm Webster tried massage.

Poughkeepsie was clearly a place throbbing with Spirit voices, numinous with the beyondness of things. You headed north, up the Hudson, and you were drawn mysteriously toward it by a power beyond your control. First there was Andrew Jackson Davis, the famous "Seer of Poughkeepsie," and then — as if that wasn't enough excitement for one place, a place of sensitive, scholarly girls attempting to concentrate on higher learning — there was Dr. Wolcott Ascharm Webster and the Webster Nervine Asylum, his clinic for extended stays. Like Andrew Jackson Davis he seemed to receive communications from another world, hear voices that no one else could hear. He certainly didn't hear *her* voice at times. What he did do was to, somehow — what was the word to use? — *encroach* upon the areas that belonged to Dr. Twemlow, her medical doctor.

(The areas belonged to *her*, to *her*.)

Dr. Twemlow — his name always made her think that he ought to have some slight speech impediment (who on earth was *she*, to t-t-talk about sp-p-peech imp-p-pediments, to *att-tt-ttempt* to t-t-talk?) — faded, retreated, before the irresistible advance of Dr. Wolcott Ascharm Webster. If she had a stutter, then he could have a lisp. If it *was* a lisp. Lisps were for "s" sounds (weren't they?), but what was the term for an inability to pronounce "r" sounds? For want of knowing the correct term — perhaps it *was* "lisp" — she continued to think of Dr. Twemlow as a lisper. (Cruel to have an unpronounceable "s" in the term that defined the condition.) His lisp, like a misspelled limp, hindered him as he staggered along in the race with Dr. Wolcott Ascharm Webster. *He*, the athletic running partner of Dr. Brown! *He*, rarely without a fine sheen of sweat — Millie tended to complain — and a smell of embrocation — she liked this even less — about him.

No, it *wasn't* "lisp." It was something to do with having a too-short tongue. Poor depwived short-tongued Dr. Twemlow, a man quite incapable of producing a juicy raspberry. On some days — looking wearily across the room at winsomely evasive, fearsomely insistent, Millie — it must be the sound he longed to produce more than any other as a summation of all he felt most deeply about her. How he must crave to evolve into one of the long-tongued! To spring into action with the most resonant of uninhibited letter "r"s, the wettest and most spectacular of raspberries! It wasn't just the desperate desire to produce the sound that conveyed the contempt that he — the verb was wonderfully appropriate — *longed* to pronounce. The creation of a dramatically drenching fall of spray — cruelly denied him — upon the face of his adversary, a Niagara Falls of derision (derrrrision!), would have been an essential part of the pleasure.

The red and yellow triangular flags were a blur as Hilde Claudia, Theodore, and Max — leaping up and down on tiptoe in their excitement — signaled success for Dr. Wolcott Ascharm Webster.

"Twemlow dwopping back! Twemlow keeling over! Twemlow withdwawing fwom the wace!"

Twemlow cwushed!

Twemlow wouted!

Twemlow overthwown!

The reader of the clouds examined her face and eyes in particular detail, as if assessing her suitability for his enthusiasm for hypnotism that followed, one of a long line of enthusiasms. If you wished to know what Dr. Wolcott Ascharm Webster had been reading recently, you did not examine his library list (though his carefully locked bookcases would have yielded clues); you studied his changing treatments of her. He commented on her pockmarks (smallpox when she was seven), and told her that her eyes were unusually dry, muttering the phrase "difficulties with tears" to himself. He tended to talk out loud as he examined her. It was not to explain things to her; patients were not in the confidence of their doctors in such matters, not a party to the mystery of their art. It was, indeed, surprising that doctors did not talk to each other (and to themselves) exclusively in Latin, the language of The Bearded Ones.

(Dr. Wycherley treated Alfred Hardie like a human curiosity as he inspected him for the signs of madness. Like Dr. Wolcott

Ascharm Webster – though Dr. Webster had much the more appropriate namesake – he had the name of an English dramatist. John Webster wrote about death and murder. John Webster wrote about madness.

("*Nullum magnum ingenium sine mixtura dementiae,*" Dr. Wycherley intoned as he examined Alfred, a man casting a spell, or drawing out demons. Here was a doctor who had the right idea, the correct sense of the dignity due to his profession. *Dementiae* didn't sound too promising, another demon unleashed from the darkness.

(When he chose not to utilize Latin, he employed multi-syllabled technical terms, equally obfuscating for the uninitiated, the beardlessly unworthy.

(Dr. Wycherley asked Alfred about his headaches, and about his inability to sleep. He asked him about his nightly visions and voices. Dr. Wycherley sounded just like Dr. Wolcott Ascharm Webster, the two dramatists peopling their stages with crowds of lunatics, derangedly speaking the words that they had written for them.)

Dr. Wolcott Ascharm Webster spoke as if he were in a lecture hall, expounding upon his discoveries to serried ranks of the behatted and bebearded rising in rows above him, or as if he were Dr. Seward in *Dracula* – what better comparison? He, also, was the owner of a private lunatic asylum – dictating his diary into a phonograph. When the public tired of the voice of Enrico Caruso, they could listen to Dr. Wolcott Ascharm Webster, tapping their feet to the infectious rhythm of his sentences. He assumed highly dramatic postures in front of his audience, as if frozen at the thrilling climax of an opera, or posing – with an expression of piercing yet caring intelligence (this took considerable concentration) – for a new painting by Thomas Eakins, *The Webster Clinic*. He'd make sure that potential patients heard all about it. *As painted by Thomas Eakins*, he'd trumpet in his advertisements, a rather racy endorsement (there was something a little – ahem – *controversial* about some of Thomas Eakins's paintings, and some of his personal proclivities), but it might well attract a more artistic –

and therefore more profitably neurotic — clientèle. Mrs. Italiaander had a painting by Thomas Eakins, depicting her late husband among a group of his fellow architects, all of them holding models of buildings they had designed, and looking like a race of giants. He was the fourth one in from the left.

"The female has difficulties with tears. Note the dryness of the eyes . . ."

Dr. Wolcott Ascharm Webster pointed with a histrionically angled forefinger, allowing ample time for Thomas Eakins to register the play of light and shadow across his noble features. There was a distinct sensation of strain in holding that slight compassionate smile for long periods.

She had made a note of the title — thank you, Oh Bearded One — in these words. *Difficulties With Tears*. This ought to be a novel, like *The Life Class*.

At first, as it had been with Dr. Severance, it had been like working on some weakness of her body, building up the strength of some frail consumptive, an Elizabeth Barrett Browning of the wall bars, curls dangling upside down as she hung suspended. "How do I love thee?" — three forward rolls on the mats — "Let me count the ways" — backward somersault on the beam — "I love thee to the depth and breadth and height" — long forward swoop on the rings, gentler glide back — "My soul can reach, when feeling out of sight" — vigorous run up to the vaulting horse, a thump of the feet on the boards, a spring into the air — "For the ends of Being and ideal Grace" — "Pant, pant, pant!" A struggle for breath. Perhaps being ill was the only way she had to show that she was a woman — frail, delicate, well-bred, too gentle for the rough world — when her body failed to illustrate the acceptable criteria for ticking. That moustache certainly gave pause for thought, pencil points hovering indecisively in the pretick posture.

Cough.

Sigh.

Look pale.

Be submissive.

Be reticent.

Be modest.

Be polite.

Be *grateful*.

Up into the air, out to the side, up into the air, out to the side: she swung the Indian clubs, synchronized with the other gymnasts stretching out in front of her, behind her, either side of her, stretching to infinity, like the floorboards, the wall bars, the gasoliers — not thinking, not seeing: there was no need to think, no need to see — part of a symmetrical pattern like the shapes viewed through a kaleidoscope, its end twisted in the hand, not a human being at all, really.

After (briefly) following in the footsteps of Dr. Severance, Dr. Wolcott Ascharm Webster had decided — he declared it like an Arctic explorer about to cross a white untracked wilderness — to enter the inner self. Long had he labored on the conscious — this was the impression he liked to give — and now it was time to take a deep breath, and plunge into the sub-conscious, the hidden chaos beneath. Instead of travelling to Poughkeepsie for short stays at the clinic, Alice now traveled the short distance across Longfellow Park to his consulting room at 11 Park Place. Every week, on Wednesday — she thought of it as Ash Wednesday — she arrived at ten o'clock in the morning, and stayed for fifty-five minutes. The House of the Interpreter. That was what she thought to herself, Christian pausing on his journey to the Celestial City. Sunday mornings were for the Reverend Goodchild, and Wednesday mornings were for Dr. Wolcott Ascharm Webster. It was as if Wednesday had become another day of worship, the day on which she bowed down and worshiped her God, confessing her sins with most Catholic-like humility. Humiliation certainly came into it. Would fifty-five minutes give her enough time? *Forgive me, Dr. Wolcott Ascharm Webster* . . . He probably relied upon her fees to pay the — considerable — cost of his brandy and cigars. He looked at Alice, and saw candlelight glinting on cut glass, a slight unsteadiness in his walk, smoke curling toward the ceiling.

He wore – it was his uniform for work – a black business suit, a shirt with a stiffly starched collar, and a black bow tie. It was like being treated by a waiter or a department-store floorwalker temporarily corralled behind a counter. He should be standing behind his desk as she entered, leaning slightly forward, his weight upon the tips of his fingers and thumbs.

"Might I recommend?" he should be saying. "This is proving to be *very* popular with our more discriminating customers," "Might I have the pleasure?" or "It is no trouble at all, Madam." She should have a list in her hand, knowing precisely what it was she had come to buy, drawing a firm line through each product as she bought it.

<hr />

It had started with hypnotism. This was the product on offer, and – although it was not on her list – she had bought it. It was Dr. Wolcott Ascharm Webster's first enthusiasm – the first *new* enthusiasm of which she was aware: electrotherapy, the baths (hot), the baths (cold), and the massage had probably all once been enthusiasms – and her initial thoughts, as he sat her so that she was facing him, their knees almost touching, enveloped in a fish-smelling miasma, were that he was going to try phrenology after all. It seemed to be the only thing he had not tried, and would have been a logical next stage: the inner self read from the outer manifestations. The cold skull would be warmed again, the undulations traced and interpreted.

When he produced the pocket-watch from his vest pocket – it was done with a consciously elegant little professional flourish, the surgeon producing his scalpel – she thought, for just a few seconds, that it was her dead father's watch, and it spun and glittered as if in the hands of the Reverend Goodchild.

". . . I come down dah wid my hat caved in.

347

Doo-dah! Doo-dah!
I go back home wid a pocket full of tin.
Oh! doo-dah day!. . ."

She would sit motionless, with her hair held away from her forehead, as if feeling for the impression left by a watch-chain, by a coin: the word *CÆSAR*, worn smooth like one of the half-erased words on the phrenology head, the profile of Venus facing right, the slumped, defeated figures of the enslaved man and woman. She became a piece of melted wax, a sealed document enclosed within her body by the pressure of his signet ring, pressed upon her by his fisted hand. Well-flexed fingertips would start to push their way through her hair, feeling for her scalp, as she held her breath, her eyes blind, like her face as a small girl in the statue in the park, gazing out and seeing nothing. *Spirituality, Faith, Trust, Wonder, Hope, Expectancy, Thoughtfulness, Grief.* Each emotion would fleetingly blossom upon her face — flickering and dying — as his fingers moved across the hidden areas of her mind, the contours of her head caressingly fondled in intense silence as he played upon her head as upon a piano. This would be how he would think of it. The instruction book — *How to Learn Phrenology* by L. N. Fowler — would be propped up with its lower edge on the back of her bowed neck, a book of sheet music propped up on a music rack.

(Mama's piano was a Chickering, in memory of Louis Moreau Gottschalk.

(A single coin would not suffice as payment for his valuable time, the solitary clunk into the metal mug held thrustingly forward by the importunate beggar. A jingling pocket full of tin was more what he had in mind, and the coins would not bear the name *CÆSAR*. He'd be *very* keen on that pocket full of tin. That would definitely appeal. He'd doo-dah, doo-dah all day long if he had that. Crisp new notes would be even more acceptable.

(His face replaced the face on the front of the sheet music she had taken upstairs, the copperplate lettering of Mama's maiden name – *Lucinda Brouwer* – faded by sunlight, the ink become a barely legible pale brown, the words written centuries ago. If she tried to play music, his would be the face watching her, immediately in front of hers like a reflection with a beard. Alice's mother, like Mrs. Albert Comstock, like Mrs. Alexander Diddecott – like, for that matter, Mrs. Humphry Ward or Mrs. Henry Wood – was always known by her husband's name: she was Mrs. Lincoln Pinkerton. Alice was unaware that it had ever occurred to her – as a small girl – that her mother might actually have a first name. She never heard her father address her mother by her Christian name. She had come across the name *Lucinda Brouwer* in books, and on music, and had asked her mother who this person was.

("That was me," – even then Alice had noticed the use of the past tense – her mother had replied, and for the first time Alice had been confronted with the idea of her mother's being Lucinda Brouwer, this person in the past who had been entirely absorbed within Lincoln Pinkerton. She had once had a name, a girl's name, a name of her own.)

Almost, she had lowered her head in front of him, bowing, offering him her head for his hands, a patient inviting him to inspect her hair for infestation. She had a picture in her mind of phrenology charts and phrenology heads, and pictured her own head divided – for his convenience – into labeled sections, like the charts in butchers' shops illustrating the different cuts of meat on the carcass of a cow or a pig all ready for the knife. He would produce his sharp little knives, and, Hamlet-like, brood awhile above her skull, planning his first incision, holding his scalpel like a ravenous Sunday luncheon diner, sensually prolonging the moment before his first crammed mouthful. Her own hands remained decorously folded in her lap.

It was the first of her ten o'clock appointments, and then – as now – there had been snow upon the ground. She was facing the window, and glanced over Dr. Wolcott Ascharm Webster's shoulders, and across the road outside, taking a last, deep breath before submerging her head under water. The water would be frozen; she would see her own reflection moving up toward her from under the ice. She must have been very prompt – doubtless driven by her uncontrollable eagerness – because the clock in the waiting room started to chime the hour as she sat down.

One . . .

First the hall.

Two . . .

Then the waiting room.

Three . . .

Then the consulting room.

In the park, snow lay upon the marble head and the marble shoulders of Albert Comstock (enough to bury a football team had accumulated in the cleavage of his buttocks), and she was conscious of averting her eyes from the ghastly sight. There might be incalculable and highly dangerous repercussions if you gazed upon such a sight in the presence of a trained alienist, one capable of discerning the secret, hidden things of the mind. Not to mention the increased pulse rate, the whimpers of desire, the drooling. There was snow upon the heads and shoulders of the statues of all the other Bearded Ones. She could see them clearly through the branches of the bare, leafless trees: Reynolds Templeton Seabright, John Randel, Jr. . . .

There was silence in the room. Dr. Wolcott Ascharm Webster did not choose to speak until he had a rapt and total stillness – *Five . . . Six . . .* – and measured his valuable time so exactly that she should not be given one second for which she had not paid.

To see statues in dreams, signifies estrangement from a loved one. Lack of energy will cause you disappointment in realizing wishes.

Nine . . .

Ten . . .

Then the pause, always that pause before the silence that followed. She was urging the hour onward, hoping to hear the chimes of eleven o'clock follow, and know that the fifty-five minutes were up, that she had – in fact – overrun her allocated time by five minutes, and should no longer be there. He'd be hurrying her out the door. Other loonies would be lined up, waiting. When G. G. Schiffendecken arrived in Longfellow Park, his waiting room was remarkably similar to that of Dr. Wolcott Ascharm Webster, and was probably modeled upon it, though – of course – you heard fewer screams of agony from the dentist's consulting room beyond, fewer sounds of metallic implements gouging and clattering.

Dr. Wolcott Ascharm Webster's hand was cold as he briefly touched her face. It was now ten o'clock. The treatment could commence. She could have her fifty-five minutes, starting *now*, on the last chime of ten, not the first. Dr. Wolcott Ascharm Webster was clearly a man capable of sharp practice, cutting corners when it suited him. Perhaps she should carry on counting, to ensure that he did not give short measure, count out all the three thousand, three hundred seconds – she'd worked this out the night before – for which she would be paying.

One . . .

Two . . .

Three . . .

There was snow on his head, on his shoulders, in his beard. He was made of marble; all night the snow had fallen upon him in the darkness. She was in a Mozart opera where something unaccountable was occurring, and Donna Anna was about to be gripped by the icy-cold hand of the statue of her father, the Commendatore, and dragged down into the depths. When he – the Commendatore, the doctor – leaned forward to make a request (*"Rispondimi: verrai tu a cenar meco?"*) she expected his breath to be clouded white, and – concentrating so much upon this – she had not really heard what he was saying, at first. He repeated what he had said, and it was then that she understood she was to be hypnotized.

Eleven . . .

Twelve . . .

Thirteen . . .

Would he say, "Look me in the white of the eyes"?

Would she be compelled to gaze into that unwritten-on blankness?

Would he count from one to ten — the counting starting all over again — as if he had administered a knockout punch?

Would he count backward, drawing her into the zero, the silence, at the end?

Behind her, the glass-covered engravings of The Bearded Ones leaned away from the wall at an angle, a gallery of hirsute, scowl-faced Mrs. Twemlows. They were all straining forward for a good view, holding their breaths, anxious not to miss a moment of this enlightening lecture. Their beards and their glum expressions demonstrated their intelligence.

Scribble, scribble, scribble.

Dark-clothed children with skates and toboggans were streaming through the gates, making the first footprints in the overnight snowfalls, the untouched whiteness that stretched down toward the lake.

To dream of finding yourself in a snowstorm, denotes sorrow and disappointment in failure to enjoy some long-expected pleasure. There always follows more or less discouragement after this dream.

<hr>

The doctor stood up, partially drew the curtains closed (it seemed odd to draw the curtains in daytime, a man hiding something) — the light dimmed, the cries of children became muffled — as if he had noticed her looking outside, her lack of complete attention.

She was to be hypnotized.

That would make her behave herself, do as she was told.

(*"Verrai?"*)

All the time, she had been aware of the children's voices from outside, a lingerer on the edge of the schoolyard, just as — in summer — she could hear the children playing under the chestnut trees as she listened from the schoolroom. Childhood — faint and far away – seemed like something she'd once heard about, not something that she'd experienced.

This had been . . .

How long ago?

There had been the other, discarded, methods first, so it would be less than seven years ago. Between six and seven years.

However long ago the precise time, she knew that it had been the time of the great rage for *Trilby*. Perhaps Dr. Wolcott Ascharm Webster saw himself as Svengali.

Trilby was fiercely denounced from the pulpit by the Reverend Goodchild and from most other places by Mrs. Goodchild and Mrs. Albert Comstock; in a rapidly changing world, certain things were comfortingly reliable. It was one novel among many (Mrs. Goodchild and Mrs. Albert Comstock were united in bigotry, if not in affection) that they had vehemently attacked as immoral and corrupting. Judging by their pronouncements, they generally preferred to attack literature or art from a position of total ignorance, as this freed their minds (those dubious organs) to focus more powerfully on the essentials.

After following this usual method of condemning a novel without having actually having read it, Mrs. Albert Comstock then – in brave and dauntless mood – read it and suffered a disconcerting sea-change. (She was certainly something rich and strange.) The portrayal of Svengali so comprehensively confirmed some of her favorite prejudices that she magisterially declared that it was, after all, a "very moral sort of book, really, when you think about it, as I – personally – have done." She was a mistress of the incisive literary judgment, her scalpel-like mind dissecting texts with a rare discrimination, laying bare their inner essence to the wonder of scholars, who felt humbled and abashed by her perspicacity.

She signaled her approval by attending a performance of the play at the Garden Theatre. She had been particularly impressed by the use of tableaux in the production, in which the actors and actresses had – at various dramatic moments – frozen for a moment, players holding a significant pose in a game of charades, in order to reproduce some of George Du Maurier's better-known illustrations from the novel. (Cue for applause from the better-informed members of the audience, Mrs. Albert Comstock ever to the fore. She'd probably shouted out the page numbers, so that everyone in the theatre should be fully aware of her mastery of the text, exclaiming at her effortless expertise.) There was nothing remarkable about such realizations to Alice. She had lived for years inside some of Sir John Tenniel's most imaginative drawings, surrounded by all the grotesqueries from *Alice's Adventures in Wonderland* and *Through the Looking-Glass*. She had received a comprehensive description of *Trilby*, laced not just with the usual exhaustive account of the costumes and hairstyles (plot came a poor second to these), but with all Mrs. Albert Comstock's gratified horror at the portrayal of Svengali. Mrs. Albert Comstock had felt threatened, demeaned, degraded: she had thoroughly enjoyed herself. There hadn't been so much shuddering since the last time Othello had kissed Desdemona, when only the exercise of the strictest self-control had prevented a booming "*Uuurgh!*" – the same sound as Charlotte's succinct summing-up of Sobriety Goodchild – from echoing around the theatre and the adjoining streets. Some coat of arms – you felt – should have been hoisted outside the theatre to mark this signal honor and emblazon the name of Comstock upon the night sky: sausages *sable* upon a steak *gules*. *Cibi Comstockianae sinceritas servitiumque.* Albert Comstock – the Colossus of the Cucumber, the Titan of the Tomato – had not been one to overlook any opportunity for publicizing his stores.

Sensing – in her turn – a marketing opportunity, and climbing ponderously onto a bandwagon, Mrs. Albert Comstock prevailed upon the head butcher at Comstock's Comestibles to launch a Trilby Sausage, with special window displays in all the branches to ensure its success. Alice pictured windows crammed with lines of sausages, all of them swaying in unison and singing "Ben Bolt" at the tops of their shrill, sausagy voices. The bigger stores in Longfellow Park, like many of its more prominent inhabitants, had a keen eye for elaborate window dressing. In the same month Mrs. Albert Comstock had graced a *Trilby* musical evening at Mrs. Alexander Diddecott's, no doubt smiling with effortful motherly pride as her daughter Myrtle played "Rosamunde" and *"L'Adieu"* (Schubert's life encompassed numerous tragedies), as Max Webster (then just beginning his career as the Infant Phenomenon of Longfellow Park) sang *"Au clair de la lune"* and *"Plaisir d'amour,"* as Dr. Wolcott Ascharm Webster played a Hungarian Dance on his banjo, as Mabel Peartree (serious competition for the sausages, and containing even more teeth) sang "Ben Bolt" . . .

Those who had been present were heard to say that it would take them a long time to forget it.

Perhaps at the next *Trilby* musical evening – this time at Château Comstock – after he had delighted everyone with his prowess on the banjo, Dr. Wolcott Ascharm Webster might contribute to the theme of the evening by hypnotizing Mrs. Albert Comstock. It would be like conquering a mountain. He could borrow the triangular flags from Hilde Claudia, Theodore, and Max, and plant them firmly at Mrs. Albert Comstock's summit as a symbol of his achievement.

"Listen to my voice," he'd say.

Grudgingly, she'd listen.

"Be still."

She'd be still, assuming the posture of a pole-axed hippopotamus.

"Empty your mind of all thought."

That wouldn't take her long.

"Sleep."

The snores would start, and the never-at-rest chandeliers of 5 Hampshire Square would tinkle piercingly.

Charlotte had brought Alice copies of *Harper's Magazine* as each installment of *Trilby* was published, discreetly smuggled into the house doubly concealed, the magazine inside sheet music, the sheet music inside her music case. This was the time before the sea-change, and Mrs. Albert Comstock had just loudly announced that she had cancelled her subscription to *Harper's* in protest against their publishing such material. All over Longfellow Park pens were dipped into inkwells, as — in their neatest handwriting — genteel ladies, who had heard what Mrs. Albert Comstock had said, discreetly wrote to *open* subscriptions.

Mrs. Albert Comstock and the Goodchilds were — as Oliver and the genteel ladies (starting to chafe a little at the restrictions imposed by gentility) had long discovered — a very good source of ideas of what to read when inspiration flagged. The same genteel ladies, wearing their most impenetrable veils, set out in groups of two and three (like wagons in a wagon train, they felt safer traveling in groups) to inspect plays, paintings, and sculpture denounced by the forces of Comstock (Anthony and Mrs.) and Goodchild (Reverend and Mrs.). Such denunciations had the power of three stars in a tourist guidebook. *Mrs. Albert Comstock: "I found it utterly repugnant!"* or *Mrs. Goodchild: "My — whatsit? — disapprobification . . ."* — an ambitious attempt at eight syllables here — *". . . is total!"* hoisted in large letters around the façade of a New York theatre should be enough to get the lines forming, fights breaking out as the number of Mrs. Goodchild's syllables increased. Her righteous fury would drive her ever onward to the heady heights of ten, twelve, fourteen syllables, and complete incomprehensibility, whatdoyoumacalliting until steam came shrieking out of her ears.

For a young woman to dream that she attends a play, foretells that she will be courted by a genial friend, and will marry to further her prospects and pleasure seeking. If there is trouble in getting to and from the play, or discordant and hideous scenes, she will be confronted with many displeasing surprises.

The more his mother and Mrs. Goodchild attacked certain books — whatever it was they attacked, whether books, paintings, or sculptures — the more Oliver sought them out. He seemed to treat their virulent rantings as thoughtful suggestions for his library list (not that the local library would risk purchasing any titles that might be thought controversial), obtained copies of them somehow or other, and carried them around with him at all times, the titles prominently on display, flaunting them in the way his mother displayed her teeth. *The Picture of Dorian Gray*, *Trilby*, Huysmans, Zola, Baudelaire (anything, in fact, vaguely French); all were sought out. He had held out *Against Nature* so that the title was clearly visible, rather in the way that Mabel Peartree held her sheet music. Dr. Wolcott Ascharm Webster had chuckled away about this to the Reverend Goodchild in that sophisticated way he had.

"It must be the Comstock training coming out, even in Oliver," he said, thinking of the window displays at Comstock's Comestibles, "to have the goods on display so clearly identified so that we know what they are."

"*Against Nature!*" The Reverend Goodchild was quick to identify that he had understood the joke.

(Pause for snigger.)

"*Against Nature!*"

(Another snigger.)

"You can say that again!"

(So Dr. Wolcott Ascharm Webster said it again.)

Alice had struggled not to intervene with a helpful clarification. "It doesn't mean *Against Nature* in *that* sense." That's what she ought to have said, helpful as ever. "Why do you open your big mouths when you don't even know what you're talking about?" That's *certainly* what she ought to have said. It was something she ought to say, loudly, at regular intervals, striking out with great force for added emphasis. She was always furious with herself when she did not say the words she was prompted to speak. *Say it! Say it!* the inner voice hissed fiercely at her, but she seldom said it. She spent much of her time, consequently, in a state of rage. Christopher Marlowe had undoubtedly had her in mind when Wrath made his appearance in *Doctor Faustus*, yet another Deadly Sin ticked on her list of shortcomings. Seven were barely enough to cope. She ran up and down the world with a case of rapiers, wounding herself when she could get none to fight withal. *I was born in hell.* That was what Wrath said, the blood dripping from his many self-inflicted wounds.

Oliver must have been only eleven or twelve when *The Picture of*

Dorian Gray had been published. It was ostentatiously seized upon, and he took great care to point out meaningfully to anyone he came across that he had the same birthday as Dorian Gray. (He did: November the tenth.) He treated it rather like a Mrs. Beeton's *Book of Household Management* for behavior, and the epigrams came thick and fast. He was — as in many other things — exceptional in this, as he was not from a family in which epigrams flowed freely. Albert Comstock had been ambitious when venturing upon a word of more than three syllables, and Mrs. Albert Comstock's bon mots — always rapturously received — included such candidates for Bartlett's *Familiar Quotations* as "Life is a funny business, isn't it?" and "It's really annoying when feathers cling to black velvet." Having half-heard the word "aphorism," she referred to these gem-like utterances as "Arthurisms" (the capital letter was clearly audible), under the impression that the term had been coined to commemorate some great wit of that name. Hard luck, Oscar Wilde, crushed into nothingness! She had probably made discreet inquiries, attempting to trace Arthur, and lure him to Hampshire Square, to dazzle delighted guests with his effortless quips. "Foreigners are not to be trusted" and "Poor people are happier than we are most of the time. I know this to be a fact." This was the sort of thing she had in mind, the sort of thing she said herself, the sort of thing she said over and over again. She had maintained this standard for years, flinging out the Arthurisms with great wet slaps. It was exactly like watching the zoo-keeper hurling the fish to walruses at feeding time: the frantic excitement, the honking sounds, the white whiskers and gleaming tusks, the faint smell of decay.

Alice had seen Oliver, when he was about seventeen — with lubricious looks and overemphatic secretiveness — carrying an obviously French, and disturbingly large, volume under the alarmed eyes of his mother.

(*French!*

(You could see the revulsion in her eyes, the frantic search for her umbrella.

(*French!*

(She'd rap its knuckles. She'd give it a good crack across its head.)

"That is a *cookery* book," Alice had whispered fiercely to him when he walked past her, and he had been blithely unconcerned.

"That had occurred to me," he said. "But Mama doesn't realize. In any case, there is a decidedly risqué recipe for *moules marinières* on page forty-seven." In a louder voice he had added, "Ah yes, the serious and even terrible responsibility writers incur when they send out to the world books full of pernicious and poisonous suggestion to contaminate the minds that have hitherto been clean and undiseased. I am a contaminated creature, trained to perfection in the lax morals and prurient literature of my day."

He had sounded quite pleased, particularly when it made his Mama shudder so spectacularly, like a gigantic earthquake-imperiled blancmange. He was determined to be the Duc Jean des Esseintes of Longfellow Park, æstheticism incarnate, and was following the instructions in *Against Nature* to the letter, with such single-minded thoroughness that it was as if this volume – also – had been a sort of cookery book. If she could find herself in Christopher Marlowe – and in numerous other volumes – he could certainly find himself in Huysmans. The Misses Isserliss were fortunate not to have had their venerable and dignified old tortoise – Septimus – kidnapped, and its shell painted gold. Oliver would have attached it to a gold-linked leash, as finely wrought as the links of a watch-chain, and gone for slow, stately walks, promenading with a sunflower in one hand, and the end of the leash in the other, though – come to think of it – it was highly unlikely that the Duc Jean des Esseintes would ever have ventured out into the swoon-inducing inhospitable vastness of the open air. He was totally *against* Nature, and kept to his room, his bed – drapes firmly drawn – as determinedly as any delicate invalid, pale and enervated as the out-of-control æstheticism roared through his fragile system. This gilding was what des Esseintes had done with his tortoise, so it was clearly – if one purported to be a true æsthete – the right thing to do with any passing tortoise. If you were to be the

Duc Jean des Esseintes — as eager to be corrupted by the character as Dorian Gray had been (this was what had awoken Oliver's enthusiasm) — you didn't draw the line at gilding the lily. Like King Midas you ran riot, not knowing when to stop. Oliver was all agog to be a Gilded Youth. Why should a tortoise grab all the glitter?

"Here comes the Gelded Youth." This was another of Dr. Wolcott Ascharm Webster's sniggered asides to the Reverend Goodchild — he was quite keen on puns (puns, like clouds, like dreams, had hidden significance) — whenever Oliver came into sight, and off the beards would go again, rutting and rearing, cacophonously copulating.

The Gelded Youth!

Snigger, snigger!

Gelded Youth!

The irony of it, when he had a son with a voice like Max's, Master Max, the shrill-voiced warbler! Huysmans hadn't explained what you were expected to do with a Pekinese or a parrot to demonstrate your æsthetic credentials, and — at this time — a Chinky-Winky and a parrot (not even a peacock!) were the only pets owned by the Comstocks, and Oliver had been left at a loss. How keenly he must have felt the lack of the lost-long-ago peacocks from the vanished Shakespeare Castle. The parrot — Hilderbrandt — was a depressed-looking, molting, moth-eaten bird, drooping disconsolately on its stand, never uttering a sound (apart from incomprehensible, foul-tempered mutterings), and occasionally given to biting chunks out of passers-by. A little æstheticism would not have gone amiss with this bright blue brute.

Oliver and the genteel ladies must have been sorely disappointed much of the time as, retired to some inner chamber — the maid dismissed for the afternoon, a chair back inserted under the doorknob to prevent ingress — they settled back, toes wriggling expectantly, a glass of reviving sherry within reach (the salacious contents might induce a momentary faintness), for a couple of hours of shocked and delighted tut-tutting. They were of the I-was-so-disgusted-that-I-had-to-read-it-four-times persuasion, but even they must have struggled to find something to shock them in the majority of the interdicted publications. In the right mood – they must possess rich inner lives unshared by the majority of the population – Mrs. Albert Comstock and the Goodchilds were probably capable of discovering covert obscenity in Mrs. Alexander Diddecott's cloyingly sentimental poems and paintings with their endless depictions of puppy dogs, fluffy kittens, and winsome waifs and urchins. (Alice would be as one with them on the waifs and urchins.) Mrs. Alexander Diddecott liked to think of her artistic endeavors as "heart-warming," though Alice opted for the term "stomach-churning." It captured the uniqueness of their vision better, she thought. If Mrs. Alexander Diddecott, and not her father, had designed the stained glass windows of All Saints', horrified martyrs would have found themselves being disemboweled by chubby, dimply-smiling cherubs, or chewed to death by cuddly, limpid-eyed lions.

Dr. Wolcott Ascharm Webster was clearly grooming Max to be the new Reynolds Templeton Seabright. Max was – he had always been – a particularly *theatrical* child, nurtured as such from infancy. The word "theatrical" irresistibly dipped into italics when used in connection with him. He spoke in everyday life with the same intensity of expression with which he performed his many – his very many – recitations and songs, stressing every syllable thrillingly. His inevitable extravagant hand movements made it impossible for him to request "a *large* can of beans" in Comstock's Comestibles without sweeping elaborately stacked displays from the counter onto the floor. Loud crashes accompanied him around all the local stores.

As soon as he was capable of speech he was wheeled out to perform "You'd scarce expect one of my age/To speak in public on the stage."

"... Where's the boy but three feet high
Who's made improvement more than I?"

This is what he would recite, laboriously ingenuous, wide-eyed and winsome, and everywhere in the room the buttocks of the more discerning members of the audience clenched audibly, with a sound like colliding cows. His pronunciation of "Demosthenes" and "Cicero" in the fourth line was much acclaimed. "Large streams from little fountains flow," he'd pipe, and you could hear the threatening roar of thunderous tidal waves engulfing everything before them, and when he informed the enthralled listeners that "Tall oaks from little acorns grow," you saw a land darkened and devastated by an impenetrably gloomy forest. Seldom had the lines "These thoughts inspire my youthful mind/To be the greatest of mankind" (received by a chorus of sentimental ahhhs) sounded more sinister and threatening, even if he did — rather grudgingly — concede that he'd be Great, not like Cæsar, stained with blood,/But only great as I am good. *Very* likely. His repertoire expanded rapidly, and no musical evening was complete without his lengthy contribution.

"What a treat!" Alice would mutter — this was the expected response — as the joyful news that Master Max was to be amongst them was revealed to the gathered throng of expectant æsthetes. One theory was that his father hypnotized him to preserve the radiant purity of his voice, though Alice embraced darker theories with enthusiasm.

Snip-snap! Snip-snap! Snip-snap!

After you with the scissors, Mrs. Albert Comstock! Make sure they're well sharpened, Mrs. Goodchild! (No, on second thoughts, file them down until their blades are as blunt as teething rings. That would be *far* more enjoyable.)

Worse was to come when Serenity Goodchild, several years younger, was launched as a feminine rival. At first, she had sought to harrow them with the most heart-rending of Mrs. Hemans's compositions. She'd tried "Alaric in Italy."

". . . Still rolls, like them, the unfeeling river,"

— she squeakily intoned, drawing to a close —

"The guardian of his dust for ever."

After what was clearly designed to be a moving pause — you could see her lips going as she counted up to ten — she bowed her head, with her hands folded in front of her eyes. Then she'd tried "The Wife of Asdrubal," killing her children and perishing in the flames of the temple. (Alice had enjoyed this. The concept appealed enormously.) A count to ten. Head bowed. Eyes covered. Then she'd tried "He Never Smiled Again," spoiling the intended effect by dissolving into giggles in mid-recitation. No. Not dissolving. The flesh involved was too too solid for dissolving, even in the most thunderous of downpours. On the occasion of the giggles, there was no count to ten, no bowed head, no covered eyes from Serenity. It was the audience who'd counted, bowed, covered, *writhed*. Whatever she'd tried, the results were always the same: audiences cramming yards of handkerchief into their mouths, falling off their seats, and struggling in vain to control their hilarity. It was as if Childe Roland — Myrtle Comstock's *fiancé* — had convulsed Flanagan's bar yet again by treating all its patrons to one of his celebrated impersonations of her Mama's doggie's farts, an unprecedentedly spectacular Chinky-Winky Krakatoa, one of those vein-bulging efforts that misted all the mirrors and rattled the light fittings. Myrtle sometimes described him as her "affianced" because she thought it sounded impressive, or, if in flirtatious mood (this, terrifying to witness, had been known to happen), as her *amoroso* (an understandably morose-looking *amoroso*). She did not know about Childe Roland's contributions to the gaiety of Flanagan's, a particularly rowdy bar, blinding with electric lights and acres of beveled glass, all of it imperiled when he let fly. This heady scent of danger set Childe Roland's pulse racing.

Sobriety Goodchild and — er — Mrs. Sobriety Goodchild (Alice

363

was not sure whether or not she had ever been allocated a Christian name), Serenity's ambitious parents, and the Reverend and Mrs. Goodchild (who pinned on their Schiffendecken's Grins like badges), the even more ambitious grandparents, had to rethink their strategy. They were prominent amongst the humorless of Longfellow Park, but decided to abandon attempts at serious declamation (Longfellow Park was clearly not in a mood to be harrowed), and demonstrate their well-hidden depths of chucklesomeness. The four of them trained Serenity to perform a whole series of nightmarish *comic* recitations, and sat there beaming with isn't-she-just-adorable? expressions on their faces as she was launched into action.

"Isn't-she-just-adorable?" was a question soon answered.

Serenity's version of "Only a 'Ittle Dirly Dirl" would have had Herod leaping into enthusiastic action, elbowing his soldiers aside so that he'd be the first in line for lopping. Dressed in a many-layered pink dress, a frog in frills (once seen, never forgotten, and — my God! – how you tried to forget), and with much roguish rolling of eyes, simpering winsomely (every gesture was painfully and pedantically rehearsed), Serenity assured her audience:

> ". . . For I'm only a 'ittle dirly dirl,
> A innocent 'ittle dirly dirl!
> With my dollies I play,
> In the nursewy I stay,
> Unless I walk out with Papa;
> Yes, I'm only a 'ittle dirly dirl,
> A good 'ittle quiet dirly dirl!
> Evwy hour in the day
> Twying hard to obey
> My dearwest, my sweetest Mama . . ."

It was the most stomach-churning rendition of baby talk since Lewis Carroll had unleashed Bruno upon the world. (What on earth could the author of the *Alice* books have been thinking of when he wrote *Sylvie and Bruno?*) Even Mrs. Molesworth's creepy cuties — lithping fearthomely — sounded like representations of courageously stark realism when you compared them with Serenity Goodchild once those eyelids of hers started batting.

Reactions were instantaneous.

("Ahhhhhh!" from the Goodchilds and Griswolds who had been hauled in to cram the rooftops.

("Ahhhhhh!" from the Goodchilds and Griswolds in the woods.

("Ahhhhhh!" from the Goodchilds and Griswolds in the music room.

("Heeeeeeave!" from everybody else within hearing. They didn't heave-ho, they just heaved, and up the nausea rose.)

Mama, Papa, Grandmama, and Grandpapa, cultivating expressions of dewy-eyed fondness, gazed upon the ogling offspring. They appeared to be convinced that the rest of the audience were as enraptured as they purported to be, clamoring crowds eager for her every coy syllable. They ignored the desperate fighting to escape, the frantic attempts at hiding under sofas or in the grandfather clock, those diving behind chairs or hurling themselves out of the windows, those pretending to faint in order to be carried from the room, the suicide attempts. These were people understandably overcome by emotion at the thought of what they were about to hear. The comic recitations signally failed to convulse the audience as much as the serious ones had done. You winsome. You lose some. No thrills from those frills. "He Never Smiled Again" had never been received in such stricken, heartbroken silence, by such still and shattered listeners. Alice survived these occasions by gazing at Serenity with an expression of rapt attention, imagining that she was fat and forty-nine, and still performing that same song, still utilizing those meticulously practiced gestures. This helped to stave off the worst effects of nausea.

On really bad days she imagined that it was the late Albert Comstock performing in front of her, miraculously restored to life as an enormous small girl, dressed like a frilly marquee all ready for an especially lavish and well-populated circus. Even Phineas T. —

"T" is for Tiny! "T" is for Trivial! "T" is for Tin-pot! – Barnum would have struggled to have filled this Colosseum-sized immensity of space. Three rings wouldn't do it; neither would four, five, or six.

> ". . . I'm six years old two weeks ago,
> An' weigh just thirty-nine . . ."

– Albert Comstock unblushingly recited (it took a Coleridgean suspension of disbelief to cope with this line; rarely had poetic faith been quite so tested) –

> ". . . My hair is short but it will gwow,
> My eyes are large and fine,
> I wear the cutest 'ittle fwocks
> That ever you did see,
> An' all the way from hat to socks,
> I'm sweet as sweet can be . . ."

On the worst days of all, Papa appeared alongside Albert Comstock, dressed in his music box ballerina dress, up on his points and wobblingly edging sidewise. He was looking straight at her.

She was an innocent 'ittle dirly dirl.

She was not going to play with her dollies; she was not going to stay in her nursewy.

She was going to walk out with Papa.

Evwy hour in the day she twied hard to obey.

Albert Comstock and Papa linked their hands and danced. This time the music was not "Narcissus." It was – such a universal favorite – "The Dance of the Gigantic Cygnets" from *Swan Lake*. As this drew to a close – "Ahhhhhh!" from all points of the compass, including even south-south-south-west, they were so sweet as sweet could be in their cutest 'ittle fwocks – Papa (he did not forget the Mary Benedict simper) assumed the third position, the heel of his right foot pressed against the instep of his left foot. It was the position in which she imagined penguins sometimes stood when they were not being observed, feeling a secret need for grace in their posture.

"Third position!" he announced, for the benefit of those who were not devotees of the ballet.

It was the position assumed by well-coached children who were about to recite in public, the position of Sobriety Goodchild in his dimpled days of yore, the position of Max Webster, Serenity Goodchild, the position that warned you that something dreadful was about to be unleashed, and — hard luck! — it was too late to escape. Mary Benedict had seemed to expect applause just for assuming the position. No recitation followed as she posed, swayingly expectant. Then the *pirouettes* would be unleashed. She'd do this with the air of Dr. Moreau demonstrating the capabilities of the Beast People. Papa clasped his hands loosely in front of him, low down, as if he were about to demonstrate the correct manner in which to twiddle thumbs, or protect himself from Miss Stammers's enthusiastically sniffing dogs. An encore had been prepared, in the correct and confident assumption that an enraptured audience would insistently demand one.

"'The Children's Hour' by Henry Wadsworth Longfellow," he announced, in the special little voice of the sentimental public speaker, as if to demonstrate that he possessed a magical rapport with the special scenes of childhood.

She began to lift her hands to cover her ears.

(She could think of only . . .

(. . . only four of Shakespeare's male characters who disguised themselves as women — and three of these were acting parts in plays, if Ariel disguised as a water nymph counted as such — curious when they were written in a time when boys acted the rôles of women. Yet she could think of . . .

(She could think of . . .

(*Seven* of Shakespeare's women characters who disguised themselves as men or boys.

(Boys disguised as girls disguised as boys. You had to concentrate on this one, and Mrs. Albert Comstock was easily confused.

(In *Twelfth Night* Viola – shipwrecked off the coast of Illyria, and trying to believe that her twin brother had not been drowned – resolved to serve Orsino disguised as a boy, and sing and speak to him in many sorts of music . . .)

She could still hear Papa.

(In *As You Like It*, Rosalind . . .)

He did not begin at the beginning.

He leaped straight in at the eighth verse.

> ". . . Do you think, O blue-eyed banditti,
> Because you have scaled the wall,
> Such an old mustache as I am
> Is not a match for you all!. . ."

Odd that he should have opted for the spelling "mustache" instead of "moustache" when – later in the poem – he chose "moulder" and not "molder."

Later in the poem . . .

He was leading up to the last two verses, the very worst verses.

The ninth . . .

The tenth . . .

The tenth was the worst of all.

His voice rose. He *was* going to recite the last two verses, and he was going to make certain that she heard what it was they had to say. He wasn't just an old moustache either. He was a Bearded One, his multi-fronded growth arranged like the foliage hiding the mouth of a pit dug in the forest, one of those innocent-looking traps whose floor was set with sharp-pointed sticks, and from which it was impossible to clamber free.

> "I have you fast in my fortress . . ."

His voice became higher, became louder, more triumphant.

He was a match for them all.

He had her fast.

— ⊗ —

She couldn't abide either Max Webster or Serenity Goodchild, but she was intriguingly tempted to enter this Battle of the Cuties as it lurched on, out of control, flattening all in its path with its pink-frilled high-voiced weaponry, threatening death by terminal nausea, and she'd begin with Max Webster. It would be easy to organize a little mischief, and Mrs. Albert Comstock's birthday was only a few months away.

The next time she arrived at 11 Park Place, just before ten o'clock one Wednesday morning (assuming that she survived her imminent incarceration in the Webster Nervine Asylum, and assuming – a fairly safe assumption – that she'd still need the – er – gentle nurturing of Max's Papa after this), she'd go up to Max in the hall with a winning, conspiratorial smile. If Max wasn't there, Theodore was bound to be. One or other of the Ichabod Cranes – lank, narrow, dangling – was always there, furtively lingering in the shadows near the staircase, as if pausing contemplatively on his way to somewhere else. They loitered about during the school holidays, always keen to discover who the loonies were who came to see their father, to seek for guidance in The House of the Interpreter. This wasn't so that they could avoid them in future – you shouldn't get too close to a loony – but so that they would have something to laugh about together. It was rare to see an uninserted index finger in the neighborhood of Theodore or Max. If it wasn't shoved up the nearest nostril (you had to be careful not to get too close, or, easily confused, they might start rummaging about in the wrong nostril), it was sure to be vigorously employed in a thorough, thoughtfully luxurious, bottom scratch. If, however, they recognized an approaching loony, the finger would be pulled out – with an audible *pop!* like a bottle of (how incongruous) cheap champagne being opened – and pointing.

369

"There's one! There's one!"

They didn't run away, with shrill cries and loping gaits, rather in the manner that Mrs. Albert Comstock and Mrs. Goodchild fondly imagined the male youth of Longfellow Park would react to the nearness of a threatening Magdalene, but – on the contrary – came lumbering closer, for a good stare, activating their nudge-nudging elbows. They'd lean forward – it was a wonder they didn't carry binoculars and notebooks about with them like conscientious ornithologists – and gape, studying this specimen for giveaway signs of madness, whispering and sniggering, crusted pointy-pointy fingers all ablur. It was a little hobby they had. They were birders, specializing in just one species, the cuckoo.

"There's one!"

"There's one!"

In the crowded cloud-cuckoo-land of Longfellow Park, their right arms would be going up and down like a lone lowly sailor's, aching with saluting in a ship full of officers, as they permanently pointed.

Cuckoo! Cuckoo! they'd blow into their bird callers. Allen's Improved Cuckoo Callers – . . . *the most natural toned, the easiest blowing, made of red cedar, silver mounted* . . . (nothing but the best for Theodore and Max) . . . *with silver reed which gives it perfect tone, the finest cuckoo call made, used in the field by all the best cuckoo shooters in America, and only $1 each* – would sound like a wallful of cuckoo clocks as they blew with reddened, ballooned-out cheeks, their guns held at the ready, all poised for potshots.

Cuckoo! Cuckoo!

"There's one!"

"There's one!"

Bang! Bang!

Two gun-toting Papagenos, they'd potshot the cuckoos as they sang, utilizing their best German accents – as taught to them by Mama – cramming their kills into the cages on their backs. What did you need with a Magic Flute when you had an Allen's Improved Cuckoo Caller, used in the field by all the best cuckoo shooters in America? Max's soprano reached eye-watering heights of piercing shrillness, and all listening men winced sympathetically, discreetly adjusting their garments with pained and thoughtful expressions.

> *"Der Vogelfänger bin ich ja,*
> *Stets lustig, heisa hopsasa!*
> *Der Vogelfänger ist bekannt*
> *Bei alt und jung im ganzen Land . . ."*

The cuckoo catchers, that's what they were, always merry and cheerful, known to old and young throughout the land. They blew into their cuckoo callers intermittently, at appropriate moments, as if making knowing cultural cross-references to Beethoven's *Pastoral Symphony*. The Websters had culture at their well-clotted fingertips. Musical instruments were picturesquely positioned about their parlor, as if awaiting the attentions of a still-life artist.

Cuckoo! Cuckoo!

"There's one!"

"There's one!"

Bang! Bang!

It was a great shame that Serenity's family had set her up as the big rival of Max – she and he had a great deal in common – but this was the position in which they found themselves, the Romeo and Juliet of Longfellow Park.

"What's in a name?" Serenity should be bawling peevishly on a well-reinforced balcony, fists clenched, in characteristically belligerent mood. "That which we call a nose . . ." – she was generally recognized as having become somewhat *obsessed* with noses since Mabel Peartree had become her Sunday-school teacher – ". . . / By any other name would – er – smell your feet" (Serenity, like her Grandmama, had a way with words), and Max – both feet primed (*Phew!*) to illustrate her epigram – would leap out to astonish her. Ahhhhhh!

"Cooee!" Alice would call in the echoing hall of 11 Park Place –

Cooee! not *Cuckoo!* — adapting the call of the Australian natives. "Cooee!"

She still felt — after all this time — oddly out of place and estranged in the realms of psychology, as if she didn't belong there, as if she had inadvertently wandered into hidden rooms, private quarters, a Masonic hall, a place where only men should be, men holding special implements, men arranged in strenuous symbolic positions like meaningful statuary. She'd plunge confidently into the center of the room — if it could be so called — that clouded antechamber to other rooms, where the secrets would be uncovered to the elected few. It was a world in which most of the vocabulary — these rooms possessed their own language, spoken like a private code to the initiated — had the sound of words not yet fully accepted into common usage. They were words to be spoken in the same way as Mrs. Alexander Diddecott employed the latest slang she conscientiously learned from her nephew, Valentine, not certain that she'd got it right. Implied quotation marks hovered in the air like fluttering wings not strong enough to remain upright. Dr. Wolcott Ascharm Webster dispensed with quotation marks. He was writing the book for the first time, and he quoted no one. He just adapted other people's words a little, tweaking the nouns, and shuffling the phrases, rattling off what he had to say like Dr. Wycherley in *Hard Cash* as he studied Alfred Hardie.

"*Therefore*" — Dr. Wycherley asserted, with emphatic italicized certainty — "dissection of your talented son would doubtless reveal at this moment either steatomatous or atheromatous deposits in the cerebral blood-vessels, or an encysted abscess, probably of no very recent origin, or, at the least, considerable inspissation, and opacity, of the membranes of the encephalon, or more or less pulpy disorganization of one or other hemispheres of the brain . . ."

Dr. Wycherley, like Andrew Jackson Davis — well, when you were a celebrated Seer (particularly one from Poughkeepsie) you could make up your own rules — was clearly (not, perhaps, the best choice of word in view of this speech) a man who made up his own words because those that already existed were inadequate to express the wonder of what he had to say. Richard Hardie, Alfred's father, had understood "talented son would doubtless reveal at this moment"; he had understood "probably of no very recent origin, or, at the least" and "or more or less," and that – er – more or less, was it. Above all, however – and this was all that really mattered – Richard Hardie had understood "dissection." This was the word at which he grabbed with considerable alacrity. He'd be all in favor of dissection, he'd wield the scalpel himself then and there, anything to get Alfred out of the way, and his hands on his money. "Hold him down whilst I hack!" that would be the order, all keen to get cleaving, a Mr. Bones, the Butcher keeping the cutting within the family, gleefully gutting Master Bones. He'd chop away, like Albert Comstock unleashed on a freshly killed cow.

(Mr. Bones, the Butcher!

(She'd remembered another Happy Family.

(Mr. Spade, the Gardener, Mr. Chip, the Carpenter, Mr. Dip, the Dyer, Mr. Soot, the Sweep, Mr. Bun, the Baker, Mr. Tape, the Tailor, and Mr. Bones, the Butcher.

(She could remember *seven* Happy Families.

(Six left to remember.

(How could she ever have forgotten the Bones family?

(They were the ones who'd always scared her the most.

(This was . . .

(This was probably why . . .

(This, *of course*, was why she'd forgotten them.

(*Thought* she'd forgotten them.

(All Happy Families resembled one another.

(Allegra simpered behind her fanned-out cards, hiding her face so that only her eyes showed.

("Master Tape is not at home."

(*Slam!*

("Mrs. Bun is not at home."

(*Slam!*

(Mr. Spade is not at home."

(*Slam!*

("Mr. Bones is not at home."

(*Slam!*

(They were there. They were all there, hidden away within the inner rooms, whispering, plotting what to do.

(Allegra had used that same teasing expression with Bayard Guilfoyle, and now she was Mrs. Bayard Guilfoyle, away playing Happy Families for real.

("Mrs. Guilfoyle is not at home."

(*Slam!*

("Mrs. Guilfoyle is not at home."

(*Slam!*

(She was very good at it. She had had years of practice, and she always won.)

"*Mad!*" Richard Hardie exulted. "*Mad!*"

He'd barely understood a word of what Dr. Wycherley had said, but "mad, mad" was the underlying meaning, and "mad, mad" was precisely what he wanted to hear. Dr. Wycherley knew where the money was, and knew what words would please. These were the words he was paid to speak. These were the words to lock Alfred into a lunatic asylum. These were the words to get him out of the way.

"Cooee! Max!"

Siren-like, she'd lure Max into her clutches with a series of seductive cooees, all the weaponry of aboriginal allure. She should be hurling a boomerang around the curve of the staircase to stun him into submission. She should be gesturing suggestively with a comatose kangaroo, drawing him toward her with an attractive duck-billed platypus.

"Cooee! Max!"

Alice would sound delighted to see him, and he'd back away, whimpering for Theodore, forgetting to point in his panic. He was very thin, but taller than she was, with lips and ears that seemed poised for flight, plucked up and fastidiously angled.

How old was he?

How old was he, *exactly*?

"*Hmmmmmm . . .*"

("It's the madwoman. It's the madwoman.")

"Cooee! Max!"

"*Hmmmmmm . . .*"

(It was Lizzie Borden, with the ax and the forty whacks, and "ax" rhymed with "Max.")

He'd not so much moved toward her as allowed her to approach closer to him, as he backed into a corner, up against a photograph of himself and Theodore holding well-polished trumpets triumphantly aloft, as if having just discovered a new method of secret signaling. Dopey, dangly-wristed, some wild creature half concealed in the dimness, he whimpered wetly at the approach of this unfettered loony.

"Max, it's Mrs. Albert Comstock's birthday on April the fifteenth . . ."

(What better, more symbolic time than this for Mrs. Albert Comstock to have been born, the time of the beginning of spring, the shy green shoots appearing through the earth after the bitter cold of winter? It was a theme that would undoubtedly have inspired Christina Rossetti. There, amidst the gamboling lambs, the tender buds, the first falterings of growth, would be Mrs. Albert Comstock clad in diamonds and daisies, smiling like a goddess of new life.)

". . . and it has occurred to me and numerous others that it would add to the happiness of the occasion . . ."

– She was such a hypocrite! –

". . . if you were able to perform for us on the day. It would be a special treat for her."

– And so good at it! –

Max was instantly all alert.

She half expected him to produce his little red-backed notebook. Max Webster liked to give the impression that he performed – he liked the sound of "performed," her chosen verb was a well-sprung trap – for the sheer joy of his art, the glorious sounds he produced, and the delight he gave to others being all the reward he sought. Money, however, always – *always* – changed hands. Papa handled the unpleasant money side of it – it was Papa who insisted on the money, because Max was, after all, a professional in his approach, and in his standards – and it was Papa who organized his engagements. (This last was another word that deeply appealed to Max, and he said it with deeply serious professionalism. This consisted of not smiling, and nodding his head twice.) The italics and the theatrical gestures sprang into action, as Max eagerly demonstrated his capabilities. In just such a way Mary Benedict once illustrated first position, second position, third position, *pirouettes*, and *pliés*, and with considerably less grace.

"I might *possibly* be available on that day. I shall need to consult my book of *engagements*." – He'd got that word in again – "What day of the week is it?"

He was hooked.

Might.

Possibly.

He never forgot his rôle as a professional, with thousands clamoring for his services. On "engagements" – ever a word to animate him – he grinned an automatic smile, and gold glinted from the suddenly exposed side teeth, canines and premolars like a rich vein in a deep mine. She must be careful not to let the glint from these hypnotize her, lull her into unprepared-for sleepiness, and ruin her Machiavellian machinations.

"We . . ."

– *We*: a carefully selected pronoun this time, a hint of those jealously competing crowds –

". . . were thinking that you might recite one or two pieces, as well – of course – as singing."

Then, casually, she'd produce the first of the poems she had copied out from *An American Anthology*.

"This is a very short one, only four lines, but we thought it might be a good one with which to begin. It's by John James Piatt."

She'd hand over "To a Lady on Her Art of Growing Old Gracefully," with wide-eyed enthusiasm. The very title would have Mrs. Albert Comstock spontaneously combusting, and blazing like a destroyed civilization. Sibyl would sizzle and spin like the most colossal of all Catherine wheels, a pinwheel whooping and exploding with hissing fire and color. The very title would spell an end to Max Webster's career at 5 Hampshire Square.

Max Webster wouldn't be able to resist.

He always began by repeating the opening words several times, like a singer finding the right pitch.

"You ask . . ."

He cleared his throat, and began again.

"You ask . . ."

He was demonstrating his professionalism.

If you wanted professionalism, you hired Max Webster. That was the message. And if you hired Max Webster, you paid an appropriate fee. ("Fee" would be another word that Max would enjoy employing.) You got what you paid for. In an appropriate mingling of themes, Max was a living embodiment of one of Mrs. Albert Comstock's favorite – er – maxims.

"You ask . . ."

He'd got it now.

He was *such* a professional.

He – he'd studied the statues in The Forum – struck an artistic pose, and started. He was away.

"'To a Lady on Her Art of Growing Old Gracefully' by John James Piatt."

"Could you stress the word 'Old' a little more forcefully?" Alice asked. Her eyes were at their widest.

As a professional, Max was not accustomed to having suggestions made to him. He gave a little professional sigh to demonstrate this point, and then tried again.

". . . Growing *Old* . . ." he said. He made it sound like a death sentence. *Aeons* stretched away, a desert landscape mistily merging into a distant horizon.

"Infinitely better, Max. You seem to know instinctively what is required."

". . . Growing *Old* . . ."

The sentence was carried out. The guillotine descended with a well-oiled whumpf.

The most celebrated of the Sibyls lived at Cumæ. Apollo fell in love with her, and said that he would give her whatever she wished. She asked to live for as many years as there were grains of sand in her hand, clutching as many as she could hold. She forgot to ask for eternal youth to accompany the passing of the centuries. She forgot to ask for eternal health and beauty. And the years began to pass.

> "You ask a verse, to sing (ah, laughing face!)
> Your happy art of growing old with grace?
> O Muse, begin, and let the truth – but hold!
> First let me see that you are growing old."

All Max could see in the poem was the unctuous flattery, and – in consequence – the pleasure he assumed it would give Mrs. Albert Comstock, and the gratifying consequences for himself. There might be a free Comstock steak pie in it for him, a Monumental, or a Gargantuan, possibly even a Colossus. He was salivating slightly at the prospect. This was not the way this poem would be seen by Mrs. Albert Comstock. After that title – *Old*! *Old*! – "ah, laughing face!" would not be the most appropriate of phrases to employ in the circumstances.

A similar choice of verse had destroyed the blossoming career of Sobriety Goodchild twenty-five years ago when he had been trundled on to perform for Mrs. Albert Comstock's fortieth birthday. (Everyone *knew* it was her fortieth birthday – Mrs. Goodchild had been busy, busy, busy – but no one dared to mention this unpalatable fact. No one volunteered to administer the forty whacks, though you could see Mrs. Goodchild's fingers twitching. She used the expression "It's not quite my forte" more than was strictly necessary.) Alice had a – er – faint recollection that she might possibly have suggested the offending piece to Sobriety.

Sobriety strode into the music room dressed as Enobarbus, an Ancient Roman in Egypt, a sight that unnerved hieroglyphics would have struggled in vain to convey. Alice had persuaded Sobriety that he would create a *sensation* – pleased smirk on his face as he visualized this – if he dressed in an appropriate costume for his performance. She had not lied. Her ideas were on a far more epic and ambitious scale than Max Webster's were today. A little cloak, a few ruffles and frills, and Max appeared to be under the impression that he was lavishly recreating the vanished glamour of the days of yore. "Sandals!" she'd whispered to Sobriety with serpent-like seductiveness. "Bare legs, and a short tunic that comes halfway down the area between your waist and your knees!" She'd avoided saying "thighs." "Thighs" would have caused panic in the lumpish dolt, though he still went slightly pink. ("Bare legs!" she could see him thinking, and he'd tugged unconsciously at the edge of his Norfolk jacket like an imperiled spinster.) "Bare arms!" Increased pinkness. Ambition had won through, however, and all pinkness was ruthlessly expunged from his glowering countenance. It was either ambition or the lure of a Comstock steak pie as reward for the sensation he'd been *guaranteed* to create, but – whichever it was – the sandals, the bare legs, the short tunic (even shorter than she'd thought possible, or – for that matter – *advisable*), and the bare arms had all appeared for the delectation of the beefy birthday girl. The *guaranteed* sensation was duly delivered. "Anyone but me would look like a Charlotte Anne dressed like this." That was what Sobriety had misguidedly persuaded himself. Perhaps, come to think of it, the startling change in Carlo Fiorelli's style of statuary may very well have been caused not by *Ben-Hur*, but by the vision of Sobriety as he had appeared that day at Mrs. Albert Comstock's, Alice's contribution to the history of art. She'd been thinking of Jane Eyre's words to John Reed. She'd been thinking of a wicked and cruel boy, who was like a murderer, a slave driver, the Roman emperors. And – even though Enobarbus wasn't an emperor – she'd persuaded Sobriety to *dress* like a Roman emperor,

379

or, at the least, in an approximation of Roman dress, a garb peculiarly unsuited to his distinctly unæsthetic anatomy. Anesthetics, not æsthetics! That was the urgent strangled cry on April 15, 1878, as the appalled audience caught its first glimpse of Sobriety Goodchild, rather *too much* of Sobriety Goodchild.

Sobriety had *very* thin legs and *very* thin arms. He had *very* large knees. Mrs. Albert Comstock (astounded, not at all enthusiastic) found herself being addressed as Cleopatra – Alice had just finished reading *Antony and Cleopatra* – as he stretched his *very* thin arms up toward her, a suppliant begging for alms. He went down on one of the *very* large knees, his perilously short tunic gaping in a way that made your eyes water, giving Mrs. Albert Comstock an extensive view of his Boys' Camel's Hair Color Drawers With Very Warm Extra Heavy Wool Fleece On Inside. It had been a very cold day, but you had to admit that the touch of camel's hair had shown a regard for detailed research that was distinctly impressive. He and his mama must have ransacked Oldermann & Oldermann's in search of drawers constructed of just the right material for historical authenticity. "By th' mass," Sobriety must have shouted in triumph, flourishing the drawers like a flag of victory, and demonstrating an unexpected knowledge of *Hamlet*, "and 'tis like a camel indeed." Oldermann & Oldermann (*Particularly To Be Recommended For Unanachronistic Underwear!*). What was brazenly displayed to the audience's disbelieving eyes – "You saw *what?*" Charlotte would be shrieking, when she told her – did, however, look *far* too warm for the banks of the Nile, *far* too comprehensively buttoned and overlapped for comfort and coolness. The embarrassing solecism of unsuitable sweatiness was an ever-present possibility for those thus clad. (". . . From many an ancient river," they'd be singing in All Saints', ever after seeing the Nile, seeing – *shudder!* – Cleopatra, seeing – another shudder – Sobriety's camel-colored sartorial sauciness vividly in front of them, "/From many a palmy plain . . .")

Alice had run all Enobarbus' appropriate speeches together, and written them out in her neatest handwriting. Sobriety had cornered her, and demanded that she supply him with something *suitable* for him to perform for Mrs. Albert Comstock's birthday *or else*. Unhesitatingly, she'd opted for *or else*. *Act Two, Scene Two,* she'd written learnedly as the heading, with *II, ii* in brackets to follow, giving – she felt – an improvingly biblical feel to her reference. Roman numerals were so much more appropriate in this context. With that underwear openly on display you needed as much improvement as you could get, prolonged exposure (a better word ought surely to have come to mind) to some of the more implacable, hectoring passages from the Old Testament. Sobriety's mute gratitude – *Grab. Grunt. Sneer. Attempt at slap* – was reward enough for her. ("A Titanic . . ." Sobriety was thinking. "A Monumental . . ." There are some certainties in life to which we clutch. Sobriety Goodchild was perpetually hungry. "Possibly even a Gargantuan . . ." He stretched his hands out further, wobbling like Mary Benedict in an over-ambitious ballet position, all ready to grab the steaming steak pies that would be generously bestowed upon him by the gratified recipient of his fulsome address.) Alice could – when in good form – construct multiple revenges that would have had John Webster applauding admiringly and feeling inadequate.

"Hail, Cleopatra!" he began, worshipful arms extended as if in a vain attempt to encompass Mrs. Albert Comstock's vastness. Prolonged exposure to the worst excesses of Dudley Dibbo's poetry had – as Alice fully expected – created in him the feeling that *real* poetry tended to have the word "Hail" in it somewhere. That's why she added it, modestly doing her bit to improve upon Shakespeare. "Hail" had created a misplaced confidence in the rightness of what he was doing, and gave a cocky swagger to his reading. ("A Gargantuan!") Otsego Lake Academy was not an establishment that approved much of poetry. It couldn't see the point. Mrs. Albert Comstock, gratifyingly, immediately looked uneasy. She'd *heard* about Cleopatra, and she hadn't liked what she'd heard.

Sobriety Goodchild unleashed himself on Shakespeare, not

understanding a word of what he was saying, apart from the occasional "the," as out of his depth as Richard Hardie listening to the words of Dr. Wycherley. His arms twitched spasmodically and his voice went up and down to indicate that he was meant to be impassioned, and the camel-colored drawers slowly crept down his right leg, the one on which he was kneeling. They had been turned back on themselves, in proud demonstration of the Very Warm Extra Heavy Wool Fleece On Inside.

It was riveting stuff.

Fingers pointed silently.

Mouths gaped.

"The barge she sat in . . ."

— he wonderingly informed them —

". . . like a burnished throne,
Burned on the water . . ."

She'd written detailed instructions all around the speeches in red ink, like a scholarly commentary on an obscure text. (It was a text that was not so much obscure as impenetrable to Sobriety.) *Pause awhile . . .* — she'd written at this point — *. . . look astonished, stare at Mrs. Comstock.* Sobriety looked astonished, as bidden, having been practicing for quite some time. Subtlety in performance was not his style. His jaw dropped, he reared back like someone attempting to save his eyebrows from the burning, his drawers dropped a further two inches, and he stared menacingly, not liking what it was he saw in front of him. His astonishment was nothing compared to Mrs. Albert Comstock's. Aghastness flexed her features almost from the very beginning. Mrs. Albert Comstock didn't like the sound of *barge*. Barges were for *commercial* traffic. Barges carried coal and ore and timber, things that were bulky and dirty and *heavy*, dumped in mountainous piles, not nicely arranged, and were employed in the more *industrial* areas of the nation. They were towed by horses, weren't they? Big horses with matted manes, not like the dainty horses that pulled carriages or ran in races, not horses that were decked in ribbons and trip-trotted nicely in pairs. There was a *distinct* lack of niceness. A barge was cumbersome and ugly and — ahem — flat-bottomed. Barge sounded like "large." She definitely took against "barge." Her face began to clench like a huge fist preparing itself for retaliatory action after an attack. A Mrs. Albert Comstock sulky expression began to take shape in front of them, a storm cloud threatening heavy rain.

". . . For her own person . . ."

— Sobriety added, warming to his task, oblivious of the lack of enthusiasm from the object of his attentions, but delightedly aware (indrawn breaths, suppressed exclamations) that the guarantee of sensation was unquestionably being honored —

". . . It beggared all description. . ."

Well, they could believe that.
That was very well put.
Splendid, Sobriety.
You could feel a surge of enthusiasm on these words.
Mrs. Goodchild had twisted herself right round so that she could see Mrs. Albert Comstock's face better. If her elbow slipped she'd project herself right into the fireplace and blaze like an out-of-season, frantically kicking, Yule log. Pleasure upon pleasure. There'd been an appalled rearing back from Mrs. Albert Comstock on "beggared." *Become more and more excited* had been Alice's helpful gloss at this point, and — it was decidedly alarming — Sobriety became more and more excited, rocking upon the bony right knee, whimpering slightly. The possibility of drooling could not be ruled out. ("Hold him down!" someone ought to be calling out, panicking. "Send for a marksman! Quick!") Sobriety was so dim that he would

have followed any instructions she had written, fondly believing that each action brought a gently steaming gravy-soaked Gargantuan ever closer. *Remove drawers. Place on head. Perform three back-somersaults, then leap on Mrs. Comstock.* If only she'd had the courage to follow her instincts and gone for broke in her instructions. Pedantic, in a way that she believed that only she could be, he would have followed every instruction to the letter. On "pretty dimpled boys, like smiling Cupids" he simpered and smirked in a way that frighteningly anticipated the worst excesses of his daughter a quarter of a century later. (*Smile*, she'd written, *and look straight into Mrs. Comstock's eyes.*) Mrs. Albert Comstock flinched visibly at his Pandarus-like leerings.

> ". . . From the barge
> A strange invisible perfume hit the sense
> Of the adjacent wharfs . . ."

They could believe *that*, also.

It was, if anything, a little *too* vivid.

On "I saw her once/Hop forty paces through the public street" Alice's instructions – in capital letters – were *STRESS "FORTY" REALLY LOUDLY*, and, ever obedient, Sobriety bellowed the word at the top of his voice, leaning so far forward for added emphasis that his nose almost prodded Mrs. Albert Comstock's aghast and upraised fan. In fact, he was so pleased with the volume he managed to achieve – it was a miracle that Mrs. Alexander Diddecott hadn't fallen backward off the sofa – that he repeated the word. You couldn't help feeling that Mrs. Goodchild had taken her son's coaching in hand at this point, enthusiastically endorsing the annotated suggestions. ("Louder, Sobriety dear, much, *much* louder!") She was watching the effects of her son's performance like the proudest of all proud mothers at a school concert. Not much chance of a Comstock steak pie, but – to his bafflement – second helpings of everything when his mama got him back home. The fan whumpfed out like the first thrust in a duel, and became threateningly agitated. The expression on Mrs. Albert Comstock's face was that of a nervous householder awoken from virtuous slumbers by suspicious noises from downstairs. Fingers tightened on fan. Knuckles whitened. There might be smites. Prods were a possibility. There could — with any luck — be uninhibitedly full-blooded bashings and ear-shattering screams. By the time Sobriety — drawing toward what he fully anticipated being a triumphant conclusion ("Humbly, madam, I thank you") — had reached "Age cannot wither her" (*STRESS "AGE", STRESS "WITHER" REALLY LOUDLY*), you could hardly see across the room for the steam coming out of Mrs. Albert Comstock's ears (the only steam Sobriety saw that day), and blurred battalions of Stephenson's *Rocket*s roared screaming across the nation's railroads with boiler-busting velocity.

Dr. Wycherley's words to Richard Hardie would have featured prominently in Mrs. Albert Comstock's — er — animated discussion with the Reverend Goodchild that must have followed Sobriety's performance. "Dissection of your talented son." Especially *those* words. *Personally* she'd have organized a more or less pulpy disorganization of one or other hemisphere of Sobriety's brain. Or *both* hemispheres. If he had two. She liked to do a job properly. The elephant's foot umbrella stand would have been ransacked for the most lethal of all the walking sticks. "Come closer, little boy, come closer," she'd have cooed, and Sobriety would have hurried closer, beaming — to the victor, the spoils! — with his hands held out Oliver-like for a Gargantuan, as if surrendering, as the gargantuan knobbly knobkerrie appeared from behind Mrs. Albert Comstock's back, and whumpfed down to brain him. *That* wouldn't take forty whacks to achieve, but she'd give him forty, just for the hell of it. She hadn't studied Her Albert's butchering technique in vain, as he whacked away fit to bust his chopping block. *Whack! Whack!* ("*Mad!*" she'd have been thinking. "*Mad!*") Sobriety's brain, and his papa's tongue. The pudding would have been a little too bland and chewy for some palates, and Chinky-Winky would have no trouble at all cadging leftovers.

Sobriety had not performed in public again. It had never occurred to him that his fall from favor was in any way connected with the assistance he had bullied out of Alice Pinkerton. Although Alice had never received the praise that was her due for this achievement, she had felt a particularly intense satisfaction in having destroyed a brute beast with the words of Shakespeare, besting the barbarian with the best of Enobarbus. It was either Shakespeare or the all-too-generously displayed Boys' Camel's Hair Color Drawers With Very Warm Extra Heavy Wool Fleece On Inside that had done for him, one or the other, and Alice preferred to think that it was Shakespeare. It was better than muffled cursing and weeping. It was better than beating pillars with a wooden head (with a head of any description, for that matter). It was better than hammering nails into a doll's head. It was better than just about anything you cared to enumerate.

She'd hooked Sobriety Goodchild, and now she'd hooked Max Webster. You could see the hook tugging at the corner of his mouth, drawing him closer, despite himself.

Any prior engagements for April the fifteenth – *You have visionary qualities, are quick-witted and perceptive, and display bubbling good humor* – that had been made by Max would be peremptorily cancelled.

Bubble, bubble . . .

The bubbles rose from the mouth of the hooked fish as it was hauled up to the surface. The visionary, the quick-witted, the perceptive, the bubblingly good-humored: this – unrecognizably – was the baffling description of Mrs. Albert Comstock on her horoscope bookmark, an unmistakable Aries in personality, it claimed, even if her looks owed more to Taurus. Well, she'd certainly ram something down Max's throat, and put a permanent end to his days of singing and reciting. The lute would fall silent in the minstrel's hall, only the tuning pegs protruding from where it had been shoved good and hard into his aghast and gagging mouth. She'd had enough of that kind of thing from Sobriety Goodchild all those years ago, and she'd soon put a stop to *him*.

Max would practice and practice, until even the Reverend Goodchild wouldn't be able to compete with him in weighing down every word with flirtatious fawning. Twinkling roguishly, eyebrows going up and down like a treeful of crows taking off into full flight, Max would give it his all — every word would ping its well-rounded vowels around the music room — and then (Alice knew he wouldn't be able to resist doing this) he'd make a low chivalric bow to the subject of his verse, confidently expecting a gurgle of delighted pleasure. He'd probably wear a little velvet pageboy cloak so that he could cast it before her. It was the sort of touch he had perfected. It would be like a sonneteer singing the praises of Queen Elizabeth I at court. The sword would appear in the royal hand, and — as he knelt proudly at her feet — she'd tap his shoulder, and knight him.

"Arise, Sir Max!"

Alice wouldn't bank on the bubbling good humor, if she were he. If a sword appeared, it would lop his head off.

Whumpf!

Thud!

Boing!

Boing!

Boing!

"There'll also be some specially written songs. I'm thinking of asking Harry Hollander . . ."

"My *fee* is a little more if I have to learn new material."

He got that in quickly.

He avoided using her name the whole time he spoke to her, though "fee" had definitely had an enthusiastic emphasis. He sounded like someone saying the name of his beloved.

"That is entirely proper, Max."

Alice had started to write one song already.

She thought it would do rather well.

It should be the first song sung, straight after "To a Lady on Her Art of Growing Old Gracefully." She'd even thought of a tune that would bring out the full beauty of the words.

"Sixty-five,
And *still* alive!
Hail,
Sibyl Comstock!"

That was as far as she'd got. It was a promising start, haunting in its simple eloquence. Mrs. Albert Comstock had been hailed as a Conquering Hero often enough, timing her entrances so as to appear in the music room to the Handelian chimes of the clock (*Dah dah dah dah dah! Daddle-daddle dah dah dah!*), so it was probably about time that she was hailed in her own right. A second verse was starting to form, somewhere at the back of Alice's mind.

"I'm not surprised you dribble, Sibyl . . ."

Would she be held legally responsible if Max Webster were slaughtered in mid-warble? It would be worth it. She'd have to ensure that Kate would be there with her camera.

It would be cruel.

Good.

It would be *very* cruel.

Excellent.

"Ichabod, Ichabod," she muttered, as if casting a curse on one of the Ichabod Cranes of Longfellow Park. "The glory is departed." The Three Weird Sisters had nothing new to teach her when it came to toil and trouble. The fire burned, the cauldron bubbled.

———

Alice had spent much time in searching through medical textbooks in an attempt to find something that might explain what was wrong with her. Something, surely, *was* wrong with her. In the absence of any clear guidance from Dr. Wolcott Ascharm Webster, who — displaying an unexpected gift for creativity — was making things up as he went along, she tried to find out for herself. Mrs. Albert Comstock – the quotation marks had been mockingly audible – described Alice as suffering from "the vapors." You could see the pale shapes forming in the air, the insubstantial smoke trails, the will-o'-the-wisps foggily floating above the marshy depths, leading unwary travelers astray. Alice had not bothered to seek out *Vapors*. *Apathy* she'd looked for, and not found. *Exhaustion. Weariness.* No success. Exhaustion and weariness did not exist, as far as the medical profession was concerned, beards perkily positioned.

Perhaps what she sought would be contained within a more spiritual volume, one less concerned with the merely physical. After this insight, she'd tried to find *Accidie*, as it described her condition so perfectly, with the added bonus of sounding appropriately confessional and mediæval, like one of the Seven Deadly Sins.

No success.

It was *tick, tick, tick* (and *tick, tick, tick, tick* again) with the Seven Deadly Sins as far as she was concerned, in intention, if not in fact, and as for the Ten Commandments . . .

She'd better not even *think* about the Ten Commandments. When she was in certain moods as a child, they'd looked temptingly like an irresistible dare, the offered possibility of a ten out of ten target. Miss Caulfeild's spelling bees had obviously had a detrimental lasting effect upon her, developing her spirit of competition (*Alice Pinkerton: The Spirit of Competition*: get that chisel sharpened, Carlo Fiorelli!) into dark and dangerous areas far beyond her control, beyond the reach of *desiccated, embarrassment, onomatopoeia*, and *graywacke*, luring her beyond even the corrupting allure of *diarrhea*. It had developed into a ravenous parasite, eating her up until nothing else of her remained, like ambition with Macbeth, or jealousy with Othello. She'd read them, Sunday after Sunday, displayed on the wall in All Saints' like a taunting challenge at a fairground shooting gallery designed to fire up the gaping peasantry, and have them digging into their pockets for their cash. *THE TEN COMMANDMENTS. How Many Can You Break? Go On! Have a Go! Splendid Prizes!*

("All manner of delight!" Mephostophilis whispered, temptingly, caressingly.

("Go on!" he was saying.

("Have a go!" he was saying.

(He'd done really well with the Seven Deadly Sins. He might as well have a go with the Ten Commandments.)

Honor – Should that be "Honour"? Would King James have spelled it "Honour"? – *thy father and thy mother: that thy days may be long upon the land which the LORD thy God giveth thee.*

That was the Fifth Commandment.

Thou shalt not kill.

That was the Sixth.

Odd that those two should be placed one beneath the other.

———— ❦ ————

Dr. Wolcott Ascharm Webster's enthusiasm for hypnotism followed so promptly upon the dramatization of *Trilby* – the year after the serialization in *Harper's Magazine* – that Alice had no doubts that he had seen the production, probably several times. She saw him in an adjoining box to Mrs. Albert Comstock's, trying to ignore her running commentary – she kept up an audible response to whatever she was viewing: she thought it encouraged the actors – and focusing his opera glasses on Trilby's bare feet, Trilby's mouth, Trilby's breasts. The nail of his right forefinger – he had long fingernails – tugged minutely at the focusing wheel, as if he were inching a coin along by clicking on its milled edge. He wanted to make the image as sharp as possible. Brian's power would wane, even with the help of the peacock feathers; Hilde Claudia – bejeweled, beside him – would be forgotten; Theodore and Max, chastely at home under the care of certain trusted servants, animatedly discussing one of the more obscure passages in *Mind and Brain*, the impish young rogues, would vanish utterly from his mind. Svengali would not be visible within the bright illuminated circle: it would be filled entirely with Trilby. He himself would become Svengali. When she spoke she would be speaking solely to him, the words of Svengali would be words from Dr. Wolcott Ascharm Webster's own mind, Dr. Wolcott Ascharm Webster's own mouth, his lips moving as if speaking the responses in a church service, his head nodding, his expression changing.

"Sit down," his lips mouthed. "I will show you something that will cure your pain better than music." They were not quite in synchronization with the words spoken, a man perpetually prompted by words that were not his own.

He brought his chair forward to where Trilby was sitting on the divan, and sat facing her, almost knee to knee.

"Look me in the white of the eyes."

He gazed intently into her eyes, and caressed her temples. (He enjoyed the "caress" bit.) Trilby could not open her eyes, could not speak, could not stand. He had total control over her.

"That is the devil's trick – hypnotism." That was what Taffy said. That would have appealed to Dr. Wolcott Ascharm Webster.

Later, in the moonlight, after he had taken the candle from Trilby's hand, and lifted it to illuminate her face, he looked into her mouth and told her that the roof of her mouth was like the dome of the Parthenon, and that her tongue was scooped out like the petal of a little pink peony. He had read *Trilby* before he attended the stage version of it, and what he heard the characters speaking on stage were some of the spicier speeches from the novel, the speeches omitted or toned down for the Mrs. Grundy spoilsports of the theatre. He told her she had a beautiful big chest. This was a line he especially enjoyed speaking. Dr. Wolcott Ascharm Webster was so absorbed that he never even noticed the appalled intake of breath from the adjoining box – *big chest!* – the frantic swishing of the fan, the agitation of the jewels rattling upon the perturbed Bosom. Svengali laid the side of his head against Trilby's bosom, the angle of his head emphasizing the – ahem – thrust of the jut. Even sharper intakes, even more insistent swishings, even louder rattlings, the sound of an endungeoned prisoner struggling in his chains, frantically fighting for freedom, the Canterville Ghost in

391

need of being oiled by the Tammany Rising Sun Lubricator (completely efficacious upon one application). A steady stream of pulverized plaster would be pattering down from the underside of the box, and powdering the pompadours beneath to an eighteenth-century whiteness. Mrs. Albert Comstock was having the time of her life.

The long white fingernail stopped where it was, arched round in mid-air, the opera glasses became very still. Dr. Wolcott Ascharm Webster was holding his breath, trying to will his thoughts into action.

("Come on, Trilby! Let's see you posing.")

("Come on, Trilby! Huh! Call yourself a figure-model!")

("Get those clothes off!")

("Let's see that *beautiful chest*!")

("That *beautiful BIG chest*!")

("*Now!*")

"Mademoiselle," Svengali said . . .

– "Mademoiselle," Dr. Wolcott Ascharm Webster mouthed –

– "*French!*" A strangled panicky cry from Mrs. Albert Comstock. This was far, far worse than her most ambitious hopes –

". . . when you have the pain, then shall you come to my little room on the seventh floor, and Svengali will play to you and take away your pain, and keep it himself because he loves you. And when we are quite alone, then will he play for you the '*Adieu*' of Schubert."

("*Little* room," Dr. Wolcott Ascharm Webster thought to himself. There wouldn't be much space to maneuver in a little room when you were crammed in with a beautiful *big* chest. They'd have to synchronize their breathing, so that he wouldn't be pushed against the wall by the size of the chest as he attempted to move in close to take away her pain.

("*Quite alone*," he thought, very still, pulse pounding as if after a good sprint up to Hudson Heights and back, in hot pursuit of Drs. Twemlow and Brown. Perhaps he might join them, a trinity of doctors sprinting gruntingly around Longfellow Park – morning and evening – elbows and knees a blur, shorts cracking with starch, arms and legs at angles of forty-five degrees, academe allied with athleticism? It might help to bring a little – er – quietude to his restlessness, subdue the avid edge of his appetites. Playing his banjo had long lost its soothing efficaciousness, but bad backs and breathlessness were ever the enemies of erotic thralldom.)

When she was hypnotized, Svengali made Trilby sing "Ben Bolt," the song she would die singing. Before she was hypnotized she was tone-deaf, incapable of singing a note in tune; hypnotized she could sing so beautifully that she cast a spell over her listeners almost as powerful as the spell which had been cast over her.

This time it was Alice's lips that were moving, as if it were she who were singing. The voice, the music, merged in her mind with those for "I Dreamt That I Dwelt in Marble Halls," and the piano music became thin, distant, echoing, like music that was indeed being played within the cavernous high-ceilinged rooms of some distant halls: tall columns, polished marble, many-paned windows. The music became "Narcissus." Dappled by the shadows of the sunlight through the palm trees, the trio of musicians – a pianist, a violinist, a violoncellist, all elderly women – in the arched hotel conservatory played as tinklingly as the teacups and teaspoons at the tables around them.

> *Ker-plunk, ker-plunk,*
> *Ker-plunkety plunky-plunk.*
> *Ker-plunk, ker-plunk,*
> *Ker-plunkety plunky-plunk . . .*

Little decorative flourishes in the piano playing reminded her of the elaborate lettering on the front cover of the sheet music, especially the *o* in *or* just before the alternative title "Oh! Don't You Remember," the *B* of *Ballad*, and the sweeping curving lines around this subtitle, and around the name of the singer, *Miss Clara Bruce*, patterned like the ripples in a pool – the patterns opening out from a dropped stone, a rising fish — like the elaborate curlicues and gold lettering on the dark blue cover of her hymn book.

If you dream you are singing while everything around you gives promise of happiness, jealousy will insinuate a sense of insincerity into your joyousness. If there are notes of sadness in the song, you will be unpleasantly surprised at the turn your affairs will take.

When she heard someone singing she saw the words in front of her, like advertisements covering a wall, or the front of a store; she saw the illustrated cover of the sheet music, as if it were being displayed in the windows of Columbarian & Horowitz, alongside the Du Rell or Du Bell Twin Brothers, "Why Did They Dig Ma's Grave So Deep?", and "Poor Wandering One."

> "Oh! don't you remember sweet Alice, —
> Sweet Alice, with hair so brown;
> She wept with delight when you gave her a smile,
> And trembled with fear at your frown . . ."

Before he first hypnotized Alice, Dr. Wolcott Ascharm Webster explained to her what he was proposing to do. This was most unlike him. She was not sure how to respond — she gazed at the gleam of the gold book titles in the dim light, unable to make out what they said — until she realized that no response was needed. Again, he was not talking to her: he was rehearsing his lectures, talking to his audience of Bearded Ones, describing himself to them in heroic language, immortalizing himself on his phonograph.

"In the case of Miss P. I followed a bold strategy . . ."

He likened himself to Orpheus (not even a trace of a smile on his face), traveling down into the underworld to bring Eurydice — herself — back from the realms of darkness. He did not regard this choice of language as being in any way in conflict with his earlier rejection of imagination, just as he did not regard a sudden blazing

394

enthusiasm for hypnotism as being in any way in conflict with his earlier usage of electrotherapy, baths, and massage. As Mrs. Albert Comstock was with art critics, so he was with alienists. He was large (though nowhere near as large); he contained multitudes (most of the population of Asia could have rambled about in roomy solitude within Mrs. Albert Comstock). He would embrace the world and everything that was in it, though – one hoped – not in so literal a manner as Walt Whitman was rumored to have done. The bardic Bearded One would not have approved of her. She looked through the eyes of the dead; she fed on the specters in books.

It seemed, however, somewhat careless of him not to be aware that Eurydice – because Orpheus broke strict instructions, and turned around to look at her face as he led her back to the surface of the earth – was dragged back into the darkness forever, into the realms of silence and uncreated things. This image of her fate did not inspire confidence that the doctor was a man who knew what he was doing, and why he was doing it. She wished she hadn't read "The Facts in the Case of M. Valdemar," Edgar Allan Poe in fine form (the flambeaux flaring, the drapes rippling along the walls), and saw herself – The Facts in the Case of Mlle Pinkerton – mesmerized at the point of death and awoken from her trance months later, to collapse into a nearly liquid mass of loathsome, detestable putridity. Franz Mesmer would smile proudly from behind her at this demonstration of the power of his art, suspended upon his piece of cord and swaying slightly, so that the reflection upon it glinted mesmerizingly. ("Turn around!" he whispered imperiously again. "Turn around!") That would make a mess of the nice thin-legged chairs with their pale upholstery, that would ruin the expensive – if florid – carpet.

"Pinkerton's Champion Stain Remover and Paragon Detergent will clean it up in no time."

This – a sentence from The Pinkerton Collection, one of Oscar Wilde's less celebrated utterances ("I knew Pinkerton would do it" was part of another sentence from "The Canterville Ghost") – was her most conscious thought as he leaned in toward her, swinging his pocket-watch from his right hand like a gold-plated grandfa-ther-clock pendulum, another Reverend Goodchild on the point of rendering unto Cæsar. If Griswold's Discovery failed to do the trick, you automatically turned to Pinkerton's.

Tick. Tock. Tick. Tock.

It was a slow, majestic rhythm, a sound too dignified for excla-mation points.

Dr. Wolcott Ascharm Webster looked like a boy who had just read the instructions for a new game of skill — not quite sure how to go about it — and who was now prematurely facing his first oppo-nent. He had that exact expression of uncomprehending concentration, that precise whiff of nervous perspiration under the American Castile toilet soap.

She half expected him to consult a little rough-papered publica-tion like a Dream Book, ungrammatical and clumsily printed in smudged misspellings, discreetly positioned in his left hand.

Mississippi Mike's Gide to Hypnoti3m.

1. Face the Subjekt.

2. Swing Wotch from side to side.

3. IMPORTANT. Do not leave go of Wotch . . .

She might well have her moustache agonizingly ripped from her face as the watch-chain became entangled, or be rendered uncon-scious by an incautiously powerful oscillation.

("How on earth did you acquire that black eye?")

("I was being hypnotized.")

He had probably practiced in front of one of the bookcases, using the glass as a mirror, striving to achieve the correctly impres-sive expression of gravitas, the properly vigorous impetus to his swing. The silent nearness of Brian, beneath the reflection, would have been a great comfort to him. He'd probably accidentally hyp-notized himself a few times as he experimented, wandering about the room like a somnambulist, bouncing off the walls and rattling the rows of Bearded Ones, until an ungraceful swan-dive off his desk (more *Nutcracker* than *Swan Lake*, and certainly no *Sleeping Beauty*) jarred him into consciousness.

He was going to show her something that could cure her pain better than music.

He did not say, "Look me in the white of the eyes."

He did not caress her temples. (Slight struggle at this point.)

He did not ask her to sing "Ben Bolt."

He just said, slowly, over and over again, as he held the watch before her eyes, "Listen to my voice. Be still. Empty your mind of all thought. Sleep . . ."

(This is the devil's trick.)

She listened to his voice.

She was still.

She emptied her mind of all thought.

She slept.

He had read the instructions properly. He could play the game and win. In the schoolyard he would take no prisoners, lord of his little domain, king of his castle, a snatcher of jump ropes.

> . . . *In the old churchyard, in the valley, Ben Bolt,*
> *In a corner obscure and alone,*
> *They have fitted a slab of granite so gray,*
> *And sweet Alice lies under the stone . . .*

"Listen to my voice. Be still. Empty your mind of all thought. Sleep."

He would say this — a notebook placed conveniently to hand — and, Wednesday after Wednesday, she listened to his voice, she was still, she emptied her mind of all thought, she slept.

The battered survivors of the princes — those who had climbed up to the tower in the abortive attempts to rescue her — could form orderly lines outside 11 Park Place to inspect the Sleeping Ugly, but who would wish to awaken her with a kiss?

She would sleep forever; she would never be awoken, and as she slept she would dream. The slab of gray granite pressed insistently upon her, stifling her breathing into shallowness.

He had talked of Orpheus and Eurydice, but – even if this myth had not had the ending it had – it was not the right comparison. She did not have the sensation of being lost somewhere inside a network of subterranean galleries, waiting to be rescued. What she felt was that the galleries were *inside herself*, and that there was a monster hidden somewhere in the depths of them. If any myth did come into her mind it would be the myth of the Minotaur, the creature at the heart of the Labyrinth that demanded the lives of the young.

This felt more like the way things were, though she balked at the thought of Dr. Wolcott Ascharm Webster as Theseus, heroically penetrating deep within the darkness to find and slay the monster. She would be Ariadne, she supposed, handing Theseus the threads so that he would be able to find his way back out of the Labyrinth after he had destroyed the creature that lived inside her. She saw the threads as being the threads of tapestries. As Theseus traveled deeper into the darkness, closer to the monster, the tapestries that she wove by night and day would be unpicked, line by line – out flew the web and floated wide – and all the pictures would unravel thread by thread: the faded king and queen playing chess in a garden (*Alice meets R.Q., Alice through Q's 3rd to Q's 4th, Alice meets W.Q., Alice to Q's 5th* . . .), and the company of hawkers carrying hooded birds on their gauntleted wrists. If Pinkerton's failed to cleanse away all the colors, all the elaboration of the pictures and patterns, she would have to rely on Webster's. Then the unstitched whiteness of the blank canvases would unravel thread by thread, in their turn, and all that would remain in her high-towered blank-walled schoolroom would be the empty frame of her loom, like a picture frame without a picture. There, exposed to view, blinking in the unexpected brightness of the light, would be the face of Bertha Rochester, no longer hidden. Theseus would abandon Ariadne on Naxos – here was another analogy that should not have been used – and there she would be, alone on the seashore, curled up in sleep, weary, tear-stained, gazed upon by Bacchus. High on the ledge outside Grandpapa's office, suddenly appearing amidst all the women, Theseus' father would wait for the return of his son, gazing out to sea, looking for the first glimpse of the sails, hoping against hope that they would be white, the linen bare, the colored threads all unraveled. Their blackness would drive him to despair and self-destruction.

Perhaps she herself was the monster, hidden away like Fair Rosamond — an unfair Rosamond (most unfair!) — the secret beloved of Henry II, in the center of the mazed corridors of the house named Labyrinth. Queen Eleanor made her way through the maze with a thread, and murdered her.

What she should have thought about, as she braced herself for hypnosis — he had made it sound potentially painful, a G. G. Schiffendecken of the mind, warning her that this might hurt just a little (*Painless Alienist* the sign buzzed and pulsed, *Painless Alienist* the sign lied in large letters) — was the opening of *Alice's Adventures in Wonderland*. This was, she supposed — thank you, Charlotte — inevitable. This was, she supposed, more like it. Here she was being hypnotized by the White Rabbit: the pocket-watch and the waist-coat pocket from which it emerged in Sir John Tenniel's illustration were identical to those of Dr. Wolcott Ascharm Webster. He certainly had pinkish eyes, and there was that way his nose sometimes twitched as it loomed through the whiskers. If the rabbit's long ears were pressed down alongside his face they would bear more than a passing resemblance to the mighty beard. She was already within Wonderland, already within the looking-glass, and it was only fitting that it should be the White Rabbit who led her into the deeper levels, a Professor Von Hardwigg of the rabbit world, leading her on her journey to the center of the earth.

Alice fell down into the darkness, becoming sleepy, clutching at the things she could remember, as if they would prevent her fall: Latitude, Longitude, the Antipathies, cats and bats. She fell past the cupboards and the bookshelves — there were many, many books — the maps and pictures hung upon pegs, and the empty orange marmalade jar, like the one that Tess of the d'Urbervilles used to hold the flowers on the grave of her dead baby, visited in secret and at night. She tried to glimpse the titles of the books, reaching her hands out toward them, tried to see the countries in the maps, the subjects in the pictures, but it was too dark — she could read nothing, she could see nothing — and she fell toward the center of the earth.

There were monsters there, at the heart of the labyrinth, and Harry Lawson, Professor Von Hardwigg, and Hans Bjelka tramped deeper inside the labyrinth of subterranean galleries inside her mind, seeking them out. All three were Bearded Ones. The novels of Jules Verne seemed to be as curiously free of women as the novels of Robert Louis Stevenson: not only writers, but also the characters of whom they wrote were most appropriate for their parts when bearded. All explorers — apart from Isabella Bird (she *knew* that there were other such women, but she could not bring their names to mind) — were in possession of a beard: beards were an essential part of the equipment (carefully ticked off on long lists), like pith helmets, compasses, and native bearers. Each subterranean discoverer bore his own stalactite — wondrously shaped and whorled — around with him in order to blend in with his surroundings, and Professor Von Hardwigg (the very name promised a hairstyle as spectacular as his beard) gave a commentary to his companions as they descended.

"The interior of the female's head is — as we suspected — strangely empty . . ."

Scribble, scribble, scribble.

Someone was taking notes.

Jules Verne had written opera libretti before he wrote novels, and she always saw his novels as operas, his characters — a stirring male chorus; there were no female voices — singing as they descended beneath the surface of the sea, floated across the desert in a balloon, journeyed to the moon, or to the center of the earth.

Harry Lawson, Professor Von Hardwigg, and Hans Bjelka were supposed to light their way with Ruhmkorf's coils — whatever they were (her ugly little head couldn't possibly know) — but she saw them in her mind (in every sense) as holding flaming torches aloft as they descended, in wanton defiance of explosive gases. They were like three bearded statues of *Liberty Enlightening the World*.

". . . Give me your tired, your poor . . ."

— they sang, as if expecting the underground corridors to be teeming with crowds of the oppressed —

". . . Your huddled masses yearning to breathe free,
The wretched refuse of your teeming shore . . ."

Mrs. Albert Comstock would certainly warm to the phrase "wretched refuse": she couldn't have put it better herself (and there was far too much of it about).

Refuse the refuse!

Verb, then noun.

That was her motto.

Alice had a photograph of herself as a little girl standing in the torch of the statue. It had been taken when the torch — all by itself — was erected in Madison Square Gardens during fund-raising for the statue, and it was oddly disconcerting to look at it now, so out of its place, and see the buildings of the city towering above the upraised hand, as if the whole immense figure of the woman had sunk beneath the surface of the earth. That was where she belonged, out of sight, buried in the darkness, hidden from light.

The men's voices echoed, drawn out and lingering, as they tramped down the underground corridors, the flames of the torches flickering on the rocky walls. It was a Wagnerian scene. Siegfried would appear shortly, and a mighty-bosomed Mrs. Albert Comstock-shaped Brünnhilde encased in iron like a battleship, full of complaints as usual: "*O feiger Mann! Falscher Genoss!/Hinter dem Helden hehltest du dich* . . ." Crystals of opaque quartz fused with drops of natural glass hung from the roof like pendants, and flared into life as they walked beneath them.

Feiger Man!

Falscher Genoss!

The words echoed and reechoed, a perpetual motion of sound in the narrow channels beneath the surface.

Down, down, they tramped, and the geological layers — neat and sharp-edged, parti-colored as a vegetable terrine — were like cupboards, like bookshelves (the bookshelves past which Alice had fallen with such curious slowness), like the diagrams in a textbook, with the little engravings of the creatures that had lived in each period, their skeletons drawn as if they had always been dead, their bones slotted neatly into straight-lined epochs as if into a dark wooden glass-fronted display cabinet, fossils with the same coiled shapes as a carefully arranged collection of seashells.

Down, down, they tramped: Holocene, Pleistocene, Pliocene, Miocene — singing the names in a bass chorus — Oligocene, Eocene, Paleocene, Late Cretaceous . . .

Through the epochs they tramped, through the periods, through the eras, through the bones of the dinosaurs, through the ammonites, the ferns, the insects and the fish. The further they penetrated to the center, the regions of eternal night, the simpler the life forms became. The rocks around them, like a layered history of architecture, buildings piled one upon the other through the centuries, as in Rome, became more primitive and undecorated as they went further down. At first they spun, like Renaissance artists lowered on the ends of ropes into the earth, through the debris of the ages and down into Nero's buried Golden Palace, hovering like descending *dei ex machina*, gods coming down to earth to bring calmness and order to the tortured lives of those who were merely human. They hung in mid-air above the earth-scattered mosaic floors, flying open-mouthed, their torches catching the glint of gold, painted flowers, the faces of nymphs and gods moving on the walls — alive — in the shifting light. Then, punching their way through the mosaics, they moved miles further down, deeper into the darkness, through the rich-veined marbles — agate gray with white, yellow with red — through schist, calcareous rocks, and red sandstone, to dark and gloomy walls, oppressive, without decoration or brightness.

Through this cavernously echoing obscurity they journeyed toward the Central Sea, huge, endless, its shores littered with the bones of the ages, edged by a forest colorless and unperfumed, overhung by flickering storm-racked clouds and the weight of their huge shadows, a place for Dante, for Virgil, for Doré. It was a silent sea, its fish blind, eyeless, in whose depths hideous monsters fought for supremacy. *Here Be Monsters.* This was the ornately scripted legend on the empty spaces of the map, of the mind. Here the monsters slept, curled up, twitching as they dreamed, awaiting their awakening. At the center there would not be just a single Minotaur. The Minotaurs would be in herds, furred and black and humped, thundering and running wild like buffalo on the Great Plains, and there was no one there to hunt them.

Like a child, Harry Lawson shut his eyes, so that he would not see the darkness.

To dream of seeing a cavern yawning in the weird moonlight before you, many perplexities will assail you, and doubtful advancement because of adversaries. Work and health is threatened. To be in a cave foreshadows change. You will probably be estranged from those who are very dear to you.

⎯⎯∞⎯⎯

Tick. Tock. Tick. Tock.

"Listen to my voice. Be still. Empty your mind of all thought. Sleep . . ." he would say.

She listened to his voice.

She was still.

She emptied her mind of all thought.

She slept.

> "Sweetly she sleeps, my Alice fair,
> Her cheeks on the pillow pressed,
> Sweetly she sleeps . . ."

The Bearded Ones swayed from side to side, they chanted, they hummed, they lulled her into sleep and forgetfulness.

This enthusiasm for hypnotism lasted for almost eighteen months.

Sometimes he used the pocket-watch, sometimes the flame of a candle, sometimes the glint of his gold ring. He fisted his hand, and held it up before her – about to strike her in the face – and angled it until the light from the window caught the gold. Thick gold watch links spread across his chest, as if he were chained down by wealth, an indulged prisoner of luxury, enthralled by his thralldom. There was a great deal of gold about Dr. Wolcott Ascharm Webster, much of it visible when he showed his teeth. When G. G. Schiffendecken appeared on the scene, Dr. Wolcott Ascharm Webster did not fall prey to the seductive power of his false teeth, the teeth that spread across Longfellow Park in wave after wave of gigantic grins, haunting the dreams of the nervous. The Maoris of New Zealand had their Queequeg-like facial tattoos, their features pressed all over with large inky thumbprints; the more remote tribes in the mountainous areas of Burma had their giraffe-necked women; and the inhabitants of Longfellow Park had their Schiffendecken's Grins ("Longfellow Park! Longfellow Park! I can tell by your teeth it's your home!"), but not at 11 Park Place.

Here – people who did not trust banks (stubbornly refusing to be seduced by the lavishness of the new branch of the Manhattan & Brooklyn Bank) – they carried their savings about with them in their mouths. The head of Charm – *Charm!* – or Cotty or Asch (whatever it was Hilde Claudia chose to call him in their queasily imagined private, intimate moments), the head of Hilde Claudia, and even the heads of Theodore and Max (running out of space in their own capacious mouths, the parents transferred assets into the mouths of their offspring) were bowed down by the weight of the gold in their teeth, the sinfulness of their capitalistic instincts, and when they talked it was like catching glimpses into a bank vault, the dull gleam in the darkness through bars.

Charm or Cotty or Asch – whatever you called him, he was still Dr. Wolcott Ascharm Webster – bared his teeth when he concentrated, and the metal gleamed in the light that shone through the small gap in the curtains. A pocket-watch, a candle flame, a ring: these did not hypnotize her; she was hypnotized by a tooth, a particularly large canine left of center at the top.

Closer he came toward her, and closer, carrying his instrument of murder before him, planning to smother her with his beard. The faint smell of fish, a very ancient and fish-like smell — Wednesday mornings were days on which he breakfasted generously on herring — would become overpowering, a man who'd been employing his beard as a seine net, strung out across the Hudson. Faintly flapping tails would slap against the side of her face, attempting to revive her after a faint. Faints were not very far away some mornings. Occasionally, there were soft-boiled egg mornings, and these — if anything — were even worse than the fish. He appeared to have developed a technique of secreting extra supplies of food within his beard, so that — without interrupting the flow of his probings — he could discreetly nibble his way through the morning when troubled by gnawing pangs of hunger. Spasmodically, he activated his jaws after slipping a few extra supplies into his mouth from his hidden stockpile, though she never seemed to catch the moment when hand made contact with mouth. Whenever he chomped, whatever he chewed, she could never rid herself of the feeling that it was she upon whom he feasted.

She should borrow Mabel Peartree's shopping basket, and one of Max Webster's little cloaks. If anything vaguely historical was selected for warbling, out came the cloaks. Max Webster pictured himself as a living embodiment of the time *When Knighthood Was in Flower*, and this particular bloom blossomed with a tropical luxuriance, a hothouse flower on the point of smashing through the glass into the colder, darker world outside. He was the hero of Mrs. Twemlow's favorite novel, a Charles Brandon *de nos jours* ("French!" Mrs. Albert Comstock shrieked, her parasol twitching into action. "French!"), and his complexion — he believed — held a tinge of beauty that the sun could not mar and a girl might envy. He was a real live man — *ha!* — full of manliness. He was almost rosy (an apple all ripe for big-teethed chomping). He was six feet (he really was, was Master Max, this Infant Phenomenon stretched on the rack of shrieking) of perfect manhood, strong and vigorous as a young lion. As she listened to him killing off his mother yet again, Mrs. Twemlow Senior's jaws rotated briskly in a counterclockwise direction as she demolished the violet creams in record time. *Vigorous. Vigorous.* Alice would wrap his red cloak about her, like some out-of-order cloak of invisibility, and then she could look the part for Little Red Riding Hood.

"Oh, Dr. Webster! What big ears you have!"

(He did. They poked out from the outer regions of his beard like glumly disporting hippopotami surfacing for air.)

"All the better to hear you with, Miss Pinkerton."

Scribble, scribble.

"Oh, Dr. Webster! What big eyes you have!"

(He did. Magnified by the lenses of his spectacles, they seemed perpetually agog, sniggeringly avid at the juicy discoveries — fat, wriggling worms — he grubbingly unearthed.)

"All the better to see you with, Miss Pinkerton."

(She'd omit the big hands. She preferred not to think about being informed that they were all the better to hug her with.)

"Oh, Dr. Webster! What a big tooth you have . . ."

(She didn't want to think about this either.)

It glinted, it winked, and it drew her in toward it.

<hr>

He was a huckster, a fast-talking showman, a carpetbagger whose carpetbag was crammed and clinking with bottles of violently colored water. He held them up in front of a wagon that emblazoned his name three-dimensionally in lurid reds and golds, and the flaring lights shone through the contents of the bottles so that his face changed color from blue to green to red. Like curiously unerotic hootchy-kootchy dancers, Hilde Claudia, Theodore, and Max wanly *pirouetted* to and fro in the flaring lights, listlessly manipulating their triangular flags like miniature fans in soporific semaphore, their minds on other things as they bumped and grinded (or should this be "ground"?).

Not much joy from hypnotism.

(Not much joy for the patient, that is. He'd quite enjoyed following in the footsteps of Svengali.)

It was time for something new.

There'd not been much joy from electrotherapy.

There'd not been much joy from baths (hot).

There'd not been much joy from baths (cold).

He'd spent most of the time with his spectacles all misted over, and he hadn't been able to see a *thing*.

There'd been no joy *whatsoever* from massage. He'd imagined that this would offer generous opportunities to caress temples, followed — almost instantly — by big chests falling submissively under his power. No such luck. He might have followed in Svengali's footsteps, but he had signally failed to achieve any measure of chesty fulfillment.

It was *definitely* time for something new.

Something New and Improved.

Something that would cause a stir.

It was time . . .

Tarantara!

It was time. . .

Tarantara!

It was time to announce the arrival of — *Tarantara!* — cloud-reading.

New!

Improved!

Cloud-reading!

Peep, peep!

Attention! The two arms were held up and away from the body at an angle of forty-five degrees — the gesture of someone in front of a runaway horse — and the flags shaken, as if a king or president was being patriotically greeted.

Peep, peep!

C. The right arm was held up and away from the body at an angle of forty-five degrees, and the left arm was held so that the flag depended from one corner in front of the center of the body.

Peep, peep!

L. The right arm was held down and away from the body at an angle of forty-five degrees, and the left arm up and away from the body, so that the two arms made one continuous line.

Peep, peep!

O. . .

If he developed a sudden fascination with carpentry, sewing, or cookery he would — she felt — somehow insinuate this into her treatment, the book of instruction open for easy reference on top of his desk.

"Make this apple pie for me, Miss Pinkerton. You will undoubtedly obtain much relief. Here is your apron. The apples are in the bowl on your right. Over there are the flour, the butter, and the other ingredients, and in that jug there is some milk . . ."

"Cook," he would say, and she would cook.

"The collar of this shirt needs repair . . ."

"Sew," he would say, and she would sew.

"Hammer," he would say, and she would hammer.

He would not say "Write."

He would not say "Paint."

He would not say "Read."

After the reading of clouds came the reading of pictures and the reading of dreams, and these arrived at about the same time, and all these methods continued into the new century. She had rather hoped that the new century, like the firm lines drawn between the epochs of geologic time, might mean the beginning of something new, something that *meant* something, but things remained the same. She did not know the names of the books that had given him the ideas for the reading of clouds and the reading of pictures and dreams, though she had her suspicions that the clouds were the result of an especially vital word being mistranslated by Hilde Claudia, for whom nouns were clearly becoming as big a problem as the werbs. The mistake might very well have happened when a word in the original German had been misread, or when – here was a possibility that surely justified a scholarly monograph from Dr. Wolcott Ascharm Webster – Hilde Claudia, hopelessly confused, had inadvertently introduced her own Cloudier self into the text she was attempting to translate.

She had asked Charlotte to try and find out which words in German were almost the same as the German word for "cloud." Charlotte actually had an English–German dictionary, but it was just the second volume – *L to Z* – of a two-volume set, not very helpful when the word sought began with "c." (Alice had toyed with the concept of someone trying to communicate without using any words beginning with the letters from "a" to "k" in the alphabet.) Charlotte had asked Emmerson, and brought back just two words – "*Wolke*" (which meant cloud) and "*Wolle*" (which meant wool) – and several phrases, including the German for "head in the clouds," "to be under a cloud" (vital for all Germanic Mrs. Albert Comstocks and Mrs. Goodchilds out Magdalene-prodding), "cloud-cuckoo land" (definitely a useful phrase if Alice was in the vicinity), and "her eyes were clouded with tears." ("*Ihre Augen waren von Tränen getrübt*": it might come in useful some day.) She must ask her to find out more words from Emmerson, and try to discover if another word ought to have been used in the translation. "*Volk*" (the German word for "people") sounded a little like the way Charlotte had pronounced "*Wolke*," and she found herself picturing cloud people, heads in the clouds, tall slow-moving beings reaching high into the sky, their shadows stretching out across the landscape.

It might well be, of course – there was always this possibility – that she had misjudged Dr. Wolcott Ascharm Webster (it was not very likely), and that no mistranslation had occurred at all. The interpretation of clouds might be at the very forefront of knowledge – pushing out a new frontier, covered wagons heading west – for those who sought to heal the minds of the lost, and bring solace to the suffering. He had borne his knowledge in triumph to Longfellow Park, like G. G. Schiffendecken bearing his false teeth (held aloft like the spoils of a conquered kingdom for the acclaim of cheering crowds), and she had cruelly spurned what he had offered to her in a spirit of Christian charity. *Ha!*

Another "ia" was evolving here, she felt, to send Mrs. Goodchild scuttling delightedly: nephophobia, a terror of clouds.

Now would be a particularly good time to provoke a Mrs. Goodchild scuttle: the sidewalks were so icy that there was the attractive possibility that she might skid (several hundred yards if she had achieved full scuttling speed) and break a leg. Alice lingered on this thought luxuriously. Mrs. Goodchild – hurtling through the park on her way home – careened across the marble surroundings of the statues in The Forum, skittling a passing group of nuns from The House of the Magdalenes (Alice generously allowed a small tingle of pleasure to Mrs. Goodchild), and collided with the plinth of Albert Comstock's marbled magnificence. Sickening crunch. First she scuttled, then she skittled, then she broke a leg. One of the Dennistons' horses had broken its leg and been shot the previous week. She dreamed. She dreamed. And if she dreamed, Dr. Wolcott Ascharm Webster would wish to know all the details.

If there were a phobia for phobias – phobiaphobia? – she probably had it, and she fully intended to hang firmly onto it.

It was her phobia.

Hers.

No one else should share it.

If she had misjudged him – reading clouds, after all, seemed no more outlandish than some of his other methods of treatment – perhaps she was helping to explore new and unknown territory, a Lewis and Clark of the mind (though Lewis and Carroll might more aptly be seen as her terrain), and "Miss P." — the very first patient — might feature heavily when the history of this new science came to be written. There would be some impressive term for it — everything Dr. Wolcott Ascharm Webster did had an impressive term for it (it would not be suitable for him to do if it did not) — and she mused a while. Nebulism? (It was nebulous in every sense.) Nephopsychology? Cloudology (not as impressive as nephopsychology)? Or perhaps they were approaching the moment when Dr. Wolcott Ascharm Webster was at last to seize his moment to be immortalized by naming what was his very own discovery after himself.

She — without knowing it — was a pioneer of Websterism, becoming one of the gods by reading the signs in the clouds, interpreting the shapes she saw in the sky. Webster's Technique would enter the textbooks, like all the diseases that were named after the men who had discovered them: Weil's, von Recklinghausen's, Hodgkin's, Bright's, Pott's, Paget's, and all the others. How very strange to give one's name to a disease, particularly when the diseases with the names of men were some of the worst, some of the most frightening. She saw their bearded faces — like the gathering of the poets, like the shareholders of the bank — looking down from the walls of the lecture theatre as she lay upon the table in front of them. The members of Dr. Wolcott Ascharm Webster's audience strained forward, moving their heads to obtain a good view, as he indicated the patient lying there below them on display, and prodded her into position. They were all glazed like framed photographs or engravings, and she couldn't see them properly for the reflections in the glass, her own warped shape reversed in front of her. Pale hands pointed, indicated.

"Note the characteristic posture of the female, with the arms crossed in front of the breasts, the knees pulled up toward the belly . . ."

Scribble, scribble, scribble.

His dubious methods, and the vigor with which they were ped-
dled, made her think of Griswold's Discovery, the revolting patent
medicine upon which the considerable fortunes of the Griswolds —
Mrs. Goodchild's sister and brother-in-law — were founded. The
boxes in which the bottles of Griswold's Discovery were enclosed
bore — as *Proof of Authenticity* (this was the expression
employed) — the grim bearded face of Josiah Griswold (not something one would imagine anyone wishing to fabricate). Even if the
bottles' swigged contents had contained the secret of eternal life,
the series of testimonials from grateful customers contained within
the box would have appeared excessive in their hysterical fulsomeness. Griswold's Discovery was heavily advertised in a way that
made the advertising for Barnum's museum appear coyly reticent,
and the face of Josiah Griswold — many feet high — peered glumly
down from heights all over New York City like a jealous god in
zealous search of sinners, to startle the unwary, and frighten nervous horses. Scowling, disapproving ("I know what you did to put
yourself in that condition!" he was booming disgustedly in his
loudest voice, so that everyone would hear him), he soared high
above *TARRANT'S SELTZER APERIENT, COLORIFIC, Boas &*
Feathers Renovated & Curled, Cigars, Painless Dentist, and *Learn to*
Waltz in Five Lessons, Guaranteed. One somehow felt that nothing
but the eager offer of ready money could compel him to allow
anyone to purchase his panacea.

If it was not the face of Josiah Griswold, it was the face of the
Griswold Girl, smiling and seductive, urging the miraculous elixir
upon the populace. Almost Schiffendeckenan in her tantalizing
toothsomeness, this buxom brunette looked nothing like any of the
frog-faced Griswolds. With the Griswolds and the Goodchilds —
the husbands and wives and tribes of children all looked identical in
their fearsome frog-facedness — one could not help feeling nervously that some deep-rooted Old Testament prohibition was being
willfully flouted, the Table of Kindred and Affinity (she had always
boggled at the thought of marrying her grandfather) plundered
for forbidden consanguinities, and bulgy-eyed twins had been

audaciously coupled in matrimony. Here was inbreeding on a Galápagosian scale to set Charles Darwin's beard aquivering yet again. Fire from heaven could not be long delayed to end this survival of the unfittest, this pedigree of perfidy.

Forget Josiah Griswold.

Forget the Griswold Girl.

Forget Griswold's Discovery.

Hilde Claudia, Theodore, and Max — recognizing that their moment had come around yet again — took up their positions to hootchy, to kootchy (kootchies always followed hot upon hootchies), to *pirouette*, to bump, to grind, to dazzle with their glitteringly hypnotic golden teeth.

Buy *these*! Buy *these*!

These — green, eight-sided, ribbed like poison containers — were the bottles flourished like rabbits from hats by Dr. Wolcott Ascharm Webster in the fairground flare in front of his wagon. In the dim interiors of the stained-glass-colored bottles, the concentrated clouds stirred and shifted, changing their meanings as they moved, very like a camel, very like a weasel, very like a whale, very like any number of things. The lettering on the bottles' labels — dark, as elaborate as that on the cover of any sheet music — read *Webster's Discovery*, and the *Proof of Authenticity* was the bearded face of Dr. Wolcott Ascharm Webster himself. There was no place here for Josiah Griswold; there was no place here for the Griswold Girl; they were elbowed vigorously aside, as the clouds swirled and pressed against the cork-stoppered narrow neck, as if they were jinnees seeking to escape, or the contents of Pandora's box eager to unleash all the troubles of the world. In *The Water Babies* Charles Kingsley, vigorously expounding his enthusiastic cold-baths muscular Protestantism to his dear little men, had — he'd meet with the wholehearted hear-hear approval of Mrs. Albert Comstock, Dr. Vaniah Odom, the Goodchilds, and, for that matter, Marie Corelli — listed Monks and Popes amongst the contents of Pandora's box, the ills which flesh is heir to, children of the four great bogies, Self-will, Ignorance, Fear, and Dirt. (He'd also listed

Quacks, Unpaid Bills, Potatoes, Bad Wine, and — in a telltale clue to the secret of his fearlessly upright fists-raised posture — Tight Stays.)

"Release me from the bottle, and I shall grant you three wishes!" cried Lust in a wheedlingly seductive voice.

"Release me from the bottle, and I shall grant you three wishes!" cried Anger, growing impatient and sounding threatening.

"Release me from the bottle, and I shall grant you three wishes!" cried Envy, whiningly furious that he was not free.

The sevenfold voices of the Sins wheedled and threatened and whined, and — behind their voices — there were countless other voices clamoring to be heard.

Me!

Me!

Me!

Hilde Claudia, Theodore, and Max were untiring.

Peep, peep!

O. The right arm was held up and away from the body at an angle of forty-five degrees, and the left arm was held flat horizontally across the front of the body.

Peep, peep!

U. The two arms were held up and away from the body at an angle of forty-five degrees. It was the same positioning as for "Attention!" — the gesture to stop a runaway horse — but the arms, this time, remained still, the king or the president ungreeted.

Peep, peep!

D . . .

S . . .

I see a "C"!

I see an "L"!

I see an "O"!

I see a "U"!

I see a "D"!

I see an "S"!
And what can I see? . . .

———⟨oᴖᴏ⟩———

"*Clouds?*" she asked, doubtfully, as he explained what it was she had
to do.

"Yes, clouds. Tell me what you can see in those clouds, Miss
Pinkerton."

Cloud-reading had arrived.

She sat in her chair at the window, and gazed up into the sky,
above the statues and the tops of the trees in the park, and told Dr.
Wolcott Ascharm Webster what it was she could see. Sometimes,
when she was not striving to read the titles of his books, she really
did try to see shapes in the sky. It was as if she were Moses on
Mount Sinai, and the LORD was coming unto her in a thick cloud.
The LORD sat behind her with his notebook, with his angelic host
behind him, buoyed up by their beards, they – also – floating high
above the world, and she read the clouds, as she would later read
the pictures. The people would hear when he spoke with her, and
believe him for ever. Hypnotism, clouds, pictures, dreams. There
would be thunders and lightnings, and a thick cloud upon the
mount, and the voice of the trumpet exceeding loud. Theodore
and Max would – slightly muffled by the intervening door and por-
tière – play their trumpets in the waiting room to ensure the
appropriate atmosphere for godlike revelations. It helped no end if
you lulled patients into the right mood. Spurning their mother's
heritage, they patriotically opted for the March King rather than the
Waltz King, John Philip Sousa rather than Johann Strauss the
Younger, and *Semper Fidelis* and *The Stars and Stripes Forever*
accompanied the ministrations of their papa.

She would draw near unto the thick darkness where God was,
and the talking cures would bring release. She would talk, and she
would be cured. The words were something bad inside her that had
to be spoken for her to feel better. In an unforeseen reversal of the

traditional arrangement, she had become a child in bed — that was how she felt — telling bedtime stories to a listening adult — week after week — as the adult listened with rapt attention, taking notes to satisfy his remembrance the more strongly.

The adult spoke no "Once upon a time."

The adult spoke no "happily ever after."

The adult was the listener, not the speaker, and it was the child who spoke of things seen in the air, things in dreams and pictures, the child who spoke the bad words, described the bad things. She spoke in the dimmed room, a room like a child's summertime room prepared for sleeping.

> *I have to go to bed by day.*
> *I have to go to bed and see*
> *The birds still hopping on the tree,*
> *Or hear the grown-up people's feet*
> *Still going past me in the street.*

As she spoke, no one else visible, she could hear the *scratch, scratch, scratch* of the pen-nib behind her, like the sound of the birds' little curved claws rattling on the bark of the tree. It was like talking to herself.

Well, that was — after all — just as it should be.

That was — after all — the first sign of madness.

That was another title she had saved, and was anxious to use before anyone else did.

It was *her* title.

The First Sign of Madness. (Or would it be "The First Sign of Madness"? Italics for a novel, and quotation marks for a short story. That was the system of punctuation she followed. She always underlined the titles in her lists, the handwritten symbol of italics, wildly ambitious to write nothing shorter than a novel, novel after novel, a Clarissa Harlowe whose quill was never at rest.)

There were so many unwritten books lined up, waiting.

She should talk more —

Scratch, scratch, scratch

— and the books would be written from her dictation.

Dr. Wolcott Ascharm Webster had been Lady Macbeth's doctor. How unlike him not to have insisted on being named, but to remain just an anonymous Doctor of Physic.

"Foul whisp'rings are abroad,"

— he'd confided in the Waiting-Gentlewoman —

". . . Unnatural deeds
Do breed unnatural troubles; infected minds
To their deaf pillows will discharge their secrets . . ."

Unnatural deeds.
Tick.
Unnatural troubles.
Tick.
Infected minds.
Tick. Tick.
Secrets.
Tick. Tick. Tick.
She possessed all the symptoms of infection.

After all those ticks came all those tics, the twitchy outer manifestations of the stricken, the nervous afflictions of the neurasthenic, the restlessness in which she could not be still (the sheets around her as ridged as a sea-washed shore), in which she could not empty her mind of all thought (thoughts swarmed upon her), in which she could not sleep. Sleep brought dreams.

These terrible dreams/That shake us nightly.

Tic. Tic. Tic.

". . . More needs she the divine than the physician."

The Reverend Goodchild — recognizing his cue — hurtled into position, panting slightly, teeth gigantically exposed. He'd (*Phew!*) know all about foul whisp'rings. He'd effect a miraculous cure by inserting a large bottle of Griswold's Discovery into her mouth, and – the tics intensified at the very thought – the laying on of his grubby, slightly clammy, hands.

Mrs. Goodchild had not liked the sound of the talking cure. It had sounded too like something – whatsit? – *Catholic* to her, the whisperings in the darkness of a confessional, crisscross bars of shadow across the face of the priest on the other side of the grille. Mrs. Goodchild would dearly love to *grill* a priest. When she barbecued something she liked it to be almost black, charred beyond recognition, like a body recovered from a conflagration, a lightning-struck sinner comprehensively sizzled by God at his tetchiest. When she grilled a sausage – "Don't play ignorant with me!" she'd start off challengingly. "You're going to answer *every* question I ask you!" – you could sketch an attractive landscape with the stick of charcoal that resulted. She'd be the most inquisitive member of the Spanish Inquisition (Protestant Division), grilling away until the atmosphere of the dungeon was black with meatily flavored clouds of smoke. There were the clouds again. There was no getting away from the clouds, and their meaning was all too clear. The thumbscrews, the rack, and the Iron Maiden (Mabel Peartree thoroughly enjoyed her little part-time position) were neatly lined up in readiness for the next stage of the torturing. The thrill of the grill, then the thrill of the kill, slow, methodical, infinitely prolonged. They'd soon get those Monks and Popes shoved back into Pandora's box, blackened and barbecued, shriveled, crisped and crackling at the edges.

"Bless me, father, for I have sinned."

Father Goodchild, his fingers raised to bless, his rosary rattling like Mrs. Albert Comstock's earrings, leaned toward her.

The talking cure had also sounded Jewish.

Neither of these was a recommendation in the eyes of Mrs. Goodchild. She did not explain why she thought it sounded Jewish, though Mrs. Albert Comstock's deeply felt description of Svengali hypnotizing Trilby had made a lasting impression upon her.

Mrs. Goodchild and Mrs. Albert Comstock always seemed to know the latest treatment that was being tried upon her, though neither Alice nor her mother told anyone what was happening. Clearly Dr. Wolcott Ascharm Webster entertained his hosts over candlelit dinners with amusing descriptions of Alice Pinkerton's latest peculiarities in the intervals when he was not playing on his banjo.

When the wine flowed with especial freedom he might very well combine the two, and sing comic songs about her, accompanying himself on the banjo. As the most fashionable treatises on etiquette explained, the most dependable manner in which to ensure popularity in Longfellow Park, the certain shortcut to a crammed-to-bursting engagement book, was to entertain all and sundry by regaling them with the most intimate and trusted secrets of other people's hearts. A guest with this to offer was guaranteed a good seat at Mrs. Albert Comstock's, and the biggest plate in 5 Hampshire Square piled high with the most enormous of all the pies produced by Comstock's Comestibles. Not just the Comstock Jumbo, Titanic, Monumental, or Gargantuan, but the Comstock Colossus, containing as much meat as Noah's Ark (including Noah himself, Shem, Ham – his very name dribblesomely weighted with promise – and Japheth, and their wives) and approximately the same size, every last cubit meat-crammed to bursting. Dr. Wolcott Ascharm Webster liked to crunch on a Colossus, and he possessed the party piece that guaranteed him guest of honor status. Mrs. Albert Comstock would keep those Colossuses (those Colossi?) coming, shunting them on like entire freight trains packed with whole herds of Chicago-bound cattle, and he'd dish the dirt as the gravy gushed down his chin, lending a youthful tinge to his beard. If he squeezed his beard out when he reached home, little Theodore and little Max could feast for a week on gallon-sized bowls of well-heated beef tea, flourishing with weed-like rapidity on the rich sustenance thus afforded them. The brazen sound of their Day of Judgment trumpets would deepen, as their ever-manlier lungs grew stronger.

He would find plenty of amusing things to sing about her.

The Goodchilds and Mrs. Albert Comstock were the audience taking notes (they'd take *plenty* of notes), the faces peering down at her from high above, elbows and sniggers fully activated, teeth glintingly on display. She was surprised that Mrs. Goodchild didn't go into more vigorous attack, bursting into the consulting room on Wednesday mornings with the air of a woman accidentally losing her bearings on some mission of mercy, those missions so movingly epitomizing her greatness of heart. She could have tiptoed through with I'm-not-really-here-don't-mind-me sort of gestures, listening avidly as she sashayed through. Mrs. Goodchild – decidedly – was showing signs of losing her subtle touch for snooping.

"I can see . . ."

"Yes?"

"I can see . . ."

"Tell me what you can see . . ."

Scribble, scribble, scribble.

She was like the poor Indian in Alexander Pope whose untutored mind saw God in clouds – a gift of discernment not exclusive to Moses – or heard him in the wind. She pictured the Indian as a Red Indian, gazing at the clouds to read the huge smoky messages – capital-lettered with eighteenth-century importance – inscribed across the sky from some vast conflagration consuming the plains, as buffalo herds thundered past in panic, hotly pursued by the ghost of Albert Comstock wielding a chopper, eagerly putting into practice his plans for the Comstock Gigantic, the Comstock Stupendous . . . *Comstock's Comestibles For A Buffalo Biggie! Grab Your Grub Now!* She thought of the same Indian in Othello's last speech, the one who threw a pearl away richer than all his tribe.

The chair in which she sat at Dr. Wolcott Ascharm Webster's was the same sort of chair as the one in which she sat in Mrs. Albert Comstock's box at the opera, with the same straight legs, the same faded figures in the tapestry of its seat and back. Sometimes – though it featured no tapestry, was without the half-discernible

groupings of gods and goddesses, the minor figures of mythology – she experienced the same sensation when she sat in the chair
in the dentist's, as G. G. Schiffendecken (smelling of peppermint,
grunting with concentration, seeing nothing but teeth: other human
beings existed solely as containers for teeth) labored in the darkness
of her mouth to extract the source of infection. He always gave the
impression of being a more hygienic version of Samuel
Cummerford, a rival for the automobile salesman, his head hidden
as he bent well down, pottering about, poking and peering under a
lifted hood with well-washed hands. It was always advisable to
count your teeth after you'd been in his chair: he was fully capable
of surreptitiously attempting to extract one or two teeth on each
visit, bringing ever closer the day when you would be driven to
purchase a complete artificial smile, and sent out into the world a
transformed person, newly toothsome in every possible meaning of
the word. Patients would stumble out into the street, their faces
curiously contorted as they – "un, ooh, ee" – touched their teeth
one by one with their tongues, making a cautious inventory of the
contents of their mouths (had he smashed? had he grabbed?) –
"oar, ive, ix . . ." In bed that night they'd be doing this over and
over, a new method of inducing slumber.

Evven.

Ate.

Ine.

En.

Dr. Wolcott Ascharm Webster should be leaning over her
with the same bright metal instruments in his hands, prod, prod,
prodding away at the lineaments of her brain, and sending her
out into the world, free from pain, and with a more radiant smile.
As she looked out of the Park Place window, she sometimes ran
her fingers beneath the seat on either side of her, feeling the
same round-headed tacks attaching the material to the wooden
frame, and felt that she was in the opera house, looking down
onto the stage. Faintly, she heard the voices of a male operatic
chorus, the glass that enclosed them muffling The Bearded Ones

in the photographs and engravings behind her as they sang with one voice. She looked up at the clouds in the way that the characters in operas looked at the painted backcloths — just a few feet behind them — like people looking at something real, seeing deep into infinite distances, far across seas, a star-filled or sun-brightened vastness that unfolded endlessly, searching for the arrival of someone they loved or hated, longing to embrace or to kill.

As she spoke, the tips of her fingers moved up and down on the smooth bright brass heads beneath her, as if she were picking out the different notes on an obscure instrument, one no longer played in a modern orchestra, accompanying herself with music. Hidden away in the darkness of the little open-fronted room, she watched the brightly illuminated figures below her live and die to music, singing. Words by themselves could not express the intensity of all the emotions that they experienced.

They sang in a language she could not understand.

In the darkness of the theatre you could not see to read the libretto, and the words were heard imperfectly, even if they were in a language you thought you knew, even if they were in the language that you yourself spoke. What you heard was not the words that were written down, the words from which meaning might be teased, but sounds, the human voice employed as another source of sound, another musical instrument.

"... *Die Strahlen der Sonne vertreiben die Nacht,*
Zernichten der Heuchler erschlichene Macht!..."

You would not hear this. You would not see these words — in a printed text — in front of you. What you heard — though you'd grasp the occasional words ("the sun," "the night"), complete phrases, hearing them, seeing them — was usually meaningless, the emotion conveyed through music, not language, and then the curtain drew across. It was time to sleep. The music had ended.

At the end of one of her fifty-five minutes of Wednesday morning cloud-reading, searching for the shapes in the sky, he told her what she was to do the following week, the fifty-five minutes of *picture*-reading. The sense of the crowded lecture theatre, the behatted and bebearded rising in tiers above her, the *scribble, scribble, scribble* of notes being taken, the voice that was always too loud for a consulting room . . . Mrs. Albert Comstock had chosen to disguise herself with a John Greenleaf Whittier false beard, which rather suited her (rarely had she appeared so pullulatingly feminine), whilst Mrs. Goodchild had favored the Oliver Wendell Holmes, cheekily curled at its extremities.

"What is happening in this picture?"

This was the new question.

This was the new enthusiasm.

New books had arrived from Vienna, whole crates of books that had to be crowbarred open, burglar-like. Hilde Claudia had been toiling night and day.

"What is happening in this picture?"

A mere description was not acceptable: the picture had to be interpreted.

(*The female — Miss P. — had it carefully explained to her what it was she had to do, and she seemed to understand. On the first occasion . . .*)

The pictures — a different picture each time — were hung on the wall alongside the window. The curtains, open for the clouds, were closed for the pictures, as they had been closed for the hypnotism. There was a light above the picture, the only illumination in the room, and she focused on this brightness, hearing only the hissing of the gas, and the voice behind her. She saw nothing but the picture, like someone concentrating prior to hypnotism.

She was surprised by the choice of pictures. Dr. Wolcott Ascharm Webster did not mention, if he indeed knew, who the artist was or what the title of the picture was — that would have compromised interpretation — but she recognized what they were, and they were better chosen than she would have imagined.

"Tell me what you can see in this picture, Miss Pinkerton."

The first picture was a Tintoretto, *St. George and the Dragon*. What a blow that Dr. Wolcott Ascharm Webster was no friend of Roland Birtle. Thus had she been prevented – no great surprise, this – from seeing Tintoretto's *Paradise* in the consulting room, probably the only picture, and the only artist, known to Childe Roland, essential components of his fascination in conversation. As he grappled with the challenging complexities of small talk, he employed that tone of voice of his, the one that almost guaranteed refreshing sleep, glazed eyes, and no exercise whatsoever for the brain. ("Did you know . . ." he would begin, in the tentative tone of voice of a tourist making his first hesitating foray into the disturbing world of Useful Foreign Phrases, ". . . that the largest painting in the world is *Paradise* by Tintoretto? It is eighty-four feet wide . . .") It would have been a stimulating challenge to interpret a picture eighty-four feet wide by thirty-three and a half feet high in fifty-five minutes. She could have gone for a refreshing stroll across it, rather in the way that G. G. Schiffendecken patrolled his "estate" from wall to wall like a sentry on duty outside a well-guarded royal palace. It might have brought a little color to her cheeks, a Wednesday morning walk in Paradise.

Here – in the chosen Tintoretto (it was considerably smaller than *Paradise*) – were clouds, the reading of clouds and the reading of pictures merging. "Sometimes we see a cloud that's dragonish." That's what Antony had said, searching for shapes in the clouds in the moments before his death, thinking that Cleopatra was dead. Well, here *was* something dragonish, and here was a fleeing princess – formally dressed in silks and jewels (the Vermeer-like gleam of pearls), clothes for a blazingly candlelit ballroom, not clothes for the open air – hurtling away from the dragon and out from the foreground of the picture toward her.

The dragonish cloud unfurled high in the sky, breathing out

smoke that opened out into further shapes, a bear, a lion, a tower'd citadel, its entrance barred and inaccessible . . .

To dream of a dragon, denotes that you will allow yourself to be governed by your passions, and that you are likely to place yourself in the power of your enemies through those outbursts of sardonic tendencies. You should be warned by this dream to cultivate self-control.

Here was a personal rebuke, a series of warnings designed expressly for her.

(*Do not be governed by your passions.*

(*Control those outbursts of sardonic tendencies.*

(*Cultivate self-control.*)

"I c-c-can see . . ."

(What she saw was Annie.)

"Yes?"

"I c-c-can see . . ."

(What she saw was a girl dressed in blue, standing in the light of an unseen window, surrounded by stillness and silence. What could Miss Pinkerton see in this picture?)

"Tell me what you can see . . ."

(What did this picture *mean*? It was the picture at which she gazed as she paused in the midst of reading, leaving words behind in an attempt to interpret the wordless.)

Scribble, scribble, scribble.

(What had Annie been trying to say, unable to communicate in words, and letting a picture carry her message? There would be a great deal of scribbling if she tried to interpret this picture: the thoughts in the girl's head, the contents of the letter.

(The nameless girl in blue — utterly still, self-absorbed, bent over in the light from the window, aware of nothing but the contents of the letter in her hand — was reading a love letter, a confession of guilt, a suicide note, a brutal rejection. Sometimes Alice thought that the girl could not read, and was staring uncomprehendingly at the writing on the paper, trying unsuccessfully to make out what it was it said, in the same way as Alice was staring at the picture. This girl wore no jewels, though Alice could just make out some pearls – pearls, again – lying on the surface of the table in front of her. Brass-headed studs hammered into the surface of the two chairs in the picture caught the light, glinted as the pearls glinted. Alice ran the tips of her fingers across the tacks hammered into the underside of the chair in which she sat, as if she had herself stepped into the picture, as if it was she who was the girl in blue.

(Had the pearls accompanied the letter? There was no joy in the girl's pose, no sense of her having received a token of love. Sometimes Alice saw resignation in the pose. Sometimes the ring-less hands seemed on the point of crumpling up the letter they held.

(Sometimes Alice thought that the girl – in her loose blue smock – was pregnant. Was this what Annie had been trying to tell her?

("Pregnant" was not a word one tended to hear in Longfellow Park. "Ahem – you know" was a favored phrase for fertility, as was "an interesting condition" – it was a condition found *most* interesting by Mrs. Albert Comstock and Mrs. Goodchild, *prod, prod* – or, voice lowered, a word most often whispered, "gravid." Mrs. Goodchild did not need to say "whatdoyoumacallit?" or "thinga-majig" or "whatsit?" when "gravid" came into it; the word came readily to her mouth. Mrs. Albert Comstock did not choose to employ an "er" in this context, though an "ahem" was invisibly inserted prior to the hissing whisper.

(Alice had never liked the sound of "gravid." It possessed an uncomfortable echo of "rabid."

(It was dangerous, highly infectious.

(It led to foaming at the mouth and madness.

(There was no cure.

(You had to shoot them.

(*Bang! Bang!*

(It was the kindest thing to do.

(They were better off dead.

("*Enceinte*" – a swooning cringe into italics at this point, for the employment of a foreign word – could not possibly be used because "*enceinte*" was French. Any girl who was "*enceinte*" had clearly neglected to marry, another brazen trollop, another candidate for The House of the Magdalenes, another Madeline, Mariana, or Elaine, hardly fair, hardly lovable, hardly the lily maid – *Ha. Ha. Ha. Ha* – of Astolat. If the word "*enceinte*" was employed, rain clouds would be sure to follow.

("*She's* under a cloud."

(*Nudge, nudge.*

(*Nudge, nudge* for *les nuages.* They were sure to be *French* clouds, extra-pendulous, extra-dark and threatening, thrusting officiously with uncorseted breasty wobblings.

("*She's* under a cloud."

(The rainfall would be heavy and prolonged.

(Sometimes words were abandoned entirely in favor of gestures, with much meaningful curving of hands in fronts of stomachs, worryingly like Alice and Charlotte's shorthand for Beard, as if The Bearded Ones carried their unborn young before them in kangaroo-like hairy pouches.

("*She's* come to grief."

(*Nudge.*

("*She's* come to grief."

(*Nudge.*

(She arrived at the place she had never seen before, and Grief was there to welcome her home.

(Something about the pose of the girl dressed in blue, about the mood of the whole painting, made her think of the other meanings of "pregnant," the sense of something rich with meaning, momentous, *teeming*, but whatever meaning there was seemed to slip through her fingers, pushed out of reach by the very hands that grasped for it. The much-folded reproduction of the painting had become torn and crumpled over the years, overlaid with a net of lines like the onset of age on the human face, cracked and crazed like the surface of an old oil painting, a phrenology head, and the crisscross lines had multiplied. Squares of color would drop out, like the pieces of a damaged mosaic, scattering fragments of brightness on the dusty floor, all that remained of a lost picture.)

The second picture had been a more recent painting, a William Holman Hunt, *The Lady of Shalott.*

What had made him select this particular picture?

Other pictures followed, and all of them contained the figure of a woman, usually alone. After a few weeks, the reading of the clouds was alternated with the reading of pictures: some weeks there were just the clouds, some weeks just the pictures. Sometimes the hissing of the gas made her feel headachy and dull, as if the gas had not been lit and she was being lulled into sleeping and forgetfulness, freed from all the troubles of the world. Beyond the drawn curtains was the stage, and on the stage the soloist awaited the moment for her song, illuminated by a circle of light in the midst of the darkness.

"I c-c-can see . . ."

"Yes?"

"I c-c-can see . . ."

"Tell me what you can see . . ."

She saw Annie.

She saw a girl dressed in blue.

The soloist began to sing.

Alice was aware of this happening. The voice was faint and distant, the voice heard from the most distant seat, the voice from a stage that was immeasurably far away so that the singer could scarcely be seen, the voice scarcely heard. Her teeth had started to seize up, dried like withered fruit, frozen in the polite rictus smile she employed in the presence of Dr. Wolcott Ascharm Webster.

It was a child's voice.

Then she realized that the distant voice was close. It was a small boy walking past outside, beneath the window and its closed drapes, on his way to the park with his mama and papa. It was like having to readjust your eyes, realizing that something you thought you were seeing far away was in fact just under your nose. There was a sense of bright illumination held temporarily at bay. After the dimly lighted room it would be dazzling when the curtains drew back, the muffled voice suddenly sharp, the brilliance blinding.

He was singing some children's rhyme, keeping his voice low, constrained by some sense of decorum. She caught the word "green," and then – a little later (she tried to shut out "Tell me, tell me . . .") – "And if this young prince chance to die."

She tried to grasp at the memory evoked.

It was something more than the voices of the children playing under the chestnut trees, the singing she heard from the schoolroom in summer through the open windows. It was something more than the figures of boys and girls on the leaf-dappled grass, more than "Walking on the green grass, / Walking side by side, / Walking with a pretty girl, / She shall be my bride . . ."

It wasn't so much the words themselves as the rhythm of the words, the timbre of the child's voice.

It was linked with her feeling cold.

As she did now.

It was linked with her sitting down.

As she was now.

It was linked with being very still.

As she was now.

It was linked with her face being fixed in one expression.

As . . .

It was . . .

She was a little girl in Carlo Fiorelli's studio, posing for the Longfellow statue. It wasn't that the memory came to her; she entered the memory, like stepping inside a painting. She was there again, all those years ago, and the unknown little boy's voice was Giorgio's voice.

She did not like to go near the statue of Longfellow and the three little girls in the park anymore, to see herself as she once was. Even if she had been in the habit of wandering about, she would have avoided it. It would have hurt her, like certain photographs hurt her, and the happier the little girl looked in the photographs – opening her mouth to be fed strawberries by her sisters, a ten-year-old holding her newly born baby brother in her arms – the more it hurt.

It was many years since anyone had said to her, "You're one of the girls from the statue!" but she and her sisters had been the models for the three girls. Carlo Fiorelli – it was rumored he had won a competition to produce a statue for the Central Park (it must have been one of the rare occasions on which John Quincy Adams Ward had not pounced) – had been a nice man. He had brought his little boy into his studio to sing to them and keep them amused as he took his photographs. They had been disappointed that the little boy, Giorgio – a tiny child, a wisp of a thing even younger than they were – was unable to sing or even speak in Italian ("Is American boy," Signor Fiorelli had said, by way of explanation), but – in his piping voice, imperfectly in tune – he had sung the words to children's games, some of them the same songs they themselves sang as they played under the chestnut trees. Without seeming to realize that he was doing it, as though it was an essential part of singing the words, Giorgio had made all the gestures of a child playing the games that accompanied the songs, holding his hands out to either side of him or in front of him, toward invisible companions, as he sang.

Longfellow had still been alive then, but he had not posed for the photographs. Carlo Fiorelli had worked from photographs of the poet collected from other sources. Papa – whose idea the statue had been, Longfellow for Longfellow Park – had been there for the early part of the sitting, before the detailed individual photographs had been taken, and he had sat in as a substitute for the poet in the group photographs.

The statue was to be a representation of the father and three daughters from Longfellow's poem "The Children's Hour," the poem from which their names had been taken – it was their father's favorite poem, he claimed, paternally, in public, though she'd never seen him reading poetry, never heard him *mention* a poem (*Moonshine*. That would be the verdict if he ever did. *Unmitigated moonshine!*) – with Longfellow as the father, and Alice and her sisters as the three daughters. This was in the days before *Ben-Hur* had taken its firm, classical, togaed grip upon Signor Fiorelli.

> "Between the dark and the daylight,
> When the night is beginning to lower,
> Comes a pause in the day's occupations,
> That is known as the Children's Hour.
>
> "I hear in the chamber above me
> The patter of little feet
> The sound of a door that is opened,
> And voices soft and sweet.
>
> "From my study I see in the lamplight,
> Descending the broad hall stair
> Grave Alice, and laughing Allegra,
> And Edith with golden hair . . ."

That was how it began. The poem was carved in full on the stone base of the statue – the statue itself was bronze – and it never failed to frighten her, especially its ending, those last two verses, like a secret story spelled out in sharply incised letters for everyone to see.

Grave, laughing, golden-haired, playing the parts they were supposed to play – she was, after all, Alice-from-the-poem – they clustered about Papa as he sat in the heavy armchair chosen by Carlo Fiorelli. Papa was holding an open book in his hands, as if interrupted at study, or as if about to read a favorite story to his eagerly expectant children.

Edith was the youngest and stood on a stool behind the chair, her arms clasped around her father's neck, leaning over his left shoulder. Alice and Allegra sat on either side of him, half on the chair, half leaning against him on his knees, their arms entwined around him, the sides of their faces against the rough hair of his beard, looking up at him. They appeared rapt in the words he was speaking, the words he was reading from the book. If they turned their heads, they would be able to read the words for themselves if they'd leaned forward a little, but they looked up at him, as if the words possessed power only if spoken by him. When she'd seen the completed statue, she'd wanted to know if Carlo Fiorelli had actually shown some words on the open pages, but the book was held up at an angle, and you couldn't see. Birds tended to sit on the top edge of the pages, and whatever was written there – if anything – would be well coated with droppings, and accumulated dead leaves. Despite these hazards, she'd been keen – for a while – to see if any words were written. All she would have to do – she plotted her route – would be to climb her way up Edith or Allegra in her best nailed boots, planting her feet firmly on their knees, waists, shoulders, and heads as she clambered. The thought of doing this had certainly added to the appeal of research, and introduced a dubious element of personal vindictiveness to her otherwise commendable quest for knowledge.

"Shall I look adoring?" she ought to have asked, anxious – like Serenity Goodchild, years later – to assume the appropriate expression for a photograph. "Shall I look adoring?"

". . . A whisper, and then a silence:
Yet I know by their merry eyes
They are plotting and planning together
To take me by surprise.

"A sudden rush from the stairway,
A sudden raid from the hall!
By three doors left unguarded
They enter my castle wall!

"They climb up into my turret
O'er the arms and back of my chair;

If I try to escape, they surround me;
They seem to be everywhere . . ."

Alice had been half afraid when Papa had told her – had called all three of them together to tell them – that they were to be the models for a bronze statue. She hadn't thought that they would be photographed – this idea hadn't occurred to her at all – and had, at first, imagined the three of them standing very still for day after day as the sculptor hammered away at a great block of bronze – she had imagined that bronze would be sculpted like marble – until their images emerged from inside it. They would have to hold their breath for all that time. Then, more frighteningly, she imagined molten bronze being poured around their bodies, a little part of them at a time, building up around them gradually until they were completely covered, until they were unable to move, unable to speak, unable to breathe, encased in decorative bronze armor from which they would never be released.

They were positioned – in and around the chair – upon a kind of turntable. Carlo Fiorelli's two assistants pulled upon ropes, and they were slowly rotated as photographs were taken of the different angles. It was as if someone – walking right the way around them – was viewing them from every angle, but it was they who were moving, not the person viewing them. It was like being on a slowly revolving merry-go-round, and they held their pose as they were – rather shakily and squeakily – moved round, wobbling slightly. The music that accompanied them was not the fairground pipes of a barrel organ, the clashing of cymbals, the swirling syrupy rhythms, but Giorgio's tiny shrill voice.

"Smile, girls! Smile!" Carlo Fiorelli urged them, himself smiling to encourage them, big, exaggerated, blissful smiles that made Allegra giggle, and Alice – the smell of Papa's tobacco-stained teeth in her nostrils – looked beyond and through the camera toward Giorgio. The little boy's arms moved, conducting a vast silent orchestra, and his high voice rose up and was absorbed by the tall-ceilinged room – it had once been a stables – with its cool

433

northern light, and its many dark angled beams, like the framework of an incomplete structure. She felt he was far, far away from her, out of reach.

She was waiting, absolutely motionless, for the liquid metal to begin dripping down upon her, to weld her to her father's body, to press upon her throat and chest and to still her breathing. It would be cold, not hot, like layers of ice freezing around her.

It would happen soon.

The day on which Carlo Fiorelli had taken the life cast of her face — she had been alone there on the day this had happened — had been like a memory of an illness when she was very young. It had been the sound of the cloth strips being prepared that had brought this into her mind. Two of the assistants had torn cloth into the right size pieces, and dipped these into a bowl of water to soak them. The sounds of water trickling into the bowl as they squeezed out the excess had been restful and soothing, the sound of Mama caring for her when she had a fever, gently tending her in a quiet house in which the blinds were lowered against the summer heat. Mama was soaking cloth in cool water to ease the heat of her brows, gently drawing back her short-cut hair and dabbing her forehead and cheeks with little wave-like motions. She listened with her eyes closed as it happened over and over, the subdued splashing that was like the sound of refreshment, Mama humming to her almost under her breath in the dim light.

Carlo Fiorelli — he wore a long white clay-spattered apron — kneeled before her (she was now in the big chair where Papa had sat, her feet not reaching the ground) and applied grease to her face, rubbing vigorously along her eyebrows. She was the exotic dish being prepared for the feast. It would have to be something Italian. Papa would not like that, because it was *foreign*, one of his most witheringly contemptuous words (and he had many), odd in a man whose fortunes were founded upon steamships crossing and

434

recrossing the oceans. She did not know the names of many Italian dishes, but thought of Veal Marsala, because she had eaten it once – her mouth half open as she chewed cautiously, suspiciously, with a sensation of experimenting, like a girl struggling with something too hot for her to swallow – and remembered the name.

14 ozs. of veal sweetbreads.
14 ozs. of veal fillet.
14 ozs. of chicken livers.
8 tbsps. of plain white flour.
4 ozs. of butter . . .

When he'd covered her face in grease, and applied the sheets of waxed paper, he'd begin to beat her face with a sculpting mallet to soften the flesh and make it into a thin layer. The butter would melt almost instantly in the hot frying pan – *Hiss! Hiss!* it foamed disapprovingly – and the flattened flesh would be fried rapidly, browning nicely.

DRINK ME. EAT ME.

If it had been ten years or so later, she would have thought of the recipe for *Coniglio con le Olive*. (She didn't know the Italian for Veal Marsala.)

2 4½ lb. rabbits.
10 tbsps. of olive oil.
2 onions.
14 ozs. black olives.
6 garlic cloves . . .

A *great deal* of garlic.

She thought of the Mrs. Albert Comstock-faced Duchess tossing the sneezing baby up and down like a howling meaty salad being prepared in the pepper-filled kitchen. The Duchess would enjoy beating that little boy to a thin layer.

> *I speak severely to my boy,*
> *I beat him when he sneezes;*
> *For he can thoroughly enjoy*
> *The pepper when he pleases!*

The Duchess sat with her toes turned in, an expression of massive disapproval on her face. Fire irons, saucepans, plates, and dishes hurtled in Alice's direction, assisting with the thinning process. She'd be a slimmed-down battered banquet in no time.

Yum-yum.

The sculptor's confident fingers moved about her face, as if they were molding her into shape, sculpting her features into those of a face he wished to create, a face better than the face she had. She was the clay on which he worked, no longer a breathing person. She could feel the tips of his fingers through the grease as he rubbed it in: they were coarse – the cut and scarred surfaces scratched her skin a little – not like the hands of an artist at all, but the hands of an artisan or a day laborer, a man who worked with tools or machines. Mama's hands had been soft and gentle, skimming her skin, barely touching her at all, a butterfly's wing touch, but these strong cold hands seemed to feel through to her bones.

(But . . .

(But . . .

(But they were *nothing* like the hands of Papa's "friend" – the friend in quotation marks – as he caressed her head, behind the high walls on the way to the Celestial City.

(Night after night.

(The wind blew, and sometimes there was snow.

(Annie was there.

(Carlo Fiorelli was *nothing* like Papa's "friend.")

The summer heat of all those years ago had long gone, and in her memory it was – as always – cold in the studio, despite the metal stove with its tall pipe, all the warmth risen uselessly far above the human figures into the high space below the angled skylights. From the place in which she was seated, she couldn't see the red flickering glow through the ornate filigree frontage, and this made her feel colder. It had been summer when the life-cast was taken – the stove would not have been lit, the air would not have been cold – and yet she somehow always thought of it as being an intensely cold day, white breath coming from within her, whiteness all around, surrounded by sculptures carved from snow. Later memories of the wintry day on which the statue had been unveiled must have overlaid her earlier memories, a coldness from the future creeping back to freeze the past.

Strait Is The Gate That Leadeth Unto Life, And Few There Be That Find It.

Through the Strait Gate was no place for the strait-laced, and through the Strait Gate the straitjackets waited.

If she started shivering uncontrollably, sensing this coldness approaching, how would this affect her, held within the rigidly expressionless, unmoving mask that was building up around her features?

This moment had come back to her, a year or so later, when she had read *Poor Miss Finch*, in which Wilkie Collins had made a passing reference to a female model "sitting" for the first time in a drawing academy, and being so nervous at the ordeal ahead of her that the only way she could be persuaded into the students' room was by being led in blindfold. This picture of the naked woman — her eyes bandaged — being stared at by the room full of clothed men as they sketched her body, had stayed in her mind, haunted her, and it may have been this that started *The Life Class*, her novel about a woman art student, developing in her mind. If the nervous figure-model had been Trilby, Svengali would have hypnotized her into confident nakedness. ("Take off your clothes, Miss O'Ferrall.") Alice had studied Carlo Fiorelli and Linnaeus Finch, and the way that they worked upon their sculptures or paintings, without knowing that she had been studying them: these observations, also, had colored her ideas. Women art students were not admitted into a life class (unless, presumably, they were as blindfolded as a frightened model, in the buff for blindman's buff). It was not suitable for them to see the unclothed human form. At the end of the novel, naked again, a woman's body had been stretched out in the dissecting room, as the men — medical students, this time — moved in toward her with their bright sharp-edged instruments. That woman with the pocket-handkerchief tied around her eyes, that woman stumbling, and cutting her fingers on the scalpels, that weeping woman, was a woman who had expressed a wish to learn to become a doctor.

As he leaned across, she gazed over Carlo Fiorelli's bowed shoulder down darkening corridors of plaster casts that seemed to stretch away for always, half-glimpsed figures from the Bible and from mythology, gleaming in the sunlessness like the obscure avenues of a graveyard at dusk. Motes of white dust spun slowly in downward-angled beams of light. More dust lay in drifts like accumulated wind-blown snow, swept away into the more remote corners of the studio, as if by a slatternly housewife who imagined that all her visitors were as unobservant or as uncaring as herself. On either side of the half-clad frozen figures, the wooden shelves stretching right up to the roof were laden with more casts, busts, miniature figures, the whiteness of the sculptures everywhere in stone, in marble, in clay, in plaster.

In a dark corner there was the life cast (*death* cast?) of a flayed criminal, a memento mori of a Marsyas, his flute forever silenced. The sculptor had not pointed this out to her — it had seemed deliberately hidden away in its semidarkness, a part of a gallery not open to the public — but she had come across it when she had been wandering about on her first visit, strolling between gods and goddesses like an awed worshiper in a pantheon. It was like an illustration in a book for a medical student, a meticulously detailed engraving to be studied late at night by candlelight, and there should have been large elaborately curled capital letters — *A*, *B*, *C* . . . — filling all the spaces of the air around it, and italicized explanations should have been printed beneath it. She had a sense of other such figures all around her, *Fig. 1*, *Fig. 2*, *Fig. 3*, many *Fig.*s from many pages, veins and organs — sharply defined, freed from the blurring obfuscation of blood — neatly laid out for scrutiny like something for sale. The student — clearly one of St. Cassian of Imola's more ambitious pupils, an eye on a career as a doctor — gestured in the air with his sharp-pointed pen, rehearsing the first incision into the flesh in front of him, perfecting the angle at which to hold his scalpel. *There*, he thought. *There.* He moved nearer, bending close to the naked, blindfold woman. ("Yes," he'd say, years later, a man noted in his profession, laden with honors, anxious to give praise where praise was due, "I had a teacher who gave me a taste for dissection. I owe so much to him. He really inspired me.")

Nearest to her were the casts of the dead, whole shelves of death masks, faces, hands, the living unable to let go, clinging on to those from whom they had been taken. Some of them were of people she had known, and not all of them were old. The still faces peered out at her from the shadows, like half-glimpsed ghosts, pausing a while in the moment before speaking, on the point of drawing the first breath. Like the faces of peaceful sleepers, they seemed to have had all emotions shushed away from them – *Shh! Shh!* (she heard the soothing whispers, felt the comforting hand) – and possessed the remote, faraway expressions of those thinking of something that had happened a long time ago, something without pain or pleasure. People came to Carlo Fiorelli to ask him to do these. He would do to the dead what he was doing to her with those same fingers, and she was as still as the dead would be, her breath half held, poised perpetually between moments of breathing. Being immortalized brought death closer, like photographs somehow seemed to do, concentrating the mind on the passing of time, the awareness of the difference between what once had been, and what now was. She had not known that art was so close to death. The artist leaned across the faces of the dead in the darkened room, a candle held in one hand, its light glowing across their features, like Psyche with her oil lamp bending down to study the face of the sleeping Eros. Time passed, and the wax dripped down onto the faces of the dead as the candle melted. More time passed, and more wax dripped down. As time passed, the death masks grew ever nearer to completion, slowly accumulating, layer upon layer. Carlo Fiorelli was the nephew of Giuseppe Fiorelli, the archeologist who had directed the

439

excavations at Pompeii, the man who had made the plaster casts of those who had died all those hundreds of years ago, the agonized dog, the fallen figures with their arms pressed around their heads, the folds of their garments ridden up around their bodies, pressed against their faces. She was one more white figure in the perpetual Pompeiian gloom of the buried streets and corridors.

Mrs. Italiaander had a plaster cast of her infant son's arm – he had been her only child – under a glass dome in her parlor. She, Allegra, and Edith had gathered around it, fortune-tellers consulting a crystal ball – *remember that you must die* – their reflections curving across the dimpled arm of the plump child they had never known. Mrs. Alexander Diddecott liked to organize her séances at Mrs. Italiaander's around it, suggesting that it acted as a conduit for the forces with which she grappled, and they had kept at a careful distance, looking, but not touching, just in case. What would little Archer Italiaander Junior (made even smaller by that "Junior") have to say to his Mama, if he had been drawn out from that other land, when all he had been able to say was that very word, "Mama"? Perhaps that was the only word she wanted to hear. It seemed so strange to have a *part* of a body on display like that.

Parts of bodies were all around her where she sat – feeling her face stiffening and growing cold – like the aftermath of some Vandal slaughter in a sacked and burning Rome, lopped-off heads and limbs littering the Forum like the parts of wrecked and (she liked to use a word precisely) vandalized statues. The faces were peaceful, however, the faces of those who had fallen asleep, their eyes and mouths serenely closed, not gaping in agony or terror. They were like the plaster casts of the bodies from a Pompeii in which Vesuvius had brought death gently, without panic, without any pain or struggle to escape. The ashes had pattered soothingly around them like gentle rain, lulling them into sleep and forgetfulness.

There were still two rusty metal horses' heads outside, above the entrance, announcing – as appropriately as they had marked out the former livery stables – that here was the domain of a sculptor in

440

stone and in bronze. Charlotte had been disgusted to hear of stables in which there were no horses. The figures of gods and goddesses, the shrouded figures from the Old Testament, the faces of the dead: these were nothing to her. You couldn't feed sugar to these! You couldn't pat them on the flank as you fed them straw! The faded *STABLES* sign still hung between the horses' heads, the letter *L* completely erased by time and the weather, the sign that gave entrance as beckoningly as *Knock And It Shall Be Opened Unto You*, but in more commanding capital letters, an exhortation that could not be ignored. *STAB ES* it now read, and the implacable demand had added a pleasing sense of purpose to some of the less eventful days of childhood.

STAB ES.

Alice studied the enigmatic summons to commit murder each time she came. It was a *portent*, she decided, seizing the opportunity to employ this word. It wasn't *MENE, MENE, TEKEL, UPHARSIN.* (Daniel, Chapter V, Verse xxv.) It was *STAB ES.* In the absence of Daniel to interpret it for her, she discussed it with Charlotte, and it was then that they had decided that the coded command – intelligible only to them – meant *STAB ENORMOUS SIBYL!* It was very satisfying when your dearest wish was emblazoned on the wall in words from heaven. They'd been following Charles Kingsley's instructions to the letter, and this Eleventh Commandment – even if painted on wood rather than written on tablets of stone – was clearly a sacred admonition placed upon them. They'd be happy to obey. It would be wrong of them not to. They could hardly miss. It certainly reconciled Charlotte to the lack of horses.

They had the brass shield (well polished).

They had the sword (carefully sharpened).

You'd think that a goatskin would be easy enough to find, but it was proving to be a real problem. The Misses Isserliss kept goats, but they were all thriving healthily – full of high spirits and goatish kicks, bouncing about with friendly butts and sheep-like bleatings – and she couldn't bear the thought of stabbing her knife into one of them to remove its skin, even when the thought of stabbing Enormous Sibyl appealed so – er – enormously. She tried to make herself believe that the goats were rams, and that she was going to be Abraham, and sacrifice one of them instead of Isaac – "The Sibyl is a ram," she told herself. "The Sibyl is an Aries" – but even this couldn't make her do it. Isaac would have to die. "STAB ES," she muttered to herself (you had to mutter loudly when capital letters were involved), memorizing an instruction from the LORD, "STAB ES," and tried to look keen. If they did it here – chisels lay temptingly about on most surfaces – it would be really convenient for the death mask, but would Carlo Fiorelli have enough plaster for the size of the face? This might be a promising opportunity for the plasterer who had plastered all thirty-four rooms of the Italiaanders' house – a man accustomed to working on an epic scale – and a way of uniting art and industry in a manner that would have gladdened the heart of William Morris.

Many and many a time they Stabbed Enormous Sibyl in the years that followed, and her failure to keel over with what ought to have been a Sibyl-shattering smash showed that the imagination – however hard you pushed it, however hard you flexed its muscles – had its limitations.

They *STABBED EVIL SINNER!*

They *STABBED EXASPERATING SWANSTROM!*

They *STABBED EXTREMELY SMELLY!*

They *STABBED ENRAGED SISTERS!*

They stabbed and stabbed again.

They had no effect whatsoever.

Carl Fiorelli chatted to her about what was going to happen.

"You will not be able to speak. If you feel you cannot breathe properly, hit me on the arm so I will know. Hit me hard!"

The studio, with its whitewashed brick walls covered by shelves and untidily painted sketches, was more like a manufactory than a place where art was created, like the interior of a warehouse, a barn. All the workers were men – they wore big boots, and these and their clothes were splashed and whitened with old, dried clay, making them look like farm laborers who had been digging in muddy fields – and Signora Fiorelli appeared only to bring lunch on a little wheeled wagon. Clay-spattered stepladders – rough, homemade, cobbled together anyhow – leaned at angles everywhere against the walls. When she first arrived, the floor had just been mopped and was blond and gleaming, but – as the floor dried – the shine went, the color disappeared, and it regained its white-spattered matte finish, like the raw floorboards of a house newly built by careless workmen. Carlo Fiorelli seemed to use anything that came to hand as an implement in his art – nails, scraps of wood, spoons, kitchen implements: these, clay-whitened, like something lumpishly exaggerated with coral or limestone accretions, lay around on every surface – and she pictured him at an evening meal in his house, overcome by inspiration, and running out to his studio, his food untasted, still carrying his knife and spoon with which to gouge and sculpt, as if it were the clay on which he fed.

One workman was preparing clay, the color and consistency of melted chocolate, in one bowl – after the Veal Marsala, the *Coniglio con le Olive*, came the Italian chocolate ice cream (boiled puddings were the usual fare at home: Papa insisted) – and the other continued to rip cloth. She pictured women in the Civil War preparing makeshift bandages for the wounded soldiers, ripping up sheets and pillowcases in the ruins of a large house. Mama's youngest brother, Edward, had been killed in the war. She still had some of his letters, with the most beautiful of handwriting, and the most inventive of spelling. Alice had seen a photograph of him in his uniform, a slight mischievous-faced young man, looking about fifteen. Grandmama had never used the word "fought" to describe what Teddy had done. It was too violent, too uncharacteristic. He had been present, and he had died. "Fought" made it sound noble and glittering and chivalric. Few of the young men would have thought of themselves as "fighting." That described what they had tried to avoid in the schoolyard, warned by their mothers: the taller, aggressive boy finding a reason to punch on the shoulders, the scuffle in the dust, the bloody nose, and the embarrassment, the stain on the shirt he had tried to wash out with cold water so his mother wouldn't find out. "My Teddy would never fight. He's a good boy." "Fighting" was not the word to describe what had happened to Teddy at Cold Harbor.

The workman ripping the cotton had started to sing something: there was a great deal of singing at the studio, all the male voices without a woman's amongst them, like those voices she had imagined from the pages of Robert Louis Stevenson and Jules Verne, though these were more like an oratorio than an opera, a dark part of a Bach *Passion*, there, amidst the pale faces of the dead. When she imagined the young soldiers singing, she did not think of them as singing sad, sentimental songs, battalions of soprano-voiced Sobriety Goodchilds trilling "Just Before the Battle, Mother." When he was unleashed upon this song, he was capable of producing more pocket-handkerchiefs than Fagin's gang, massed white handkerchiefs flourishing like the surrenders of entire armies, and thunderous nose-blowings. She was far more moved when she imagined the soldiers singing comic songs. She had heard children, emerging from the park on a Saturday afternoon, singing "Goober Peas" as they chewed peanuts, and wondered if they even knew that they were singing a Confederate soldiers' song.

> ". . . When a horseman passes, the soldiers have a rule,
> To cry out at their loudest 'Mister, here's your mule!'
> But another pleasure enchantinger than these,
> Is wearing out your grinders, eating goober peas!
>
> "Peas! Peas! Peas! Peas! Eating goober peas!
> Goodness how delicious, eating goober peas!. . ."

The voices of children were the voices of the soldiers as they wished the war was over, when, free from rags and fleas, they'd kiss their wives and sweethearts, and gobble goober peas.

The first strips of cloth were the size of playing cards. They were dipped in plaster of Paris, and Carlo Fiorelli — humming, whistling under his breath, the opera tunes the band played in the park – began to cover her face. He sang a few lines now and then in Italian, with great fervor, intense moments from something larger, oddly out of scale in isolation. She had been wounded and was being bandaged, mummy-like layers being wound around her head to make her better. ("Wound around a wound," she whispered under her breath, liking the two different pronunciations of the same word in one short sentence.) It was a bad head, and thought bad thoughts, and must be cured. A few years later, after she had seen Oscar Wilde at the theatre, she had imagined Louisa May Alcott, Oscar Wilde, and Walt Whitman talking together in quiet voices about *Hospital Sketches*, and Walt Whitman – never one to be elbowed aside by the writings of another – beginning to quote from one of his Civil War poems: "Straight and swift to the wounded I go,/Where they lie on the ground after the battle brought in . . ." Louisa May Alcott and Oscar Wilde nodded their heads; this confirmed a point they had been making. Smaller pieces of cloth – the size of postage stamps (she imagined rows of miniature bearded presidents lined up across her face, preparing her to be mailed) – were placed carefully on one side, reserved for around her eyes and nostrils. She would be white like a monument, standing high above the fields of the dead.

As the first layer began to dry, she could no longer feel the fingers of the sculptor applying further layers, and she felt enclosed within metal, peering out through the eyeholes, encased within bronze. She was within the statue looking out; she herself had actually become the statue. She was the Girl in the Bronze Mask, or the benighted heroine of *The Curse of the Capitoline*, the first of the two Reverend Goodchild novels published in 1876, and the mask had become a part of her face, not fastened on separately. "This is really interesting" had been her main thought. Her face had become something heavy, and she felt herself drawn downward as if by sleep, a sensation of languor, a wish to lay the head down, and drift away. It was a strange feeling – the curious feeling of being separate from her body – but she never felt that she was having any difficulty in breathing. Carlo Fiorelli was applying clay to her hair, all round the back of her head, the sculptor molding her into shape. Between bursts of song, he had talked to her a little at first, but then — as her mouth was covered — he stopped talking to her. He and the workmen exchanged little comments, instructions and observations. It was just because they had become absorbed in what they were doing, but she felt that she had ceased to be there, was already a statue. As he covered her ears, silence closed in upon her. She tried very hard not to swallow. If she did so, her whole face seemed to shift uncomfortably.

The second layer of cloth was dipped in blue plaster of Paris.

(*Paris.*

(Mrs. Albert Comstock staggered back a little, reaching for her umbrella with which to defend herself.

(Paris, *France.*

(*Blue* plaster.

(*Sacre bleu!*

(*French* blue plaster.

(What monstrosity was being brought into being practically within her purlieu?)

He used blue plaster so that he would know when he had covered the whole face twice, but — it occurred to her a year or so later — she must have looked like Oscar Dubourg, the blue-faced twin in *Poor Miss Finch*. How would Charlotte have reacted to seeing her like that, bringing literature to life?

After the clouds came the pictures, and after the pictures came the dreams. After the fifth or sixth picture had been read came the first reading of a dream, with the considerable difference that — this time — she did not interpret; she merely described, and Dr. Wolcott Ascharm Webster did the interpreting.

There was a distinct change in the atmosphere of the morning on which this first happened. He had experienced another vision:

446

something he himself had read in the clouds, something huge and tumultuous unfurling above St. George and the Dragon, something that was going to change the way in which he saw things, and send him down into different caverns. He was the artist, and she was the artist's model (Trilby again), hired for the day, placed in the position that he chose, the raw — naked, shivering — material from which he created his works. Sometimes she felt like a victim of Burke and Hare, an anonymous corpse sold to an anatomist for dissection. Burke and Hare merged again in her mind with Jekyll and Hyde, though here there was no Jekyll — Jekyll had vanished altogether — but two Hydes, linked like a monstrous birth, doubled in power, moving in unison, searching through suffocatingly dark alleyways, sniffing the air, seeking for those to kill.

If he be Mr. Hyde, I shall be Mr. Seek.

Even more books had arrived from Austria — the crowbars were never at rest — and Hilde Claudia had been busy translating. It would soon be time to buy yet another bookcase, to find room for yet another key in his vest pocket, which bulged, which chinked, like an inadequately concealed layer of chain mail positioned to protect the heart from assault, to shield it from feeling. Alice hoped Hilde Claudia was more careful with her dictionary this time, though she was still always trouble having with her werbs.

Dreams seemed the most perverse area yet into which she had been led.

She could understand the reading of meaning into pictures; she could even understand the reading of meaning into clouds. Mistranslation or not, there seemed to her a certain validity in reading what one saw in certain shapes. What you were in your mind colored everything that you saw, and to read what that mind saw in shapes was to reveal what was hidden inside that mind. When the lawyer, Mr. Utterson — in *The Strange Case of Dr. Jekyll and Mr. Hyde* — had studied Henry Jekyll's will, in which Edward Hyde had been made his heir, he suddenly had a vivid picture of Hyde, the man he had never seen. *Out of the shifting, insubstantial mists that had so long baffled his eye, there leaped up the sudden, definite presentment of a fiend.* In such a way would thoughts from deep within her mind come walking toward her through the shapes of the clouds.

After he had glimpsed his shape in the mists, the man he had never seen began to enter Mr. Utterson's dreams, walking into them in the way that he walked out of the mists. *He would be aware of the great field of lamps of a nocturnal city; then of the figure of a man walking swiftly; then of a child running from the doctor's; and then these met, and that human Juggernaut trod the child down and passed on regardless of her screams. Or else he would see a room in a rich house, where his friend lay asleep, dreaming and smiling at his dreams; and then the door of that room would be opened, the curtains of the bed plucked apart, the sleeper recalled, and, lo! there would stand by his side a figure to whom power was given, and even at that dead hour he must rise and do its bidding.*

In such a way would figures walk into her dreams, make her rise and do their bidding. In clouds, in dreams, she would see the subjects that possessed her mind. That which was already in the mind was all that the eyes saw, and – sometimes – what was in the mind was a girl at a window, bathed in light, bowed over, a letter in her hands.

Beneath the pillow of each of the fallen girls in The House of the Magdalenes there would be a crumpled Dream Book, pressed flowers – flat and colorless – between certain pages, the cheap, coarse-textured paper stained slightly by sap. Each dream interpretation was like a spell, holding within its words the promise of better things to come.

Dream Books were the province of the impoverished, the unhappy, the eternally hopeful. Their interpretations seemed to find hidden enemies everywhere, false friends, threatened reputations, interspersed with hints and warnings to small tradesmen. She imagined Albert Comstock at the beginning of his glittering career in comestibles – unlikely though it was that it would ever have occurred to anyone to describe him as a *small* tradesman –

beached upon his bed like Moby-Dick in a nightcap, a long, weary day of sausage stuffing at an end, snoring thunderously, with his well-thumbed Dream Book neatly stacked by his bed on top of his accounts book. This would be years before the magic moment when Mrs. Albert Comstock — his mirror image, her bosom as big as his beard — hove into view, and she made him her own.

"I had a dream last night."

Annie closed her eyes, clenched her hands, praying that she would hear the words she wished to hear as Alice read to her, explained the meaning of what she had dreamed.

Rosobell, their servant now, had two such books — *What's in a Dream* and *Pearson's Dream Book* — in the cutlery drawer, and consulted them religiously, as if looking up symptoms in a medical book. She read both books, and chose the interpretation she preferred. That was where Dream Books belonged: in the kitchen, their corners curled and browned, pushed up against the knives and forks next to handwritten recipes.

—— ⌘ ——

Rosobell had loaned Alice her copies of *What's in a Dream* and *Pearson's Dream Book* — it had a bright yellow cover patterned with red poppies — in case she wished to consult them. She was a kind woman. The one interpretation from *Pearson's Dream Book* that had remained in Alice's mind — because of its startlingly incongruous randomness — had been: *To dream of a cameo brooch, means that you will achieve success as a pianoforte player.* "Of course! Of course!" Alice had muttered to herself, sardonically. "Why go to the expense of buying a book when the meaning is so *obvious*?"

She was recklessly choosing to ignore the clear advice she had been given as a dreamer of dragons.

She was allowing herself to be governed by her passions.

She was placing herself in the power of her enemies through those outbursts of sardonic tendencies.

She had been warned to cultivate self-control.

On the inside cover of the Dream Book was an advertisement for another publication from the same publisher, *Things a Woman Wants to Know, with an Illustrated Section on The Folding of Napkins.* These two titles usefully covered just about everything a woman wanted (or, indeed, needed) to know in life, Alice thought: dreams, and the folding of starched white table napkins. Unusually great-hearted men must have written them. What more could a woman hope to do but spend her time in dreaming as she folded napkins, bent over day after day like a denizen of an unusually genteel sweatshop (a perspiration emporium, possibly), "The Song of the Napkin" rather than "The Song of the Shirt." The symmetrical, elaborately crafted linen constructions would creep out of the kitchen and begin to mount up and cover the stairs, creeping into every space in the house like stiff-edged oversized lavender-scented orchids, or elaborate party hats for a celebration at the end of a gathering of popes. They would fill the corridors, flood the carpets of all the rooms, rise to press against the windows and the ceilings, rising up, rising up, pale, white, peculiarly proportioned, fungi from beneath dark stone and rotting wood, growing and multiplying in dark cellars with insistent urgency. She would be lifted up, pressed against the skylight in the schoolroom, suffocated, scrabbling at the glass.

Peep, peep!

Attention! The two arms were held up and away from the body at an angle of forty-five degrees, the flags shaken from side to side, and Hilde Claudia, Theodore, and Max — seeing an opportunity — leaped into action, anxious to demonstrate their numerous esoteric skills. As an encore, they'd give a demonstration of their yodeling. They could clear a room in fifteen seconds once they were launched into this. People who had suffered for years from sinus trouble were miraculously cured in no time.

They were holding the two-color napkins, divided from corner to corner into a triangle of red and a triangle of yellow, one in each hand.

Peep, peep!

It was the time for The Folding of the Napkins.

Illustrated.

"The Miter!" Max announced, singing in his admired but somewhat troubling boy soprano voice. Was "boy" quite the word to use for Max these days? Were there such things as "youth sopranos"? (Yes, there were. They raised their arms in shrill acclamation, and sang "See the conquering hero comes!/Sound the trumpets, beat the drums . . ." They called for sports to be prepared, for laurel to be brought, for songs of triumph to be sung. They were tall, they were thin, and they were squeakily insistent.)

"Fold the napkin in three lengthwise, and in doing this turn the last fold backward . . ."

It was the voice of a solo in a church choir, the shrill voice of the white-clad chorister penetrating to the mysteries of faith. There should be an antiphonal chant, to complete the effect – "Verily lengthwise! Verily backward!" – from the gathered congregation of Women Who Wanted to Know.

". . . *Thus!*" Hilde Claudia and Theodore chorused, and all three simultaneously performed the appropriate actions like department store demonstrators, professional smiles upon their faces that also looked like the demonstration of a product, moving their heads a little in order to glint their gold. (Hilde Claudia – if she had possessed Schiffendeckens – would no doubt have seized the opportunity to demonstrate how to slip them in, once she had disposed of the intricacies of how to fold napkins into a miter.)

". . . Do not put it over the other!"

("Verily!" chorused The Women Who Wanted to Know.)

"Double and make a crease to mark the half, and open it out again. Take the left-hand point at the top . . ."

". . . *Thus!*"

". . . and fold it diagonally to the center crease, pressing the divisions well; then take the right-hand point at the bottom, and fold it the reverse way. Now take the figure produced . . ."

". . . *Thus!*"

The napkins were flourished, smilingly — the smiles, like the napkins, folded only so far, a precise part of a predetermined pattern — held aloft for all to see, to learn, to emulate.

(All in the most martial manner
Marching double-quick;
While the napkin like a banner
Waves upon the stick!

(Willie, Johnnie, Mary Jane, and Peter marched like Grenadiers deeper and deeper into *A Child's Garden of Verses*.)

". . . and fold it in two, lengthwise and backward, along the line AB . . ."

"*AB! AB!*" chanted Hilde Claudia and Theodore, running their index fingers caressingly along the designated line for folding, to clarify Max's instructions, proud to demonstrate that they knew AB, they knew CD, they knew EF, they knew all the letters of the alphabet, and the gestures by which to signal them.

("Verily!")

". . . and turn back the right-hand point, so that the points shall be outside . . ."

"*Thus!*"

". . . Twist the napkin round the fingers to make it like a cap in shape, and tuck the ends at the base into the grooves made by the folds in order to keep them secure . . ."

Accompanied by thuses and verily, the antiphonal chanting of the believers, the shapes of three bishop's miters had mysteriously evolved in the hands of Hilde Claudia, Theodore, and Max. They held them out in front of them for inspection, like priests displaying holy relics to the faithful on a designated day, and then — not sure what to do with them in the absence of a dining table — placed them upon their heads. They looked as if — playing some literary parlor game, a sort of Mrs. Jarley's Waxworks — they were attempting a partial reproduction of the illustration of the chess pieces from the first chapter of *Through the Looking-Glass*, the bishops down in the hearth walking about among the cinders with the kings and queens and castles. Alice had just climbed through the mirror, and jumped down into the room beyond the looking-glass.

The Women Who Wanted to Know applauded with enthusiasm, an encore-demanding acclaim.

(Yes, there would be an encore. Yes, the yodeling would soon begin.)

At last their lives had been given a purpose. At last they knew all that they wanted to know. At last they were initiated into the mysteries of The Folding of Napkins.

"W.Q. to Q.B.'s 4th!" Mabel Peartree shouted, waving her shawl, a little overexcited.

You could see the bafflement in the faces of The Women Who Hadn't a Clue What She Was Talking About.

("*Double your cue?*"

("*Cubies?*"

("Was she speaking in code?")

Mabel Peartree claimed to be able to play chess, and always had a *Mary Celeste* game, abruptly terminated in mid-move, laid out on display in her front parlor, carefully copied from a book of puzzles. It was a little still life economically indicating that you were in the presence of scintillating intelligence, like Mrs. Albert Comstock's proudly displayed novels. She'd look at it knowingly, challenging visitors to unlock the secret of the right move to make.

Hilde Claudia looked annoyed as the shawl twirled and spun in the air, and tugged her miter tighter. *She* was the one for secret signaling, *she* was the one who knew the right moves.

"We three kings of Orient are. . ."

They held the second, unfolded napkin in front of them, to cover the gifts they carried, in the way that Annie enfolded her Book of Dreams in silk. They didn't need a red and white striped pole.

453

They didn't need a telescope ("All the better to see you with, Miss Pinkerton") or a tripod. They didn't need to sing about the fountain in the park, the roguish pair of eyes, the poor heart stolen away. The King of Light offered gold for royalty, the White One offered frankincense for divinity, the Lord of Treasures offered myrrh for death. What they carried bore a disconcerting resemblance to Portia's caskets at Belmont in *The Merchant of Venice*. The thought had occurred to Alice at a Christmas pageant, and she had covered her mouth, to erase the sinfulness of the thought. The more she had tried to think of something else, the more she had thought of those three caskets, gold, silver, and lead. *What many men desire. As much as he deserves. Give and hazard all he hath.* Reading Shakespeare was encompassed about with dangers to the soul. The scroll bearing the words of poetry was pushed into the empty eye socket of a skull. Gilded tombs did worms infold. The world was still deceiv'd with ornament.

". . . Bearing gifts we travel so far . . ."

(Should it be "travel so far" or "traverse afar"?)

The Magi's miters wobbled slightly as they walked. The folded napkins were too small for their heads, and so they walked like the socially ambitious undertaking deportment exercises, the miters balanced upon them. They walked very upright, their shoulders straight, their arms slightly out to each side. Once they had mastered deportment they — developing a taste for social advancement — would turn to Miss Winterflood to improve their elocution. She was a very aged lady now (one sometimes felt that she might very well have played Gertrude to Reynolds Templeton Seabright's Hamlet), but her vowels continued to be a source of astonishment and envy.

". . . Fiiieeeld aaand fooouuntaaaiiin, mooor aaand
    mooouuuntaaaiiin,
Fooollooowiiing yooondeeer staaar . . ."

454

They would have the vowels of bishops, the vowels of kings, of Melchior, Gaspar, and Balthazar.

It was time for the encore.

The yodeling began, and The Women Who Wanted to Know applauded with Reynolds Templeton Seabright thunderousness. "*Geschichten aus dem Wienerwald*" (they'd *certainly* have some tales to tell), followed by "*Morgenblätter*" (and they'd make headlines in the morning papers). It was a time for waltzing, not for marching. The Waltz King was at last given an opportunity to set all feet tapping to his insistent one-two-three, one-two-three rhythm. When it came to culture, you couldn't beat what Vienna had on offer.

The applause was the sound of a thunderstorm about to unleash its first tree-shattering fork of lightning, the flames and the smoke, the earth-shaking smash.

Up on the hill, Benjamin Franklin braced himself as he flew his kite, drawing the lightning toward him with the key — small, glinting in the intermittent flashes — that dangled below the silk kite tacked to the cross of thin laths.

("*Unter Donner und Blitz*" from the quick-to-spot-a-cue Websters.)

This was a key to unlock the mysteries of the storm-clouded skies, a key to release the knowledge locked away, the mysteries hidden in the box.

———

On the morning when Dr. Wolcott Ascharm Webster had told her that she should begin to tell him her dreams he hadn't actually announced "I am a disciple of the Dream Books," he hadn't used the expression "oneiromancy" — she was beset about by "ancies"; after the "ias," the "ancies" — but he had been all fired up. Hilde Claudia had been working overtime, werb-grappling all the hours that God sent, hemmed in by sharp-cornered, acutely angled dictionaries, strips of ripped paper protruding from the more significant pages. Alice had again seen him as at the start of a race, running on the spot, flexing and unflexing his fingers. He took deep breaths; he stretched up into the air as far as he could reach, and his arms mimicked the number 11 on his shirt; he reached down and touched his toes; what lay ahead was a marathon, not a sprint, and he was going to elbow his way to the front, come what may. His shirt was blindingly white. His starched shorts — they were rigid enough to stand up by themselves like a baffling manifestation at one of Mrs. Alexander Diddecott's séances — had an ironed-in crease that was sharp enough to crack a walnut.

Hilde Claudia's, Theodore's, and Max's arms were a blur, the flags spinning as if their lives depended upon it, shipwrecked mariners on a waterless island signaling to a passing vessel, the first they had sighted in seven years of searching.

"You tell me your dream," he had started to explain, and she had tottered on the verge of singing, "I'll tell you mine."

That would have set him scribbling: perhaps the interpretation of music might have arrived after all. It was a song, a dreadful sentimental song *as Sung by Miss Etta Butler* that she remembered Charlotte playing on the piano three or four years ago — "You Tell Me Your Dream, I'll Tell You Mine" — the little boy and the little girl singing coyly to each other. The perfect song for herself and Dr. Wolcott Ascharm Webster.

If "Ben Bolt" was the song for hypnotism, this would be the song for dream-reading. They would sit — in the position prior to hypnotism — facing each other, with their knees almost touching, but he would not produce his pocket-watch. Instead he would go down on one knee — a suitor making a formal proposal — and implore her in song.

> "You had a dream, well, I had one too,
> I know mine's best 'cause it was of you.
> Come sweetheart tell me, now is the time,
> You tell me your dream, I'll tell you mine . . ."

It would almost be enough to make her look forward to Wednesday mornings.

("Sweetheart"?

(Hmm.

(She wasn't too sure about "sweetheart.")

What he said would depend upon which Dream Book he used. Perhaps she might be offered a choice of interpretations. Shelves would be crammed with brightly colored books, far jollier than the usual somber volumes. The title *What's in a Dream* had made her think of "what dreams may come": there was Hamlet again, cloud-reading, dream-reading. *What's in a Dream* was the book to which Alice referred most frequently, seeking out the meanings of the past, the dreams that Annie had dreamed all those years ago.

One of the two quotations she could remember from De Quincey was the one about crocodiles; the other was one about dreams. She would have thought that the words were not especially memorable or significant, but they had remained in her mind, speaking to something inside her, random as all things remembered. They were: *It gave him pleasure that he could reach me in the very recesses of my dreams*. Each time she brought these words to mind, she saw the face of Dr. Wolcott Ascharm Webster — with an expression of drooling pleasure on his face ("You tell me your dream!" *Snuffle! Snuffle!*) — snuggling up close beside her, he become the crocodile, about to kiss her lingeringly with cancerous kisses, sucking out all her breath, and embracing the most private thoughts within her.

In the second half of the sentence — she abruptly remembered (the words must have lain dormant within her) — De Quincey imagined himself lying amongst reeds and Nilotic mud (she'd enjoyed discovering the word "Nilotic") with "unutterable slimy things," and in that last phrase — unmistakably — was Dr. Wolcott Ascharm Webster being described yet again. She couldn't remember the identity of the "him" to whom De Quincey referred, the taker of pleasure from the secret dreams of others (it may even have been the crocodile), but she always thought of "him" as a fervent-faced father, rampant with twitching, overgrown with beard, avid for the most inaccessible of recesses, though De Quincey's father had died when he was very young.

Dr. Wolcott Ascharm Webster was seeing himself as a Joseph, a Daniel, a biblical dream-reader from one of those Old Testament stories thought most suitable for children, once taught each week to her Sunday-school class by Kate, and now taught – Alice still felt a sensation of baffled incredulity – by Mabel Peartree. Alice should follow the lead of Joseph's brothers, for whom she had a certain sneaking regard, as she had for the Prodigal Son's brother. She knew just how they felt.

Maggie Tulliver had merely pushed the irritatingly pink-and-white Lucy into cow-trodden mud. When Alice Behaved Worse than She Expected – she had felt, as a girl – she intended to get full value. If there had been a convenient pit in the wilderness of Longfellow Park, her sisters Allegra and Edith would have been cast into it – it would have been deep; it would have had steep sides – at regular intervals throughout childhood. A passing company of Ishmaelites from Gilead would have been offered two trussed bundles to strap onto their camels, alongside the spicery and balm ("Miss Stein! Miss Stein! This is surely symbolic!") and myrrh. She would have killed a kid of the goats of the Misses Isserliss with enthusiasm and dipped the wine-colored woolen coats of her sisters in the blood. *An evil beast hath devoured her; Allegra is without doubt rent in pieces*: she had found these words wonderfully satisfying to repeat to herself, especially "rent in pieces." She should – like Joseph's brothers with Joseph – hate Dr. Wolcott Ascharm Webster yet more for his dreams, and for his words.

It gave him pleasure.

Yes.

Oh, yes.

Alice was the butler, the baker, Pharaoh (she had certainly experienced her seven years of famine at 11 Park Place), Nebuchadnezzar, describing her dreams to the one man who could interpret them. Avoiding the risky "You tell me your dream," and the ever-present danger that she would enthusiastically relive Miss Etta Butler's triumphs, he should echo Jacob's words, "What is this dream that thou has dreamed?" ("Behold, this dreamer cometh," he would utter unto himself as she arrived for her consultation.) Verily, she should reply in Joseph's words to the butler and baker: "Do not interpretations belong to God?" This would not have had the desired effect, however, this would not have prevented the eternities of fifty-five minutes in which clouds, pictures, and dreams were interpreted. Dr. Wolcott Ascharm Webster was — in his own view — a God of gods, a Lord of kings, and a revealer of secrets, listening to the thoughts of her heart. His patriarchal Old Testament beard — well gritted from desert sandstorms, sand trickling down and mingling with the talcum powder beside his bookcase — marked him out as a man at one with the prophets, his visionary eyes searching the clouds on the horizon for camels, weasels, whales. Shepherds with beards as big as sheep watched their flocks by night, clutching their crooks in case crooks came rummaging through their rams.

One of the blue Dutch tiles around the fireplace in her room showed Daniel in the den of lions. The picture — in reversal of the Elphinstone Dalhousie Barton technique — showed a very large Daniel, and three very small lions, looking like Chinky-Winky in triplicate, a sulky Cerberus. Not even Daniel would have survived a night in a sealed den (Darius' signet came down on the stone like Papa's Roman coin on Kate's forehead) with three farting Pekinese. On the tile next to Daniel — standing in a row in the burning fiery furnace — were Shadrach, Meshach, and Abed-nego, with their legs firmly planted, like the bottom layer of a troupe of acrobats, waiting for others to clamber on top of them. The little figures moved in the flickering of the flames, as if the furnace were lapping at them uselessly, unburning, unconsuming.

She should consult *What's in a Dream* and *Pearson's Dream Book* and see what they had to say about the sheaves; the sun and the moon and the eleven stars; the vine and the grapes; the baskets of bread and the birds; the fatfleshed and the leanfleshed cattle and the corn; the great image of gold, silver, brass, iron, and clay. She would see which of the interpretations Joseph and Daniel would have favored if they'd had those books to guide them in their seeking. The pictures of the dreams were bright on the walls of the Sunday-school room, with the ark, Jonah and the whale, Moses in his little ark of bulrushes among the flags, the crossing of the Red Sea, the nativities, the crucifixions, the fishermen on the Sea of Galilee, the Sermons on the Mount, the miracles. She'd felt quite superior in Sunday-school when most of the other children had made the usual mistake, and drawn baby Moses lying *amongst* bulrushes, not lying amongst flags in an ark made *out of* bulrushes. Sobriety Goodchild – not properly grasping what "flags" meant – had gone one stage further, and patriotically drawn a gigantic redfaced baby almost smothered by a massed Fourth of July display of Stars and Stripes, using up most of his red and blue crayons in the process. Moses (very odd to see a Moses minus a beard), a presidential candidate in the making, flourished a flag in each hand, and – mouth agape – looked as if he was giving his all to "And this be our motto, 'In God is our trust,' / And the star-spangled banner in triumph shall wave . . ." How remiss of John Philip Sousa not to have written *The Stars and Stripes Forever* yet; here was the perfect illustration for the front cover of the sheet music. There'd be massed flags in the windows of Columbarian & Horowitz, patriotic bunting cheering along with this jingoistic juvenile. ("Very – er – *interesting*, Sobriety," Miss Augusteena had commented faintly. "Why don't you show it to Dr. Odom, Miss Augusteena?" Alice had asked, a teacher's pet of helpful suggestion – "Er . . . Er . . ." from Miss Augusteena – and Sobriety had smirked proudly.) *The Star-Spangled Banner* would have suited Moses as his little personal anthem, like Mrs. Albert Comstock and her "See the Conquering Hero" chiming clock. Huckleberry Finn had thought it was Moses and the "Bulrushers," probably envisaging cowboy-like rodeo cavortings, stampeding crowds of check-shirted matadors throwing themselves upon rearing Brahman bulls. He lost interest when he heard that Moses was dead. He didn't take no stock in dead people. Alice had had to resist a Miss Watson-like shudder at the double negative when she first read the novel. *A tolerable slim old maid, with goggles on.* That was Miss Watson. No need to search too far to find Mark Twain's source of inspiration for that character. Longfellow Park fairly *hummed* with literary richness. Semicolons were utilized with a comma-like profligacy, and the pluperfect tense was readily employed in the most casual of conversations.

First you had a dream, then you looked in a book. This, more or less, was Alice's understanding of what would be involved in reading dreams. Instead of being locked away behind glass, the books consulted — grease-spotted, flour-dusted — would be spread out like recipe books across a well-scrubbed kitchen table, the corners of the pages turned down like overshuffled playing cards. The dream was described, a Dream Book was consulted, and the dream was interpreted. Dreamers of cameo brooches would play the piano superbly, or they would be overwhelmed with sadness.

("Alice . . ."

(Faintly, she heard a voice calling her name, the dreams drawing her toward them, embracing her into their many-leveled immensities.)

It was as simple as that.

This was how Dr. Wolcott Ascharm Webster had made it sound, though he seemed to suggest (by what she could grasp from his Swanstromian vagueness) that dreams were images of the past — what had already been — and not of the future. Nothing could be changed, and things would remain as they were. This was hardly encouraging. It sounded all wrong. Depressed cooks and servant-girls would be deprived of their dreams, forced back into the past from which they had been struggling to escape.

("Alice . . .")

"I had a dream last night."

("Alice . . ."

(The voice was *singing*.)

Annie had always sounded hopeful, as if the dream had been something given, a little gift from which better things might begin.

Peep, peep!

M.

Peep, peep!
S.
I see a "D"!
I see an "R"!
I see an "E"!
I see an "A"!
I see an "M"!
I see an "S"!
And what can I see?. . .

("Alice, where art thou?. . .")

Caliban at the window, she waited for the clouds to open and show riches ready to drop upon her as she dreamed.
She waited.

(". . . I've sought thee by lakelet . . .")

She waited.

(". . . I've sought thee on the hill . . .")

What could she see in those clouds?

(". . . And in the pleasant wild-wood
When winds blow cold and chill . . ."

(The wild-wood was not very pleasant now, and the trees were tall and dark, shutting out the light, grouped closely together so that the paths could not be seen, a maze grown to rankness, uncontrolled thickets spilling over onto – and blocking – the way out into the open air. The winds were rising, with a low moaning, agitating the branches into restlessness.)
The electrotherapy, the baths (hot), the baths (cold), and the massage had failed to cure her.

The hypnotism, the reading of the clouds, and the reading of pictures and dreams had failed.

She knew what would be coming next.

Soon.

On Wednesday.

On Wednesday morning she'd walk through the looking-glass into the cold dark room beyond, dark and cobwebbed (she'd be caught in Webster's web like a sucked-dry housefly's drained and rattling corpse), with the wall lined with fake books. The time would have come to take her away to the Webster Nervine Asylum in Poughkeepsie for an extended stay of weeks, months. It would be time for the rest cure, the S. Weir Mitchell method. That would be the new shape discerned in smoke and shadows. After the talking cures that were not cures, it would be the turn of the silent cure, in which she did not speak, was not spoken to, was not allowed to read or write. If she mentioned that she wrote she'd probably have to burn all that she'd written. That was what she felt. There'd be a cleansing blaze to burn the past out of her, like cauterizing a wound, a moment's pain for lasting health. A smell of burned flesh, fragments of black burned paper falling from the sky. She'd be freed from the malady of thought.

Like Mrs. Archbold in *Hard Cash*, like Dr. Severance of Staten Island, Dr. Wolcott Ascharm Webster knew that a whistle was an essential piece of equipment when you were grappling with loonies. He'd blow upon it — when the necessary time arrived (it was only a matter of waiting) — and two men would come quietly into the room.

One of the men would begin to speak to her.

"Be calm, my dear young gentlewoman . . ."

"Shh! Shh!" the other man said to her soothingly. (He should be patting her on the back. He should be saying, "There, there!")

". . . Don't agitate yourself. You have been sent here for your good; and that you may be cured . . ."

"What are you talking about? What do you mean?" she'd cry. "Are you mad?"

"No," one of the men would answer. "No . . ."

"Shh!" said the other man again. "Shh!"

(*Pat, pat.* "There, there!")

". . . *We* are not . . ."

They'd advance toward her, their arms extended on either side of them, like farmers shooing their animals down the tunnel into the slaughterhouse, cutting off the avenues of escape. Now they'd both be making little "Shh! Shh!" sounds, men attempting to calm a troubled sleeper. *There! There! There* was where they wanted her to go, down into the dark, brick-lined straw-strewn tunnel that was the entrance to the labyrinth, *pat, pat* on her back as they guided her the way they wanted her to go.

(She would not – in fact – be walking across to 11 Park Place on Wednesday morning next week.

(She would not be surrounded by men who had been summoned by a blown whistle.

(She would not be *taken away* to the Webster Nervine Asylum.

(She would be traveling there voluntarily, carrying her bags, a woman setting off for an eagerly anticipated and much-needed holiday, walking down the zigzag path to the Hudson – crossing and re-crossing, slightly further down each time, the places where she had already been – on her way to the tunnel under the railroad-track that led to the boat landing. The last time she had made this journey, her mother had gone with her. This time she would be alone.

(S. Weir Mitchell's method was waiting for her. Then she would be alone no longer. By electing to make this journey, by choosing to go to what she knew would be waiting for her, surely she was providing the definitive proof that – despite her private protestations – she *was* mad, mad in a way that could not ever be cured?

(At the rail of the boat, as it began its journey up the Hudson, she'd look back the way she had come. News – as it had a habit of doing at Longfellow Park – had got around, and the zigzag path was lined with crowds, fluttering with white handkerchiefs.

("Goodbye, Alice!" Mrs. Albert Comstock was booming, her handkerchief flapping like the mainsail of an Indiaman. "Have a nice time with the loonies!"

("Goodbye, Alice!" Mrs. Goodchild was shouting. To demonstrate her sadness, she dabbed at her eyes with her handkerchief between waves.

(Dab.

(Wave.

(Dab.

(Wave.

(Each brisk flick of the handkerchief dried it efficiently in time for the next dab.

("Goodbye, Alice!" the Reverend Goodchild bellowed beside his wife. His handkerchief was so squelchily soiled, so heavily cargoed with unidentifiable lumpishness, that it was incapable of waving. Like a flag in mourning, it tastefully demonstrated the sincerity of his sadness. It hung heavily from his hand, swaying slightly, a dangling and dangerously overloaded diaper, like several hundredweight of cheese curdling slowly into full-flavored maturity.

("Goodbye, Alice!"

("Goodbye, Alice! Good luck with the gibbering!")

"Be calm . . ."

"Don't agitate yourself . . ."

"Shh!. . ."

"Shh!. . ."

"You have been sent here for your good . . ."

"You may be cured . . ."

"*We* are not mad . . ."

"Shh!. . ."

"Shh!. . ."

"Listen to my voice . . ."

"Be still . . ."

"Empty your mind of all thought . . ."

"Sleep . . ."

(There was a *buzzing*, like the electric bell at 11 Park Place. The door opened, and she was in the dimness of the hall, the lesser light on the other side of the looking-glass. Max and Theodore — *bekannt*

465

bei alt und jung im ganzen Land — scampered closer at her approach, fingers rummaging thoughtfully up their noses. Long-legged and disheveled-haired, skipping and leaping, rich in dubious habits, they looked like the illustration for a new set of verses in *Struwwelpeter*. What was going to happen to them would not be good.

(Good.

(Each *Vogelfänger* faced an uncertain future, a dark fate.

(*Cheerful Stories and Funny Pictures for Good Little Folks*. That's what Heinrich Hoffman — a man who obviously understood what brought a smile to the faces of young children — promised, as he lopped and mutilated and drowned and, especially cheerful and funny, this one, set light to entire classrooms full of naughty juveniles.

(*Cuckoo! Cuckoo!*

(Cooee! Max!

(Cooee! Theodore!)

> All night long in the dark and wet,
> A man goes riding by . . .

("Alice . . .")

> Late in the night when the fires are out,
> Why does he gallop and gallop about?

(*Buzzzz!*

(The buzzing intensified.

(It was . . .

(It was . . .

(It was *their* electric bell.

(It was . . .)

Loud and clear, shrilly insistent, it finally burst free from the brackets that had muffled it.

It was Charlotte, ringing at the front door, singing "Alice, where art thou?"

Arm in arm, she and Charlotte would walk to All Saints'. That afternoon they would say goodbye to Ben. It might still be light.

It was time for church, time to brace herself for Dr. Vaniah Odom ("back by popular request") and the Reverend Goodchild.

It was time for the last service in All Saints' before the church was demolished.

It was time for . . .

Three

THE WICKED SHADOWS

. . . The shadow of the balusters, the shadow of the lamp,
    The shadow of the child that goes to bed —
All the wicked shadows coming, tramp, tramp, tramp,
    With the black light overhead.

From Robert Louis Stevenson, "Shadow March,"
A Child's Garden of Verses

I

It was time for Alice to go to bed. She had survived the combined forces of Dr. Vaniah Odom and the Reverend Goodchild – it had been a near thing – and now it was time for bed.

It had been a little later, a little darker, than she had imagined when they had said goodbye to Ben, some time ago. The darkness had made it seem later than it was. Kate had been there, wearing the Roman scarf that Ben had brought back for her from the time he had been in Italy with Joseph. Vivid in crimsons and blues, it had added a little color to a dull day. Ben had promised to bring back each of them something pretty from Japan: a screen, a vase, a kimono.

As she walked upstairs, *A Child's Garden of Verses* was in her head again, as it had been that morning. She had gone down in darkness, and now it was dark again as she made her way back without turning up the gas. The darkness had barely lifted all day, and the lack of light had oppressed her. She had gone down without candlelight in the dark morning, but now candlelight accompanied her on her way back up the stairs. She had lighted it from the pilot light. The almost full moon shone through the colored glass of the landings, but drained away all the color.

The moon has a face like the clock in the hall.

That was how Robert Louis Stevenson had described it, a clock-face that was brilliantly illuminated, but so far away that the time could not be read.

All of the things that belong to the day
Cuddle to sleep to be out of her way.

This clock-face had no *II*. No *IIII*. No *VI* or *IX*, and no hands with black ace-of-spades-shaped tips — like miniature versions of the railings outside Miss Iandoli's house — moving round and round the dial, muted chiming every quarter of an hour. Lewis Carroll ought to have written an *Alice* story about time, beginning with Alice searching for a missing kitten — it would be the black kitten, and not the white kitten — by stepping inside the tall case of a pendulum clock. Lewis Carroll would play with the concepts of memory and things already seen: he'd rehearsed this in Alice's conversation in the dark wood with the White Queen — every single thing crooked, all over pins — in *Through the Looking-Glass*. Strangely reduced in size, as if — yet again — she had drunk from the little bottle labeled "DRINK ME," she would stand in the echoing wood-scented darkness of the base, with the dimly glinting machinery of the weights, chains, and pendulum suspended high above her, as Alice entered the world of Edgar Allan Poe.

". . . Ninety years without slumbering . . ."

— she sang under her breath (terrible dreams shook them nightly, they were troubled with thick-coming fancies that kept them from their rest, the written troubles of the brain weighed upon the heart) —

". . . Tick, tock, tick, tock,
His life seconds numbering,
Tick, tock, tick, tock,
It stopped short
Never to go again,
When the old man died . . ."

No tick.

No tock.

Silence.

The old man had so much blood in him.

She should have been stained first red, and then green, and then green, and then blue. She studied her hands, the hands that were filled with darkness in the flickering candlelight and should have been changing color, step by step; she studied her shadow. The moon was big and bright, but the sky seemed utterly black, as empty of stars as the angel-guarded ceiling of All Saints'. The wind had barely abated all day, and was still howling around the house. The candleflame fluttered. She'd memories of Lady Macbeth-like moments on the stairs, wandering up and down, like someone sleepwalking, carrying a candlestick.

"From breakfast on all through the day,
At home among my friends I stay . . ."

— she was thinking, as she approached the schoolroom door —

". . . But every night I go abroad,
Afar into the land of Nod . . ."

Tick, tock, tick, tock.

Nod was where Cain went in the Bible after he had killed his brother. He was the son of Adam and Eve, the first murderer. Adam and Eve stood hand in hand on one of the Dutch tiles around the fire, but they were pictured when they were still childless, before they were driven out of Paradise. The LORD told Cain that he was cursed from the earth, which had opened her mouth to receive his brother's blood from his hand; when he tilled the ground, it would not henceforth yield unto him its strength; a fugitive and a vagabond would he be in the earth. Cain said unto the LORD that his punishment was greater than he could bear, because he had been driven from the face of the earth, and hidden from the face of the LORD. There was a mark upon him so that everyone

473

would know who he was. Because they knew who he was, they would not kill him, not bring his suffering to an end.

She had imagined him when she was a little girl, bent over in the land of Nod, east of Eden, his hands covering his face like someone ashamed to be seen. It was a desert place, where a reddish dust blew in the wind which darkened the sun and brought night closer, irritating the eyes so that tears ran down the dirty face of the man who had killed his brother, leaving smudged lines. In the land of Nod he dreamed bad dreams, and wept. No one would kill him, and he had to go on living.

In *Hard Cash*, when Alfred Hardie was taken to the third private lunatic asylum, a huge old mansion fortified into a jail, he was conducted through passage after passage, through door after door, and along a covered way to the noisy ward, to the singing, the roaring, the howling like wolves. As he lay on his filthy truckle bed, one of the maniacs sang, and shouted, "Cain was a murderer! Cain was a murderer!" all night long, over and over, the one thing he still knew.

> ". . . All by myself I have to go,
> With none to tell me what to do –
> All alone beside the streams
> And up the mountain-sides of dreams . . ."

I had a dream last night.
Tell me your dream, Miss Pinkerton.
She stepped into the schoolroom. The drapes had not been drawn across the windows, and the cold moonlit pattern of the windowpanes was thrown across the floor, and angled onto the bed. A shadow moved before her. *And I see him jump before me, when I jump into my bed.*

She lit the lamp, and turned up the flame, driving the shadows into the corners of the room, fading the moonlight.

She blew out the candle.

The curl of the smoke, its smell.

Soon she would not hear voices anymore.
Soon she would be still.
Soon she would empty her mind of all thought.
Soon she would sleep.
And when she slept, she would dream.

"... Try as I like to find the way,
I never can get back by day ..."

She bent her head to one side, and then the other, as she removed her earrings.

"... Nor can remember plain and clear,
The curious music that I hear."

One Ash Wednesday, these words had gone through her mind over and over at Dr. Wolcott Ascharm Webster's, in the way she used to repeat words to herself when she was memorizing them, or trying to shut out thoughts.

"Listen to my voice," he was saying. "Be still. Empty your mind of all thought. Sleep ..."

"Try as I like to find the way," she was hearing inside herself, "/I never can get back by day,/Nor can remember plain and clear,/The curious music that I hear ..."

Curious Music. That was one on her list of titles. Another one, from "Keepsake Mill" was *A Sin Without Pardon.* "Here we shall meet and remember the past" was the last line of this poem, as if the place existed only as a source of memory, and would not be there without the weight of what once had been.

It was night. It was windy.

Here he came again.

"Whenever the moon and stars are set,
    Whenever the wind is high,
All night long in the dark and wet,

A man goes riding by,
Late in the night when the fires are out,
Why does he gallop and gallop about?. . ."

Her fire was not out. Rosobell had newly laid it, to give her warmth and flickering light in the darkness.

Now in the falling of the gloom, / The red fire paints the empty room . . .

If you tell anybody, the wind will get you.

". . . Whenever the trees are crying aloud,
 And ships are tossed at sea,
By, on the highway, low and loud,
 By at the gallop goes he.
By at the gallop he goes, and then,
By he comes back at the gallop again."

All night long, he would be there.

Ben had thought that a child had written the verses, just as she had thought that a girl had painted herself standing at an unseen window, totally absorbed in reading a letter. They were words spoken with the voice of a child, not of an adult.

Down in Chestnut Street a grotesque little figure, wearing clothes too big for it, was bringing darkness to the street, doing things the wrong way round, his feet crunching through the snow. Gradually, one by one, the lights were being extinguished, the darkness coming closer and closer toward her, the street darker and darker, until the ladder clunked against the lamppost outside their house. The misshapen figure scuttled spider-like up the ladder, and put out the light. Put out the light, and then put out the light. She did not want it to look up and see her at the window. She did not want to see Leerie's leering face, staring up at her, illuminated in moonlight.

". . . And now at last the sun is going down behind the
 wood,

And I am very happy, for I know that I've been good . . ."

That was from "A Good Boy." It was like a prayer written for children.

"... I know that, till tomorrow, I shall see the sun arise,
No ugly dream shall fright my mind, no ugly sight my
    eyes . . ."

Behind his back, the good boy had his fingers crossed. "I've been *good*," he said aloud, repeatedly, as if it was his task to convince someone. "I've been *good*. I *know* that I shall see the sun arise. I *know*. I *shall* see the sun. No ugly dream shall fright *my* mind, no ugly sight *my* eyes. I *know*."

Good things of day begin to droop and drowse,
Whiles night's black agents to their preys do rouse.

"I *know*," Macbeth repeated. "I *know*."

She had – more or less (rather less than more) – kept darkness at bay throughout the day. Not for much longer. The darkness she had tried to escape was now around her, inside her, and the silence made it darker. It was time for the ugly dreams, the ugly sights.

("No more *sights*!" Macbeth had begged.)

The wicked shadows would be coming, tramp, tramp, tramp.

2

Halitotic Herbert had been the first person she had actually heard calling her the madwoman in the attic. He was, in fact, the *only* person she had heard call her the madwoman, but he had said it several times, often in gatherings where he smiled at her in the most obsequious manner. His enormous artificial grin was too large for his mouth, as if he had swallowed a smile that was trying to escape from the hostile vessel of his body: he shared his wife's delicious sense of fun. How their house must rock with laughter!

As he grinned his gigantic fawning grin, his teeth were misaligned, so that his smile was facing to one side, like a squint in the teeth. It was oddly disconcerting, and she tended to lean to one side, to balance things out a little, when she found herself being talked to by him. With the Reverend Goodchild, one did not experience a conversation: one was talked to, talked *at*.

His filthy teeth — it had never occurred to him to clean them since he had purchased them; they were as furred and thickened as limestone rock formations in a damply dripping cavern — were the exact same dirty yellow as the Goodchilds' toilet bowl. Long yellow-brown streaks ran down and through *Edwardson, Boyd & Sons, Sanitary Appliances*, and she half expected to read these words printed across his grin whenever it expanded hugely before her. The blue lettering — a little washed away and faded — looked like veins just discernible beneath the skin, old tattoos on the point of vanishing. G. G. Schiffendecken clearly failed to provide long-term care for his products in the obsessively possessive manner of Samuel Cummerford, the owner of the first automobile showroom in the area. Samuel Cummerford sold his products sulkily and reluctantly, giving the impression that he parted with them against his better judgment, and under great duress, to those who were unworthy of possessing them. He was like the parent of a spendthrift son, brokenheartedly compelled to auction cherished family heirlooms after years of his increasingly uncontrollable profligacy. Even after he'd sold an automobile, he'd still maintain a jealously proprietorial interest in it. He carried a large soft cloth and a tin of polish around with him in an inner pocket, and always stopped to inspect his automobiles — they remained "his" automobiles, even after being sold at handsome prices — whenever he came across them, to ensure that they were being maintained in a manner that met with his approval. They never measured up to his strict requirements. Out would come the cloth, out would come the polish, and the owner would emerge from the shop, or the church, or – indeed – his own home, to discover his automobile gleaming, the polished brass dazzling in the sunshine, and a little gold-lettered card – *Samuel Cummerford, for the Aristocrats of Automobilists* – prominently displayed upon the windshield. (*I trusted you, and you let me down!* was the unspoken accusation.)

If only G. G. Schiffendecken could be persuaded to emulate these praiseworthy standards of care! He would not be able to resist stopping the Reverend Goodchild in the street whenever he came across him, and – without saying a word – peeling back the lips from the grubby grin, breathing heavily upon the teeth thus exposed, and polishing away with a soft cloth in a vigorously circular clockwise motion, whistling tunelessly all the while. When he'd completed the job that clearly needed to be done – a final, head-on-one-side, critical appraisal, to ensure that the correct intensity of gleaminess had been achieved – he'd let the lips snap back with a reverberating elastic twang, and continue on his way with a spring in his step, and the satisfied air of a man at peace with himself, a man never known to let his high standards slip. The Reverend Goodchild, his beard vibrating with the after-shocks, would be left clutching a card that had mysteriously appeared in his hand. *G. G. Schiffendecken. Purveyor of Grins to the Gentry.*

The smell of the Reverend Goodchild's breath – a (*Teuch!*) potent combination of cabbage and tobacco (Great heaven! Had she stumbled across the secret ingredients of Griswold's Discovery?) – reinforced the lavatorial image in a repellent multi-sensory experience, to which might be added the sense of touch. He tended to touch the back of her hand caressingly as he talked, and his fingers had – the image of the toilet bowl seemed to lead her irresistibly to this image – the faintly disturbing clammy warmth of a recently vacated toilet seat.

She was not destined to be a genteel lady, or an Ideal Mother, when such thoughts came unbidden into her mind. She would banish such vulgarity, simper at her clergyman, yield flutteringly to his flattering blandishments.

"Tee-hee, your reverence!" she should snicker shyly at his effortful flirtatiousness, holding out her mama's best china teapot to offer him a refill for his cup, coyly averting her eyes. That's what spinsters were supposed to do, wasn't it, launch themselves into blushful vicar-snickering? "Tee-hee!"

Ha!

She most certainly would *not*!

She did *not* revere this Reverend.

The madwoman in the attic.

That was who she was.

That was *what* she was.

She heard the phrase, in the accents of the Reverend Goodchild – she had been at Mrs. Albert Comstock's – as clearly as if it had been the only thing said in a silent room, the way you could hear your name spoken in a room crowded with speakers, and she knew that it was describing her. She had instantly seen the creature in the inner room, the hidden door behind the tapestry, and it was like facing the wrong side of a painting or a mirror, like (she had that feeling again) the underside of the gold-embroidered purple coverlet that concealed the portrait of Dorian Gray.

She was in the room without windows, she was the thing that scrabbled and bit, the sound on the rising gale of a dog howling at a distance. She was the figure in the deep shade, at the farther end of the room, the thing that ran backward and forward, that groveled on all fours, that snatched and growled like some strange wild animal covered with clothing, that had its head and face hidden, the clothed hyena that she knew had her face: dark-skinned, pocked with smallpox scars, hairy. Words once spoken were spoken forever, and she listened for it again all the time, straining to catch her own name, her own description. As a minister with a high opinion of his own preaching he was unused to speaking in lowered tones.

For a while she had suddenly seen herself through the eyes of someone else, and had faltered. Then pedantry had taken over.

Not the attic: the schoolroom.

Not the attic: the schoolroom.

That had been her foremost thought, as if he were more wrong about the room than about the madness. Grace Poole had given Rochester a cord, and he had pinioned the arms of the madwoman behind her, and bound her to a chair with more rope.

"Now that I have your *full* attention, Miss Pinkerton, we may begin . . ."

Would it be hypnotism?

Would it be clouds?

Would it be pictures?

Would it be dreams?

Would it be . . .

Would it be . . .

Would it be time for her to be taken away?

3

. . . Grace Poole.

She remembered the name of the other novel that contained a character named Poole, the one she had been trying to call to mind early that morning. It was a novel she'd been thinking about — on and off — for much of the day, as though teasing herself with the nearness of the knowledge that she had possessed all the time without realizing.

The Strange Case of Dr. Jekyll and Mr. Hyde.

Poole was the name of Dr. Jekyll's butler, the elderly man who had seen the dwarf, and heard the pacing up and down within the locked room. With the corpse of Mr. Hyde lying on the floor of Dr. Jekyll's cabinet, Poole and Utterson had searched the chamber, looking into the depth of the cheval glass with an involuntary horror. It was so turned that it showed them nothing but the rosy glow playing on the roof, the fire sparkling in a hundred repetitions along the glazed front of the presses, and their own pale and fearful countenances stooping to look in.

It was a room that looked rather as her room was looking at that moment.

Come in, or the fog will get into the house.

She heard the words as clearly as if they had been spoken, as clearly as if they had been "the madwoman in the attic." For a moment they sounded like something she herself might have uttered, seized by a rebellious impulse – "Come in, or the frogs will get into the house" – as she locked all doors and barred all windows against the entrance of the Goodchilds and Griswolds. An incautious peer through the green glass at their massed approach had pushed her over the edge (*Aaaaghhhh!*), and driven her to acts of desperation.

"Come in, or the fog will get into the house."

For a while she thought that they must have been words spoken by Poole to Utterson, as he admitted the lawyer to Dr. Jekyll's house, the house in the fog-shrouded square of ancient, handsome houses decayed from their high estate, and let in flats and chambers to map engravers, architects, shady lawyers, and the agents of obscure enterprises. The fog still slept on the wing above the drowned city, where the lamps glimmered like carbuncles through the muffle and smother of these fallen clouds. Then she remembered that the words were spoken in *The Picture of Dorian Gray*, and were not spoken by a butler. Dorian Gray had a valet – Victor – rather than a butler, but the words were spoken not by Victor, but by Dorian Gray himself to Basil Hallward as he let him into his house in that same fog on the night he murdered him.

Victor was probably an incognito Victor Frankenstein, wandering between two more novels in order to observe Dorian Gray and Dr. Jekyll and pick up a few tips. No wonder people seemed to confuse Frankenstein's creature with Mr. Hyde, seeing Mr. Hyde as something huge and monstrous, when he was something far more frightening than that. The name "Hyde" was so well chosen, hidden away as Hyde was, hidden away like Bertha Rochester and Dorian Gray's portrait, but hidden in a far better place, hidden not within a locked inner room, but inside another person like something

482

trapped within the brain, impossible to find unless the brain itself were entered.

If he be Mr. Hyde, I shall be Mr. Seek.

Dr. Wolcott Ascharm Webster demonstrated his celebrated sense of fun.

The blindfold went around her eyes, and the teasing voice called out to her from some far corner of the room.

"Tell me what you can see, Miss Pinkerton."

She was led in like the frightened figure-model, naked and blind in front of the room full of staring men.

It was birthday party game time. The candles had been blown out to make it even darker, and there was the lingering church interior smell of just-snuffed candlewicks, the air hazy, stinging the eyes. She could smell it, she could feel it. The one wish had been made.

"Miss Pinkerton!"

"Miss Pinkerton!"

"Miss P-P-P . . ."

"Miss P-P-P . . ."

"The madwoman in the attic!"

Dressed in their birthday party best, they called out to her from everywhere around her, and she could not see where they were. She recognized the voices. The blindfold was very tight, as tightly knotted as a gag to prevent screaming. In her birthday-suit bareness, this was the only cloth in contact with her body.

"Miss Pinkerton!"

"Miss Pinkerton!"

"Miss P-P-P . . ."

"Miss P-P-P . . ."

Lips were puckered for the "P-P-P" all about the room, as if prepared for kissing, big soggy smacks to make the eyes of the seers bug out and bulge.

"Madwoman!"

"Attic shape!"

Not only was the Reverend Goodchild under the impression

that Bertha Rochester was imprisoned in an attic, he was also one of those who thought that the picture of Dorian Gray was in the same place, and she remembered when she had heard him say this. It came to her all at once. It had been after an afternoon he had spent sniggering and simpering with Mrs. Albert Comstock at Comstock Castle. She had been – even by her high standards – on repellently poisonous form. So had he. It was one of the things at which they both excelled.

As they left 5 Hampshire Square, the Goodchilds had been just in front of Alice and her mother. It had been one of the last occasions on which she had been visiting with her mother, before her mother's collapse into invalidism. An antimacassar had caught on the stud of the Reverend Goodchild's collar, and it lay across the back of his shoulders like a lace-edged surplice, giving him a provocatively priestly, Roman Catholic appearance. It was neatly arranged, as if he'd done it on purpose, with an artist's eye for symmetry. It probably matched the lace in his combinations. Alice – as, of course, was only right – said nothing. He was smuggling out Mrs. Albert Comstock's complete antimacassar collection, piece by piece, to add to the sophisticated ambience of The Old Pigpen, and who was she to stifle the commendable ambitions of another? They'd be carrying out the furniture next, preferably beginning with a piece still occupied by Mrs. Albert Comstock. If she could be persuaded to activate her fan, the three of them would create a scene possessing all the elegance of the bygone days of the sedan chair, an incident from an eighteenth-century novel brought to life to charm all beholders. They might be persuaded to race around Hampshire Square a few times, a sedate and genteel counterpoint to the whip-crackingly underdressed sweatiness of a chariot race (though there'd be plenty of sweat from the Reverend H. P. – Howled *Phews!* – Goodchild).

On the doorstep, he had whispered piercingly to his wife, "I wouldn't have thought it possible, but that woman is more *grotesque* than ever. Just imagine what the picture in the attic must look like." This had gone down very well with Mrs. Albert Comstock's great friend. "Ooh, you really are *dreadful*" — "dreadful" was accompanied by much donkey-like heehawing ("dreadful" was good, "dreadful" was to be commended) — "H.P.! *Dreadful!*"

Naughty old H.P.!

He was — inevitably — one of those who couldn't distinguish between Frankenstein and his creature, and she'd also heard him refer to Mrs. Albert Comstock as "Frankenstein with a bosom." "A *dreadful* thing to say, H.P.!" — the thunderously echoing heehaws were out in force — "*Dreadful!*" "Dreadful" was what she wanted. "Dreadful" was what she craved to hear. "Say it again, *louder!*" was the unspoken command as the heehaws reverberated. He'd mentioned a bosom! And, of all the bosoms in the world to mention, he'd mentioned THAT bosom! H.P. — Heehawingly Perceptive — was quite incorrigible! Ostrich feathers whizzed in all directions as the fan was vigorously activated. It was like Icarus working himself up for the moment of launching, that first leap out into space. Go on, Mrs. Goodchild! Jump! If Mrs. Goodchild had understood the reference to the portrait in the attic, it must have become a common expression.

Alice had not realized that *The Picture of Dorian Gray*, like *The Strange Case of Dr. Jekyll and Mr. Hyde*, had become mythic so quickly. The attics of Longfellow Park — it was no wonder that the Goodchilds and Mrs. Albert Comstock boasted of the immense size of theirs (The Old Pigpen was a wilderness of echoing garrets) — must be preternaturally crowded with grinning grotesqueries, discordant with screaming madwomen, dreadful with terrifying portraits. "O Attic shape! Fair attitude!" Keats had rhapsodized in "Ode on a Grecian Urn." He'd have soon changed his tune after an eye-opening stroll in *her* neighborhood. There wasn't much beauty in the truth he'd find in that vicinity. That was all she knew on earth and all she needed to know.

She had almost leaned forward and corrected the crowing clergyman, "Not the attic: the schoolroom." She'd also struggled not to say, "Not Frankenstein: Frankenstein's creature." She'd struggled even more not to add, "What an excellent description, H.P.!"

She could have knowingly nudged him with her elbow as she said "H.P." – Hugworthy Pal – as a sign of their growing closeness, leering horribly with an intimacy born of a shared revulsion. (*Hyde's* Pal, more like!) It would have been worth it, just to see the expression on his face, torn between pleasure and panic. Her main thoughts at the time, however – apart from gratification that her belief that Mrs. Goodchild and Mrs. Albert Comstock could not bear the sight of each other had been confirmed – was astonishment that Mrs. Goodchild had read (or at least knew something about) *The Picture of Dorian Gray*. Perhaps she had furtively perused Oliver's copy, filched from Mrs. Albert Comstock's – concealed under an antimacassar – and there had been another sea-change in Longfellow Park, not so rich, not so strange as the other.

As Oliver stood at the landing stage below Hudson Heights, the music would creep by him upon the water.

"Full fathom five thy mother lies . . ."

"Jolly good!" Oliver would announce, cheerfully. "Could you possibly make it deeper?"

"Of her teeth are coral made . . ."

"Splendid!"

The Great Barrier Reef would have a rival in the Hudson River, and stunned divers would swim around the immense flooded structure, marveling at the soaring arches and dazzling underwater whiteness. The surface of the river would bubble as if it were boiling as their cries of amazement seethed upward. Out-of-their-depth pearl divers, seduced by the tales of the gleaming riches – pearls already released from the drab, stained confinement of their shells, pearls of unparalleled size and value – would hitch up their – ahem – loincloths and prepare to plunge.

Those are pearls that were her eyes.

"Au fond du temple saint, paré de fleurs et d'or,
Une femme apparaît! Je crois la voir encore!. . ."

Unaccountably, these Ceylonese pearl fishers would be expressing themselves in French. Not only that, but they'd be *singing*, and that was what they'd sing as they took deep breaths. This would be the exercise to expand lungs to their maximum capacities. This would be the song to carry them down to the deepest depths, to the biggest pearls. This is what they *always* sang. You'd think Bizet would have given them another decent melody, but this one always went down well.

Down, down, the divers dove.

A woman appeared!

They could see her again!

> *"O vision, ô rêve!"*

This is what they'd bubblingly exclaim – with mounting excitement – as they drew within sight of Mrs. Albert Comstock's false teeth. This was a dream to feature in the latest edition of all the Dream Books, prominently featured on the covers in large print. Dr. Wolcott Ascharm Webster unscrewed the cap of his fountain pen and turned to a new page in his notebook.

"You tell me your dream . . ." he began to say, in his most soothing, you-can-trust-me, I-want-*every*-detail, don't-miss-out-the-mucky-bits manner.

> "Oui, c'est elle! C'est la déesse plus charmante et plus
>   belle! . . ."

The fountain pen began to race scratch-scratchingly across the page.

Mrs. Albert Comstock!

Charmante.

Belle!

(Charming!

(Beautiful!

(Mrs. Albert Comstock!)

He couldn't avoid involuntary cries of revulsion and disbelief. He must practice more to suppress them. They almost always seemed to lead to a certain loss of confidence on the part of his patients, often at points where it was becoming really interesting.

He looked again at his notes.

Charmante!

Belle!

Mrs. Albert Comstock!

Unobtrusively, he shifted his chair a little more securely behind his desk so that he was well shielded by a pile of leather-bound books.

Hell's bells!

These were men with *enormous* mental problems.

He felt about under the heaps of papers that littered the ink-stained red-leather surface, feeling for the handbell that he kept for just such an emergency. A brisk burst of the prearranged signal — the first line Papageno sang in *The Magic Flute* — and Theodore and Max would shoulder-charge their way into the room to grasp the lunatic pearl fishers with the killer hold around the neck that paralyzed all normal movement, the one that they practiced on their mother every Thursday night under careful supervision. His two sons — they were so keen — would sometimes ask if they could practice on Mama on other nights when they were bored, and (eager to encourage enthusiasm: Hilde Claudia should surely be capable of recognizing that this was what he was doing) he always agreed to their demands. They'd stand there, flexing their knuckles, leaning forward. "Go on, Papa," they'd wheedle insinuatingly. "Go on. We've nothing else to do. Go on. We're *bored*. Let us strangle Mama."

The pearl fishers warbled away, unaware of the furtive rustlings as their doctor frantically sought for the means of summoning assistance.

("Der Vogelfänger bin ich ja . . .")

488

(*Ja!* Bring the straitjackets with you!)
(*Ja!* Bring the big sticks and the gags!)
(*Ja!* Alert Poughkeepsie!)
(*Ja!* Send urgent messages to the Webster Nervine Asylum!)
(*Help!*)
(*Ja!*)

"... Oui, c'est elle! C'est la déesse qui descend parmi
   nous! ..."

They were simple men, who'd led sheltered Ceylonese lives,
with not much to get the pulses racing except an occasional passing
elephant of unusual attractiveness.

Unleashed on Longfellow Park they'd create carnage. No
woman with G. G. Schiffendecken false teeth would be safe from —
ahem — untoward familiarity.

Up on Morningside Heights, work had started on the Cathedral
of St. John the Divine, but here — peering over the rails of the
many boats as they made their way up and down the river — astonished observers caught glimpses of something even more
spectacular, rippling with quivering columns of insubstantial sunlight, dappled by the swarming shadows of shoals of fish. It was
another cathedral, a drowned cathedral, with its submerged stone
angels, its carved memorial tablets, its sodden books, dwarfing the
tallest structures in the city.

(Poole was the name of Bertha Rochester's keeper.

(Poole was the name of Dr. Jekyll's butler.

(There was another name ...

(There was another name shared by characters in two different
novels, another name ending in an "e" ...

(It hovered on the edge of memory ...

(Rooke.

(That was it.

(Rooke was the name of the nurse in *Persuasion*.

(Rooke was the name of the head keeper in Drayton House

Asylum in *Hard Cash*, the third lunatic asylum in which Alfred Hardie was imprisoned. In this madhouse the name of the doctor was Dr. Wolf. He'd rook him, all right, he'd move across the squares of the chessboard, leaping across the unoccupied ranks and files, moving ever closer to his goal.

(A rookery of Rookes. A rookery of seals. They slithered on the wet rocks on the edge of the cold, gray sea in a remote place where they had never seen a human being.)

4

"Come in, or the fog will get into the house."

Dorian Gray – with his pure, bright, innocent face – had murdered Basil Hallward on November the ninth, the eve of his (and Oliver Comstock's) birthday. He had sat in his library with him, smoking, his own fog creeping up around him and into the room, and then taken him up to the top of the house – to the schoolroom – and shown him the hideous face on the canvas. Basil Hallward had asked him to pray, to say the prayer that he was taught to say in his boyhood – "Lead us not into temptation. Forgive us our sins. Wash away our iniquities" – and Dorian had picked up a knife he had used to cut a piece of cord, and dug it into the great vein behind Hallward's ear, crushing the man's head down on the table, and stabbing him again and again. When his servant woke him in the morning, he looked like a boy tired out with play, or study.

Poole led Utterson across the yard to the building that was known as the laboratory or the dissecting rooms. Inside the dingy windowless structure they crossed the theatre once crowded with eager students and now lying gaunt and silent, the tables laden with chemical apparatus, the floor strewn with crates and littered with packing straw, and the light fell dimly through the foggy cupola. At the further end, a flight of stairs mounted to a door covered with red baize; and through this Mr. Utterson was at last received into the doctor's cabinet.

It was a large room, fitted around with glass presses, furnished, among other things, with a cheval glass and a business table, and looking out upon the court by three dusty windows barred with iron. Outside, the block of building thrust forward its gable on the street. It was two storeys high; showed no window, nothing but a door on the lower storey and a blind forehead of discoloured wall on the upper; and bore in every feature the marks of prolonged and sordid negligence.

("Storeys" and "storey" – like "discoloured" – were the spellings used by Robert Louis Stevenson. She preferred "stories" and "story," liking the idea this gave of a building that was constructed out of words, levels of a building that were created within the imagination, and took physical shape. There was the first story, and the second story. There was the hidden third story.)

The door, which was equipped with neither bell nor knocker, was blistered and distained. The fire burned in the grate; a lamp was set lighted on the chimney-shelf, for even in the house the fog began to lie thickly; and there, close up to the warmth, sat Dr. Jekyll.

The fog thickened, seeping through the cracks in the glass roof above the dissecting rooms. Alice was the female on the dissecting table, and she looked up, up past the pale faces of the peering, bearded men, feeling curiously listless, devoid of will or energy.

"This is the female . . ." the voice of the lecturer intoned, describing her malady as much as her sex.

She studied the jagged threads in the dirt-encrusted glass, seeing shapes in them, like the shapes you saw in lines and stains on ceilings (or in clouds). After Tess had murdered Alec d'Urberville at The Herons in Sandbourne, the lodging house in the new-sprung city of pleasure beside the sea, his blood had drip, drip, dripped through the floor of the bedchamber, and on the ceiling of the room below the redness grew from the size of a wafer to the size of the palm of a hand, held out for its fortune to be read. The oblong white ceiling, with the red stain at its center, had looked like a gigantic ace of hearts. It wasn't spades that brought death, it was hearts. "Off with her head!" shrieked the Queen of Hearts, and Tess bowed down on the morning of her execution, allowing the rope to be slipped around her neck in the prison at Wintoncester. From West Hill, Tess's husband and sister — Angel Clare and, 'Liza-Lu — looked down toward the red-brick building with its rows of short barred windows, and as they watched, a black flag — like the one Captain Nemo had unfurled at the South Pole — moved slowly up the staff of the flagpole. They bent themselves down to the earth, speechless, and remained thus a long time, absolutely motionless. The lines and stains opened out into faces, landscapes, cracked like the surfaces of old oil paintings, or old glass negatives, as if she were lying beneath the conservatory in a decaying, abandoned house.

As a little girl she had always confused the two meanings of the word "conservatory," and had imagined that music students studied inside glass-enclosed structures, bent over their instruments like the mediæval women over their tapestries, their dark-clad bowed bodies reflected in the gleaming glass above and around them as they sang their scales, tuned their instruments, practiced. She heard the music now, faintly, in the distance, the voice of a soprano — Almina, the sleepwalker, clad all in white — singing an aria from *La sonnambula*. The fog was swirling in, circling around the gaslights, darkening the room, blurring the boundaries, thickening the edges out of focus as if in the moments before sleep, and she saw shapes in these, as she saw shapes in clouds. It was — indeed — like having clouds there inside the room. The fog had got into the house, all right, confusing the eyes, confounding the mind, and the fallen clouds had smothered with their shifting shapes.

This was what she saw all the time when she removed her spectacles and everything became misty. She had bad eyes. They were eyes that saw bad things, things that weren't really there.

Lead us not into temptation.
Forgive us our sins.
Wash away our iniquities.

5

Saturday morning fog.

Mist rolling up the Hudson.

Shapes in the clouds.

It was a few weeks after Mary Benedict had departed with her family for Lac Qui Parle.

Mama was in her own room, the door purposefully closed. Dr. Twemlow had already been that morning, and would be there again. Alice would soon — very soon — have a baby brother or sister, just like Charlotte had Linnaeus, and Myrtle Comstock had Oliver. Allegra and Edith were at Grandmama's and Grandpapa's, and she had luxuriated in their absence. She had been practicing on the piano under the eyes of Louis Moreau Gottschalk, quietly, thinking of Mama. She would go and fetch the sheet music she had put on one side to loan to Charlotte.

It had been the music for "Carry Me Back to Old Virginny" — then a fairly recent song — in a collection with other James Bland songs, the one from which Mama had been playing the night before, the one with "Oh Dem Golden Slippers," the one with the cover illustration of the monstrous caricatured man and woman with the small sharp teeth and crocodile-jawed boots. Her revulsion at the illustration had come later. She had no recollection of its having made any impression upon her at the time. The book — in any case — was probably folded back to a particular song, with the cover illustration hidden. All that mattered was the music and the words. "Oh Dem Golden Slippers" was not a song Mama played with any frequency.

Alice, as she picked up the sheet music, had found herself at the back window of the schoolroom. She looked up toward Hudson Heights. All morning, the bluffs had been shrouded in fog, and as she watched, they began to reappear — little by little — reclaimed from vagueness as the mists faded. She looked up and became aware of something missing, a gap in the sky. It had been a little while before she realized what had happened.

The tower of the Shakespeare Castle was no longer there. It had been a Potemkin palace — built of paper, built of ice, beautiful but transitory — to surprise and delight Catherine the Great. The paper — an appropriate image — had been ripped and torn down, destroyed by the winds; the glittering pleasure domes and pillars of ice had melted away into rippled pools, a dirty detritus of gold and red paints muddied together into a desolate nothingness.

She stared for a while, wondering if her eyes had become even worse than usual overnight, and polished the lenses of her spectacles, thinking that might help. She focused carefully, as if there was just one stubborn area of fog that was refusing to move, hoping that the tower might spring back into being with a snap, like a mirage in the desert taking detailed form, studying the blurred, shifting sky as intently as if — even then — she was seeking for shapes in the clouds. The tower, however, remained not there, and smoke was billowing up from above the trees. Alice thought of all the possible permutations of literature contained in thirty-seven pinkish panels.

She came to a decision.

"I'm venturing unto yon Hudson Heights, to espy Mistress Charlotte, O menial one," she informed Annie, who was arranging some drooping white flowers in a vase in the parlor. Mama usually arranged flowers, but Mama had done little in recent weeks, made fragile by the carefulness needed in carrying an unborn child. Even the weight of a flower might be too heavy for her to lift. Alice had known where to find Annie. She had listened at the fireplace in the schoolroom, and heard her singing.

Annie made an elaborate curtsy, and assumed an expression of vacuous servility.

"Verily, your ladyship. Wouldst thou honor mine humble self by accepting a simple token of my esteem?"

Annie held out a pleasingly mediæval-looking hothouse lily, her head bowed, abashed to gaze into the splendor of the face of the lady of the manor, the Lady Alice.

"It p-p-pleaseth me well," Alice informed her, with an imperious gesture, and took the lily. She had been cultivating her imperious mien for some time, and Annie was always willing to abase herself before it. "Thou hast done well, O simple but loyal p-p-peasant."

"Verily, I am not so enthusiastic about the use of the word 'simple,'" Annie added.

". . . your ladyship," Alice corrected her.

"Verily, I am not so enthusiastic about the use of the word 'simple,' your ladyship."

"It seemeth to me the p-p-perfect choice of adjective for one as low as thou art."

"And few could be lower, your ladyship."

Annie warmed to her rôle, once they got going.

"How true that is. Farewell, menial but p-p-pleasing p-p-peasant."

"Farewell, your ladyship. Cook hath prepared thy favorite viands for the banquet. Be not late."

"I shall return in good time, and in splendor. P-P-Perchance I shall encounter thee again this day."

"Verily." Annie tended to overdo the verilys, but her curtsies were splendid.

Holding her lily, and a copy of "Carry Me Back to Old Virginny" – she was humming "There's where the cotton and the corn and taters grow" – Alice swept from the room, out through the front door, and up past the orchards toward Hudson Heights, and the pillar of smoke by day.

And the ruins of the Shakespeare Castle.

6

The gates were wide open, and she walked through them to find herself amid ruins, walking into the remains of Thornfield Hall, and within her memories of *Jane Eyre*. She looked with timorous joy toward a stately home; she saw a blackened ruin. No need to cower behind a gatepost, indeed! – to peep up at chamber lattices, fearing life was astir behind them! No need to listen for doors opening – to fancy steps on the pavements or the gravel walk! The lawn, the grounds were trodden and waste: the portal yawned void. The front was, as she had once seen it in a dream, but a shell-like wall, very high and very fragile-looking, perforated with paneless windows: no roof, no battlements, no chimneys – all had crashed in.

For a moment she had a picture of Reynolds Templeton Seabright on the roof, standing, waving his arms above the battlements, shouting – some of the more declamatory passages from *King Lear* might have been a good choice of text – his hair streaming against the flames as he stood, giving his very last performance. Then she realized, after a while, that the castle had not been destroyed in a fire. It was being demolished, rapidly and methodically, and this must have been going on for weeks. Timbers were lined up along a low wall, organized in size and usability, and other materials were stacked all around the wreckage of the garden: tiles, bricks, paving, but not the windows, not the panels. Scavengers had been waiting to pounce, besiegers to burst through defenses.

The smoke was billowing out of a huge bonfire in the middle of where the topiary had been, a half-blackened ragged knight rearing through the haze. There was no sound of peacocks. They were probably barbecuing on spits at the bonfire, an exotic feast for the workmen, of whom there was – she noted – no sign. They must have just left. They had probably gone to find some fine wine to complement their newly acquired taste for peacock flesh. They'd sit there with the feathers stuck attractively in their hair (bold pioneers of the æsthetic movement), youthful King Lears with peacock feathers instead of flowers, munching on meat. The whole place seemed abandoned to ruin and destruction, as sacked as Troy.

For the first time, she walked up the shallow flight of steps, and through the flung-open front doors. For the first time she walked on the decorative tiles of the hallway she had never seen before, open to the sky, and broken glass crunched under her feet. She looked up to where the tower had been. In the late afternoons and evenings of fall and winter, the setting sun had caught and reddened the glass in its windows and she had looked up at them. The windows had been of leaded stained glass, and it had been difficult to make out what the figures in them had been from a distance. They were too high up. She'd always meant to ask to borrow the Finches' telescope, and now it was too late. The arches had been clouded in greens, reds, and blues, like the high windows of All Saints', the figures taking on the luminescent radiance of saints or angels.

She was walking on the fragments of the stained glass, the narrow sad-eyed Burne-Jones and Rossetti faces, the flowing hair and gesturing hands, the attenuated bodies of Imogen, Titania, Hermione, Portia, unidentifiable faces and figures. All around her were the broken pieces of the panels, the scattered figures, and — she knew with certainty — they would not be there for much longer: Juliet, on her balcony, like a prisoner behind bars, but no Romeo; Henry the Fifth's head; Antony reaching out to embrace a dismembered Cleopatra; Prospero without his staff. She wandered round the shattered walls and through the devastated interior. Winter snows had drifted through that void arch, winter rains beaten in at those hollow casements, upon those drenched piles of rubbish, those stones and fallen rafters like a desecrated church.

She imagined Rochester in the ruins. She knew that Jane found him at Ferndean Manor, but she thought of him as at Thornfield Hall, sitting unseen in the cool darkness. His blindness, his mutilation, would be hidden in the shifting shadows thrown by the branches of the trees. The fire had destroyed the hall at harvesttime the previous year, but the trees had been growing amidst the ruins for years, and their leaves hissed, sea-like, wave-like, as the wind blew in from the Hudson through the blackened and broken walls and the crumbled mullions. Rochester would emerge stumblingly, advancing slowly and gropingly, pausing, as if he knew not which way to turn. To him all was void darkness. He seemed to wish by touch to gain an idea of what lay around him: he met but vacancy still. He tried to walk about: vainly – all was too uncertain. He stood quiet and mute in the rain now falling fast on his uncovered head.

Fragments of partially burned paper fell down on her from the bonfire, a blizzard from a blazing library, flames roaring up walls of books. She picked a piece from her shoulder, charred but readable. . . . *The sun/Has turn'd to ice! – There is a haze in the sky,/Chilly and thick, that ne'er will clear away!/The earth is wither'd grass, leaves, flowers, and all!.* . . . This seemed very apposite. Perhaps Mrs. Alexander Diddecott was right. This was one of the ways she had – there were many – of discovering what the future had to bring. She would open a book at random – the Bible was the best choice – and read the message lying there for her within. Mrs. Albert Comstock probably utilized Marie Corelli novels. Alice had tried this once with the Bible, but the message – . . . *The families of the Gershonites shall pitch behind the tabernacle westward. And the chief of the house of the father of the Gershonites shall be Eliasaph the son of Lael* . . . – had not been very helpful. She seemed to have wandered into Carlo Fiorelli statuary territory. She caught another piece of paper as it floated down in front of her. . . . *Hold on, old Robert! That's the mood! Hold on! Rail at her! Spurn her! Curse her! Drive her mad!.* . . . Hmm. Not very encouraging. The next fragment that fell seemed to be the handwritten opening of a story, "Templeton the Phrenologist". *It was the winter of 18-——, and I found myself* . . .

She stood there in the ruins amidst the broken figures, the shattered glass, with the burned pieces of paper falling upon her. She was filled with an urge to rescue something, but there seemed to be too much to do, and she did not know where to start. What was still there would not be there for much longer. Her imperious mien would have to be at its mienest. The workmen would soon return, and she wanted no witnesses to what she was going to do.

She went back out through the gates and set out for the Finches' house, further along the Heights, running, still clutching the lily and the sheet music, her hair and shoulders confettied with black-ened paper, a guest fleeing a sad wedding. She tried to hold her lily in the style adopted by the angel hoisting Little Nell in the final illustration in *The Old Curiosity Shop*. The tiny, nervous-looking waist-high angel in *The Girlhood of Mary Virgin* stood alongside a lily that was as tall as he was. It was placed in a vase on top of a stack of huge books, rigidly upright. Dante Gabriel Rossetti seemed to have a supply of sturdy specimens. Lilies, too often – especially in warm rooms (though there was hardly this excuse here and now) – drooped sloppily over, dragged down by the weight of their heads, like ill-postured pale consumptives, like – indeed – pale-faced, thin-limbed angels. Those haloes could be heavy. Perhaps they were singing the song she was singing now. She visualized the stiff-stemmed lily being utilized as a baton, keep-ing strict time in the heavenly choir. They were carrying Little Nell back to Old Virginny, to the cotton and the corn and the taters. What a surprise that would be for her. "Taters!" she would exclaim, as her eyes fluttered open to glimpse her first view of heaven. "The very things of which I dreamed!" (*Dreaming of potatoes, brings incidents often of good.*)

> "Carry me back to old Virginny,
> There's where the cotton and the corn and the taters grow,
> There's where the birds warble sweet in the spring-
>   time . . ."

There were no birds singing now. The sedge had wither'd from the lake, and no birds sang. (*To dream of rotting potatoes, denotes vanished pleasure and a darkening future.*) Here – near the ruins of a castle – was where she would meet a knight-at-arms, alone and palely loitering, dreaming of pale kings and princes, pale warriors. She could be a *Belle Dame sans Merci* if the need arose – well, per-haps not very *Belle*, but most decidedly *sans Merci* – holding her lily with emblematic coolness, like a drawn weapon.

"Have at thee, varlet!"

She made merciless thrusts with the flapping white-fleshed flower. Verily.

> ". . . Carry me back to old Virginny,
> There let me live till I wither and decay,
> Long by the old Dismal Swamp have I wandered . . ."

She and Charlotte were singing the same song as they emerged from Delft Place ten minutes later, side by side, pushing Linnaeus's baby carriage with no Linnaeus inside, running back toward the ruins of the Shakespeare Castle. Any witnesses would have feared for the imperiled speeding infant they supposed was inside. When Mama produced her baby brother or baby sister, she and Charlotte could have races with the baby carriages. It must have been then that she first had the idea of reenacting a scene from the Reverend Goodchild's awful (but Alice-free) novel *The Curse of the Colosseum* (1876), the two chariots hurtling round in front of the baying crowds of Ancient Romans. The only things worse than Ancient Romans — in the poison-soaked, stab-mutilated world of the Reverend Goodchild's novels — were modern Romans.

"Hasten unto the castle!" Alice cried, still thinking of her conversation with Annie.

"Pray heaven we come not too late!" Charlotte could pick up a cue quickly.

"Verily!" She'd reversed her previous opinion that Annie overdid the verilys. There could never be too many verilys.

> ". . . Massa and Missis have long gone before me,
> Soon we will meet on that bright and golden shore,
> There we'll be happy and free from all sorrow,
> There's where we'll meet and we'll never part no more."

Alice wasn't too keen on that double negative in the last line. She had her grammatical standards.

When they arrived they moved with speed, rescuing possessions from a sinking ship or a burning house. They would not have much time. Charlotte had seen the workmen walking away about half an hour earlier, and they would soon be back. They immediately realized that there was to be no choice about the panels. They would be able to carry only one away in the baby carriage, and the only one that was loose and undamaged — apart from its name being broken away from the bottom edge and one decapitated Sister — was the one for *Macbeth*, lying propped up against the front wall like a target in the butts.

Alice had run along the front of the building, and down the nearest side, but all the others were fixed firmly in place. They had all been mutilated, by the look of it, the broken figures lying on the ground beneath. It was like an illustration of Ancient Rome after the carnage of an invasion. She thought of her stories, destroyed, trodden into the earth. She had faint memories of grim-faced Roundheads despoiling statues in churches, shooting up at inaccessible angels and virgins, broken figures falling down to earth, shattering. Rocks burst through hallelujahing hosts, saints exploded, and cold bright light illuminated the dimness. The Roundheads would have liked this demolition of the Shakespeare Castle, competitively jostling to become involved in the destruction. They didn't like the theatre. They'd closed all the theatres in England, and silenced all those voices of grief and joy.

Panting, staggering, Alice and Charlotte lowered *Macbeth* into the baby carriage, which dipped noticeably under the weight.

"You've been overfeeding this child," Alice complained.

"Quadruplets," Charlotte corrected, maternally patting Macbeth and the Three Weird Sisters.

"I hope Mama doesn't have quadruplets." Alice visualized her mother with her arms vastly extended out at each side, two infants under each arm, all scowling like miniature sour-faced Mrs. Twemlows, or a surfeit of Chinky-Winkies. (Was that the plural for Chinky-Winky?) Nursing them didn't bear thinking about. Whole teams of wet-through wet nurses — bosoms alertly poised for instant access — would work tirelessly night and day.

Charlotte tickled Macbeth under the chin.

"Coochi, coochi, coo! What an adorable child!"

Her last two sentences — if the former had been a sentence — were Mrs. Alexander Diddecott's verdict on Linnaeus. They were still awaiting Mrs. Albert Comstock's verdict. The suspense of not knowing whether the child would be allowed to live.

Alice had heard Mrs. Albert Comstock described as being "of the Jonathan Swift school of child management." She hadn't known what this meant, but it had not sounded good. She thought it was something to do with Mrs. Albert Comstock's size, a reference to the Brobdingnagians.

A vastly magnified illustration from *Alice's Adventures in Wonderland* came into her head, the same one that she had recalled yesterday afternoon: a gargantuan Duchess with a gargantuan baby on her knee, the pose Mrs. Albert Comstock adopted with her succession of sulky-faced Pekineses. Myrtle Comstock — slightly older than she and Charlotte were — was, there was no doubt about it, verging on the Brobdingnagian.

"Coochi, coochi, coo! What an enormous child!"

She must try that the next time she saw her, rail at her, spurn her, curse her, drive her mad. Alice believed in using her time usefully. Come to think of it, Myrtle displayed an unmistakable facial likeness to the Pekinese: this, surely, must awaken maternal feelings deep within the Comstock Bosom. Oliver, her baby brother, looked nothing like the rest of the family, and was a pretty child whom Alice could quite enthusiastically have coochi-coochi-cooed in the absence of his mother. Mrs. Albert Comstock regarded him with distinct distaste: perhaps this was Jonathan Swift's sub-Herodian attitude to male infants. *Speak roughly to your little boy, / And beat him when he sneezes* . . .

All the girls she knew were being presented with baby brothers. Perhaps Mama might have a boy this time, and Papa would love him more than he loved her and her sisters. She would like to have a brother.

Macbeth was safely stowed in the baby carriage. They scurried

about, rather hopelessly scooping up whatever came to hand, figures broken from the panels, larger pieces of stained glass. The
hall tiles were beautiful, and undamaged, but so firmly fixed that it
was impossible to remove them. She kneeled down, and pulled at
the edges, trying to insert her fingernails, but she could not loosen
them. They had words written upon them, illustrations. *And by
and by a cloud takes all away*. She did not recognize these words.
You and I are past our dancing days. These she recognized, and felt
wise. *I know thee not, old man*. All the words were sad. They
stretched all around, beneath her feet — she walked across the
speeches — strewn with dirt and debris, and would soon be shattered
by sledgehammers. There was no time to read anymore, and she
ran back down the steps into what had once been outside. Now
there was no longer any distinction between what was inside and
what was outside. She scrabbled about in the broken fragments of
terra-cotta, with a particular purpose in mind, wishing that there
had been passing idlers to pause and ask what she was doing.
"What the deuce is she doing?" That's what they would ask each
other. (They would be men.) "I'm looking for a witch's head, of
course!" was what she would have replied, a sentence she was rarely
given the opportunity to employ. She found one head, the size of a
broken chess piece, but it was not the head of a witch. It wore a
crown, and looked like a king. There had been a small execution a
short while earlier, the death of a deposed monarch in the ruins of
his overthrown castle. *Reenter MACDUFF, with MACBETH'S
head*.

"For God's sake let us sit upon the ground / And tell sad stories
of the death of kings," she said, showing the head to Charlotte,
picking at the crown to remove the mud. ("For God's sake!" tended
to be Allegra's response — if Mama was not in the room — when she
quoted Shakespeare, but Charlotte was ever ready to look
impressed.) She'd just read *Richard II*. Richard hadn't been executed with pomp and formality on a high-raised stage; he'd been
stabbed to death in the dungeon where he had been imprisoned at
Pomfret Castle. She'd looked for Pomfret on a map of England, so

that she could see where Richard had been killed, but she had been unable to find it. It wasn't in the index. She knew that it was somewhere in Yorkshire. Perhaps it was near Thornfield Hall. "I wasted time, and now doth time waste me." That's what Richard said. He'd been listening to music and crying as he said this, because the music was a sign that someone loved him, and soon afterwards Exton had come in with the other murderers and killed him.

"We can't take anything else," Charlotte said, as Alice added the head to what they had salvaged. She sounded out of breath, and looked — as Alice must herself — dusty and crumpled.

It was not just a matter of time. The baby carriage was packed to capacity, and weighed down. It looked bowlegged — if wheels could be so described — an unfortunate camel conveying Sphinx-like Mrs. Albert Comstock in the direction of the Pyramids during her Egyptian holiday.

Alice made a gesture to embrace the building in front of her.

"Goodbye," she said, not feeling in the least foolish. She felt — part of her surveyed what her feelings were — obscurely tearful.

"Goodbye," Charlotte said, equally solemnly.

She remembered the *Hamlet* panel, and looked up above the entrance. She would have wanted to rescue this, if she could have reached it — it was on a higher level, it might not have been damaged — but it was no longer there. It was larger than the other panels, and there was a deep space where it had once been. It seemed to have been neatly and properly removed: there were no broken fragments of terra-cotta left in the stone. She ran back inside, looking at the bottom of the wall, searching for an angled pink piece of statuary. Nothing. She ran back down to the front, looking in places where she had looked already. She didn't know why she was searching for it; it would have been too large, too heavy, for them to move, but she knew she wanted to see it again. She knew that there would be nothing left to save the next time they came there.

"We couldn't take it, in any case," Charlotte said, knowing what Alice was doing. She was arranging a little blue blanket on top of what they had rescued, making comfortable a sleeping overweight infant. "It's time we went." It was one of the few occasions on which Charlotte had been the one taking the initiative.

As they pushed the baby carriage through the gates – one of them, they saw, was detached from its moorings, and leaning back against the wall – Alice was looking backward all the time, like Mary Benedict in reverse. She was looking at the shadowed space above the entrance, as though she could read the shape of the missing figure in the recess, straining her eyes to see, straining her ears to hear the vanished cries of the peacocks.

Ten years later, at the funeral of Albert Comstock in Woodlawn Cemetery, she wandered away from her father and mother and sisters, her little brother, the other relatives, in search of Reynolds Templeton Seabright's grave. She had been disappointed by Albert Comstock's elaborate tomb, completed for him months before his demise. (Mrs. Albert Comstock – energized and full of enthusiastic ideas – had overseen the construction, like an ambitious houseowner constructing a costly summer house.) Despite persistent rumors, it had not possessed a space for advertising the latest bargains at Comstock's Comestibles, a useful service for economically minded mourners. Like Green Wood Cemetery, Woodlawn had been designed for Marvellian green thoughts in green shades, the serene contemplation of the pattern of life and death, the transience and the persistence of being. Philosophically inclined picnickers could pack a skull in their hamper, neatly positioned next to the thinly cut sandwiches and well-polished apples, and could contemplate it in some rural glade amidst the tree-shaded gravestones, lost in deep musings on all that had gone before. And this was all that had come into her mind: day-old pies handsomely reduced in price for the shrewd and observant purchaser.

She had found the gravestone of Reynolds Templeton Seabright.

It bore the *Hamlet* panel from the Shakespeare Castle – this was the purpose for which it had been removed – and a quotation from Edgar Allan Poe: *Ah, broken is the golden bowl! the spirit flown forever!* They must have started the demolition of the castle the moment that the old actor was dead. Alice hadn't known that he was dead on the morning she had come across the almost completed demolition. She wouldn't have been surprised if they had started to demolish it with the old man still inside, a premature destruction, his heartbeat still sounding within the shell.

Alice and Charlotte had to push hard, and keep the wheels aligned straight ahead. There would be no turning corners with this overloaded wagon. They saw the workmen — a group of about seven of them — walking up the footpath from Longfellow Park, and tried to look as if they were innocently strolling past, perambulating some well-behaved and well-nourished child. One of them waved. Alice had a momentary picture of a shortsighted laborer kindheartedly reaching into the baby carriage and gently chucking a miniature Richard the Third or a miniature Henry the Fourth under the chin. ("He's very small, isn't he? Why is he wearing a crown?") It would probably be the first time ever that Richard the Third had been coochi-coochi-cooed. ("What an adorable king!")

Charlotte saw the expression on Alice's face. She waved back to the workman, and the two of them began to increase their pace, trying not to show how much they had to exert themselves to do this. The wheels were creaking alarmingly. ("What do you feed him on?")

"The two little girls walked away from the Shakespeare Castle in the late morning of a day in the winter," Charlotte prompted, looking at Alice.

They walked on a little way farther.

"The two little girls walked away from the Shakespeare Castle in the late morning of a day in the winter."

Charlotte was determined.

After a while, Alice spoke.

"Counterclockwise," she said. A ghost story in daylight.

She began.

"The two little g-g-girls walked away from the Shakespeare Castle in the late morning of a day in the winter . . ."

She could still tell her stories, clockwise and counterclockwise. She knew the details of every panel, and the order in which they had been positioned around the walls.

First, *Macbeth*.

Second . . .

The workmen were behind them now, walking across toward the opening in the wall, to complete the job they had started. Alice and Charlotte, instead of heading back to Charlotte's house, were starting down the road past the orchards toward Alice's house. They gripped the handle of the baby carriage firmly, their hands side by side, about to begin a duet at a piano, leaning back at an angle to prevent it from hurtling down the descent. One of the workmen was whistling a tune Alice recognized. Workmen always whistled. She stopped speaking, and listened, turning back a little in the direction of the music.

Charlotte answered the unasked question.

"'Shew! Fly, Don't Bother Me,'" she said. There were few songs she didn't know.

After a pause, in which Alice did not continue with the story, Charlotte spoke the first line of the song, again prompting.

"I think I hear the angels sing . . ."

". . . I think I hear the angels sing . . ." Alice picked up the cue, but she sang, instead of speaking. Charlotte joined in.

". . . I think I hear the angels sing,
I think I hear the angels sing,
I think I hear the angels sing,
The angels now are on the wing.
I feel, I feel, I feel,
That's what my mother said . . ."

"That's beautiful, girls!" the workman who had been whistling called across to them. "I think it's me can hear the angels sing."

They giggled, as girls must – girls must giggle, workmen must whistle – and left, as they arrived, pushing the baby carriage and singing, but walking slowly, not running. They were not – in fact – pushing the baby carriage, so much as being drawn downhill by its weight, digging in their heels to prevent it from running away with them, dragging them downward to their doom. They felt like tiny Miss Stammers, being taken for a walk by her enormous dogs.

"... I feel, I feel, I feel,
I feel like a morning star,
I feel, I feel, I feel,
I feel like a morning star ..."

(It would be the workmen who would wield the morning stars as they destroyed what remained of the Shakespeare Castle, obliterating the surviving figures, splintering the unbroken glass, the spiked balls swinging around on chains until they were just blurs, wrecking as the walls roared down in clouds of dust.

(With the goddess of beauty they would destroy. They would destroy with the mother of love, the queen of laughter, the mistress of grace and of pleasure.)

"... I feel, I feel, I feel,
I feel like a morning star ..."

Their singing became increasingly breathless. They stopped as they approached Chestnut Street, some time later, feeling like morning stars. They didn't want anyone to hear them, and to come out and see what it was that was burdening the baby carriage. It would be too much of a surprise to peel back that blue blanket and see what lay within, a baby with the face of King Lear. ("That beard really suits him, bless him!") If they'd taken Linnaeus with them, they could have laid him protectively across the top of the smuggled haul of Shakespearean refugees. There he'd have wobbled, Linnaeus the First, precociously encouraging his teeth to emerge by chewing gummily on Richard the Third's hump, the hindquarters of Henry the Fifth's horse, and throwing any inquisitive peerer off the trail by being what ought to have been there, a baby in a baby carriage.

They entered the garden via the back entrance, and went into the stables, the cobblestones bright with newly scattered straw, as if packing cases had been prized open. They had a visitor. Dr. Twemlow's horse was chomping away like a creature never fed, the carriage angled across awkwardly. He himself was probably in the kitchen, also chomping. He had a tendency to wander into kitchens, exclaiming at the delicious smells he had detected with the aid of his trained medical nostrils, and cooks could take a hint. His mama did not feed him properly. That was the general opinion.

There was a pause as Charlotte seized the opportunity to lavish endearments upon an unfamiliar horse. She'd dart into the road to launch herself upon any promising-looking beast, and no stables remained unexplored. "Promising" encompassed all horses that looked sad, neglected, or unwell; "promising" encompassed *most* horses. She'd convinced herself that her loving attentions were all that could draw them back from the very brink of death at the hands of a cruel master, cramming straw into their panicky resisting mouths. Dr. Twemlow's horse looked as unimpressed as most others, and attempted to bite her. Charlotte patted away for a little while longer, drew her fingers lover-like through its mane, muttered "There's a good boy! There's a good boy!" and only desisted when a determined lunge from the good boy almost knocked her off her feet. She behaved throughout as if nothing that happened had come as any surprise to her. As it happened most times she sought to persuade passing horses that she alone loved them and cared for them, this would have been fairly easy to do. You traced her progress down the street by listening for the sounds of whinnying and rearing, as cursing riders came crashing down to earth. "There's a good boy!" she muttered once or twice more out of habit – from a safe distance – as the good boy rolled his eyes and lashed out with his back legs.

They unloaded the baby carriage, and set out what they had rescued in neat rows in a disused stall. Someone had produced far more than quadruplets. The stall still bore — on a little brass plaque — the name of Jessica, a horse Alice could remember well.

They were emerging from the stable, carrying *Macbeth* between them wrapped in the blue blanket, looking like participants in some small religious procession in a Mediterranean country, when Dr. Twemlow emerged, carrying his bag. Yes, he had been on the chomp. There were crumbs in his beard, and down the front of his vest. They were pausing for a moment, awkwardly angled, as Alice attempted to suck the pad of her thumb. She'd cut it on a piece of the stained glass, a Katherina or a Beatrice slicing neatly through her flesh, and she looked up at the doctor through a latticework of fingers, with the salty taste of blood in her mouth. She hoped he didn't think she still sucked her thumb.

He looked not at them but beyond them, seeing the baby carriage.

"My," he said. "You do come prepared."

When Alice appeared not to understand what he meant, he indicated — with a flurry of flaky crumbs — what he was looking at.

He hovered on the verge of saying, "Unto us a child is born" for several tottering seconds. Then, lurching back onto — more or less — normal usage, he disappointingly changed his mind.

"Your mama has been blessed" — he liked to give the impression that he was accompanied on his missions by well-drilled annunciating angels (a man who *knew* he heard the angels sing) — "with a child. You have a little brother." (A *brother*!) He made a vaguely clerical gesture with a soap-scented hand. The smell of the soap was the thing she remembered most, that and the weight of *Macbeth*.

(A *brother*!)

She and Charlotte had carried the panel right up to the top of the house, to the schoolroom. Then Charlotte had returned home with the empty baby carriage, and she had gone to see her baby brother, Benjamin Franklin Pinkerton, and told him that he would learn Latin. They had had the name all ready in case Mama had a baby boy. Papa had chosen it. They had not had a girl's name ready. It seemed a lot of name for such a small baby. The baby had clasped her proffered fingers firmly.

"There's bonus, a gift."

She had lain with her arms around Mama for a while, her pocket-handkerchief wrapped around her thumb because of the dripping blood, and then transferred the rest of the figures and the glass to the schoolroom in several journeys, trudging up the stairs with Ophelia, Imogen, Bottom, the figures of kings and queens, tyrants and lovers.

Now, apart from the panel in Woodlawn Cemetery and an imagined shape in the sky, they were all that was left of the Shakespeare Castle. She had returned, a day or so later, and nothing at all was left, just plowed-up earth. Even the topiary had been grubbed out like a well-rooted dandelion.

7

The *Macbeth* panel was propped against the wall, at one side of the mansard window facing onto Chestnut Street. She turned away from it, and moved toward the fireplace, her reflection advancing in the mirror above the mantelpiece. In the center of the mantel, along from the sheet music bearing the face of Louis Moreau Gottschalk, its back reflected in the mirror, was the clock with the moon dial. She had watched it throughout her childhood, waiting for the full moon, waiting for the cold light to flood into the room through all the windows, as if all that brightness, draining away color, came from within that little wooden case. With this clock she had tried to hold back time.

When the time of a full moon approached, she would open the glass front of the clock — its small silver key, like a charm from a bracelet, was kept hidden in an old cigar box with other treasures – and push the moon back a few days. She'd thought it would be like trying to hold back a planet, but she was able to do it with the tip of her little finger, a slight counterclockwise push, the action of someone easing an eyelash out of the corner of an eye.

It had never worked. The full moon had still appeared in the sky on the predicted night, just as the almost full moon had appeared tonight, and the cool silvery light had still spread the outlines of the windows on the floor, like reflections on ice.

The man who went riding by, late at night when the fires were out, when the wind was high, the man who galloped and galloped about, had a face that she knew when she was a little girl. When the trees were crying aloud, when the ships were tossed at sea, he went by at a gallop, and then came back at the gallop again, and he had the face of Papa's "friend." Papa was not the kind of man who had friends – it was a word she had never heard him use – but she could not think of any other term to define the man she meant. There were many possibilities – "colleague," "associate," "acquaintance" – but she always thought of the word "friend," and she always thought of this word in quotation marks, at a time when Oliver Comstock was a new-born baby, and it would be years before Mrs. Albert Comstock began to refer to Arthur Vellacott as Oliver's "friend." She only ever saw Papa's friend – Papa's *"friend"* – in darkness, and it seemed he appeared when – like tonight – there was a powerful wind blowing, and, it seemed so in her memory, when – like tonight – there was a bright full or near-full moon, a man drawn out by wildness and the cold phosphorous brightness. She never knew his name. He was just Papa's "friend," a man with a beard who smelled of tobacco and drink, and money was involved with it. When he came, something entered the house that should have remained outside, and it was Papa who had brought it in.

He had started coming to the house in the months before Ben was born. The two men – before they arrived – seemed to spend most of the early evening in drinking at their club. Mama said so –

a fierce, frightened whisper in the hall — and she could smell that smell when they came toward her. Papa was at home less and less, working late, absent at weekends, and when she saw him that was the smell that she began to notice. She couldn't have said if it was whisky ("whisky" if the drink came from Scotland, "whiskey" if the drink came from Ireland) or brandy, or whatever it was: it was just the smell that she knew as "drink." That was the word used by Mama, the word she wasn't supposed to have overheard, and that was the way he smelled now, of that, and of the strong cigarettes that he smoked, the ones that made her cough, and tears come into her eyes. The way he talked was different, the way he moved was different: both speech and movement seemed drawn out and fastidious, with an underwater slowness. Throughout the glimmering green-lit, aquatic summer evenings, throughout the early fall, he slid his feet across the tiled floor of the hall with careful, conscious daintiness. It was the same sort of movement as the careful, over-controlled way he slid the back of his finger across the inside of his top lip to remove loose grains of tobacco, or enunciated words with absolute precision from those same wet lips.

There was this particular night.

Mama was on her way out somewhere — Alice could not remember where — and her anger (she was angry again, the same intense whispering in the echoing hall) was partly because Papa had made her late by spending longer than he had said he would at the club, and (Alice felt) partly because he had brought his "friend" home with him again. He had been coming repeatedly for several weeks by this time. Allegra and Edith were not there — she could not remember, either, where they were — and she was alone in the house, apart from Annie, with Papa and his "friend," the two bearded men.

She did not have a nurse anymore. Nurse had been dismissed. She had not been a young woman, and she had been kind, patient and affectionate with her, showing her photographs of her sister's children, and talking about them. Alice couldn't even remember her name — she had always known her as "Nurse," and that was how she had addressed her — and she had never known how and why she had left. She had been there, and then she had not been there, without even saying goodbye to her. It was something to do with Papa. Like Miss Ericsson, she would go quiet, and concentrate on some small task when Papa came into the room. "Good evening, Mr. Pinkerton," she would say — it was usually evening when he appeared, bored, on the lookout for some source of distraction — and then she would busy herself with something trivial, folding some of Allegra's clothes very precisely, or finding the right toy for Edith. She could remember Nurse showing her a photograph of a boy and a girl, her nephew and niece, standing outside a barn in Kansas or Nebraska, somewhere like that. The boy was holding a puppy, and the puppy was called Patch. She could not remember the boy's name or the girl's name, but she knew that the puppy had been called Patch. "The barn is painted red," Nurse had said, "and that cart is yellow," and her finger had indicated a barn and a cart that were the color of bruised late-evening clouds, clouds that you saw in your memory.

She did not know where her mama had gone; she did not know where her sisters were; she did not know the exact date (though she knew it was the late summer, sometime before she had started to encircle the Shakespeare Castle with Charlotte, and Mary Benedict): her memories were a curious mixture of the utterly precise, and the mistily vague. Sometimes she could read the labels on every can and bottle on a shelf in a memory, or the headlines in a newspaper in the hand of a passerby; other times she could not see the face of the person in front of her, recognize where she was in the house, or know whether it was night or day. In memory as in life, she was sometimes wearing her spectacles, and sometimes not. Between the sections of intensely detailed recollections there was nothing at all. Why did some things — little things, trivial things — remain in the memory for years, forever, and other things — things you thought you'd never forget, or things you never even thought of memorizing because they were so completely a part of you — vanish without trace?

This particular night she would not forget. Something had changed.

They were in the front parlor. The drapes were not closed, and the gaslights were on so low that the light of the moon — it was a full moon — was bright enough to cast the shapes of the windows right across the carpet, and partly up the wall, long pale shapes like reflections in water, glimmering, shifting, and there were shadows in the corners of the room. The gas-lamp outside had not been lighted. She remembered that, but did not know if it was because the lamplighter had not come — letting the full moon do the work that he should have done — or because it was broken. She should have looked out, and down the street, to see if other lamps had been lighted. Then she would have known. She usually looked out for the lamplighter, but that night she had forgotten. It must have been well past her usual bedtime. It had been windy all day, and the force of the wind increased with the coming of darkness. The curtains — with a faint *whoosh* — shifted a little into the room and back again with the currents of cold air, like something breathing.

The men's cigarettes glowed as they inhaled. She didn't know that this was what was happening; she just knew that the ends of the cigarettes glowed red, and then the men would blow, long, thoughtful clouds of smoke into the air, into her face, making her cough. It was as if they had come to the end of a banquet — one of those hour after hour multi-coursed monstrosities favored by Papa, course after course after course, every course piled high on the plate, and every course accompanied by wine. Stained and crumpled napkins had been cast down on the table, belts had been loosened and vests unbuttoned, and the inebriated and overfull feasters sprawled back unsteadily in their chairs. Papa's "friend" eyed her speculatively. She was one of a range of desserts and he was trying to decide whether or not he had the appetite for a few mouthfuls more.

They did not speak much. They seemed to be waiting for something, each waiting for the other to make a beginning. There was a sense of some written agreement being put to the test for the first time by two businessmen who did not trust each other, each on the alert for a strict adherence to every sub-section, every paragraph, every *word*, each — with scrupulous politeness — attempting to interpret each word, each paragraph, each subsection in a way that would bring a triumphant sensation of superiority over the other. They were two equally matched chess players about to begin a long-awaited game. One player would hold his two clenched hands in front of the other player, his hands side by side, one hand holding a hidden black piece and one holding a hidden white piece, like a father about to surprise his child with an unexpected gift, returning home after a long journey. "Choose," he would be saying. "Go on. Choose." Was it the queens he held, or two pawns, or could any piece be used for the selection of the color to play? There was a special language involved, a mixture of languages like (the image had come to her years later) a Volapuk of the chess board: *zugzwang, j'adoube, kriegspiel, en prise.* "Go on. Choose." There was just the glow from where their mouths were, and then the smoke around their beards and in front of their eyes, making them even more difficult to see in the dim light. She was standing in front of Papa, as he held her loosely at the waist — he often did that — and made her strike matches to light their cigarettes for them. It was like a game, when the matches went out, or the cigarettes failed to light. Sometimes Papa's "friend" would deliberately blow out the match. The more she giggled, the more they laughed, not really an amused laugh, a different kind of laugh.

She was pretty that night. They told her she was pretty. Then there were those laughs again, because they were laughing at themselves for having said this. They knew it wasn't true. Why her, and not Allegra? This was what she couldn't understand. Allegra *was* pretty. Why not Allegra, if prettiness was what they wanted? This was the question she kept asking herself, then, and later, going over it again and again when she was alone in the schoolroom. Was it because she was the one who happened to be there, or had she been *chosen*?

They were passing her between each other — this had happened before — half throwing her little distances into two outstretched hands, and sometimes it hurt, jarring the breath out of her, when they caught her under her arms. She was laughing when they began, slightly excited, and then she fell quiet when she became breathless. They held their cigarettes in their mouths to leave their hands free, and ash tumbled down onto her head as they caught her with a jerky upward motion. Papa held her so that her ear was against his watch-pocket, and she could hear his watch ticking, feel its small vibration, and the watch-chain pressed against her cheek.

As she was pressed closer against them, she smelled other smells above the smell of the cigarettes and the alcohol. There was a meaty, sweaty kind of smell — old sweat, drawn out by warmth — and, stronger than this, the smell of cinders and smoke. They both had the fire and brimstone smell of fallen angels cast out of heaven. The elevated railway did not, at this time, travel as far out as Longfellow Park, but they must have been on it that day. The smoke from the train had blown upon them, scattered them with ashes, and they smelled as if they had been toiling all day in a foundry, pouring out the molten metal whilst dressed — oddly formal — in dark suits, their faces gleaming red in the darkness, or laboring in a vast, darkened manufactory, fitfully illuminated by the flames from furnaces as they tossed in shovelful after shovelful of crumbling, wet coal, the metal edge of the shovel scraping against the concrete floor in a way that made her shudder. It was like the high-pitched shriek of chalk on a blackboard, as the answers were written up after a test. The smoky, industrial smell gave her the feeling that their hands would be calloused and dirty, and that she would have hand-prints upon her clothes and body. She didn't want her dress to be spoiled.

Papa's "friend" was humming a tune, absent-mindedly, in the same sort of way that people chewed gum or whittled at pieces of wood. She was one of a long line of burdens being thrown from hand to hand by workmen loading a steamboat or a freight car, or the same burden being thrown over and over, and he was passing the time, lulled out of boredom and forgetfulness by the music, the same piece repeatedly. It was one of the tunes from Papa's pocket-watch. Perhaps he had heard it a short while earlier, and it had stayed in his mind.

Beautiful dreamer . . .

— he hummed, rather tunelessly —

. . . wake unto me,
Starlight and dewdrops are waiting for thee . . .

After a while Papa started to whistle it. She heard it shrill against her ear, felt the warm breath blowing against her. Then they were both whistling, loitering idlers in the street, men with time to kill and nothing to do, indolently waiting for some source of amusement to catch their attention. They were men in the mood to place wagers on the first bird to alight on a telegraph wire, the first dog to bark or growl, the first raindrop to reach the bottom of a windowpane.

. . . Sounds of the rude world heard in the day,
Lull'd by the moonlight have all pass'd away . . .

"Pass the Parcel!" Papa's "friend" suddenly shouted, making his mind up about something. She opened her eyes, and the white exploding fireworks shapes became black exploding shapes. She tried to turn her head, to see what was happening across the room, and Papa's "friend" was clapping his hands, making inward gestures, like a player in a game wanting the ball to be passed to him. Papa laughed until ash fell down the front of his vest and into her hair, and threw her across to his "friend."

. . . Beautiful dreamer, queen of my song,
List while I woo thee with soft melody . . .

"When the music stops . . . !" his "friend" said, and – behind her back – she felt him, holding her with the upper parts of his arms, mime the actions of someone playing a piano. His whistling stopped, and he pulled off one of her shoes without unbuttoning it properly, hurting her. They were her favorites, red tanned goatskin, buttoning up the side, with a little tassel on the front.

(*Goatskin* shoes!

(All this time – without realizing it – she had possessed the goatskin for which she and Charlotte had long sought to suppress Mrs. Albert Comstock. They could have killed her *ages* ago. Barefoot, she could have walked through snow to administer the fatal blow, carrying her coal scuttle and Grandpapa's Japanese sword. The shoes would have been on the small size for the task assigned to them, but they would have sufficed, if she'd held them carefully in the right place. *When you come near her look not at her herself, but at her image in the brass; so you may strike her safely. And when you have struck off her head, wrap it with your face turned away, in the folds of the goat-skin on which the shield hangs.* It was important that she avert her face. She must not look upon that which she was killing.)

Papa's "friend" began to whistle again, and threw her across to Papa.

> *. . . Gone are the cares of life's busy throng,*
> *Beautiful dreamer, awake unto me . . .*

Papa immediately threw her back, given something he did not want.

> *. . . Beautiful dreamer, awake unto me . . .*

"When the music stops . . . !"

Papa's "friend" pulled off her second shoe, and threw her straight back. They were becoming clumsier in the way they were throwing her. It did not matter if she should fall, if she did not remain upright, and it was beginning to happen more and more quickly. She was to be hurtled across a white line, part of a pattern painted on grass, a smear of grass-stains and whitewash down the whole length of her body, an object being used in order to win a game with strict predetermined rules. Somewhere, faint in the distance, an unseen crowd roared encouragement to the players. There would be the shrill sound of a blast on a whistle, an infringement of the rules detected by an alert referee, and someone would start booing. She was feeling giddy, her vision blurred, her sense of direction lost. It was like the time on the roundabout when she had been sick, and Mama had held her, patting her back, whispering words of comfort because she was crying.

She was not crying now. She did not protest, did not utter a word.

Surreptitiously, Papa's "friend" touched her face lingeringly, caressingly, like someone attempting to make out the profile of a queen or a president on the heads side of a newly minted coin, recognizing the person depicted solely by touch. She had become a coin like the coin on Papa's watch-chain, a small unit of currency.

It happened this particular night, and then it happened every time he came, and he came often.

Something made her feel that she ought to become still, silent, make herself invisible, weightless, not really there at all.

8

It was what she learned to do in the weeks that followed, when Papa's "friend" began to sit her down upon his knee. He just held her, very still, very close, seeming to freeze, and hold his breath. When Papa left the room – he had started to leave the room, *click, click, click* across the hall to his study on the opposite side, another *click* as he closed the door behind him – she felt that she was on the edge of a vertiginous drop, poised like the statues of the watching women on the ledges of Grandpapa's office, waiting for their men to return from the sea.

She had seen the backs of some of them from Grandpapa's windows, as new and unweathered as if they were standing in Carlo Fiorelli's workshop. Penelope was to the right of the biggest window facing onto South Street, and, even though it could not be seen from the street, the back — the tumbling hair and falling folds — was as fully detailed as the front, like the figures high in the roof of a mediæval cathedral, invisible to the human eye far below, finished on all sides because God could see everything.

God could see everything.

She, too, held her breath, in case Papa's "friend," in case she herself, might somehow forget that she was there. If she should move, she felt, she would fall, turning over and over to smash upon the ground.

"You're one of the girls from the statue," he whispered.

That was all he said, and he said it every time, the necessary words of a ritual, like a password that promised reward.

She imagined Papa in his study, the room on the other side of the front door, bent over lists of numbers and symbols — dollar signs, pluses and minuses — bent over the close-written papers with tiny writing. He was like a clerk totting up his totals in a banking hall, adding up the same numbers over and over in order to arrive at the same answer each time. There was no money in the study, just records of where it had been, where it was going. Discreetly, he bent certain fingers slightly over, or sketched downward strokes — like the beginnings of a matchstick figure — in tight symmetrical blocks like the markings-off of the days of an imprisonment, as he calculated in all the redness of the ink.

She let herself become stone, become bronze, become her own figure in *The Children's Hour*, the blind-eyed girl. Each time Papa's "friend" came into the house, he would sit with her upon his knee in the front parlor, like a man waiting for something, and Papa would leave the room, *click, click, click* to his study, *click* as the door closed. It always, she came to realize, lasted for exactly an hour, like something that had been paid for, like — later — her fifty-five minutes with Dr. Wolcott Ascharm Webster on Ash Wednesdays.

At first she had felt that she might be expected to say something — the silences seemed awkward, impolite, the frigid emptinesses of one of the more unsuccessful afternoons at Mrs. Albert Comstock's (there were plenty of these) — but she had somehow sensed that silence was all that was expected, even though the silences had become difficult to endure. She would spoil it — though she wasn't sure what *it* was — if she spoke. She sat, stone, bronze, unmoving, unspeaking, listening to the hiss of the gaslights if it was in darkness, or the sound of Celia Iandoli practicing her piano-playing, or the fluttering wings of a trapped butterfly, if it was daylight, wanting to pick it up in her cupped hands and release it from an opened window. If you rubbed the dust from its wings it would die.

She must not speak for this one hour.

She must not move.

She must not think anything, or feel anything.

The hour would pass.

Sometimes Papa came in and sat beside them, angled slightly inward, and the silence continued, this time with the slight wheeze of Papa's breathing, the suffocating smell of just-smoked cigars.

"You're one of the girls from the statue."

9

There was another particular night.

By now it was late in the summer, or early fall; it was growing darker earlier, and some of the nights were cold. She must have imagined the sound of the butterfly's wings. It had been too late in the year for that, not high summer, unless she'd heard one of the last survivors, living a little while longer in the warmth indoors, fluttering its wings as it slowly died. Sometimes, quite late in the year, she'd be surprised by the faint whirring sound, the slow, struggle to return to life of something she had imagined long dead. It was still the time before fires were set every day, but she sometimes awoke in the middle of the night because of an unexpected coldness, shivering under the inadequate coverings upon her bed. This night, however, was the end of a day that had been warm. It was another full moon, another night when the wind was blowing, another night in the front parlor with Papa and Papa's "friend."

The gas-lamp outside had been lighted a short while before. We are very lucky, with a lamp before the door. She had sat with her head back, watching the lamplighter climb up the ladder above her, Dr. Vaniah Odom mounting up to sway in his pulpit on his tower of hymnbooks.

"I see hell!" he would declaim, staring into the flame as he lighted it, and it bloomed purply-white, illuminating his face like a pumpkin lighted from inside.

O Leerie, see a little child and nod to her tonight.

It was time to begin.

"Pass the Parcel!" Papa's "friend" said, matter-of-fact now, confident. The first time he'd said it, it had almost been a question, though there had been no question mark, no upward inflexion of the voice. It was not a question now. He sounded like a man ordering his favorite dish from the menu in a restaurant, his little treat to himself after a week of toiling. She saw herself in the ice-cream parlor with a tall glass towering in front of her, taller than she was as she sat down. She had a long thin spoon, long enough to reach to the very bottom of the glass, as silvery and narrow as a dueling weapon. From above, like threatening thunder, she could hear the feet of Mary Benedict, of Myrtle Comstock, of all the girls in the ballet class as they leaped up and down, as they spun and galumphily *glissaded*. The voice of the ballet teacher – a Madame something, *another* of the all-conquering Mesdames – was shouting with a metronomic incantation. *Thud! Thud! Thud!* Myrtle Comstock hit the floorboards like an ill-tempered avalanche. *Thud! Thud! Thud!* ("That'll show you!" she was grunting. "That'll teach you a lesson." For Myrtle Comstock, ballet was an advanced martial technique.) Alice shut out all sound, and concentrated on the frosted surface of the glass, the dark cherries like lips poised for kissing, the ice cream still solid, still preserving the shape of the scoop. She was prolonging the moment before she started, a delicious delay before she began to dip into the whipped cream, slowly, the little strands of dark chocolate that crunched between the teeth and melted in the mouth.

Again there was that smell of smoke and cinders. They belonged near flames, and ashes were upon their heads, pattering down. They were trapped in Pompeii, or Sodom and Gomorrah. Abraham had asked the LORD if he would destroy the righteous with the wicked. He was but dust and ashes. Two angels came to Sodom at even, and Lot rose up to meet them, and bowed himself with his face toward the ground. The *LORD* rained upon Sodom and upon Gomorrah brimstone and fire from the *LORD* out of heaven; and he overthrew those cities, and all the plain, and all the inhabitants of the cities, and that which grew upon the ground. But his wife looked back from behind him, and she became a pillar of salt.

Alice imagined wet, slurping tongues licking her lingeringly, as if she were a Savory Special from Comstock's Comestibles, with a yum-yum taste to her flesh. (The weapon-like spoon made its first foray into the cream and chocolate. You had to be careful, or melting ice cream would overflow, and run in thin rivulets down the outside of the glass.)

The smoke of the country went up as the smoke of a furnace. Lot went to dwell in a cave with his two daughters. There was not a man in the earth to come unto the daughters after the manner of all the earth. They made their father drink wine that night.

Alice — recklessly revealing that she had been surreptitiously browsing through the Bible in Sunday-school when she was supposed to be listening to a discussion of how sweet Little Baby Jesus was — had asked Miss Augusteena what this curious story meant, Lot behaving like a tippling caveman as his daughters poured booze into him. A cave and wine seemed such a curious combination. You'd have expected gin or beer. Miss Augusteena had come over all pink and confused in a mother's-womb-untimely-ripp'd sort of way (imagine the expression on Miss Swanstrom's face if *that* passage had been printed in their edition of *Macbeth*!), and ignored the question. "Little Baby Jesus! Little Baby Jesus!" she repeated, desperately, bouncing her brother's baby up and down on her knee vigorously until all his features blurred. She'd pilfered Dixon Augusteena – a particularly annoyed, truculent-looking infant who deeply resented being kidnapped – to add a little winsomeness to her teachings, and all the girls had cooed. Loud sentimental sighs drowned Alice's insistent questioning. *Why* did they make their father drink wine?

Alice thought that she felt grit against her cheeks from the two men's clothes, and imagined dirt streaks down her face.

> *. . . Beautiful dreamer, out on the sea*
> *Mermaids are chaunting the wild Lorelei;*
> *Over the streamlet vapors are borne,*
> *Waiting to fade at the bright coming morn . . .*

Annie had come into the room.

She was watching them, unseen by the men, from the doorway. Alice had not told her about Papa's "friend," and she felt embarrassed that she should see what she was seeing. She felt foolish.

Annie said something to Papa. It might have just been his name, but there was a sharpness in the way she spoke that made Alice hold her breath. The words of the song went from her mind. There had been something different in the way that Annie looked at Papa in recent weeks, the way she held herself when he looked at her. Alice had seen him, some mornings, some evenings, looking at her as she polished the furniture or scrubbed the floor. As the time for the birth of the new baby came closer, Mama spent longer and longer in her room, with the drapes drawn, like someone ill. Having a baby was an illness, something that wasn't talked about. Mama seemed not to be around so much to speak to Annie, and Papa had watched Annie, checking – so it appeared – that she completed her given tasks satisfactorily.

Something had changed; something gone away or something come closer. Annie would never have dared to speak to Papa like that – it was the tone of voice, not the words used – only a few weeks previously, when the earlier darkness of the evenings was still taking people by surprise. Annie had polished and scrubbed, polished and scrubbed, so that – by concentrating on removing every fingerprint, making every surface shine, removing all the evidence from the scene of some crime – she could somehow avoid having to look at Papa.

Annie came right into the room, up closer to them.

Papa's "friend" had just said, "When the music stops . . . !" and they were all standing still, in silence. It was like a game of Statues. You froze in position when the music stopped, in some exaggerated Reynolds Templeton Seabright posture, and the first person to move – however slightly – lost the game. Whenever he said, "When the music stops . . . !" she kept on singing the words of the song inside her head, so that the music did not really stop, as if by doing this she could prevent there being a silence.

. . . Beautiful dreamer, beam on my heart,
E'en as the morn on the streamlet and sea;
Then will all clouds of sorrow depart . . .

Annie walked right up to Papa's "friend," and held out her hands, to take Alice away from him. She wasn't that much bigger than Alice herself, but she held out her hands with the intention of taking her in her arms, and carrying her away with her. Her hands were held out only a small distance away, the fingers splayed out like someone expressing grief, an unspoken demand. They were the hands Alice had watched raking up ashes, polishing cutlery, holding out the material of a skirt in a curtsy.

The two men stood motionless for the longest time, the wind louder in the silence, a loose pane rattling, the hems of the curtains slowly swaying backward and forward, hissing against the floor, the sound of women hurrying into or out of a room, their skirts dragging. The thing that surprised Alice the most was not that Annie had said something, but that Papa had said nothing in reply.

When Papa's "friend" made no move to hand her over to Annie, Annie said something again – it was something polite, something conciliatory, she said "Please," she said "sir" – and began to move forward. Papa's "friend" made a clumsy sideways movement, hunching around with the top half of his body, his arms tightening around Alice, like a spoiled child refusing to show something he wanted to keep all for himself, like Sobriety Goodchild with his new baseball bat, that only he could hold, only he could use. Annie spoke yet again – "Please, sir . . ." she said – holding out her hands like a suppliant, and Alice felt the tips of her fingers beginning to grasp the top of her arms. She had to reach up, on tiptoe, she was so small. Alice began to turn around to face her, to reach out her own hands.

Then Papa spoke. He said something to Annie, something short and coarse, something that made his "friend" laugh loudly. The "friend," still laughing, with a spiteful little movement like a brat stamping his foot, petulantly threw the shoe he had just removed from Alice at Annie's face. With equal eagerness he would willingly have cast the first stone at anyone who happened to be around, aiming very carefully for the head. This was a shoe with a buckle. It made a little Christmassy jingling sound, and cut Annie just below the eye.

She continued to hold out her hands.

"Please, sir . . ."

10

They were outside the house, in the windy moonlight, walking in the darkness between the flickering pools of gaslight. It was a surprisingly mild night for early fall, though the wind had a sharp edge to it. This must have been on the same night, because it was the night of a full moon.

What happened that night happened again and again over the next few months. There was not enough time left to wait another month for the next full moon, because it started to become too cold to go out. There was a gap for a time, and she thought it had finished, but it started again in the spring. What happened was always the same.

The full moon was very large and very bright, and seemed to grow in size, its light becoming more intense – heavy, oppressive, catching stiflingly in the throat like pale floating thistledown, or the pollen of heavily scented lilies – as they moved out of Chestnut Street, down Chestnut Hill, and along Rivers Street, away from all the lighted streets, and down toward the far side of the park. Her shoes had not been put back on her, and she was not wearing her new winter coat – Mama was always most scrupulous in dressing her up warmly when she went outside in the colder weather: her coat, gloves, scarf, hat – but Papa had his arms tightly around her. He was carrying her now, not his "friend," holding her against him, with her legs wrapped around him, to keep her warm by the nearness of his body, carrying her upstairs to her room. Annie was walking beside them, her hand reaching up and touching Alice's back, to let her know that she was there. Papa's "friend" was on the other side of Papa, whistling again, waiting for the moment when the music would stop.

"Beautiful dreamer," Alice sang inside herself, "wake unto me."

The music would not stop; she'd keep the music from stopping, keep it inside her. Though she was not beautiful, she felt she was the dreamer; motion seemed dreamlike, slow and underwater in the heavy light.

> . . . *I had a dream de udder night,*
> *When ebryting was still;*
> *I thought I saw Susanna dear,*
> *A coming down de hill . . .*

She opened her mouth with a little pop, looking for the bubbles that she thought would emerge, rising in a stream to the surface of the dark water. It was very quiet. There was a distant dog barking somewhere over on the other side of the park, lonely as a nighttime prairie train whistle. Sounds of the rude world heard in the day,/Lull'd by the moonlight have all pass'd away.

> *. . . The buckwheat cake was in her mouf,*
> *De tear was in her eye,*
> *Says I, I'se coming from de souf,*
> *Susanna, don't you cry . . .*

The previous week – Saturday morning – Papa had made Annie sing "Oh! Susanna." Annie hadn't wanted to, but Papa had made her. He had come out of his study when Annie was in the hall. He said he'd heard her singing when she thought he was out of the house. He'd heard her – several times – from his study, and she had a nice voice. He was sometimes in the house, he told her, when she thought he wasn't there. He saw more than she realized. He heard more. He had made her sing it properly, correcting her pronunciation in the approved Mrs. Albert Comstock fashion. "Properly" was "de" and "udder" and "ebryting." "Properly" was "de" and "mouf" and "I'se" and "souf." *Susanna, don't you cry*. Alice had been in the front parlor, sitting at the piano. Unused to asking, Papa had ordered Annie to sing. Alice had wanted to play the music as Annie sang, to let Papa know that she was there, in the next room, and could hear them.

Annie was *hers*, not Papa's.

Alice looked over Papa's shoulder and up at the moon. That gave her a reference point to the world she knew, and she might know where she was as long as she saw that, gazing at it as if she was memorizing it. The way that he was holding her, she could not see the direction that they were going, only the places where they had just been. Papa and his "friend" walked without speaking, knowing where they were going.

"We're going to the Celestial City," Papa had said.

The Goodchilds lived in a former farm on the far side of the park, near the shore of the lake. Longfellow Park still had the feel of being on the edge of open countryside at this time, far from the city, upstate rather than uptown, with Hudson Row and the streets leading out of it, and the new mansions along Park Place, looking oddly urbanized and out of place, forerunners of what was to come. On the western outskirts there were working farms enclosed within rows of new houses, built out at odd angles next to the out-buildings — here it was the farms that were beginning to look out of place — and cattle and pigs browsed and rooted about freely, con-sidering the new streets to be a natural extension of the farmyard. The Goodchilds' house — near which no animals ventured — had extensive grounds containing orchards and pastures, two cottages, and numerous former henhouses, cowsheds, stables and pigsties, the whole enclosed within a tall brick wall. Beyond the wall, the landscape that led to the Celestial City was being built: the work had started toward the end of the summer, and — by the following summer — performances of *The Pilgrim's Progress* were to become a permanent feature of life in Longfellow Park.

Alice had never, at that time, been inside the Goodchilds' house, had never been inside the walls that enclosed it — though the Reverend and Mrs. Goodchild were often in her parents' house — but she knew which house was theirs. Everything she knew about their house she had heard from others.

"That's where the Reverend and Mrs. Goodchild live," Mama had said, as they walked past — a long, looping detour — on their way to see Mama's friend Mrs. Italiaander, the widow of the archi-tect who had designed All Saints' and Park Court, she and Allegra hand in hand, Mama pushing Edith in her reed and maple baby carriage, the lace edge to its parasol wobbling.

"That's where the Goodchilds live," Nurse had said, resting on the oars for a moment, as they looked across the lake from the row-boat toward the back of the house.

"That's where Sobriety Goodchild lives. *Uuurgh!*" Charlotte had said, screwing her face up in revulsion, as they dawdled through Verbrugge Woods, which ran down one side of the house toward the lake.

She was never sure whether these observations were made as proud demonstrations that the speakers were in possession of privileged information, or whether they were meant as warnings, though she preferred to think that they were warnings. Lizzie Galliant, the heroine of the childhood adventure stories she had invented, gazed at the walls and the half-hidden house beyond, and planned to unmask the dark secrets that none but she suspected.

The lights were on in the Goodchild house, but — to her disappointment — they did not swing open the tall ornate gates and go up to the front door. By then, she'd started walking around the Shakespeare Castle with Charlotte, and Mary Benedict, and visualized a similar circling. It would be counterclockwise. Instead, they walked past the gates, and — it was quite a long walk — around to the side of the house that adjoined Verbrugge Woods. They were much more exposed now, and the wind became stronger, louder. Alice hadn't been there since the time with Charlotte, and much had changed.

It took her a while to realize this, and then she felt all a small child's resentment at the fact that — for no good reason — things had not remained the same. A proper paved surface — quite wide — had been laid down the side of the wall: she heard the heels of the men's boots clicking on the stone, the sound echoing back from the brickwork. The loudest sound, however, almost drowning the sound of the footsteps, was that of the wind whistling through the trees in the woods.

The wildness of the night was becoming exciting: the teachers at school always complained that the girls became noisy and hard to control when there was a storm. She couldn't see the trees — Papa was holding her so that her back was to them — but she could see the huge swaying shadows of branches grappling against the wall, the color of the ivy that covered it all bleached away by the bright moonlight. The shadows seemed to stagger, an exaggerated version of the way that Papa and his "friend" had been walking. They moved a little further, and then she could see trees, the tops of other trees, the trees beyond the wall, moving from side to side in the wind. She heard their leaves hissing, a sound different from that made by the nearer trees outside the wall. Sounds were different there; different trees grew. The leaves were already beginning to fall — the men's feet sometimes crunched through accumulated heaps, individual leaves made little scampering sounds against the paving-stones like small, wild creatures — and now they descended in a blizzard as the wind tore them from the branches, flicking against her face like taunting fingernails (this was one of Sobriety Goodchild's many specialties), quite painful.

It was then that she saw the first of the newly painted boards that had been affixed to the wall. The moonlight was bright enough to read by, but the shadows hid some of the words. The only words she could read on the first board were *The Wilderness Of This World*. The words seemed to pulsate as they were hidden and revealed, hidden and revealed, by the undulating shadows. She read them over Papa's shoulder, leaning a little for the best angle.

On another board the words she could read were *Strait Is The Gate*. It was like being inside Mrs. Italiaander's front parlor, where framed and glazed biblical texts lined the walls, reflecting and making more visible the plump little marble arm in the glass dome that was precisely positioned in the center of the table. For a moment she felt the sensation of being inside an immense roofless room, flooded with moonlight, the brightness reflecting on the polished glass surfaces, turning the texts into wordless mirrors. Then she realized where they were going: to the green-painted door in the wall, a door almost hidden by trailing sprays of untrimmed ivy that hung down like a loose and swinging curtain. She and Charlotte had noticed this, imagining a secret garden within, and dared each other to try to open it. They had turned the round knob, but the door had been locked.

Papa pulled her so that she was facing forward. Without speaking a word to her, he clasped his two hands together, enclosing her within a kind of seat, her back against the inner side of one arm, the upper parts of her legs against the inner side of the other. Now the door that she had seen with Charlotte was in front of her. It had been repainted – it was impossible to tell the color in the moonlight – and the ivy had all been cut away from around it. Above it was another painted sign, on which she could read every word: *Knock And It Shall Be Opened Unto You.* She tried to remember a story she had once read, in which a hidden door in a wall had led to a different world. She had certainly told stories in which Lizzie Galliant had found her way through such doors, into magic kingdoms, forgotten lands.

The wall, to which other painted boards had been fastened, stretched away to right and left, shadowed by the shapes of trees, as sharp-edged and distinct as shadows made by sunlight. She almost expected it to feel warm, so sun-like were the shadows. She imagined crowds lining beside the wall to enter, brightly lighted in the cool moonlight, the hugely magnified shadows of hands lifting to knock and have the Gate – that was the word painted upon the board – Opened Unto them.

But Papa's "friend" did not knock. He produced a key from an inside pocket – Alice was surprised that it was he who had the key, and not Papa – and unlocked the Gate.

"The Celestial City," he said, and Papa sniggered, thinking he had said something witty.

They went through the Gate and into the place where there was to be no more crying, nor sorrow, for he that was the owner of the place would wipe all tears from her eyes, a place peopled with thousands, none of whom was hurtful, but loving, and holy, every one walking in the sight of God, clothed with immortality, as with a garment. Round and round she'd walk in the sight of God within the walls, clockwise and counterclockwise.

Papa and his "friend" – she remembered this clearly – removed their hats before they stepped inside, and Papa's "friend" locked the door behind them. They entered like respectful visitors stepping inside a place of worship.

533

In the shelter of the wall it was, for a while, stiller and quieter.

In front of them the landscape of *The Pilgrim's Progress* stretched away into the distance, sloping downward in the direction of the lake, brightly lighted in the moonlight, each structure – each tree, each stone – casting a shadow that lent it a peculiarly tactile three-dimensional quality in the softly radiant light. Behind them, beyond the wall, the place from which they had come, was the City of Destruction, peopled by the damned who would burn with fire from Heaven (Mrs. Albert Comstock with an intensity that would have sizzled a salamander); before them was the way to the Celestial City, a chance of salvation.

Immediately on their left was the House of the Interpreter, which looked as though it was being used as a sign-painter's temporary workshop. Moonlight flooded in through the open door to illuminate the bottom ends of some signs propped up inside: *. . . Dreamed A Dream*, *. . . Wrath To Come*, *. . . His Holy Pilgrims*. A paved path, the Wall of Salvation on either side of it, led upward away from this to where a great mound of earth – the Hill Called Difficulty – was taking shape. Further back, a little to one side, wheelbarrows, spades and picks were stacked against the near wall of the Palace Called Beautiful. A workman had left his jacket hanging over the handle of one of the spades, and it fluttered, bat-like, casting a long shadow.

Beyond that – this whole area was still a building site – the ground, as far as it could be seen, was being cleared for the Valley of Humiliation and the Valley of the Shadow of Death: felled trees lay on their sides, and there was a long, deep swath of raw earth, with huge piles of excavated soil. The trees must have been felled that same afternoon, though there was something ragged and shattered about them, the remnants of a wood destroyed in a storm, torn down, snapped and ripped rather than cut. The wood was still fresh and white where they had been axed, and there was a smell of sap and greenness, like the time when the apple trees had been pruned in the orchard. She thought of the smell of apples, soft brown, overripe fruit slippery and bursting beneath her feet, a rotting Eve-peopled Paradise in which there was too much fruit, too much knowledge. Vanity Fair, the Plain Called Ease, Doubting Castle, the Mountain of Error, and the Celestial City itself could not be seen, but were probably still being constructed. In daylight, the whole area must heave with swarming Goodchilds and Griswolds, frogs pushing laden wheelbarrows, frogs endlessly arcing up and down with picks like chain-ganged prisoners, characters from a children's story created to induce nightmares, a kingdom in which the kings were frogs. The starlight and dewdrops were waiting for her, loitering with no virtuous intent. The River of the Water of Life could be heard faintly, running through the grounds and down toward the lake.

Papa held her face firmly in one hand, hard enough for his fingers to dig in, and pushed her head back until she was looking directly at the moon. She blinked, and tried to pull away a little: it was bright enough to dazzle. Papa spoke gently (no, not "gently," *quietly*, *intensely*) but his hand hurt.

"You're my Little Woman," he said — it was something he had often said before — "My Little Woman, and you must make me a promise. You'll make your Papa a promise, won't you?"

He asked as if she had a choice.

("That's a rhetorical question," she said to herself in the pause that followed.)

He couldn't manage the correct tone of voice for a request. He was unaccustomed to making requests.

She tried to nod her head, but she couldn't because of the way he was holding it, but he must have felt her chin push against the palm of his hand a little.

"Say it. Say it." ("Gently" was not at all the right word.) "Say you'll promise." He was very firm, very insistent.

"Please, sir . . ." Annie started to say.

Alice hadn't noticed her come forward. She had been standing against the entrance to the House of the Interpreter, with *Dreamed*

A Dream behind her. She spoke hesitantly, like a child in school unsure of the answer to a question. Alice would not have been surprised if she had held her arm into the air, slightly down at an angle because she was not entirely confident.

"Please, sir . . ."

"*Be quiet!*"

Papa did not turn to face Annie, did not even raise his voice. The two words were hissed out. He continued to focus his attention on Alice.

"Say you'll promise."

She managed to speak.

"Yes, Papa."

"This is what I want you to promise."

He moved his head down so that the side of it was resting against the side of her head — the bristles of his beard were sharp and rough, she almost expected them to draw blood — and tilted his head at the same angle as he had tilted hers, so that they were both looking at the moon.

"I want you to promise me that every time you look up at a full moon you'll think of me, your Papa. Will you promise me that?"

He was speaking very quietly, whispering, as though he wanted no one to hear him but herself, though his "friend" was listening. Alice saw him lean in a little closer toward them, wishing to share in a moment of private communion, longing to nuzzle in his beard on the other side of her face. The moonlight caught the lenses of his spectacles, and he seemed to have no eyes. The light dazzled her, like the reflection from a Perseus-polished shield, though this was one that would turn her into stone.

"Please, sir . . ."

"*Be quiet!*"

Alice whispered in reply. She said it quickly, to stop Papa speaking to Annie in that way again.

"Yes, Papa."

"Say it. Say it to Papa."

"Every time I look at the full moon I shall think of you, Papa."

"For always."

"For always."

She looked at the moon, staring at the bright pale circle, though it hurt her eyes, and saw the details of Papa's face gazing down on her from the nighttime sky, filling her field of vision. It was like an adult's face thrusting forward to peer in at an infant in a baby carriage, blotting out the whole of the rest of the world.

Coochi, coochi, coo.

What an adorable child.

"There's my Little Woman."

Then, and only then, he turned to face Annie. He did not speak to her — he had said nothing to her the whole time except for the two "Be quiet!"s — but pointed up toward the Palace Called Beautiful, in the way he pointed out the place where he detected Annie had missed some dust when she was cleaning a room, or not positioned a drape symmetrically enough. He usually snapped his fingers when he did this, but he did not do so now. Alice had rarely heard him speaking to Annie until recently. The time he had made her sing "Oh! Susanna" remained clearly in her mind because it was so unusual. It was as if it was years later, and he was giving instructions to Rosobell — who had not come to them until years after his death — using the movements of his body instead of words because she could not hear. Annie looked back at Alice. She appeared to be about to say something, but this time Papa did snap his fingers, gesturing upward again, and Annie began to walk to the Palace Called Beautiful, with Papa — after some whispering consultation with his "friend" — following behind her.

Then Papa's "friend" took her into the House of the Interpreter. They went in amongst the pots of paint and the signs resting against the walls, their feet crunching through the piles of leaves that had drifted in through the door. It was like moving through layers of broken cups and plates, with the sound of the large, fragile leaves shifting. They were in the Potter's Field, the final resting place of strangers and the unclaimed, unrecognized dead, a landscape composed entirely of tilted heaps of matching crockery, plates, saucers, and bowls neatly fanned out like packs of playing cards across the surface of a table, their whiteness glinting in the cloud-darkened dimness.

(Side by side, Mesdames Sylvie, Etoile, and Roskosch – the Three Fates; Madame Roskosch was Atropos, the one who cut the thread of life – leaned forward to interpret the shuffling of the patterned plates, studying the shifting shapes. Alice stood before them, facing the Three Weird Sisters, waiting to hear her fate. They could see the past, the present, and the future. They had never been known to fail.

("*La Maison de Dieu*," Madame Sylvie intoned, in her exotic Brooklyn French accent.

("(The Tower Struck by Lightning)," Madame Etoile interpreted (in whispered brackets).

(Madame Roskosch did not say anything, but leaned closer toward the pictures on the plates.

("*L'Amoureux*."

(A little snigger here.

("(The Lovers)."

(Another snigger.

("*Le Bateleur*."

("(The Magician)."

(She knew what the next cards were going to be. The three of them were grouped together, as if they were a set.

("*Le Soleil, La Lune, et L'Etoile*," Madame Sylvie muttered, virtually incomprehensibly, even slipping in an "*et*" to demonstrate her fluency in French.

("(The Sun, The Moon, and The Star)."

("*La Lune*," Madame Sylvie whispered, letting her breath out in a low hiss, as if this were the card for which she had long been waiting, the card that would win the game, the card that she could snap down on top of the others with a triumphant cry.

("The Moon."

(The brackets had disappeared, and the moon seemed larger.

(Card number XVIII was a large serving plate – one big enough to allow ample room for John the Baptist's head, with a generous accompaniment of vegetables – poised to eclipse all other cards by sheer size. The two battlemented towers loomed hugely, the two howling dogs seemed more ferocious than ever, and the parasite crawled closer out of the deep, dark pool.

(Madame Roskosch, for the first time, seemed on the point of speaking. She pointed at *La Lune*, and began to open her mouth. Her teeth were sharp and pointed.

(A secret was about to be brought to light.)

It was impossible to walk without breaking the plates, though you tried not to, placing your feet with infinite care, and scarcely breathing. The rafters were exposed in the ceiling of the House of the Interpreter, and cobwebs trembled on the underside of the tiles. Papa's "friend" sat on a pile of stacked signs not far from the entrance, and when she sat on his knee she could see the moon from the angle at which they were, and the tops of trees writhing against the sky. There was a little copse of them near the entrance.

She should feel safe, here, protected – *The orchard walls are high and hard to climb* – but she did not feel so.

And the place death, considering who thou art.

The wind was shrieking through these trees so loudly – they were now some distance away from the shelter of the walls – that she almost expected the moon itself to be flipped over and sent spinning away, leaving the world in utter darkness. She listened to the noise made by the wind through the trees, using that sound to overcome all other sound.

The usual words were spoken. She could still hear them.

"You're one of the girls from the statue."

12

She felt again that sensation of being on the verge of a fall, out on the ledge outside Grandpapa's office. She sat and thought of the bronze sculpture in the park, near the children's play area and the aviary, repeating sections of poetry in her head to pass the time until Papa returned.

She was sitting on the man's right knee, in the same place and position as that of her bronze figure in *The Children's Hour*. Papa's "friend" did something he had not done before. He pushed her head back, just as Papa had done earlier outside, until she was looking directly at the moon. He moved his head down so that the side of it was resting against the side of her head, again like Papa. He had been watching what Papa had done so that he could copy it. Like Papa's, his beard rubbed against the side of her face. As Papa had done, he tilted his head at the same angle he had tilted hers. She waited for him to ask her to make the same promise that she had made to Papa, but he did not do this.

He did something else he had never done before. He began to feel the surface of her skull with the tips of the fingers of both his hands, searching for something, mussing her hair. As he did so, he began to recite the names of some of the features of the surface of the moon — she recognized that was what they were: craters, plains, ranges of mountains, rilles — as eager to demonstrate his astronomical knowledge as Mary Benedict was. All the time he was looking upward, a man who could see what he was naming. His eyes could see things that were very far away.

"Plato, Copernicus, Julius Cæsar, Agrippa, Tycho . . ." he began, almost in a chant, a memorized list repeated like the conjugation of an irregular verb, liking the sound the words made, but not knowing their meaning. Mary Benedict had a telescope, and knew all the names of the places on the moon. The moon was an area in which Mary Benedict's knowledge was undoubtedly ahead of Alice's, and she had great skill in shifting conversations moonward. Alice wondered whether to nod, to show that she understood, that Mary Benedict had made sure she understood, but it might jerk his fingers away from the contours he seemed to be studying, and might make him angry in the way that Papa was sometimes angry. Papa was always controlled in his anger, absolutely controlled. He always knew exactly what he was saying, planning out what to say before-hand, freed from the tyranny of choice.

". . . Aristotle, Archimedes, Kepler, Hercules . . ."

It was a curious list of names, a mixture of the historical and the mythical. She must not move. She must not think anything, or feel anything.

She was stone.

She was bronze.

She was a figure in a statue.

The hour would pass.

This was the House of the Interpreter, the place where things were explained, and made clear, where Christian was shown excellent things to help him in his journey. The Interpreter went with him into a private room, and explained the meaning of the picture that hung there against the wall. He told Christian what it was he could see in that picture, the picture of a man whose work was to know and unfold dark things to sinners, a forerunner of Dr. Wolcott Ascharm Webster, a pioneering John the Baptist of alienists. In another room the Interpreter showed Christian two little children, Passion and Patience, and explained their behavior to him. *For the things that are seen, are temporal; but the things that are not seen, are eternal.* These things did ravish his heart; he could have stayed at that good man's House a twelvemonth, but that he knew he had further to go.

". . . Oceanus Procellarum, Palus Epidemiarum, Lacus Somniorum . . ."

Because they were in Latin, they were like the words of Doctor Faustus, the words of an apothecary, words to make the impossible happen: gold from lead, eternal life, the calling up of devils.

The Ocean of Storms. The Marsh of Disease. The Lake of Sleep.

It was like Christian's journey to the Celestial City infinitely extended with many new dangers. It would be a long time before he and Hopeful drew near the presence of the Shining Ones and the Gates, and the bells that rang for joy.

". . . Mare Frigoris, Mare Crisium, Mare Imbrium, Mare Nubium . . ."

There, floating high above them, was a huge hollow phrenological head, brightly illuminated – bright enough to cast shadows – with all its features marked and labeled, all the labels to what lay beneath the surface, the things that were hidden from sight like something secret beneath the unstable, shifting, volcanic emptiness. She had just read *The Last Days of Pompeii*, and the tips of his fingers pattered upon her head like descending ashes. From his clothes, from his beard, there was that Sodom and Gomorrah, that Pompeii, that *Paradise Lost*, that fallen angel smell of smoke and cinders.

As his fingertips moved across her head, he was reciting what it was he could feel, identifying his findings from the lettering in the sky, the words large enough to read from earth, an Interpreter guided by a higher source of knowledge. Coldness, he found, Crises, Showers, Clouds . . .

Next, he would tell her what his findings meant.

Everything had a hidden meaning. That was what Mrs. Alexander Diddecott had told Mama.

She imagined Annie, beyond the Hill Called Difficulty, in the Palace Called Beautiful, sitting upon Papa's knee, just as she was sitting on the knee of Papa's "friend." She, too, would be looking up at the moon, at the seas that were not seas, at the cracked and crazed surface where the lettering was fading. Like Christian and Charity in *The Pilgrim's Progress* they would discourse together till late at night. Annie would be in a large upper chamber, whose window opened toward the sun rising, and the name of the Chamber would be Peace, where she would sleep till break of day.

On the day after this she would see the Delectable Mountains. She would be taken to the top of the house, and bade look south, and she would behold, at a great distance, a most pleasant mountainous country, beautiful with woods, vineyards, fruits of all sorts; flowers also, with springs and fountains, very delectable to behold. Then she would go on her way, into the Valley of Humiliation.

"Conscientiousness, Justice, Integrity . . ." Papa would be saying, seizing an opportunity for phrenology, forcing Annie's face against his watch-chain, and away from the light of the moon. "Hope, Hope Future, Hope Present, Spirituality, Faith, Trust, Wonder . . ."

A long time seemed to go by when there was silence inside the little brick building.

The House of the Interpreter, like the Palace Called Beautiful, had once been a place where animals were kept. Papa's "friend" had stopped naming the features of the moon, and the only near sound was the sound of his breathing. During a lull in the wind, she heard footsteps coming toward them, and then Papa's voice just outside.

The hour had passed.

"There's something I must tell you," he was saying to Annie. He never called her by her name, just as he had never called Alice by her name the whole time. He had forgotten who they were. "Are you listening?"

"Yes, sir." Annie's voice was low. It sounded as if she had been crying. He had been rebuking her — cold and sarcastic — for not completing some job properly, hurting her for being a bad girl.

The moon became large and liquid, slightly distorted, Alice seeing it through the showers, through the clouds, and the drops of moisture blurring her vision.

"You must not talk about tonight," Papa was saying to Annie. His voice became quieter, but more intense. He paused, to ensure that he had Annie's full attention. "If you tell anyone what has happened, the wind will get you."

After a pause, he spoke again. Alice imagined him holding Annie under her chin, so that she would look into his face.

"Do you understand?"

"Yes, sir."

"If you tell anyone what has happened, the wind will get you."

Papa's "friend" went outside, and Papa came toward her again. Annie did not look at her. She was standing, very still, with her head lowered, the bad girl standing on a chair at the front of the class for all to gaze upon. The two men seemed to forget that she was there. Papa picked Alice up in the way he had been holding her before, in a sort of seat, and moved out into the open air again, standing under the little clump of trees. Papa's "friend" followed close behind, as though he wished to hear every word that would be spoken, so that he could memorize them and repeat them later, mimicking the gestures, echoing the words. She could see the moon reflected on the surface of the River of the Water of Life. The darkness in the water, the wind in the trees, seemed to enter her mind. Fir trees sobbed and moaned, holly whistled, ash hissed, beech rustled. Papa seemed very calm, very controlled, as he always did. Whatever he wanted to happen, happened. "Choose *me!*" she'd once wanted to call out when he came into the schoolroom, to gaze at her and her sisters. "Choose *me!*" She'd thought that it would be a sign of love. He took her face in his hand as he had done before, grasping her under the chin. Again he rested the side of his head against the side of her head, and again he tilted her head back until they were both gazing at the moon.

"The Sea of Coldness," she thought. "The Sea of Crises. The Sea of Showers. The Sea of Clouds."

"What did you promise Papa?" he asked her softly.

"Every time I look at the full moon I shall think of you, Papa."

"For always."

"For always."

"There's my Little Woman."

It became a formula, just like "You're one of the girls from the statue."

She didn't know why — perhaps it was something to do with the way Annie's head was bowed — but she began to cry, a little burst, short and intense, like a sneeze.

He did not pat her back in the way that Mama would have done. He stood, waiting for her to stop, patiently, a man with all the time in the world — though she knew that the patience lasted only so long, that time had a predetermined end to it — and she soon stopped.

A sudden, stronger blast of wind howled through the branches of the trees, a scream at a pitch it hurt to hear, and she jerked convulsively in Papa's arms, trying to press her hands against her ears, trying to shut out the noise. Sharp-edged leaves rushed at her face, and she shut her eyes. With his right hand, Papa pulled her hands away from her ears, and put his face close to hers. When she opened her eyes, his face was all she could see. It filled the whole world in front of her, like the moon had.

"You must listen to the wind," he said.

Then he shouted across to Annie. "Remember what I told you about the wind?" It seemed to be more of a question than a command, but Annie did not answer in words. She nodded her head once, up and down, though Alice could still not see her face.

Then Papa and Papa's friend took her and Annie back home, because it was late, it was well past Alice's bedtime, even Annie's bedtime, and it wouldn't be good for them to stay out longer.

That was the first time it happened.

13

It happened numerous times over the months that followed – Papa, Papa's "friend," and Annie – through the fall (the fall in which she had walked around and around the Shakespeare Castle with Charlotte, and Mary Benedict), stopping temporarily for the winter. It happened again in the spring and on into the summer, the summer when *The Pilgrim's Progress* landscape was finally completed, and the performances began. It continued after the performances finished for the year, through into a second fall, and the beginnings of a second winter, and then it stopped because Annie was not there anymore. It happened for more than a year. It happened one last time after Annie had gone, and then it never happened again, and Papa's "friend" stopped calling. On that last time, there were no indications that it *was* the last time. Nothing was said, there were no promises made to let her know that she was now free, that she need not sit in unmoving silence for those hours, and – for a long time, on into the summer and the following fall, for a year, for years, for long after Annie had gone – she continued to expect that Papa would find her, when she was alone, and tell her that she was going to the Celestial City. That was how it always began.

When Ben was five or six years old she wondered if Papa ever took him for walks to the Celestial City, to meet his "friend" or another "friend," in the way that he had done so often with her. She looked at her sisters, and wondered about them, trying to catch a hidden expression in their eyes, especially Allegra's, but it was something she could never ask them. It only ever happened on the way to the Celestial City, or – when the winter set in, and if Mama was not there – in the house, where it had started. Alice would be with Papa's "friend" in the front parlor, and Papa would take Annie elsewhere in the house. In the evenings – particularly the spring evenings, as they moved away from winter – he would tell her that they were going to the Celestial City, Papa and his Little Woman, Papa's "friend" and Annie, and, putting down what she was doing – the book she was reading, the piece of music she was trying to learn – she would obediently go into the hall and put on her coat, trying to fill her mind with the words from the book, the sound of the music. These words, this music, would go through her head as she sat on the "friend"'s knee, the girl from the statue.

She was stone.

She was bronze.

Sometimes Papa came in the night, and woke her from sleep. This was her sign that spring had arrived, that the evenings were milder.

They would walk towards the Goodchilds' house, and go down the side adjoining Verbrugge Woods, toward the door with *Knock And It Shall Be Opened Unto You* on the painted board above it. The color of the newly painted door was green, a slightly darker shade than the original faded green, she had discovered, the first time she was taken there in daylight.

The painted board nearest to the right of the door had the words *I Am Directed By A Man Whose Name Is Evangelist To Speed Me To A Little Gate That Is Before Us, Where We Shall Receive Instructions About The Way*, and the one nearest to the left of the door had the words *Strait Is The Gate That Leadeth Unto Life, And Few There Be That Find It*. She read those words many times, just before they stepped inside the door.

They were painted by the same signwriter who had painted the signs for Comstock's Comestibles, and he had used the same colors and the same style of alphabet. She half expected to see *SERVICE WITH SINCERITY!* painted on a board upon the gate, a promise of polite and courteous attention from Mr. Worldly Wiseman, Apollyon, and Giant Despair. Perhaps the signwriter had a limited repertoire. She had seen the same colors — red and black — and the same ornate lettering on *Beware Of The Dog* signs all round Longfellow Park, and on all the signs in the park. Papa never knocked on the door. He had a key of his own on every occasion after the first time, and that was how it was Opened Unto him. Always, he removed his hat before they stepped inside. He would feel bad if he forgot to do this.

Sometimes Papa's "friend" would be waiting on the other side of the Gate. Sometimes he would come with them, meeting them on the way there, loitering somewhere so that Mama would not see him. It was the way that children made assignations with disapproved-of friends, friends — the Huckleberry Finns of Longfellow Park — made all the more attractive by that disapproval. The door would be locked behind them, and they would begin to move out into the world beyond the wall, further and further into the world of *The Pilgrim's Progress* that had taken shape around them during the first winter, and continued to grow throughout the spring that followed. The Hill Called Difficulty was completed and the excavated earth from the Valley of Humiliation and the Valley of the Shadow of Death was transported nearer the lake to make the Delectable Mountains. The Valley of Humiliation and the Valley of the Shadow of Death were completed almost simultaneously, and it was on another night of a full moon that they had walked through these valleys for the first time.

They walked through the Valley of the Shadow of Death, and past the mouth of Hell, along a narrow pathway with a deep ditch on the right-hand side, and a quagmire on the left-hand side.

They left the Valley of the Shadow of Death and went into the cleared space in the middle of a group of former stables, where Vanity Fair was being constructed. Carpenters had fitted shop frontages into the buildings, and market stalls – the wood of them still raw and unpainted – were lined up in the little cobbled square.

As the landscape unfolded in the course of the next few weeks, the year moving on toward summer, they traveled further into it – the Plain Called Ease, Lucre Hill, the Pillar of Salt (the big wet tongue slurped yum-yummily), By-Path Meadow – until, in the very early summer, Papa and Papa's "friend" took her and Annie inside the Celestial City for the first time, crossing the River of Death to reach it. The River of Death was the same small stream that formed the River of the Water of Life further upstream, but here it was wider, spreading out into the flatter land before it began to flow into the lake. There was a stiff evening breeze on this particular evening, and – in the nighttime quietness – they could hear the water of the lake slapping against the shore, like waves on the edge of a small sea, and the leaves of the trees rustling.

Papa was watching Annie closely as they made their way back, sensing her apartness. When they paused, just inside the wall, before they went back through the door and onto the path opposite Verbrugge Woods, he began his catechism. There was always a catechism, unfailingly undergone. It went with the key turning in the lock, the men's hats being placed back on their heads, the surrounding silences.

"What will happen if you tell anyone what has happened?"

"The wind will get me, sir."

Annie had been told that a silent nod was no longer sufficient. Papa needed to hear her voice now.

"And will you ever tell anyone what has happened?"

"No, sir."

"You cannot escape from the wind. You know that, don't you? Wherever you try to go, whatever you try to do, the wind will always find you. Even a gentle wind, even a breeze, barely enough to ruffle the leaves on the trees."

He lowered his voice, and whispered.

"Even a whisper."

"Yes, sir."

"Especially a whisper."

"Yes, sir."

14

The Pilgrim's Progress landscape was finally completed, one month after Alice and Annie had been taken all the way to the newly converted Celestial City for the first time by Papa and his "friend," and the annual summer performances began. "We're going to the Celestial City," he had said the first time they'd gone through the Gate — back in the previous fall — but the City had not been built then, and they had moved only gradually through the pages of the book, journeying further and further as the toiling frogs labored ever closer to the edge of the lake.

The Pinkertons were invited to the very first of the week's performances, a gala opening, as special guests of the Goodchilds. The whole family went. Servants were also invited. It was felt to be a wholesome and educational experience, particularly suitable for the servant class, although — as the Reverend Goodchild delicately phrased it — "Our dusky brethren would, I am sure, be more comfortable within a religious experience with their own people." They had no servants with them, however. Annie had stayed at home to care for Ben. The Finches also went — baby Linnaeus, like baby Ben, remaining at home in the care of a servant — and Alice was pleased when Charlotte came up beside her as they stood in the forefront of the crowd near the door in the wall. She'd much rather be with her than with Allegra and Edith, who — unaccountably, most annoyingly — were still there. She had really been counting on the company of Ishmeelites from Gilead to arrive with their camels bearing spicery and balm and myrrh (she'd wanted to find out what myrrh looked like: she'd seen gold and — less easy to find, this — frankincense) to carry them away to enslavement in Egypt. They could so easily have been rolled up in carpets — feet kicking furiously — and slotted conveniently between a camel's humps, but the merchantmen had let her down, the wicked, quaint fruit-merchant men.

The Reverend Goodchild was making a speech, but she heard little of what he was saying.

She was looking at what she had once seen by moonlight.

The crowds she had imagined lining beside the wall to enter the door were now there. The *Hudson Valley Chronicle* had given extensive publicity to the opening. The previous week's edition had contained a long interview with the Reverend Goodchild. It was strange to see those crowds, something she had pictured in her head, happening in front of her in reality: imagination given physical shape. She had tried to make Lizzie Galliant real — she had concentrated really hard to make her appear — but had never succeeded. "No," Lizzie would say, like the Lizzie in "Goblin Market," "no, no, no." "You're Bet, You're Betty, You're Lillibet," Alice would hum, "(But You'll Always Be Lizzie to Me)." "What ails you, child?" Lizzie Galliant would ask. "Be not afeard. I am Lizzie Galliant. Strong men fall powerless before me!" The crowds were thickest in front of the door in the wall, overflowing into the spaces beneath the trees in the nearest part of Verbrugge Woods. Boys had climbed into the lower branches. Once she had expected warmth from the cool light of the moon; now she thought the summer sunshine should chill.

Knock And It Shall Be Opened Unto You.

Everyone was staring at the painted board above the door. There was a burst of applause as the Reverend Goodchild finished his speech. He said something to the reporter at his side, who had been scribbling furiously in his notebook throughout the speech — *a long-cherished dream, sharing with our neighbors in Longfellow Park, a Goodchild heritage, spiritual, moving, should be regarded as Pilgrims, Pilgrims with a capital "P," our journey through life, Goodchild, great tradition of the Mystery Plays in Europe, a sort of miracle, enter as in a church, Gate with a capital "G," gentlemen's hats should be removed, Goodchild, the Lord walking amongst us*: this was more or less the gist of it — and then moved up to the door.

A hush fell as he lifted his hand, casting a hugely magnified shadow on the surface of the door. The photographer from the newspaper arranged the legs of his camera tripod carefully, and then disappeared under the black cloth. Something always made her think of ostriches when she saw photographers doing this, particularly when they had long, lanky legs like the one in front of her. There was something of a lacuna, as the Reverend Goodchild gave muttered instructions — he seemed to have definite ideas about the photographs that he wanted taken — and the crowd waited.

Charlotte wriggled, and stared about her, waving at people she knew. Well-behaved children, in the care of their parents, made small, constrained gestures in reply, like secret signals. The Reverend Goodchild stood motionless, smiling, each time the photographer prepared to take a picture. His smiles were always exactly the same size and shape. He was like Washington Thoroughgood in his bakery store, who had the gift of being able to divide a cake into perfectly equal segments, like a mathematical diagram in a schoolbook, over and over. Mama sometimes threatened to bring him to the house when she and Allegra quarreled, unable to agree who had the larger portion of pie.

When the photographer expressed himself satisfied, the Reverend Goodchild, the smile once more in position — it was one of those beneficent, glowing smiles, the sort favored by the artists who illustrated the colored pictures of saints that were distributed by Sunday-schools — gave a signal, an upward gesture with his outspread arms, like someone bestowing a blessing, and stood, waiting for something to happen. He did not have to wait long.

Faintly, through the trees from an inner part of Verbrugge Woods, the voices of a choir could be heard. People began to turn round, to face in the direction from which the voices were coming, and those on the outer margin of the woods began to move to one side. A boy fell out of one of the trees in a shower of leaves, probably shot down. The voices became louder, the words clearer, as the choir drew near.

"Who would true valor . . ."

— *valour* —

"... see
Let him come hither;
One here will constant be,
Come wind, come weather.
There's no discouragement,
Shall make him once relent,
His first avowed intent,
To be a pilgrim . . ."

(A problem with accuracy belatedly occurred to Alice. *Would* the spelling be "valor," when the words were *spoken*, with an American accent? Spelling and punctuation were set about with hazards to trip up the unwary. She was never quite sure when to use "as if it was" or "as if it were" — that sort of construction — and this niggled away, somewhere at the back of her mind. She felt much happier when things were right and wrong with a mathematical purity, to know that she had written something that was precisely right, as if she was — as if she were — a singer knowing that her voice was singing perfectly in tune. As if she *was* . . . As if she *were* . . . Sometimes, what ought to be the right alternative seemed *wrong*. The spelling of "minuscule" had long bothered her.)

Charlotte leaned forward, peering through the trees, and then squealed, tugging at Alice's sleeve.

"Sobriety Goodchild! Sobriety Goodchild!"

Mama frowned a little, looking down at her, but Alice and Charlotte stood like girls transfixed, staring as the massed ranks of the Goodchilds and Griswolds advanced through the trees, like an army of frogs into Egypt, singing "To Be a Pilgrim." They were ready for anything that Satan might throw at them, braced to repulse diabolical attack.

Having heard rumors that the vast majority of the Goodchild family would be taking part in the performance, they had been on the alert for any sign of Sobriety, but had not expected to be rewarded quite so soon. They had come hoping to be amused by the sight of Sobriety looking unaccustomedly bashful and self-conscious, forced into a public display by his ambitious parents, like a shy child (though Sobriety Goodchild was anything but this) made to recite a comic monologue in front of assembled guests. What they saw was even funnier, far better than they had hoped for, something to hold onto and treasure the next time he hurt them or made them cry. He was one of the big boys at school – lumpish, grunting – and preserved a ruthless hierarchy. Henry Collis, the supposed bad boy of the school, protected them from him with a courtly, gentlemanly grace.

The choir, as it emerged from between the trees, was composed entirely of Goodchilds and Griswolds dressed as angels, and Sobriety Goodchild was one of the angels. It was the worst sight they'd seen (they realized, with delight) since Stephanotis Fassenden – Henry Collis always said that her first name sounded like a disease caught by cattle – recited "I'm a Little Wittle Girlie, and the World's a Big, Big Place" (to great acclaim) in front of the assembled parents at school whilst dressed as a baby. (Given half a chance, Alice would have brained the Little Wittle Girlie with a Biggy Wiggy Boulder, smashing it down on her Little Heady Weddy until it was a Bloody Pulpy Wulpy. She got *really* annoyed sometimes.) The memory of the Little Wittle Girlie had darkened Sobriety's mind, lingering there jealously for all those years until he had launched Serenity upon an aghast world, not so Little, not so

Wittle, but gruesome in her Girliness. Now, however, it was he who was Little, he who was Wittle, he who was an angel choiring angel sounds. He was wearing a long white gown, holding a golden harp, and a halo, the rim of a straw hat painted gold, was placed at a rakish angle upon his head.

Sobriety was attempting to cultivate an expression of pious innocence, large-eyed and limpid, like a homeless puppy on a sentimental calendar, or one of Mrs. Alexander Diddecott's soulful waifs. His hands were clasped prayerfully against his chest, his fingers daintily tucked in, and his head was slightly lowered, like that of a modest pupil pretending to ignore the exclamations of wonder at his precocious brilliance. His eyes were shifting about, looking for old ladies to send into ecstasies. When he caught sight of Alice and Charlotte his expression briefly altered to the one they recognized from the schoolyard – his lower lip protruding with sulky belligerence – but he (unlike Henry Collis) would be entering Otsego Lake Academy at the end of the summer, and would not be lying in wait behind the chestnut trees anymore.

"What an adorable child!" Charlotte remarked to no one in particular.

Charlotte!

Miss Ericsson pressed her pocket-handkerchief against her lips.

She heard Charlotte's voice from what seemed like long ago, indicating a faded green-painted door, and saying, "That's where Sobriety Goodchild lives. *Uuurgh!*" His voice, very loud, and very flat, was audible above all the others, bellowing, "Nooo liiion caaan him friiight!" He showed far more expression, far more *enthusiasm*, but – sadly – little more tunefulness, when he sang – as he often sang – about the premature death of a mother. His inadequately anchored wings – slightly grubby – wobbled noticeably on the higher notes, and dipped to one side. He passed quite close to them – "Coochi, coochi, coo!" from Charlotte – and aimed a surreptitious blow with his harp, but missed.

"He looks . . ."

Charlotte stopped, and began to giggle, overcome by the daring of her imagination.

"He looks . . . He looks like . . ."

She struggled vainly for a while, and then managed to complete her sentence, ending with a shriek, and then collapsing into quivering, whimpering laughter.

"He looks like *a constipated sheep!*" "Constipated" – *really*, Charlotte, and just before *The Pilgrim's Progress!* – was a decidedly risqué choice of word.

Charlotte shook helplessly beside her, uttering stifled choking sounds, tears coursing down her cheeks. She could be – at unpredictable moments – a terrible giggler, and – several times in church – had received glares from Dr. Vaniah Odom that would have felled a lesser being, that would – in fact – have poleaxed a constipated sheep. When this happened Alice felt sure that Lizzie Galliant did walk on earth after all, in the shape of Charlotte Finch.

"*A constipated sheep!*" Charlotte wailed, barely able to speak.

The angels were now gathered in front of the Reverend Goodchild, like carol singers informally greeting a householder. There was a memory from the previous year, of three little girls standing at the bottom of a flight of steps, as a door swung silently open, and a shadow reached down toward them to the sound of the wind in the branches of the trees. In action how like an angel, in apprehension how like a god. The Reverend Goodchild paused, savoring the moment, a man posing to be photographed again, and the photographer took the hint. Once more a hush fell upon the crowd. An infant was crying somewhere at the back of the crowd, and the Reverend Goodchild frowned a little, fearing the photographer might record the sound, and spoil the effect at which he aimed. Alice could feel Charlotte far-gone in giggles.

As he had done before, the Reverend Goodchild raised his hand. As he had done before, he cast a huge shadow on the surface of the door. He knocked three times, each knock carefully spaced out and weighted with authority, and Mrs. Albert Comstock, Looking

Delighted, boinged out like a gigantic jack-in-the-box — some of those springs were *really* strong — and opened the Gate Unto him. "Looking Delighted" was the phrase that the *Hudson Valley Chronicle* — the editor, by a remarkable coincidence, was her brother-in-law — always employed to describe her reaction on one of the many occasions when she was being presented with a bouquet at some church festivity (this was before she had transferred her allegiance to a more fashionable Fifth Avenue church), or just lending the radiance of her presence to an otherwise unremarkable event.

Mrs. Albert Comstock, looking delighted, presented the prizes.

Mrs. Albert Comstock, looking delighted, listened to the choir.

With that same expression she would, if asked — had Longfellow Park offered such opportunities to shine — have launched ships, welcomed visiting heads of state, or (Looking Particularly Delighted on this occasion) declared war. No one seemed surprised that it should be Mrs. Albert Comstock presiding at the first performance of *The Pilgrim's Progress.* ("How unexpected," Mr. Brittain muttered behind them, dryly, in the voice of a man whose worst fears were being realized.) There was a burst of applause, loudest from those who were nearest to the Goodchilds and Griswolds. Mrs. Goodchild, Looking Not Quite So Delighted, appeared behind her and attempted to thrust her face into any part of the gateway — or Gateway — that was not blocked by Mrs. Albert Comstock. This did not leave her with much space, and she was driven to jumping up and down, and appearing intermittently in the top left-hand corner, a woman demonstrating the bounciness of a newly purchased springboard, her hair gradually falling loose. There he was again, that little boy with the iron pen aiming for St. Cassian of Imola. If his target had been the size of Mrs. Albert Comstock the poor, deprived lad would have been in with a chance of a decent stab. The pen nib would have made quite a squelch.

The door remained open, and the Reverend Goodchild disappeared inside. The angels now became "guardian angels" — "We are your guardian angels," they kept saying helpfully — and began to organize the crowd's orderly entry through the door. "Please remove your hats, gentlemen Pilgrims," they added from time to time, together with — most emphatically of all — "Have your money ready, Pilgrims." They gave the distinct impression that they'd knock the hats off the insufficiently pious, and extract wallets from the innermost pockets of the unforthcoming. They took great care to pronounce the capital letter "P" in "Pilgrims" (a slightly aggressive popping sound, a faint mist of spray), to remind everyone that it was there. They guided the crowd the way they wanted them to go, firmly making sure that everyone remembered to pay. People began to swarm in, pressing closer together. Alice clutched Mama's hand tightly when the time came to go in through the door, and — once more — begin the journey to the Celestial City, though this time there was — when she began it — no wind, and no moon.

15

Mrs. Goodchild's mother — she had been half titillated, half scandalized, when Henry Collis described her as "the Froggiest of all the Frog People" — was sitting at a large kitchen table collecting admission money with undisguised enthusiasm, and placing it in a metal cash box, big enough and formidable enough to contain the week's takings from A. T. Stewart's or Arnold, Constable's department store. The main pleasure of her life must have been removed when her daughter — within a year or so — replaced her as the one to collect the admission fees. No wonder she had died shortly afterward. There was no point in going on. Alice could see what Henry Collis meant about her, and would not have been the slightest bit surprised if Mrs. Goodchild's mother — she did not know her name — had casually shot out a long coiled tongue and whipped a passing bluebottle into her mouth as a tasty snack, crunching away vigorously.

Alice watched her face carefully as Mama paid the price of their admission, waiting for a telltale unpursing of the lips. Mama had the money all ready: the Reverend Goodchild had said that they were to be "his very special guests," but Mama knew the Reverend Goodchild of old. An automatic smile came to the lips of Mrs. Goodchild's mother at regular intervals – up, down, up, down, like the flame in a gaslight being adjusted – but it was not co-ordinated with what her eyes were seeing, so she sometimes smiled when there was no one in front of her. She may have been smiling at the money, rather than the – er – Pilgrims. A heavily built Goodchild angel stood on either side of her, presumably – as they took no part in the selling of the tickets – as bodyguards to safeguard the takings, holding their harps at slightly aggressive angles. They looked like men riding shotgun on a stagecoach, and their haloes – hanging low over their foreheads – gave them the furtive air of riverboat cardsharps wearing peaked eye-shades.

"We're inside the wall!" Charlotte whispered, standing on tiptoe to try to see above the adults all around, and Alice did the same, trying to give the impression that she was seeing everything for the first time, trying to look surprised. She looked back hopefully at Mrs. Goodchild's mother, but her tongue remained uncoiled and unseen. She had the sort of mouth that could have contained a tongue big enough to leap out and wrap itself around anything that flew, and the look of a woman who would crunch contentedly on whatever she caught: a buzzard, a golden eagle, an innocent passing angel. Telltale feathers – crumpled and crestfallen – would poke out of the corners of her mouth, as if she had swallowed Geronimo. With any luck, he'd have his tomahawk with him, and would be able to hack his way to freedom.

The crowd was shepherded – "Step this way, Pilgrims! Step this way, Pilgrims!" – by the guardian angels, all of whom possessed the same unco-ordinated (she did not co-operate with Noah Webster when it came to spelling "co-ordinated") smile as Mrs. Goodchild's mother. It was mildly disorienting, though the flames of these gaslights gave out no warmth. You imagined that they'd have rehearsed the smiles, just as they'd rehearsed the singing of "Who Would True Valour See" and whatever else they'd be performing. "Smile!" their director would order, and they'd smile, preparing for the Schiffendeckian smiles in the photographs of the future. "Smile!" Again they'd smile. "Smile!" The edges of their mouths would begin to ache. There'd be an increasing sense of strain. One last look behind her at the Froggiest of all the Frog People. Still no signs of a tongue, and – more of a blow, this – still no signs of a tomahawk dramatically emerging from her midriff. They were drawn together in a small paved square in front of the House of the Interpreter. Celia Iandoli – a tall, clever girl who had just left Miss Pearsall's School for Girls; she could play the piano beautifully – was there with her parents; there was Miss Ericsson, who always spoke nicely to Alice; the full complement of Dibbo Daughters with their parents; Mrs. Courlander and her sister, whose daughter was in the same class as Alice at school . . .

Across from them, and blessedly not too close, the Comstocks were holding court in a little circle that included Mrs. Goodchild (ah, that's why her mother was raking in the cash), Mr. (a rare sighting) and Mrs. Alexander Diddecott, and Mabel Peartree. They regarded themselves as the main attraction of the evening (Mrs. Albert Comstock was Looking Comprehensively Delighted, the cords on her neck – she had a neck in those days – standing out like the framework of a bridge: *Look at me! Look at me! Look at me, Being Delighted!*) and were being strenuously vivacious. You couldn't help feeling that – as the unchallenged (who would dare?) guest of honor – she ought to have been clasping a gigantically vulgar bouquet (huge ugly heads, livid colors, the brighter the better) thrust wobblingly upward in both hands by a stammering minute child, lost from sight beneath The Bosom. Heads would roll for this unforgivable oversight, and sharply administered Comstockian cracks from her tightly clenched fan would unleash the *boing, boing, boing*s as it whacked sharply down to hack. "Off with their heads! Off with their heads!" she'd scream, crimson with fury, the Queen of Hearts with her heart-shaped fan, vigorously decapitating, pointing her finger to unleash thunderbolts.

Myrtle, slightly eclipsed by her mama, and seeing Alice and Charlotte, adopted – as if by a natural feeling for ungainliness – various peculiar postures to show off her expensive new dress. It was a dingy shade of green, and she looked like something inadequately disguised to blend in with the undergrowth. She assumed her poses – a model for one of the more fearless modern artists – with an expression of fierce concentration on her face, the same expression she used when she was tying the laces of her boots, a task that clearly challenged the utmost resources of her intelligence. It was probably one of the few things she was allowed to do without close supervision. Intermittently, when she caught Alice's eyes, she thrust out her large wet tongue. It would have fed a family of five. Hmm. Big tongues, like big buttocks, were a favored feature of the Comstock breed. Myrtle Comstock would have no difficulty whatsoever in pronouncing the letter "r."

There was a lot of "*Ooh-look!*"ing going on.

"Ooh, look! Look at all those nice signs!" Mrs. Albert Comstock boomed.

"Ooh, look! What delightful lettering!"

Boom.

"Ooh, look!"

Boom.

"Ooh, look!"

Boom.

("Ooh, look at *me*! Ooh, look at *me*! Ooh, look at *me*!" That's what all these "Ooh, looks!" were saying.)

Boom.

Boom.

("Ooh, look!" came a faint faraway voice from the direction of Lac Qui Parle, the lake itself speaking, rippling the surface, the sky-tinted waters. "The Ocean of Storms, *Oceanus Procellarum*."

"Ooh, look! I decidedly approve!"

Boom.

"Charming signs."

(He'd used a *great deal* of paint.)

People obediently ooh-looked about them as they waited for everyone to be assembled, pointing out — slightly subdued, crushed by the boom of the Comstockian exuberance — the newly-painted signs to each other (there was a strong smell of fresh paint): *The House Of The Interpreter, As I Slept I Dreamed A Dream . . ., To The Wall Of Salvation.* On the wall opposite Alice was a sign she hadn't seen before. *I Seek An Inheritance, Incorruptible, Undefiled, And That Fadeth Not Away; And Is Laid Up In Heaven.* She began to think of other signs around Longfellow Park, with the same style of lettering, the same colors, as many as she could think of, as quickly as possible. *Beware Of The Dog, To The Tropical Aviary, To The Bandstand, Boats For Hire, Keep Off The Grass . . .*

Keep Off . . .

Keep Off . . .

Nearby, somewhere out of sight, a trumpet sounded, and everyone fell silent as *The Pilgrim's Progress* began.

"Ooh, listen! A trumpet!"

Boom.

Not much escaped Mrs. Albert Comstock's notice.

They ooh-listened.

Dr. Vaniah Odom appeared above them ("Ooh, look!") on the roof of the House of the Interpreter, like a spokesman in a beleaguered city appearing on the walls to parley, the Citizens upon the walls of Angiers in *King John.* ("Hear us, great kings," he should be declaiming, "vouchsafe awhile to stay,/And I shall show you peace and fair-fac'd league . . .") Dr. Vaniah Odom was the sort of man who went in for vouchsafing. He raised his hands in the same gesture that the Reverend Goodchild had employed outside the wall, as if in blessing — Alice suppressed the awful, irresistible thought that he looked like a picture she had once seen of the pope on the balcony of the Vatican in St. Peter's Square — and then began to speak in his special, holy voice, the one that went up at the end of sentences, and in which he made the words all long and drawn out, stretching his vowels. He had two voices: the holy voice, and the

561

angry voice, and it was the angry voice that people heard most on Sundays at All Saints'.

"As I walked through the wilderness of this world, I lighted on a certain place, where there was a den; and I laid me down in that place to sleep: and as I slept I dreamed a dream . . ."

As they all gazed upward at Dr. Vaniah Odom, perched in his aerial pulpit, Alice heard Mr. Brittain — a quiet, respectable old man who lodged with Mrs. Barnhouse — urge, distinctly, in an imploring, heartfelt whisper, "Go on, jump! Jump! Why don't you jump?" Mama turned round to look at him, with an expression of mild reproof. "I didn't mean to say that *quite* so loudly," he whispered to her piercingly. He then said it again, much more quietly. He was a very polite old man, and one with such good taste. ("I'm really looking forward to Vanity Fair," Alice heard an equally elderly friend confiding to him. "I hear that Becky Sharp is in it, and that she's something of a *naughty girl*!" Here was a man doomed to disappointment, breathlessly anticipating wanton displays of drawers and corsets. He and Mr. Brittain — every man should have a hobby — shared their collection of Lindstrom & Larsson catalogues companionably between them, helpfully indicating pages of particular interest as they made new acquisitions. "Page 284, top line, third from left." *Nudge.* "Now *there's* a *naughty girl*!")

". . . I dreamed a dream, and behold I saw a man . . ."

The Reverend Goodchild moved through the crowd and stood in the center of the little square.

"Ooh, look!"

Boom.

He was clothed in rags (nicely cut in symmetrical tatters), was carrying a book, and had a great burden upon his back. It didn't weigh very much, but — when he remembered — he attempted to look burdened. He opened the book, read, and began to weep (his face going all boo-hoo, his shoulders going up and down in a regular rhythm), as the voice of Dr. Vaniah Odom faded away in a manner that he clearly regarded as rather poetic. There's nothing

Reynolds Templeton Seabright can do that *I* can't do! This was the message. The Reverend Goodchild's shoulders went up and down like those of someone coughing, and he assumed a woe-is-me attitude. His spectacles caught the late afternoon sun, like two small circular mirrors.

"What shall I do?" he lamented.

Alice hoped that Mr. Brittain might suggest something suitable, but he failed to do so, even though she'd moved helpfully to one side so that her presence in front of him wouldn't muffle his voice. She'd wanted whatever he had to say to come across loud and clear.

The Reverend Goodchild was Christian, about to begin his pilgrimage. How on earth would they be able to distinguish the actor from his rôle? "Christian" with a capital "C," "Pilgrim" with a capital "P"; it was all capital, capital with the Reverend H. P. – Highly Punctuated, Holiness Personified, Hallowed Pilgrim – Goodchild. Capital!

"He's very good, isn't he?" Mrs. Albert Comstock boomed, louder than the Reverend Goodchild was speaking – it wasn't a question, despite the punctuation – getting her approval in early, and inspiring the actors into scaling ever-higher heights of humbuggery. (This sounded the right sort of word to use.)

Alice began her journey to the Celestial City, her first journey without Annie, without Papa and Papa's "friend," holding the hands of Mama and Charlotte. Papa, who had been standing on the far side of Mama, did not go with them. He was taking part in the production, and, as soon as they were inside the wall, he had left them to go in the direction taken by the Reverend Goodchild.

They were guided from place to place – "Step this way, Pilgrims! Step this way, Pilgrims!" Up, down, up, down, the brightness of the gaslight intensified and faded – by the whispering frog-faced angels, as they followed the Reverend Goodchild on his pilgrimage to a better world, accompanied by ooh-lookings, ooh-listenings, a continuous cacophony of booms. Gaslight on a warm evening always made her feel headachy and unwell, the hissing like that of unlit escaping gas, the fumes overpowering her, drawing her into drowsy forgetfulness.

16

At the end of the journey, as dusk began to fall, she stood with the others just outside the Celestial City, as the flames of torches fluttered in a breeze from the direction of the lake, and the moon became faintly visible, pale, and smudged by clouds. The Goodchild and Griswold angels had become a choir again, and stood in rows – the tallest in the rear – on the roof of a vaguely ecclesiastical structure that had once been a boat shed. Their white gowns glimmered against the dark water of the lake as they began to sing the same song with which the performance had begun.

"Whooo sooo beeeset him rouuund!" Sobriety Goodchild positively howled. Charlotte started to giggle again. She did not make a sound, but Alice could feel her shaking uncontrollably.

Just as the Reverend Goodchild was Christian in this first year of *The Pilgrim's Progress*, so Papa was Hopeful. Side by side, Papa and the Reverend Goodchild sank to their knees, their hands clasped in prayer, their eyes bright and lifted up to the heavens, a radiance around them, their expressions ecstatic (or as near as they could manage). The Reverend Goodchild's ecstasy was surprisingly convincing; he was probably thinking about the money that had been raked in by the Froggiest of all the Frog People. She must have held up the cash box and rattled it for him as he walked past, to demonstrate its well-crammed cash-filled condition.

The lenses of their round wire-framed spectacles caught the light. Sometimes flames flickered there, sometimes the cool tones of the moon's reflection.

Papa was nowhere near where she was, but she could smell his breath as if he was breathing into her mouth. It smelled overpoweringly of the sickly-sweet pink cachous he chewed in an unsuccessful attempt to mask the smell of his decaying teeth. Perhaps it was those very cachous that rotted his teeth in the first place. He shared them with his "friend." Their jaws moved rhythmically as they chewed the small lozenges, making tiny crunching sounds, crushing the bones of small birds in their mouths. They passed the patterned tin between them, its jewel-bright colors like one of her Huntley & Palmers tins, moving it across from hand to hand without speaking, like the way they passed her.

Crunch.

Crunch.

Crunch.

Tinted bubbly foam glistened on their thick lips, and dribbled into their beards.

The flames of the torches made flapping noises, like sheets on a row of washing lines, as the breeze caught them, and the angels' gowns fluttered.

The moon had sharpened, become clearer, fully emerged from the clouds like a large, cold eye staring down on her.

It was a full moon.

She and Annie would be brought back again tonight – she found herself thinking, though it had not happened for three weeks (they must have been busy rehearsing) – when the crowds had left, accompanied by Hopeful and Faithful (she had recognized Papa's "friend"), walking through the churned-up earth and the discarded candy wrappings ("Pilgrims! Pilgrims!") to the Celestial City. Christian and Faithful had been led up and down in chains at Vanity Fair, and placed in a cage. Faithful had been put to death. First they scourged him, then they buffeted him, then they lanced his flesh with knives; after that they stoned him with stones, then pricked him with their swords; and last of all they burned him to ashes at the stake. This was the part of the performance that she had enjoyed the most. This was the part where she had struggled against a strong inclination to shout "Bravo!" and applaud enthusiastically.

Charlotte's shaking intensified. She was doubled over, still holding Alice's hand with one of her hands, but cupping her other hand over her mouth to stifle the frantic whooping sounds she was making.

Alice looked at the moon, listened to the wind. There were things she ought to say in the Celestial City, things she ought to say wherever she was.

Every time I look at the full moon I shall think of you, Papa. For always.

She clutched Mama's hand tighter.

If you tell anyone what has happened, the wind will get you. You cannot escape from the wind. You know that, don't you? Wherever you try to go, whatever you try to do, the wind will always find you. Even a gentle wind, even a breeze, barely enough to ruffle the leaves on the trees.

Even a whisper.

Especially a whisper.

For always.

For always.

The wind would take Annie. Annie would disappear, like Nurse had disappeared, without saying goodbye, without Alice knowing that the last time they had spoken together was the last time.

Trumpets sounded, angels came out of the Celestial City to greet Papa and the Reverend Goodchild, and the choir sang even more loudly.

Papa and the Reverend Goodchild were led through the Gate and into the Celestial City by angels, and everyone poured in after them. It was a squash inside, and Pilgrims were angling their heads or attempting to stand on tiptoe so that they could see properly. It was like being at the back of a crowd as a procession went past. Some Pilgrims, showing their teeth in smile-shaped snarls, because that made it all right, shoved their way firmly through to the front. It was a technique they had perfected at rummage sales.

Faithful, like one of the Shining Ones, reappeared to welcome Christian and Hopeful. He wasn't dead, after all. He walked on like one of those actors who expected applause at his every entrance

("It's me again! It's me! *Me!*"), and looked annoyed when it didn't happen. In such a way, one felt, would Reynolds Templeton Seabright have entered, Mrs. Albert Comstock-Conquering-Hero-fashion, dah-dah-dah-dah-dah-daddle-daddling, delaying his first line until the thunderous applause had somewhat subsided, so that his vowels might be heard to their best advantage.

As Papa and the Reverend Goodchild kneeled in the central courtyard of the Celestial City they looked like communicants kneeling at the altar. Raiment was put upon them that shone like gold, and angels placed crowns upon their heads, and harps into their hands.

The frog-faced angels suddenly produced hand-bells from behind their backs with abracadabra flourishes, and bells began to peal, echoing out across the lake. You could tell by their expressions of agonized concentration that this bit — like the smiles — hadn't been rehearsed often enough. Many of them were fortunate not to have an eye out as the ringing became animated to the point of foolhardiness, the sharp silvery lips of the bells flashing up and down like murder weapons being used to beat out brains.

Alice clung tightly to Mama's waist, never wanting to let go, her whole body shaking. The thin summer coat smelled slightly of lavender, and a button pressed against the upper part of her cheekbone, as sharp as any Roman coin. She pressed harder, to feel the button dig in more.

"*There will I keep you for ever,*" she thought. "*Yes, for ever and a day.*"

17

On the last time she was taken to the Celestial City, the time just after Annie had gone, she had not wanted to go, but Papa had made her go, to where his "friend" was waiting for them behind the wall, even though it was winter, even though it was so cold. They had left footprints in the freshly fallen snow, as they trailed out to The Old Pigpen. Papa had left them, and wandered down to the edge of the lake to wait there for an hour. The rowboats would be frozen together now in the shallows at the edge of the lake, locked in ice. People would be skating soon, whissshing, and spinning round. Papa would have his pocket-watch with him. Once or twice, his "friend" had started to complain that they had not been there for the full time, a man who had been hiring something for a set period, like a rowboat on the lake. A peevish, pettish note would come into the "friend"'s voice, that of an aggrieved customer whom a scheming merchant had unwarrantedly cheated of his rightful due. *No one applauded when I came on again at the end!* You could still hear the resentment in his voice, months later. He had been a *very* good Faithful. He had been *excellent.* Everyone had said so. That was the note you heard in his voice, that fretful whine that things were not as they should be.

In the Celestial City his voice had become contented again. The correct goods had been supplied. She felt that he ought to be sucking his thumb, making little noises like her baby brother sleeping. She was the pacifier, the thumb, and he was the gurgling child, clad in his newly washed diaper, his silent rattle fallen upon the floor. A fire had been lighted in the room at the back, where the little kitchen once had been, and it had the look of a children's secret den prepared for some feast, the flames crackling, and sending up sparks. You thought it would be driftwood, a fire lighted on whitened pebbles at the edge of the sea. There should be skates hanging from the wall, hot drinks, marshmallows to toast.

"You're one of the girls from the statue."

It was a clouded night, and no moon was visible.

He began, as he always began, with her head. Each time the beginning was the same words, in the same order, and she would brace herself for the moment when things began to change, as they always did. He was very methodical in what he did. Even though the moon was not visible, he would begin by naming the features of the moon, as he had done the first time they had passed through the

Gate. They had not knocked, but it had been Opened Unto them. This had been going on for over a year now. The hour would pass. After a while, she would not feel his fingers. She would peep out through the eyeholes of the statue she had become. She was — she felt sometimes — more afraid of what didn't happen than what did, the sense of considered possibilities.

"Plato," he said, "Copernicus . . ."

First they scourged him . . .

Down at the lake's edge she imagined Papa, becoming bored, tentatively beginning to place first one foot, then the other, upon the thin covering of ice that ran a few yards into the lake from the bank. There'd be a creaking, the straining sound of something on the point of snapping, echoing all around the silence of the lake. The surface of the lake would vibrate, held on a resonant note. Emboldened, Papa would take another step out upon the dangerous crust of ice, lured into Jesus-like walks upon the water after his performance as Hopeful. He had fed the five thousand, and sent the multitude away. He had gone up into the mountain apart to pray, and when the evening was come, he was there alone, lost in Gethsemane musings. He walked on the sea, out to the disciples on the ship, ignoring the waves and the wind. "Be of good cheer," he said, "it is I; be not afraid." The wind ceased. Papa took another step further out onto the lake. Hope gave you strength. With Hope you could do anything.

She had hated Bruno's 'ittle-dirly-dirl-like mispronunciations in *Sylvie and Bruno*. "Hurted mine self *welly* much!" he sobbed, cutely curly-headed, posing awhile as Mrs. Alexander Diddecott leaped upon her watercolors with ecstatic cries; "Not as much as *I'd* like to hurt you," Alice had muttered mutinously. (*Welly welly* much *indeed*! That's how much she'd have liked to have hurted him.) How *could* Lewis Carroll have ventured so far out into the treacly, feet-squelching depths of Mrs. Molesworth territory? One of the mispronunciations had, however, lingered in her mind as a potentially useful expression. "River-edge." That was Bruno's version of "revenge." "Revenge is a wicked, cruel, dangerous thing!" the narrator had cried. (*Moral Lessons Effortlessly Inserted for the Instruction and Betterment of the Young Person.* In *The Water Babies,* Charles Kingsley, following this golden rule to ensure the Betterment of the Young Person, named the worst ills of all in Pandora's box as *Naughty Boys and Girls.* "I must be clean," Tom said. "I must be clean," and he pulled off his clothes, and went to the river-edge to throw himself beneath the clear, cool water.) *"River-edge?" said Bruno. "What a funny word! I suppose you call it c'ooel and dangerous because if you went too far and tumbled in, you'd get d'owned."* River-edge. Papa moved closer toward where the ice became darker, the soft, dangerous edge. If he went too far and tumbled in, he'd get drowned. Or he'd freeze to death, clutching at the soft sorbet ice-edge as it turned to slush and spurted between his grasping, feeling-deadened fingers. The c'ooeler the better. That was her position on the matter.

"... Aristotle, Archimedes ..."

... then they buffeted him ...

She tried to think of Annie.

All week she had been searching for Annie in the snow.

She could see the last two verses of the statue's stone base, the lettering that was like that on a newly cut gravestone, as clearly as if they were painted on one of the stacked signs in the House of the Interpreter. She couldn't stop herself reading them, the verses that could not be true, the verses that must not be true, her mouth pressing against the metal, frozen, unable to speak, unable to move away, but breathing, seeing. The man playing the music took all the children away, and into the mountain.

The next-to-last verse.

> "... I have you fast in my fortress,
> And will not let you depart,
> But put you down into the dungeon
> In the round-tower of my heart ..."

The ...

The last . . .

The last verse.

She saw it like something written on a blackboard, a task to be learned by heart.

> ". . . And there will I keep you for ever,
> Yes, for ever and a day,
> Till the walls shall crumble to ruin,
> And molder in dust away!"

There will I keep you forever.

This was what the father had said to his three daughters.

I will not let you depart.

They were put down in the dungeon of his heart.

Goneril strained blindly upward, to whisper into her father's ear.

> "Sir, I love you more than word can wield the matter,
> Dearer than eyesight, space, and liberty;
> Beyond what can be valued, rich or rare . . ."

Regan's whispered words overlapped with those of her sister's.

> ". . . I am alone felicitate
> In your dear Highness' love."

"N-N-Nothing, my lord," Cordelia said. "N-N-Nothing."

N-N-Nothing would come of n-n-nothing.

The bodies of the three sisters lay – in homage – in front of the body of their father at the end of the play.

> . . . *We that are young*
> *Shall never see so much nor live so long.*

". . . Kepler, Hercules . . ."

. . . then they lanced his flesh with knives . . .

She thought of Annie again. She had walked round and round The House of the Magdalenes, Pettifar's Orphanage, and the North River Lunatic Asylum, coming across her own footsteps like those of some polar explorer as she circled round in the untrodden snow. Then, as if concentrating on something bright with which to hypnotize herself, she thought of the brightness of the left side of her breast in the sculpture. Moving very slowly, so that Papa's "friend" would not know that she was moving – she had to keep still, he became annoyed if she moved – she placed her right hand upon the same place on her own body, to ease an ache by its warmth, to feel an alteration in the rhythm of her heart.

On the fragile carapace of ice, Papa took a step further out across the lake, swaying slightly like a man on a flimsy windblown bridge. He stood with his arms extended out on either side of him, balancing. One step too many, and he would fall through into the dark icy water beyond the edge. He paused for a moment, feeling the shifting surface beneath his feet. One more step, and the ice would still support him. One further step. He stood there a long time, like someone unable to continue, someone unable to turn back. It was intensely cold. He would feel the ice thickening beneath him, the surface of the water becoming misty and opaque like a breathed-on mirror. One step closer to the edge. River-edge.

> *. . . "O father! I see a gleaming light,*
> *O say, what may it be?"*
> *But the father answered never a word,*
> *A frozen corpse was he.*
>
> *Lashed to the helm, all stiff and stark,*
> *With his face turned to the skies,*
> *The lantern gleamed through the gleaming snow*
> *On his fixed and glassy eyes.*

Then the maiden clasped her hands and prayed
That savèd she might be;
And she thought of Christ, who stilled the wave
On the Lake of Galilee . . .

". . . Oceanus Procellarum, Palus Epidemiarum, Lacus Somniorum . . ."

Storm. Disease. Sleep.

The thing that she had feared would happen, had happened. The molten bronze had been poured around her body, a little part of her at a time, a thin layer of metal, decorative armor plating slowly encasing her whole body, gradually becoming thicker, gradually becoming rigid, until the living girl within was covered, overwhelmed and stifled by the work of art that contained her.

". . . Mare Frigoris, Mare Crisium, Mare Imbrium, Mare Nubium . . ."

She couldn't move, she couldn't speak, she couldn't breathe.

Coldness. Crises. Showers. Clouds.

. . . after that they stoned him with stones . . .

She had turned into her own bronze figure in *The Children's Hour*, like a ventriloquist's dummy poised forever upon the knee of the man who manipulated her, made her move in the ways he wanted, put his words into her mouth.

18

The Children's Hour statue was sited near the children's play area in the park, and the bedraggled survivors of the exotic birds from the aviary. In a winter storm — it was the second winter of the Celestial City, just before Annie had gone — a branch from an overhanging tree had crashed through the aviary's glass roof, and most of the fragile birds had been blown out — or had willingly flown out — from the rarefied warmth of their ornate little pavilion into a nighttime blizzard. Small brightly colored frozen corpses had littered the neighborhood for days.

Alice had been awake, sobbing, alone in the schoolroom at the top of the house, terrified of the wind, and of Papa and his "friend." She – suffering from a cough – had been left behind when Papa had taken Allegra and Edith to Charlotte's birthday party. Papa had taken them because Mama was away from home, taking Ben to be seen by his grandparents. Mama would never have left Alice alone in the house when she was ill, even if Annie was there, but Papa did not see children when he looked at her and Annie. A Little Woman was not a child. Charlotte had promised to come and see her the following day, and Allegra had taken her birthday present to the party for her, to give to Charlotte.

Her sobbing was interrupted by bouts of coughing, and when she tried to shut out the sound of the wind by hiding her head beneath her pillows, she felt that she was suffocating, and that was how she felt those times perched upon the knee of Papa's "friend." She thought that she heard a more distinct, closer sound than that of the wind, a sharp tapping, like fingernails against glass, and the glass vibrated slightly in the wind. She thought of a sudden crash, and the cold air bursting in.

If you tell anyone what has happened, the wind will get you.

They had not said a word to anyone, *anyone*, and the wind was howling outside her window.

If she screamed, she felt that Papa, even though he was up on Hudson Heights, would somehow come back into the room. She thought that he had hidden himself somewhere in the house with his "friend," their jaws rotating clockwise in unison as they crunched the cachous, as the pinkness dribbled down into their beards. *Tick, tock* went the crunching clockwork, *tick, tock*.

Annie would be in her room near the kitchen. In novels, servants had rooms in the attics of houses, but Annie's room was downstairs. It was Alice and her sisters who had the rooms at the top of the house. She wondered if Annie would be sleeping. The wind would not be so strong where she was. Perhaps she had managed to fall asleep. Perhaps she would have a dream to interpret in the morning, though she seemed to have had no dreams for a long time now.

Timidly, she tried to summon Lizzie Galliant, Lizzie Galliant who lived inside her, and who was afraid of nothing. She would know what to do. She had never let her down, until Papa and his "friend" had started to take her to the Celestial City. Papa was stronger than even Lizzie was. She was half afraid to call Lizzie's name in case, this time, she ignored the summons, and whom would she have then to help her? Alice knew that she herself possessed special powers, and that she was capable of summoning Lizzie to her assistance. She also knew that she must not use these powers until the right time came, otherwise she would lose them. Unlike Aladdin with the ring and with the lamp, she could not summon a jinnee again and again to do her bidding when she was in danger, or when she needed help. It had to be the right time to use her powers, and she would know when that time had come. She would have only one chance.

"Lizzie!" she called quietly, and even the mention of her name in that room seemed to be louder than the noise of the storm: even her name was strong, the name that Alice had given to her. She said it again, and again, more like an incantation than a summons – "Lizzie! Lizzie! Lizzie!" – and felt herself become stronger.

Lizzie would come, Lizzie was coming, and her mien would be at its most imperious.

The wind was inside the room itself: the night-light flickered, almost guttered, and threw tall swaying shadows across the walls, like the gas-lamp outside the front parlor window casting moving patterns on the wallpaper, shifting, glowing, never at rest.

She heard Lizzie's voice, calm, soothing. "What ails you, child?"

Lizzie was tall, Lizzie was older and wiser than she was, and sometimes she said "you," and sometimes she said "thee."

"I am afeard that something is amiss. Be of good cheer. I am here beside you, and we shall face this stern summoner together. Let us

575

arise and show we fear not this dark and tortuous imbroglio. Be not afeard. We shall drive this varlet back whence he came, a broken and pitiful remnant of his former self. I am Lizzie Galliant. Strong men fall powerless before me! I have the power that alone belongs to women! Men's beards will burst into flame at my approach and flare wondrously!"

Alice had a particular fondness for this last sentence. She would have given a great deal to possess this power, and had practiced for ages, exercising to build up muscles. No glimmer yet within any of her chosen targets. She had focused her powers like a burning glass upon Dr. Vaniah Odom's beard on Sundays, but there had not been even the faintest of faint flickering red glows from within its tenebrous depths.

She picked up her night-light and cautiously moved closer to the window that looked out from the front of the house, a lull in the storm suggesting for a moment that even the forces of nature quailed before the power of Lizzie Galliant. She saw her reflection glowing in the darkness of the window when she drew back the drapes, and realized that the tapping on the window was a snowstorm.

She shaded the light and peered outside into Chestnut Street, her forehead against the cold glass. In the circles of light from the gaslamps, huge flakes dizzyingly gusted and spun, and miniature drifts had formed upon the windowsill and in the corners of the window. Then she saw, lying on the sill, up against the glass like someone seeking refuge, a tiny red bird, a little tropical flame of warmth, its claws tightly gripped to prevent itself from crying out. Emboldened by the temporary cessation of the wind, she hurriedly opened the window, and reached through the bars to pick up the almost weightless scrap of color.

Back in her bed, the window closed again, and the drapes tightly drawn, she — with a vague memory of something she had read or heard — placed the little corpse within the bosom of her nightgown. It had been as cold as a glacier-smoothed pebble, recovered after years buried deep within the ice. For several hours she had lain awake, like a young nursing mother, still, hardly daring to move, thinking that the warmth of her body might bring it back to life. It was what Lizzie Galliant would have done. A little pool of water gathered in the hollow at the base of her neck, and wet the edge of her gown.

She was awoken suddenly by a tremendous crash, and leaped up in her bed as the wind screamed around the nursery.

The wind will get you.

She felt something leap within her breast, a tremendous beating of wings, confusedly remembered the red bird, and clutched at the front of her gown. Suddenly they had become huge wings, the wings of an eagle or a swan beating in her face, leaping up and away from her, blundering about the room, crashing against the mirror and thudding into the walls, sweeping the Shakespeare Castle figures and the fragments of glass to the floor with a smash, sweeping down the fallen golden stars, a sense of swarming shadows, the sound of deafening wings. The wind howled again, and she arched back against her pillows, the wings pounding against her chest. Then she realized that the pounding, the beating, was from within herself, was the pounding of her own frightened heart, and that the bird was dead – had been dead ever since she had lifted it into the room – its torn red feathers strewn all down the front of her nightgown and across her sheets.

She began to pick at the red feathers down the white front of her nightgown – so many feathers for so small a bird – and found that what she thought were feathers was in fact blood. During her sleep – perhaps in holding the small body, fragile as an egg, comfortingly against herself, perhaps in unknowingly convulsing as the sound of the renewed storm increased – she had crushed it. The blood was everywhere, and the little corpse – seemingly made entirely of blood – had disappeared in a spray of redness.

Holding her hands away from herself, a feeling that it was they that were stained, they that would mark what she wore (though they were clean, it was what she wore that was soiled), she slid out of bed on the side toward the squat, windblown candle. She was drawn toward the light, and made herself sit still for a moment, trying to decide which of the noise was from outside the house, and which of it was from inside herself. Gradually, her breathing and her heartbeat steadied, though looking at the rapid flickering of the little flame made her want to breathe more quickly. As she bent toward it, long shadows bowed around the walls and in the mirror. The fire was now ashes, burned out by the intensity of the wind, and the room was very cold.

She didn't call for Lizzie Galliant again. The right time had not yet come. There would be another time, a worse time, and then would be the time to call for her, the time for the two of them to face the stern summoner side by side, the time when strong men would fall powerless before them, and beards would burst into flame and flare wondrously. She held out her hands a little, palms upraised, to feel a faint warmth from distant flames.

Annie.

Alice picked up her night-light, and moved toward the door. There was such a downdraft from the chimney as she passed the fireplace that she shielded the candle, and hunched protectively around it. The snow would come down there first and advance into the room, creeping forward, accumulating in the corners . . .

Annie . . .

She had not done this before, but she had not been alone in the house at night before with Annie.

She wanted Annie to cover her warm, to pray to the angels to keep her from harm. She wanted Annie to tenderly kiss her, to fondly caress her. She wanted to fall gently to sleep on her breast, deeply to sleep from the heaven of her breast.

She had read about it.

Now she wanted to do it.

She began to make her way downstairs. On the landings the storm seemed to be all around her. The night-light gave such a small area of illumination. She could barely see down to her feet moving on the stairs, and had to feel her way downward. The house was a different place in darkness. She ought to have lighted a lamp. There were no colors on the stairs, no colors anywhere. She should close her eyes, find out what sleepwalking was like, gain an insight into Lady Macbeth, and impress Charlotte by her knowledge. Charlotte was a good friend, and always prepared to be impressed.

"This is 'slumb'ry agitation,'" she thought. It was always satisfying when words left the page and became real.

"'She has light by her continually; 'tis her command.'"

That was another example. She was conscious of visualizing two sets of quotation marks for this sentence as she thought of herself speaking it, but there should only be one. The words had ceased to be an extract from a text; they had become a description of what she herself felt.

She couldn't rub her hands together without putting the night-light down on the stairs, and she didn't want to do that.

"Yet here's a spot." There were many of those. She was a guilty woman after a bloody death. One set of quotation marks.

"Wash the blood-stains from your fingers," she chanted, interposing a little Longfellow into the Shakespeare. "Bury your war-clubs and your weapons."

The tiles of the hall, and then of the kitchen, were cold under her feet. She could feel the edges of the individual tiles, the rough lines of cement between the smooth tiles. She slid the soles of her feet about, trying to see if she could distinguish between white tiles and black, and feel which color was the colder. She imagined that the white ought to be the colder, the slippier. It was as if she was walking a great distance across a sheet of ice. She ought to be holding her hands in front of her if she was sleepwalking, but she held them out to the side, like a novice skater taking her first tentative steps out onto a frozen lake. Would she have been able to read words painted on the tiles with the tender skin at the sides of her feet, in the way that her fingers had traced the raised or incised letters of a gravestone?

Infant Daughter of Lincoln and Lucinda Pinkerton.

She slid the soft rounded edges of her feet – first one, then the other – gently across the cold surface in a long looping curve, attempting to balance herself preparatory to Mary Benedictine balletic cavortings.

And by and by a cloud takes all away.
You and I are past our dancing days.
I know thee not, old man.

The raised candle flame was reflected in the dimly visible cups and plates of the dresser, and in the glass of the kitchen clock.

It ticked sonorously. When you couldn't see properly, sounds were louder.

"One, two; why then 'tis time to do't."

One set of quotation marks.

"Annie . . ."

She started to say the name far too early, and said it so quietly that Annie would not have heard her in any case, but – as she felt when she called the name of Lizzie Galliant – she felt stronger for saying it. She wanted Annie to know that it was she who was coming, so that she would not hear a knock on her door, and think that it was Papa, come to take her out to die in a Sea of Coldness on the way to the Celestial City. It was a frozen sea in which the multitudes of the damned – their heads diminishing away into a distance too far to see – were enclosed in the ice up to their nostrils, unable to cry out, unable to call the name of someone who would come and save them. Their eyes were full of despair, of realization that this was what eternity would be like; this was all they would ever know, ever again.

Hell is murky.

No quotation marks.

"Annie . . ."

She had a name to call. She had someone who would save her. She would not cry out, "Help!" The word she would call would be "Annie."

She held the night-light closer to her face, to prevent ice from forming in front of her mouth, inside her mouth, so that she could go on calling. There was a slight warmth, enough to free a Northwest Passage through the Arctic wastes. The center of the stumpy candle had all been burned away, and there was a thin, almost transparent, glowing wall of wax around the flame. She held it close to her eyes. It was like the moment when the surface of a long-frozen lake was on the point of dissolving into liquid. Anyone who tried to walk upon it would plunge through into darkness, icy coldness.

Annie's room was off a little corridor that ran away from the kitchen. Alice could see the outline of the door illuminated by candlelight from inside. Even though the wind was not quite so violent lower down, it was still keeping Annie awake. Good. She hadn't liked the thought of approaching a door in darkness. If she had frightened Annie in awakening her, she would have frightened herself further.

"Annie . . ."

She said it again, louder.

"Annie . . ."

It was as if there were other people in the house, sleeping, and she could not raise her voice above a certain level.

"Annie, it's m-m-me, Alice . . ."

She walked closer toward the thin flickering lines of light.

Yet who would have thought the old man to have had so much blood in him?

No quotation marks at all.

19

Ten years or so later, a dark early morning during another storm, this nighttime scene had come into Alice's head when she had pushed open the door of Papa's study to find Papa's body after he had killed himself.

The 1888 blizzard had started the week before her twentieth birthday. Mama, and her brother and sisters, had been spending the weekend at Grandpapa and Grandmama's, and had expected to return home on the Monday morning. The storm had started as Monday had started, and they had not managed to reach home through the snowdrifts and blocked roads until several days later, summoned by the news of a death.

In the early hours of the Monday morning, as on the night when the birds were killed, Alice was awoken by the sound of a storm, though it was a storm far worse than the earlier one had been. In the glow of the night-light – she still had a night-light – she had looked at the time on her pocket-watch as it hung on its stand – three forty-eight, the minute hand edging towards the X – and gone back to sleep. She had been writing into the early hours, vaguely aware of the sound of the storm, and had fallen asleep only an hour or so earlier. Some hours later, she had woken again, and walked over to the window looking out from the back of the house. She had, for years now, kept all drapes firmly closed, to keep out the darkness (it would be a long time yet before she began to leave them open), and she bobbed down a little, to stand up inside the little covered space with the drapes resting against her back, the cold glass in front of her. It must feel like this for a photographer, bent over under his focusing cloth, about to take a winter photograph of bare trees. There was – she discovered, as she attempted to look out – no view to capture on this side of the house, no counting up to three or five. There was nothing to see. It would have been difficult enough at night in normal circumstances – there were no street lights yet on that side; it was still all fields and orchards – but the panes of the window were encrusted with snow that looked packed thick enough to keep out daylight. If she hadn't seen the time on her watch – it was now a few minutes past six – heard that it was ticking, she would have experienced the slightly suffocating feeling that it was broad daylight, and all the windows of the house – the whole of the interior like the bottom of a well, all light excluded – blocked by snow.

The fire was still glowing, and she added more coal before she walked across to the mansard window at the front, and, standing behind the drapes as she had done before, she was enclosed in a little alcove with a seat. She always felt like ten-year-old Jane Eyre at the beginning of the novel when she did this, a child needing to acquire a more sociable and childlike disposition, a more attractive and sprightly manner. Until she could speak pleasantly, she should remain silent, cross-legged like a Turk in the window seat, hidden behind red moreen curtains, studying a book with descriptions of the death-white realms of the Arctic Zone, those forlorn regions of dreary space, that reservoir of frost and snow, those firm fields of ice, the accumulation of centuries of winter, those scenes that were so like the scenes hidden deep inside herself, ice frozen for so long, and at so low a temperature, that it would never melt, the glass-like splinter of ice lodged within the heart.

The scenes from the book, the scenes from inside Jane's head, were the scenes outside the window, the white pages ripped from a book that never ended, and flung out to bury an entire landscape. A tremendous blinding snowstorm was raging down from the north, had been raging for some time, enveloping and burying the countryside. It was one of those great natural phenomena – like witnessing a comet or a meteorite shower – when those who saw it felt that they had to go on watching, because what they were seeing was so spectacularly out of the ordinary. Perhaps this was how people reacted during earthquakes or volcanic eruptions, unable to tear themselves away as the buildings collapsed upon them, the ash buried them, hypnotized and destroyed by the most intense moment of their lives, memorizing what they were seeing, believing that they would be talking about it for years to come, made interesting by what had happened to them. That was how they had died at Pompeii – arms guarding their heads, reaching out toward safety, rehearsing the words of witness that they would never speak – their whole lives reduced to the eternal gestures of their silenced bodies. The snow was not so much falling – the flakes were huge, flakes to bury, to smother, spinning and unfolding like leaves, they seemed to slow down time – as being *hurled* against the houses like a barrage of missiles by the gale.

The "tumultuous privacy of storm," she thought, enfolded in the little space between the drapes and the window, the pocket of silence. This was what Ralph Waldo Emerson must have experienced, to make him write those words.

She sat on the window seat and watched the red-stained snow surge through Prospero's cloak, and accumulate in red drifts against the house, across where Chestnut Street had been the previous day. The cloak vibrated slightly, and there was a humming, like a wineglass on a high note. You wet your fingertip, and circled round and round the rim, faster and faster. Mrs. Alexander Diddecott and Mrs. Italiaander reversed a wine-glass, and pressed their fingers against the upturned base. The wineglass slid with a squeaky sound across the polished surface of the table, faster and faster around the glass-enclosed white plaster arm in the center, impelled by a force outside the control of the lightly resting fingers. It spun from letter to letter of the alphabet spread out on cards in a circle around it, a concentric shape within the circle of the table, spelling out troubling, riddling Delphic messages from beyond. The sliding discordant stridency of the glass rim spelled out imperfect messages like flawed chalk, when the downward or the upward strokes did not mark the blackboard. The messages were elaborately analyzed, searched for secret messages. *No harm. I have done nothing but in care of thee, of thee, my dear one, thee, my daughter.* The blood-colored snow piled high.

The snow — with the direction in which the gale was blowing — should have been drifting up against the opposite side of Chestnut Street (as it was, all the steps up to the front doors on that side of the street were already covered), but it was funneling round onto their side. Through the howling of the wind, she could hear a high-pitched humming — shriller than the sound made by the vibrating glass in the window — that kept changing in pitch.

BEWARE, the wineglass message spelled out, sliding rapidly across from letter to letter with its piercing chalk-on-blackboard shriek. *DANJER. DARKNES.* The cards were always arranged — it was a little hushed ritual, Mrs. Italiaander clutching her necklace —

in the same order, solemnly positioned around the table in a counterclockwise direction as if they were playing cards being dealt out before a game with high stakes. The little loosely curled white fingers of Archer Italiaander Junior always pointed – discreetly indicating a private communication – at the letter *M*. *MAMA*. Was that what he was saying? His mama did not seem to notice, but each time the fingers silently pointed. *DETH*. *BLUD*. That's what the wineglass spelled out, but *M* was the real, the hidden message, the one that no one but she had noticed. They always drank red wine from the glasses first – it gave an uncomfortably holy communion sort of feeling to the ceremony – and some was always left in the glasses, dribbling down slowly as they were inverted, and leaving long wet streaks, quicksilver-like with their curved rims, across the polished table as they slid from place to place. It was like another hidden message – in handwriting this time – as the curved outer surfaces of the loops and swirls and beads of redness scribbled out across the table and caught the dim light.

The humming wineglass sound would keep Miss Iandoli awake, even if the storm didn't, and it was loudest outside her house. It was the sound of the wind through the telegraph wires, and a telegraph pole stood right outside Miss Iandoli's bedroom window. You looked up toward the sky, and every city street – these days – was enclosed within a tight network of wire, level upon level, like thick washing lines strung between tenement buildings, to prevent the birds from flight. Some of the poles had so many arms – was that the word? – upon them that they had the look of wide skyward-pointing ladders with which invaders from another element could storm the upper levels of the skies, each rung of the ladder with an odd dark shape silhouetted upon it at each side, like roosting, motionless birds, caught within the traps, all in the exact same position, all the exact same size. From these, the wires led across from pole to pole like rigging from the masts of a ship.

There were no lights on in any of the houses, as if she was the only person awake, yet she thought of everyone she knew, imagining him or her awake and watching as she was watching, visualizing the windows at which he or she would be sitting. For this you had to sit, a spectator at a play or the opera, not stand with one hand resting negligently against the wall on one side. Charlotte would be calling to Linnaeus to come and look, come and look, as the storm shrieked around Hudson Heights. It was like a summer beach, the tide coming in, and coming in, and the sandcastles losing their shapes and vanishing, though this was a beach where the sea would freeze, the waves held in their descent, as the moving landscape changed out of recognition beyond, a place in which the only things that were fixed were those that were held within the mind of the observer. She wondered if Papa was sitting looking out across the wildness at the back, where the fields and orchards would be buried under huge windblown drifts, or facing the same way she was facing, out across the street, losing track of time in his study. She had heard a door click in the hall long ago, before she had gone to sleep, a sound that had echoed right up the stairs, before the snow had started.

When the dark early morning had come – nothing to show that it *was* morning, except for the time on her pocket-watch – the street was still deserted, no one daring to venture out, and the blizzard howled. It was going to snow all day; the snow was never going to end. There were not many children in Chestnut Street, but she doubted that – in an hour or so – there would be any streets and parks in the city noisy with shrieking children tugging sleds and rolling great balls of snow down slopes, heads bowed against the gale. What was happening outside was too extreme, too dangerous, for children – for anyone – to be out, and she had a sense of being marooned, out of reach of anyone else. She was not sure whether she was barricaded in against the blizzard, or whether the storm had trapped her in the house. In the back of her mind, she ticked her way through a little list. Mama and the others would not be getting back today; travel was impossible, and the whole city would have shuddered to a halt. All streets would be the same as the street in front of her, a deserted snow-blocked canyon down which winds howled. Karin, their maid, had gone with them.

There was plenty of coal, plenty of oil, candles, food. If Papa had not also been in the house, she would, tentatively, have started to feel a little exhilarated, a desert island sense of freedom, even if the island did happen to be surrounded by a frozen sea across which intruders might approach. Slowly, tentatively, bulkily well-swathed figures would begin to feel their way across the undulating solidified surface of the waves.

She built the fire up again, wrapped her gown around her, and began to go downstairs, carrying a candle. On some days she felt that the stairs were like the stairs in the caves of Kôr in *She*, the stone stairs that had been worn down from seven and a half inches to three and a half inches, by the feet of the same woman walking up and down them, up and down them, like a prisoner in a cell, for century after century. If she was feeling like this in the week before her twentieth birthday, what on earth would she be feeling like in the week before her *thirtieth* birthday? (Now, thirty *was* old. It was only a short step from thirty to the two thousand and more years of Ayesha, pronounced Assha.)

Snow had frozen into a solid sheet on the outer side of the windows, as at the back of the house, and she found herself walking down a staircased corridor lined with the blurred reflections of fake mirrors.

Looking-glass, looking-glass, made out of ice.

The whole of the mountain of Kôr was filled with the countless embalmed bodies of the dead, and nearly all of them were perfect.

Tell me, please tell me, that I look really nice.

Faithful besotted native girls did not survive long in the novels of H. Rider Haggard. Once they became enamored of the white intruders, they were doomed. Alice blamed the beards that the men brought with them. Beards and guns. These were the two essentials for possessing power over swaying, feverishly inferior natives. These were the symbols of supremacy. Depending on their geographical location, the cowed natives bowed or salaamed or kowtowed – a thoughtful element of choice was involved here – but they always fell down when the guns and the beards were whipped out to astonish them. (Native bearers held the beards high in the air, to preserve their dryness amidst the tropical foliage so that they could retain their power.) Ustane: doomed by the presence of the beard. Foulata: doomed by the presence of the beard. The beards were poisonous outgrowths flourishing beneath strong suns, and one touch brought death to the unwary.

In the kitchen the water was bubbling in the side boiler of the stove. The fire must have been roaring in the wind, though it was, by now, almost burned out, and the farther parts of the room were already starting to feel cold. Warmth lasted for such a little time.

She began to feed in small pieces of coal, squatting down, listening to the wind in the chimney, gradually adding larger and larger pieces. She had caught it in time, and with the fierce draft it soon began to glow again. Intermittently, the glass over the face of the kitchen clock caught the flickering of the flames, and she watched as the minute hand moved down the right-hand side, from *IIII* (why *IIII*, and not *IV*? she wondered, not for the first time) to *V* to *VI* (painted upside down), and then up the left-hand side, from *VII* to *VIII* to *IX*. The Roman numerals made her think of Shakespeare's kings. Richard II. Richard III. Henry IV (not IIII), Parts One and Two. Henry V. Henry VI, Parts One, Two, and Three. There was no VII. Henry VIII. No IX. No X. No XI. *XII Night?* Possibly.

The ace-of-spades-shaped pointer on the end of the minute hand edged round and round, tick-tocking from minute to minute. She saw it as the ace of hearts, of clubs (she always thought of these as being blackberry-shaped), of diamonds, time moving past as a game of solitaire passed the lonely moments. "You're nothing but a pack of cards," she'd sometimes whispered (without the exclamation point) as a little girl, hoping that – by saying this – all that was happening around her would collapse into nothingness, shrivel away into nothing but a dream from which she would awaken. "You're nothing but a pack of cards." She whispered this to Sobriety Goodchild, to Mrs. Albert Comstock, to Dr. Vaniah Odom, waiting for the toppling to commence, the first vital card slipping silently sideways, the slow inevitability of the total collapse that followed. "You're nothing but a pack of cards." She whispered it to Allegra, to Edith, to Euterpe Dibbo, to Myrtle Comstock, to Mrs. Goodchild. There were not enough cards in the pack. She'd have to open further packs, fifty-twos after fifty-twos – like weeks, like years – too many spades, too many court cards staring at her, preparing to play multi-packed elaborate games with complicated rules, games with *French* and *foreign* names, games that did not inspire confidence in the nervous gambler – *rouge et noir* (there was Stendahl, recklessly tossing a huge wad of notes on *noir*), *bezique, baccarat* – games that no one could follow, the sort of games that inevitably led to violent quarrels.

"Off with her head!" the Queen of Hearts would scream, quick to spot an opportunity for pleasure.

"Nonsense!" Alice would reply, very loudly and decidedly, and the Queen would fall silent.

"Off with her head!" the Queen would shout, and Alice would grow to her full height again.

"Who cares for *you?*" she'd ask the Queen, invincible as Lizzie Galliant, looking down from her eminence. "You're nothing but a pack of cards!"

She'd borrowed packs of cards from Papa's study without his knowing, and shot the cards high into the air like an incompetent overambitious shuffler. She'd used more than one pack to ensure a storm of cards upon her, raining down with light, glancing touches upon her head and shoulders, a bride assailed by aggressive confetti.

"Let the jury consider their verdict," the King said.

"No, no!" said the Queen. "Sentence first – verdict afterwards."

"Stuff and nonsense!" said Alice loudly. "The idea of having the sentence first!"

"Hold your tongue!" said the Queen, and she'd turned purple, the appropriately imperial shade of someone choking.

"I won't!" said Alice.

("Stuff and nonsense!"

("I won't!")

("Who cares for *you*?")

(Alice had said these words over and over, as if learning the language of defiance, the incantation against evil. Were parents really unaware of how dangerously subversive the *Alice* books were? It wasn't just logic that was under attack.)

"You're nothing but a pack of cards!"

As the cards fluttered down, she struck at them with her fists, with spurts of genuine revulsion, feeling that she was under attack from crowding, choking, fluttering giant moths or bats, shouting out the defiant words, cuffing them away from her. Sometimes she'd catch at a card as it fell, a member of the audience invited to choose a card – any card – by a magician, or one of the superstitious picking out a card in which her fortune lay. Mrs. Alexander Diddecott told her that the worst cards in the pack were spades, cards of unhappiness and loss. The sharp edges of the spades, the slight gleam glimpsed in the dark crumbly earth, cut down deep, scraping against the soft wood of the rotting coffin. The ace of spades – the card that showed the passing of time on the kitchen clock – was the death card, but the very worst card of all was the nine of spades. "Spades! A grave!" That was what Carmen had said, and every card she drew was spades. ("Hearts! A grave!" Tess Durbeyfield whispered, seeing her fate in the stain upon the ceiling, and in every card she drew, where every card was hearts. The Queen of Hearts passed her sentence. It was death. It was off with her head, and Tess did not know the words of defiance.) In one of Tchaikowsky's operas a character stabbed himself to death after the card he turned up was revealed as the Queen of Spades, spades digging another grave. The metal cut like a well-honed knife into the damp wood, through into the small dark space beneath, bringing to light that which had long been buried. Dante Gabriel Rossetti's earth-filled fingernails thrust through to reach for the manuscripts he had buried with his wife's body years earlier, urgently holding the stained pages close to the lantern, straining to see if the scrawled words were still legible, to glimpse words and phrases.

. . . a toad within a stone he read.

. . . Time crumbles on . . .

. . . its cold circle charmed . . .

. . . vanish as smoke . . .

The manuscript had survived.

The poems could still be read.

The cards rose up into the air, and came flying down upon her, and she gave a little scream, half of fright and half of anger, and tried to beat them off. They were Happy Families cards, smothering her, pressing down upon her with all the weight of the slab of gray granite laid upon sweet Alice. Did they remember sweet Alice, buried in the old churchyard, in a corner obscure and alone? The Spade family, the worst of all the suits, was upon her, eager to be digging: Mr. Spade, the Gardener, Mrs. Spade, the Gardener's Wife, Master Spade, the Gardener's Son, Miss Spade, the Gardener's Daughter. Their eyes were intent, their purpose firm. The task before them would give them no particular pleasure but it was a task they were there to do. Spades. A grave. The blood-soaked Bones – the Sweeney Todds of the card world, eager to grab the headlines with every new excess of butchery (*BONES BUTCHERY! BONES BLOOD BONANZA! IT'S DEM BONES, DEM BONES!*) and conveniently based in Fleet Street, happy, happy, happy – were not far behind them, and moving closer. It gave a disturbing new meaning to the expression *Family Butcher's*, particularly if you weren't too fussed about the apostrophe. Dem Bones had their bright sharpened instruments – unlike Madame Roskosch, they *did* use injurious instruments – eagerly positioned to start their snip-snap disconnecting. Bones. A death. The Tape family edged competitively upon them, the Happy Families fighting for precedence like scavengers around a corpse. Mr. Tape, the Tailor, and Master Tape, the Tailor's Son, moved forward, swarming upon her as if to peck out her eyes, fluttering like wings against her face.

"Could I have Mr. Tape, please?"

Mr. Tape was at home.

Mr. Tape lunged at her eyes with his needle, absently attempting to put them out, or stitch her lids together, a long thread curving out in the air behind him. He was cross-legged in the air, seated upon an invisible magic carpet, stitching away at a garment, every outward thrust casually aimed at her face, a duelist with a tiny but deadly weapon, Lemuel Gulliver's Brobdingnagian wasp-stings.

Stitch-stitch-stitch.

"Could I have Master Tape, please?"

Master Tape was at home.

Master Tape — *Struwwelpeter* hair, dead eyes, a simian, scowling face — opened and shut a pair of scissors that were as tall as he was. He'd snatched the scissors from the scissor-man, lopped off his long legs, and snip-snapped him into silence. He snipped, he snapped, his expression unchanging, he himself the scissors, the implements become the whole of himself, the stiff bright blades moving up and down, up and down, goosey, goosey gander goose-stepping like an invading army intent on death, upstairs and downstairs and in my lady's chamber. If he met an old man who wouldn't say his prayers, he'd take him by the left leg and throw him down the stairs. Then he'd enter my lady's chamber, slamming the door shut behind him. That was whither he wandered.

Snip-snap! Snip-snap! Snip-snap!

Just behind him, Mrs. Tape, the Tailor's Wife, and Miss Tape, the Tailor's Daughter, were donning large white aprons with the slightly weary air of those with yet another messy and wearisome — but necessary — night's work ahead of them. A woman's work was never done. *Stitch-stitch-stitch.*

> *. . . Stitch — stitch — stitch,*
> *In poverty, hunger and dirt,*
> *Sewing at once, with a double thread,*
> *A Shroud as well as a Shirt . . .*

"Could I have Mrs. Tape, please?"

"Could I have Miss Tape, please?"

Mrs. Tape and Miss Tape were at home.

Mrs. Tape, the Tailor's Wife, and Miss Tape, the Tailor's Daughter – Mrs. Goodchild and Serenity to the life – unleashed a tape measure like a lasso, and wrapped it around her throat, pulling at opposite ends, tug-of-war fashion.

"Neck measurement is thirteen inches," Mrs. Tape announced to an unseen assistant busily taking down the details. The measurements of the body needed to be taken, so that the shroud could be made the correct size for the burial.

Tug, tug.

"Neck measurement is twelve and a half inches," Miss Tape corrected.

Tug, tug.

"Twelve inches."

"Eleven."

Alice was now the one turning purple.

They whirred around her with kite-tail snappishness, and the stitch-stitch needle and the snip-snap scissors drew closer.

Tapes.

A shroud.

The Happy Families were upon her in full force.

All happy families resemble one other, but each unhappy family is unhappy in its own way.

If she didn't play Happy Families, she could always play Old Maid. Even in children's card games, spades was the suit to avoid. If you were the player left with the Queen of Spades in Old Maid you wouldn't meet a Tchaikowskian death, but – an even worse fate, some thought – you were the one who would end up by being the old maid. Allegra and Edith had shrieked with horror if any game threatened to leave either of them with the dreaded card, and they'd conspired to edge it toward Alice. "Old maid! Old maid! Alice is going to be an old maid!" They chanted it in a way that made death sound merciful. There were truth and hidden meanings

593

even in schoolroom playing cards. Mrs. Alexander Diddecott would be sure to announce this with a meaningful nod.

"Stuff and nonsense!"

"I won't!"

"Who cares for *you*?"

Those were the powerful words. Those were the words to drive away her assailants.

They were nothing but a pack of cards — hearts, clubs, diamonds, Happy Families — all the spades beaten down to litter the floor around her.

"Take that! Take *that!*"

She'd find herself lying on a bank with her sister, a bank on which no wild thyme blew, dead leaves fluttering down upon her face, the fall suddenly chilling a summer's day as time leaped abruptly onward. The Fall. She felt the capital letter, a different shape in her mouth. The icy winds blew away the fragile veil of modesty, and Eve cowered in her discovered nakedness.

"Wake up, Alice dear!" her sister would say. "Why, what a long sleep you've had!"

Alice told her sister — her strangely nameless sister — all that she could remember about her dream, and then Alice left, moving away into the whiteness where there was no more print, out of the pages of the book, and her older sister remained behind, thinking of what Alice had described to her.

When Alice had completely refueled the stove she filled her ewer with hot water, and made her way back out of the kitchen, into the echoing coldness of the hall. The candle-flame was reflected in the glass of the inner door opposite her. *That light we see is burning in my hall. How far that little candle throws his beams!* That was what Portia had said to Nerissa, as they arrived back at Belmont. *So shines a good deed in a naughty world.* The one flame was repeated many times, but this did not make it feel any warmer. The front door would be completely covered by the drifting snow, and green snow, blue snow, red snow, would be pressing against the colored glass, pushing at the flap of the mail slot, to force its way through, push open the inner door, and engulf the hall.

At the bottom of the steps, she paused. There was something wrong. She had known it when she first came down, and she had ignored it.

She stopped to listen.

It was partly something to do with sound.

She thought of placing the ewer on the side of the bottom step, but held it against herself, both arms wrapped around it as if she needed to feel the warmth. She turned around, straining to see, and the candle-flame blew horizontally, almost snuffed out. She had to put the ewer down after all, doing it with extreme care, as if the stair was not level, and the jug might slide off. She was holding the candle in her left hand, and when she turned around, she cupped her right hand around the jumping, fluttering flame.

It was partly something to do with what she could see, what she could *feel*.

She held the candle higher, near the side of her head, peering forward, and it seemed that her cupped hand was protecting her eyes from the too-close flame, as much as it was protecting the flame from the draft, the distinct draft that was almost extinguishing it. She took a step forward, and then another, straining to see in the darkness, the reflected light in front of her confusing her sense of distance, confounding the near and the far. She concentrated to see so fiercely that little white stars pinged in the blackness of the hall, and she felt that it was snowing inside the house, pulsating pinpoint flakes suspended in the air in front of her.

For a moment – only a moment – she thought that she was imagining this, but then she realized that it was really there.

Her bare feet *were* walking through snow.

It *was* snowing inside the house.

She felt as if she had not slept all night through – concentrating unblinkingly on the white blankness of the drifting snow outside throughout the night – and this made her feel lightheaded, her surroundings become unreal and distant, retreating as she moved closer to them, a faint rising ringing sound in her ears. It was like the seconds immediately before a faint.

The feet were moving. She watched them. Bare feet, like a penitent's.

They were *her* feet.

She looked down, and behind her, seeing her footprints leading to her from the foot of the stairs, the imprint of her feet distinct in a thin layer of snow across the tiles, so close, so far away. It was her footprints in the snow – circling around and around Pettifar's Orphanage, The House of the Magdalenes, and the North River Lunatic Asylum – never erased by later falls of snow, later sun, in all the years between.

"Do you hear the snow against the window-panes, Kitty? How nice and soft it sounds!"

This was what Alice had said to the black kitten, just before she had climbed up onto the chimney-piece and through the looking-glass. The snow this morning sounded anything but nice and soft, *felt* anything but nice and soft. In front of her, it was becoming deeper. It was *moving*, she realized, it was moving toward her. She stood still for a while, and felt wind against her feet and the lower part of her legs, felt the snow slowly accumulating. She would walk on, and into deeper and deeper snow, drifts inside the house like the ashes burying Pompeii. She would look up, and as the morning gradually lightened to a dull grayness, the snow would be black against the sky, flakes large enough and blown fiercely enough to hurt the eyes and blur the vision, like the windblown leaves at the Shakespeare Castle, the Celestial City. Her limbs, her body, would gradually be numbed as she sank down, stoned like St. Stephen. On the feast of Stephen she sank into the snow, lost, buried within the whiteness.

Deep.

Crisp.

Even.

Brightly shone the moon.

It was coming from the direction of Papa's study.

She moved forward, through the deepening snow, like a paddler on a winter beach heading for the sea. There was a gap between the bottom of the study door and the tiled floor – they had to remember to be quiet when Papa worked in there – and the snow was being blown through this into the hall from the study, this room the source of coldness, the Snow Queen's palace that froze the hidden chambers of the heart. Now that she was nearer, she could see the outline of the door illuminated by a flickering light from inside, too strong to be from a candle. The door seemed to strain in time with the gusts of wind from outside, and with each gust more snow was blown beneath it, and – she noticed – through the keyhole. A bank of snow had accumulated in the corner to one side, and there was snow right the way across the hall to the door of the front parlor.

Behind that other door, Faithful would be waiting, still faithful after ten years and more. He'd always be there, always waiting, after ten years, after twenty, after twenty-five. He would turn to face her, half frozen, ice in his hair and eyes, looking yearning and hopeful (though Hopeful was in the other room), and she'd watch as the yearning and the hopefulness rapidly died.

"*You're* not one of the girls from the statue," he'd say, disappointed and accusing. "You can't be Alice."

He'd hold up his ice-covered hands to prevent her entrance, to drive her away. His eyes were iced over, and he gazed blindly, his head not turned at quite the right angle for seeing, not seeing yet knowing what it was he saw.

"You're too *old*."

It was toward the other door, the study door, that she leaned her head.

"P-P-Papa . . ."

She said it again, louder.

"P-P-Papa . . ."

She waited to hear a reply.
She waited for "P-P-P."

20

"Annie . . ."
She said it again, louder.
"Annie."
She waited to hear a reply.
She thought for a moment, and then an idea occurred to her.
"Annie, where art thou?" she sang.
Annie would have heard the way that Charlotte greeted her.
"Annie, where art thou?"

The light quivered all around the door, seemingly on the point of being blown out into darkness. She cupped her hand around the night-light, so that the illumination from the door would appear brighter. Most light spilled from beneath the door, and she moved her bare feet into the little pool of brightness, to warm them. One birthday-cake whoosh of breath, one wish, and the tiny candlelit area would be gone.

"One year back this even . . ."

Annie spoke the line, and her voice was so close; she was standing on the other side of the door, her head pressed against it as Alice's was. The wood vibrated minutely, like the resonant fragile body of a violin. There would be a soundhole on either side of her head, inclined inward, one like an elongated "f" on her left-hand side, and one like a reversed drawn-out "s," those old-fashioned esses in Shakespeare, with a horizontal line through the middle like an "f," or a European "7," on her right-hand side. Light would glow through them from some miniature inner room, close to the heart of the music.

". . . And thou wert by my side . . ."

She spoke, also. The two of them spoke the alternate lines to the end of the first verse, conducting a conversation.

"... And thou wert by my side ..."

"... Vowing to love me ..."

"... One year past this even ..."

"... And thou wert b-b-by my side ..."

"... Vowing to love me, Alice ..."

It was Annie who spoke the last line, and as she spoke it she pulled the door open. She had still used the name "Alice" in the words of the song, even though Alice had changed it to "Annie." For the first time, Alice saw Annie's room, and didn't know what to say. She had not planned that far ahead. She ought to say something about the way in which they seemed to have been avoiding each other, the way they had stopped talking, stopped finding the meanings of dreams, the words of songs.

"... Whate'er might betide," she continued, after too long a pause, the next line of the song, and then added, "Annie ..."

"I art here," Annie said, in answer to the question that Alice had sung.

"Did I wake you?" It was a silly question to ask, but she could think of nothing else. What would she say if Annie said yes? (Should she have said, "Didst I wake thee?"?)

Annie didn't say yes.

"I was awake," she said. "I was thinking."

She noticed the front of Alice's nightgown.

"Bloodstains," she said. "Cold water. Salt."

She sounded like a maidservant who had been summonsed to obey her mistress's command in the middle of the night, called out to solve an urgent problem with the laundry. Cold water and salt would have cleansed away the nightmares from Lady Macbeth, soothed away the candlelit walking in darkness, the rubbing of the hands. Cold tears from deep within her would have washed away the blood. The tears would not have been warm. They would not have fixed the stains irremovably in the hands. A little cold weeping would clear her of the deed. Come, come, come, come, give me your hand. What's done can be undone. To bed, to bed, to bed. There she would sleep in dreamless sleep, curled up like a tired baby.

Without the weeping there would be an eternity of sleeplessness. Weep, and then sleep.

Weep, weep, weep, and be well.

In silence, they watched as a red feather — it must have been caught up in Alice's hair — floated down between them, spiraling around and around. It danced for a moment in the heated air above the night-light, and then — like another small, doomed bird, an exotic moth — it fell into the flame, hissed briefly, and ceased to exist. There was no flare, no little spurt of light like a struck match. It just melted away.

"Burned feather," Annie said, as the acrid smell passed fleetingly between them, as short-lived as the sound of the hiss. "I won't faint now."

She was pointing at the bloodstains. Alice doubted that Annie would ever have been in danger of fainting at the sight of blood, even without the smell of burning feathers. She was too practical, too down-to-earth, and would have stepped over massed piles of swooning Mrs. Goodchilds and Mrs. Albert Comstocks (more of a running jump than a step would be required for this latter obstacle; that, and a carefully angled springboard) in search of cold water and salt, in order to wash away the stains, resolutely failing to recognize any need to denude passing parrots of their plumage.

Annie grasped Alice's face gently, and peered closely at her nose, her mouth, searching for the source of the blood. Her breath smelled of tooth powder. She was wearing a fresh nightgown, and there were two sharp creases down the front — like shoulder straps — where she had ironed it. There was a smell of lavender, like something newly unwrapped, the way Mama sometimes smelled.

She pressed the fingers of both her hands against the sides of Alice's mouth, to open it up so that she could see inside, and the mouth became a long elongated oval. It was like being examined by a dentist.

"It was a b-b-bird," Alice began to explain, as another red feather spiraled down. It sounded like "It was a g-g-gird"; her mouth was so misshapen. It was a large, fluffy feather, almost weightless, and it moved slowly, floating across the air like something on the surface of water. ("Down, down, down the down descended," Alice thought, experimentally.)

"A gald gird, obviously," Annie said, imitating the way she spoke to make her laugh, and not moving her fingers away. "A gald *shivering* gird."

She put one hand on Alice's back, manipulating her like a ventriloquist's dummy, and Alice moved jerkily, like Dum-Dum the Dummy.

"The g-g-glood," Alice explained. "It's not my g-g-glood. It's a g-g-gird's."

"It's like a murder," Annie said. "All this glood everywhere."

"A very g-g-gloody murder."

"You need to wash your mouth out," Annie said, seemingly shocked by Alice's venture into controversial language. It made her sound even more like a dentist. She'd be asking her to spit next. There was always something mildly scandalous about being encouraged to spit by an adult, though Annie was no adult.

The feather continued its slow descent.

This time, Alice met the descending feather halfway, saving it from the flame, and caught it neatly between her thumb and first finger like the tiniest of fans. Thinking of this image, she raised her head at an aristocratic angle, and fanned genteelly away with the single feather.

"Your ladyship," Annie said, seeing her cue, released her hands, and curtseyed deeply.

It was the first time she had done this for what seemed a long time. Alice looked at the crown of Annie's bowed head, the hair all tied up with little white bows for bedtime, and – though Annie couldn't see her – fanned the feather in her direction, a servant hot after hard work and needing cooling. Annie looked up, and – seeing what Alice was doing – closed her eyes, and leaned back at an angle, driven back by the force of a powerful gale.

It was a room without windows.

Like Bertha Rochester's room.

There should have been a tapestry hung on the wall to conceal the door and the little gleams of light, a keeper to control her and keep her silent.

She was like something stored away in a cupboard — slightly larger (though not much) than most — like another item of equipment, a sewing machine (she was partly this), or a carpet sweeper (and also partly this). She had placed her candle behind the piece of colored glass from the Shakespeare Castle that Alice had given her, a figure that Alice thought might have been Marina, partly because she was in an attitude of singing, her hands held out before her. She had told Annie the story of *Pericles*, how at the end Marina had sung to her lost father on board his ship — he not knowing her, she not knowing him — and drawn him back from grief and silence. Music had brought him back to life, as it had brought back to life Pericles' lost wife, Thaisa, Marina's lost mother, brought back Hermione in *The Winter's Tale*, brought back Lear from madness.

"What song did she sing?" Annie had asked.

"It doesn't give the words. It just says *Marina sings*." ("I am a maid / My lord, that ne'er before invited eyes, / But have been gaz'd on like a comet.")

"It's a lovely story, but it's sad," Annie had said. "All those lost years."

"Fourteen years."

"Fourteen."

When his daughter was restored to him, Pericles had heard the music of the spheres — the music that Lorenzo and Jessica had been unable to hear, as they sat in the moonlit garden at Belmont — like a man who had been granted immortality, and the muddy vesture of decay had slipped from his mortal body. Soft stillness and the night became the touches of sweet harmony. He had fallen asleep, and seen a vision that had led him to the lost wife, the lost mother.

A band of blueness was cast across Annie's narrow bed and partly onto the wall through the glass of Marina's gown. The color made the air seem colder. The white-painted wooden walls were bare, blue-tinged, and they were inside a room cut into ice, a little square-edged space of shelter contrived inside a glacier. There were no pictures from magazines pinned neatly to the walls, as Alice had once imagined, pictures of faces, faces that were not looking at Annie, but turned away from her, reading books that they held up before them, with a consciousness that they knew things that were unknown to her. She had forgotten her spectacles, and couldn't see clearly. Everything was hazy. Perhaps it was like this when you couldn't read. She didn't know whether she ought to look on Annie's one private place, but she looked around, memorizing, recognizing the clothes hanging on hooks beside the door. There was the dress Annie had worn when she had gone to see her brother the previous week. Her working clothes hung above the head of the bed, swaying slightly like a lonely suicide. They were both shivering, and Alice started to cough again, doubling up with her hand to her mouth. It *really* hurt.

"Come on."

She climbed into bed beside Annie. There was not much room in it for the two of them. They were like Lizzie and Laura, the two sisters in "Goblin Market."

("No," said Lizzie: "No, no, no . . .")

"I was looking at Diamond," Annie said, opening the copy of *At the Back of the North Wind* that Alice had loaned her. The book had been lying on top of the blue-tinted bedspread. They had to turn almost onto their sides to be able to face each other to talk. "This is the picture I like best."

She opened the book at Chapter XVI, the picture of Diamond sitting in an upright wooden chair — the back of his head just reached the top of it — with his baby brother on his knee, singing to him. His arms were wrapped tightly right around the baby as the infant faced him, and he was leaning forward toward him, almost touching foreheads. Behind them was a white-clothed breakfast table, set with a teapot and crockery, and there was a teakettle on the hearth in front of them. It was an image of domestic peace.

603

"It's the only picture in the whole book where he's smiling," Annie said. "Had you noticed?"

This wasn't true, but she knew what Annie meant. There was a picture of Diamond – still weak after his illness – being carried by his uncle to a pony-cart so that he could be taken down to the seashore for a few hours. The next picture after this one was of Diamond resting his head in his mother's lap as she read a book on the sand beside the sea. He might have been smiling in both these pictures, also, but they were sad smiles, absent smiles; he was smiling at something else that only he could see, something that was not there, a memory of long ago. In the picture with his brother he was smiling into the baby's face to make him smile, and there was no one in the world but the two of them. In this picture it was a real smile. In this picture Diamond was not being protected, he was protecting someone else. He sang like someone singing a lullaby.

(". . . And if that diamond ring turns to brass,
Papa's going to buy you a looking-glass . . .")

She wondered if Annie would want her to read part of the story to her, as she sometimes did. She hoped she would.

"Diamond, just hold the baby one minute. I have something to say to your father."

Those were the first words she could see, if she peered closely, her nose pressed against the page of the book. The words of the song he was singing – "Baby's a-sleeping . . ." – came shortly after this. When there were songs in the novel – especially "I know a river" – the words ran down the middle of the page, and there were big areas of unprinted whiteness on either side, like those beside the illustrations, and at the beginnings and ends of chapters. It was soothing, quieter, when there were no words there.

Alice touched the picture of Diamond. *"I have something to say to your father,"* she practiced inside herself, ready for reading. *"I have something to say to your father,"* but, this time, Annie did not ask her to read. Sometimes she asked Alice to tell her stories, in the way she had told stories to Charlotte, and Mary Benedict as they walked around and around the Shakespeare Castle. Annie would ask for certain features to be included in the stories: a long straight road, empty fields, trees in the fall. Things like that. This time, she didn't ask her to tell a story, either.

There was a newspaper, neatly folded, open at the personals, on a shelf at the side of the bed. The printing was blurred — Alice thought that it was the printing, rather than her eyesight — and it was as if Annie had been touching the paper, attempting to read by touch like a blind person, searching for someone who could predict her future for her, as she was always doing. There may have been words she recognized, words that she wished to touch, and bring closer, words she wanted to know by feel as much as by sight, like Macbeth with the dagger he saw before him. Next to it, wrapped in the silk scarf, was her Dream Book, alongside a neatly stacked pile of Reuben's letters. They were propped against Annie's Dancing Bear Bank like a solitary support at the end of a row of books. She ought to have appeared in Annie's room with her nightgown pocket filled with enough chinking cents for a nighttime of listening, someone weighing herself down prior to drowning. They could lie there side by side, watching the organ-grinder's arm turning, and the bear dancing, listening to the Duke of Mantua's song from *Rigoletto*. "*La donna è mobile, qual piuma al vento . . .*" Women were fickle, like feathers flying in a wind, always changeable, never constant, like stars falling from the sky. It was the opera in which the hunchback caused the death of his daughter, Gilda. He opened the sack he was about to throw into the river, and found her, stabbed and dying.

The Dream Book, so conveniently to hand, was there for a purpose, awaiting her arrival in the room, to read, to interpret what had been dreamed. She wondered if Annie would say, "I had a dream last night." Perhaps she had stopped dreaming.

The songs in *At the Back of the North Wind* were words without

music. There probably had been music written for them, but she did
not know it. All she knew was the words.

"I know a river
whose waters run asleep . . ."

That was how "I know a river" began.

". . . run run ever
singing in the shallows
dumb in the hollows
sleeping so deep
and all the swallows
that dip their feathers . . ."

There were feathers again, feathers falling from the sky instead
of stars.

The newspaper and the feathers (the feathers in the song, and the
feathers that had fallen through the air) made her think of Annie in
the kitchen, carefully renovating black gloves with an eggcup full of
black ink and olive oil, and feathers as brushes. She had lined up
feathers across the newspaper with which she had covered the
kitchen table, and was breathing shallowly, so that they wouldn't
blow away, laboriously dipping a feather in the eggcup, and dabbing
at the seams of the gloves, one by one. The gloves were spread in
pairs across the table, spaced out with the tips of their thumbs
touching, fingers outstretched, like the wrong-colored gloves fluttering in the air during the chorus of a minstrel song. Doo-dah.
Doo-dah. The song Annie had been humming would not have
been a minstrel song – minstrel songs were for white people, white
people with their faces painted black – but one of the songs she had
learned from Reuben, a song Alice hadn't recognized. Perhaps he
had sung it to her when she had seen him. It was hearing this
through the schoolroom fireplace that had drawn Alice down into
the kitchen.

Alice had watched Annie from the doorway, wondering what the words to the song would be. When you knew that there were words to accompany a piece of music, when you knew these words, it was quite different to hearing music that was nothing but music. The words seemed to get in the way, interposing themselves between you and the music.

Annie hadn't known that she was there. Alice had watched her in the way that she had watched her when she had been practicing her curtsies.

"Gracious. What a lot of teeth!"

Annie had not smiled anymore when she curtsied, after Mrs. Albert Comstock had said this, not even when she was making a mock curtsy for Alice. She curtsied with eyes lowered, her face serious, making a nervous obeisance to an uncertain-tempered queen.

"Off with her head!" screamed the Queen of Hearts, her left arm rigidly horizontal in front of her, her index finger pointing accusingly.

"Off with her head!" screamed Mrs. Albert Comstock and Mrs. Goodchild in chorus.

"Off with her head!" screamed Alice.

They pointed at Annie like the Three Weird Sisters facing Macbeth, the Thane of Glamis, the Thane of Cawdor, the King hereafter.

The severed heads danced in the air, foretelling Macbeth's fate, further apparitions rising up from the cauldron.

To dream of a head severed from its trunk, and bloody, denotes that you will meet sickening disappointments, and the overthrow of your dearest hopes and anticipations.

She blew the red feather high into the air above the bed.

When she had seen Annie dabbing black ink onto gloves with feathers, she had been seized with the desire to emulate her, and had gone upstairs to copy what she was doing in every particular, taking her oldest pair of winter gloves out of the drawer. They were going to Mrs. Albert Comstock's that afternoon, and she would look impressively smart. She had taken the previous week's newspaper up to the schoolroom, teased some extra-large feathers out between the stitches in her pillow – she'd been Jane Eyre often enough; she might as well try *Wuthering Heights* and be Catherine Linton in a delirium for a while (though she would not have been able to identify the different feathers, as Catherine had) – and settled down with a bottle of Sanford's ink, unwisely choosing the indelible ink that was used to mark the laundry. She didn't have any olive oil, and used ink entirely. It would not make any difference.

Catherine Linton had said that you couldn't die if there were pigeons' feathers in a pillow. Were any of her feathers pigeons' feathers? She had dabbed away happily along the seams, in the way that she had seen Annie doing, in the places where the leather was rough and abraded. She paused occasionally to add black eyes and augment beards on the faces (all were bearded) on the front page. The one flaw in her enjoyment was that Mrs. Albert Comstock was not pictured Looking Delighted that week; otherwise she could have given her an extra-generous outgrowth of whiskers to balance The Bosom. This required advanced mathematical capabilities. It would have helped her through the afternoon, to gaze at Mrs. Albert Comstock's face, and remember how much it had been improved by the addition of a gigantic beard. Perhaps she might suggest it to her, as a Beauty Hint, though she was the sort of woman for whom hints – even when capital-lettered – were too subtle to have much effect.

At Mrs. Albert Comstock's – impatient to flaunt her gentility – she had removed her renovated gloves with ostentatious elegance, to reveal hands that were striped like a zebra's bottom with indelible ink, where the undried ink had seeped through.

"Gracious."

As with zebras' bottoms, so with teeth, as Mrs. Albert Comstock conveyed her amused disapproval by revealing – *click!* – her size sixteen smile. Ha, ha, ha, ha could not be far behind. Alice tried to explain what had happened, and ha, ha, ha, ha had – she had been correct in her assumption – made its tee-hee-heeingly infuriating snorting sound.

Later, she'd heard them – Mrs. Albert Comstock and Mrs. Goodchild – making sniggering remarks to each other about Annie, and feathers, and black ink. Alice had learned to cultivate the art of looking in a different direction as she listened in to their conversations. Mrs. Albert Comstock and Mrs. Goodchild appeared to be under the erroneous impression that ears were like eyes, and needed to be focused on what they were noting to be able to work. Between their sniggers, Alice had picked up certain phrases, not fully understanding what they meant, as she stared across at the painting of Albert Comstock, lost in the contemplation of its enormous loveliness.

"A *large* bowl of black ink."

Snigger.

"Do you think he needs to use an ostrich feather?"

(Extra-loud snigger at this point.)

"*Several* ostrich feathers, I should imagine."

Snigger.

"Can you imagine?"

Snigger.

"Keep her fresh and shining."

Snigger.

"I think *she's* under a cloud, don't you?"

(That expression again, and it caused another extra-loud snigger.)

"She's *come to grief.*"

Snigger, snigger, snigger.

'Twas summer, the darkie was gay.

No. This darkie had come to grief. No gaiety for her.

Snigger.

All coons look alike to me.

("Coons" rhymed with "tunes." Sing those tunes, coons! Sing those tunes! Make sure that you pronounce the words *properly*!)

Gracious.

Whatdoyoumacallit?

My word.
Thingamajig.
If I might be permitted.
(She would be.)
Whatsit?
Darkie.
Darkie.
Snigger.
Snigger, snigger.
(*Snigger* sounded – *Snigger, snigger, snigger* again – like "nigger." *Snigger.*)

Annie walked amidst the sunshine, but rain rained on her alone, a little black cloud that followed her about, and cast her shadow before her, so that people moved away to avoid the darkness.

A little water hadn't cleared Alice of the deed of zebra-bottomed hands. She was so covered in ink that if she'd applied Eureka Ink Eradicator she'd have disappeared completely from sight. She had rubbed, rubbed away for what seemed like weeks – Yet, here's a spot – a Lady Macbeth ensanguined with black blood, slaughtering an entire court in a *Titus Andronicus* bloodbath as she enthusiastically sang minstrel songs. She dreamed – *Stab!* – of Mrs. Albert Comstock – *Stab!* – with the light brown – *Stab!* – hair. The more she remembered the sniggers she'd heard, the more enthusiastically she imagined the stabbings, in the way that she'd found that to thump herself on her breast helped to take away the pain of certain thoughts.

Ha – *Stab!* – ha – *Stab!* – ha – *Stab!* – ha – *Stab!*

"V" is for Vengeance.

"V" is for Villainy.

"V" is for Very Enjoyable Indeed.

It was always Mrs. Albert Comstock and Mrs. Goodchild she stabbed, as she thought of the way they'd sniggered about Annie. The wooden doll's head was mashed to the texture of well-chewed licorice root when there was no flavor left, the tongue all black, and

610

the fibers whitened to the color of long thin whiskery leeks' roots. "Lickerish" meant greedy, lustful, lecherous. She imagined a big red tongue licking wetly, noisily, slurpily turning black as it licked away the ink on her hands, the ink in all the books, until everything was white again, and no written words remained.

After the stabs, the slurps.

She'd been stabbing Papa also, though he was someone they had been sniggering about, not someone doing the sniggering. She stabbed extra hard when she thought of him. In most productions of *Hamlet*, Hamlet "pranced about" (this was Mrs. Albert Comstock's insightful phrase: she was a woman who possessed a keen critical mind, a rare grasp of the essentials of world literature) for nearly four hours. After an hour and a half, the mighty Mrs. Albert Comstock buttocks would be shifting restlessly, and her corsets creaking like the timbers of a sailing ship in a storm, and she would be talking even more — and even more loudly — than usual.

In Alice's production (she had thought about it in lingering detail), the Ghost of Hamlet's Father — after his demand for revenge, after his description of his murder — would say "Remember me" and Hamlet would leap upon him and stab him to the heart with a cry of "Then, venom, to thy work." It was a dagger that he saw before him, and — unlike Macbeth's — this one *was* sensible to feeling as to sight.

Curse him!

Stab!

Curse him!

Stab!

Curse him!

Stab!

STAB ELSINORE'S SOVEREIGN!

The play would be over before the end of Act One, Scene Five, and everyone could leave the theatre in ample time for a decent meal without having to sit through the rest of it. Mrs. Albert Comstock would be thrilled. The venom was slow-working, but it poisoned the heart.

"V" is for Venom.

Hamlet's Father was also named Hamlet.

Hamlet stabbed through the breath-stained glass of the looking-glass and destroyed the misty reflection of himself. It was what Dorian Gray had done. It was what Frankenstein's creature had done. It was what Dr. Jekyll had tried to do. It was what she had tried to do, telling Dr. Wolcott Ascharm Webster what she saw in clouds, what she'd seen in dreams, the distorted images of her inner self. She'd talk, and she'd be cured. The rest would be silence, and in the silence there would be a long-sought-for stillness.

(Rather silence than the voices she heard, through the walls and up the chimney, the music in the distance. Rather blank white paper than the written troubles of the brain.)

In her version of *Macbeth* (this was the result of much studying of the panel in the schoolroom: scholarship took many forms) the Third Apparition — the Bloody Child — instead of prophesying that "none of woman born shall harm Macbeth" said (this was a *much* better idea than Shakespeare's was, Alice thought, and so did Charlotte) "no man of woman born shall harm Macbeth." In her version the Witches' trick was with the word "man." It was (the idea had been like a revelation) a *woman* — Lady Macbeth, in her madness, his own loving wife — who killed him, lopping off his head, not a man at all!

First "Give me the daggers!"; then *Boing! Boing! Boing!*

Who would have thought Macbeth to have had so much blood in him?

Those hands would ne'er be clean.

What was done could not be undone.

Macduff's late revelation that he was not "born" because he was "from his mother's womb untimely ripp'd" always struck her as cheating, feeble playing with words, certainly not one of Shakespeare's better efforts. No wonder Macbeth was annoyed. She'd have been *furious*. At Miss Pearsall's School for Girls these words were tactfully not explained. At Miss Pearsall's School for Girls these words were not even *printed* in their edition. It was the very words that were untimely ripp'd. Wombs did not exist at Miss Pearsall's School for Girls, where the human form was comprehensively lopped of all dubious portions, all possible sources of not-very-niceness, Mrs. Albert Comstock and Mrs. Goodchild shriekingly unleashed, weighed down with razor-sharp scissors and chisels, demolishing great swathes of Ladies' and Gentlemen's Districts like the most uninhibited of New York City's property developers. In their edition Macduff announced – it was rather self-important of him to employ the third person – "let the angel whom thou still hast serv'd/Tell thee Macduff was untimely born," leaving most of the class baffled. You felt, in their edition, that Macduff (a perpetually embarrassed Dr. Twemlow of Fife, scarlet and twitching as the wind whipped at his kilt) would have blushed a becoming pink, and diffidently informed Macbeth that Macduff was – ahem – untimely – ahem – born, with much embarrassed hesitating and spluttering on the ahems. Mary Benedict and (less convincingly) Miss Swanstrom did their best to look knowing at this point.

Another red feather circled between them, and landed on the white bedspread. It was the wrong color to be a pigeon feather, the feather escaping from the sleeper's pillow and so permitting death to follow. Now – she continued to look around her – she was inside the little wooden box she had imagined from the other side of the door, inside the illuminated interior of the violin, and the sound-holes – the italic "f" and the reversed "s" – now opened into darkness.

That "f" shape always made her think of music, and of the use of the long "s" in the old eight-volume edition of *Clarissa* – *Clarifsa* – that she had read, the events of the novel taking place to the sound of chamber music, sad sounds in small rooms. The wind was louder in the room than she had imagined it would be. She felt small and tucked away, like a doll stored by a child who had become too old, something hidden inside a cigar box beneath the elaborately decorated, brightly colored lid. She did not like this image, thinking of the smell of cigar smoke on clothes and beards. It was a time to talk, to share confidences and tell stories, not a time to think of Bearded Ones.

She explained about the bird, and began to feel tearful again.

"Have you had a d-d-dream?" she asked Annie, to change the subject.

Annie shook her head. No dream.

Alice unwrapped the Dream Book from the scarf, the ritualistic beginning of an interpretation, as if Annie had said yes. Annie asked her if *she* had had dreams, and she said no, wondering if Annie was lying to her, as she was lying to Annie. She flicked, apparently casually, through the little book – *Album, Dragon, House, Morgue, Pulpit, Stone Mason* (all things had hidden meanings) – and stopped at *Wind*.

She could not remember, years later, what it had said, but Rosobell's *What's in a Dream* said: *To dream of hearing the wind soughing, denotes that you will wander in estrangement from one whose life is empty without you.* It was disconcerting when something in which you did not believe told something that seemed like a truth, like a prayer being answered when you did not believe in God. For a moment, the feeling had come across her that she should ask Mrs. Alexander Diddecott to take her to one of her séances, so that she could call up Annie and talk with her again. Annie would be a little girl, and Alice would be an ugly, peculiar spinster, a madwoman in a schoolroom. Annie would be frightened of her. "It's *me*, Annie. It's *me*." Like she had imagined happening with Papa's "friend," like Faithful, Annie would turn away from her, shuddering at the sight of the person she had become, turning away from her empty open arms.

"Are you *sure* you haven't had a d-d-dream?" she asked Annie. "A while ago, if not last night?"

She was hoping that Annie would say yes, and then Alice would lie to her. She knew that she was going to lie to Annie. It came to her all of a sudden.

Annie said yes.

"Well . . ." she began.

She paused, struggling, wanting to use the same formula. It had to be the same words, or — Annie felt — it wouldn't work, and she had said that she hadn't had a dream.

"I had . . ." Alice prompted, letting her know that she understood.

"I had a dream last night . . ."

It was said in a rush. The two of them were hurrying toward each other.

She looked straight at Alice, the direct look of the dark eyes.

For a moment, Alice saw her at a distance, far away and out of reach, a small figure alone in bright moonlight with a painted board behind her bearing the words *Dreamed A Dream*. It was like a sign — *Take care. She bites* — that she should wear upon her back like a knapsack, or like the burden upon Christian's back, a sign defining what she was, what she had done.

"It *was* last night."

"Liar," Alice said teasingly, meaning not that she was lying now, but that she had been lying when she had said that she hadn't had a dream. It was a word that could be used only with someone to whom you were very close. Annie knew what she meant.

"Disgraceful," she said. "A corrupting influence on a young child."

"So much now becomes clear."

Annie reached between them, to pick up the red feather, and then picked at Alice's hair, plucking an exotically colored — Turkey red — turkey. She pulled away so many feathers — they tugged; it felt like they really were being plucked from her skin — that Alice thought she must look like a Red Indian brave ready for war on the shores of Gitche Gumee. Her war paint would smudge the sheets.

> . . . *Wash the war-paint from your faces,*
> *Wash the blood-stains from your fingers,*
> *Bury your war-clubs and your weapons,*
> *Break the red stone from this quarry,*

615

Mold and make it into Peace-Pipes,
Take the reeds that grow beside you,
Deck them with your brightest feathers . . .

"Deck them with your brightest feathers."

She quoted the line from *The Song of Hiawatha* as Annie fanned out four or five feathers against her nightgown. She hadn't known then that the aviary had been damaged in the storm, and that the little dead bird from outside her window was one of many, though she knew that the aviary was the place where she'd seen it. She tried to visualize the signs that identified the birds, trying to recall the name of the little red bird. As you stood with your back to *The Children's Hour*, you could see the little paintings of the birds in front of the glass structure, and the black and red lettering saying what they were.

Annie held the feathers up above her face, and blew at them, scattering thistledown or dandelion seeds. She smiled at Alice as they floated between them.

". . . and this is what I dreamed."

She pointed at the feathers, quick little stabbing motions, setting them spinning around and floating upwards again.

"Feathers were falling downward, all around me, many more than these, as if I'd burst the mattress when I was making the bed. It was like being out in a snowstorm, like being out tonight. There was a wind howling, but the feathers weren't being blown. They were falling straight down, and mounting up around me. I thought that I was going to be buried under feathers, suffocated. I looked upward . . ."

She moved her head, looking up toward the white boards of the ceiling, as the feathers fell unnoticed on the bedspread, closing her eyes. She always reenacted what she had dreamed, making Alice feel what she had felt.

". . . and had to close my eyes because the feathers were falling into them. It felt nice. They were warm, not cold. I opened my eyes again, and shaded them . . ."

She brought her hands up above her eyes, shielding them from bright sunshine, a dazzle on fallen snow.

"... and saw that there were birds in the sky, and the feathers were falling from them. The birds weren't singing. The birds couldn't sing. They were opening and closing their beaks, but everything happened in silence. The feathers fell more and more thickly, and after a while they became cold. I thought that the birds could have no more feathers, and that they must be cold, and I felt that coldness. I wanted to make them warm again, to make them sing."

She stopped, looked across at Alice, with the usual self-deprecating shrug of her shoulders, the rueful twist to her mouth, expecting that Alice would laugh at her for sounding so serious, for thinking that dreams had meanings. There was an opening formula, and there was a closing formula, and now she spoke that.

"That was my dream."

She added a little more.

"And now you have come, and brought my dream in with you."

She moved her hands over where the feathers had settled, stirring them into motion.

"I am your d-d-dreams come true!"

"My dreams come true! Though you haven't brought enough feathers."

"It was a very small b-b-bird."

Alice opened the Dream Book. She actually turned to what would have been the right page for *Feathers*. There was no entry for this subject, but she was not going to read what was written in the book. She remembered to bring the book close to her face, peering, like someone struggling to read without her spectacles. On the left-hand side, halfway down, was an entry for *Father*. She refocused her eyes, so that the words on the page were even more blurred, and pretended to read.

"To d-d-dream of feathers is a very g-g-good omen," she said, trying to use the right sort of language. "It foretells happiness after a p-p-period of sadness, when all that you have been hoping for

617

comes about." Annie had seemed so sad recently. She even remembered to struggle over certain words — "omen," "sadness," "hoping" — a short-sighted struggler who couldn't see them the first time, and had to reread them.

She also remembered to look into Annie's eyes as she lied, smiling to show that she was pleased for her with the interpretation.

She riffled forward nearer to the beginning of the book, to the page with the word *Birds*. Alice had developed a system of looking up the meanings of all the elements of the dreams, and trying to construct a meaning for all the different interpretations put together. "It is a special gift, to be able to reconcile the variant readings into a true interpretation," she had said impressively, like the seventh child of a seventh child, one with powers granted to a favored few. This time there was an entry, but she did not read it. Opposite it, on the right-hand page, were *Birth*, *Birthday*, and *Birthday Presents*, the flickering candles on the cake blown out. She knew that she had not looked up *Feathers* before, but could not remember about *Birds*. Annie would remember what she had said. She would have to be careful. Annie had not responded to her smile.

"To d-d-dream of b-b-birds is to d-d-dream of freedom," she said. This sounded convincing. This must surely be true. She hadn't linked the feathers with the meaning she had given to them, though most of the interpretations seemed oddly arbitrary. The more arbitrary, the more convincing, perhaps. For some reason, the image of Roman household gods came into her mind, briefly. "You will fly away to a new p-p-place where you will be happy . . ."

The happier she tried to make the meaning of the dream sound, the sadder Annie looked. She began to improvise further, trying to make her voice sound matter-of-fact, someone reading symptoms from a medical encyclopædia, so that an illness could be diagnosed. She was saving a life. Alone, in a snowbound cabin, miles from anywhere, only she could take the necessary steps.

"In this new p-p-place you will be able to b-b-begin a new life where your d-d-dreams really will come true. Many p-p-people will love you. All the old unhappiness will be left in the p-p-past. You must not forget all the p-p-people you leave b-b-behind when . . ."

"Freedom," "happy," "new," "true," "unhappiness," "forget": these were the words on which she pretended to struggle, holding the page even closer to her face. She was trying to give Annie the dream she wanted to have, the meaning for a dream she'd never dreamed, though she had used too many words that made her stutter. She'd used too many words altogether. Should she have mentioned becoming more beautiful, and being respected – she had mentioned being loved – or would Annie remember that this was the meaning for a dream about geraniums, not birds, not feathers? She saw Annie's face as it had been throughout the whole of a summer's day, sun-filled, eyes half closed, staring at the red petals so closely that it was as if she was the one who was shortsighted, and not Alice, concentrating as she was concentrating now. The meaning she had hoped for hadn't happened in sunshine; Alice might be able to make her believe that the meaning had happened in coldness and snow.

She had gone on for far too long. The interpretations in Annie's book tended to be enigmatically brief, and of an oracular vagueness that could be stretched to mean most things. Annie was smiling at her, rather sadly.

"'Where your dreams really will come true,'" she quoted, the inflexion of her eyebrow, if not of her voice, making this a question.

"That's what it says," Alice said, not sounding convincing even to herself. "Your d-d-dreams really will come true." She said it without the quotation marks, trying to make it sound like something that was going to happen. She did not succeed.

"Liar."

This time it was Annie who said the word. She said it fondly, lovingly.

"Your d-d-dreams really . . ."

"Liar."

Alice faltered to a close.

Annie picked up the feathers, and blew them into the air again.

"'Happiness after a period of sadness,'" she said. "'All that you have been hoping for comes about.'"

She reached across, and took the book from Alice, touching the words on the page in the way that Alice had visualized her touching the newspaper.

"No," she said. "Those aren't the words I can feel here."

She touched her breast, the gesture Alice often found herself making, and repeated what she had said, stressing the last word.

"Those aren't the words I can feel *here*."

(She should have bowed down upon herself.)

(She should have had her arms clasped tightly across her stomach, attempting to warm and soothe a new source of pain.

("I feel it *here*," she should have been saying. "I feel it *here*.")

She touched Alice's face. The transferring of her hand from her breast to the face — it was a cold, dry little hand — was like a gesture that meant love. It was oddly dignified.

"You're kind, Alice. You've always been kind to me."

"Isn't Mama kind?"

"She brought me this comforter."

Annie lifted up the bedspread, and they touched the comforter underneath it, all those feathers. The tiny sharp quills dug into their fingers like the grip of small birds' claws, or pens with which to write in miniature books, handwriting that could barely be read.

"*That's a turkey's,*" Catherine Linton murmured to herself, "*and this is a wild duck's; and this is a pigeon's . . . And here's a moorcock's; and this — I should know it among a thousand — it's a lapwing's. Bonny bird; wheeling over our heads in the middle of the moor . . . we saw its nest in the winter, full of little skeletons.*"

The first things Alice had looked up in *What's in a Dream*, twenty-five years later, had been *Feathers* and *Birds*. Then she had looked up *Wind, Moon*, other things.

620

To dream of seeing feathers falling around you, denotes that your burdens in life will be light and easily borne.

That was the first meaning she had read, very like the one — she had remembered every word — she had invented.

To dream of molting and songless birds, denotes merciless and inhuman treatment of the outcast and fallen by people of wealth.

That was the second meaning she had read.

It was a special gift, to be able to reconcile the variant readings into a true interpretation.

21

"Look."

Alice leaned across, and picked up the top letter from the pile written by Reuben. There was something she wanted to show Annie. She imagined touching the letter, and then touching her breast, in the way that Annie had just done with the Dream Book. The name was printed in large capital letters on the envelope, so that Annie would recognize it more easily because of this.

MISS ANNIE CLEMENT, In care of Mr. and Mrs. L. Pinkerton, 7 Chestnut Street, Longfellow Park, New York City . . .

The band of blue light from the colored glass went right across the deep blue paper as she held it, like something being illuminated for an important scene.

"May I write on this?"

Annie looked doubtful.

"I won't spoil it."

Alice looked for a pen or pencil, and then picked up one of the struck matches from the base of the candlestick. Using this as a writing implement, her face close against the envelope, she printed her own name in charcoaled capital letters, exactly beneath Annie's. There was a good wide space.

ANNIE

Then Alice became a little embarrassed, not sure of how to continue, how to explain the point that had seemed so important when she had first noticed it. She knew Annie would understand.

"Can you see?" she asked. "Your name, and my name?"

Annie took the envelope from her.

"They begin with the same letter," she said. "They end with the same letter. They have the same number of letters in them." She smiled at Alice. "They *belong* together."

She understood.

"We begin the same, and we end the same." The next bit was more difficult to say, but she had thought it out beforehand. "You are my heart, containing me," Alice said. "I am your heart, containing you."

She was reaching out toward an emotion she had never experienced, trying to grasp it in her hand, and feel it. She wanted to know what it was like. She had read about it. Often, she had read about it.

Annie hadn't laughed, hadn't looked puzzled.

"Of course, it doesn't work with 'P-P-Pinkerton' and 'Clement,'" Alice added. She let Annie know that she knew she had a second name. "I tried to do something with them."

(She'd tried numerology with "Alice Pinkerton" and "Annie Clement," trying to reduce the letters of the two names to the same number. She'd copied out the table of interpretation from one of Mrs. Alexander Diddecott's books. "A," "J," and "S" had a value of 1, "B," "K," and "T" had a value of 2, and so on, and – though she'd labored long, struggling with a baffling arithmetical puzzle, trying to cheat – she had never been able to produce any final name number but 8 for her name, and 7 for Annie's, numbers with different meanings.)

Annie picked up another spent match, and drew a line through the two opening "A"s and two closing "E"s.

"Can you make a word out of the letters that are left?" she asked, as if this might confirm a kinship.

Alice looked dubious, and thought.

"You can almost make 'CLINIC,'" she said, after a while. This didn't sound too hopeful.

"I don't like 'CLINIC,'" Annie said.

If you dream that you are a patient in a hospital, you will have a contagious disease in your community, and will narrowly escape affliction. If you visit patients there you will hear distressing news of the absent.

She rubbed where she had drawn through the "A"s and the "E"s.

"Is it better if you use the full names? Do they make a word?"

She picked up the newspaper from beside where the Dream Book had been, and smoothed it on the bed between them. There wasn't really a "between," they were so jammed in, and the opened personals pages rested upon them both. Alice thought that Annie was asking her to read something, and began to lean forward, screwing up her eyes.

"I'm trying to find a space, for you," Annie said, "a space where you can write."

She turned the page over, and a Griswold's Girl hovered over a bottle of Griswold's Discovery, a large area of whiteness between the two of them, reaching out toward it like God on the point of giving life to Adam. The Griswold's Girl beamed rapturously as Alice thought for a moment, and then wrote – underneath *DISCOVER GRISWOLD'S! THE PURE CURE!* – "ANNIE C" and "ALICE P."

"'IN A NICE P-P-PLACE,'" she announced eventually.

"'In an ice place'?" Annie asked, mishearing. "Is that what it says?"

"A *nice* p-p-place, but I like 'ice p-p-place.' I *p-p-prefer* 'ice p-p-place.'"

"Is this where we are?"

"Ice."

"Aren't you warm yet?"

"My toes are wriggling with coziness."

"Nice, not ice. Tell me that poem again. The Annie Collection."

"'For Annie'?"

"No, the other one. 'Annie of Tharaw.'"

> "Annie of Tharaw, my true love of old,
> She is my life, and my g-g-goods, and my g-g-gold . . ."

"My life, my goods, my gold," Annie repeated.

"You said it wrong. You didn't say g-g-g."

"G-g-good."

"I don't know it all by heart," Alice admitted. "I read it to you from a b-b-book."

"Do you remember the part about the wind?" Annie asked. "The wind and the bad weather?"

The wind seemed to be penetrating down the interior corridor, blowing through and dipping the candle-flame downward.

> ". . . Then come the wild weather, come wind or come
> snow . . ."

Alice started, uncertainly. This wasn't right.

> ". . . We will stand by each other, however it b-b-blow . . ."

"'We will stand by each other.' That's the bit I remember."

"There's another b-b-bit, about hail b-b-beating down, and rains falling."

"'The more it beats, the more they fall, the stronger grows the love . . .' Something like that."

"Yes."

"There's something about forests and ice. I'll follow you through forests. I'll follow you through ice. Not that, but something like that."

"In an ice p-p-place."

The wind in the corridor outside Annie's room shrieked again. It was like the end of "The Eve of St. Agnes," as Madeline and Porphyro escaped from the mansion, gliding like phantoms. *The arras, rich with horseman, hawk, and hound, /Flutter'd in the besieging wind's uproar; /And the long carpets rose along the gusty floor.* Annie shivered. She was so close that Alice felt her shaking, and shivered alongside her.

She opened *At the Back of the North Wind* at Chapter IV, "North Wind," the right place to read, words that might work better than the interpretation of the dream had done.

"... There was a great roaring, for the wind was dashing against London like a sea; b-b-but at North Wind's b-b-back, Diamond, of course..."

– "'... of course...'" Annie mouthed –

"... felt nothing at all. He was in p-p-perfect calm. He could hear the sound of it, that was all..."

The page had been marked with a neatly cut strip of pretty patterned paper, a place at which Annie had often opened the novel, to look at the picture of Diamond curled up on North Wind's back. He was not hanging on, clutching at her shoulders to remain safe, but lay against her – small as a new-born baby – warm and half-asleep in bed, his eyes open but sleepily unfocused, his hands loosely cupped beneath his chin. She was young, she was beautiful, her left hand rested against the place where her heart was, and her eyes – also – seemed to be seeing something far away. North Wind's long flowing hair swept around both of them like the swirling eddies of water in a fast-flowing stream, filling the greater proportion of the illustration. He was lying beneath a pool of deep, clear water, curled up very still amongst the smooth pebbles at the bottom, perfectly at peace, drowned in a bath of the tresses of Annie, like Tom in *The Water Babies*, sunk down into the cool, cool water, hearing the sound of church bells in his head. Annie would lie on her side in bed, looking at this scene, until it filled her eyes so completely that sight overwhelmed the other senses, and she did not hear the wind outside, did not feel the drafts that rippled the candle-flame. As she looked at this picture, she would touch the words that Alice had just read, and she would feel the words here on the page, and *here* in her heart. She would recognize the feel, the sight, of certain words.

. . . Diamond . . .

. . . of course . . .

. . . perfect calm . . .

Alice flicked further forward through the novel, to the end of Chapter IX, to a passage she did not read aloud. North Wind had taken Diamond to the north side of an iceberg, and placed him on a ledge of ice in a cave near the water. A page or so further on, and Diamond was walking on the shore of a land made of ice, begging North Wind to let him go into the country at her back. To do this, he had to walk on, treat her as an open door, and go right through her. He walked toward her instantly. When he reached her knees, he put out his hand to lay it on her, but nothing was there save an intense cold. He walked on. Then all grew white about him; and the cold stung him like fire. He walked on still, groping through the whiteness. It thickened about him. At last, it got into his heart, and he lost all sense. Whereas in common faints all grows black about you, he felt swallowed up in whiteness. It was like a death, a letting-go, like Tom slipping beneath the surface of the water because he must be clean, he must be clean, washing away his blackness. She felt swallowed up in whiteness herself, in the unprinted sections of pages at the beginnings and ends of chapters, on both sides of the illustrations, in the wide margins of the short-lined songs where there were no words, and – most of all – in the whiteness of the unwritten-on pages of her journals. She wondered if Annie felt the silence that she felt in these places.

Crunch.

Crunch.

Crunch.

The feet crunched through the ice, like Papa's feet crunching through the bones of the babies she imagined were buried secretly in their garden. Frankenstein's creature, after he had leaned over Frankenstein's lifeless body and asked him to pardon him, sprang from the cabin window out on to the ice raft, and the waves bore him away. The last sight of him, like the first sight of him, was of a solitary figure surrounded by ice, moving away into darkness and distance.

Alice wanted to look around for photographs in the little room, to peer into the blurry vagueness to see if there were any likenesses of Reuben, a mother and father, on the shelf beyond the letters. That was where photographs would be, so that someone who couldn't read could see them, someone lying in bed listening to the wind. She hadn't liked to ask Annie about a mother and father, in case it was something she did not want to talk about, and she had never mentioned them. Did she *have* a mother and father? The only letters that ever arrived for Annie were letters from Reuben. If you couldn't read, if you couldn't write, how could you let people far away know that you loved them?

She shouldn't look. She stared down at the Griswold's Girl.

THE PURE CURE.

Cures Loneliness!

Cures Sadness!

Cures Orphanhood!

The engraved face was all crinkled, like the cracked surface of an old oil painting. She sniffed the sheet of newspaper, and the strongest smell – stronger than the smell of cheap inky paper – was the smell of onions. If she sniffed for long enough, tears might come into her eyes. This reminded her that this was a page that Annie had saved, a page that she might have been waiting to have read to her. She had unwrapped the onions, and found the page waiting for her, a little unexpected extra on a dark morning. Alice turned it over to the personals on the other side, the crackling of the paper loud in the small room, to the world of Madame Etoile and her like.

"Shall I shed light on the tenebrous?" Alice asked.

This was another formula they went through.

"'Tenebrous'?" Annie asked. This was the password, the word repeated with a question mark.

"Dark, shadowy, hidden by fog."

"And ice."

"And windblown snow. Shall I read them out?"

She was smoothing the paper, already as well smoothed as if Annie had ironed it after she had finished the sheets. Perhaps there would be a faint smell of onions on the pillow shams, bringing tears to the eyes, sad dreams to the sleeper.

"Yes," Annie said. "Yes, please. That was one of the things I've been thinking about. I've been trying to work out what some of the words might say."

"Madame Etoile is here again."

Madame Etoile was always there, always telling all you wanted to know, always seeing the past, the present, and the future, always using the same words in her advertisements, and Alice did not read out what she had to say. They knew already. Her address was one of those that she had printed out for Annie. Alice imagined Annie approaching Madame Etoile's to discover what her future was going to be, and then forgetting the address. She would stop kind-faced passers-by, and point at the printed details she was unable to read for herself. There were beggars like that, people who never spoke, too proud to put their pleas into speech, silently indicating the words on the notices they held up before them. *PLEase HElp* the words would say, moving in and out of capital letters like the sign in George Cruikshank's illustration for *Oliver Twist*. *MY CHild is ILL and I AM HUNgry.* They held the words before them, people Particularly Recommending Oldermann & Oldermann For Boys' School Attire, their heads bowed. Alice sometimes gave them a few coins, if Mama said she could, and was embarrassed if they thanked her, and embarrassed when she felt annoyed if they did not.

She read out the personals for a long time, this time genuinely struggling to read some of the blurred words. Annie nodded, and occasionally asked questions, but did not ask Alice to write down any addresses. She was waiting for something. After a while, Alice strayed across several columns into a new area, one that she still thought was advertising fortune-tellers, seers of what the future would bring. These seemed to be even more rigidly exclusive of gentlemen than Madame Etoile, and Annie became awkwardly alert.

This was what she had been waiting for.

"A LADIES' SPECIALIST," Alice began, and had read the advertisement all the way through, without especially noticing what it was she was reading, when Annie asked her to read it again. "A LADIES' SPECIALIST," she repeated, "with many years' (more than fifteen) success in this city, g-g-guarantees certain relief to ladies, with or without medicine, at one interview. Unfortunates please call. RELIEF IS CERTAIN. Delightful rooms available if required. Dr. Argersinger. Residence . . ."

For the first time, Annie asked her to write down the name and the address. On the back of one of Reuben's envelopes, she printed the details with the heads of spent matches.

The wording of the advertisements tended to be similar, sharing a common restricted vocabulary, to ease communication with those they sought to find. They made great use of capital letters; they were pronouncements from the LORD. They presented themselves as important announcements, not something as vulgar as advertisements. Each time, Annie asked Alice to write down the name and the address.

"IMPORTANT TO FEMALES," Alice read, "Dr. and Madame . . ." – the Mesdames were out in force where beauty, clairvoyance, and certain relief were involved – ". . . Unthank (TWENTY YEARS' P-P-PRACTICE IN THIS CITY) g-g-guarantee certain relief to ladies, with or without medicine, at one interview. Ladies from a distance p-p-provided with p-p-pleasant rooms. ELECTRICITY scientifically applied . . ."

Electricity was always a guarantee of scientific respectability, a place at the farthest frontier of progress. You'd be warm, you'd be well lighted, you'd lie there — slumbering beatifically — as arcs of power pulsed and sparked around you. There'd be no need for spills or matches, no acrid skeins of smoke to make the tears well up.

Another one she read — they filled about a quarter of a column — was: *SURE CURE FOR LADIES IN TROUBLE. Consultation and advice FREE. Certain to have THE DESIRED EFFECT within twenty-four hours, without any injurious medicines or instruments used. ELEGANT ROOMS. Madame Roskosch . . .*

Madame Roskosch was scarcely a French name, yet Alice — as she used to do with the advertisements for Madame Etoile (perhaps it was the shared "Madame" — with an "e" on the end — that made her do it) read out this last with an exaggerated French accent, raising her voice for the capital letters. "LADIEES IN TROUBAIL" — she read — "'Ave ze dezaiyaired" — she'd giggled a little over her version of "desired," though Annie had remained serious-faced — "effect" she read, "wizzout any enjuriars medeecines or enstruments used. ELEGAINT ROOMS . . ."

Dr. Argersinger.

Dr. and Madame Unthank.

Madame Roskosch.

These were the three that Annie settled on. She listened as Alice reread the advertisements she had picked out, and narrowed them down to these. Alice underlined and starred them on the back of the envelope, and then rewrote them neatly on the back of another envelope. Just like *Album*, *Dragon*, *House*, *Morgue*, *Pulpit*, and *Stone Mason*, some of the words and phrases — *certain relief, unfortunates, interview, scientifically, sure, desired effect* — had hidden meanings. This much she could sense. She did not like the three names she had marked. Argersinger, Unthank, & Roskosch. They had the sound of one of those shadowy, corrupt businesses in a Charles Dickens novel — *Bleak House* or *Our Mutual Friend* — lurking on an upper floor at the head of a darkened staircase in one of the decaying and squalid courts or alleys of the city: Whitechapel or St. Giles, places where the mud was deepest, the fog densest, and the poverty the most desperate. It would be something to do with the legal profession, with corruption, with years of litigation, and squandered inheritances.

She put two stars beside Madame Roskosch, because Annie asked her to. "'Sure,'" Annie had repeated in her usual voice, not attempting to copy Alice's French accent. "'Free,' 'certain,' 'desired,' 'elegant.'" The word "ladies" was clearly a worry to her, but whether this was because of her age or because of her class, Alice was unable to decide. *TROUBLE* was the word that registered most with Alice (the capital letters were like a shouted warning), and *injurious* and *instruments* were also vaguely alarming. Fortune-telling seemed attended by hazards that she had never noticed before. No instruments were used, so she knew that there would be no music, and everything would happen in silence. This idea of silence worried Alice more than anything else. If there were instruments, they would lie, dull and dusty with disuse, propped at angles against cane chairs, and not shiny and sparkling with vigorous polishing, reflecting the features of a proud and careful owner bent over them and making beautiful music.

Annie closed her eyes, clenched her hands in the way she did when she was willing the meaning of a dream to come true, and chose Madame Roskosch. It was like a nonreligious version of Mrs. Alexander Diddecott's random consultations of the Bible, drawn to the right words by a power greater than she was.

On another envelope Alice wrote out Madame Roskosch's name and address all by themselves, this time with three stars in front of them, under the heading *THE DESIRED EFFECT*. She repeated them several times until Annie knew them by heart, just as she knew "For Annie."

"Madame Roskosch," she said. "Madame Roskosch," nodding, learning a new word, dark, shadowy, hidden by fog. "Read me the address again. What was the number?"

Alice read her the address again. The number was thirty-seven.

Alice handed her the envelope, and Annie folded it carefully and placed it within the bosom of her nightgown, like a girl in a novel secreting a forbidden smuggled-in love letter, one that she would take out, unfold, and reread – over and over – whenever she felt sad or lonely.

In this way, without knowing it, using a funny French accent, she helped Annie to die.

22

"P-P-Papa . . ."

The snow would mount up the stairs, like the cool blue-green light of the afternoons, and fill the house, until everything was ice. It hissed through the keyhole and beneath the door of the study, like the exhalation of frozen breath from a giant sleeper. It did not occur to her that it was odd to have snow inside the house. It was there, that was all. In the flickering glow of her night-light, she was standing in the snow outside a stranger's house, about to begin the words of a carol.

"We three kings of Orient are . . ."

"Orient" would not go down well in Longfellow Park. "Orient" was seething with the troops of Midian, all of them well armed with sharp-edged primitive weapons. "Orient" was where the faces were inscrutable, but what they held in their hands was all too readily scrutable. "Orient" was where they bowed down to wood and stone, gods that were in the plural, and without capital letters, and too brightly decorated. *Idols. Graven images.* That was what they worshiped, and the words sounded ominously Old Testament, something violently objected to by the LORD. There'd be flames and smiting, and the earth would gape beneath the ungodly. *Thou shalt not bow down thyself to them, nor serve them: for I the LORD thy God am a jealous God, visiting the iniquity of the fathers upon the children unto the third and fourth generation of them that hate me . . .* (The

LORD had a propensity for punishing children for the sins of the fathers.) "Orient" was where you couldn't get a decent night's sleep because of the constant hammering of nails — such people had no consideration — for the nonstop night and day crucifixions. "Orient" was where they didn't even possess a proper alphabet or proper music, a place of opium-induced nightmares, a place fastidiously avoided by God. "Orient" was where it was far too hot, in preparation for the flames of hell that awaited the pagan hordes that dwelt there. They wouldn't bring gold; they wouldn't bring frankincense and myrrh. They'd bring the means of death with them, cunningly disguised as gifts, learning from the wanton excesses of the under-clad knee-flaunting Greeks.

> . . . *Bearing gifts we traverse afar*
> *Field and fountain, moor and mountain,*
> *Following yonder star . . .*

"P-P-Papa . . ."

Again, there was the high singing sound in her ears, the sensation of being distant from all that was around her, in a dream, observing things happening to herself with a cool, dispassionate interest. After a night with little sleep, the dreams were arriving with the morning, and she was sleepwalking whilst wide awake. She felt disassociated from everything around her, remote in time as much as remote in place. There was no star to follow. All the stars had fallen, and she was lost and wandering in starless darkness. There were no futures to foretell in the heavens. Gemini had faded from the sky. There was no Aries, no Pisces in the floor of heaven.

> . . . *O star of wonder, star of night,*
> *Star with royal beauty bright . . .*

It was a star of night, without beauty or brightness, leading her on into a deeper darkness, without Virgo, Libra, or Sagittarius.

633

"P-P-Papa . . ."

Papa was not to be disturbed. This was known as firmly as if he had hung a sign on the doorknob outside the room, like a guest in an hotel, and yet Alice knocked on the door. It was not a tentative tap, but a firm well-knuckled rap; he was a man who had ordered that he should be awoken for an important appointment at a certain time.

She did not call his name again.

The feast of Stephen.

She looked behind her, trying to make out the figure of a page – small, bowed over – placing his feet in her footprints, and following behind her, laden with flesh, wine, and pine logs. *Sire, the night is darker now,/And the wind grows stronger;/Fails my heart I know not how;/I can go no longer.*

> . . . *Westward leading, still proceeding,*
> *Guide us to thy perfect light . . .*

The figures on the terra-cotta panel were not representations of the Three Weird Sisters facing Macbeth. They were of herself, Allegra, and Edith, singing their carol to Papa. They were herself, Charlotte, and Mary Benedict, singing to Reynolds Templeton Seabright. They were herself, Annie, and Annie's child, Desiderata – not Joshua; she knew the child would be a girl – singing to . . .

Singing to . . .

Singing . . .

When she pushed the door, it resisted, something pushing against it from the other side. She was pushing it backward through a drift of snow, still loose and lightly packed, so that – with slight pressure – it opened into the study with a crunching sound, slowly and more slowly as it compacted the snow behind it. As it opened, looser snow gusted out like a blizzard inside the house, and her night-light was blown out. In the smoky, flaring light of a windblown gaslight, her nightgown snapped out behind her in an icy blast, she took her first steps inside the snow-filled room. Sleety drizzle drenched her hair and the front of her nightgown, gathering in her eyebrows and eyelashes, blurring all she saw, and scraps of torn paper blew into her and stuck to her cheeks and clothes, like confetti at a wind-blasted wedding. The light suspended from the ceiling swung, hissing, like that of a ship on a stormy sea, and she saw what she saw like someone blinking, darkness and brightness in rapidly flickering succession. There seemed to be more darkness than brightness, and what she saw she saw in glimpses, hurtling past lighted upper windows on the elevated railroad at night. She closed the door behind her, pushing it back without turning around, and the wind blowing through the room eased. Snow, not fire, filled the grate — the fire had long since died — and snow had drifted in through the open window — the upper sash of the left-hand window was almost fully lowered — to accumulate everywhere.

What she saw was somehow remote, far away from her, and yet the detail was intense.

It was a dark subterranean room beneath the level of the snow, like a room cut into ice, as she had once imagined Annie's room. The windows were almost totally blocked by a snowdrift, stifling the sound and power of the wind, or the door would otherwise have been slammed back. The drift continued down into the room through the opened window, a continuous smooth slope, half burying the desk, down onto and across the floor. In the top left-hand corner of the left-hand window, a little gap — the only part not yet blocked — was funneling more snow through, but all that could be seen through the panes — they were a multiplicity of small dark-backed mirrors — was the deep, windblown, layered snow. The heavy velvet tobacco-smelling drapes of the open window had fallen, or been pulled down, and the brass pole lay at an angle, projecting from the snow, as if hurled there. Snow was everywhere, incongruously heaped upon everyday domestic objects, and she felt like a survivor after an avalanche, trapped in the ruins of her home, listening for rescuers, distant, muffled voices calling her name.

"I'm here!" she should be calling, to guide them to her. "I'm here!"

She had no thoughts of what had happened, the how or why of it, the bitter cold of outside breaking through into the inside, like the strange reversals that occurred when carefully decorated inner walls — walls for displaying pictures and photographs in quiet rooms — were exposed to the elements during the demolition of a building. Forgotten drapes flapped from broken windows, and rain-drenched wallpaper hung down in strips. Her house had collapsed around her, and she was walking through snow. The books, the shelves, were buried under snow; snow covered the carpet, the chairs against the wall, the cigar lighter, the inkstand, and papers. What had once been there was hidden from view, and only her memory made her see it now. There was nothing but the snow, a continuous, untrodden swathe of smooth snow that swept in an unbroken arc from Hudson Heights, through the orchards, through the house, across the room, through the window, across the street, and down Chestnut Hill. The globes of the unlit wall lamps were filled with snow, and the photograph of the office on South Street had a miniature drift of snow across its lower half. An out-of-season storm had invaded that sunlit summer scene. Papers slapped wetly from the mantel and shelves, and were stuck at angles where they had been blown in crumpled layers against the glass of the mirror, the pictures, the windows, like fly sheets advertising cheap goods pasted to the dark exterior of a failed business. They were startlingly white in the dim underground light. Around them, and everywhere in the room, were fragments of torn paper. Papa had made his own artificial snowstorm in the room before the real snow started, tearing up page after page, ripping them up small so that no word should be legible, and throwing the pieces high into the air, so that a blizzard whirled around in the wind through the open window.

She was treading blood into the whiteness as she moved forward. She looked down and saw this. Her bare right foot had stepped through the torn wet paper and the snow into the broken

636

glass of a smashed bottle. She couldn't feel this — her feet were numbed — but she saw the blood.

All these thoughts, these impressions, happened in moments.

All she was aware of was of opening the door, stepping into the room, and seeing her father towering above her, over her, half buried in snow and paper, his swivel chair on top of his desk, as if he had placed it there in preparation for hanging himself, ready to leap out into space.

The chair had swung right round so that he was facing her, and what she saw was a tableau — a *tableau vivant* in which nothing was living — silent, motionless, a Mrs. Jarley's Waxworks where the spirit of Madame Tussaud — there was another Madame — was at its strongest. On one side of the desk, the four drawers had been pulled out from top to bottom — a little further out each time — so that they formed a set of library stairs from the floor to the desktop. It was like an ascent to a guillotine where he could do a far, far better thing than he had ever done, even if he would not find a far, far better rest. *A Tale of Two Cities*! She had been the first to guess what the tableau was representing, and had won the game.

The accompanying music — she heard it distinctly; Miss Iandoli, recklessly throwing her windows open in the blizzard, was playing the piano transcription — was not from an opera this time, though the fourth movement, the most significant one, had been filched from an opera. It was the music from a symphony, the *Symphonie fantastique*, "Episodes in the Life of an Artist." Berlioz had, with sympathetic appropriateness for the subject, the two featured cities — *Paris et Londres (Paris and London)* — named the five movements in French, and helpfully translated these names — whisperingly enclosed in brackets — into English.

1. Rêveries, passions (Daydreams, Passions).

2. Un bal (A Ball).

3. Scène aux champs (In the Fields) . . .

He had not hanged himself.

He had . . .

He had cut his throat, and there was

(STAB EVIL SINNER!)
far more blood than the blood from her foot.
(La Maison de Dieu (The Tower Struck by Lightning).
(L'Amoureux (The Lovers).
(Le Bateleur (The Magician).
(Le Soleil (The Sun).
(La Lune (The Moon).
(L'Etoile (The Star) . . .)

The snow had poured in upon him, piling up across his shoulders and tumbling down, and his blood had poured down his chest and stomach, accumulated in his lap, mingling with the heaped snow, and down his legs, across the desk, and down to the floor toward where she was standing. All the red ink from all those torn sheets of papers, all the redness from all those columns of scribbled and slashed-out figures, all that infinity of years of numbering, profit and loss, had burst out from within him into a single mass of darkly clotted gleaming blackened scarlet. She pulled away some of the confetti-sized pieces of wet paper stuck to her face, looking at what was written on them, a woman searching for something to read to pass the time. Faintly, she recollected reaching up and catching fragments of burned paper as the Shakespeare Castle fell in ruins, and smoke billowed around her. *The sun/Has turn'd to ice! — There is a haze in the sky,/Chilly and thick, that ne'er will clear away!/The earth is wither'd grass, leaves, flowers, and all!* The torn paper was all covered with handwritten figures in columns, and the red ink stained her hands. Her face, also, would be streaked with smudged redness, and dabbed with an excess of scarlet-smeared white beauty spots, like the face of an unskilled boy who had overambitiously attempted to shave away a nonexistent beard.

4. Marche au supplice (March to the Scaffold).

It was a rapid march she heard. He was hastening toward his execution; he was leaping into space, eager to be dead, or being pushed forward from behind, through the study, up the four steps, onto the top of the desk, struggling to free himself, but overpowered.

She moved forward for a close look, her head leaning back to see.

His head had fallen back, something severed and gazing up at the ceiling from a drenched basket, and the great gash in his throat grinned at her like a huge red-lipped mouth. His frozen beard, blood seeping pinkly through the ice, stuck vertically upward like wild, surprised hair above the dripping lips. He looked like King Lear, *fantastically dressed with wild flowers.*

"I will die bravely," he should be saying, "like a smug bridegroom. What! I will be jovial."

("I never expected this to happen!" the grinning mouth was exclaiming, giggling. "How astonishing!")

"O my dear father!" she should be saying, kissing those lips. "No cause," she should be saying, "no cause," and weeping.

(She said nothing – nothing came of nothing – and tears were frozen inside her. Attempts to weep would damage her eyes, rupture her tear ducts. Even then, she was experiencing Difficulties With Tears, had been having difficulties for years.)

Blood soaked through the full depth of the half-melted layer of ice and snow, the color of pale, water-soaked raspberries. A refreshing fruit sorbet cleanses the palate between the courses of a rich meal, enabling one's guests to appreciate the subtle, delicate flavors with more discernment.

Yum-yum, say they.

(*STAB EVIL SINNER.*)

The *idée fixe* – so much more satisfying a term than leitmotiv, so much more *psychological* – was insistently emphasized each time it appeared, guiding her toward the correct answer. Think of something French! Something French! The guillotine blade glinted, fell.

THWUNK!

5. Songe d'une nuit du Sabbat (A Witches' Sabbath).

Fair is foul, and foul is fair.

Ay, sir, all this is so.

His head was angled back toward the open window behind him, like the head of someone trapped inside a structure filling with icy water, not snow, and straining for the only remaining source of air, opening his mouth wide to suck. His arms, like those frozen in mid-gesture by rigor mortis, seemed to be held out yearningly behind him, reaching for something beyond his reach, the swimmer in rising water. He appeared to be filling his lungs before a plunge into the depths of dark water, sucking the air desperately into his mouth. He was as wet as someone who had plunged repeatedly, searching for something over and over, scrabbling to find what he wanted, trying to identify it by the sense of touch alone, unable to see, a broken-nailed pearl fisher tearing at the oyster shells with bruised hands. Something about his posture made her see him as Lockwood or Heathcliff, his hands moving past a window ledge covered with names scratched into the paint — the same names repeatedly, like the pages of old schoolbooks filled with hour upon hour of handwriting exercises — breaking through the glass of the casement to snatch at the hand of a lost, sobbing child outside in the snow. "Let me in — let me in!" the child begged. He was reaching blindly back, his hands over his shoulders. He would pull the child's wrist — the child was "it," not "her" — onto the broken pane, and rub it to and fro till the blood ran down.

"Who are you?" Lockwood asked frantically, as the small ice-cold hand clung on to his.

"It's twenty years," mourned the child's voice, "twenty years, I've been a waif for twenty years!" There was her face, reflected in the dark interior of the window, looking in from outside. Twenty years. Her whole life. If she spoke, she would speak with the voice of a child; she would gurgle with the sound of a child not yet able to speak coherently.

She'd be like Archer Italiaander, Junior, summoned back from the realms of the dead to greet his mama.

"Mama," she'd be saying. "Mama."

Archer Italiaander, Junior, was *very* young for speech, even for the speaking of a single word. You imagined him as Archer Italiaander (Junior), the "Junior" enclosed in brackets like something whispered and suppressed, barely audible. His mother insisted that this was the word she had heard him speak. Quite distinctly. More than once. He'd *looked* at her as he said it.

"Mama."

"I'm very surprised to be dead," Papa would say, with a note of dissatisfaction. He never demonstrated an emotion, but always identified the one he purported to be experiencing. "I'm very angry indeed," he would say, in that same calm, unraised voice, as if he were casually remarking, "Pleasant weather for the time of year," or, "Rather cooler than yesterday." "I'm happy," that's what he would have said in order to alert observers to the presence of happiness, had he ever been happy. It was not an expression he had, in fact, ever been known to use, but he would have spoken it in that same cool tone of voice, a voice tentatively attempting to give a name to something faintly recollected from long ago.

The piles of books in front of the window moved; thrusting forward, as if a character in a novel were bursting through into real life.

She moved forward like a Madame Defarge – yet another Madame – hastening for a closer look, click-click-clicking with her knitting needles, careful not to drop a stitch, using her time constructively – not wasting a moment – to shape warm garments in the icy coldness as the tumbrels rolled. *Click, click, click*: the knitting needles were the sound of iced-over twigs rattling together in a storm. If it wasn't stitch-stitch-stitch, it was click-click-click.

She couldn't see his face, but snow would be filling the open eyes, the open mouth, the nostrils, the seashell convolutions of the ears, layered across the miniature landscape of the pale face, Madame Tussaud forming wax around the dead features to make a death mask. The blind white faces of the dead were all around her in Carlo Fiorelli's workshop. She heard the ripping of the cloth for the life cast, all the fabrics in the room being torn up like the papers, removing everything that was soft or comforting. She should close her eyes, not move, breathe slowly, as the layers were constructed upon her face; the muted splashing sound as Mama dabbed her face, soothing away pain.

When a horseman passes, the soldiers have a rule . . .

Her heavy-laden face was pulled downward, fixed in one place, incapable of expression. Her mouth was covered, her ears; she could not speak, could not hear.

But another pleasure enchantinger than these . . .

Marche au supplice (March to the Scaffold) began to play again, louder, faster, enthusiastic crowds encoring the orchestra, as an opera rapidly approached its great, climactic death scene. It was strange to know the endings in opera and in Shakespeare, to watch the characters, and wait for the deaths of those who were going to die. From the time that they appeared, you knew that they would die, and every word they sang or spoke drew them closer to that moment.

Papa was slumped back, exhausted, after his death, after the demanding final aria at the end of a long night of singing. He had sung of his approach to death, of his crossing through the dark borderlands into silence, and the crowds applauded his dying, and the manner of his death. In the moonlight, he had invited the statue of the man he had murdered to a banquet, and the statue had appeared. The cold of an Arctic December had spread throughout the room, as the marble hand of the statue had seized hold of his hand.

"Repent!" the statue had ordered. "Repent!"

Death had drawn close, and the words had been the words of a foreign language.

> *"Chi l'anima mi lacera, —*
> *Chi m'agita le viscere!*
> *Che strazio ohimè! Che smania!*
> *Che inferno! Che terror!"*

This was what he was singing, as the demons dragged him down to hell like another Doctor Faustus. Just as *"Sie kommt! Sie kommt!"* in *The Magic Flute* made you feel fluent in German, so *"Che inferno! Che terror!"* sounded comfortingly comprehensible to those who had once thought they couldn't understand a word of Italian. Mozart wrote in a language that a citizen of any nation could understand. Sometimes his librettist wrote in German, sometimes he wrote in Italian, but Mozart's unchanging language of music was universal, and words were not needed, barely heard. Liking Mozart was a slightly odd, esoteric taste, something that might perhaps be better not expressed if you wished to impress.

There was the end of a plug of absorbent cotton sticking out of Papa's nearer ear, his left. It looked like something inserted hastily, with no thought for how it looked, no attempt to press it neatly out of sight. The inner part was darkened, yellowed with oil, the outer part as fluffy and white as the edges of springtime clouds. I wandered lonely. The daffodils fluttered and danced, beside the lake, beneath the trees. He must have been in pain from an earache. The cotton was as smooth and bright as the snow that settled around it, upon it, but it would be soft and warm. It would soothe and lull into sleep, and deaden sound. If she called his name, he wouldn't hear her. The cotton would deafen him, his ears sealed so that he could not be disturbed, so that he could sleep, a Ulysses freed from temptation as the Sirens sang alluringly. For many years he wandered, and after all his years of wandering his own child would eventually kill him.

She knew he could not hear her, but she still called his name.

"P-P-Papa," she said. "P-P-Papa."

(Alice leaned toward the black kitten, as she wound the knitting-wool into a ball, like an Ariadne drawing her way close toward the monster at the heart of the labyrinth.

("I was watching the boys getting in sticks for the bonfire – and it wants plenty of sticks, Kitty! Only it got so cold, and it snowed so, they had to leave off. Never mind, we'll go and see the bonfire tomorrow . . ."

(The ball of wool grew larger, as she drew in the thread and wound it round and round.

("You know I'm saving up all your punishments for Wednesday week – Suppose they had saved up all *my* punishments? What *would* they do at the end of a year? I should be sent to prison, I suppose, when the day came."

(She drew in the thread, drew in the thread, tugging as she pulled.

("Do you hear the snow against the window-panes, Kitty? How nice and soft it sounds! Just as if someone was kissing the window all over outside. I wonder if the snow *loves* the trees and fields, that it kisses them so gently? And then it covers them up snug, you know, with a white quilt; and perhaps it says 'Go to sleep, darlings, till the summer comes again.'"

(If the kitten was not a good kitten, she would put it through the looking-glass into the Looking-glass House.)

She was Miss P-P-Pinkerton, the Shipping Merchant's Daughter. That thought came to her again, as it had that morning.

As you gathered the members of your Happy Family you had to say "please," you had to say "thank you." If you forgot, you were not given the card, and you lost your turn. This thought kept going through her head. You had to be polite. Whatever happened, however much Allegra cheated, you had to be *polite*. Miss Ericsson had been very firm about this, a doomed attempt to instill civilized behavior into Allegra and Edith.

"What is the magic word?" Miss Ericsson would ask.

The answer was not "Abracadabra!" or "Open, Sesame!"

"What is the magic word?"

Please.

That was one of the magic words.

Thank you.

Those were the other magic words.

Please.

Thank you.

You spoke those words, and the spell-bound door was opened, revealing all the treasures hidden within.

With the help of Charlotte that morning, she had been able to

644

recollect twelve of the Happy Families, the happy families that all resembled one another. Who were the members of the thirteenth and final family, the Mr., the Mrs., the Master, and the Miss? She had known eight before Charlotte had called, and – between them – they'd managed to recollect two more before they'd gone to All Saints', and two more in the church (such was their concentration on the spiritual guidance offered by Dr. Vaniah Odom and the Reverend Goodchild).

There was Mr. Bun, the Baker's family. Everyone could remember the Bun family.

"Could I have Miss B-B-Bun, the B-B-Baker's D-D-Daughter, please?"

The magic word.

(She sometimes stuttered more with nouns. It was as if she could feel their solid shape in her mouth, blocking the movement of her tongue, an impediment to fluency. Perhaps her stuttering was caused by the perpetual coldness, her shivering slurring the words she tried to speak.)

"Miss Bun is at home."

"Thank you."

The other magic words.

There was Mr. Mug, the Milkman's family.

"Could I have Miss M-M-Mug, the M-M-Milkman's D-D-Daughter, please?"

The magic word.

"Miss Mug is at home."

"Thank you."

The other magic words.

There was Mr. Chip, the Carpenter's family, Mr. Soot, the Sweep's family, Mr. Grits, the Grocer's family, Mr. Bung, the Brewer's family, Mr. Block, the Barber's family . . .

There was . . .

There was . . .

There was Mr. Spade, the Gardener's family, Mr. Tape, the Tailor's family, Mr. Pots, the Painter's family, and Mr. Dip, the

Dyer's family. They were a little apart from the other families, the darkest grouping. They were four-fifths of the innermost circle, and it was in a circle that they were gathered, their backs turned to observers, either to shield from sight what it was they were watching, or because they could not bear to tear their eyes away from whatever it was that drew them there. There was a sense that it was something they should not be watching – a bare-knuckle fight, a cockfight, a summoning of the dead or of demons – or something more exciting, more secret and shameful than these were. The Masters and the Misses had pushed their way through to the front to ensure themselves a good view, and were almost hidden from sight by the backs of the Misters and the Mistresses. ("Mistresses" added to the sense of the forbidden.)

They had gathered around the fifth family of the inner five. They were watching Mr. Bones, the Butcher's family, as they prepared to play music and sing.

Most of the Bones family was left-handed.

Mr. Bones, the Butcher, his face averted, his eyes closed (more, you felt, to luxuriate in the sensation of slicing than to express revulsion), was carving through a great red cut of raw meat with a huge broad-bladed knife held in his left hand. The mightily bosomed Mrs. Bones, the Butcher's Wife, the very spit of Mrs. Albert Comstock – *Spit! Spit! Spit!* – towered like the *Alice in Wonderland* Duchess turned homicidal. She'd spoken roughly to her little boy, she'd beaten him when he sneezed, and now she was all agog for slaughter, her appetite roused for stronger meat. She held aloft a great joint of blood-flecked flesh, and in her left hand grasped a cleaver with an air of enthusiasm. That large apron straining across the lower part of her body would not retain its pristine whiteness for very much longer. Master Bones, the Butcher's Son, the only dextral member of this sinister family, whistled insouciantly as he walked along with a gigantic squelchy joint – it contained more meat than the whole of his body, and *oozed* blood – resting over his right shoulder. He looked like a murderer – happy and fulfilled in his work – ambling along to dispose of a body, a Burke or a Hare on his way to pay a call upon Robert Knox and claim his seven pounds, ten shillings. He had the same hairstyle as his father: a dark upturned flick of hair on either side of his face, like horns. Miss Bones, the Butcher's Daughter, was feasting upon a bone the size of a baby. She clutched it in both hands (it was hers, hers, *hers*) – a distinct possibility of ambidextrousness (was there such a word?) here – and was applying the end of it to her mouth. She was like someone about to play one of the larger brass instruments – a euphonium or a serpent – though you felt that what was going on here was sucking rather than blowing, a determined attempt to extract the marrow from the bone that was bigger than her two legs combined. The meat had been nibbled entirely away from the surface of the bone, and now it was time to slurp out the jellied tissue inside it. *She sucked and sucked and sucked the more* . . . Her eyes were almost crossed with concentration. You could imagine her tongue rooting ruthlessly about in its quest for fresh sustenance, seeking that elusive raspberry seed in the hollow tooth at the back of the mouth. She was a figure from one of the darker Central European fairy stories. She was an infant Samson, musing a while in pensive thought, resting from her slaughterous labors with the well-wielded jawbone of an ass. *With the jawbone of an ass, heaps upon heaps, With the jaw of an ass have I slain a thousand men.* She smote them hip and thigh – she especially enjoyed smiting them on the thigh, the satisfyingly fleshy *thwack!* – with a great slaughter. *Heaps upon heaps! A thousand men!* The bone was the exact shape of one of the bones on a pirate's skull-and-crossbones flag, as white, as bare, as symmetrical. She'd have them walking the plank, as she chewed all the while. She'd have them skewered on cutlasses, ready for a barbecue, dribbling in toothsome anticipation, cannibalistically keen. She'd have them hauled off and keelhauled. *She sucked until her lips were sore. . .* Her dress was dyed a deep uniform red, the blood seeped out of the chewed-off meat and into her clothing. She should have been sitting in a spreading pool of blood, dabbling her fingers, holding up her bloodstained palms for inspection. They were a Happy Family. Everyone could remember the Bun family, but — once she'd called them to mind — it was the Bones family she remembered in most detail, Brudder Bones and his brooding brood playing dementedly in their blood-soaked minstrel show.

The hand of the LORD was upon her, and carried her out in the spirit of the LORD, and set her down in the midst of the valley which was full of bones, and caused her to pass by them round about: and, behold, there were very many in the open valley; and, lo, they were very dry. And he said unto her, Daughter of man, can these bones live? . . . Then he said unto her, Prophesy unto the wind, prophesy, daughter of man, and say to the wind, Thus saith the Lord God; Come from the four winds, O breath, and breathe upon these slain, that they may live. So she prophesied as he commanded her, and the breath came into them, and they lived, and stood up upon their feet, an exceeding great army, and each of them had the face of Papa.

All the Daughters in the Happy Families pack had her face, a fearsome pack of thirteen plain-faced Daughters, more than enough of them to vanquish the complete set of Dibbo Daughters, and each of them fully armed with the symbol of her father's trade, but they were heavily outnumbered by the exceeding great army.

Can these bones live? Oh, yes. They could live all right. They could move, they could dance, and they could spin and turn and rattle up and down in an urgently insistent xylophonic rhythm. The music began quietly, almost inaudibly, designed merely as the background noise to the more important business of talking, the Mrs. Albert Comstock attitude to music in all its forms.

> "Ezekiel connected dem dry bones
> Ezekiel connected dem dry bones
> Ezekiel connected dem dry bones
> I hear the word of the Lord . . ."

It was the Bones family who were playing, the Happy Families playing card players. They were a chamber quartet, a refreshing infusion of highbrow culture into the generally unashamedly populist approach of the majority of minstrel show performers. Mr. Bones, the Butcher, sliced his knife through the raw meat like a left-handed cellist possessed by the music as he sawed away with his bow. Mrs. Bones, the Butcher's Wife, wielded her cleaver vigorously against the joint, playing one of the more obscure instruments of the percussion section. Master and Miss Bones, the Butcher's Son and Daughter, added their own multi-textured layers to the rich tapestry of sound produced by their parents: he percussive in his instrument of choice, she opting for wind.

All around them, the other Happy Families swayed in unison to the rhythm, and joined in the singing.

> ". . . Your toe bone connected to your foot bone,
> Your foot bone connected to your ankle bone,
> Your ankle bone connected to your leg bone,
> Your leg bone connected to your knee bone . . ."

Dem bones may have been dry, but the instruments they played were soaked, and a fine red mist of blood drizzled down upon their audience. The Masters and Misses in the front row held up their faces in eyes-closed bliss, drinking in the gentle rain from heaven after a long drought, something for which they had been dreaming and praying for a long, long time. Blood stained their clothes, ran down their faces in rivulets, trickling down from where it gathered above their eyebrows and in their hair, and pooled in the palms of their loosely curled upturned hands. Miss Pots – the looking-glass-changed Alice – found a bloody redness to coat not just her face but the whole of her, seeping in deep, and Master Pots proudly displayed his reddened tongue: he'd been licking the blood from the butcher's implements. Miss Dip held her stained left hand away from her, in Lady Macbeth revulsion, but Master Dip – huge-headed and smiling broadly – held his dripping hands away from his sides, in proud display of a blooding, a symbol of manhood achieved. It was blackness, not redness, that dripped down, as if he'd zestfully slaughtered the Soot family, or massacred a minstrel-show challenge to the musical supremacy of the Bones.

They heard the word of the Lord.

"Could I have Miss D-D-Dip, the D-D-Dyer's D-D-Daughter, please?"

The magic word.

"Miss Dip is at home."

"Thank you."

The magic words.

"Could I have Miss B-B-Bones, the B-B-Butcher's D-D-Daughter, please?"

The magic word.

Slam!

(The door reverberated, its knocker activated into an almost out-of-hearing resonance, the windows rattled.)

"Miss Bones is not at home."

Slam! Slam!

(Bolts were shot firmly home. The key turned in the lock.)

The magic word had not worked.

No "Abracadabra!" No "Open, Sesame!"

The door remained closed against her. It was not Opened Unto her.

It was a looking-glass door, and as it closed against her she saw why Miss Bones was not at home, why the Miss was missing. She saw the reflection moving toward her.

She was Miss Bones, knocking on the door and asking for herself.

She was Miss . . .

She . . .

It was only then that she realized that she was shivering, in great uncontrolled waves like spasms. It was like that time when she was trembling with fever once, the time when Mama had been bathing her face with cool water. Then she had been too hot; now she was too cold. There would be no soothing trickling sounds, no washing away of the pain. Water would be frozen in the bowl, a miniature part of that landscape of ice. An ice place. The spasms were like cramps in bed at night, that same sensation of coldness, an inward-pulling tightness in the veins, her body completely out of her control, her knee bone connected to her thigh bone, her thigh bone connected to her hip bone, her hip bone connected to her back bone, her back bone connected to her shoulder bone . . .

She heard the word of the Lord.

She would press the thumb and first finger of her right hand tightly together (about to kiss their tips, and hold them cupped upwards, a connoisseur's gesture of approval after a tasting), and grip the end of the cotton fibers protruding from Papa's ear with her fingernails. But she couldn't. Her hands were shaking too much. She'd be unable to make them do what she wanted them to do. She would tug at the cotton, as slowly and carefully as if she were drawing a splinter of wood out of her other hand. But she couldn't. Caroline Renwick had called such splinters "spells," a term her Yorkshire grandmother had used. She was drawing out a spell.

By the pricking of my thumbs, something wicked this way comes.

It was the spell that was pricking her thumb, the spell that twitched as it sensed the nearness of wickedness, the wood swelling in the steady drip-drip of falling tears, just before they froze into ice. She could do it, if she could keep her fingers still, without having to touch the cold flesh, pulling it out in the way she had done to — most satisfyingly — disembowel her smug-faced doll, Lumpety.

Yard after yard of stuffing had emerged in a continuous chain from the small rent in the stitching near where the bellybutton would be. ("Bellybutton" was a slightly daring choice of word.) It was as if — the image had come into her mind yesterday — Roland Birtle really had — in the interests of being interesting — drawn out his not-so-small intestine, to the wonder of Miss Wouldhave, to demonstrate its length, to prove the veracity of the Fascinating Fact with which he had regaled her.

"Twenty-three feet!" he exclaimed, his voice rising, a performer drawing toward the climax of his act.

"Gracious!"

"Twenty-four feet!"

"Gracious!"

"Twenty-five feet!" This was his moment of triumph, as he pulled out the last few inches with a squelchy plop, and collapsed in upon his hollow self. (And that was the *small* intestine!) He had died being interesting. It was what he would have wanted. (I *told* you it was twenty-five feet long!)

"Gracious!" Miss Wouldhave exclaimed yet again, keeling over dramatically, stealing the limelight from Myrtle. Myrtle, knee-deep in small intestine, looked *furious*.

After the *mwah!* kiss of the fingertips (*This is absolutely delicious!*), the initial cautious tug with the fingernails, the slight resistance, she would haul out the contents of the cotton-filled head hand over hand, like a winner in a tug-of-war contest. She'd yank away – right hand, left hand – yo-ho-heave-hoing in her deepest voice with the Volga Boatmen (matted beards, depressed expressions, bent forward at angles of forty-five degrees as they pulled ropes as thick as suspension bridge cables straining over their shoulders). She'd demonstrate a vivacious sense of fun as she yo-ho-heave-hoed away. It would warm her up nicely, bring the sensation back into her frozen and shaking hands, drawing the sunshine toward her, the Alabama warmth, the Georgia warmth of Dixie, of Macy.

"... Oh, Lawdy, pick a bale of cotton ..."

she'd trill, heaving fit to bust, picking, picking, picking at the cotton, like a tarry-fingered oakum-picking prisoner settling into the rhythm of a life sentence, and the Volga Boatmen, seizing upon a less dirge-like incantation than the usual repetitious yo-ho-heave-ho (this tended to pall after a decade or so), joined in with a thrillingly incandescent intensity, approaching some thuribleswinging, climactic Hallelujah moment in a Russian Orthodox service (if they went in for Hallelujahs), the interior of the cathedral as impenetrably cloudy with incense as the opening of *Bleak House* was with fog. Their sonorous voices thundered above a timorous *Tum, tum, tum, tum, ti-tu* or *Tum-ti, tum-ti, tum-ti, tum* into a deeper, darker world elsewhere, where *tum*s, *ti-tu*s and *tum-ti*s faltered into shamed silence.

> ". . . Oh, Lawdy, pick a bale a day.
> Oh, Lawdy, pick a bale of cotton,
> Oh, Lawdy, pick a bale a day.

> "Jump down, turn around . . ."

Down they'd jump, round they'd turn, holding the harvested contents of the hollowing head high above them ("Look what we've picked!"), and the hands of the Volga Boatmen (the only parts of them visible through the dense fog) would force their way skyward, all of them maypole dancers spinning cat's cradle patterns with their ropes in the air, singing away in de land ob cotton as the Volga (oh, Lawdy) became, from bank to bank, an impenetrable entanglement of jammed boats, barges, and rafts stacked high with wood.

> ". . . To pick a bale of cotton,
> Jump down, turn around,
> To pick a bale a day . . ."

Papa's face would sag inward like a leaking balloon, and become a flimsy crumpled mask – a shriveled death mask – with no head to wear it. The head caved in, ceased to exist, whooshed into nothingness, melted in warmth.

Look away, look away, look away, Dixie land! *Macy! Macy!* Lawks-a-mercy, it was Macy.

Old time dar am not forgotten.

653

"... Me and my Papa can
Pick a bale of cotton.
Me and my Papa can
Pick a bale a day.

"Oh, Lawdy, pick a bale of cotton,
Oh, Lawdy, pick a bale a day . . ."

"Look at what happens when you pick your nose!" she would
cry warningly, demonstrating to an eagerly appalled audience, as
they leaned forward to obtain the best view. There were gasps —
horrified, rather pleased — and the thunderous applause started.
"Bravo!" someone shouted, clearly one of those embarrassingly
demonstrative enthusiasts from the opera. "Bravo!" If the defunct
nose-picker had been a woman, he would have shouted "Brava!"
You just knew he would be pedantically correct in his expressions
of acclaim. It took one pedant to recognize another, to admire his
technique with a certain cool jealousy.

She leaned forward, going up on to tiptoe to try to see the death-
changed face more closely, straining over the giant toothless grin of
the neck.

Seldom went such grotesqueness with such woe;
I never saw a brute I hated so . . .
Me and my Papa . . .
Me and my Papa . . .

Curse him! Curse him! Curse him!
She should be chanting these words in a double-double-toil-
and-trouble incantation, circling counterclockwise, pointing her
finger the whole time at the body of the suicide around which she
moved.

She should grasp an ear in each hand, and tilt the bald head forward, adjusting the swivel, to see if her reflection still swam darkly
within it as in a looking-glass.

Tilt. Tilt. Tilt.

It would creak with the wetness and the snow.

Alice moved her face closer to the curve of the skull, dropped forward at her tugging, to make out the details of the creased flesh in the whiteness of a little limb beneath the surface of glass, the tiny fingernails of a snow-colored arm.

("Let me in – let me in!" a child's voice sobbed. "I'm come home, I'd lost myself on the moor! . . . It's twenty years . . .")

Tilt. Tilt. Tilt.

If she tilted the head too far forward, if . . .

If the gash . . .

If the gash had been too deep . . .

The head would fall forward, bounce, and roll across the floor . . .

Me and my Papa . . .

Me and my Papa . . .

She would find herself looking into the smooth hairless surface above his left eye, the tips of her fingers letting go of the ears and reaching forward to touch the polished bumps. The main areas began just above the eye. She avoided looking at the eye, the dead eye of a mackerel glaring accusingly at her from a plate at lunchtime and spoiling her appetite. Mackerel sky, mackerel sky,/Not long wet, and not long dry. The clouds – cirrocumulus and altocumulus – patterned the sky, and what the weather would bring could be read within them. That's what you could see in those clouds.

I have died so that you might eat me!

That was what the eye was saying. It made her feel guilty if she did eat the fish, and made her feel guilty if she didn't.

("Eat me, drink me, love me."

(That was what Lizzie said to Laura in "Goblin Market."

(She had tasted the forbidden fruit for her sake.)

She wished cook would cut off the heads before she served them.

Just above the eye, left of center – his left, her right: she had to reverse everything in her mind, looking in a mirror — there was *Order*, *Neatness*, and *System*. That was Papa, all right. There should be a huge bump there, like a cyst bulging out. She couldn't bring herself to touch it, to see, in case it burst into sticky wetness. Her fingers hovered above the other nearer areas. *Locality* and *Exploration*. That was one. Further back, and a little more to the right, there were *Humor*, *Mirthfulness*, and *Wit*. Her hand would sink into a hollow up to her wrist, her fingernails digging at the walnut of the brain. The body would twitch restlessly, like Frankenstein's creature starting to come alive, as she activated areas of stimulation. Behind that, an area twice as large, was *Blandness*, *Agreeableness*, and *Youthfulness*. In the middle of the very back of the head, in the place where a murderess would place the barrel of a gun before she pulled the trigger, there were *Parental Love*, and *Love of Children*.

She flexed her index finger.

Her *trigger* finger.

Bang!

Bang!

Bang!

"What horror is he in!" Belford had written of Belton in *Clarissa*. "His eyes look like breath-stained glass!"

She had often pictured eyes like breath-stained glass when she looked in mirrors. She had stared at the dark surface of night-backed windows, trying not to breathe, so that she could see. *Moving thro' a mirror clear/That hangs before her all the year/Shadows of the world appear.*

"His malady is within him," Belford had written earlier, "and he cannot run away from it."

He must be wicked to deserve such pain . . .

Would there still be a luster on the gleaming dome, or would it have clouded over in death, become reflectionless breath-stained glass?

Out vile jelly! Where is thy luster now?

Lustre.

All's dark and comfortless.

The raised foot stomped down, and passers-by disappeared under lumpy piles of squirted strawberry jelly. They licked their red-clotted lips, unable to stop themselves, and shuddered with delighted revulsion as they sucked the fruits from that unknown orchard.

We must not look at goblin men, we must not buy their fruits.

Yum-yum.

Above them, at the window above the jelly-encrusted railings, the strawberry-smelling scene of carnage, one of Miss Iandoli's pupils — a beginner — was falteringly making an overambitious attempt at *Narcissus.*

After a few notes, there was silence.

The pupil was bent over, looking at the hands that would not do what she wanted, that would not produce the music that she could hear inside her head.

She should find a looking-glass, hold it to her father's lips, punish him, thrust him through into the Looking-glass House.

If she held it to his lips, and then looked into it and saw her reflection clearly, this would mean death.

Edward Hyde would pass away like the stain of breath upon a mirror.

That was what Dr. Jekyll had believed, that image of breath-stained glass again. It was such a revealing image, this linking of the hidden inner monster with the picture of someone looking into a mirror, Dr. Jekyll seeing the reflection not of his face but of the being inside himself, hating and fearing the brute that slept within him. The mirror had the power of Dorian Gray's portrait. With it he was able to follow his mind into its secret places. It was the most magical of mirrors.

The drug he took had no discriminating action; it was neither diabolical nor divine; it but shook the doors of the prison-house of his disposition; and, like the captives of Philippi, that which stood within ran forth.

That was how Dr. Jekyll described what had happened to him, though she wished that Robert Louis Stevenson had dispensed with all the apparatus of the drug. No drug was needed to draw out the darker self. It slept until it was woken, and then it roared forth. The mirror in which Dr. Jekyll looked was the perfect mirror for all alienists to employ.

Look in this mirror, Miss Pinkerton. Tell me what you can see.

If she looked in such a mirror she would see her true self.

Dr. Jekyll believed that the evil would pass away, as transient as breath, as breathing, because life was such a fragile thing, lasting for so short a time.

She was alone in the house with a dead man.

Me and my Papa.

Me and my Papa can . . .

Me and my Papa can . . .

She was alone.

Snow was piled up in drifts, darkening the lower windows, blocking all the doors of the house. She could not leave, was unable to seek help. There was no one to see her, no one to hear her, if she opened one of the upper windows and tried to shout above the noise of the storm.

(Lizzie.)

She had almost heard the name being called, a voice far away across fields, a voice from the upper room of a distant house. Her own faint voice calling, calling across time, and not distance.

(Lizzie Galliant.)

She almost called for Lizzie Galliant, summoning up herself as a child to call for the comfort she had craved from someone stronger than she could ever be. The time had come, the one time she could use her powers, like a bee defending itself and killing itself by the use of its sting . . .

She did not call out the name.

She was made out of frozen metal, weathered bronze, and should take her place upon Papa's knee for *The Children's Hour*, not moving for year after year, her breathing stilled, just aging slowly as the snow raged around her. He was there, high above her, ready, in the correct pose, waiting for her. There she stands, a lovely creature, who she is, I do not know; I have caught her for her beauty.

She was one of the girls from the statue.

There should be a large book for Papa to hold, to complete the pose. Often, she had wished to read the words within the book, if words were there to read. Now she could choose the book. His account book would be somewhere close beneath the snow, its pages ripped out, its thick covers — wet and warped — closed upon emptiness. What had once been there was numbers, not words. That could be the book he was reading to her, teaching her all her lessons of addition and subtraction, all the calculations that needed to be made. He'd be more at home with numbers. One, two, three . . . He'd be Moses, reading the Ten Commandments as his bedtime story. "Thou shalt have no other gods before me. Honor thy father and thy mother," he'd be saying in an unfamiliar once-upon-a-time voice. "Thou shalt not kill."

"Why not, Papa?"

"Because it's what it says in the book. You have to have things the same as they are in the book, otherwise they're wrong."

She sat beneath the flapping cloth, like a corpse covered by an enfolding sheet, as the snow steadily pattered upon it, deepening over their bodies, the three blind little girls and the blind bearded man frozen together, waiting in the darkness for another little girl to unveil them.

> Between the dark and the daylight,
> When the night is beginning to lower . . .

Brightness would fall upon them, and there they would be exposed, all of them dead, all of them blind, as an unseen crowd applauded, and — to the sound of the *idée fixe*, marching to the scaffold — the massed schoolboys of Otsego Lake Academy, their buttons glinting with the red glow of the setting sun, too many buttons to count, would chant the last verse of "The Children's Hour."

The same red glow would shine from the bright, golden area of her breast, the worn part near her heart, as she listened to the words she could not read.

> ". . . And there will I keep you for ever,
> Yes, for ever and a day . . ."

She saw the fortress rising high above her, dark, windowless, its many levels of stone blocking out the light.

> ". . . Till the walls shall crumble to ruin,
> And moulder in dust away!"

As it crumbled, the grit hissed and pattered down upon her, crunching under her feet like spilled sugar, making her hair itchy, and her reddened eyes water, tears blurring her vision to give an underwater sway to everything she saw.

There he would keep her for ever, Yes, for ever and a day.

The first thing she had said to Mama, when she and her sisters and brother finally managed to reach the house, was, "Promise me you won't marry again." She'd insisted that Mama make the promise, insisted that she sign a piece of paper.

Mourning had been a strain, remembering to look decorously sad, and speak in a low, brave voice. The black clothes of full mourning put on each morning – mourning for morning, mourning for night – were a useful reminder of what would be appropriate behavior, a tactful little nudge that no one saw happening, and the solemn expressions were assumed (a too-revealing choice of verb) with the dark clothes. It was like a ritual for which you had to wear special clothing, an assigned task. Soldiers wore special clothes to kill. Butchers wore special clothes to hack meat. Sweeps wore special clothes to clean chimneys. The Happy Families pack was a guide to appropriate fashions, miniaturized fashion plates helpfully gathered together. Miss Pinkerton, the Mourning Daughter. *LOOK SAD* she was reminded by the carefully ironed memento mori. *DON'T*

LAUGH. SIGH INTERMITTENTLY AND GAZE INTO THE MIDDLE DISTANCE, as incipient tears poised in the about-to-fall position. Sometimes she believed that she felt these feelings. Surely — as a demonstration of her real, deep, and sincere grief — she ought to have blacked her face as well, in decorously tasteful minstrel show mourning, applying the burned cork with slow, thoughtful movements between sighs? How those movements would have moved Papa and impressed Mrs. Albert Comstock, a suitable Symbolic act of homage.

"Gone are the days . . ."

— ". . . *de* days . . ." Mrs. Albert Comstock corrected firmly, but Alice ignored her —

". . . when my heart was young and gay . . ."

— She might manage a sad little quaver in her voice —

". . . Gone are my friends from the cotton fields away:
Gone from the earth to a better land I know . . ."

("Some folks like to sigh,
Some folks do, some folks do . . ."

(It began quietly, far away in the distance, but drew closer, became louder.

(". . . Some folks long to die,
But that's not me nor you.

("Long live the merry, merry heart
That laughs by night and day . . .")

After a while, Dr. Severance of Staten Island was drawn on like more dark clothing. Then, heaviest and blackest of all – as thick as winter clothing, but failing to keep out the cold – the deepest of deep, deep mourning, it was time for Dr. Wolcott Ascharm Webster. Miss Pinkerton, the Madwoman in the Attic.

23

Twenty-five years ago, as a blizzard raged around the house, she had walked down the stairs in darkness to see Annie, and helped her find the woman who would kill her. Fifteen years ago, in another blizzard, she had gone downstairs to find her father's body.

She had felt that she had watched all night during the 1888 blizzard – her short periods of sleep had been shallow – and some words of Robert Louis Stevenson had kept going through her head. She half drowsed as she sat and watched the storm, hypnotized by the featureless whiteness. In the morning – a morning scarcely distinguishable from the night; it was as dark, as bleak – the storm was raging as fiercely as ever, and the words were still in her head, like a tune that could not be shaken off.

> *. . . among the desert sands*
> *Some deserted city stands,*
> *All its children, sweep and prince,*
> *Grown to manhood ages since,*
> *Not a foot in street or house,*
> *Not a stir of child or mouse,*
> *And when kindly falls the night,*
> *In all the town no spark of light . . .*

There had been a profound silence inside and outside the house, beneath the sound of the gale. The obliterating snow was still hissing across as thickly as ever, looking as if it would never end. Chestnut Street was blocked, with a huge drift piling up toward their side, and Chestnut Hill, running downward beyond, was impassable. The telegraph poles, the elements torn from their positions, lay collapsed all the way down the street like the masts and spars of shipwrecked galleons — a destroyed armada of *Hesperus*es and *Hispaniola*s in the midnight and the snow — crashed down through the ice from the sky into a lower, colder, element, their snow-thickened wires thrumming like storm-torn rigging.

The pole outside Miss Iandoli's house had fallen right across the street to their house, dragged down by the weight of the snow, and she looked down upon it, expecting to see a frozen corpse, still clutching a telescope, staring up at her from a smashed crow's-nest, its dead eyes all iced and glittering. She saw it as distinctly as a Doré engraving of the Ancient Mariner as he once had been, a young man leaning against a mast, his head bowed and his arms extended out from his sides, like an exhausted crucified figure.

She could lean down from her window, and press her lips against that cold face, so that they would freeze against it as she had once imagined them doing against the buttons of a uniform, against a bronze statue, as the snow beat against her, closed her eyes and mouth, and penetrated to the inner parts of her ears.

The skipper's daughter, the salt tears in her eyes, was wrapped in her father's seaman's coat, and he had bound her to the mast with rope cut from a broken spar. He had lashed her tightly, though he had left her hands free.

Her hair fell and rose in the wind, as if her body was still breathing.

24

She knelt down to be in the warmth close to the fire, and began to brush her hair. She hadn't undressed yet, but wished to begin the ritual of counting, to drive all other thoughts out of her head. She'd laid her nightgown on the chair beside her to warm. The wintry moon shining through the stained glass of the casement might have thrown a glory like a saint on Madeline's hair as she kneeled in prayer on St. Agnes' Eve – Porphyro growing faint at her purity, her freedom from mortal taint – but she certainly neglected its care, failing to brush it before she slept.

> Brush hair, brush,
> The men have gone to plow . . .

– *plough* (should it be "plough"?) –

> . . . If you want to brush your hair,
> Brush your hair now . . .

"One, two, three . . ."

Time for the nighttime brushing of her hair to begin, the repeated one-to-a-hundred ritual that she completed automatically, without looking into a mirror. She found herself becoming anxious if she did not brush, tugging out the elf-locks, unable to sleep without removing them.

Looking-glass, looking-glass, on the wall.

". . . twenty-five, twenty-six, twenty-seven . . ."

It was soporific, counting up to a hundred, over and over, a certain soothing monotony, just right before bedtime, emptying her mind of everything but the repeated numbers, free even from the image of leaping flocks of sheep soaring over five-barred gates. Nothing but numbers. The poppied warmth of monotony oppress'd her soothed limbs.

". . . sixty-three . . ."

– *Crackle!* (Her hair was bulking out like thunder-filled storm clouds.) –

". . . sixty-four. . ."

– *Crackle!* –

". . . sixty-five . . ."

– *Crackle!* –

664

They had once had a cook who had timed whole recipes by singing set numbers of verses of hymns, favoring specific hymns for specific recipes, like an evangelical pot-rattler, a *cordon bleu* of the canticle. (Mrs. Goodchild was under the impression that Gordon Blue was the name of a famous chef. "It was as good as Gordon Blue," she would say loftily, of any half-digestible meal she had wolfed down in an expensive restaurant, anxious to inform them how much it had cost.) Alice still found herself salivating — hard to explain this away to observant strangers — as the congregation of All Saints' launched into "Let us, with a gladsome mind, / Praise the Lord, for he is kind." This had always meant that they would be having beef and potato hash for lunch, and this — Mrs. Freeborn's advanced culinary skills had been the making of a sophisticated and discriminating palate — had been Alice's favorite meal. She was always gladsome when she heard this hymn.

> ". . . The hornèd moon to shine by night,
> 'Mid her spangled sisters bright!. . ."

Mrs. Freeborn's voice — hollow and echoing — sometimes boomed out from the schoolroom fireplace toward lunchtime, and *Dribble! Dribble!* went Alice. Beef and potato hash! Tomato ketchup would flow like a bloodbath.

> ". . . All things living he doth feed,
> His full hand supplies their need! . . ."

sang the fireplace.

This verse qualified for meaningful emphasis. They were lucky to have Mrs. Freeborn, and Mrs. Freeborn — "His *full* hand supplies *their need*!" — made certain that they were made aware of this.

Dribble! Dribble!

Annie had used the same technique, singing a section of a song that lasted exactly three and a half minutes as she cooked a soft-boiled egg. Alice heard Annie's voice, the words of the song, as she spooned out the firm white, the runny yolk, from the egg in the eggcup decorated with painted squawking hens.

"Her bright smile haunts me still," she would sing to her distorted reflection on the back of the spoon — high-foreheaded, narrow-faced and narrow-nosed, not much of a bright smile, like a fun-free Flemish face in a religious painting — blurred on the curved yolk-smeared surface. It wasn't only the hens that squawked. She held the spoon like a miniature hand mirror, a mermaid in her turn, singing sadly to her reflection as she sat uncomfortably on the damp, cold rocks.

> Looking-glass, looking-glass, in the spoon,
> Tell me who's fairest, and make it soon.

More worrying than the elongated Low Country face, the reflection of a sulkily big-lipped Easter Island statue occasionally stared back at her, a Mrs. Albert Comstock gloomily impending over the breakfast table, stifling her appetite, and casting a cloud over the rest of the morning. Sometimes Alice had tried to balance her egg in a toothpick holder, as they were made in more interesting shapes than the eggcups, and was always surprised if it fell off and rolled across the table, leaving a yolky trail across the cloth. She was particularly drawn to one in the shape of a witches' cauldron — it was described as being a gypsy kettle — and absentmindedly cast spells, as she and the two other Weird Sisters dipped thin slices of buttered bread into their egg yolks. The grilled kidneys made quite respectable poison'd entrails, and the broiled herrings definitely tasted of swelt'red venom. The finger of birth-strangled babe was more of a problem, especially when ditch-deliver'd by a drab, but she had hopes of the tiny new beef sausages from Comstock's Comestibles. They looked perfect for the part.

"Double, double toil and trouble . . ."

She muttered the words,; what she said was secret. She saw

Albert Comstock, quite distinctly, standing over the cauldron, his face illuminated by a lurid glow from the flickering flames, as he mixed the ingredients for the latest monstrous pie he had concocted. In went the fillet of a fenny snake, the eye of newt, and toe of frog.

"*Plop!*" went the wool of bat and tongue of dog.

"*Plop! Plop!*" from the sow's blood that hath eaten her nine farrow, and the grease that's sweaten from the murderer's gibbet.

Albert Comstock rubbed the fingers of his right hand daintily against his thumb, adding some rare and precious spice, saffron ground like gold dust.

"Make the gruel thick and slab!" he chanted.

Knives and forks could stand up unaided in Comstock's Celebrated Gravy – *It's Thick! It's Comstock!* Now, there was a sentiment with which she could enthusiastically concur! – like miniature rows of Excaliburs waiting for modest-faced long-haired Arthurs to draw them squelchily forth.

("Please, sir," Oliver hastily interjected, as the ladle drew closer to his basin, "I'd rather not have any more." Horror was depicted on every countenance.)

Alice had tasted of the Comstock Bargain Counter. She knew of what she spake. She could still taste the Tartar's lips from that last cutlet, revolted by the flavor. She very much doubted that Porphyro would have produced some Comstock's pies out of the closet to add to his pile of goodies lined up for his Eve of St. Agnes midnight munchings with Madeline, thudding them down with soggy plops next to the spiced dainties, the delicates, on the golden dishes and the baskets bright of wreathed silver, filling the chilly room with perfume light. "Delicates" was not the word that sprang to mind to describe Comstock's pies, robust fare designed for the ambitious, salivating, trencherman who hadn't eaten for a month or two, and enjoyed the sensation of teeth crunching on bones, marrow spraying out for several feet in all directions.

That juice was wormwood to her tongue, she loathed the feast.

". . . Fire burn, and cauldron bubble . . ."

(*Hiss!* from the dripping saliva, trying to attract her attention.)

"What was that?" Allegra asked suspiciously.

". . . Cool it with a baboon's blood . . ."

(*Hiss! Hiss!*)
"Eh?" from Edith.

". . . Then the charm is firm and good . . ."

(*Hiss! Hiss! Hiss!*)
"How now, you secret, black, and midnight hags!"
"What was that?"
"Eh?"

The Two Weird Sisters stared at her across the breakfast table, the ends of their spoons protruding from their mouths, not really interested, but affecting a response just to be irritating. They had shoved the egg-yolk-darkened silver apostle spoons — baptismal presents — so far into their mouths that only the bearded heads on the handles were visible, upside down: St. James and St. John, the sons of Zebedee.

Laughing Allegra, and Edith with golden hair.

Laughing! Golden!

The pigeons swarmed around *The Children's Hour*, and the heads of Allegra and Edith vanished, whirring with fluttering wings.

Plop! Plop! Plop!

The birds defecated copiously, grunting with effort.

Plop! Plop! Plop!

Heave! Heave!

Symbolism was such a comfort.

"Eh?"

"Eh?"

The heads of St. James and St. John — in vigorous agreement with each other — bobbed up and down in time with her sisters' grunts.

Being cultured was ever a burden, and communication with the rude majority difficult.

". . . ninety-seven, ninety-eight, ninety-nine . . ."

She stood up, still brushing, beginning a new section.

"One, two . . ."

Another of Curdie's songs from *The Princess and the Goblin* came to her, like a memory of something she'd done a long time ago. Hard to imagine that she'd ever chanted to herself as a child, watching her face in the mirror as she brushed her hair, that Shetland pony's of a mane! She'd liked the comparison of Maggie Tulliver to a Shetland pony, and seen it as quite a compliment, perhaps influenced by Charlotte's breathy sighings over horses. A copy of *Black Beauty* and a good supply of chocolate, and Charlotte was in heaven. It was the illustrations of the horses that she'd liked best in *At the Back of the North Wind*.

> "One, two —
> Hit and hew!
> Three, four —
> Blast and bore!. . ."

— It wasn't quite Christina Rossetti —

> ". . . Five, six —
> There's a fix!
> Seven, eight,
> Hold it straight!. . ."

— But it was verse to drive away goblins —

> ". . . Nine, ten —
> Hit again!

669

Hurry! Scurry!
Bother! Smother!
There's a toad
In the road!
Smash it!
Squash it!. . ."

The Goodchilds – mouths open, hands held up in horror – toppled slowly beneath the road-roller that effortlessly flattened them with neither pause nor wobble. (She could savor it more if it happened slowly, and lingered over the expressions of outraged disapproval.)

Smash them!

Squash them!

Serenity – you had to admire the girl – gave a good shove to her mama and papa, in an attempt to jam its works and save herself. When it had engulfed them – she paused for a moment to enjoy the view of their twitching legs frantically bicycling in the air (she couldn't prevent a little giggle) – she shoulder-charged Grandmama and Grandpapa, and the Reverend H. P. – Hideously Pressed – Goodchild and Mrs. Goodchild were flattened like (here was a really satisfying simile) dried cow-dung. Then it was Serenity's turn. Like a Juggernaut, the road-roller continued on its way with an epic religious-procession dignity about it, the fringes jiggling on its howdah. In its wake it left a set of *five* life-sized Happy Family cards flapping in the breeze. Here was an interesting variation of a traditional game. Reverend Goodchild, the Preacher; Mrs. Goodchild, the Preacher's Wife; Mr. Goodchild, the Preacher's Son; Mrs. Goodchild, the Preacher's Daughter-in-Law, and Miss Goodchild, the Preacher's Granddaughter, nothing but a pack of cards.

They'd been smashed.

They'd been squashed.

They were toads in the road, incommoded, exploded.

Their aggrieved expressions attained a height of hitherto

unachieved frogginess; their flattened faces were – captured forever – the froggiest of all possible frogs, the toadiest of all possible
toadies. This was not a very happy-looking Happy Family. Tolstoi
had got it all wrong. You expected better from a novelist of his cal-
iber. *All happy families resemble one another . . .* It took all that time
to read *Anna Karenina*, and he couldn't even get the first sentence
right! At least *War and Peace* had a few battles to look forward to
during the boring bits. *And* he had a title! Huh! He was clearly a
count on whom you could not count. In the flat, papery right hands
of the compressed cards, other, smaller cards were still grasped.
They were invitation cards. Mrs. Albert Comstock was holding an
"At Home" at that very moment. It was toward her house that the
Goodchilds had been hastening. It was toward her house that the
road-roller was heading now, increasing its speed slightly in its
eagerness to demolish Hampshire Square and everyone within it.
Max Webster was promised for today's entertainment, together
with Dr. Wolcott Ascharm Webster. The red velvet portières' rings
shot right across the pole as the next act was announced for another
afternoon's feasting on culture, teeth splintering on the bones,
hands glistening with grease.

Rattle, rattle, rattle.

"Dr. Wolcott Ascharm Webster and Master Max! High-pitched
Shrieks and a Banjo!"

Applause!

Dr. Vaniah Odom had promised to demonstrate his hootchy-
kootchy dancing with Myrtle Comstock. His head would be about
level with her waist.

Rattle, rattle, rattle.

"Dr. Vaniah Odom and Myrtle Comstock! The Thrill of the
Forbidden! Erotic Entanglements! See Hell and Live to Tell the
Tale!"

Applause!

Mabel Peartree would be there. Mabel Peartree was *always* there.

Rattle, rattle, rattle.

"Mabel . . ."

Outside, through the red-stained windows there was a curious grinding, crushing sound . . .

Outside, beyond the heavy curtains, something was lurching inexorably toward them . . .

Outside . . .

Those *rattle, rattle, rattlings* were — Gracious! — about to become death rattles.

Thunderous applause!

Encore!

Bravo!

Brace yourselves!

Howdy, Howdah!

"... Fry it!

Dry it!

You're another!

Up and off! . . ."

Her reflection gazed back at her, next to the face of Louis Moreau Gottschalk. He had the same face as Edgar Allan Poe, as Roderick Usher. It was like looking at puzzle pictures, designed to fill the empty hours, in which two apparently identical pictures were printed side by side. Armed with a soft-leaded pencil, the viewer studied the illustrations in order to find the ways in which they differed, circling the changes in the altered version. She imagined Dorian Gray — the mirror and the picture the same size side by side — reaching out with a thick BBB pencil to circle all the changes in the picture, like a tailor marking out his material to start crunching through with his heavy-bladed shears. He grasped the pencil with his whole hand, a knife with which he was about to stab, the technique he'd employed so successfully when he'd murdered Basil Hallward. He drew circle after circle, moving his hand in upon himself over and over. There were so many changes that the blackness grew, like the shadows of a growing darkness that obliterated all features, all colors, until nothing remained of the painted face.

"B" is for Badness . . .

"B" is for Brutalization . . .

"B" is for Blackness . . .

He'd look into the picture, as into a mirror, and see only darkness. He'd look into the mirror, and see the same thing, poised between two counterbalanced darknesses, darkness on his left side, darkness on his right side, a Doctor Faustus with no Good Angel to whisper the words of repentance and redemption. He would have ceased to exist, swallowed up as Dr. Jekyll was swallowed by Mr. Hyde, scribbled out by the BBB of the soft lead, become cancelled writings, obliterated variations.

She'd done this with the Sir John Tenniel illustrations for *Through the Looking-Glass*, the two from the very beginning of the novel. One depicted the back of Alice as she disappeared through the looking-glass, her right arm held up as if to steady herself against the surface of the glass – the glass that was melting away like a bright silvery mist ("Tell me what you can see in that mist") – and the other the same moment from inside the Looking-glass room, as the front of Alice emerged into it, her left arm – as if for balance – held in front of her. In the Looking-glass room, the altered picture, the reversed world within the reflection, the clock and the vase on the chimney-piece – both beneath glass domes – had curious, wide-mouthed, smiling faces, and Tenniel's initials – in the bottom right-hand corner of the first picture – were in the bottom left-hand corner, in reversed Leonardo da Vinci mirror writing. It was not a particularly entertaining exercise, as there were not all that many differences, the world through the looking-glass only a minor variation of the world it reflected.

The Alice in the novel was not the same Alice as in *Alice's Adventures in Wonderland*. Here, also, there were alterations. In the later novel, the Alice band appeared for the first time, and the stripes on Alice's stockings. She looked like someone who had been tightly tied around her legs and bound to a chair, and these were the marks that remained. The broad dark band across her head was like a bandage. As the injurious instruments cut into her brain, she

673

struggled to free herself from the knotted cords that bound her, and they cut in deeper.

Tighter!

Tighter!

Grace Poole gave Dr. Wolcott Ascharm Webster a cord, and he pinioned the arms of the madwoman behind her, and bound her to a chair with more rope. Panting, sweating, he bound her legs. Grace Poole held another cord ready, silently, without waiting to be asked. She knew what was expected of her.

"*This* is what I wished to have," he said, "this young girl, who stands so grave and quiet at the mouth of hell, looking collectedly at the gambols of a demon. I wanted her just as a change . . ."

"We don't blame you!"

That's what the watching Bearded Ones were supposed to reply.

"We'd have felt the same!"

Tighter!

Tighter!

She reached her hand up toward her reflection, as if, in her turn, to draw circles – more like elongated ovals – at the top of the high forehead, beneath the eyes, across the top lip, with a sharpened BBB. With a more discreet – attractively feminine – moustache, Madeline Usher would look exactly the same as Louis Moreau Gottschalk, Edgar Allan Poe, her twin brother . . .

Who is the fairest one of all?

The disease of the lady Madeline had long baffled the skill of her physicians. A settled apathy, a gradual wasting away of the person, and frequent although transient affections of a partially cataleptical character, were the unusual diagnosis.

Alice traced the ovals upon her reflection in the looking-glass, at the top of the high forehead, beneath the eyes, across the top lip, blurring the image. She had read "The Fall of the House of Usher," and had caught the disease from the words on the page – that was what had happened – the settled apathy creeping up inside her, the black ink upon her fingertips like the first telltale symptoms of a plague, the words that had poisoned her when touched. She peered at the tips of her fingers, her hand held palm-first in front of her face, looking for the blackness there, tracing for a meaning in the lines. *A settled apathy. A gradual wasting away. Transient affections.* Whatever it was that Madeline Usher had had, she – unmistakably – suffered from it, also.

We have put her living in the tomb!

She peered shortsightedly at her face, gazing upon the House of Usher and its landscape, the rank sedges, the white trunks of decayed trees. They were like the first sight of Treasure Island: the gray – *grey* – melancholy woods, the wild stone spires, the peculiar stagnant smell hanging over the anchorage, the smell of sodden leaves and rotted tree trunks, the clouds of birds wheeling and crying over the woods, and the surf foaming and thundering on the steep beach.

The worst dreams Jim Hawkins ever had were when he heard the surf booming, or started upright in bed, with the sharp voice of Captain Flint still ringing in his ears: "Pieces of eight! Pieces of eight!"

Hush, little baby, don't say a word,
Papa's going to buy you a mockingbird.

If that mockingbird won't sing,
Papa's going to buy you a diamond ring.

If that diamond ring turns to brass,
Papa's going to buy you a looking-glass.

25

Tentatively, she reached out the little finger of her right hand toward the glass front of the moon-dial clock on the mantel, as if it was unlocked, and she was about to flick it open with the edge of her nail, like Papa flicking open his pocket-watch to listen to one of the tinkling music box tunes. A little flick with her little finger, a push with her pinkie, an appropriate enough action for a Pinkerton. "Pinkie" was what some of the boys at Otsego Lake Academy had called Ben, not in a particularly friendly way. She wiggled her little finger. *Pinkie*. She wiggled her index finger. *Trigger*. One slight movement with each finger, and there would be peace, an end to moonlight and voices.

Perhaps it might work this time. The slight counterclockwise push with the very tip of her finger, barely denting the flesh, and the cold illumination would slowly retreat from the room as the near-full moon was rolled away into the darkness, until only the stars remained.

> All of these things your Papa will do,
> Because of the way that he loves you.

She turned up the lamp a little more. The moonlight on the floor was driven completely away from the room, and light bloomed outward.

High up as she was, she did not always draw her drapes as she once had, and she was enclosed by looking-glasses on all four walls: the dark-backed windows, the glazed surfaces of pictures, the bookcases. All, in the light of the lamp, reflected her standing in front of the biggest looking-glass in the warm glow from the flickering fire, her hand pressed against her breast. It was a gesture she kept repeating unconsciously. It was starting to snow heavily again. She could hear it against the windowpanes, see the whiteness swarming against the dark outer corners away from the reflections. Her looking-glasses were Dr. Jekyll's, not Dorian Gray's, and her reflections in the windows and bookcases – she was surrounded by herself, all the Alices from all the books, in a gloomy winter park crowded round by grotesque frost-protected statues – were distorted, warped into ugly, unrecognizably disfigured shapes, displaying ugliness, not beauty. Perhaps they were a mirror of what she really was, enclosed within a Coney Island mirror maze, wasting her entrance money by failing to laugh at the blurred, flaw-changed images, alone in a crowd of misshapen strangers, pointing, laughing, all of whom had her face and body. She should be a vampire, looking into a mirror and seeing nothing there. Now that *would* be a true reflection of what she was, what she would be.

There was something she ought to remember about a mirror, something that had occurred to her earlier that day. She had written it down. She would find it, read it, and add more to it. It was an idea for a story, a beginning from which something was starting to develop. It had been inside her all day, and it would be growing. Something about a mirror. Once she had been scared not to write things down, in case she forgot them. Now she let them grow until the right time came.

Looking-glass, looking-glass, on the wall.

If that looking-glass gets broke . . .

If that looking-glass got broke, Ice Queen splinters would freeze her heart within her, putting an end to all attempts at weeping.

Crack! Crack!

Beneath the thin layer of ice was the cold dark water.

She was below the ice, seeing light, hearing faint sounds, but unable to break through, unable to take a breath.

Inside the copy of *A Child's Garden of Verses* that she had given to Ben when he was a little boy, she had written *From your loving sister.* "*The children sing in far Japan,*" picking out this line from "Singing," seemingly knowing that Ben would travel to that country one day. It was a book without pictures, and when she had read the verses she had seen scenes from her own childhood, feeling that the poems had been about her. She wondered if he had the book in his room somewhere. There was still a "his" room. The previous lines of the poem, with even more seeming prescience, were *The sailor sings of ropes and things / In ships upon the seas,* but she had written what she had written because she had just been to see *The Mikado* with Charlotte.

"When the bright lamp is carried in,
The sunless hours again begin . . ."

She reached her hands up and over her shoulders, and began to unhook the back of her dress.

". . . O'er all without, in field and lane,
The haunted night returns again.

"Now we behold the embers flee
About the firelit hearth; and see
Our faces painted as we pass,
Like pictures, on the window-glass.

"Must we to bed indeed? Well then,
Let us arise and go like men . . ."

— like men, like men, she must be like a man —

". . . And face with an undaunted tread . . ."

— she must be undaunted, she must summon up the spirit of Lizzie Galliant, protectress from childhood —

". . . The long black passage up to bed.

"Farewell, O brother, sister, sire!. . ."

She let her dress slip down, and there were words . . .
There were words . . .
The words were — for a while — just out of her reach like the name of a snatch of remembered music, and then they came to her.
Her rich attire creeps rustling to her knees . . .
Something like that.
Well, "rich" was wrong, but the sound was right. It was "The

Eve of St. Agnes" again: Madeline preparing for sleep, hoping to receive visions of delight, as — unknown to her — Porphyro watched. *Her rich attire crept rustling to her knees: half-hidden, like a mermaid in sea-weed, pensive awhile she dreamt awake.*

For a long time she had thought — it must have blighted many an afternoon at Miss Pearsall's School for Girls — that Porphyro had taken Madeline away to murder her. "Porphyria's Lover" had somehow become conflated with Porphyro — Robert Browning fused with John Keats (a testament to the clarity of Miss Swanstrom's teaching) — and she had pictured Madeline being strangled by her own hair on another night on which the wind blew. The feast that Porphyro had prepared in the chamber — especially the candied apple, the jellies, and the lucent syrops — had sounded ominously like the seductive, corrupting fruits of the goblin men. Her lover found a thing to do, and all her hair in one long yellow string he wound three times her little throat around and strangled her. He propped her head up on his shoulder, and all night long, as the wind raged, he sat unstirring with her corpse beside him.

These lovers fled away into the storm.

". . . O wind, a-blowing all day long,
　　O wind, that sings so loud a song!

"I saw the different things you did,
But always you yourself you hid.
I felt you push, I heard you call,
I could not see yourself at all —
　　O wind, a-blowing all day long,
　　O wind, that sings so loud a song!

"O you that are so strong and cold,
O blower, are you young or old?
Are you a beast of field and tree,
Or just a stronger child than me?. . ."

She knew the answer to this one.

She held up her hand in the childless schoolroom — *I know! I know! Ask me! Ask me!* — but nobody asked her.

She saw the different things it did.

She felt it push.

She heard it call.

It was strong and cold.

It was not young.

It was a beast.

It was stronger than she was, and it was not a child.

26

She shifted her face a little to the left, and again studied the face of Louis Moreau Gottschalk, the face of Edgar Allan Poe next to her reflection — she was drawn to the eyes — in the way that people had studied the face of her new baby brother twenty-five years ago. There was a special way of looking at the faces of babies, at the faces in old photographs, searching for likenesses between what was and what once had been. This was how she was looking at herself, trying to recognize someone she had once known.

Why had Lewis Carroll kept to the usual red and white chess pieces, instead of changing them to black and white, to echo the black and white kittens, a Black Queen, a Black Knight? She imagined the king and queen playing chess on the Flemish tapestry in Dorian Gray's schoolroom as black and white pieces, a white king holding a white king, and a white queen holding a black queen, as if shifting into her shadow. They moved across the tiles of the kitchen floor at nighttime, when everyone was asleep, creeping out like mice or cockroaches into the clock-ticking stillness.

Sometimes, in darkness, in candlelight, she had looked into the mirror in an attempt to see Annie's face, the dark reflection looking back into her eyes, the white piece opposite the black piece, like an object and its shadow. Shadow gave depth to substance. That was what her drawing teacher had told her.

You had to have shadows, as if no day were sunless.

To dream of seeing yourself in a mirror, denotes that you will meet many discouraging issues, and sickness will cause you distress and loss in fortune.

It was Annie's eyes that she could remember best.

She felt like Madeline on St. Agnes' Eve – January the twentieth: no wonder it had been so cold, no wonder it had been snowing – carrying out all the correct rituals in order to see the face of her beloved, the murderer who would carry her away to his haunted palace. Mrs. Alexander Diddecott always claimed that Halloween was the best night for this sort of thing, the night to produce the best results. You leaned over a bowl of water with a lighted candle – it had to be at midnight, as the clock was chiming – allowing the molten candle wax to drip into the water, and (she assured them) the fallen wax would harden into the initial of the man with whom you would fall in love, or (at the least) marry. You had to complete the action within the time that it took for the clock to strike twelve. If you failed to achieve this, you had to wait a whole year until the next St. Agnes' Eve before you could do it again.

Surely there'd be an excess of lovers whose names began with "I" or "O," the most likely shapes for falling wax to form, eager jostling crowds of Ians and Osberts, Irwins and Orvilles, pushy lips confidently pursed for kissing? Were you allowed to move about a bit, attempting to write, like naughty, frostbite-defying small boys writing their names in the snow as they urinated (she sometimes saw rather more than she bargained for when she looked down from her high window), or was that cheating?

"Me! Me! *Me!*" chorused the crowds of Ians and Osberts, the bustling throngs of Irwins and Orvilles.

I am the man of your dreams!

I am the lover foretold in the mystic midnight ceremony!

In candlelight you leaned across the water, struggling to make out letters in the dimness, in Mr. Brczin's consulting room on Indian Woods Road, in dire need of new spectacles.

"I think it might be a 'C.' No, a 'Q.' It *could* be a 'Q.' Unless it's a 'D,' or an 'O' . . ."

The lenses grew thicker and thicker, the size and shape of portholes. You saw the dim reflection of yourself glinting on the surface of the water, a distant figure at the bottom of a well.

Bong! the clock chimed hollowly, down in the hall.

Bong!

Twelve seconds, that was the only time you had in all the year to discover that name.

Bong!

Bong!

Did you attempt (another part of the All-Hallows' Eve fun, self-consciously preserving old traditions like a participant in a mummers' play, a bell-jingling English morris dancer, or the choir in *Under the Greenwood Tree*) to sink your teeth into apples floating in the same water, risking mouthfuls of wax – *Teuch!* – chewing death masks, cannibalistic teeth closing on the initials of one's beloved?

Bong!

Bong!

Economically uniting two traditions in one, you could – in one continuous piece – cut the peel from the apple you'd retrieved from the water (removing it from your mouth first made this significantly easier), and throw it over your shoulder. It would fall – Madame Diddecott assured them – into the initial of the man who was the one for you, the Ian or Irwin or Isaac, the Osbert or (preferably not) Orville, the Ivor or (even worse) Oswald.

Brace yourself, Ivan!

Purse those lips, Oscar!

You bear names with a favored letter.

How likely was it that apple peel would form an "H" or an "E" or a "B"? Determined girls would peel and peel away if they'd set their hearts on Harold or Edward or (an interesting choice, this one, from a girl who liked a challenge) Brian – how many apples had Dr. Wolcott Ascharm Webster crunched his teeth into, like an Adam enthusiastically embracing sinfulness, waist-deep in browning, cidery-smelling peel? – and their families would be eating apple pies for months.

Bong!

Bong!

They should have sent in Dr. Wolcott Ascharm Webster when they were demolishing the apple orchards. He'd have chewed his way through them in no time, peel hurtling over his shoulders, a combine harvester at full throttle, wrecking the little lost pockets of Paradise as comprehensively as a whole galaxy of Mrs. Albert Comstocks crashing cataclysmically to earth.

Bong!

Bong!

Madeline leaned over the bowl of water, searching for the face of the man who was going to murder her. It was so difficult to see clearly. Behind her, on the casement high and triple-arch'd, St. Agnes was depicted in the glass, three times over, with her threefold malformed lambs hugely leaping, their hooves sharpened for killing. In bed, supperless, lying upon her back, Madeline would look like the sculptur'd dead in the chapel, emprison'd in black, purgatorial rails: knights, ladies, praying in dumb orat'ries, aching in icy hoods and mails.

There were only a couple of seconds left!

She peered closely, almost immersing her face in the water.

She could see something!

P!

P!

She could definitely see a "P."

Bong!

Bong!

Just in time.

The man who would murder her had a name that began with a "P."

In another room, a similar room, a room not far away, Dr. Jekyll gazed into a cheval glass, weeping like a lost soul, searching for changes in his face, for the hidden monster that came from within him. He had the intense focused stare of a Narcissus who loathed his reflection, yet could not look away, mesmerized by his own eyes. *Ker-plunk, ker-plunk, ker-plunkety plunky-plunk* . . . In a room beyond this one, through the wall from Dr. Jekyll, each seeing the other as his own reflection, Dorian Gray stood in front of his portrait with a mirror, also searching for changes, the signs of aging. As it had revealed to him his own body, so it would reveal to him his own soul. Dr. Jekyll sobbed in front of his reflection, seeing the dreadful thing he had become, and Dorian Gray smiled in front of his, seeing nothing but unchanging, ageless beauty. Order was reversed in his schoolroom, a place from within the Looking-glass House, and it had become a room in which a work of art aged, and a human being never altered. There should have been a portrait of himself in Dr. Jekyll's cabinet alongside his cheval glass, a portrait that never changed in the way that Dorian Gray's changed, an image of himself as he had once been. The reflection in the mirror would change, day by day it would change, altered by that which grew inside, even if the only change was that caused by time, and still he would sob, as the — this time — unchanging nature of art intensified the sense of his own fragile transience.

The Reverend Goodchild was not just wrong about Mrs. Rochester, and about Dorian Gray's portrait. He was wrong about Mr. Hyde. Mr. Hyde was not something huge, Frankenstein creature-like, as she had heard him claim. He was ever made uneasy by that "stein" (she had heard some of his comments about wonderful, ardent, dark-eyed Miss Stein) and it was probably this that had led to his also being wrong about Frankenstein's creature. He thought that the unnamed creature was itself called Frankenstein, having assumed the name of its creator, absorbed him within itself, as Mr. Hyde had absorbed Dr. Jekyll. Mr. Hyde, however, was something far more disturbing than this.

Mr. Hyde was not a shambling monster, lurching clumsily within the unfamiliar clothing of its body.

Mr. Hyde was the size of a child, a hunched and hideous *child*.

He was the size of a deformed child dressed in adult clothing enormously too large for it – the trousers hanging on the legs and rolled up, the waist of the coat below his haunches, the collar sprawling wide upon his shoulders – like the ill-dressed lunatics in *Hard Cash*. It was as if – like Dorian Gray – he had had his childhood stolen from him, and this had turned him into something misshapen and revolting, horrible – most horrible – to look upon, his stunted body reflecting the ugliness of his malnourished mind. There was no mention of Henry Jekyll's childhood in *The Strange Case of Dr. Jekyll and Mr. Hyde*, apart from the brief comment – just after he had thought himself saved – that he had thought of his life as a whole, following it up from the days of childhood, when he had walked with his father's hand. That was the one memory of his childhood: himself as a child walking hand in hand with his father.

Walking where?

Walking to what?

The descriptions of Edward Hyde were the descriptions of a child – smaller, slighter, younger, than Henry Jekyll – in whom something had gone horribly wrong, and made him monstrous, a thing with a haunting sense of unexpressed deformity.

That child of Hell had nothing human.

That was what Henry Jekyll had said.

(Father Hell, the sinful priest come forth to acknowledge his sin-born child – this thing of darkness he acknowledged his – stepped out from the shadows with Franz Mesmer. He was holding steel implements in both hands, and they glinted slightly. They'd dazzle in full light, perfect for the application of mesmerism. Once you'd got them to take their clothes off, it wasn't too difficult to get them to agree to having the steel applied to their naked bodies. *Turn around!* That was what they were whispering in unison. *Turn around!* They whispered so quietly that anyone hearing them would turn around, thinking that they were responding to promptings from within their own minds.)

Child.

"*Young* Hyde" was what Mr. Utterson, the lawyer, called him, as if his youth were the most horrible thing about him.

"*Master* Hyde" was what he called him.

The first time Mr. Hyde entered the novella, he calmly crushed a girl of eight or ten under his feet, and left her screaming on the ground, a man attempting to destroy what reminded him of childhood, though – in truth – he scarcely seemed aware of what he had done, trampling through her as if she were not there at all, a childhood that had never been. Mr. Utterson had nightmares about him, and saw the little figure glide stealthily through sleeping houses, or move the more swiftly, and still the more swiftly, even to dizziness, through the wider labyrinths of a lamp-lighted city, and at every street corner crush a child and leave her screaming. And still the figure had no face by which he might know it.

He did not have the mirror that Dr. Jekyll had, the mirror unstained by breath, in which he might see the reflection of that for which he sought, the thing that was pale and dwarfish, the thing that gave an impression of deformity without any namable malformation.

Mr. Hyde entered Dr. Jekyll's house through the blistered and stained door that was on the dark, hidden side of the house, in a by-street, the door without bell or knocker, the door that led into the dissecting-room. That was how *The Strange Case of Dr. Jekyll and Mr. Hyde* began, with the section entitled "Story of the Door." That was the *Knock And It Shall Be Opened Unto You* door, the door that she sometimes saw as the door of their house on Chestnut Street, the looking-glass door of Dr. Wolcott Ascharm Webster's house on Park Place, the door that was every door in Longfellow Park, with gleaming, grinning, G. G. Schiffendecken false-teeth door knockers.

She had knocked.

The door had been Opened Unto her.

It was a door that was opened in the way that the lid of Pandora's box was lifted, driven open by the powers of what lay within.

She saw the small grotesque figure — Mr. Hyde, Dorian Gray — bent over in the schoolroom, at the desk, its face hidden, very still, conscious of wrongdoing and not wishing to be seen, flooded in red light. When it moved, it would be a crab-like scuttling from shadow to shadow. It was writing and writing and writing, as obsessively as a thing that could never stop, the one task that remained for it to do.

Scribble, scribble, scribble.

The only part of his original character that remained to Henry Jekyll, when he changed into Edward Hyde and was unable to change back again, was his handwriting. Perhaps he was writing his name over and over, to remind himself of who he really was, though the shriveled child he saw in the mirror was not that person. In this, wasn't he like anyone else, looking into a mirror and seeing a strange reflection that was not the person inside, feeling this more and more powerfully as the years went by, as the reflection aged?

Henry Jekyll.

Henry Jekyll.

Henry Jekyll . . .

"That's me," Henry Jekyll thought, lingering over the curve in the letter "J" and the "y"s, touching the loops of the "k" and the "l"s, as though the handwriting were more real than he was. He wrote slowly and carefully, lingering over each letter caressingly, like someone who had to think about the spelling, trying to write in his most beautiful handwriting, attempting to create an attractiveness about the name that had vanished forever from the person it had once defined.

Henry Jekyll.

Henry Jekyll.

Henry Jekyll . . .

That's *me*. That's *me*.

(*Edward Hyde.*

(That's what he heard from the whispering inside himself.

(*Edward Hyde.*

(*Edward Hyde* . . .

(That's what he saw reflected in the mirror.)

Henry Jekyll.

Henry Jekyll.

Henry Jekyll . . .

He wrote the same words over and over, like a badly behaved schoolboy set a copying task by a schoolmaster as a punishment, writing the same lines repeatedly for hour after hour. They were the words of a lesson he had failed to learn, or an admonition to be memorized and never forgotten, Hyde-bound by the malformed and terrifying child that he had become. He tried to write his name exactly the same each time he wrote it, the letters precisely the same size, the angles and whorls as identical as thumbprints or fingerprints repeatedly impressed from the same hand.

Henry Jekyll.

Henry Jekyll.

Henry Jekyll . . .

(*I must NOT* . . .

(That's what he should have been writing, carrying out the imposition he had been given to avoid further chastisement.

(*I must NOT* . . .

(*I must NOT* . . .

(That was the lesson that ought to have been learned by heart.

(As he wrote out the lines he became less and less conscious of what it was he was writing, seeing nothing but the unwritten whiteness between the words, rather than the words themselves.)

He existed in what he had written, not in who he was.

What he had written he would leave behind him, and what he was would cease to be.

As he wrote, he wept, and it was not the weeping of a child. It was the sound that Poole had heard through the locked door of his master's cabinet, the sound that was like the weeping of a woman or a lost soul, the weeping that came away upon his heart, and made the butler himself wish to weep.

When the bright lamp is carried in,/The sunless hours again begin. These were night thoughts.

27

All that she could hear was the wind, and the windblown snow pattering against the windows. Linnaeus's painting, hanging on the wall opposite, was reflected in the mirror. There it was, above and beyond the face of Edgar Allan Poe, the face of Louis Moreau Gottschalk, like a glimpse into another room, distant, out of reach, hanging in a corridor in the Looking-glass House, its emptiness deepening a sense of inner silence.

She turned, and walked over to it.

Most nights, most mornings, she stood in front of it for a while.

It was not a painting that became unseen in the room, a part of the furniture, not seen because seen so often. Like a window, like a door, it was something of which she was always aware, opened anew each day to something different. It was not there for its size, for its color, for its blending in with what was already present.

She felt the sensation that she had felt that morning in the hall, just after she had imagined the copy of the *Hudson Valley Chronicle* lying on the tiles, with the engravings of The Bearded Ones, and thought of the words of "Goblin Market," the two sisters, Lizzie and Laura.

> *. . . That night long Lizzie watched by Laura,*
> *Counted her pulse's flagging stir,*
> *Felt for her breath,*
> *Held water to her lips, and cooled her face*
> *With tears and fanning leaves . . .*

"I am Lizzie Galliant," she said, repeating the words she had said before she had gone down to Annie's room on another night of snow, the words she had not said for years. "Strong men fall powerless before me! I have the power that alone belongs to women! Men's beards will burst into flame at my approach and flare wondrously!"

It would be like the scene of the dancing in *She*, where the mummified corpses of the long-dead were set ablaze like enormous flaming torches to act as illumination, or the scene in *Quo Vadis?* where Nero illuminated his pleasure gardens with the blazing bodies of living Christians. The Bearded Ones – a more entertaining spectacle – would, after flaring wondrously, explode like Guy Fawkes Night fireworks. Dr. Wolcott Ascharm Webster, Dr. Vaniah Odom, G. G. Schiffendecken, the Reverend Goodchild, Papa: all would fizz like Roman candles, flaring stars rocketing up into the sky.

"Did you say *Roman*?" Dr. Vaniah Odom hissed waspishly as he ignited, not pleased, not pleased at all, as he shot skyward.

Whooosh!

Whooosh!

Whooosh!

It was the apocalyptic end of *Through the Looking-Glass*, as Alice pulled the tablecloth with both hands, crashing plates, dishes, and guests to the floor, as bottles flew about, and candles soared up to the ceiling, exploding into stars, as if Alice had slept right through to the following night, the night of the fireworks.

Whooosh!

Whooosh!

Whooosh!

It was the wrong ending, from the wrong book, but she wanted to say the words she had said so often as a child, lashing out with clenched fists at the air in front of her.

"Stuff and nonsense!"

"I won't!"

"Who cares for *you*?"

"You're nothing but a pack of cards!"

She was taller now, more of a height with her adversaries, and she should grow her nails long, like Dr. Wolcott Ascharm Webster. She should unclench her fists, and lash out with her nails, aiming at throats, at eyes. They would be within reach now.

As she stood in front of Linnaeus's painting, the crackling and the explosions, the oohs and the aahs, the acrid gunpowder smell, the frightened shouted words, all faded away. She was aware of nothing but the scene in front of her, a painting of the room in which she stood, the large painting another mirror, reflecting an interior in which she did not exist. Her breathing was stilled — breath misted glass — as she looked into the Looking-glass House of the painting. She did not stand too close to it, holding back a little, feeling that she was above a great height, and might fall into it.

Like all Linnaeus's paintings, the scene contained no human figure, but its title was a person's name. All the pictures hanging in Delft Place had this same style. They were conversation pieces without the human figures, paintings of silence, and most were of interiors. *Charlotte* — his painting of his sister — showed the window at which Charlotte sat as she looked out on to the Hudson, sewing, reading, writing letters, sorting her little collections. *Mother* was the piazza on a summer's day, a cane chair, and the telescope. *Father* was a painting of an empty field — the cloud-filled sky seemed to go on forever — near a small copse, a place she did not recognize. The painting that bore his own name, his last painting — he had named it *Linnaeus*, and not *Self Portrait*, making it appear that he was not Linnaeus — was yet another of the empty, drapeless, bare-boarded, white-doored rooms at Delft Place, the rooms he painted over and over, rooms lined with his own paintings. You did not feel that the paintings were of the interiors around them; you felt that the interiors were designed to match the paintings, a representation of some inner place, close, just out of reach. The rooms became stiller as they were gazed upon. There was no sound, no movement, and

691

all around became suffused with their unpeopled emptiness. If she looked hard enough at the empty rooms and deserted landscapes, if she concentrated on the unpopulated places where people once had been, she sometimes felt that she would be able to see these absent people. If she didn't see Charlotte, if she didn't see Mother or Father, she might begin to see Linnaeus in every painting, even if the paintings bore the names of other people.

He had not sold any of his paintings. They were not the sort of paintings that people wished to buy. He had sometimes made a little money — as with the cloud-covered skies for Henry Walden Gauntlett, the glories of the angels for the Reverend Calbraith — by carrying out little jobs that required some artistic ability, like Miss Iandoli adding to the earnings she made from teaching piano-playing by hand-coloring photographs. She imagined Linnaeus walking about at first light, when no one would see him, carrying a palette with only two colors upon it, and renewing the red and the black of the signs all around Longfellow Park. *Keep Off, Keep Off,* he'd paint over and over. *Beware.* If he'd still been alive, it would probably have been Linnaeus who would have been hired to paint the giant Mozart on Megoran Road. He would have painted the right music in the sky. He had been meticulous about that sort of thing.

> *Soave sia il vento,*
> *Tranquilla sia l'onda . . .*

The breezes would be gentle, the sea would be calm, as the two young women prayed for those they loved.

The paintings reminded her of Ida Brook's room after she had died. She and Charlotte had gone to see Ida's mother, to express their condolences. Ida hadn't really been a friend of theirs, and that was one of the reasons why they had gone: feelings of remorse, things they had said, things they hadn't said (this last above all). Ida had seemed in perpetual hopeful search of a close friend.

"Would you like to see the room in which she died?" the

mother had suddenly asked — not waiting for a reply — after their faltering attempts at conversation had faded into silence, and they had been led upstairs to gaze in silence, another silence, at a room in which they had never been before, trying to feel something, that someone had died there, trying to think of what to say. The drapes had been partially closed across the slightly opened window, the blind partly lowered, as if an invalid was still there, shielded from too bright a light, and the bed was neatly made, the sheets and blankets so tightly drawn across that no one could have lain inside them. *Tip-tap. Tip-tap.* She had spent the time trying to detect the source of the slight tapping she could hear, and then realized that it was the pull on the end of the blind cord. The little wooden acorn was rattling against the sash bar. *Tip-tap.* *Tip-tap.* Death was silence.

"Ida Brook! Ida Brook!" She faintly heard Miss Swanstrom's voice raised for one last time in weary expostulation at the unparalleled dimness and clumsiness of Ida Brook.

For one last time she heard Ida Brook's voice.

"Oh dear," she said. "I've died. Oh dear. How on earth did that happen? Mama will be so upset."

She would never hear Ida Brook's voice again, never see that clumsy, galumphing girl clodhopping about with tousled hair and ink-stained fingers. The mother had closed the door behind them as they entered, and Alice had felt stifled, oppressed, despite the open window. It was too tidy a room for Ida Brook to live in. That was the main thing she thought. How little she'd been affected by the death of someone she'd known. How small a space was occupied by the living.

Alice always closed the door of any room in which she found herself, but the doors at Delft Place — like the doors in the paintings — were always left open, leading into further rooms beyond, and rooms beyond those, illuminated by the light from unseen windows. Someone was expected to call at any moment, and no barrier was to be placed in his way as he stepped into the interior.

Alice — Charlotte had given her the painting for her thirtieth birthday — was a meticulous representation of the schoolroom, the room in which she lived her life, though a room from which she was absent. It was as if she was being remembered by what she had left behind her after she had ceased to exist: the windows, the mirror, the bed, the bookcases, the golden stars from All Saints', the broken figures and pieces of glass from the Shakespeare Castle, the papers, the Huntley & Palmers tin, the writing materials, the unpublished novels and stories. She loved this painting, seeing her surroundings, without herself being there, a great weight lifted – a great oppression toppled – by her absence.

28

She walked across to the window that looked out from the back of the house, and took up the position she had assumed that morning. As the wind gusted, snow was flung against the windows, like handfuls of gravel thrown to gain attention.

She opened her hand as she stood there, and looked at her reflection in the mirror on Annie's ring, as she sometimes did at Mrs. Albert Comstock's, when it seemed to take away the sound from all around her. She held it up close to her face, so that all she could see was her own eye looking back at her. It was her Pinkerton badge of office, flourished imperiously to open doors that would otherwise be barred. *We Never Sleep*, that was what the unblinking eye promised, a future of perpetual dreamlessness, in which all nights would be spent watching those who were suspected, taking notes, thinking, building up evidence.

Scribble, scribble, scribble.

When you'd seen the right things, heard the right words, you moved in to put an end to what had to be stopped, the guilty vanishing from the world as the narrow barred windows closed in around them.

She brought the looking-glass ring closer, closer, until the eye began to blur. She was looking for a little white reflection on the iris, as if it would be there at nighttime, the memory of the light that had been shining in through a window in daylight. In photographs, in paintings, windows that were not visible were sensed in that tiny glimmer, opening out the enclosed room into the wider world beyond. The subjects of Henry Walden Gauntlett's photographs – grouped in front of their cloud-filled skies – all had this brightness in the upper part of the eye, a little to one side, on the verge of tears. He said that it brought them to life, gave them humanity, and discarded any photographs in which he had failed to capture this effect. They had died without that light.

He had told Kate this when she was learning about photography from him, one of the mysteries of his art. Alice remembered the occasions on which she had been to his studio, to be photographed with her family, feeling that she and her sisters were back at Carlo Fiorelli's being photographed for *The Children's Hour*. She tried not to think of these photographs. She had thought that people would live longer since photography had been invented, their faces remaining after they were dead, but – somehow – the opposite was true. There was a new sadness now because of photographs, even of the living. You seemed to be more aware of change, the perpetual impermanence of being, the ever-aging reflections in the looking-glasses. In the Looking-glass world of the White Queen the inhabitants lived their lives backward, and memory worked both ways. Memories of the future intruded into the present. The Queen – she practiced believing in impossible things – screamed before the brooch pricked her finger; the bleeding came later, with no screams, as the pain had already been experienced. In a similar looking-glass reversal, Alice felt – it was what Dr. Wolcott Ascharm Webster made her feel – that her past lay before her, and not behind her. All that would happen, all that she would become, was shaped by what had already been, and what had already been could not be changed. She would travel through her life, to find her past moving backward toward her from the future, and she would relive all that had already happened. She looked for the little gleam of whiteness, a glimpse of an emptiness within, trying to remember if there had been a similar gleam in Annie's eyes, a similar emptiness.

"Only it is so *very* lonely here!"

That was what Alice had said to the White Queen.

She gazed at the little dot of whiteness on the iris, gazing into this void, until the whiteness seemed to move out toward her, and the features of the face dissolved. Whoever was there in the photograph could no longer be seen, and all she saw was the whiteness, like a nothingness inside them, this little gleam that gave them life. Emptiness and absence drew memories out of her, like magic-lantern projections onto a white screen: the former orchards, now featureless snow-covered building lots; the space above the trees, where the tower of the Shakespeare Castle had once been. It was an image captured on a photograph, one of those blurred ghost figures — not fully there, not quite absent — of someone walking in a street whilst it was being photographed, someone who had not stayed motionless for the duration of the exposure. She had seen such photographs, some of Kate's studies: the sharply delineated buildings, the transparent, transient, fading human beings. It was strange to see ghosts walking in sunlight, their faint outlines, their blurred features. Ghosts should disappear in sunshine, the way that shadows disappeared with the coming of clouds. Ghosts were shadows, thrown by the shape of the person who saw them. New York City was changing so rapidly that anyone who had been there for some time would see all streets like this, the buildings become as ghostly as the human figures, as short-lived. In street after street, block after block, the buildings — demolished, swept away in weeks, days — would exist only in the memory, people seeing what had once been there, mistily superimposed over what now existed. If she went back to Grandpapa's office, retraced her Gulliver's journey on the day she had traveled into the realm of The Bearded Ones, she would become another Rip Van Winkle (beardless, deprived of power) as she wandered lost amongst the vanished buildings, the vanished streets, the whole districts that had vanished forever, unable to recognize where she was. There would be rows of houses which she would never have seen before, and those which had been familiar would have disappeared. There would be towers in the sky that had not been there before, a deeper darkness in the ghost-crowded streets. Strange names would be over the doors, strange faces at the windows, everything would be strange. She'd be staring around, speechless and lost.

She had seen such photographs, also, when Mrs. Alexander Diddecott produced alleged evidence that ghosts existed, and manifestations during séances (Alice wasn't sure whether these, also, qualified as ghosts), pointing triumphantly at the semitransparent misty figures of men and women awkwardly posed on twilight staircases or in empty rooms. When they appeared alongside the living they appeared to be superimposed from another dimension, unaware of the others around them, their introspective eyes not quite looking in the right direction, not quite looking at the right angle. All of them had a blurry radiance around their faces, like the glowing nimbuses of the saints in the stained glass windows of All Saints', sanctified because they were dead. When they spoke – Mrs. Alexander Diddecott assured her that they sometimes spoke (she had tried to persuade Charlotte to come with her, to speak with her dead brother) – Alice imagined that they spoke with the voice of a ventriloquist's manipulated figure, the voice of Dum-Dum the Dummy.

You can't stop me talking.
You can never stop me talking.
Dum-Dum says what must be said.
The dead have to speak.

It seemed that – seeing these images in the other, outdoor photographs – the streets were ghost-crowded, the figures of the dead passing unseen in daylight amidst the living they outnumbered.

The Reverend Goodchild had a line of similar photographs in the Sunday-school room, a whole row of Children Who Had

Found the Lord and Been Saved. They looked not unlike Mrs. Alexander Diddecott's winsome waifs, but with added smugness. "I've been saved!" they were declaring. "And *you haven't!*" Only considerable self-control, you felt, kept them from thrusting out their tongues mockingly at the doomed, like – a daunting visualization, possible only in the most capacious of minds – massed mocking rows of Serenity Goodchilds and Myrtle Comstocks. Alice – her soul was undoubtedly damned, and she'd end up comparing notes in hell with Dr. Faustus, both of them sulky and complaining, like ill-mannered captains of losing teams – couldn't stop herself seeing "Saved" in sporting terms. In photograph after photograph she imagined mud-stained men – dressed for football or baseball (many of them favored stripes), blurred with movement in front of a net or beside a white line – triumphantly holding up the Children Who Had Found the Lord. "Saved!" they were shouting, breathless but triumphant. "Saved!" Being Saved seemed, unfortunately, to result – almost immediately – in death. The realization grew upon you as you studied the details of the Saved beneath each photograph, the throb-throbbing details of virtuous deathbed speeches unparalleled since the time when Dickens had shamelessly committed Nellicide (though Little Eva had jealously tried her best in *Uncle Tom's Cabin*). This was not much of an incentive for good behavior to the seething mob of juveniles crammed into the Sunday-school. No wonder Mabel Peartree had such difficulty in controlling them.

Annie had not been photographed. There were no photographs of Annie, unless – somewhere – she was captured in a ghost-photograph as she trudged toward Washington Square, a wraith like a shadow in the street, barely seen against the sidewalk. Alice thought again of the lack of photographs in her room, she and her family people who had never been. There was the memory of a voice, eyes in a fading face.

She . . .

She couldn't . . .

She couldn't really . . .

She couldn't really remember Annie all that well, though she attempted to persuade herself that she could.

There.

She'd put it into words.

Annie, where art thou?

Her eyes were as dark as the pips of a pear.

"Pretty Polly Perkins of Paddington Green."

That was the title of the song she had been trying to remember, though now that she remembered the song she didn't think that the line about the eyes being as dark as the pips of a pear came from it. She had been convinced that it did. She could hear the voices singing from across Park Place.

> "I am a broken-hearted milkman, in grief I'm arrayed
> Through keeping of the company of a young servant maid
> Who lived on board and wages the house to keep clean,
> In a gentleman's family near Paddington Green.
>
> "She was as beautiful as a butterfly
> And proud as a Queen
> Was pretty little Polly Perkins
> Of Paddington Green . . ."

Pretty little Annie Clement of Longfellow Park.

> *. . . With a smile upon her countenance*
> *And a laugh in her eye.*
> *If I thought that she loved me*
> *I'd have laid down to die . . .*

> ". . . The man that has me must have silver and gold . . ."

— that was what Polly Perkins had said —

". . . A chariot to ride in and be handsome and bold.
His hair must be curly as any watch-spring,
And his whiskers as big as a brush for clothing . . ."

The skylight was covered in settled snow, as it had been on the night she had gone down to Annie's room, and on the morning after the 1888 blizzard had begun. She felt that the whole house was buried beneath a huge drift. If she opened the window, snow would avalanche inward, and fill the room, hissing briefly on the lamp before bringing darkness. It would be like an icy version of the ashes that covered Pompeii, bringing death by eternal winter, and she would be found curled up within, perfectly preserved with her possessions scattered about her, just as she had imagined Annie that morning, lying choked with cinders. Their two bodies should be side by side, their arms wrapped around each other protectively, a statue caught forever in a frozen moment.

Hush, little baby, don't say a word.

Did you miss me?

Come and kiss me.

Never mind the bruises, hug me, kiss me . . .

There would be a great, white silence, and the wide swathes of snow with no footprints. Mama and Papa would be many feet above them, wrapped in furs, watching as the men that they had summoned dug down through the thick-packed snow. The horses hitched to the sled, sensing the atmosphere, frightened by the approach of the wolves, shied nervously, and their bells jingled.

"My daughter!" Mama was calling. "Save my daughter!"

Allegra and Edith had been thrown to the circling wolves, anything to keep them at bay a little longer, to buy the time necessary to save her favorite child. The wolves munched halfheartedly. What they were eating didn't taste very appetizing, but they were hungry. The spades of the diggers became a frantic blur. They knew that they were racing against time. Papa would be hurtled wolfward next. It would be their last chance. Apart from the sheer pleasure of

700

seeing him being devoured – *Munch!* went the wolves' salivating jaws. *Munch! Munch! Crunch!* (the *Crunch!* was the first mouthful of head) – there was the distinct possibility that his flesh would poison them, and that they would choke on the mighty snow-stiffened beard. The munching and howling would be replaced by retching, reeling, and writhing, so much more enjoyably alliterative. After Reeling and Writhing there would be Ambition, Distraction, Uglification, and Derision. Papa was so educational. Alice squatted amongst the rocks, looking up at the Gryphon and the Mock Turtle. Her feet were *tiny*.

From below her, deep within the house, she heard the muffled chiming of a clock. It had been hours since she'd settled Mama for the night. She'd been upset, thinking of Ben going away. Alice didn't count how many chimes there were, but it was a prolonged sequence, a late-night eleven or twelve o'clock chime.

Tick, tock, tick, tock.
His life seconds numbering,
Tick, tock, tick, tock.
It stopped short
Never to go again,
When the old man died.

No clock had stopped when Papa had died, not even the wall clock with the snow-obliterated face in his study. Unseen behind the glass the hands had turned the same as always, the pendulum swung from side to side with the same regular rhythm.

Tick, tock, tick, tock.

29

The Reverend Goodchild had made himself sound unusually beneficent when he had explained that the bodies of those buried in All Saints' graveyard were to be exhumed and reinterred in the fashionable new cemeteries. It was most magnanimous of him: the bank – having bought the land – might have been prepared to pay extra for the novelty of sinking its vaults amidst the bodies, the sides of the coffins forming unusual paneling for a subterranean boardroom. Every business benefited from new and novel ideas, and there would have been an undoubted *frisson* from handling dazzlingly polished gold bars and crisp new bank notes amidst the decay of the dead. Here the Websters would feel at home. They would rent a vault for private use, and grin unrestrainedly, unleashing their golden gleams with no fear of their smiles being smashed and grabbed by opportunist thugs. They would save up their jokes for these safe, private moments. Dr. Wolcott Ascharm Webster's upper canine – more and more fully displayed – would lull Hilde Claudia, Theodore, and Max into hypnotized forgetfulness. Their red and yellow flags would droop.

In the spring, when the ground was no longer too frozen to dig, the coffins would be removed, and it would be like the Day of Judgment in the graveyard, as the mounds of fresh soil mounted amidst the gravestones, and the bodies were drawn up out of the earth.

Papa would be rising from his grave, as if he'd never been dead.

Albert Comstock was buried – safely at a distance – over at Woodlawn Cemetery, like Reynolds Templeton Seabright, where the monuments were bigger and grander, more worthy of the colossi therein interred, but Papa was at All Saints', only a short walk away. She would be able to go across to the graveyard during the exhumations and prod his bones, to make sure that he was dead. Just in case. She did not see them as white bones, bright in the blackness. They were thick and darkly furred, partially gnawed, meat still adhering, shunned by retching predators.

Papa would be rising like a resurrection, a Lazarus who had lain in the grave for fifteen years, not four days – "Lord, by this time he stinketh" – bound hand and foot with graveclothes, and his face bound about with a napkin. Faintly, warningly, there was – on the very edge of hearing – the sound of a chamber quartet playing on odd instruments, a tune that brought its words inescapably to mind.

Toe to foot, foot to ankle, ankle to leg, leg to knee, knee to thigh, thigh to hip, hip to back, back to shoulder . . .

Dem bones. Dem dry bones.

Your shoulder bone connected to your neck bone,
Your neck bone connected to your head bone,
I hear the word of the Lord!

Dem bones, dem bones, gonna walk aroun'
Dem bones, dem bones, gonna walk aroun'
Dem bones, dem bones, gonna walk aroun'
I hear the word of the Lord!

There were only two bodies with their family name that she knew in the graveyard at All Saints'. One of them was Papa's, and one of them was the body of someone she had never known in life, someone who had died at the moment when she herself had been born. It was the body of her unnamed twin sister.

The Pinkertons were lucky, Alice supposed, in losing only one child, unless there were others that Papa did not think worthy of remembering, others that he had long since forgotten. He seemed to have forgotten those who were living, so why not those that were dead?

Perhaps she did have the gift, and really *was* the seventh child of a seventh child (there were aunts and uncles of whom she had never been told, though it was a struggle to think of Papa as a child). The little skeletons buried in the garden – they would be there somewhere, in the earth beneath neatly labeled plants, *crunch, crunch, crunch* – were not the skeletons of birds, not the forgotten nest that Catherine Linton had discovered in the wintertime. This was why she had the power to interpret dreams, the power to read clouds and pictures. Her twin sister's gravestone was the size of a milestone, the few words upon it as terse as an indication of distance: *Infant Daughter of Lincoln and Lucinda Pinkerton* (this was the only place where she had ever seen her parents' Christian names side by side) *19th March 1868*. If she were the seventh child of a seventh child, there would have to be five others buried in the garden to make up the total of the six sisters who had been born and died before her.

She saw them all as sisters.

The Seven Sisters.

Nine, with Allegra and Edith, a threefold set of Weird Sisters, with treble the power, the Dibbo Daughters comprehensively vanquished by their ignominious failure to achieve a full complement of muses. She had been the younger of the twin girls, and her unnamed older sister had died. It would have been the only time that Papa would have shown an interest in gardening, as he laid the bodies beneath the earth, patting down the soil in a way that looked like, but was not, affection, Mr. Spade, the Gardener, burying his children in the darkness. Beside him, assisting him by the flickering light of lanterns, was Mrs. Spade, the Gardener's Wife, and – the sole surviving offspring – Master Spade, the Gardener's Son, and Miss Spade, the Gardener's Daughter. All of them wielded their gardening implements – dirt-encrusted, well used and worn, not new and glinting in the circles of illumination – with the eagerness of *Treasure Island* fortune seekers. They were Burkes and Hares frantically hiding bodies beneath the soil, not unearthing them to sell, Dante Gabriel Rossettis burying the poems that must never be read, Injun Joes and Muff Potters piling more earth on Hoss Williams's body as young Dr. Robinson lunged despairingly toward it with his bright dissecting knives, his shadow huge across the gravestones in the moonlight. Papa looked as though he would rather be using his bare hands than a spade, eager to feel the dirt sliding between his fingers and pushing beneath his nails, in the way that she had preferred to grasp weeds when she was gardening, liking the faint tug of resistance from the roots. Sounds would be muffled and furtive: the rattling slide of metal into gravelly ground, hissed whispering. The tiny skeletons would have been like those of chickens after a farmhouse meal, the fragile bones stripped of all flesh.

Crunch.

Crunch.

Crunch.

Years later, after she had read *Tess of the d'Urbervilles*, remembering these thoughts, she had imagined – in the far corner of the garden, beyond the apple trees – a line of Keelwell's Marmalade jars, each with its little bunch of flowers, at the head of each grave, as neatly arranged as if they were on a shelf at Comstock's Comestibles. She should collect all six jars together, and recreate the geometrical exactness of a Comstock's display, the positioning that of circus tumblers: three jars on the bottom row, two jars on the middle row, and one jar on top. On top of that one, precariously aligned, there would be a seventh jar, her jar. She would be on top. She would be like Pip in *Great Expectations*, studying the grave of his father and mother, late of this parish, and the five little stone lozenges, each about a foot and a half long, that were arranged in a neat row beside it, in memory of his five little brothers. Her thoughts traveled out to the marsh country, down by the river. She saw it as she had seen it many times before, a churchyard that was a bleak place overgrown with nettles in the midst of a dark flat wilderness, and the tiny graves of Alexander, Bartholomew, Abraham, Tobias – without an angel – and Roger. She saw a sixth little lozenge, a sixth tiny grave, the one for her baby sister, the one without a name.

The angel Raphael helped Tobias to overpower the king of the demons, and to marry Sarah.

"Hold your noise!" cried a terrible voice. "Keep still, you little devil, or I'll cut your throat!" and Magwitch rose up from amongst the graves, the king of the demons returned to seek revenge. "What fat cheeks you ha' got," he said. "Darn Me if I couldn't eat 'em, and if I han't half a mind to 't!" He tilted Pip further and further, and the church rolled right over. His heart and his liver would be tore out, roasted and ate. Perhaps if Pip forestalled him, ripped out his own heart and liver and roasted them himself, the awful stench might drive Magwitch away. He'd be heartless and liverless, but otherwise unharmed. It had worked for Tobias with the demon Asmodeus, though the name *Tobias* on that little stone lozenge was a worry. Perhaps the young man had got him. There was a young man hid with Magwitch, in comparison with which young man he was an Angel. Even the angel had abandoned him, led him down into his grave. The young man had a secret way, pecooliar to himself, of getting at a boy, and at his heart, and at his liver. A boy might lock his door, might be warm in bed, might tuck himself up, might draw the clothes over his head, might think himself comfortable and safe, but that young man would softly creep and creep his way to him and tear him open. He was a Dorian Gray, a Mr. Hyde sort of young man, small in stature, tenacious of purpose, with long thin dangling fingers, artist's fingers. Magwitch picked his way among the nettles and brambles, eluding the hands of the dead people, stretching up cautiously out of their graves, to get a twist upon his ankle and pull him in.

Marcus Stone had illustrated *Great Expectations*, as he had illustrated *Our Mutual Friend*. She'd often tried to imagine what the five little gravestones for Pip's brothers had looked like, but Marcus Stone had not illustrated this scene from the novel. It became very important to see it, but all she could see was an unillustrated whiteness, the graveyard buried beneath untrodden snow. In her mind, the little lozenges became tinier and tinier, the size of cachous to fit into mouths for sucking, to set pink foam dribbling down into beards.

Crunch.

Crunch.

Crunch.

Alice studied the long lists of children who had not survived childhood, carved out on the tombstones of other families, and tried to believe that the Pinkertons were fortunate, with only one acknowledged loss. Charlotte and Linnaeus had two dead little brothers, and a little sister. Some assumed that the more children that were lost, the easier it became with each new death. They were wrong. The Reverend Goodchild, one such assumer, made his feelings clear at funerals with small coffins, rattling through the service at a great rate. Babies couldn't understand what you were saying, could they? Why take your time?

Next one, please!

Bring on the next one!

There was always a next one.

Quickly!

After she had read *Tess of the d'Urbervilles*, she had thought back to her secret visits to her sister's grave when she was a little girl, the time when she had been like Tess Durbeyfield sneaking out in darkness to visit her baby's grave, the shameful secret buried amongst the nettles in the shabby corner by lantern light, with the drunkards, the suicides, all those that were damned. It was the way Mama had looked – like someone ashamed (there was something wrong that, clearly, was all her fault) – when she had gone (always alone) to the grave with a posy of flowers in her hand, taking a trowel and a wooden basket – there was a special name for it that she couldn't bring to mind – as if she were going gardening. Gardening was – indeed – what she did, tidying the tiny plot in the corner beside the wall, digging out the moss from the letters in the gravestone with the edge of the metal implement so that they could still be read. Alice, unseen, had followed her, watched her, and found the gravestone that bore her own date of birth, a sister of whom she had never heard, her silent, nameless, stillborn twin.

She saw Dr. Vaniah Odom – flinching fastidiously – leaning over the pinched face of a dead child, scooping his hand down into the blood-filled font, belatedly christening the child without a name.

"Ask, and ye shall have," he was saying, not making it sound very likely, "seek, and ye shall find; knock, and it shall be opened unto you . . ."

He gabbled the words in the same way that he gabbled the words for weddings and funerals (though he enjoyed funerals more), an actor who had grown tired of the part he was playing, speaking the same words over and over, in a run that had gone on for far too long. He was a Reynolds Templeton Seabright weary of gesturing. "I see hell!" he was rumored to have shrieked absentlymindedly at the Comstocks' wedding as Sibyl lifted her veil, allowing his attention to wander for a small, but vital, moment. He was also the seventh child of a seventh child, a member of the freemasonry of the prophetic, a seer gifted with a special insight into what the future would bring.

Her lost sister had been one of the great secrets of her childhood, something she had not told to Charlotte. She had wanted to talk to Mama about it, to ask her about her sister, but Mama had never taken her to see the grave, as she had taken her to Louis Moreau Gottschalk's. Her sister had never existed.

"So give now unto us that ask; let us that seek find; open the gate unto us that knock . . ."

They knocked on the green-painted door, and the Reverend and Mrs. Goodchild jack-in-the-boxed out of it, teeth a hard white blur. "Welcome, Pilgrims!" they chanted in unison. "Have your money ready. The Celestial City awaits! This way, Pilgrims! This way!"

Why had they never spoken about her dead sister?

For a while, a particular time, she had gone to stand at the grave, not to talk – she had seen Mama's lips moving, though she had never been able to make out what it was she was saying – but to stand and look at her own date of birth. Sometimes she had laid her hand upon the stone. It had been a time of the year when the stone had usually been sun-warmed, as it had been on some of the times when she had been searching for Annie, laying the side of her face against the outer walls up on Hudson Heights. She had tried – her hands upon the stone, she had to kneel down to touch it – to feel something, to think that she had already lived and died, that she was a ghost come back to earth.

She tried to think of a name that could be a name for her nameless sister, as she had later tried to think of another name for herself instead of Alice. "Victoria," she had sometimes said, or Ruth, or Rebecca, or Maggie, or Jo, speaking the name as she touched the stone. If she said the right name, she might bring her sister into being, like Mrs. Alexander Diddecott speaking in a séance, and would hold the tiny speechless baby in her arms. For a while, after she had read *The Comedy of Errors*, snow on the ground outside the window as she read, the name she spoke had been Alice, summoning herself back from the dead. They were twins, identical in every way, even their names the same. At the very end of the play Dromio of Ephesus and Dromio of Syracuse had at last met the twin brother that each of them had long given up for lost. Dromio of Ephesus had taken his brother's hand, refusing to walk in front of him. "We came into the world like brother and brother," he had said to him, "/And now let's go hand in hand, not one before another." They were the last words spoken in the play.

Linnaeus would not be rising. The Reverend Goodchild had not allowed him to be buried at All Saints' because he thought there was something *ambiguous* – that was his choice of adjective – about his death. He had refused point-blank when Charlotte begged him, so that Linnaeus could be buried with his parents. "*Ambiguous . . .*" he had repeated. "*Ambiguous . . .*" – the dot-dot-dot was unspoken, but audible, inviting her to answer an unasked question in the lingering silence after the word had been spoken – and he had scarcely showed his teeth at all when he said it. "No. *Quite out of the question.*" There had been nothing whatever ambiguous about what he had to say, or of the manner of his saying it. The place for Linnaeus would have been amongst the empty marmalade jars, a place of nettles where the damned were, the uncared-for corner where Sunday visitors dumped dead flowers as they tended graves and where the untrimmed branches of the trees hung down close to the ground so that there was bare earth and the grass did not grow, a place for smoky bonfires as darkness fell. There was no place for *ambiguity* in the neat well-tended places, where the graves were all facing the same way in mathematically correct lines between carefully raked graveled walks (you could see the marks made by the prongs of the rakes), where the grass was short, and the flowers fresh and prettily arranged.

The death of Linnaeus – like the death of her sister – was something that she and Charlotte had never discussed, though they had hovered on the verge of the subject once or twice recently. They had been close to saying something in church that morning, after the service. Charlotte and Linnaeus had lived on in Delft Place since the deaths of their parents, and now Charlotte lived alone in that huge house, with her brother's paintings on the walls. When she thought of them together, she thought of them as wearing mourning, the black clothes for the deaths of their parents, the white, shocked faces. They had been very young when it happened. When you saw them in the street, you could not forget the reason why they were wearing black.

Wide-eyed, his mouth slightly open and surprised, Linnaeus always had the look of someone startled from sleep.

30

In the course of the day, and now of the night, the shape of the unbuilt streets had changed, was changing, and it was as if what was in her mind could also be smoothed away, obliterated, reshaped into unmarked whiteness like what was outside, the mind itself as transient, as temporary a thing. It was, somehow, like twilight, the time when darkness had entered the house gradually, and the words on the page in front of her gradually became unreadable in the dusk. The shadows grew longer and thinner, and unnoticed details sprang briefly into unusual prominence, seen for the first time. The shapes of the furniture around her, the shapes of the trees outside in the garden, fuzzily blurred in the way that they did when she removed her spectacles, and then – slowly – assumed darker and more solid substance, quite unlike what they were in daylight. They were almost like the moments before sleep, that letting go of control, those quarters of an hour, those half-hours, before the lamps were lit, and the light returned. She'd sit, unable to read anymore, feeling the darkness silting in, wrapping itself around her. *Now in the falling of the gloom/The red fire paints the empty room:/And warmly on the roof it looks,/And flickers on the backs of books.* She thought of desert sands advancing to bury a lost Ozymandian city, or, again, of the snow transformed into ashes descending to bury Longfellow Park like Pompeii.

The ashes were not like the small, light residue of a domestic fire, the sort of ashes that Annie had been instructed to collect and use again to start a fresh blaze, kneeling on the rug before the grate in her long sacking apron, gathering them like a harvester into a special bucket, Tess Durbeyfield laboring at some repetitive task, bent over in the drab desolation of Flintcomb-Ash. These ashes would not have hurt anyone, just left a dusty mark on their clothing like a symbol of sadness, a sackcloth-free mark of mourning. The other — lethal — ashes (ashes grown monstrous) fell from the darkened sky like a shower of meteorites, thundering, shattering, collapsing. The fleeing population was being stoned to death for sins of Old Testament proportions, after Bearded Ones had passed pitiless judgment upon them, beaten about the head with the very stones on which the Ten Commandments were neatly inscribed like the lettering on expensive gravestones.

Here Lies . . .

"Liar! Liar!"

They were from Sodom.

They were from Gomorrah.

They must die.

The rocks pounded down like the toppled debris of earthquake-shattered structures, as those without sin enthusiastically seized upon one of the perks of their condition, casting the first stone with tremendous force, hurling the baseball during a vital league game. *Thou shalt not kill, Thou shalt not commit adultery, Thou shalt not steal, Thou shalt have no other gods before me, Honor thy father and thy mother, Thou shalt not bear false witness* broke in bloodstained fragments as they smashed upon skulls and fragmented limbs. *Honor, Thou shalt,* and *Kill* were now the words on rocks all by themselves, seized – they were such handy smite-sized chunks – and used again, and again.

Honor.

Honor.

Honor.

Thou shalt.

Thou shalt.

Thou shalt.

Kill.

Kill.

Kill.

Commit adultery. (Though they would rather – if it were all the same – kill.)

Steal. (Killing would be better.)

Bear false witness. (Killing would be far more enjoyable.)

Exodus XX, XXI, and XXII (all those exes in Exodus, as God marked them out for destruction with a cross, like rotten trees in a corrupted orchard) fell to earth, homicidal hailstones blackening the sky, and the piled bodies of an overwhelmed city were lost from sight and buried beneath them. A finer ash pattered and sifted down, drifting through the apertures, and filling every remaining space.

Thwack! Thwack! Thwack!

A hit!

A very palpable hit!

The crowd roared.

Mount Sinai was altogether on a smoke, because the LORD descended upon it in fire: and the smoke thereof ascended as the smoke of a furnace, and the whole mount quaked greatly. And all the people saw the thunderings, and the lightnings, and the noise of the trumpet, and the mountain smoking: and when the people saw it, they removed, and stood afar off, and Moses drew near unto the thick darkness where God was.

Miss Swanstrom had not killed *The Last Days of Pompeii* for Alice. It had been dead already when she had first read it, interested to find the faults that had made Mrs. Albert Comstock declare that Lord Lytton – together with Sheridan Knowles – was her favorite playwright. (If she couldn't find one of his plays, she'd read one of his novels.) It had soon become clear that a major part of his appeal – it could not have been based upon his subtlety as a writer (not that Mrs. Albert Comstock would recognize subtlety) – was that (like Tolstoi) he possessed a title. Almost as impressive, his other name – Bulwer-Lytton – employed a hyphen. English lords – as Shakespeare's history plays confusingly demonstrated – seemed, like characters in Russian novels, to possess two or three different names, usually simultaneously. Alice had had to draw up a list of characters, and their various names, on her bookmark when she had read *War and Peace*, and family trees had sprouted like the spidery multi-rooted notes of an amateur gardener.

The names of the characters in Lord Lytton's novel – they existed more as names, as labels, than as characters – were in her head. After nearly seventeen centuries – Lord Lytton had written, in the final chapter of his novel – the city of Pompeii was disinterred from its silent tomb all vivid with undimmed hues; its walls fresh as if painted yesterday – not a hue faded on the rich mosaic of its floors.

There had been a special-shaped cloud that marked the destruction of the city. The mother of Pliny the Younger had noticed it at about one o'clock on the afternoon of that day in August, a cloud of unusual size and appearance hovering above Vesuvius in the shape of a mushroom or an umbrella pine tree, its trunk extending to a great height, opening out into branches at the top. Pliny the Elder had gone to investigate the strange formation, and had been amongst those killed.

The lines of gas-lamps were smaller and fainter as they stretched farther away across the places that had once been fields and orchards, and the snow whirled around in the pools of light. Once they had lived – or so it had seemed – far beyond the farthest north, then – for a while – on the half-shaped raw edge of things, the shanty-towned frontier; now they were being engulfed, their apartness forever ended. The open countryside had become rough-edged, muddy, unpicturesque, a desolate debris-scattered wildness with an air of utter abandonment, unsuspected so close to a huge city, with straggling farms and small accidental groupings down rutted roads, and the occasional houses of the rich, unused for most of the year, on the higher ground or looking out over rivers. There were still hills and trees, all that had been there before, rocky mounds, wooden shacks, grazing goats, like scenes from rural Montana. It was like the time when she and Charlotte had gone to see Grant's Tomb a year or so earlier. Across the road from the shining new structure, the pillared Roman Pantheon, the empty fields had stretched away like something on the wrong side of a city, the outer edges where people came under cover of night to dump what they no longer wanted. Away from the Hudson and the swarming crowds of sightseers, amidst the rubbish-strewn lots, were the blank backs of billboards, ragged clumps of bare winter trees, a few scattered amateurishly half-demolished buildings, all waiting to be swept away. Amidst the fields and farms, isolated high-stooped row houses were being built here and there – with no discernible pattern – amongst raw earth, as if they were all that remained after some unforeseen cataclysm had swept everything else away. Sagging wooden palings gave a rural ambience to dis-tricts with metropolitan pretensions. Behind them, in ill-tended truck farms, sad-looking vegetables – most of them cabbages – were planted out like geometrical patterns in rows as stiff and straight-edged as the new streets. Their leaves were pale and limp, all the color faded out of them. They'd wither in the mouth like Dead Sea fruit, produce that no one would ever wish to eat. Roads petered out, led nowhere. Half-completed churches reared up in areas excavated so extensively for foundations that the roads seemed like bridges across the chasms of a wasteland, and the raised metal frameworks for the elevated railroads stretched out across wastelands of mud and desolate fields in the early twilight, to places where it seemed that there would never be anyone living.

She experienced the same sensation as she had that morning,

that the featureless mounds of snow in the darkness between the lamps marked the buried ruins of a lost city, and not the site of a city that was yet to be built. The place where nothing had been built had become the place where something once was. The wooden signposts, the fenced-off sections, marked the areas claimed by archeologists, the places in which to dig. In its forum were the half-finished columns as left by the workman's hand, – in its gardens the sacrificial tripod, – in its halls the chest of treasure, – in its baths the strigil, – in its theatres the counter of admission, – in its salons the furniture and the lamp, – in its cubicula the perfumes and the rouge of faded beauty, – and everywhere the bones and skeletons of those who once moved the springs of that minute yet gorgeous machine of luxury and of life.

From these skeletons, from the condition and position of the bodies, the novel had been constructed, inventing names and lives for them: Burbo, Calenus, Diomed, Julia, Arbaces. When the dead had completely crumbled away, they left a space where they had once been amidst the solidified ashes. If plaster was poured into this space, like a cast being made for a statue, the faces and figures of those who had once been there were recreated. This was what Giuseppe Fiorelli had done at Pompeii. As she looked at Linnaeus's painting of herself, the painting that bore her name, but in which she did not appear, she thought of this idea of a nothingness where a life had once been lived, where all that remained was what once had been around it.

She thought, most of all, of her writing materials – outside her family, Charlotte and Linnaeus were among the few people who knew (or "had known" in Linnaeus's case: death demanded a whole new grammatical construction) that she wrote – the Huntley & Palmers biscuit tin in the shape of a bundle of leather-bound books tied together by a strap. It was in here that she kept her ink and pens, her lists of titles.

The Shape of the Clouds.

The title had come to her that morning. It was one that she had to use. Late last night, and in the course of the day, what would be the first sentences had started to form in her head. She thought of it as being a story, but it might develop into something more. She felt the impulse, the weight, of something more substantial inside her. She waited until a sentence was perfect: then she could write it down, her scratching pen the only sound in the silent room. Once she had started, the words flowed, at least five hundred words a day. That was what she aimed to achieve every day.

She looked at the reflection of her face in the dark glass of the night-backed window, and smoothed her just-combed hair, hearing the voices of the maidens in *The Mikado*, preparing Pitti-Sing for her wedding day, dressing her hair, and painting her face and lips.

> "Braid the raven hair –
>   Weave the supple tress –
> Deck the maiden fair
>   In her loveliness –
> Paint the pretty face –
>   Dye the coral lip –
> Emphasize the grace
>   Of her ladyship!
> Art and nature, thus allied,
> Go to make a pretty bride."

She looked at her face reflected in the dark glass, the reflection without braiding, without paint.

Supple.

Fair.

Loveliness.

Pretty.

Grace.

Pretty.

Six crosses in a row.

This raven had brought an unkindness.

Pitti-Sing's voice sang the next part as a solo.

"Sit with downcast eye —
   Let it brim with dew —
Try if you can cry —
   We will do so, too.
When you're summoned, start
   Like a frightened roe —
Flutter, little heart,
   Colour, come and go! . . ."

This she *had* managed.

She had cried.

She had started in fright when she was summoned.

Her heart had fluttered; her color had come and gone.

An unkindness of ravens.

A desert of lapwings. It stretched away before her, and there was no birdsong.

A tittering of magpies.

Titter! Titter!

The magpies sniggered about what they knew, as they flew across against the clouds.

One for sorrow.

Two for joy.

Three for a wedding.

Four for a death.

Five for silver.

Six for gold.

Seven for a secret never to be told.

A Secret Never to be Told.

A Sin without Pardon.

(Hide thy face from my sins, and blot out all mine iniquities.)

A child should always say what's true.

Robert Louis Stevenson said this in "Whole Duty of Children," the fifth poem in *A Child's Garden of Verses*, just after "Young Night Thoughts."

All night long, and every night,
When my mamma puts out the light,
I see the people marching by,
As plain as day, before my eye.

"*Ihre Augen waren von Tränen getrübt.*"
Her eyes were clouded with tears.
She knew that sentence would come in useful.

"*I, blinded with tears . . .*"

The words came to her from far away and long ago.

". . . *Still strove to speak: my voice was thick with sighs*
As in a dream. Dimly I could descry
The stern black-bearded kings with wolvish eyes,
Waiting to see me die . . ."

31

She went across to the fireside, and pulled her warmed nightgown on over her head, then returned to her usual place standing at the window. She'd disordered her hair, and would need to brush it again. Her hairbrush was where she had left it, precisely aligned on the window ledge.

Intermittently, the moon emerged from behind the snow-filled clouds. It had still been daylight – however dark and wintry – when she, Charlotte, and Kate had waved goodbye to Ben, another version of the terra-cotta *Macbeth* figures. He'd said his goodbyes to Mama, alone in her bedroom, trying to understand what she was attempting to say to him. She'd held her hand to the side of his head, and wept. They had stood at the parlor window, waving their hands tiltingly in the way that children waved. It had been too cold to stand at the front door, a gray, dark day without shadows, and the snow had started again.

Charlotte and Linnaeus had been waiting for her in the moonlight when she had returned with Mama from her first stay in the
Webster Nervine Asylum. She and Mama had left the boat — like
people disembarking after a day's pleasure cruise up the Hudson:
voices across the water, laughter, fireworks — and Charlotte and her
brother had come out of the shadows to greet them. They must
have waited for a long time. Arm in arm, they had walked up the
slope beneath the trees, and Charlotte had started them all singing,
singing to the moon, the song from *The Mikado*. Alone on stage,
dressed and painted for her wedding, Yum-Yum sang about the
sun and the moon.

> ". . . She borrows light
> That, through the night,
>   Mankind may all acclaim her!
> And, truth to tell,
> She lights up well,
>   So I, for one, don't blame her!
>
> "Ah, pray make no mistake,
>   We are not shy;
> We're very wide awake,
>   The moon and I!"

She looked at the moon now.

When she looked at it, she tried to work out what it made her
think, how she felt, wrinkling up her eyes as if she were staring into
the brightness of a midday sun, waiting for an eclipse to begin. If
she waited there long enough, if she waited there all night through,
she might see the moon fade, and the morning star appear. When
the moon was lost for a while, she looked at the reflection of her
face in the dark glass.

"'Yes, I am indeed beautiful!'" she said aloud, quoting Yum-Yum's
words. "'Sometimes I sit and wonder, in my artless Japanese way,

why it is that I am so much more attractive than anybody else in the whole world.'"

The moon appeared again, the moon that was so nearly a full moon. She should be in fine cackling form by Wednesday morning, when she began her journey to the Webster Nervine Asylum for her second stay there, her mind crammed – her eyes dazzled – with all the empty whiteness of full-moon lunacy.

La Lune! La Lune!

She was such a card!

A carriage would be waiting for her at the boat landing when she arrived at Poughkeepsie. It would drive along beside the edge of the river, and then up through the trees, through the open gate and into the grounds. Dressed all in white, she'd be driven through the whiteness of the snow, into the wordlessness and the silence that was waiting for her in the margins.

She'd enter the handsome hall.

They'd be there, smiling professionally – "Such a pleasure to see you again, Miss Pinkerton!" – as they angled the visitors' book toward her, a regular guest checking into a sun-filled summer hotel, one to which she returned year after year to relive the memories of happier times, her luggage positioned on the floor at her side, at precisely the same angle as the visitors' book on the desk.

She'd be directed up the left-hand staircase, and through an open door into what appeared to be a drawing room. A servant would lead the way – though she knew the way – carrying her bags for her.

The servant would lead her across the drawing room and open a concealed door that was disguised as a looking-glass, and they would walk through the looking-glass into the cold bare room beyond, dirty and cobwebbed, its nearer wall lined with the fake books.

The matron of the asylum would walk toward her, flanked by Allegra and Edith.

"Calm yourself," her sisters would say, linking their arms in hers. "There is no wonder nor mystery in the matter: *you were expected.*"

The matron would pull at a gold chain that was hanging around her neck, and draw out an ivory whistle. She would blow upon it until she achieved the right key, the cue for the three of them to begin singing.

> "Three little maids from school are we,
> Pert as a school-girl well can be,
> Filled to the brim with girlish glee,
>   Three little maids from school!
> Everything is a source of fun . . ."

— At this point they would begin to chuckle —

> ". . . Nobody's safe, for we care for none!. . ."

— The chuckling would become louder, more discordant —

> ". . . Life is a joke that's just begun!. . ."

The chuckling would become loud laughter, uncontrolled, high-pitched, echoing around in the emptiness.

"Calm yourself," the matron would say, laying a hand on her arm. There'd be no sign of Allegra and Edith — Allegra and Edith would never have been there — and Alice would continue singing all by herself.

> ". . . Three little maids from school!
> Three little maids who, all unwary,
> Come from a ladies' seminary,
> Freed from its genius tutelary — . . ."

The matron would pull at the gold chain again, and draw out the ivory whistle. When she blew upon it, two men would come quietly into the room.

". . . Three little maids from school!. . ."

One of the men began to speak to Alice.

"Be calm, my dear young lady; don't agitate yourself. You have been sent here for your good; and that you may be cured . . ."

"What are you talking about? What do you mean?" Alice cried. "Are you mad?"

"No," one of the men answered. "*We* are not . . ."

They and the matron drew closer toward her, reaching out.

It was for her own good.

To bed, to bed.

And not to read.

The books would not be real books.

And not to write.

There would be no pens, no paper.

To bed, to bed, to bed.

And not to think.

The mind would be emptied of all thought.

And not to talk.

The tongue, like the writing-hand, would be stilled.

To bed, to bed, to bed.

And not to sew.

No stitch-stitch-stitch.

No sharp-edged pens or needles.

Safest not to have them around.

Just sleeping.

Just dreaming.

She wouldn't escape the dreams.

Drifting listlessly away.

Drifting.

Nothing else.

Because nothing else mattered.

Sometimes, when a full moon took her by surprise – looking up, seeing it through the skylight – she felt someone had climbed up on to the roof and was watching her.

What did she think about, looking up at the full moon?

"Dot. Dot. Dot," she said.

The text was moving into silence. Out in the North Pole wastes of whiteness, where there were no more words, the characters struggled and died in those margins beyond the text, stifled by that silence.

Dot. Dot. Dot.

Sometimes – on rainy afternoons, on winter evenings – she had been tempted to read *The Mystery of Edwin Drood* for the first time, the Dickens novel she had been saving as – this was how she sometimes felt it – the last book she would read. She had had *Our Mutual Friend* saved as well, but – with a sensation of luxurious abandon – she had read it when she returned from her first visit to the Webster Nervine Asylum. (Only one unread Dickens novel left!) *The Mystery of Edwin Drood* was the one she had chosen to save until last because, of course, it was the last one Dickens had written, the one he had left incomplete when he died. She had hovered around the book several times. There were only 155 pages in her edition.

It wouldn't take long to read . . .

It wasn't one of his better books . . .

She'd looked at Luke Fildes's illustrations – twelve of them – telling herself that this wasn't cheating, it didn't count as reading, trying to decide what she could deduce about the novel from them. It was a place of darkness and deep shadows, figures lying dead or unconscious on beds in squalid rooms, fashionable young men leaning upon pianos or mantel-shelves, a girl cowering away from a man in an overgrown garden, a girl – the same girl? – nervously sitting in a boat with three men in the middle of a river. This last reminded her, though the girl was not doing the rowing, of Lizzie Hexam in *Our Mutual Friend* unwillingly guiding the boat for her father as he sought for corpses in the Thames.

Charlotte had bought her an edition of Charles Dickens – complete, except for *A Tale of Two Cities* – from a secondhand bookstore the previous year, and inside every book, on the first blank page, was written *Edward Gwynne Lawrence. From his loving brothers Frank & Jack on his 21st Birthday. March 28th 1900.* Charlotte had remembered her saying that she would have liked to own a uniform edition, instead of the oddly assorted volumes she had accumulated over the years. The pages had not been cut in any of the volumes, and she had spent a stormy day working through them with a letter-knife, sometimes pausing to study the illustrations or read passages as the wind beat at the windows. It was then that she'd looked at *The Mystery of Edwin Drood*. She had been going to leave the pages of this novel uncut, to keep her out, to leave the cutting until the reading, but she hadn't been able to stop. After she'd looked at the illustrations, she'd looked at some of the headings at the top of right-hand pages – *Mad Love, Rosa flees for Protection, A Preux Chevalier, The Thorn of Anxiety* (it sounded quite promising) – and then she'd turned to the final page, *The Last Addition to the Score*, to see the final words that Dickens had written. She imagined him at his desk, thinking, writing a few words, pausing, writing a few words more, and then the pen falling from his fingers and rolling across the floor. Most of page 155 was blank, but – above the whiteness – there were a few lines of type.

"Know him! Better far than all the Reverend Parsons put together know him."

Mrs. Tope's care has spread a very neat, clean breakfast ready for her lodger. Before sitting down to it, he opens his corner-cupboard door; takes his bit of chalk from its shelf; adds one thick line to the score, extending from the top of the cupboard door to the bottom; and then falls to with an appetite.

It was disappointing that the last sentence was complete. She'd hoped that it might have ended in mid-sentence, or part-way through a word, though the use of the present tense added an intriguing tension to those final words.

Appetite.

The last word written.

When she'd read *The Last Addition to the Score* she'd imagined something to do with music, the last few notes added to something appropriately Schubertian and Unfinished, but now saw that all it meant was "twenty." This was not as promising, though still intriguing: twenty-one lines drawn in chalk. Perhaps she didn't want to read the incomplete novel after all. ("I'm brooding on Drood," she thought to herself.) The explanation for those chalk lines could never be as interesting as the puzzled speculation, the not knowing. The stained glass windows were wiped clean as she wielded the magic wand of Pinkerton's Champion Stain Remover and Paragon Detergent; the Shakespeare Castle was utterly destroyed; the tapestries were unthreaded like a wiped-clean blackboard with all the chalked words gone.

The thing was . . .

The thing was that when blackboards *were* wiped clean — the waving goodbye motion of the hand with the cloth — the words being erased were already committed — *ha!* — to memory, and could not be forgotten, learned by heart, written troubles of the brain.

There was no dot-dot-dot after the point at which *The Mystery of Edwin Drood* had come to a premature stop, but there was a row of nine stars below the last line. Then there were no more words, and silence began in blank white paper.

32

Japan, the country to which Ben was traveling, was a country without shadows, even on days of sunshine, a country without clouds, even when it rained.

She had studied the prints in Grandpapa and Grandmama Brouwer's house, the ones Grandpapa had brought back with him from the time when he had been in Japan. The artists ignored clouds and shadows (and perspective), and this was how she had found herself — as a girl — imagining the country. She didn't know whether all artists followed the same conventions, but, in those she knew, far and near seemed to exist — like past and present — in the same place, at the same moment, and that which was far away assumed as large a shape as that which was near, as in a child's drawing.

Ben, blinking in the bright light, held his hand up above his eyes as he looked up into a cloudless sky, shapes forming within his eyes as the sun dazzled. Around him were the people without shadows, the Japanese, their parasols hiding their faces. They were ladies of Japan: on many a vase and jar, on many a screen and fan, they figured in lively paint, their attitude queer and quaint.

They did not appear to see Ben.

It was as if he — also — were a cloud, or a shadow.

33

She had the feeling again, as she saw her pale reflection in front of her, and — she had been back at the window for no more than a few minutes — went to her writing journal where it lay on the bed, her pen lying within the hollow between the opened pages.

She read again what she had written most recently. She always dated what she wrote, so that she knew the day on which she had written it. This was her nearest approach to a diary.

I saw another ghost last night. They come at twilight, the in-between-time, not in full darkness, gathering like starlings in a public square as the light fails, but in silence, with none of the gregarious groupings and noise of the birds. They live in the mirrors. Sometimes — & always one at a time — they emerge from the mirror, & walk into the room.

Her head slightly on one side, concentrating to hear that distant dictating, she unscrewed the top of her pen, and began to write in the blackest of black ink.

As if restless, they never stay long in one place, wandering about as if searching for something, something they'd lost & were anxious to find again. They make a sound like moths' wings . . .

She paused, listening more carefully, and then added two insertion arrows in the incomplete final sentence. After *They* she wrote *never speak, but they,* and before *sound* she wrote *rustling.* Without any further pause, she completed the sentence she had started.

. . . fluttering against glass, as if drawn in toward illumination as daylight fades. It makes them seem insubstantial & brittle, as if they were made out of thin paper, rising up out of the pages as the words were read . . .

She inserted *of a book* after *pages,* and added *as the pages were turned* at the end of the sentence.

One particular ghost comes again & again, never losing that intensity of searching, the eyes fixed intently upon the floor in front of her, as if what she sought might be there. She leans right down, as if that which she seeks is small, and precious to her. She never sees me. None of them ever sees me. It's as if I'm not there, as if I'm the one faded & half effaced.

A pause.

Something not quite right.

She changed the period after *None of them ever sees me* into a comma, added an insertion arrow, and wrote *just as they never seem to see each other. They swarm, they gather, but they are always alone, not seeing their surroundings, but seeing only something within themselves.*

Without pausing, she altered the period after *half effaced* into a comma, and added *& as if they exist alone, without me, though I feel that it is my presence that gives them shape, as if they were the reflection I make in the mirror —* she was writing more and more rapidly, the unseen dictator speaking with increasing urgency and speed — *a self I cannot recognize & have never seen before, something hidden emerging from an inner room, the Alice-Through-the-Looking-Glass room beyond the one visible in the mirror, & never seen.*

After a short pause, she crossed through *& never seen.*

She paused.

She paused.

In the space above the first line – it was the top of the left-hand side of a double-page spread – she wrote *The Shape of the Clouds.*

Scribble, scribble, scribble, she thought.

She paused.

She paused.

She knew she hadn't written five hundred words yet for that day. Five hundred words would fill two pages of the journal, and her handwriting was just starting to reach down the right-hand side. She sometimes wrote a great deal more than five hundred words; she never wrote fewer.

She waited a little while longer, in that listening stance.

After a while – it was one of her drawing-to-a-close actions at the end of each day – she began to count the words she had written, her lips moving, the whispered numbers just audible. A further pause, and then she replaced the journal and the pen exactly where they had been, and went back to the window.

There was an ink stain on the side of her face. She touched it, feeling the blackness entering inside her.

There was a Young . . .

– Young! –

. . . Lady in White,
Who looked out at the depths of the Night;
But the birds of the air,
Filled her heart with despair,
And oppressed that Young . . .

– Young! –

. . . Lady in White.

The crows, the starlings, the choughs, the parrots, the herons, the hawks, the owls, the peacocks, the woodpeckers, the finches, the ravens, the lapwings, the magpies: all the birds of the air fell a-sighing and a-sobbing as they swarmed upon her, she become another St. Francis, vanishing beneath the falling feathers.

Soon it would be time to put out the lamp and go to bed. It would be time to dream again.

How she had longed for one day of cloudless skies, one night of dreamless sleep. She had thought – as a young child – that clouds were not there in the nighttime, that they swarmed away to sleep like birds, but they were always there, hidden in the darkness, vague shadows obliterating the stars, blurring the changing shape of the moon, absorbing the muted circle of light.

She stood at the window. With her left hand she gripped one of the iron bars, and with her right hand she picked up her hairbrush.

"One, two, three . . ."

She had written three hundred and thirteen words.

Three hundred and *eighteen* words if she included the title.

She always included the title.

The day had not been entirely wasted.

She had to write at least a hundred and eighty-two words before she could go to sleep.

She rested her bowed head against the upraised arm, her face hidden, her eyes closed.

". . . four, five, six . . ."

ACKNOWLEDGEMENTS

I wish to avoid one of those long, exhaustive, look-how-hard-I've-worked lists of references, but I am anxious to acknowledge how grateful I am to the many writers I consulted during the writing of this novel, especially the novelists, poets, dramatists, and song-writers from whom I quote, or to whom I make reference. Any reader will recognize how essential a part they play in this novel, and how much I owe to them. The dream interpretations are taken from *What's in a Dream* by Gustavus Hindman Miller (1901). Harry Graham's poem "Tender-heartedness" (from *Ruthless Rhymes for Heartless Homes*) is quoted by kind permission of the Trustees of Mrs. Virginia Thesiger. I am not conscious of having quoted from any other copyright text, and apologize if I have inadvertently done so. I have tried to be true to the period about which I have written, though I have adapted some things to suit my purpose. I am grateful, also, to the friendly and efficient staff of the North Yorkshire Library Service – especially Ivy Summons, Shena Hugill, and Liz Luxmoore – for their tireless and interested help in finding what were sometimes elusive texts for me during my research. Numerous other people have helped and encouraged me, and I owe particular thanks to Gerard Galloway, and – most of all – Paul Barton.